MIGHTY MARVEL MASTERWORKS

PRESENTS

CAPTAIN AMERICA

VOLUME 1

COLLECTING

TALES OF SUSPENSE Nos. 59-77

STAN LEE • JACK KIRBY

COLLECTION EDITOR
Cory Sedlmeier

BOOK DESIGN
Nickel DesignWorks

ART & COLOR RESTORATION
Michael Kelleher & Kellustration

COLLECTION COVER
Michael Cho

VARIANT CLASSIC COVER
Jack Kirby & Dick Ayers

VP PRODUCTION & SPECIAL PROJECTS
Jeff Youngquist

SVP PRINT, SALES & MARKETING
David Gabriel

EDITOR IN CHIEF
C.B. Cebulski

MIGHTY MARVEL MASTERWORKS: CAPTAIN AMERICA VOL. 1 — THE SENTINEL OF LIBERTY. Contains material originally published in magazine form as TALES OF SUSPENSE (1959) #59-77. First printing 2022. ISBN 978-1-302-94615-9. Published by MARVEL WORLDWIDE, INC., a subsidiary of MARVEL ENTERTAINMENT, LLC. OFFICE OF PUBLICATION: 1290 Avenue of the Americas, New York, NY 10104. © 2022 MARVEL No similarity between any of the names, characters, persons, and/or institutions in this book with those of any living or dead person or institution is intended, and any such similarity which may exist is purely coincidental. **Printed in Canada.** KEVIN FEIGE, Chief Creative Officer; DAN BUCKLEY, President, Marvel Entertainment; JOE QUESADA, EVP & Creative Director; DAVID BOGART, Associate Publisher & SVP of Talent Affairs; TOM BREVOORT, VP, Executive Editor; NICK LOWE, Executive Editor, VP of Content, Digital Publishing; DAVID GABRIEL, VP of Print & Digital Publishing; MARK ANNUNZIATO, VP of Planning & Forecasting; JEFF YOUNGQUIST, VP of Production & Special Projects; ALEX MORALES, Director of Publishing Operations; DAN EDINGTON, Director of Editorial Operations; RICKEY PURDIN, Director of Talent Relations; JENNIFER GRÜNWALD, Director of Production & Special Projects; SUSAN CRESPI, Production Manager; STAN LEE, Chairman Emeritus. For information regarding advertising in Marvel Comics or on Marvel.com, please contact Vit DeBellis, Custom Solutions & Integrated Advertising Manager, at vdebellis@marvel.com. For Marvel subscription inquiries, please call 888-511-5480. **Manufactured between 3/25/2022 and 4/26/2022 by SOLISCO PRINTERS, SCOTT, QC, CANADA.**

10 9 8 7 6 5 4 3 2 1

CAPTAIN AMERICA
TALES OF SUSPENSE NOS. 59-77

WRITER:
Stan Lee

PENCILERS:
Jack Kirby
Dick Ayers
George Tuska
John Romita

INKERS:
Chic Stone
Frank Giacoia
Dick Ayers
George Tuska
Joe Sinnott
John Tartaglione
John Romita

LETTERERS:
Sam Rosen
Art Simek

EDITOR:
Stan Lee

SPECIAL THANKS:
Ralph Macchio

CAPTAIN AMERICA CREATED BY JOE SIMON & JACK KIRBY

CONTENTS

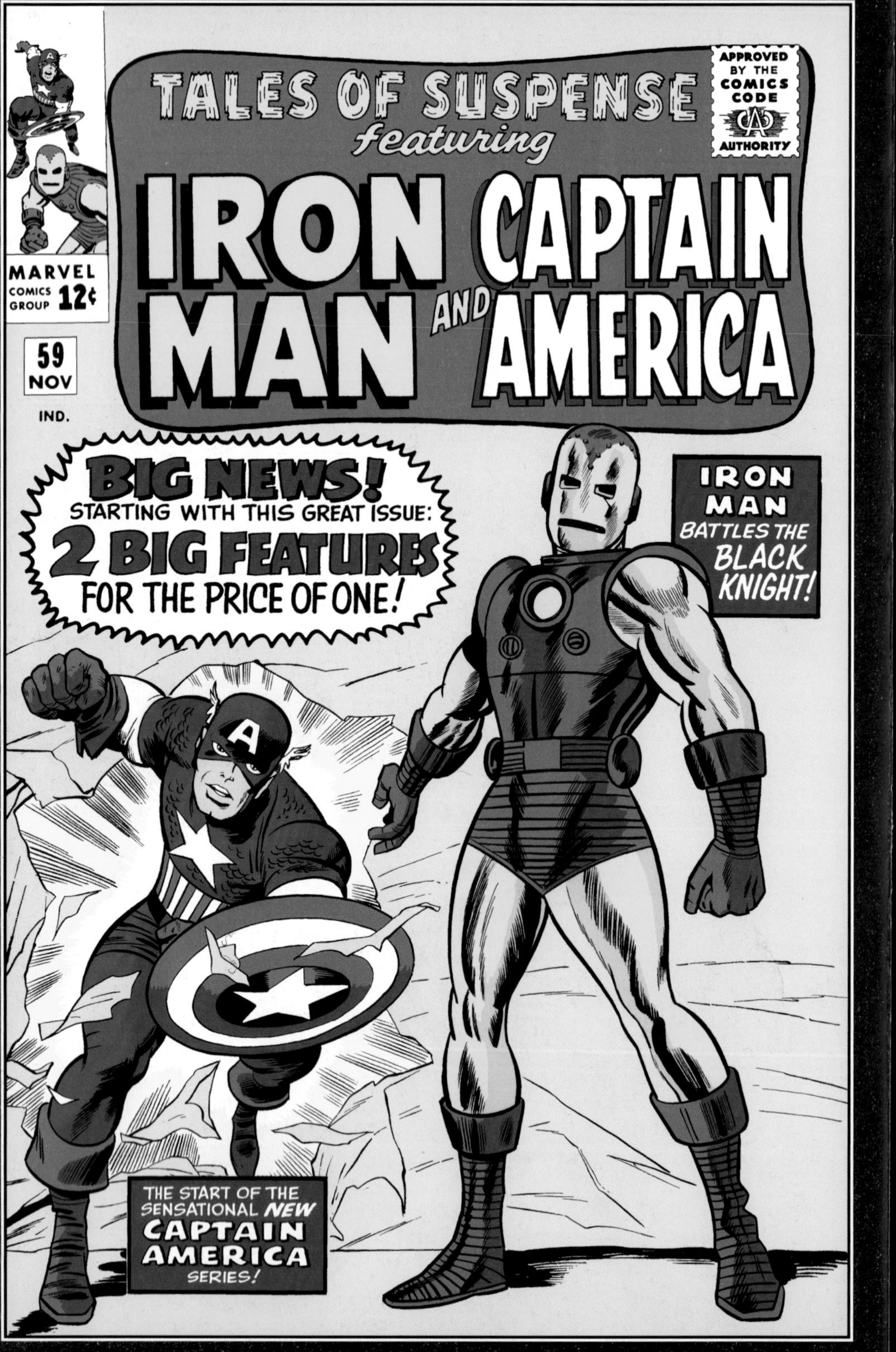
TALES OF SUSPENSE
featuring
IRON MAN
AND
CAPTAIN AMERICA
APPROVED BY THE COMICS CODE AUTHORITY
MARVEL COMICS GROUP 12¢
59 NOV
IND.
BIG NEWS!
STARTING WITH THIS GREAT ISSUE:
2 BIG FEATURES
FOR THE PRICE OF ONE!
IRON MAN BATTLES THE BLACK KNIGHT!
THE START OF THE SENSATIONAL NEW CAPTAIN AMERICA SERIES!

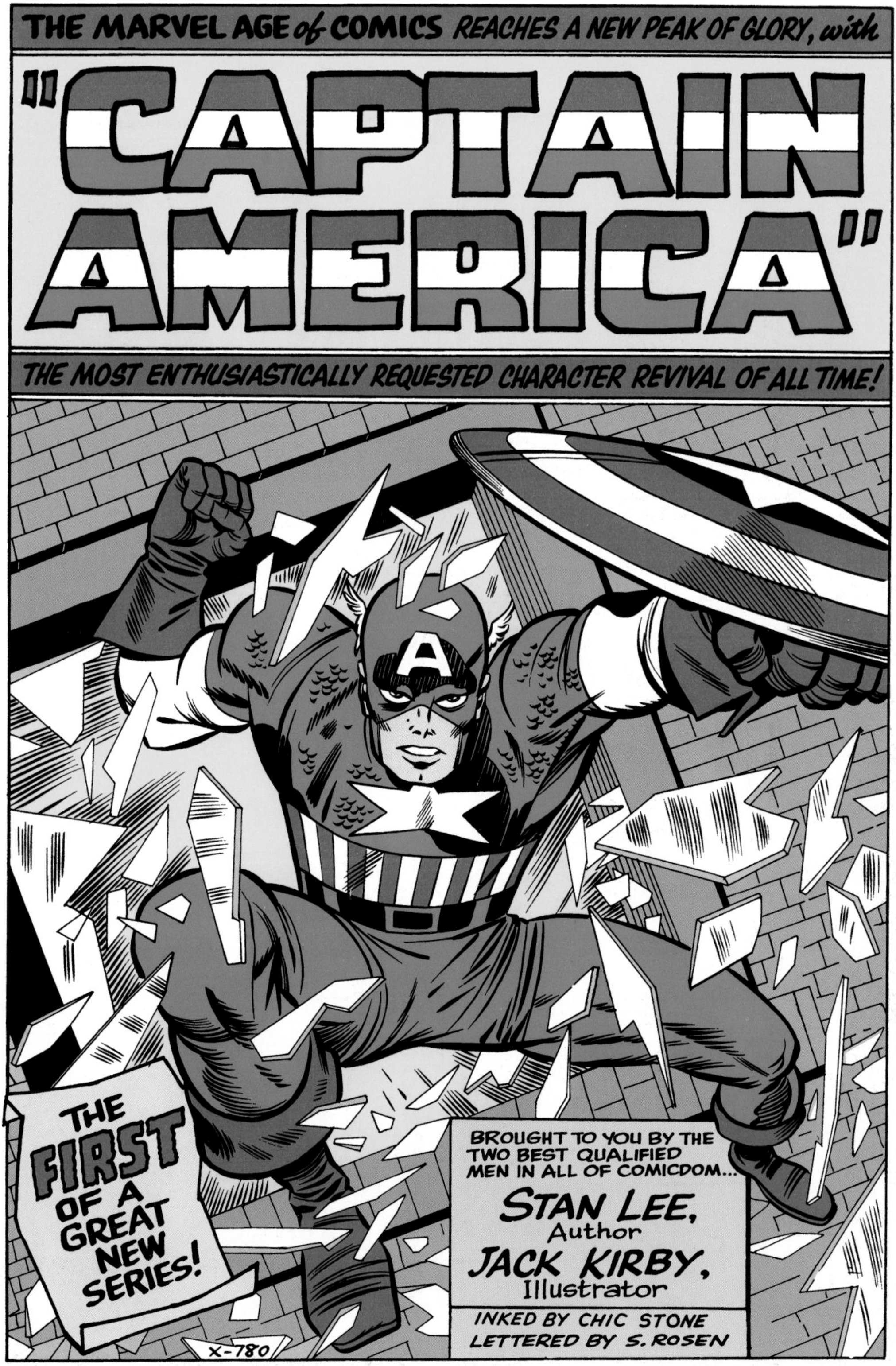
THE MARVEL AGE of COMICS REACHES A NEW PEAK OF GLORY, with
"CAPTAIN AMERICA"
THE MOST ENTHUSIASTICALLY REQUESTED CHARACTER REVIVAL OF ALL TIME!
THE FIRST OF A GREAT NEW SERIES!
BROUGHT TO YOU BY THE TWO BEST QUALIFIED MEN IN ALL OF COMICDOM...
STAN LEE, Author
JACK KIRBY, Illustrator
INKED BY CHIC STONE
LETTERED BY S. ROSEN
X-780

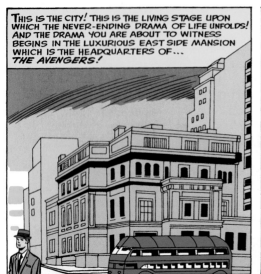

THIS IS THE CITY! THIS IS THE LIVING STAGE UPON WHICH THE NEVER-ENDING DRAMA OF LIFE UNFOLDS! AND THE DRAMA YOU ARE ABOUT TO WITNESS BEGINS IN THE LUXURIOUS EAST SIDE MANSION WHICH IS THE HEADQUARTERS OF... *THE AVENGERS!*

ACTUALLY, IT WAS ONCE THE RESIDENCE OF MULTI-MILLIONAIRE ANTHONY STARK, BUT HE DONATED IT TO THE WORLD'S MIGHTIEST FIGHTING TEAM AS A PUBLIC SERVICE...

BEFORE I LEAVE FOR THE EVENING, SIR, I THOUGHT YOU MIGHT LIKE SOME FRESHLY BREWED COFFEE!

WHENEVER POSSIBLE, THE AVENGERS LEAVE ONE OF THEIR MEMBERS AT THE MANSION IN THE EVENT THAT SOME EMERGENCY SHOULD OCCUR! TONIGHT, THE DUTY ASSIGNMENT HAS FALLEN TO THE MAN KNOWN AS... *CAPTAIN AMERICA!*

THANK YOU, JARVIS! I WON'T REQUIRE ANYTHING ELSE!

IT WAS CERTAINLY GENEROUS OF STARK TO PROVIDE US WITH A *BUTLER*, IN ADDITION TO THE MANSION ITSELF!

NOT EVEN THE AVENGERS THEM-SELVES SUSPECT THAT TONY STARK IS REALLY *IRON MAN*, ONE OF THEIR OWN MIGHTY MEMBERS!

FINALLY, THE BUTLER DEPARTS, LEAVING THE BROODING COSTUMED ADVENTURER ALONE WITH HIS THOUGHTS...

THESE TOURS OF DUTY CAN BE MIGHTY LONELY, ESPECIALLY TO A MAN WHO THRIVES ON ACTION!

PERHAPS I CAN MAKE TIME PASS MORE QUICKLY BY LOOKING THROUGH THIS OLD SCRAPBOOK ALBUM OF MINE!

BUT, CAPTAIN AMERICA IS DUE FOR MORE ACTION THAN HE SUSPECTS! FOR, NOT FAR AWAY, A MEETING IS TAKING PLACE WHICH IS SOON TO SHATTER THE QUIET OF THE STALWART AVENGER'S EVENING...

BUT HOW CAN A MOB LIKE *US* MANAGE TO PUT ANYTHING OVER ON THE *AVENGERS*, BOSS?

JUST HOLD THAT CHAIN TIGHT, AND I'LL *SHOW* YA...!

2.

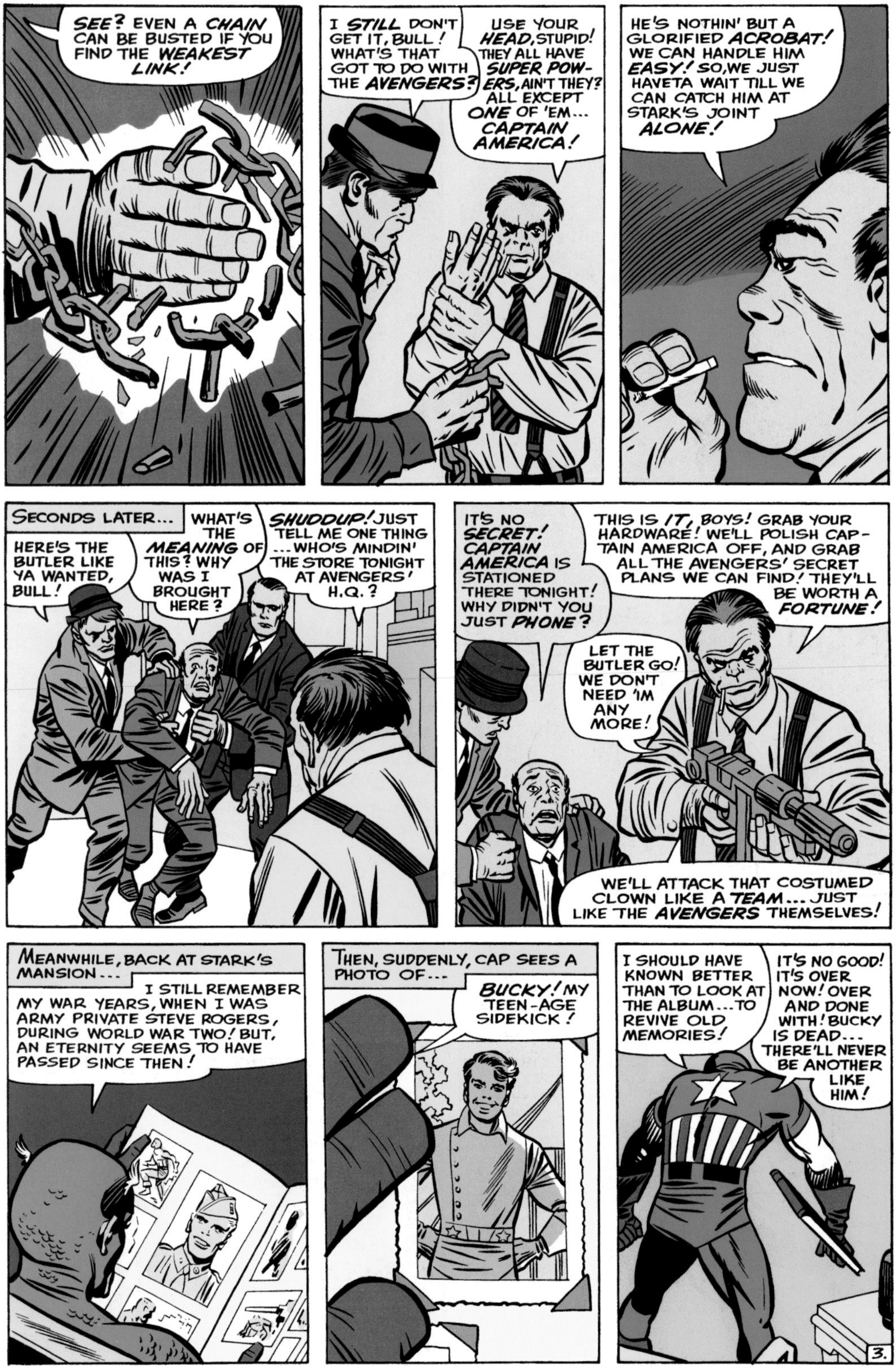

SEE? EVEN A CHAIN CAN BE BUSTED IF YOU FIND THE WEAKEST LINK!
I STILL DON'T GET IT, BULL! WHAT'S THAT GOT TO DO WITH THE AVENGERS?
USE YOUR HEAD, STUPID! THEY ALL HAVE SUPER POWERS, AIN'T THEY? ALL EXCEPT ONE OF 'EM... CAPTAIN AMERICA!
HE'S NOTHIN' BUT A GLORIFIED ACROBAT! WE CAN HANDLE HIM EASY! SO, WE JUST HAVETA WAIT TILL WE CAN CATCH HIM AT STARK'S JOINT ALONE!
SECONDS LATER...
HERE'S THE BUTLER LIKE YA WANTED, BULL!
WHAT'S THE MEANING OF THIS? WHY WAS I BROUGHT HERE?
SHUDDUP! JUST TELL ME ONE THING ...WHO'S MINDIN' THE STORE TONIGHT AT AVENGERS' H.Q.?
IT'S NO SECRET! CAPTAIN AMERICA IS STATIONED THERE TONIGHT! WHY DIDN'T YOU JUST PHONE?
THIS IS IT, BOYS! GRAB YOUR HARDWARE! WE'LL POLISH CAPTAIN AMERICA OFF, AND GRAB ALL THE AVENGERS' SECRET PLANS WE CAN FIND! THEY'LL BE WORTH A FORTUNE!
LET THE BUTLER GO! WE DON'T NEED 'IM ANY MORE!
WE'LL ATTACK THAT COSTUMED CLOWN LIKE A TEAM... JUST LIKE THE AVENGERS THEMSELVES!
MEANWHILE, BACK AT STARK'S MANSION...
I STILL REMEMBER MY WAR YEARS, WHEN I WAS ARMY PRIVATE STEVE ROGERS, DURING WORLD WAR TWO! BUT, AN ETERNITY SEEMS TO HAVE PASSED SINCE THEN!
THEN, SUDDENLY, CAP SEES A PHOTO OF...
BUCKY! MY TEEN-AGE SIDEKICK!
I SHOULD HAVE KNOWN BETTER THAN TO LOOK AT THE ALBUM...TO REVIVE OLD MEMORIES!
IT'S NO GOOD! IT'S OVER NOW! OVER AND DONE WITH! BUCKY IS DEAD... THERE'LL NEVER BE ANOTHER LIKE HIM!
3.

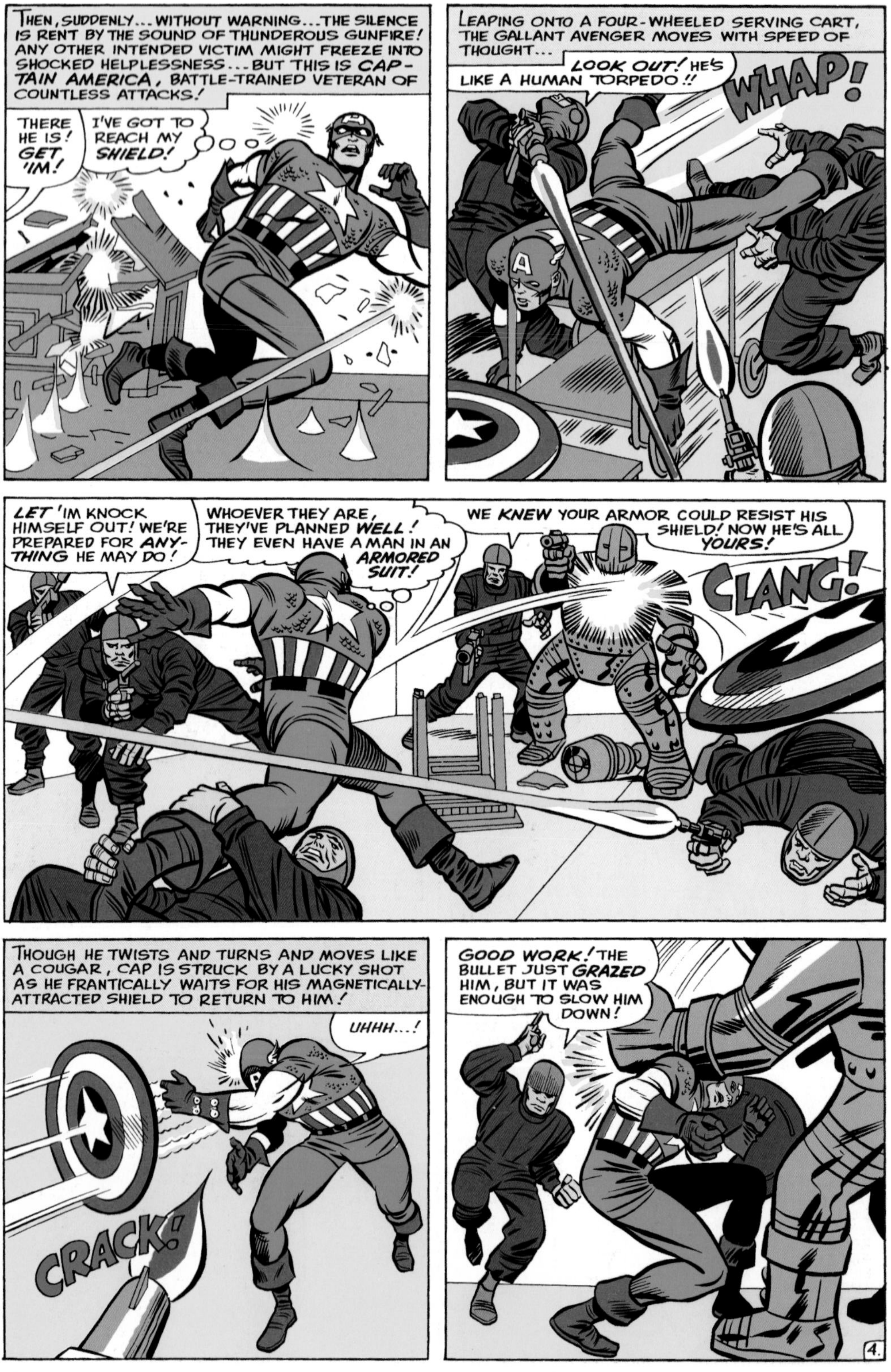
THEN, SUDDENLY... WITHOUT WARNING... THE SILENCE IS RENT BY THE SOUND OF THUNDEROUS GUNFIRE! ANY OTHER INTENDED VICTIM MIGHT FREEZE INTO SHOCKED HELPLESSNESS... BUT THIS IS CAPTAIN AMERICA, BATTLE-TRAINED VETERAN OF COUNTLESS ATTACKS!
THERE HE IS! GET 'IM!
I'VE GOT TO REACH MY SHIELD!
LEAPING ONTO A FOUR-WHEELED SERVING CART, THE GALLANT AVENGER MOVES WITH SPEED OF THOUGHT...
LOOK OUT! HE'S LIKE A HUMAN TORPEDO!!
WHAP!
LET 'IM KNOCK HIMSELF OUT! WE'RE PREPARED FOR ANYTHING HE MAY DO!
WHOEVER THEY ARE, THEY'VE PLANNED WELL! THEY EVEN HAVE A MAN IN AN ARMORED SUIT!
WE KNEW YOUR ARMOR COULD RESIST HIS SHIELD! NOW HE'S ALL YOURS!
CLANG!
THOUGH HE TWISTS AND TURNS AND MOVES LIKE A COUGAR, CAP IS STRUCK BY A LUCKY SHOT AS HE FRANTICALLY WAITS FOR HIS MAGNETICALLY-ATTRACTED SHIELD TO RETURN TO HIM!
UHHH...!
CRACK!
GOOD WORK! THE BULLET JUST GRAZED HIM, BUT IT WAS ENOUGH TO SLOW HIM DOWN!
4.

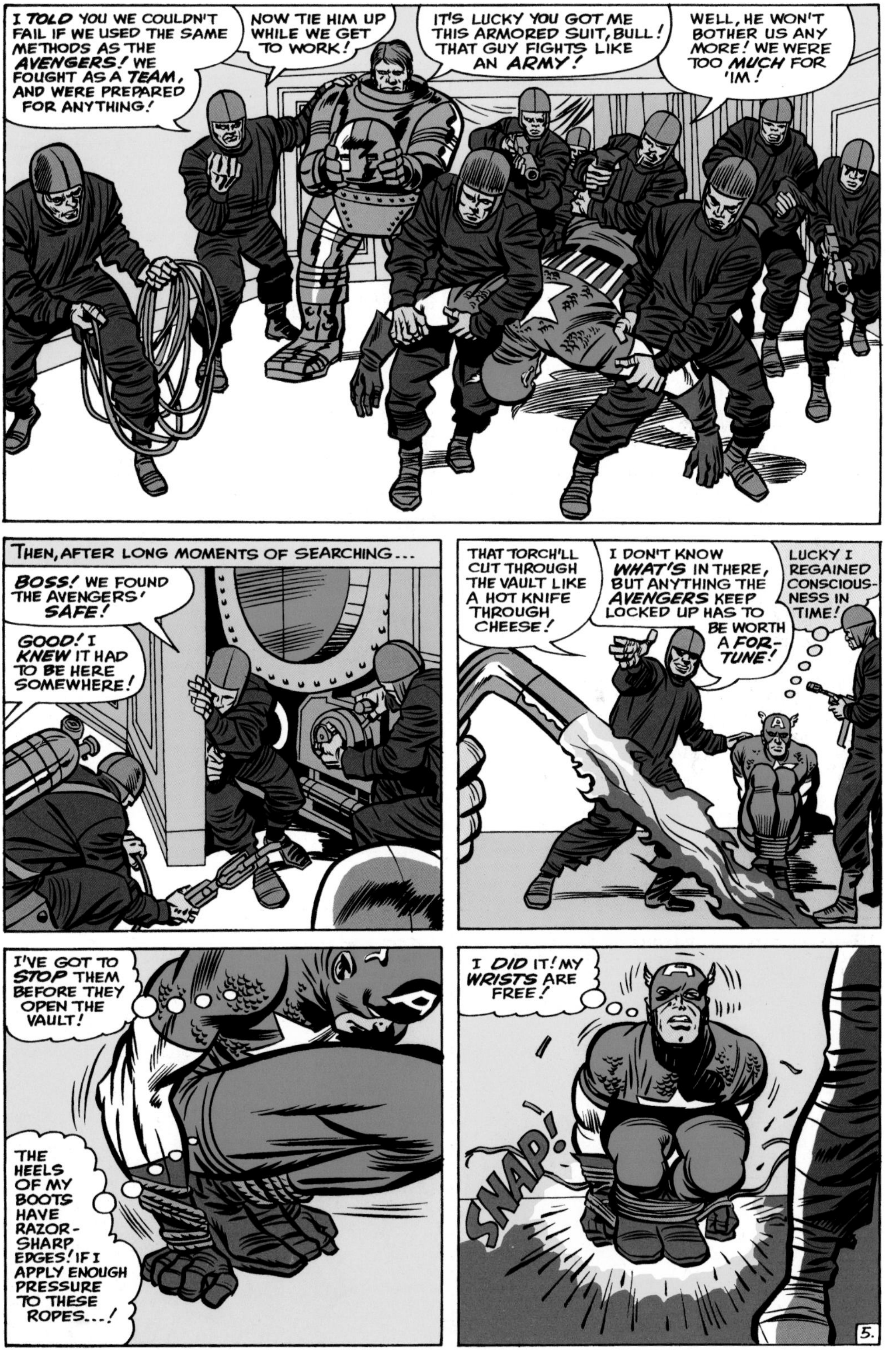

I TOLD YOU WE COULDN'T FAIL IF WE USED THE SAME METHODS AS THE AVENGERS! WE FOUGHT AS A TEAM, AND WERE PREPARED FOR ANYTHING!
NOW TIE HIM UP WHILE WE GET TO WORK!
IT'S LUCKY YOU GOT ME THIS ARMORED SUIT, BULL! THAT GUY FIGHTS LIKE AN ARMY!
WELL, HE WON'T BOTHER US ANY MORE! WE WERE TOO MUCH FOR 'IM!
THEN, AFTER LONG MOMENTS OF SEARCHING...
BOSS! WE FOUND THE AVENGERS' SAFE!
GOOD! I KNEW IT HAD TO BE HERE SOMEWHERE!
THAT TORCH'LL CUT THROUGH THE VAULT LIKE A HOT KNIFE THROUGH CHEESE!
I DON'T KNOW WHAT'S IN THERE, BUT ANYTHING THE AVENGERS KEEP LOCKED UP HAS TO BE WORTH A FOR-TUNE!
LUCKY I REGAINED CONSCIOUS-NESS IN TIME!
I'VE GOT TO STOP THEM BEFORE THEY OPEN THE VAULT!
THE HEELS OF MY BOOTS HAVE RAZOR-SHARP EDGES! IF I APPLY ENOUGH PRESSURE TO THESE ROPES...!
I DID IT! MY WRISTS ARE FREE!
SNAP!
5.

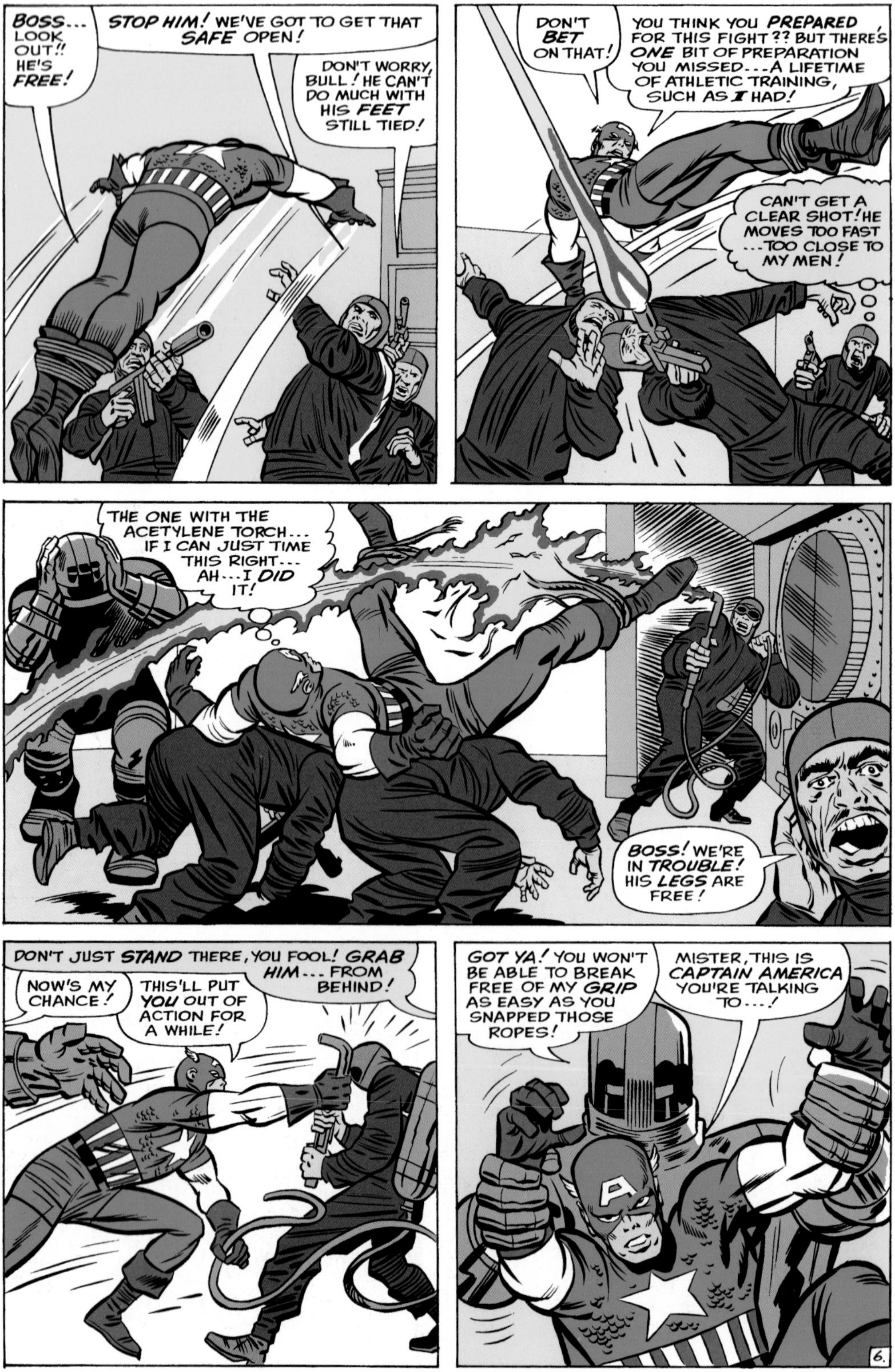
BOSS... LOOK OUT!! HE'S FREE!
STOP HIM! WE'VE GOT TO GET THAT SAFE OPEN!
DON'T WORRY, BULL! HE CAN'T DO MUCH WITH HIS FEET STILL TIED!
DON'T BET ON THAT!
YOU THINK YOU PREPARED FOR THIS FIGHT?? BUT THERE'S ONE BIT OF PREPARATION YOU MISSED...A LIFETIME OF ATHLETIC TRAINING, SUCH AS I HAD!
CAN'T GET A CLEAR SHOT! HE MOVES TOO FAST ...TOO CLOSE TO MY MEN!
THE ONE WITH THE ACETYLENE TORCH... IF I CAN JUST TIME THIS RIGHT... AH...I DID IT!
BOSS! WE'RE IN TROUBLE! HIS LEGS ARE FREE!
DON'T JUST STAND THERE, YOU FOOL! GRAB HIM... FROM BEHIND!
NOW'S MY CHANCE!
THIS'LL PUT YOU OUT OF ACTION FOR A WHILE!
GOT YA! YOU WON'T BE ABLE TO BREAK FREE OF MY GRIP AS EASY AS YOU SNAPPED THOSE ROPES!
MISTER, THIS IS CAPTAIN AMERICA YOU'RE TALKING TO...!
6.

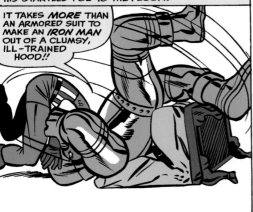

MOVING WITH THE EASY CAT-LIKE GRACE OF A TRAINED JUDO MASTER, CAP SUDDENLY SHIFTS HIS WEIGHT, THROWING HIS HEAVIER, SLOWER OPPONENT OFF BALANCE! AND THEN, APPLYING JUST THE RIGHT AMOUNT OF LEVERAGE, HE HURLS HIS STARTLED FOE TO THE FLOOR!

IT TAKES *MORE* THAN AN ARMORED SUIT TO MAKE AN *IRON MAN* OUT OF A CLUMSY, ILL-TRAINED HOOD!!

THEN, REMOVING THE MOBSTER'S HELMET IN ONE SWIFT MOTION, CAP SENDS HIM TO DREAMLAND WITH ONE WELL-PLACED BLOW!

I'LL HAVE TO CUT THIS SHORT NOW! IT SOUNDS AS THOUGH THE *REST* OF YOUR LITTLE GANG WANTS TO GET IN ON THE ACTION!!

I KNOW HOW *EAGER* YOU ARE, BOYS... BUT JUST GIVE ME A SECOND TO REGAIN MY *SHIELD!* I FEEL KINDA *LOST* WITHOUT IT!

OKAY... THANKS FOR WAITING!

AND NOW, I'LL TRY TO MAKE UP FOR LOST TIME! HOW'S *THIS* FOR A STARTER?!!

PILE ON!! HE CAN'T BEAT US *ALL!*

NO? I'M BEGINNIN' TO WONDER!

BAH! MISSED HIM!

HE SHIFTED HIS WEIGHT AGAIN! HE'S GONNA *TRY* SOMETHIN'...!

7.

13

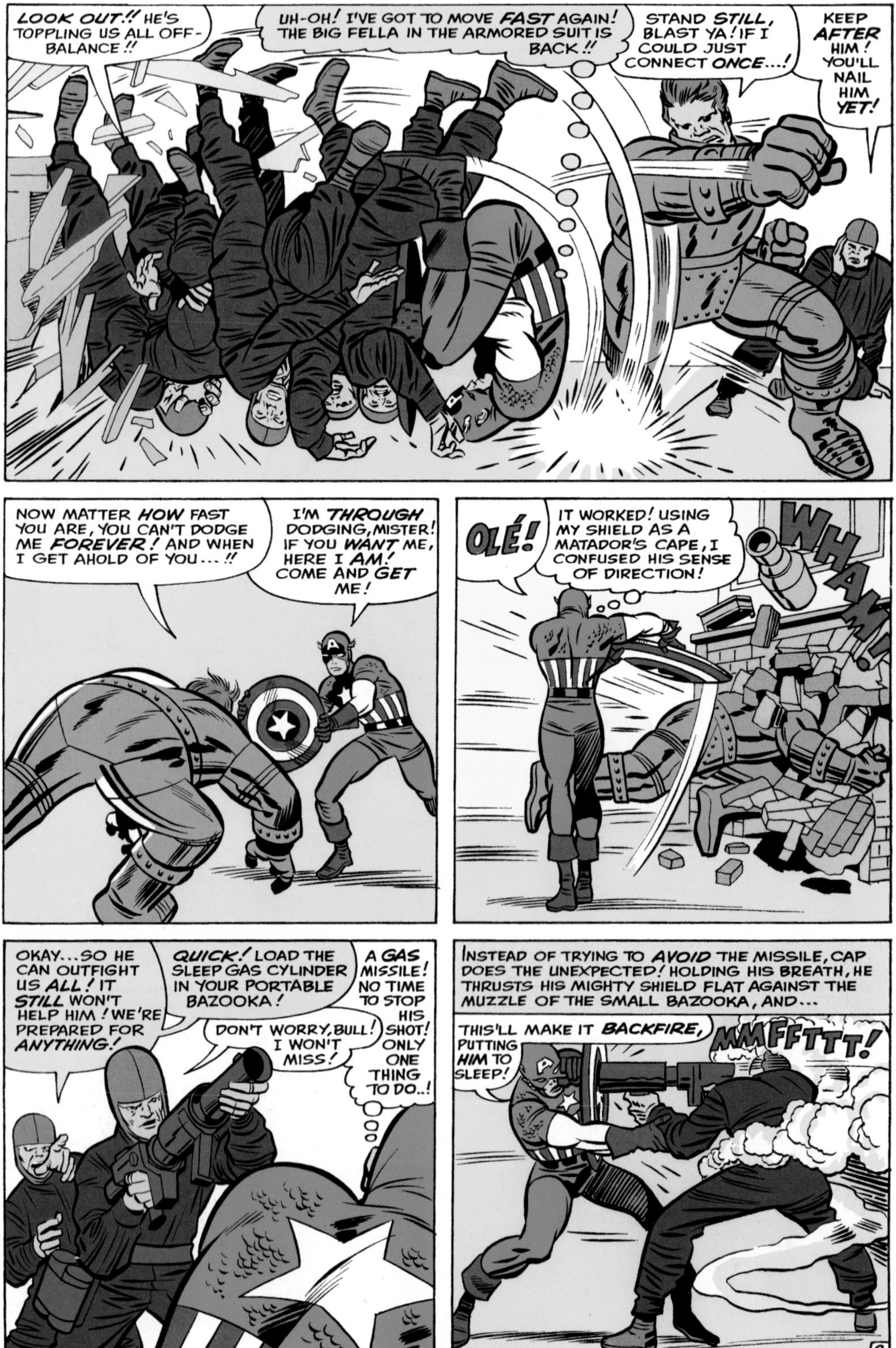
LOOK OUT!! HE'S TOPPLING US ALL OFF-BALANCE!!
UH-OH! I'VE GOT TO MOVE FAST AGAIN! THE BIG FELLA IN THE ARMORED SUIT IS BACK!!
STAND STILL, BLAST YA! IF I COULD JUST CONNECT ONCE...!
KEEP AFTER HIM! YOU'LL NAIL HIM YET!
NOW MATTER HOW FAST YOU ARE, YOU CAN'T DODGE ME FOREVER! AND WHEN I GET AHOLD OF YOU...!!
I'M THROUGH DODGING, MISTER! IF YOU WANT ME, HERE I AM! COME AND GET ME!
OLÉ!
IT WORKED! USING MY SHIELD AS A MATADOR'S CAPE, I CONFUSED HIS SENSE OF DIRECTION!
WHAM!
OKAY...SO HE CAN OUTFIGHT US ALL! IT STILL WON'T HELP HIM! WE'RE PREPARED FOR ANYTHING!
QUICK! LOAD THE SLEEP GAS CYLINDER IN YOUR PORTABLE BAZOOKA!
DON'T WORRY, BULL! I WON'T MISS!
A GAS MISSILE! NO TIME TO STOP HIS SHOT! ONLY ONE THING TO DO..!
INSTEAD OF TRYING TO AVOID THE MISSILE, CAP DOES THE UNEXPECTED! HOLDING HIS BREATH, HE THRUSTS HIS MIGHTY SHIELD FLAT AGAINST THE MUZZLE OF THE SMALL BAZOOKA, AND...
THIS'LL MAKE IT BACKFIRE, PUTTING HIM TO SLEEP!
MMFFTTTT!
8

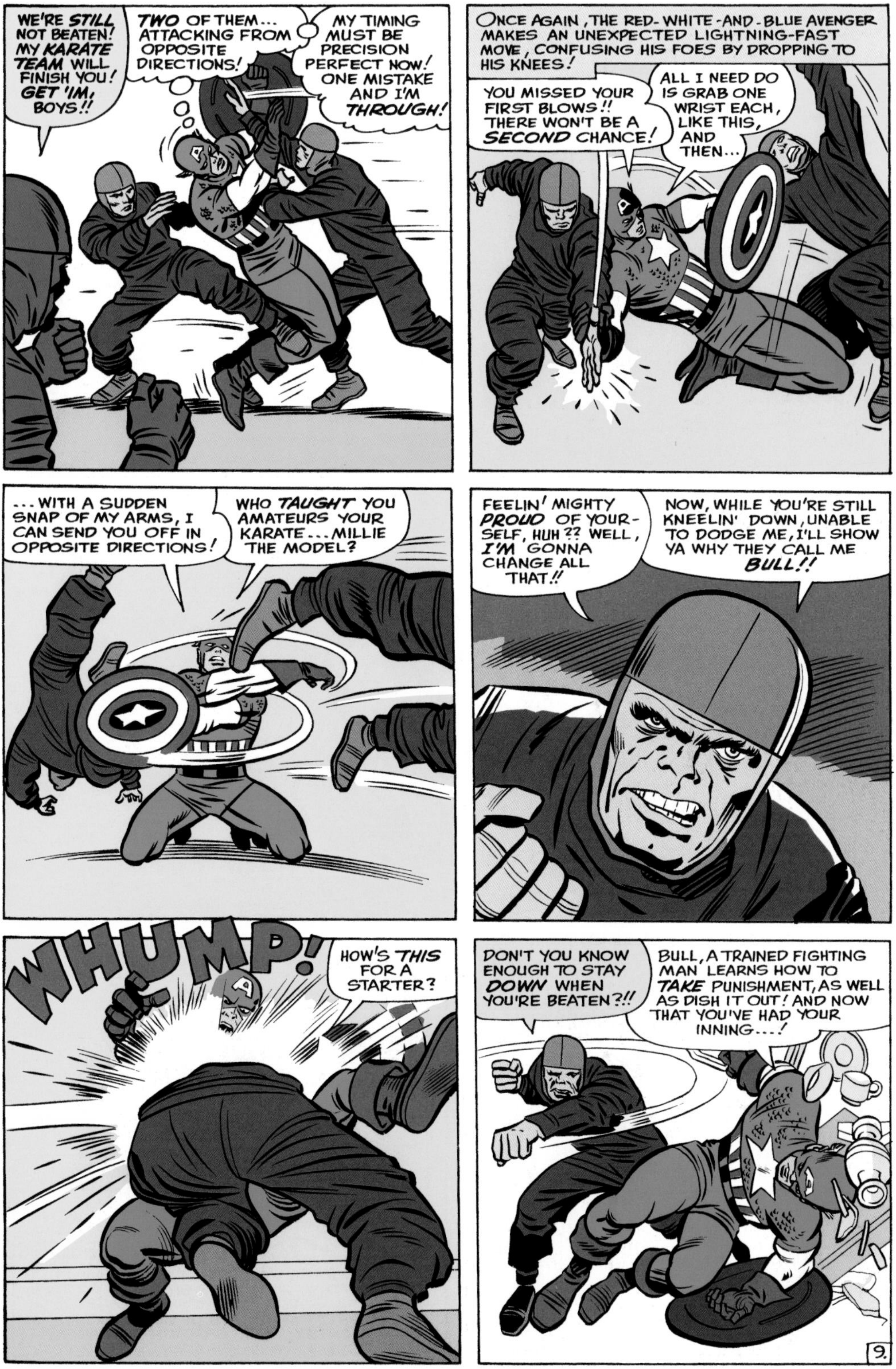
WE'RE STILL NOT BEATEN! MY KARATE TEAM WILL FINISH YOU! GET 'IM, BOYS!!
TWO OF THEM... ATTACKING FROM OPPOSITE DIRECTIONS!
MY TIMING MUST BE PRECISION PERFECT NOW! ONE MISTAKE AND I'M THROUGH!
ONCE AGAIN, THE RED-WHITE-AND-BLUE AVENGER MAKES AN UNEXPECTED LIGHTNING-FAST MOVE, CONFUSING HIS FOES BY DROPPING TO HIS KNEES!
YOU MISSED YOUR FIRST BLOWS!! THERE WON'T BE A SECOND CHANCE!
ALL I NEED DO IS GRAB ONE WRIST EACH, LIKE THIS, AND THEN...
...WITH A SUDDEN SNAP OF MY ARMS, I CAN SEND YOU OFF IN OPPOSITE DIRECTIONS!
WHO TAUGHT YOU AMATEURS YOUR KARATE... MILLIE THE MODEL?
FEELIN' MIGHTY PROUD OF YOURSELF, HUH?? WELL, I'M GONNA CHANGE ALL THAT!!
NOW, WHILE YOU'RE STILL KNEELIN' DOWN, UNABLE TO DODGE ME, I'LL SHOW YA WHY THEY CALL ME BULL!!
WHUMP!
HOW'S THIS FOR A STARTER?
DON'T YOU KNOW ENOUGH TO STAY DOWN WHEN YOU'RE BEATEN?!!
BULL, A TRAINED FIGHTING MAN LEARNS HOW TO TAKE PUNISHMENT, AS WELL AS DISH IT OUT! AND NOW THAT YOU'VE HAD YOUR INNING...!
9.

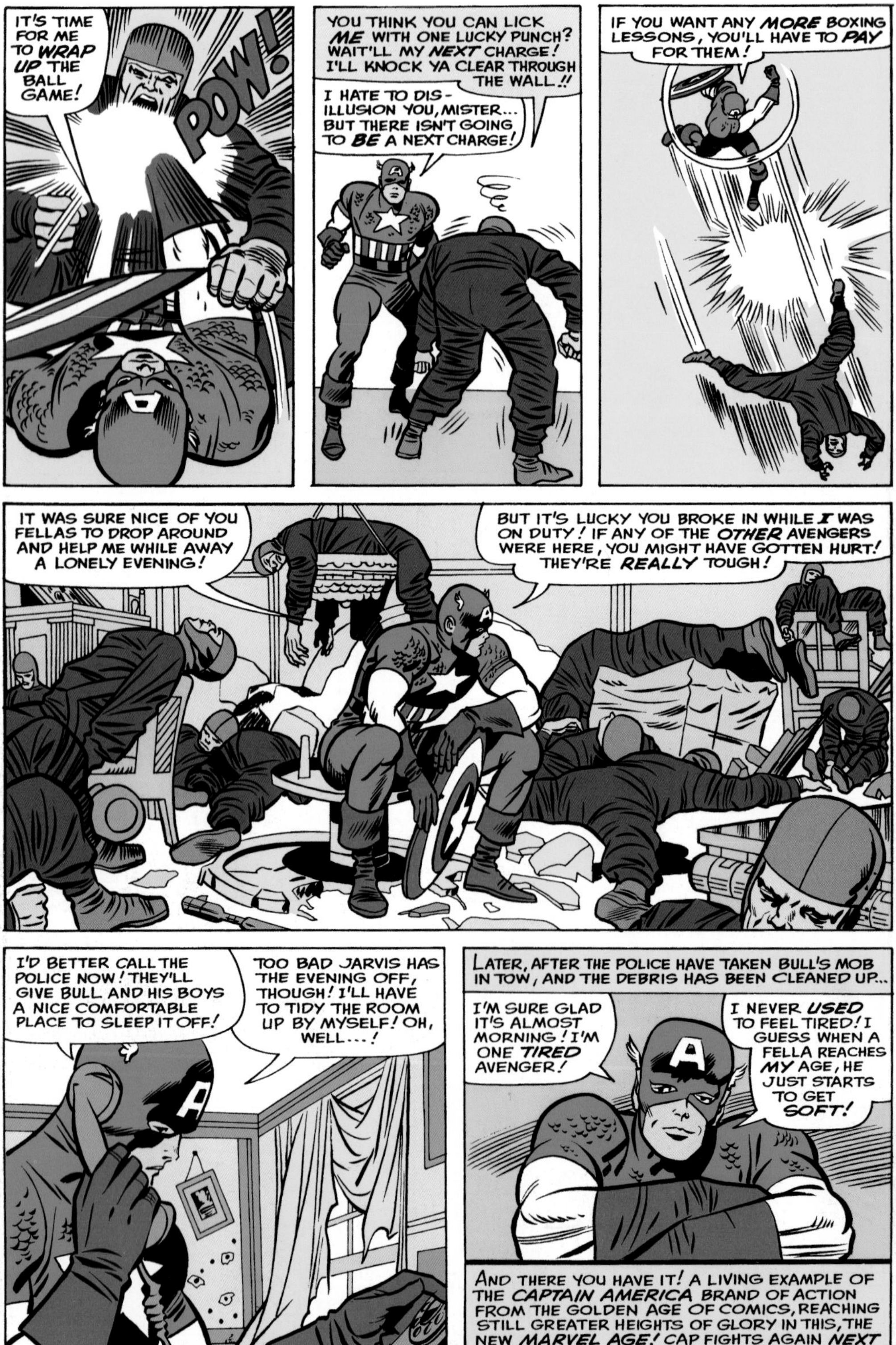

IT'S TIME FOR ME TO WRAP UP THE BALL GAME!
POW!
YOU THINK YOU CAN LICK ME WITH ONE LUCKY PUNCH? WAIT'LL MY NEXT CHARGE! I'LL KNOCK YA CLEAR THROUGH THE WALL!!
I HATE TO DIS-ILLUSION YOU, MISTER... BUT THERE ISN'T GOING TO BE A NEXT CHARGE!
IF YOU WANT ANY MORE BOXING LESSONS, YOU'LL HAVE TO PAY FOR THEM!
IT WAS SURE NICE OF YOU FELLAS TO DROP AROUND AND HELP ME WHILE AWAY A LONELY EVENING!
BUT IT'S LUCKY YOU BROKE IN WHILE I WAS ON DUTY! IF ANY OF THE OTHER AVENGERS WERE HERE, YOU MIGHT HAVE GOTTEN HURT! THEY'RE REALLY TOUGH!
I'D BETTER CALL THE POLICE NOW! THEY'LL GIVE BULL AND HIS BOYS A NICE COMFORTABLE PLACE TO SLEEP IT OFF!
TOO BAD JARVIS HAS THE EVENING OFF, THOUGH! I'LL HAVE TO TIDY THE ROOM UP BY MYSELF! OH, WELL...!
10.
LATER, AFTER THE POLICE HAVE TAKEN BULL'S MOB IN TOW, AND THE DEBRIS HAS BEEN CLEANED UP...
I'M SURE GLAD IT'S ALMOST MORNING! I'M ONE TIRED AVENGER!
I NEVER USED TO FEEL TIRED! I GUESS WHEN A FELLA REACHES MY AGE, HE JUST STARTS TO GET SOFT!
AND THERE YOU HAVE IT! A LIVING EXAMPLE OF THE CAPTAIN AMERICA BRAND OF ACTION FROM THE GOLDEN AGE OF COMICS, REACHING STILL GREATER HEIGHTS OF GLORY IN THIS, THE NEW MARVEL AGE! CAP FIGHTS AGAIN NEXT ISH! BE HERE...WE'LL BE LOOKING FOR YOU!!

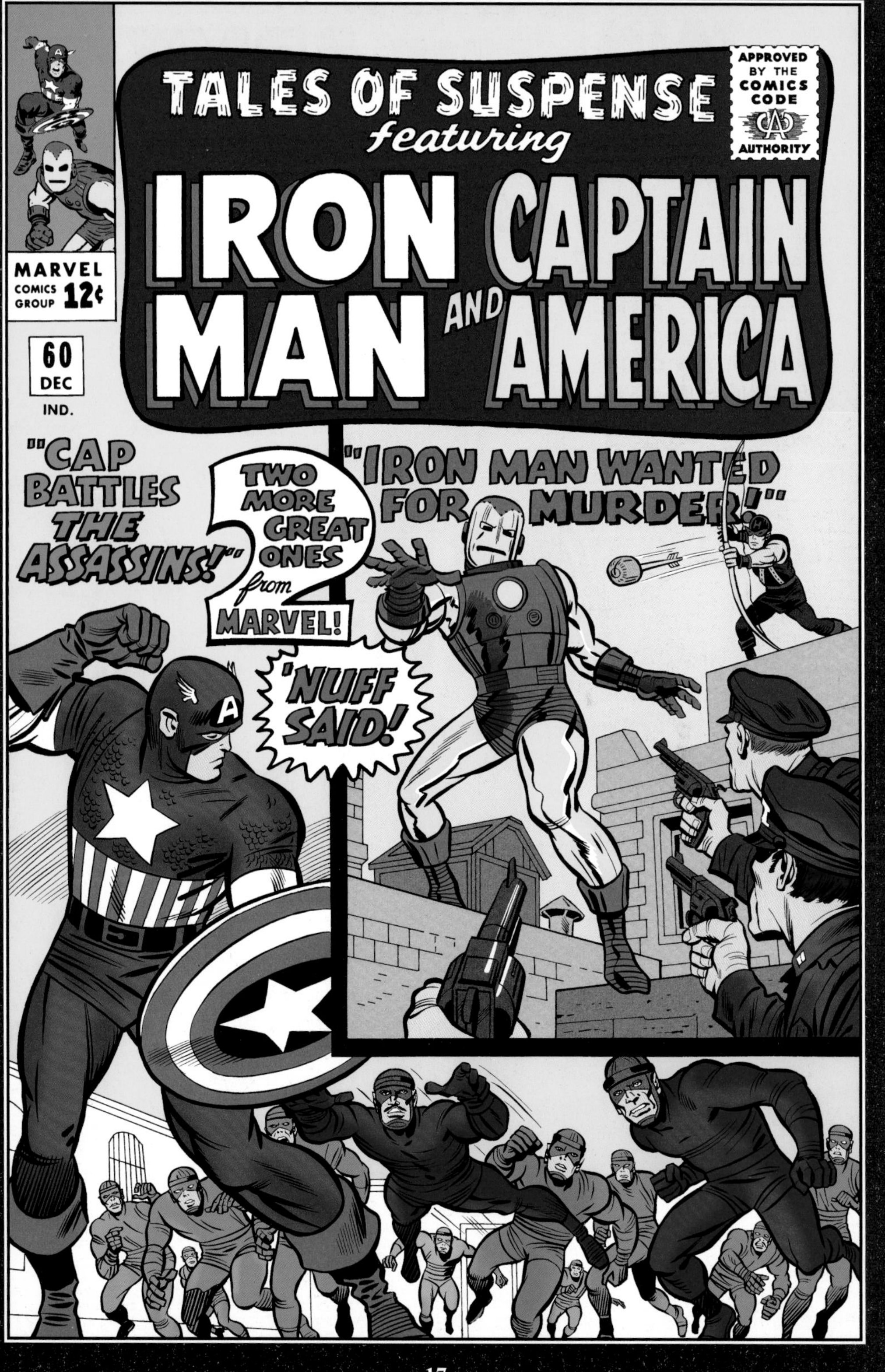
TALES OF SUSPENSE
featuring
IRON MAN AND CAPTAIN AMERICA
APPROVED BY THE COMICS CODE AUTHORITY
MARVEL COMICS GROUP 12¢
60 DEC
IND.
"CAP BATTLES THE ASSASSINS!"
TWO MORE GREAT ONES from MARVEL!
"IRON MAN WANTED FOR MURDER!"
'NUFF SAID!

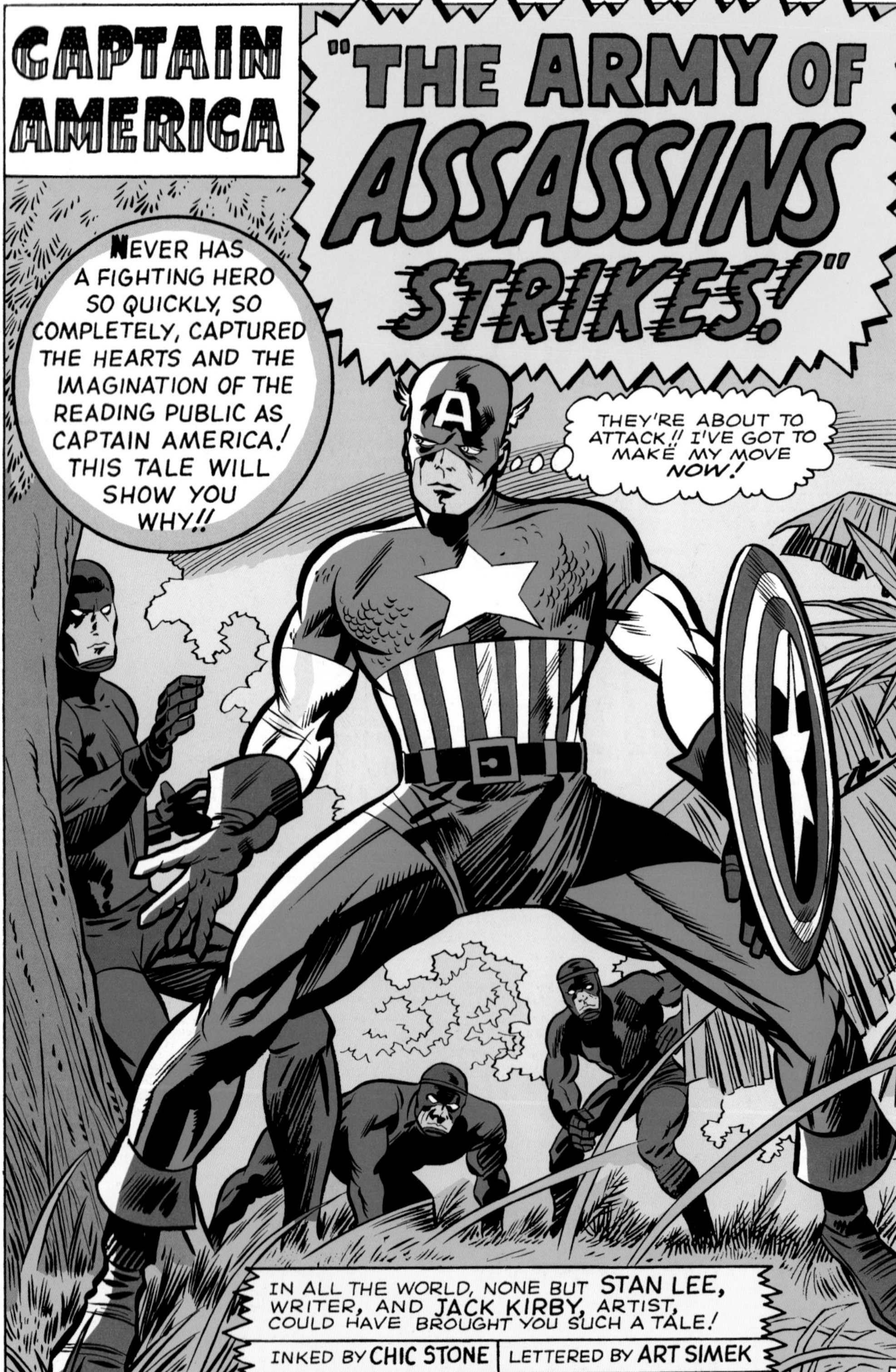
CAPTAIN AMERICA
"THE ARMY OF ASSASSINS STRIKES!"
NEVER HAS A FIGHTING HERO SO QUICKLY, SO COMPLETELY, CAPTURED THE HEARTS AND THE IMAGINATION OF THE READING PUBLIC AS CAPTAIN AMERICA! THIS TALE WILL SHOW YOU WHY!!
THEY'RE ABOUT TO ATTACK!! I'VE GOT TO MAKE MY MOVE NOW!
IN ALL THE WORLD, NONE BUT STAN LEE, WRITER, AND JACK KIRBY, ARTIST, COULD HAVE BROUGHT YOU SUCH A TALE!
INKED BY CHIC STONE
LETTERED BY ART SIMEK
X-784
1

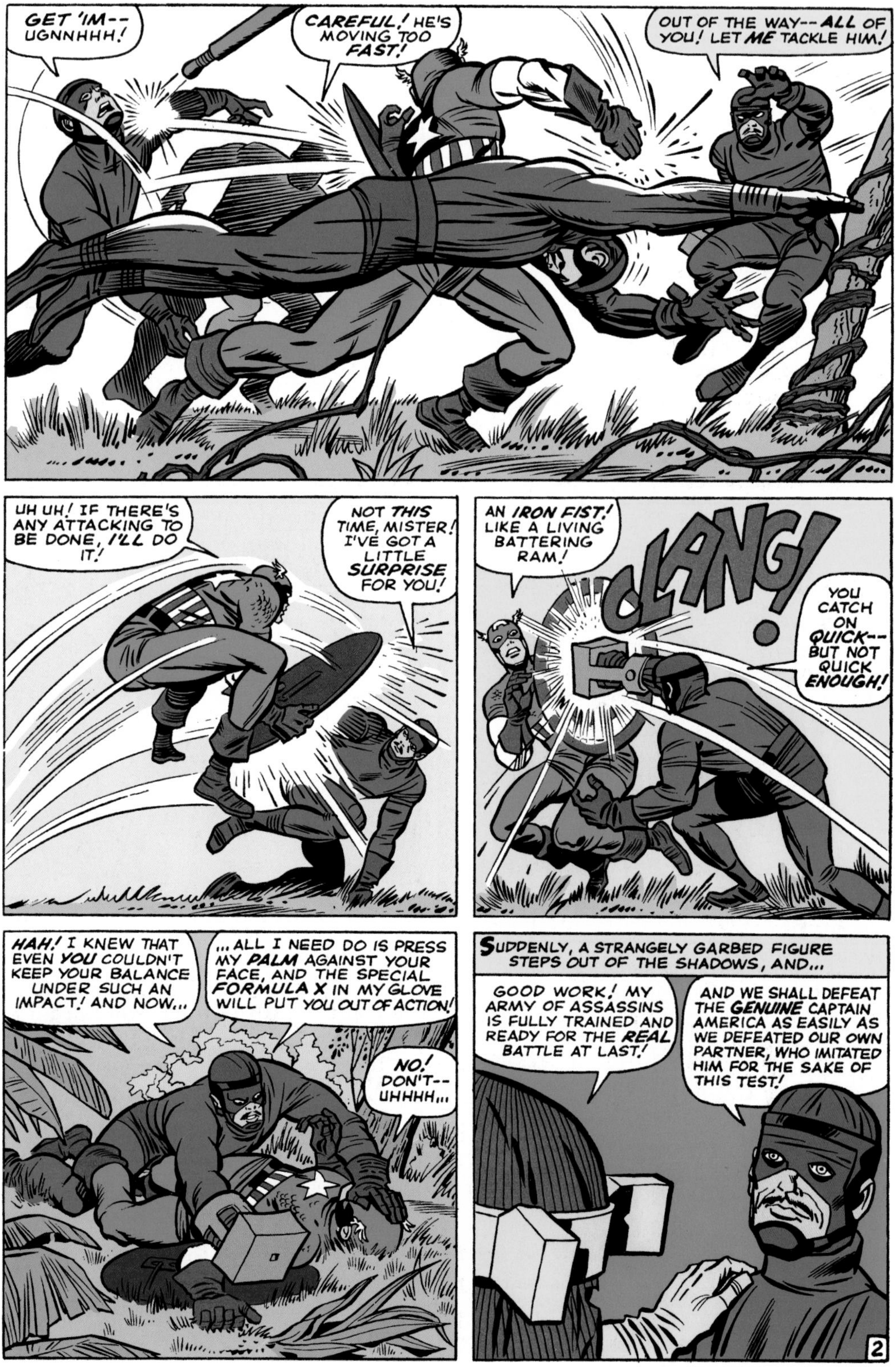
GET 'IM--
UGNNHHH!
CAREFUL! HE'S MOVING TOO FAST!
OUT OF THE WAY--ALL OF YOU! LET ME TACKLE HIM!
UH UH! IF THERE'S ANY ATTACKING TO BE DONE, I'LL DO IT!
NOT THIS TIME, MISTER! I'VE GOT A LITTLE SURPRISE FOR YOU!
AN IRON FIST! LIKE A LIVING BATTERING RAM!
CLANG!
YOU CATCH ON QUICK--BUT NOT QUICK ENOUGH!
HAH! I KNEW THAT EVEN YOU COULDN'T KEEP YOUR BALANCE UNDER SUCH AN IMPACT! AND NOW...
...ALL I NEED DO IS PRESS MY PALM AGAINST YOUR FACE, AND THE SPECIAL FORMULA X IN MY GLOVE WILL PUT YOU OUT OF ACTION!
NO! DON'T--UHHHH...
SUDDENLY, A STRANGELY GARBED FIGURE STEPS OUT OF THE SHADOWS, AND...
GOOD WORK! MY ARMY OF ASSASSINS IS FULLY TRAINED AND READY FOR THE REAL BATTLE AT LAST!
AND WE SHALL DEFEAT THE GENUINE CAPTAIN AMERICA AS EASILY AS WE DEFEATED OUR OWN PARTNER, WHO IMITATED HIM FOR THE SAKE OF THIS TEST!
2

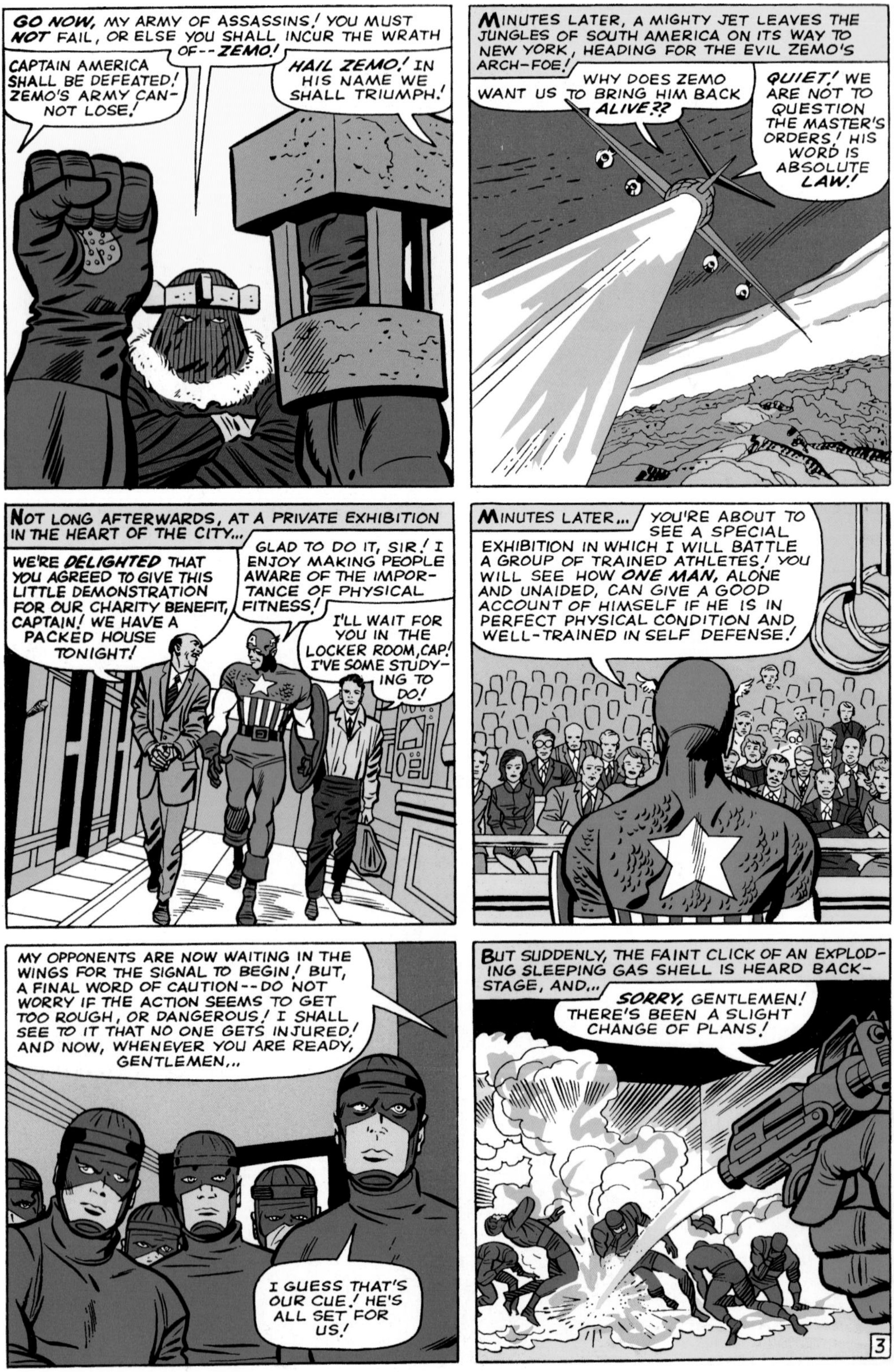
GO NOW, MY ARMY OF ASSASSINS! YOU MUST NOT FAIL, OR ELSE YOU SHALL INCUR THE WRATH OF--ZEMO!
CAPTAIN AMERICA SHALL BE DEFEATED! ZEMO'S ARMY CAN-NOT LOSE!
HAIL ZEMO! IN HIS NAME WE SHALL TRIUMPH!
MINUTES LATER, A MIGHTY JET LEAVES THE JUNGLES OF SOUTH AMERICA ON ITS WAY TO NEW YORK, HEADING FOR THE EVIL ZEMO'S ARCH-FOE!
WHY DOES ZEMO WANT US TO BRING HIM BACK ALIVE??
QUIET! WE ARE NOT TO QUESTION THE MASTER'S ORDERS! HIS WORD IS ABSOLUTE LAW!
NOT LONG AFTERWARDS, AT A PRIVATE EXHIBITION IN THE HEART OF THE CITY...
WE'RE DELIGHTED THAT YOU AGREED TO GIVE THIS LITTLE DEMONSTRATION FOR OUR CHARITY BENEFIT, CAPTAIN! WE HAVE A PACKED HOUSE TONIGHT!
GLAD TO DO IT, SIR! I ENJOY MAKING PEOPLE AWARE OF THE IMPOR-TANCE OF PHYSICAL FITNESS!
I'LL WAIT FOR YOU IN THE LOCKER ROOM, CAP! I'VE SOME STUDY-ING TO DO!
MINUTES LATER...
YOU'RE ABOUT TO SEE A SPECIAL EXHIBITION IN WHICH I WILL BATTLE A GROUP OF TRAINED ATHLETES! YOU WILL SEE HOW ONE MAN, ALONE AND UNAIDED, CAN GIVE A GOOD ACCOUNT OF HIMSELF IF HE IS IN PERFECT PHYSICAL CONDITION AND WELL-TRAINED IN SELF DEFENSE!
MY OPPONENTS ARE NOW WAITING IN THE WINGS FOR THE SIGNAL TO BEGIN! BUT, A FINAL WORD OF CAUTION--DO NOT WORRY IF THE ACTION SEEMS TO GET TOO ROUGH, OR DANGEROUS! I SHALL SEE TO IT THAT NO ONE GETS INJURED! AND NOW, WHENEVER YOU ARE READY, GENTLEMEN...
I GUESS THAT'S OUR CUE! HE'S ALL SET FOR US!
BUT SUDDENLY, THE FAINT CLICK OF AN EXPLOD-ING SLEEPING GAS SHELL IS HEARD BACK-STAGE, AND...
SORRY, GENTLEMEN! THERE'S BEEN A SLIGHT CHANGE OF PLANS!
3

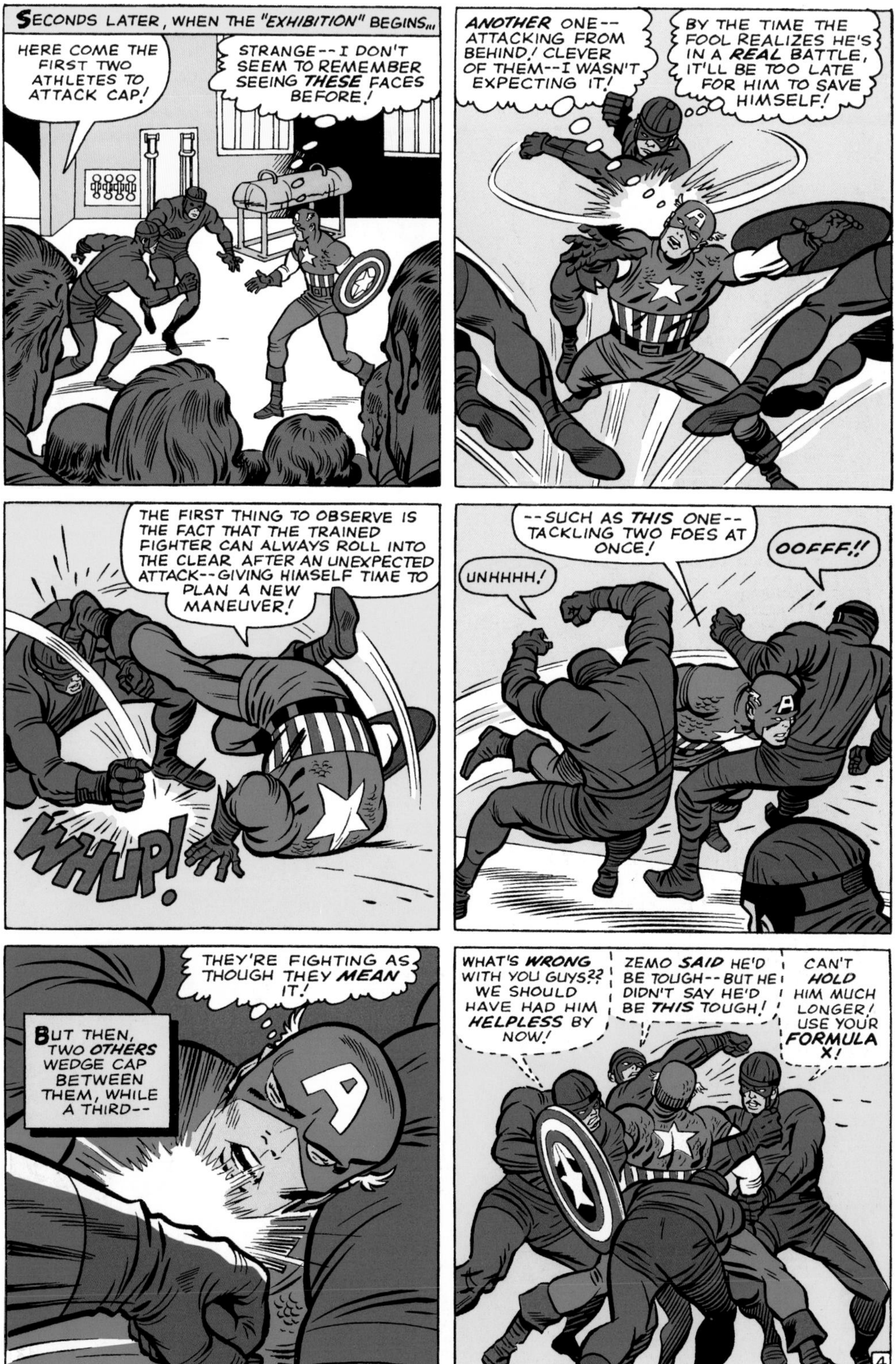
SECONDS LATER, WHEN THE "EXHIBITION" BEGINS...
HERE COME THE FIRST TWO ATHLETES TO ATTACK CAP!
STRANGE--I DON'T SEEM TO REMEMBER SEEING THESE FACES BEFORE!
ANOTHER ONE--ATTACKING FROM BEHIND! CLEVER OF THEM--I WASN'T EXPECTING IT!
BY THE TIME THE FOOL REALIZES HE'S IN A REAL BATTLE, IT'LL BE TOO LATE FOR HIM TO SAVE HIMSELF!
THE FIRST THING TO OBSERVE IS THE FACT THAT THE TRAINED FIGHTER CAN ALWAYS ROLL INTO THE CLEAR AFTER AN UNEXPECTED ATTACK--GIVING HIMSELF TIME TO PLAN A NEW MANEUVER!
WHUP!
--SUCH AS THIS ONE--TACKLING TWO FOES AT ONCE!
UNHHHH!
OOFFF!!
THEY'RE FIGHTING AS THOUGH THEY MEAN IT!
BUT THEN, TWO OTHERS WEDGE CAP BETWEEN THEM, WHILE A THIRD--
WHAT'S WRONG WITH YOU GUYS?? WE SHOULD HAVE HAD HIM HELPLESS BY NOW!
ZEMO SAID HE'D BE TOUGH--BUT HE DIDN'T SAY HE'D BE THIS TOUGH!
CAN'T HOLD HIM MUCH LONGER! USE YOUR FORMULA X!
4

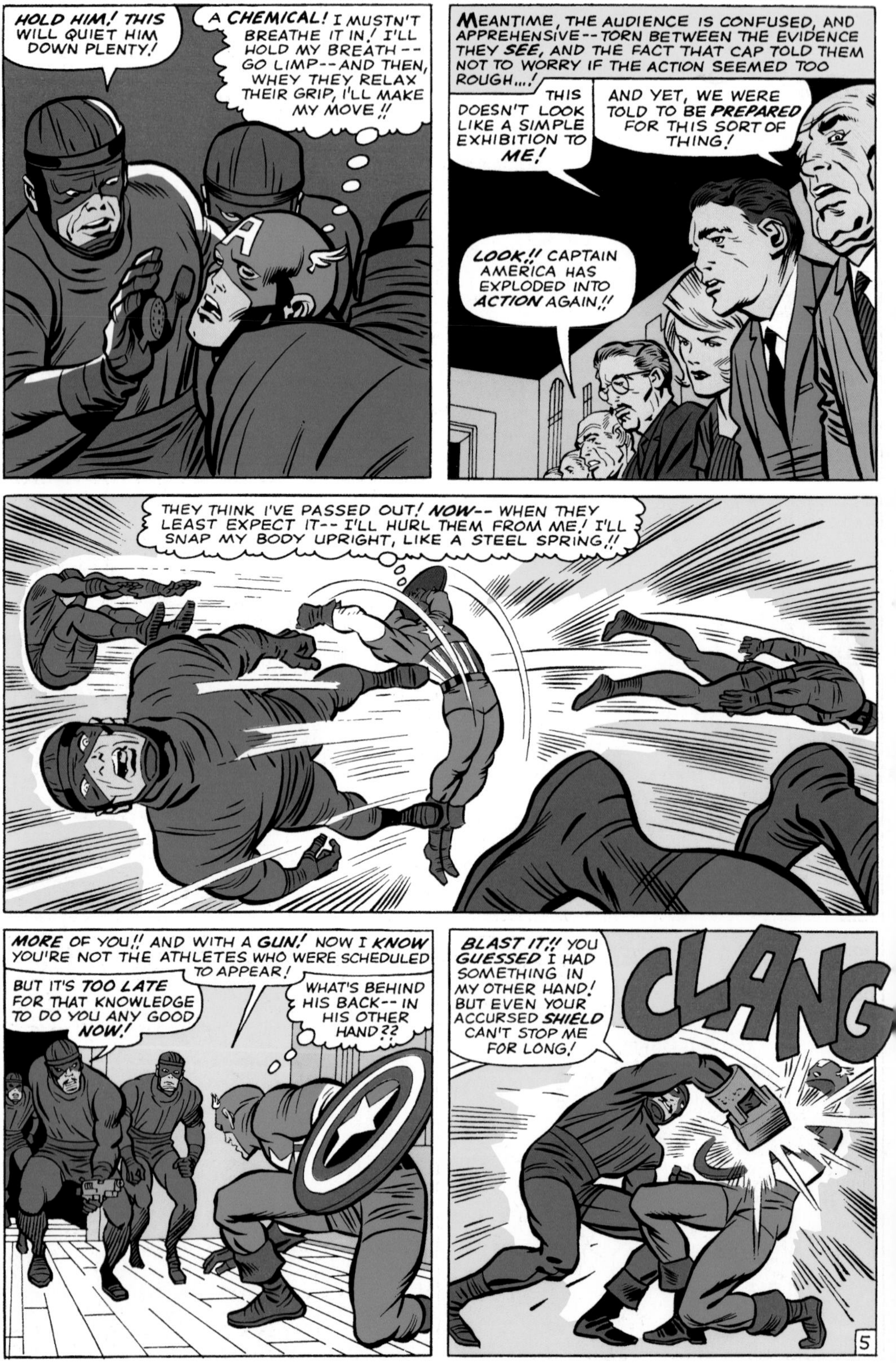

HOLD HIM! THIS WILL QUIET HIM DOWN PLENTY!
A CHEMICAL! I MUSTN'T BREATHE IT IN! I'LL HOLD MY BREATH -- GO LIMP -- AND THEN, WHEY THEY RELAX THEIR GRIP, I'LL MAKE MY MOVE!!
MEANTIME, THE AUDIENCE IS CONFUSED, AND APPREHENSIVE -- TORN BETWEEN THE EVIDENCE THEY SEE, AND THE FACT THAT CAP TOLD THEM NOT TO WORRY IF THE ACTION SEEMED TOO ROUGH...!
THIS DOESN'T LOOK LIKE A SIMPLE EXHIBITION TO ME!
AND YET, WE WERE TOLD TO BE PREPARED FOR THIS SORT OF THING!
LOOK!! CAPTAIN AMERICA HAS EXPLODED INTO ACTION AGAIN!!
THEY THINK I'VE PASSED OUT! NOW -- WHEN THEY LEAST EXPECT IT -- I'LL HURL THEM FROM ME! I'LL SNAP MY BODY UPRIGHT, LIKE A STEEL SPRING!!
MORE OF YOU!! AND WITH A GUN! NOW I KNOW YOU'RE NOT THE ATHLETES WHO WERE SCHEDULED TO APPEAR!
BUT IT'S TOO LATE FOR THAT KNOWLEDGE TO DO YOU ANY GOOD NOW!
WHAT'S BEHIND HIS BACK -- IN HIS OTHER HAND??
BLAST IT!! YOU GUESSED I HAD SOMETHING IN MY OTHER HAND! BUT EVEN YOUR ACCURSED SHIELD CAN'T STOP ME FOR LONG!
CLANG
5

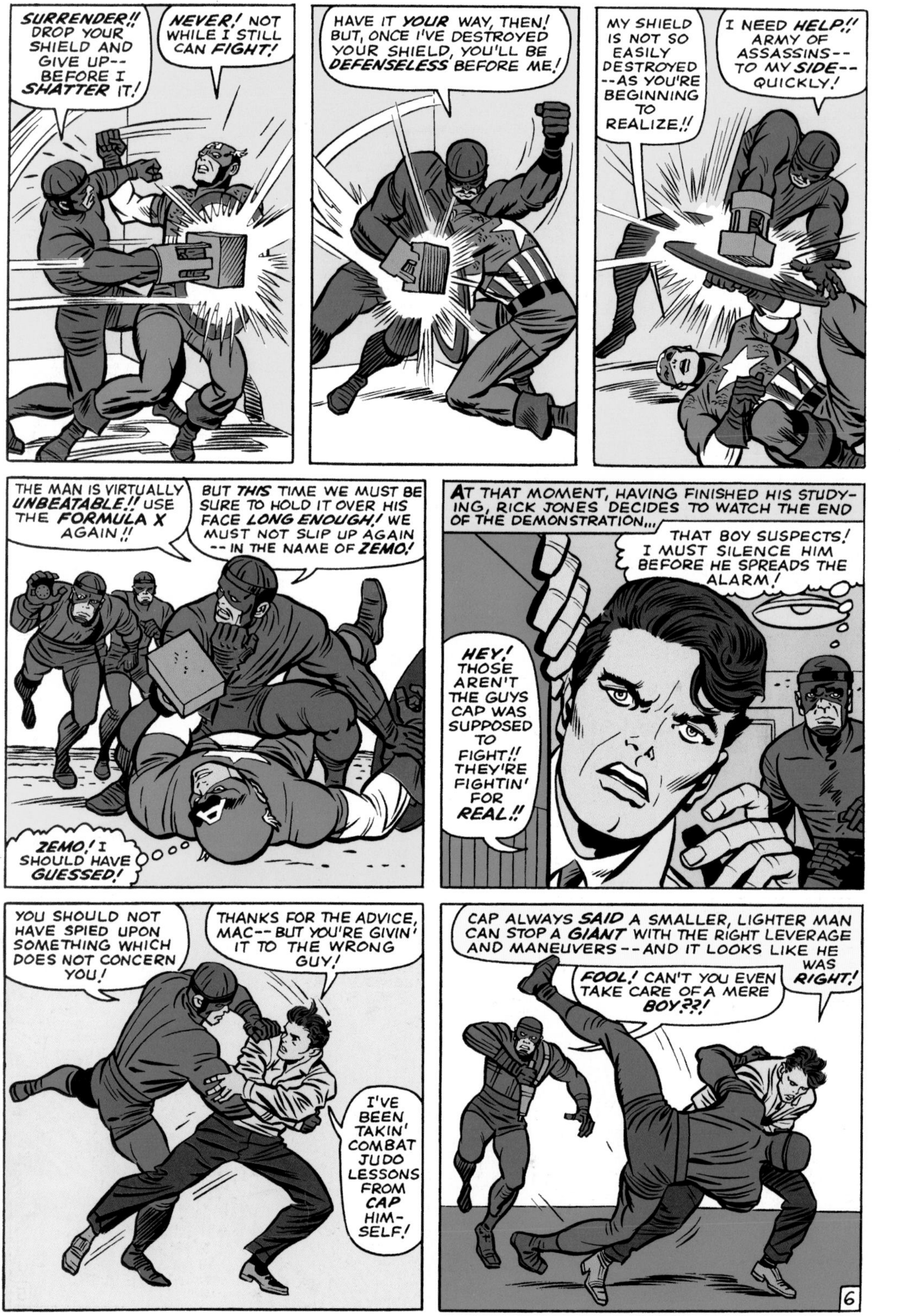
SURRENDER!! DROP YOUR SHIELD AND GIVE UP-- BEFORE I SHATTER IT!
NEVER! NOT WHILE I STILL CAN FIGHT!
HAVE IT YOUR WAY, THEN! BUT, ONCE I'VE DESTROYED YOUR SHIELD, YOU'LL BE DEFENSELESS BEFORE ME!
MY SHIELD IS NOT SO EASILY DESTROYED --AS YOU'RE BEGINNING TO REALIZE!!
I NEED HELP!! ARMY OF ASSASSINS-- TO MY SIDE-- QUICKLY!
THE MAN IS VIRTUALLY UNBEATABLE!! USE THE FORMULA X AGAIN!!
BUT THIS TIME WE MUST BE SURE TO HOLD IT OVER HIS FACE LONG ENOUGH! WE MUST NOT SLIP UP AGAIN -- IN THE NAME OF ZEMO!
ZEMO! I SHOULD HAVE GUESSED!
AT THAT MOMENT, HAVING FINISHED HIS STUDYING, RICK JONES DECIDES TO WATCH THE END OF THE DEMONSTRATION...
THAT BOY SUSPECTS! I MUST SILENCE HIM BEFORE HE SPREADS THE ALARM!
HEY! THOSE AREN'T THE GUYS CAP WAS SUPPOSED TO FIGHT!! THEY'RE FIGHTIN' FOR REAL!!
YOU SHOULD NOT HAVE SPIED UPON SOMETHING WHICH DOES NOT CONCERN YOU!
THANKS FOR THE ADVICE, MAC-- BUT YOU'RE GIVIN' IT TO THE WRONG GUY!
I'VE BEEN TAKIN' COMBAT JUDO LESSONS FROM CAP HIMSELF!
CAP ALWAYS SAID A SMALLER, LIGHTER MAN CAN STOP A GIANT WITH THE RIGHT LEVERAGE AND MANEUVERS--AND IT LOOKS LIKE HE WAS RIGHT!
FOOL! CAN'T YOU EVEN TAKE CARE OF A MERE BOY??!
6

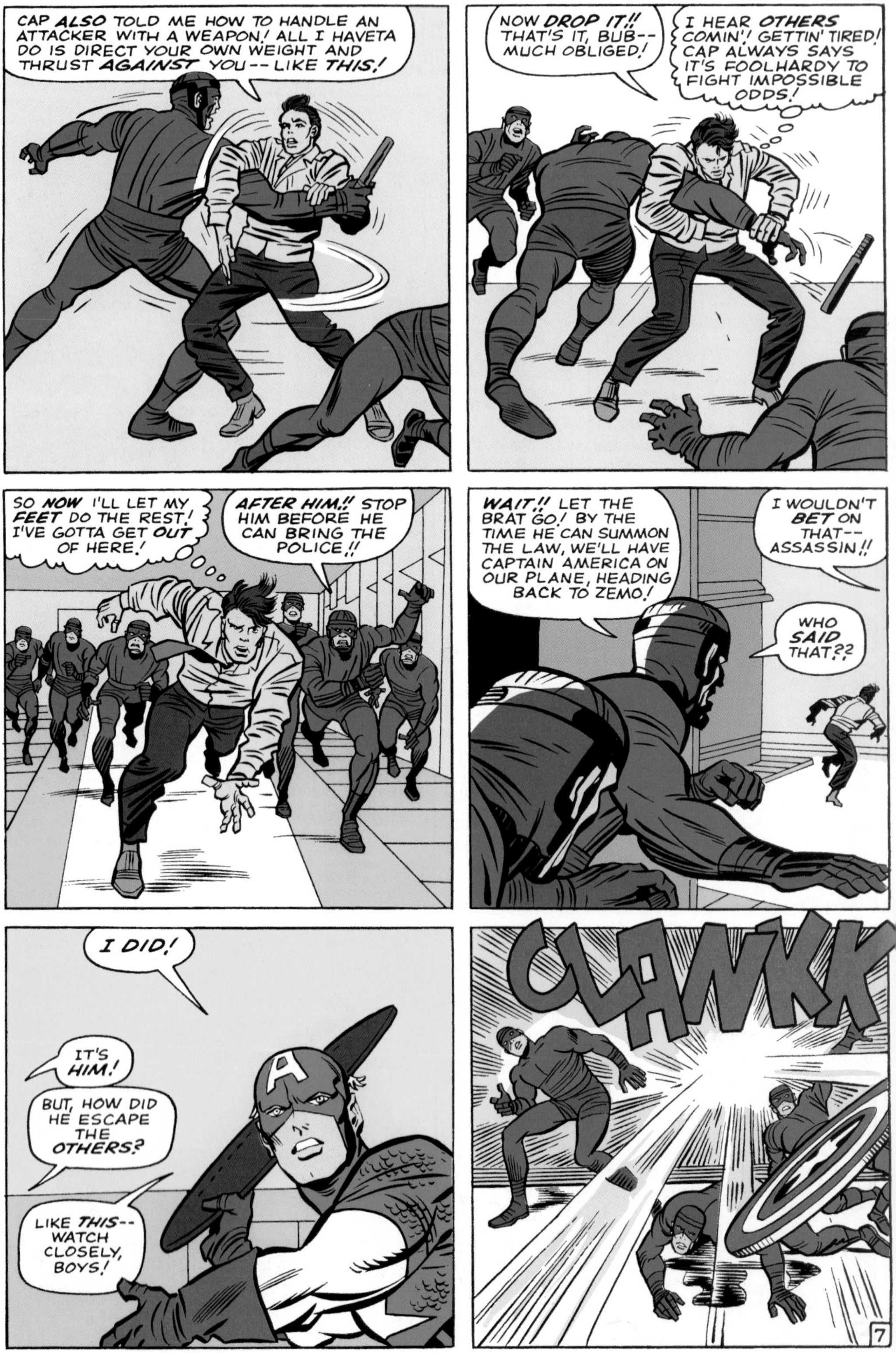
CAP ALSO TOLD ME HOW TO HANDLE AN ATTACKER WITH A WEAPON! ALL I HAVETA DO IS DIRECT YOUR OWN WEIGHT AND THRUST AGAINST YOU--LIKE THIS!
NOW DROP IT!! THAT'S IT, BUB--MUCH OBLIGED!
I HEAR OTHERS COMIN'! GETTIN' TIRED! CAP ALWAYS SAYS IT'S FOOLHARDY TO FIGHT IMPOSSIBLE ODDS!
SO NOW I'LL LET MY FEET DO THE REST! I'VE GOTTA GET OUT OF HERE!
AFTER HIM!! STOP HIM BEFORE HE CAN BRING THE POLICE!!
WAIT!! LET THE BRAT GO! BY THE TIME HE CAN SUMMON THE LAW, WE'LL HAVE CAPTAIN AMERICA ON OUR PLANE, HEADING BACK TO ZEMO!
I WOULDN'T BET ON THAT--ASSASSIN!!
WHO SAID THAT??
I DID!
IT'S HIM!
BUT, HOW DID HE ESCAPE THE OTHERS?
LIKE THIS--WATCH CLOSELY, BOYS!
CLANKK
7

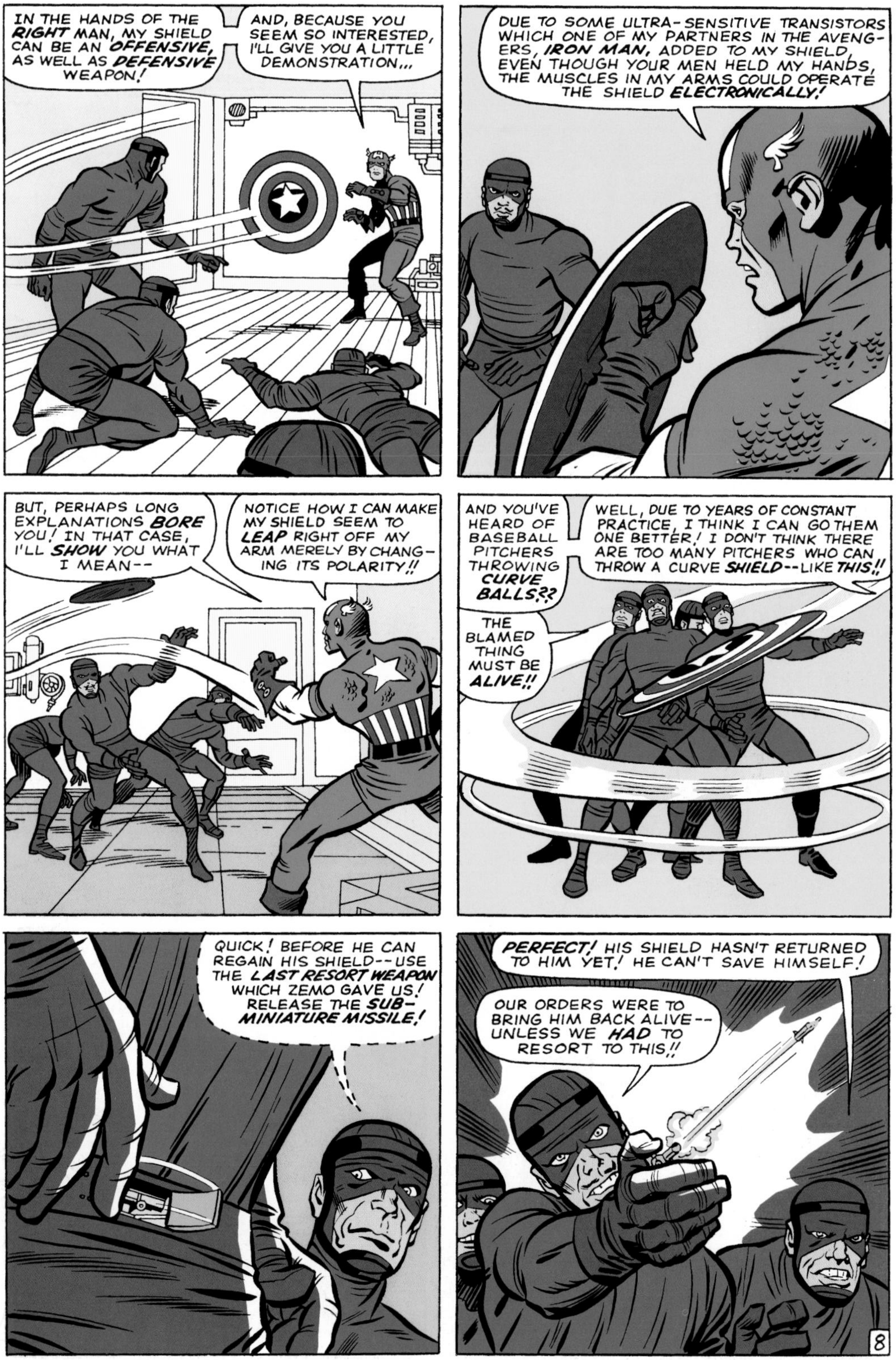
IN THE HANDS OF THE RIGHT MAN, MY SHIELD CAN BE AN OFFENSIVE, AS WELL AS DEFENSIVE WEAPON!
AND, BECAUSE YOU SEEM SO INTERESTED, I'LL GIVE YOU A LITTLE DEMONSTRATION...
DUE TO SOME ULTRA-SENSITIVE TRANSISTORS WHICH ONE OF MY PARTNERS IN THE AVENGERS, IRON MAN, ADDED TO MY SHIELD, EVEN THOUGH YOUR MEN HELD MY HANDS, THE MUSCLES IN MY ARMS COULD OPERATE THE SHIELD ELECTRONICALLY!
BUT, PERHAPS LONG EXPLANATIONS BORE YOU! IN THAT CASE, I'LL SHOW YOU WHAT I MEAN--
NOTICE HOW I CAN MAKE MY SHIELD SEEM TO LEAP RIGHT OFF MY ARM MERELY BY CHANGING ITS POLARITY!!
AND YOU'VE HEARD OF BASEBALL PITCHERS THROWING CURVE BALLS???
WELL, DUE TO YEARS OF CONSTANT PRACTICE, I THINK I CAN GO THEM ONE BETTER! I DON'T THINK THERE ARE TOO MANY PITCHERS WHO CAN THROW A CURVE SHIELD--LIKE THIS!!
THE BLAMED THING MUST BE ALIVE!!
QUICK! BEFORE HE CAN REGAIN HIS SHIELD--USE THE LAST RESORT WEAPON WHICH ZEMO GAVE US! RELEASE THE SUB-MINIATURE MISSILE!
PERFECT! HIS SHIELD HASN'T RETURNED TO HIM YET! HE CAN'T SAVE HIMSELF!
OUR ORDERS WERE TO BRING HIM BACK ALIVE--UNLESS WE HAD TO RESORT TO THIS!!
8

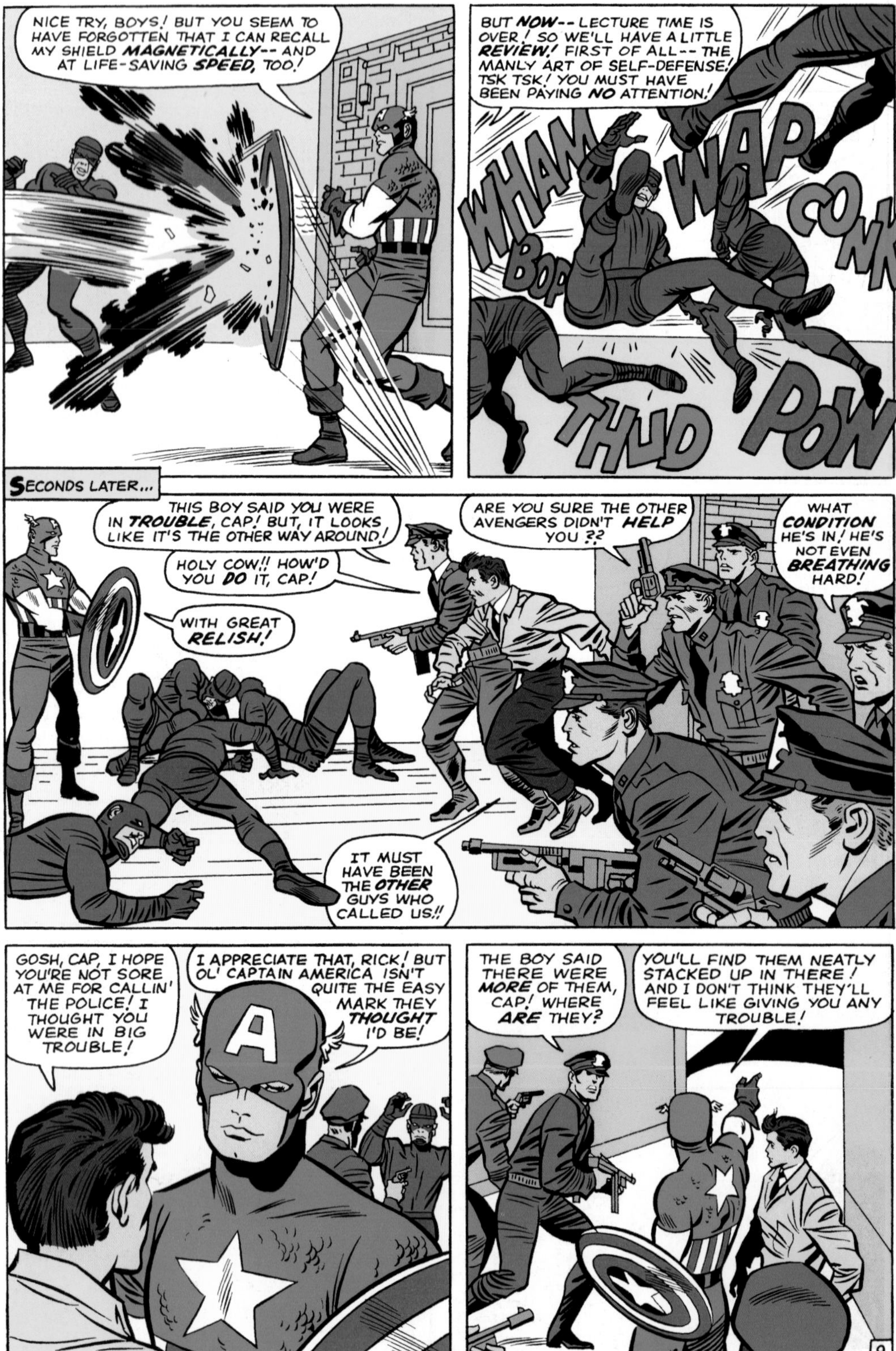
NICE TRY, BOYS! BUT YOU SEEM TO HAVE FORGOTTEN THAT I CAN RECALL MY SHIELD MAGNETICALLY-- AND AT LIFE-SAVING SPEED, TOO!
BUT NOW-- LECTURE TIME IS OVER! SO WE'LL HAVE A LITTLE REVIEW! FIRST OF ALL-- THE MANLY ART OF SELF-DEFENSE! TSK TSK! YOU MUST HAVE BEEN PAYING NO ATTENTION!
WHAM
WAP
CONK
BOP
THUD
POW
SECONDS LATER...
THIS BOY SAID YOU WERE IN TROUBLE, CAP! BUT, IT LOOKS LIKE IT'S THE OTHER WAY AROUND!
HOLY COW!! HOW'D YOU DO IT, CAP!
WITH GREAT RELISH!
ARE YOU SURE THE OTHER AVENGERS DIDN'T HELP YOU ??
WHAT CONDITION HE'S IN! HE'S NOT EVEN BREATHING HARD!
IT MUST HAVE BEEN THE OTHER GUYS WHO CALLED US!!
GOSH, CAP, I HOPE YOU'RE NOT SORE AT ME FOR CALLIN' THE POLICE! I THOUGHT YOU WERE IN BIG TROUBLE!
I APPRECIATE THAT, RICK! BUT OL' CAPTAIN AMERICA ISN'T QUITE THE EASY MARK THEY THOUGHT I'D BE!
THE BOY SAID THERE WERE MORE OF THEM, CAP! WHERE ARE THEY?
YOU'LL FIND THEM NEATLY STACKED UP IN THERE! AND I DON'T THINK THEY'LL FEEL LIKE GIVING YOU ANY TROUBLE!
9

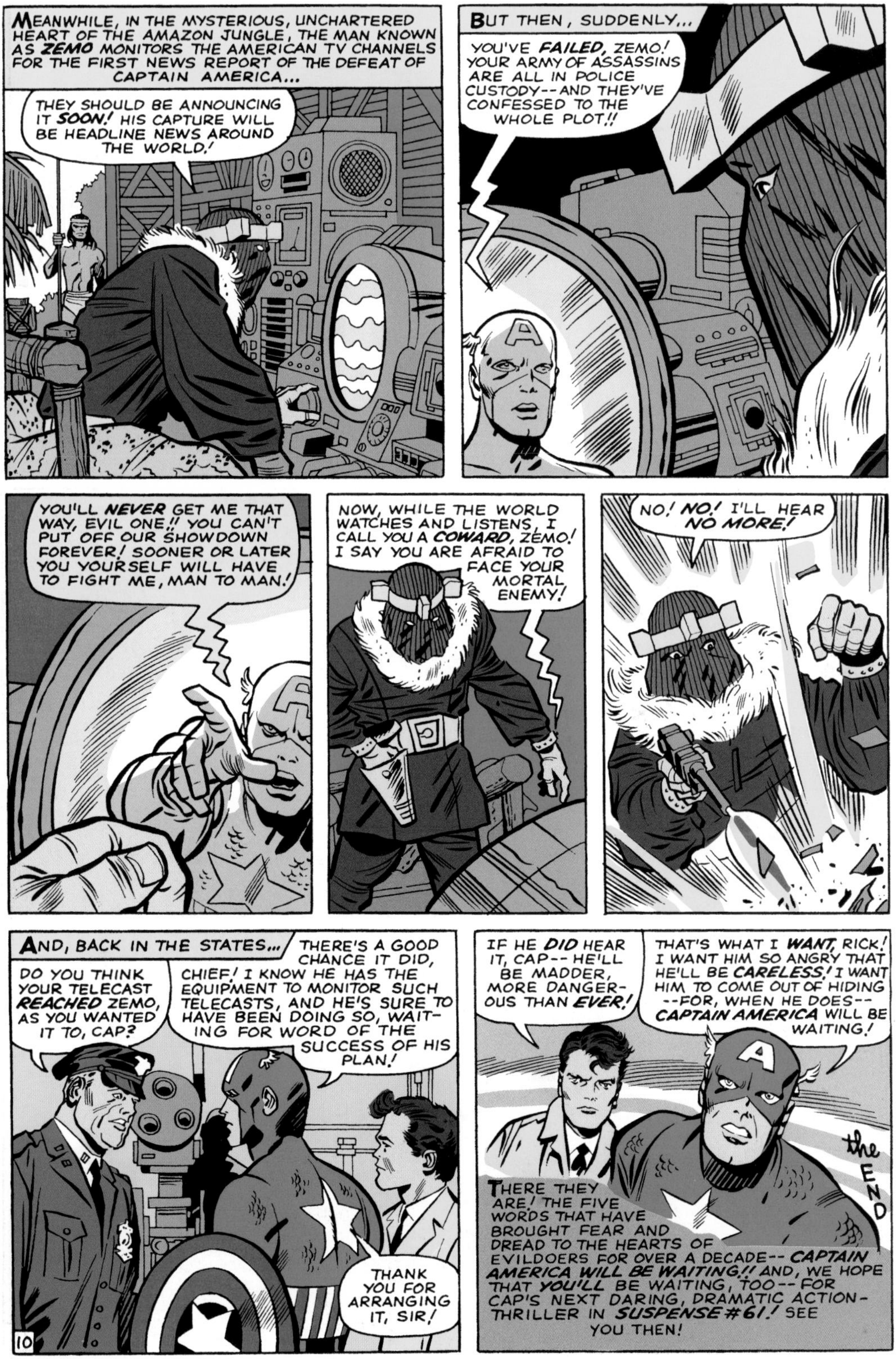
MEANWHILE, IN THE MYSTERIOUS, UNCHARTERED HEART OF THE AMAZON JUNGLE, THE MAN KNOWN AS ZEMO MONITORS THE AMERICAN TV CHANNELS FOR THE FIRST NEWS REPORT OF THE DEFEAT OF CAPTAIN AMERICA...
THEY SHOULD BE ANNOUNCING IT SOON! HIS CAPTURE WILL BE HEADLINE NEWS AROUND THE WORLD!
BUT THEN, SUDDENLY...
YOU'VE FAILED, ZEMO! YOUR ARMY OF ASSASSINS ARE ALL IN POLICE CUSTODY--AND THEY'VE CONFESSED TO THE WHOLE PLOT!!
YOU'LL NEVER GET ME THAT WAY, EVIL ONE!! YOU CAN'T PUT OFF OUR SHOWDOWN FOREVER! SOONER OR LATER YOU YOURSELF WILL HAVE TO FIGHT ME, MAN TO MAN!
NOW, WHILE THE WORLD WATCHES AND LISTENS, I CALL YOU A COWARD, ZEMO! I SAY YOU ARE AFRAID TO FACE YOUR MORTAL ENEMY!
NO! NO! I'LL HEAR NO MORE!
AND, BACK IN THE STATES...
DO YOU THINK YOUR TELECAST REACHED ZEMO, AS YOU WANTED IT TO, CAP?
THERE'S A GOOD CHANCE IT DID, CHIEF! I KNOW HE HAS THE EQUIPMENT TO MONITOR SUCH TELECASTS, AND HE'S SURE TO HAVE BEEN DOING SO, WAITING FOR WORD OF THE SUCCESS OF HIS PLAN!
THANK YOU FOR ARRANGING IT, SIR!
10
IF HE DID HEAR IT, CAP-- HE'LL BE MADDER, MORE DANGEROUS THAN EVER!
THAT'S WHAT I WANT, RICK! I WANT HIM SO ANGRY THAT HE'LL BE CARELESS! I WANT HIM TO COME OUT OF HIDING --FOR, WHEN HE DOES-- CAPTAIN AMERICA WILL BE WAITING!
THE END
THERE THEY ARE! THE FIVE WORDS THAT HAVE BROUGHT FEAR AND DREAD TO THE HEARTS OF EVILDOERS FOR OVER A DECADE-- CAPTAIN AMERICA WILL BE WAITING!! AND, WE HOPE THAT YOU'LL BE WAITING, TOO--FOR CAP'S NEXT DARING, DRAMATIC ACTION-THRILLER IN SUSPENSE #61! SEE YOU THEN!

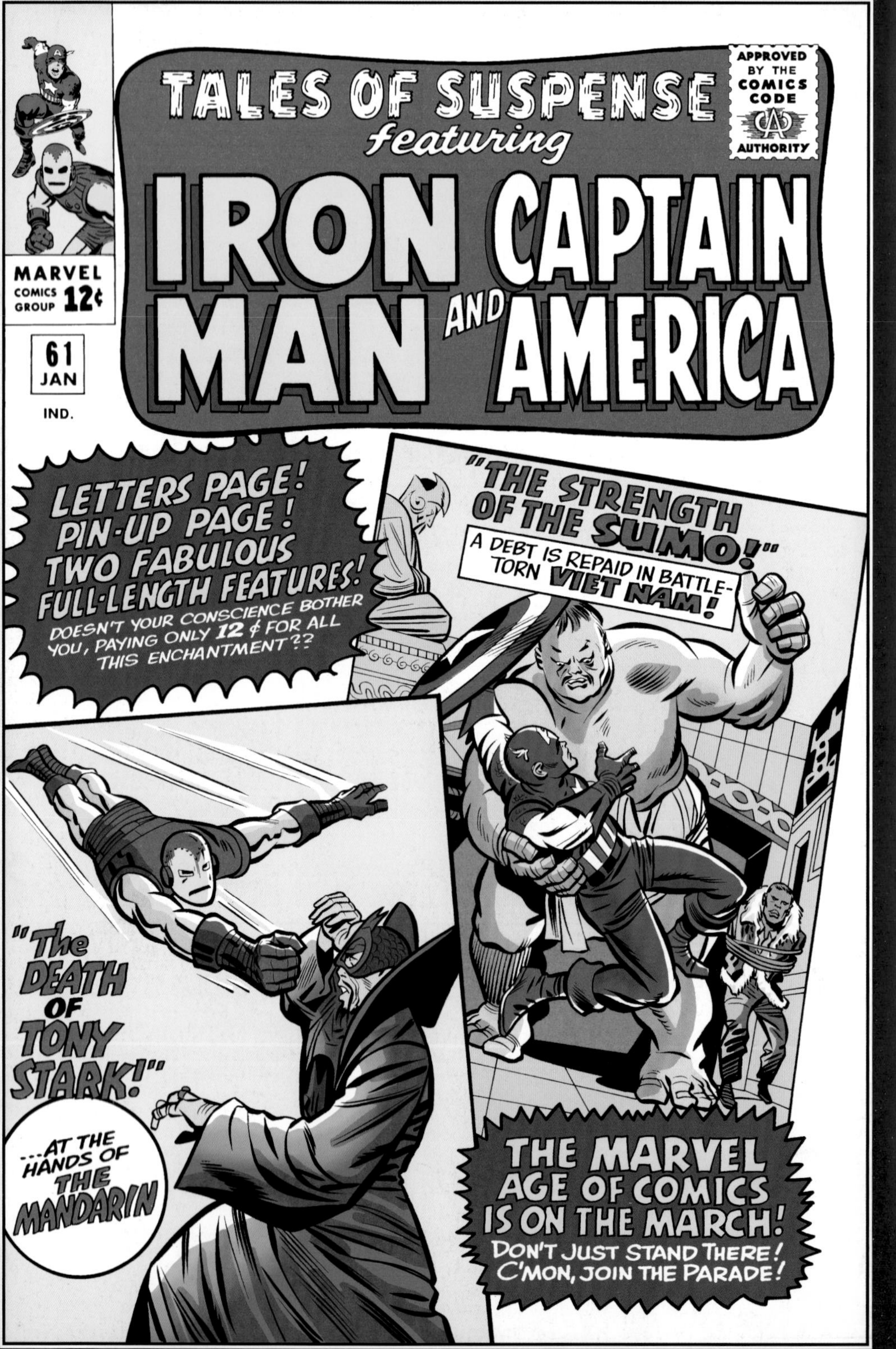

TALES OF SUSPENSE featuring
IRON MAN AND CAPTAIN AMERICA
APPROVED BY THE COMICS CODE AUTHORITY
MARVEL COMICS GROUP 12¢
61 JAN
IND.
LETTERS PAGE! PIN-UP PAGE! TWO FABULOUS FULL-LENGTH FEATURES!
DOESN'T YOUR CONSCIENCE BOTHER YOU, PAYING ONLY 12¢ FOR ALL THIS ENCHANTMENT??
"THE STRENGTH OF THE SUMO!"
A DEBT IS REPAID IN BATTLE-TORN VIET NAM!
"The DEATH OF TONY STARK!"
...AT THE HANDS OF THE MANDARIN
THE MARVEL AGE OF COMICS IS ON THE MARCH!
DON'T JUST STAND THERE! C'MON, JOIN THE PARADE!

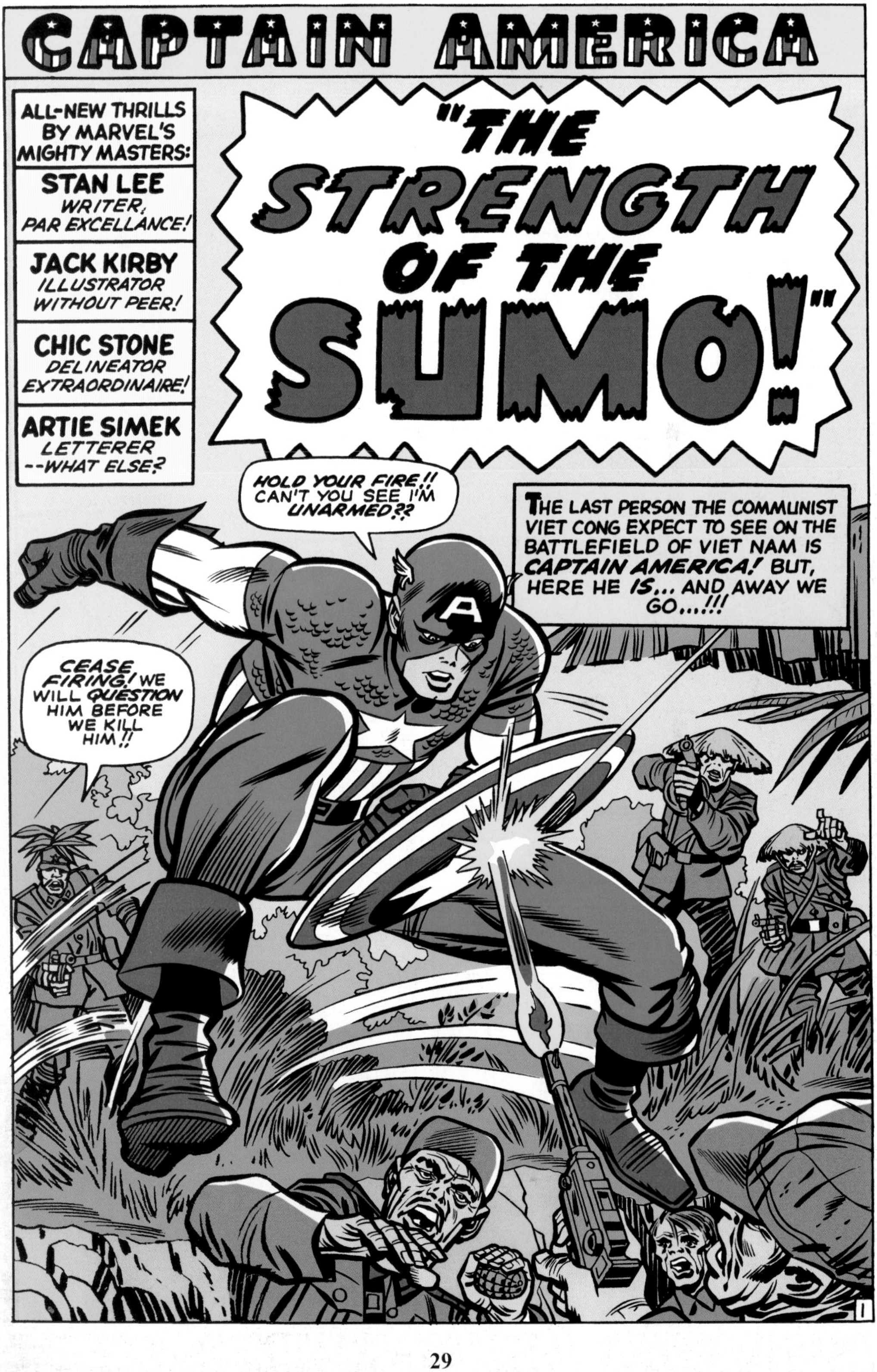
CAPTAIN AMERICA
ALL-NEW THRILLS BY MARVEL'S MIGHTY MASTERS:
STAN LEE WRITER, PAR EXCELLANCE!
JACK KIRBY ILLUSTRATOR WITHOUT PEER!
CHIC STONE DELINEATOR EXTRAORDINAIRE!
ARTIE SIMEK LETTERER --WHAT ELSE?
"THE STRENGTH OF THE SUMO!"
HOLD YOUR FIRE!! CAN'T YOU SEE I'M UNARMED??
THE LAST PERSON THE COMMUNIST VIET CONG EXPECT TO SEE ON THE BATTLEFIELD OF VIET NAM IS CAPTAIN AMERICA! BUT, HERE HE IS... AND AWAY WE GO...!!!
CEASE FIRING! WE WILL QUESTION HIM BEFORE WE KILL HIM!!
1

IS THE COMMUNIST FIGHTING MAN SO WEAK, SO UNSURE OF HIMSELF, THAT HE FEARS ONE LONE AMERICAN?? IS *THIS* THE MUCH-VAUNTED POWER OF THE VIET CONG??

I HAVE COME TO SEE YOUR *GENERAL*-- OR IS *HE*, TOO, AS FEARFUL, AS *YOU!*

STILL YOUR TONGUE, COSTUMED ONE! EVEN *WE* HAVE HEARD OF THE PROWESS OF CAPTAIN AMERICA! WE WILL NOT BE AS EASY TO *TRICK* AS YOU MAY HOPE!

I SAY SHOOT HIM *NOW!*

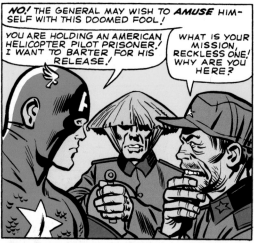

NO! THE GENERAL MAY WISH TO *AMUSE* HIMSELF WITH THIS DOOMED FOOL!

YOU ARE HOLDING AN AMERICAN HELICOPTER PILOT PRISONER! I WANT TO BARTER FOR HIS RELEASE!

WHAT IS YOUR MISSION, RECKLESS ONE! WHY ARE YOU HERE?

HE MUST BE MORE *IMPORTANT* THAN WE GUESSED IF *YOU* WOULD COME TO THIS PLACE TO TRY TO FREE HIM!

HE *IS* IMPORTANT-- TO *ME!* I OWE HIM A VERY GREAT DEBT!

COME--FOLLOW ME! AND MAKE NO RASH MOVE IF YOU VALUE YOUR LIFE!

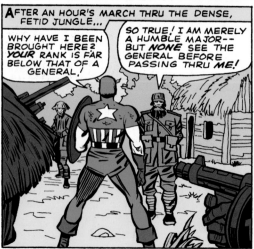

AFTER AN HOUR'S MARCH THRU THE DENSE, FETID JUNGLE...

WHY HAVE I BEEN BROUGHT HERE? *YOUR* RANK IS FAR BELOW THAT OF A GENERAL!

SO TRUE! I AM MERELY A HUMBLE MAJOR-- BUT *NONE* SEE THE GENERAL BEFORE PASSING THRU *ME!*

HMMMM...THERE IS *STRENGTH* IN YOUR ARM! I ALWAYS BELIEVED CAPTAIN AMERICA TO BE MERELY A YANKEE *LEGEND*-- UNTIL NOW!

BEFORE YOU ARE BROUGHT TO THE GENERAL--YOU MUST FIRST PASS A LITTLE TEST!

A *TEST?*

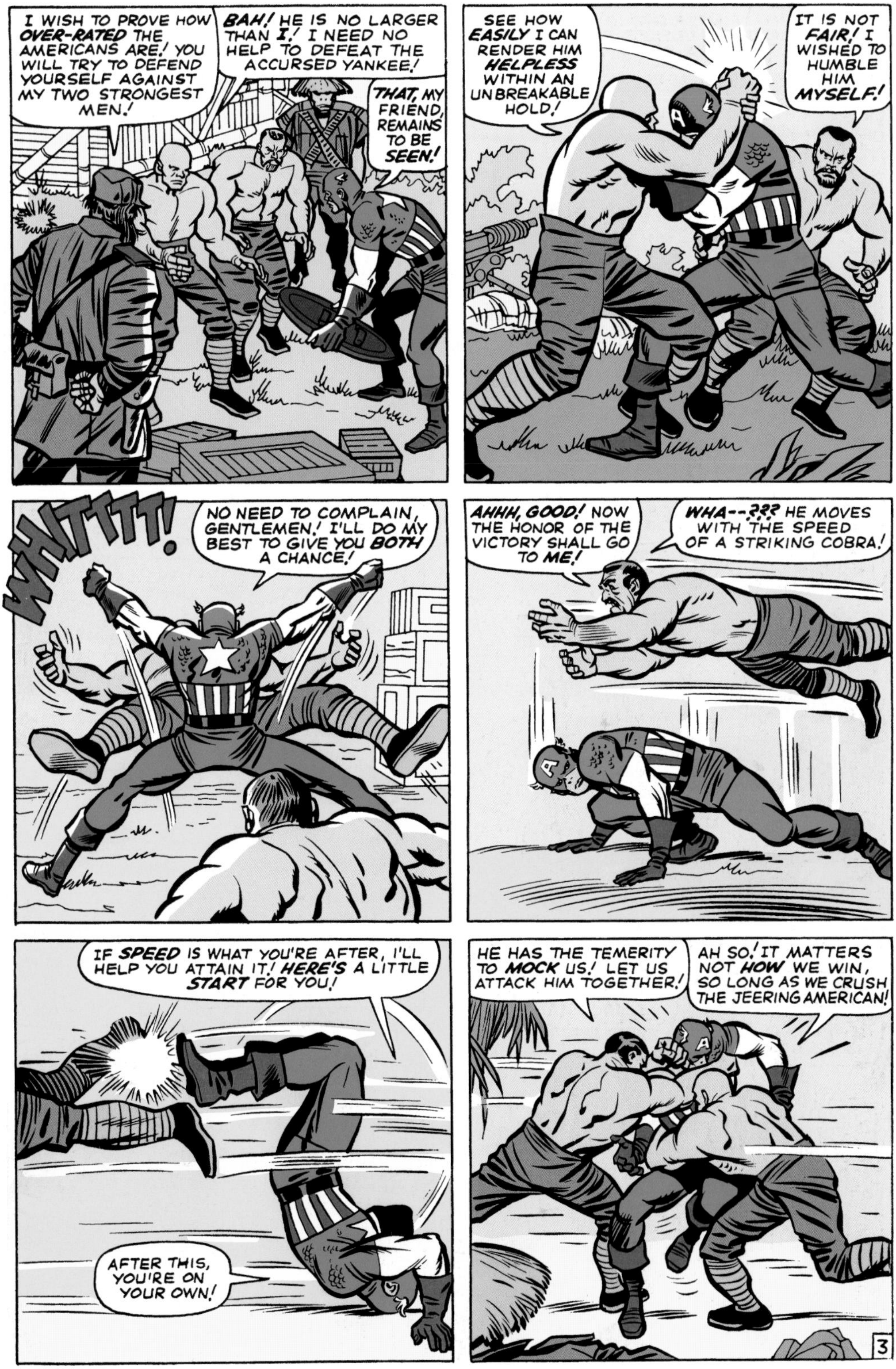
I WISH TO PROVE HOW OVER-RATED THE AMERICANS ARE! YOU WILL TRY TO DEFEND YOURSELF AGAINST MY TWO STRONGEST MEN!
BAH! HE IS NO LARGER THAN I! I NEED NO HELP TO DEFEAT THE ACCURSED YANKEE!
THAT, MY FRIEND, REMAINS TO BE SEEN!
SEE HOW EASILY I CAN RENDER HIM HELPLESS WITHIN AN UNBREAKABLE HOLD!
IT IS NOT FAIR! I WISHED TO HUMBLE HIM MYSELF!
WHTTTT!
NO NEED TO COMPLAIN, GENTLEMEN! I'LL DO MY BEST TO GIVE YOU BOTH A CHANCE!
AHHH, GOOD! NOW THE HONOR OF THE VICTORY SHALL GO TO ME!
WHA--??? HE MOVES WITH THE SPEED OF A STRIKING COBRA!
IF SPEED IS WHAT YOU'RE AFTER, I'LL HELP YOU ATTAIN IT! HERE'S A LITTLE START FOR YOU!
AFTER THIS, YOU'RE ON YOUR OWN!
HE HAS THE TEMERITY TO MOCK US! LET US ATTACK HIM TOGETHER!
AH SO! IT MATTERS NOT HOW WE WIN, SO LONG AS WE CRUSH THE JEERING AMERICAN!
3

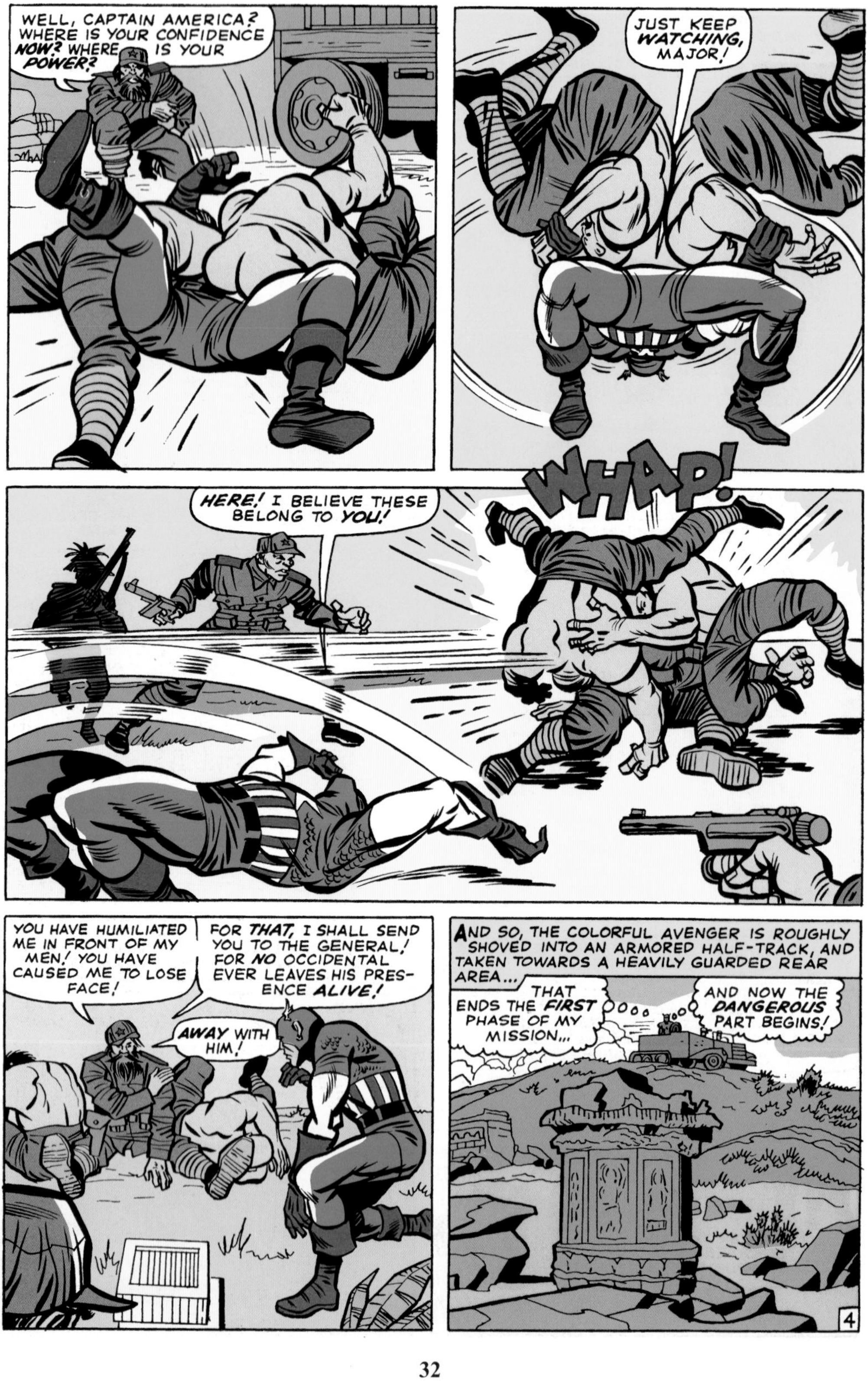
WELL, CAPTAIN AMERICA? WHERE IS YOUR CONFIDENCE NOW? WHERE IS YOUR POWER?
JUST KEEP WATCHING, MAJOR!
WHAP!
HERE! I BELIEVE THESE BELONG TO YOU!
YOU HAVE HUMILIATED ME IN FRONT OF MY MEN! YOU HAVE CAUSED ME TO LOSE FACE!
FOR THAT, I SHALL SEND YOU TO THE GENERAL! FOR NO OCCIDENTAL EVER LEAVES HIS PRESENCE ALIVE!
AWAY WITH HIM!
AND SO, THE COLORFUL AVENGER IS ROUGHLY SHOVED INTO AN ARMORED HALF-TRACK, AND TAKEN TOWARDS A HEAVILY GUARDED REAR AREA...
THAT ENDS THE FIRST PHASE OF MY MISSION...
AND NOW THE DANGEROUS PART BEGINS!
4

FINALLY, AFTER HOURS OF RIDING...

THIS MUST BE THE PLACE!

I AM CAPTAIN AMERICA! I DEMAND TO SEE--!

I KNOW WHO YOU ARE! WE COMMUNISTS MAKE IT OUR BUSINESS TO KNOW ALL OUR DEADLY ENEMIES!

BUT, YOU ARE IN A POSITION TO DEMAND NOTHING!

WE'LL LET THE GENERAL DECIDE THAT! FIRST, I WANT SOME ASSURANCE THAT OUR CAPTURED PILOT IS STILL ALIVE!

THAT IS SIMPLE ENOUGH TO ARRANGE! GUARDS! BRING THE PRISONER FORTH!

JIM BAKER! I'VE FOUND YOU AT LAST!

CAP! THEY'VE CAUGHT YOU TOO! I-I CAN'T BELIEVE IT!

I'M NOT CAUGHT, SON! I'VE COME TO FREE YOU!

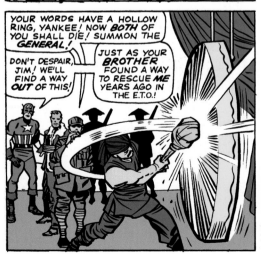

YOUR WORDS HAVE A HOLLOW RING, YANKEE! NOW BOTH OF YOU SHALL DIE! SUMMON THE GENERAL!

DON'T DESPAIR, JIM! WE'LL FIND A WAY OUT OF THIS!

JUST AS YOUR BROTHER FOUND A WAY TO RESCUE ME YEARS AGO IN THE E.T.O.!

I OWE THIS TO HIM, LIEUTENANT-- AND TO YOU! AND BY ALL I HOLD DEAR, I SWEAR TO YOU THAT MY DEBT WILL BE PAID!

BUT THE ENTIRE FREE WORLD NEEDS YOU, CAP--!

IT NEEDS YOU TOO, SON! IT NEEDS ALL OF US!

SILENCE! THE GENERAL COMES!

5

IT LOOKS TO *ME* AS THOUGH THE GENERAL HAS SEEN TOO MANY CECIL B. DEMILLE MOVIES!

ONLY A GLORY-HUNGRY, POWER-MAD POTENTATE WOULD EMPLOY SUCH A RETINUE! WHO IS--?

CAP! LOOK OUT! BEHIND YOU--!

SO,!! THAT IS MY MOST WORTHY VISITOR! LET ME TEST HIS METTLE!

AH! I FEAR THE FAMOUS CAPTAIN AMERICA WILL NOT BE IN A POSITION TO RESCUE EVEN *HIMSELF* THIS TIME!

FORGIVE THE MOST UNSEEMLY BEHAVIOR OF THIS UNWORTHY PERSON! I AM THE LEADER OF THESE LOWLY ONES-- BETTER KNOWN TO *YOU* PERHAPS AS --THE *GENERAL!*

THE GENERAL-- A GIANT *SUMO WRESTLER!* I NEVER SUSPECTED....!

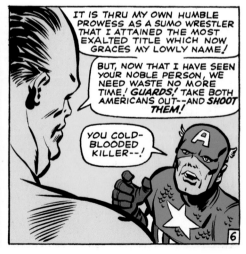

IT IS THRU MY OWN HUMBLE PROWESS AS A SUMO WRESTLER THAT I ATTAINED THE MOST EXALTED TITLE WHICH NOW GRACES MY LOWLY NAME!

BUT, NOW THAT I HAVE SEEN YOUR NOBLE PERSON, WE NEED WASTE NO MORE TIME! *GUARDS!* TAKE BOTH AMERICANS OUT--AND *SHOOT THEM!*

YOU COLD-BLOODED KILLER--!

6

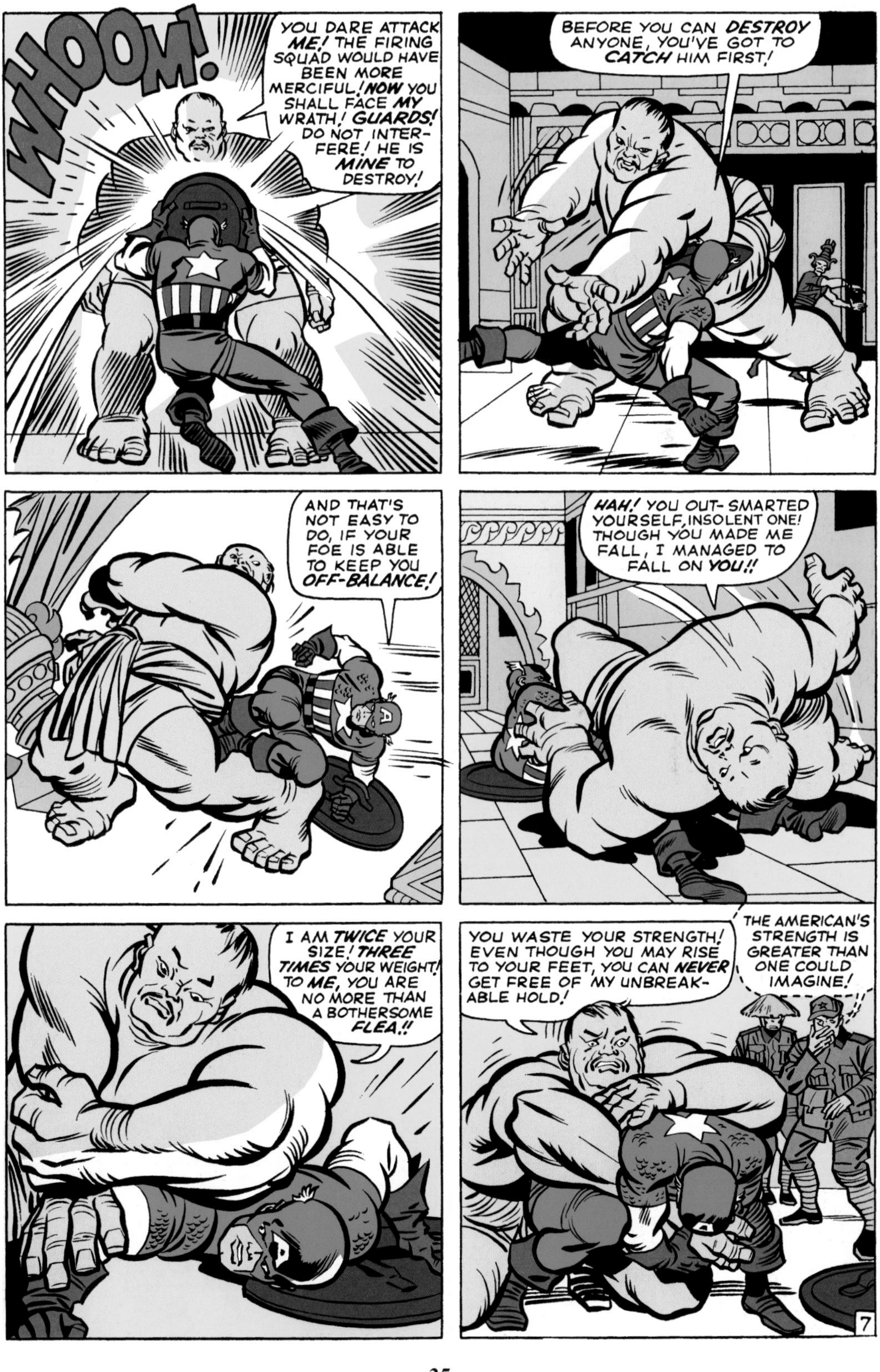
WHOOM!
YOU DARE ATTACK ME! THE FIRING SQUAD WOULD HAVE BEEN MORE MERCIFUL! NOW YOU SHALL FACE MY WRATH! GUARDS! DO NOT INTERFERE! HE IS MINE TO DESTROY!
BEFORE YOU CAN DESTROY ANYONE, YOU'VE GOT TO CATCH HIM FIRST!
AND THAT'S NOT EASY TO DO, IF YOUR FOE IS ABLE TO KEEP YOU OFF-BALANCE!
HAH! YOU OUT-SMARTED YOURSELF, INSOLENT ONE! THOUGH YOU MADE ME FALL, I MANAGED TO FALL ON YOU!!
I AM TWICE YOUR SIZE! THREE TIMES YOUR WEIGHT! TO ME, YOU ARE NO MORE THAN A BOTHERSOME FLEA!!
YOU WASTE YOUR STRENGTH! EVEN THOUGH YOU MAY RISE TO YOUR FEET, YOU CAN NEVER GET FREE OF MY UNBREAKABLE HOLD!
THE AMERICAN'S STRENGTH IS GREATER THAN ONE COULD IMAGINE!
7

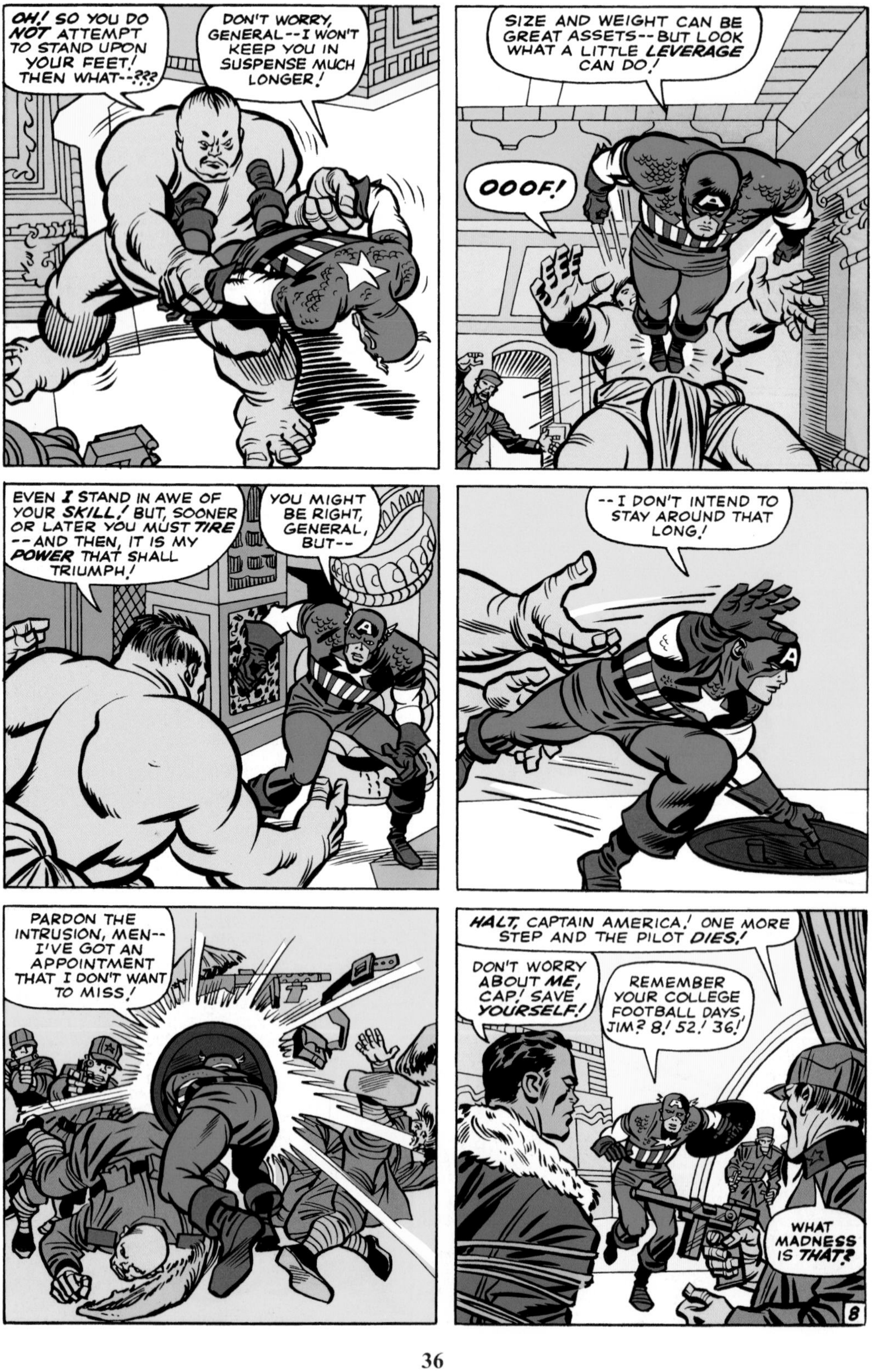
OH! SO YOU DO NOT ATTEMPT TO STAND UPON YOUR FEET! THEN WHAT--???
DON'T WORRY, GENERAL--I WON'T KEEP YOU IN SUSPENSE MUCH LONGER!
SIZE AND WEIGHT CAN BE GREAT ASSETS--BUT LOOK WHAT A LITTLE LEVERAGE CAN DO!
OOOF!
EVEN I STAND IN AWE OF YOUR SKILL! BUT, SOONER OR LATER YOU MUST TIRE --AND THEN, IT IS MY POWER THAT SHALL TRIUMPH!
YOU MIGHT BE RIGHT, GENERAL, BUT--
--I DON'T INTEND TO STAY AROUND THAT LONG!
PARDON THE INTRUSION, MEN-- I'VE GOT AN APPOINTMENT THAT I DON'T WANT TO MISS!
HALT, CAPTAIN AMERICA! ONE MORE STEP AND THE PILOT DIES!
DON'T WORRY ABOUT ME, CAP! SAVE YOURSELF!
REMEMBER YOUR COLLEGE FOOTBALL DAYS, JIM? 8! 52! 36!
WHAT MADNESS IS THAT?
8

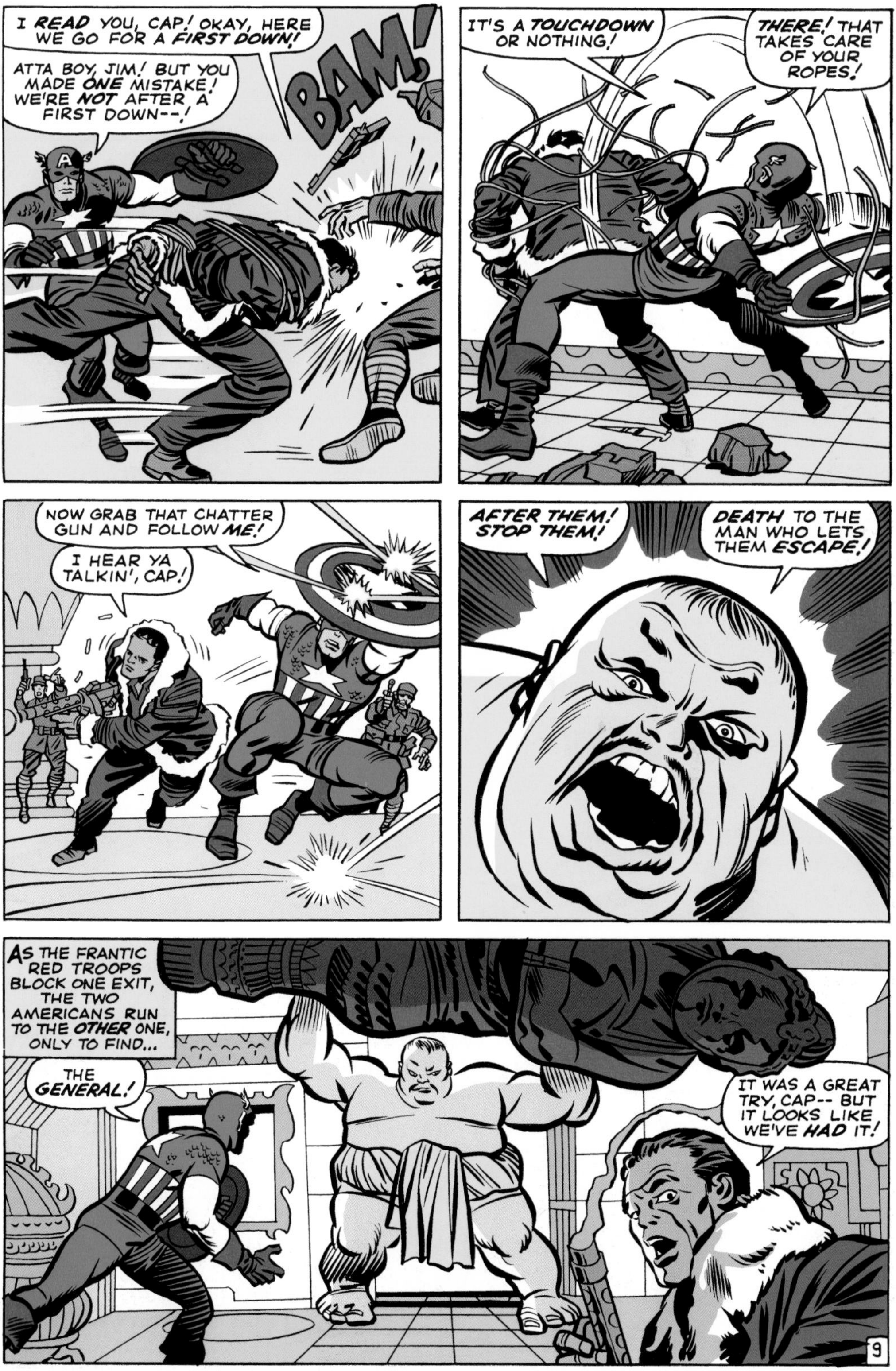
I READ YOU, CAP! OKAY, HERE WE GO FOR A FIRST DOWN!
ATTA BOY, JIM! BUT YOU MADE ONE MISTAKE! WE'RE NOT AFTER A FIRST DOWN--!
BAM!
IT'S A TOUCHDOWN OR NOTHING!
THERE! THAT TAKES CARE OF YOUR ROPES!
NOW GRAB THAT CHATTER GUN AND FOLLOW ME!
I HEAR YA TALKIN', CAP!
AFTER THEM! STOP THEM!
DEATH TO THE MAN WHO LETS THEM ESCAPE!
AS THE FRANTIC RED TROOPS BLOCK ONE EXIT, THE TWO AMERICANS RUN TO THE OTHER ONE, ONLY TO FIND...
THE GENERAL!
IT WAS A GREAT TRY, CAP-- BUT IT LOOKS LIKE WE'VE HAD IT!
9

KEEP PITCHIN', BOY! WE'RE JUST *BEGINNING* TO FIGHT! GET READY TO *SPRINT!*

NOW! I'LL BLIND HIM WITH MY SHIELD WHILE YOU RACE BETWEEN HIS LEGS! GO, JIM!

I'M NEXT! NOT *BAD* FOR AN OLD-TIMER, EH?

HOW *ABOUT* THAT?!!

KEEP RUNNING! IN HIS BLIND RAGE, HE DROPPED THE IDOL RIGHT ON *HIMSELF!*

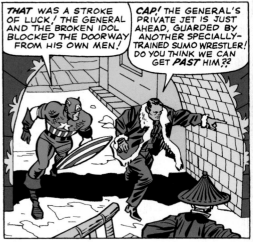

THAT WAS A STROKE OF LUCK! THE GENERAL AND THE BROKEN IDOL BLOCKED THE DOORWAY FROM HIS OWN MEN!

CAP! THE GENERAL'S PRIVATE JET IS JUST AHEAD, GUARDED BY ANOTHER SPECIALLY-TRAINED SUMO WRESTLER! DO YOU THINK WE CAN GET *PAST* HIM?？

THIRTY SECONDS LATER...

I THINK SO!

LOOK SHARP, JIM! THIS IS A *MIG!* WE DON'T WANT OUR OWN FLYBOYS TO GUN US DOWN!

NOT A CHANCE, CAP! AS SOON AS WE GET WITHIN RADIO RANGE, I'LL GIVE THEM THE WHOLE SCOOP!

CAP, I DON'T KNOW HOW TO *BEGIN* TO THANK YOU FOR--

STOW IT, BOY! THE PLANE'S SO NOISY, I CAN'T HEAR A WORD YOU'RE SAYING!

the END

MORE OF THE SAME *NEXT* ISH--AS IF YOU DIDN'T KNOW! *SPECIAL!!--* CAP GUEST STARS IN *SGT. FURY #13,* NOW ON SALE! LEARN WHY HE WAS THE GREATEST HERO OF ALL DURING THE GOLDEN AGE OF COMICS! DON'T MISS IT!

10

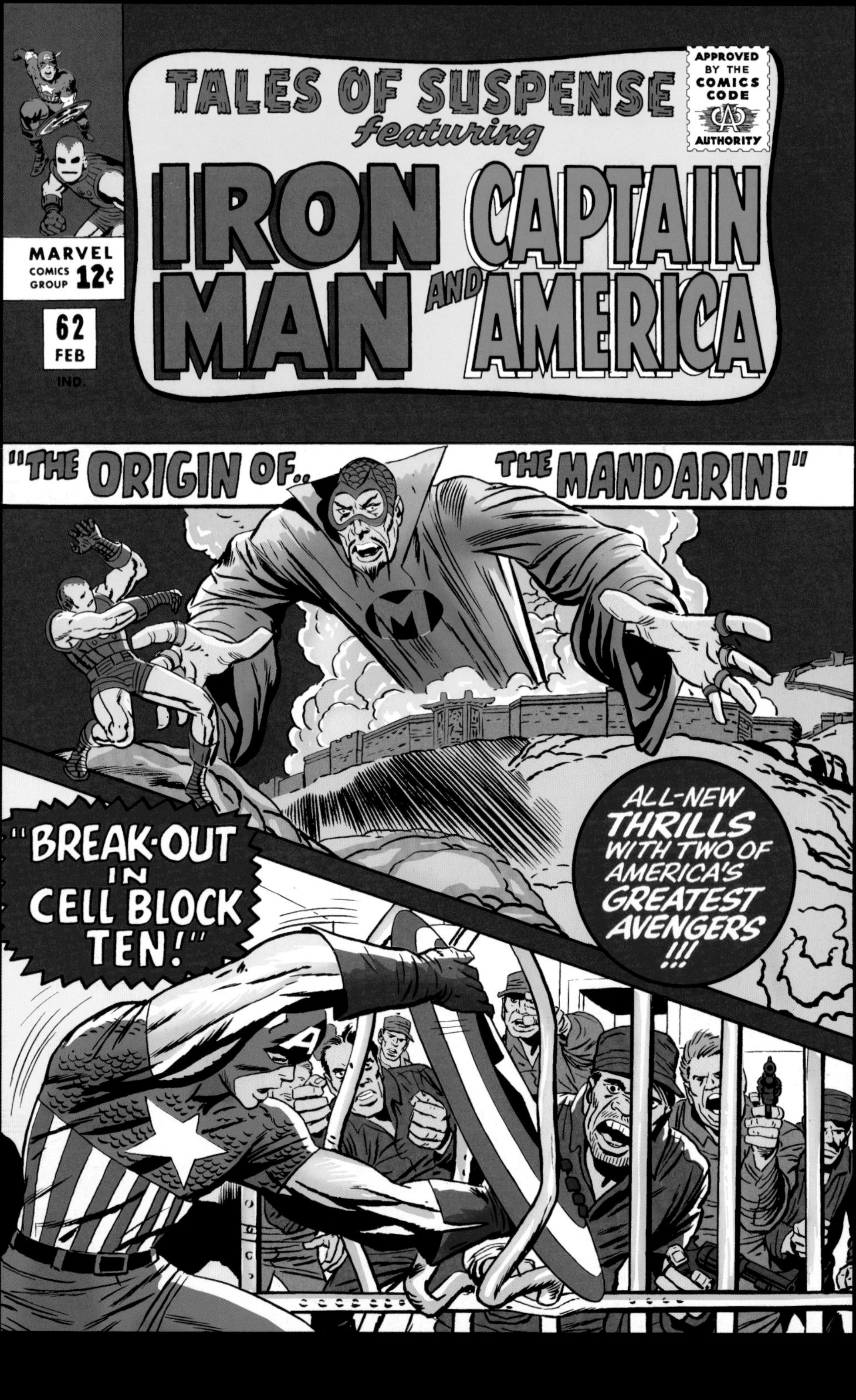
APPROVED BY THE COMICS CODE AUTHORITY
TALES OF SUSPENSE
featuring
IRON MAN AND CAPTAIN AMERICA
MARVEL COMICS GROUP 12¢
62
FEB
IND.
"THE ORIGIN OF.. THE MANDARIN!"
"BREAK-OUT IN CELL BLOCK TEN!"
ALL-NEW THRILLS WITH TWO OF AMERICA'S GREATEST AVENGERS !!!

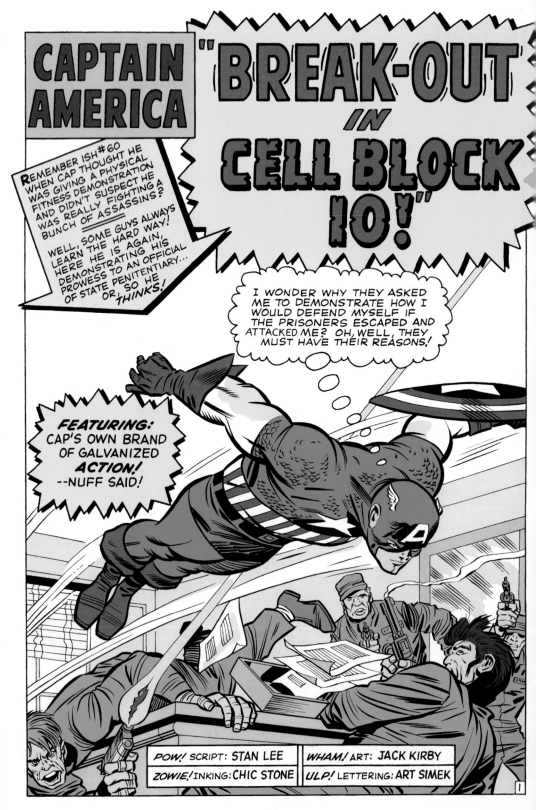

CAPTAIN AMERICA

"BREAK-OUT IN CELL BLOCK 10!"

REMEMBER ISH #60 WHEN CAP THOUGHT HE WAS GIVING A PHYSICAL FITNESS DEMONSTRATION AND DIDN'T SUSPECT HE WAS REALLY FIGHTING A BUNCH OF ASSASSINS?

WELL, SOME GUYS ALWAYS LEARN THE HARD WAY! HERE HE IS AGAIN, DEMONSTRATING HIS PROWESS TO AN OFFICIAL OF STATE PENITENTIARY... OR, SO HE THINKS!

I WONDER WHY THEY ASKED ME TO DEMONSTRATE HOW I WOULD DEFEND MYSELF IF THE PRISONERS ESCAPED AND ATTACKED ME? OH, WELL, THEY MUST HAVE THEIR REASONS!

FEATURING: CAP'S OWN BRAND OF GALVANIZED ACTION! --NUFF SAID!

POW! SCRIPT: STAN LEE

WHAM! ART: JACK KIRBY

ZOWIE! INKING: CHIC STONE

ULP! LETTERING: ART SIMEK

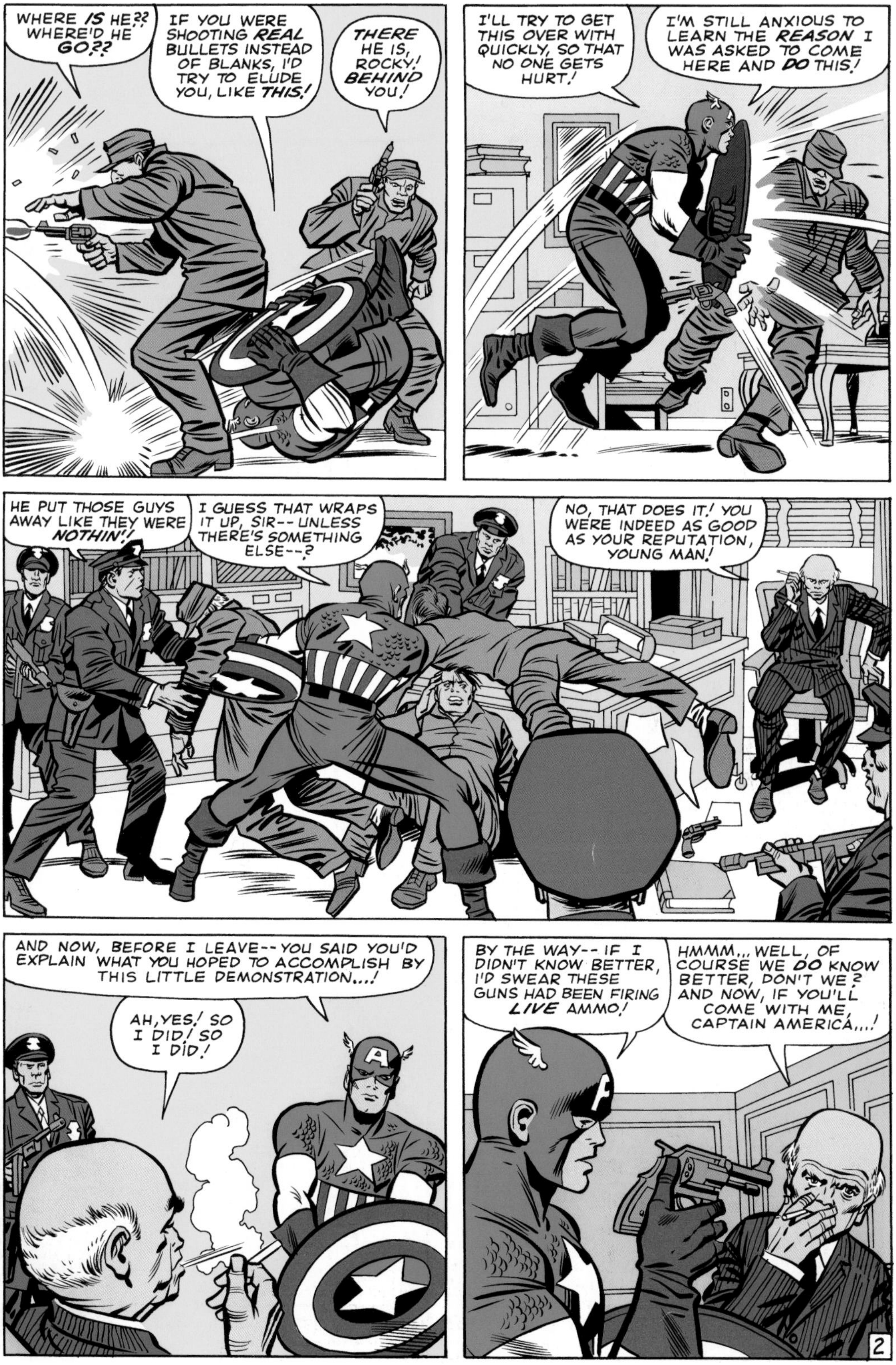
WHERE IS HE?? WHERE'D HE GO??
IF YOU WERE SHOOTING REAL BULLETS INSTEAD OF BLANKS, I'D TRY TO ELUDE YOU, LIKE THIS!
THERE HE IS, ROCKY! BEHIND YOU!
I'LL TRY TO GET THIS OVER WITH QUICKLY, SO THAT NO ONE GETS HURT!
I'M STILL ANXIOUS TO LEARN THE REASON I WAS ASKED TO COME HERE AND DO THIS!
HE PUT THOSE GUYS AWAY LIKE THEY WERE NOTHIN'!
I GUESS THAT WRAPS IT UP, SIR-- UNLESS THERE'S SOMETHING ELSE--?
NO, THAT DOES IT! YOU WERE INDEED AS GOOD AS YOUR REPUTATION, YOUNG MAN!
AND NOW, BEFORE I LEAVE-- YOU SAID YOU'D EXPLAIN WHAT YOU HOPED TO ACCOMPLISH BY THIS LITTLE DEMONSTRATION...!
AH, YES! SO I DID! SO I DID!
BY THE WAY-- IF I DIDN'T KNOW BETTER, I'D SWEAR THESE GUNS HAD BEEN FIRING LIVE AMMO!
HMMM... WELL, OF COURSE WE DO KNOW BETTER, DON'T WE? AND NOW, IF YOU'LL COME WITH ME, CAPTAIN AMERICA...!
2

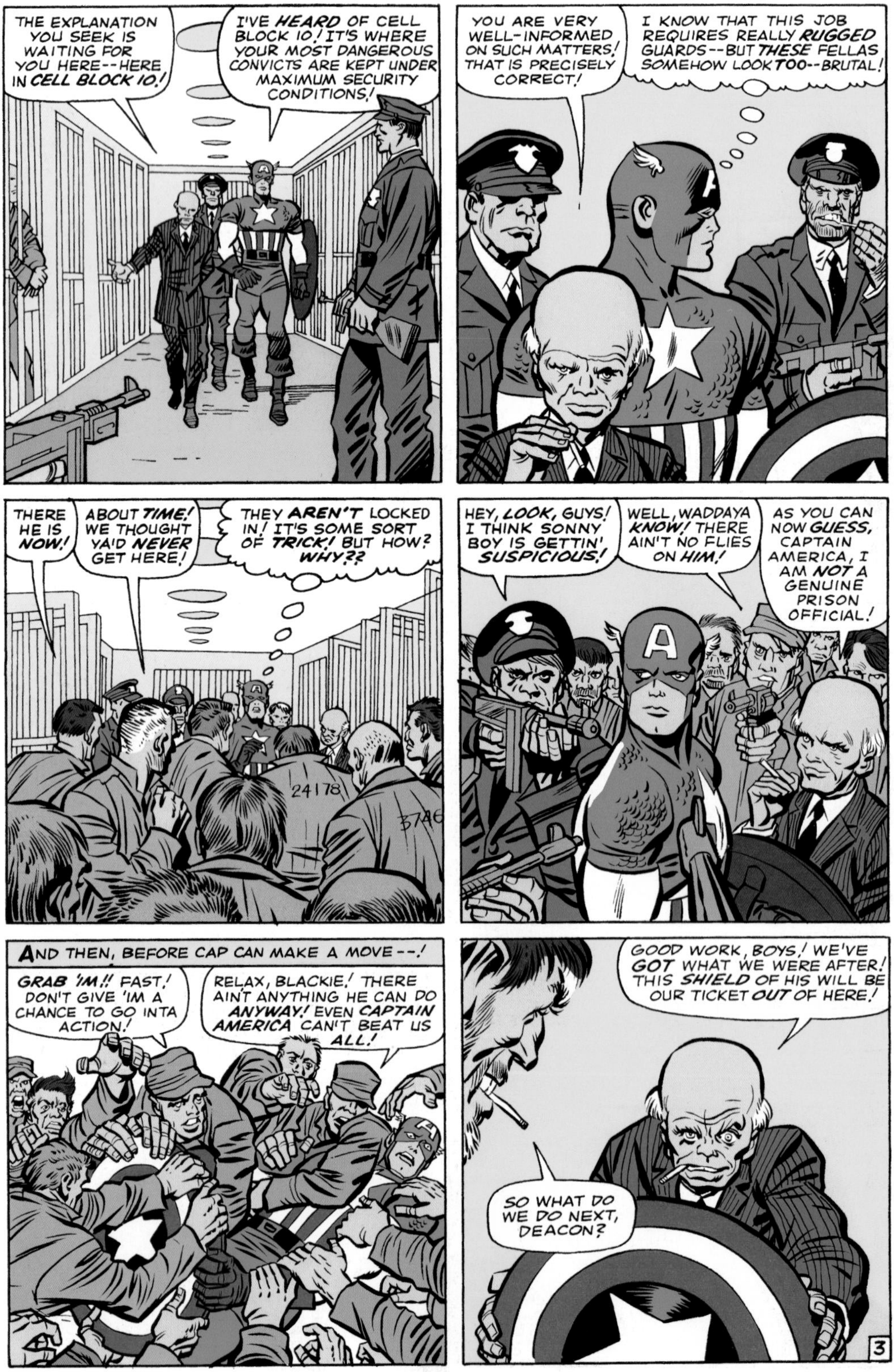
THE EXPLANATION YOU SEEK IS WAITING FOR YOU HERE--HERE IN CELL BLOCK 10!
I'VE HEARD OF CELL BLOCK 10! IT'S WHERE YOUR MOST DANGEROUS CONVICTS ARE KEPT UNDER MAXIMUM SECURITY CONDITIONS!
YOU ARE VERY WELL-INFORMED ON SUCH MATTERS! THAT IS PRECISELY CORRECT!
I KNOW THAT THIS JOB REQUIRES REALLY RUGGED GUARDS--BUT THESE FELLAS SOMEHOW LOOK TOO--BRUTAL!
THERE HE IS NOW!
ABOUT TIME! WE THOUGHT YA'D NEVER GET HERE!
THEY AREN'T LOCKED IN! IT'S SOME SORT OF TRICK! BUT HOW? WHY??
24178
3746
HEY, LOOK, GUYS! I THINK SONNY BOY IS GETTIN' SUSPICIOUS!
WELL, WADDAYA KNOW! THERE AIN'T NO FLIES ON HIM!
AS YOU CAN NOW GUESS, CAPTAIN AMERICA, I AM NOT A GENUINE PRISON OFFICIAL!
AND THEN, BEFORE CAP CAN MAKE A MOVE--!
GRAB 'IM!! FAST! DON'T GIVE 'IM A CHANCE TO GO INTA ACTION!
RELAX, BLACKIE! THERE AIN'T ANYTHING HE CAN DO ANYWAY! EVEN CAPTAIN AMERICA CAN'T BEAT US ALL!
GOOD WORK, BOYS! WE'VE GOT WHAT WE WERE AFTER! THIS SHIELD OF HIS WILL BE OUR TICKET OUT OF HERE!
SO WHAT DO WE DO NEXT, DEACON?
3

PUT HIM IN THE CELL WITH THE *REAL* DEPUTY SUPER-INTENDENT! NOW THAT WE HAVE HIS *SHIELD*, HE'S NO GOOD TO US ANY MORE!

DON'T JUST *STAND* THERE! GIVE US A *HAND*! HE'S LIKE A *TIGER*!

HOLD 'IM! DON'T LET 'IM GET AWAY!

IT AIN'T *EASY!* THERE'S ONLY ABOUT A *DOZEN* OF US!

NO SENSE TRYING TO RESIST *NOW!* I'LL WAIT TILL I LEARN MORE ABOUT THEIR PLAN!

--WHEW!--QUICK--SLAM THE DOOR ON 'IM!

CAPTAIN AMERICA! I'M ACTING SUPERINTENDENT CARLSON! I WISH I COULD HAVE *WARNED* YOU--!

DON'T WORRY ABOUT *THAT, SIR!* SUPPOSE YOU FILL ME IN ON WHAT'S *HAPPENING* HERE?

THE CONS MANAGED TO OVERPOWER A GUARD, TAKE HIS KEYS, AND GET CONTROL OF CELL BLOCK 10! *BUT*-- THEY CAN'T BREAK THRU THE MAIN GATE TO FREEDOM! THEY'RE KEEPING *ME* HERE AS HOSTAGE TILL THEY FIND A WAY--!

I SEE! AND THEY MUST THINK MY *SHIELD* HAS SOME SPECIAL POWER WHICH MAY *HELP* THEM!

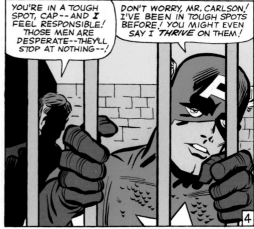

YOU'RE IN A TOUGH SPOT, CAP--AND *I* FEEL RESPONSIBLE! THOSE MEN ARE DESPERATE--THEY'LL STOP AT NOTHING--!

DON'T WORRY, MR. CARLSON! I'VE BEEN IN TOUGH SPOTS BEFORE! YOU MIGHT EVEN SAY I *THRIVE* ON THEM!

4

43

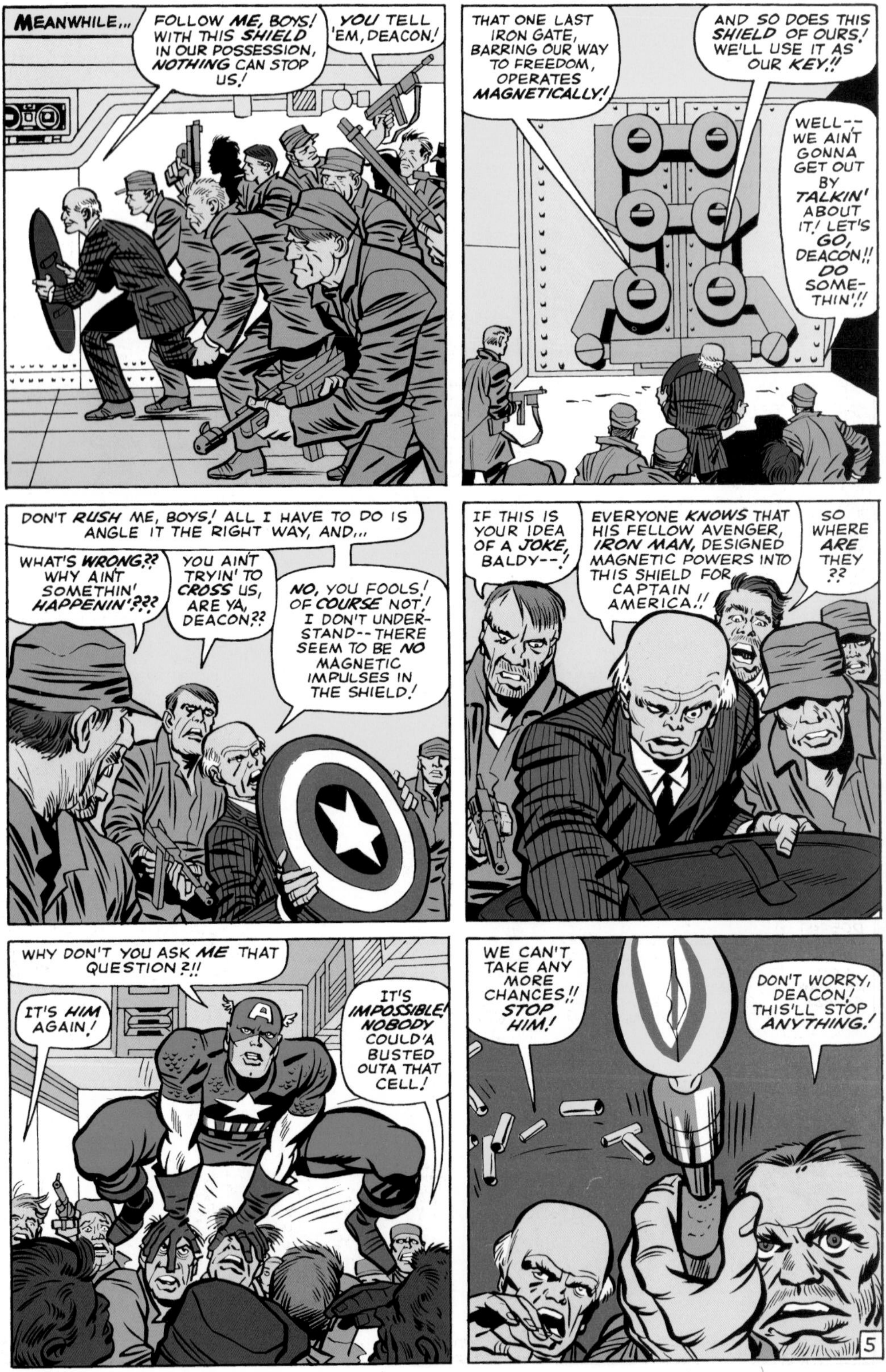
MEANWHILE...
FOLLOW ME, BOYS! WITH THIS SHIELD IN OUR POSSESSION, NOTHING CAN STOP US!
YOU TELL 'EM, DEACON!
THAT ONE LAST IRON GATE, BARRING OUR WAY TO FREEDOM, OPERATES MAGNETICALLY!
AND SO DOES THIS SHIELD OF OURS! WE'LL USE IT AS OUR KEY!!
WELL-- WE AIN'T GONNA GET OUT BY TALKIN' ABOUT IT! LET'S GO, DEACON!! DO SOME-THIN'!!
DON'T RUSH ME, BOYS! ALL I HAVE TO DO IS ANGLE IT THE RIGHT WAY, AND...
WHAT'S WRONG?? WHY AIN'T SOMETHIN' HAPPENIN'???
YOU AIN'T TRYIN' TO CROSS US, ARE YA, DEACON??
NO, YOU FOOLS! OF COURSE NOT! I DON'T UNDER-STAND--THERE SEEM TO BE NO MAGNETIC IMPULSES IN THE SHIELD!
IF THIS IS YOUR IDEA OF A JOKE, BALDY--!
EVERYONE KNOWS THAT HIS FELLOW AVENGER, IRON MAN, DESIGNED MAGNETIC POWERS INTO THIS SHIELD FOR CAPTAIN AMERICA!!
SO WHERE ARE THEY ??
WHY DON'T YOU ASK ME THAT QUESTION ?!!
IT'S HIM AGAIN!
IT'S IMPOSSIBLE! NOBODY COULD'A BUSTED OUTA THAT CELL!
WE CAN'T TAKE ANY MORE CHANCES!! STOP HIM!
DON'T WORRY, DEACON! THIS'LL STOP ANYTHING!
5

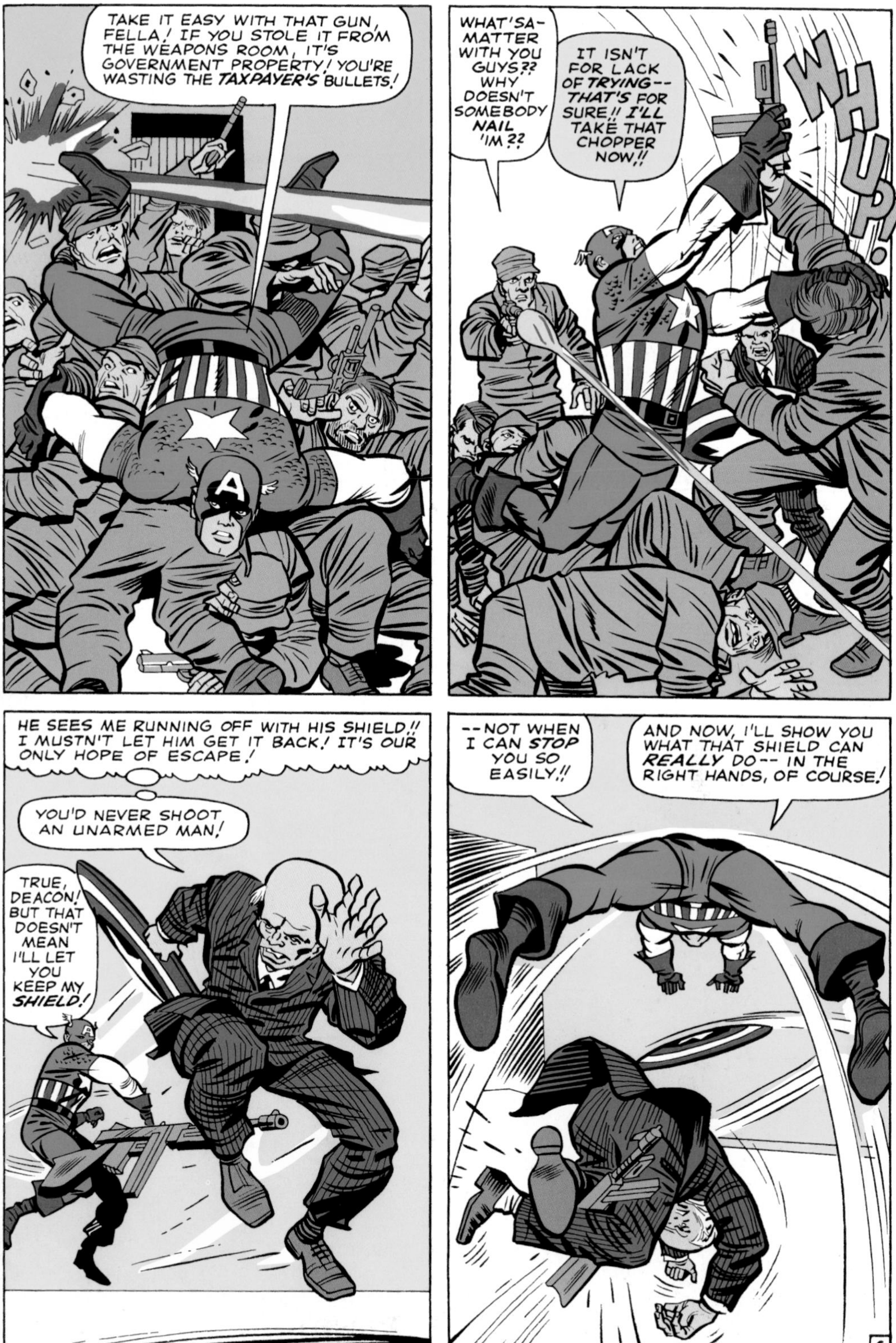
TAKE IT EASY WITH THAT GUN, FELLA! IF YOU STOLE IT FROM THE WEAPONS ROOM, IT'S GOVERNMENT PROPERTY! YOU'RE WASTING THE TAXPAYER'S BULLETS!
WHAT'SA-MATTER WITH YOU GUYS?? WHY DOESN'T SOMEBODY NAIL 'IM??
IT ISN'T FOR LACK OF TRYING-- THAT'S FOR SURE!! I'LL TAKE THAT CHOPPER NOW!!
WHHUP!
HE SEES ME RUNNING OFF WITH HIS SHIELD!! I MUSTN'T LET HIM GET IT BACK! IT'S OUR ONLY HOPE OF ESCAPE!
YOU'D NEVER SHOOT AN UNARMED MAN!
TRUE, DEACON! BUT THAT DOESN'T MEAN I'LL LET YOU KEEP MY SHIELD!
--NOT WHEN I CAN STOP YOU SO EASILY!!
AND NOW, I'LL SHOW YOU WHAT THAT SHIELD CAN REALLY DO-- IN THE RIGHT HANDS, OF COURSE!
6

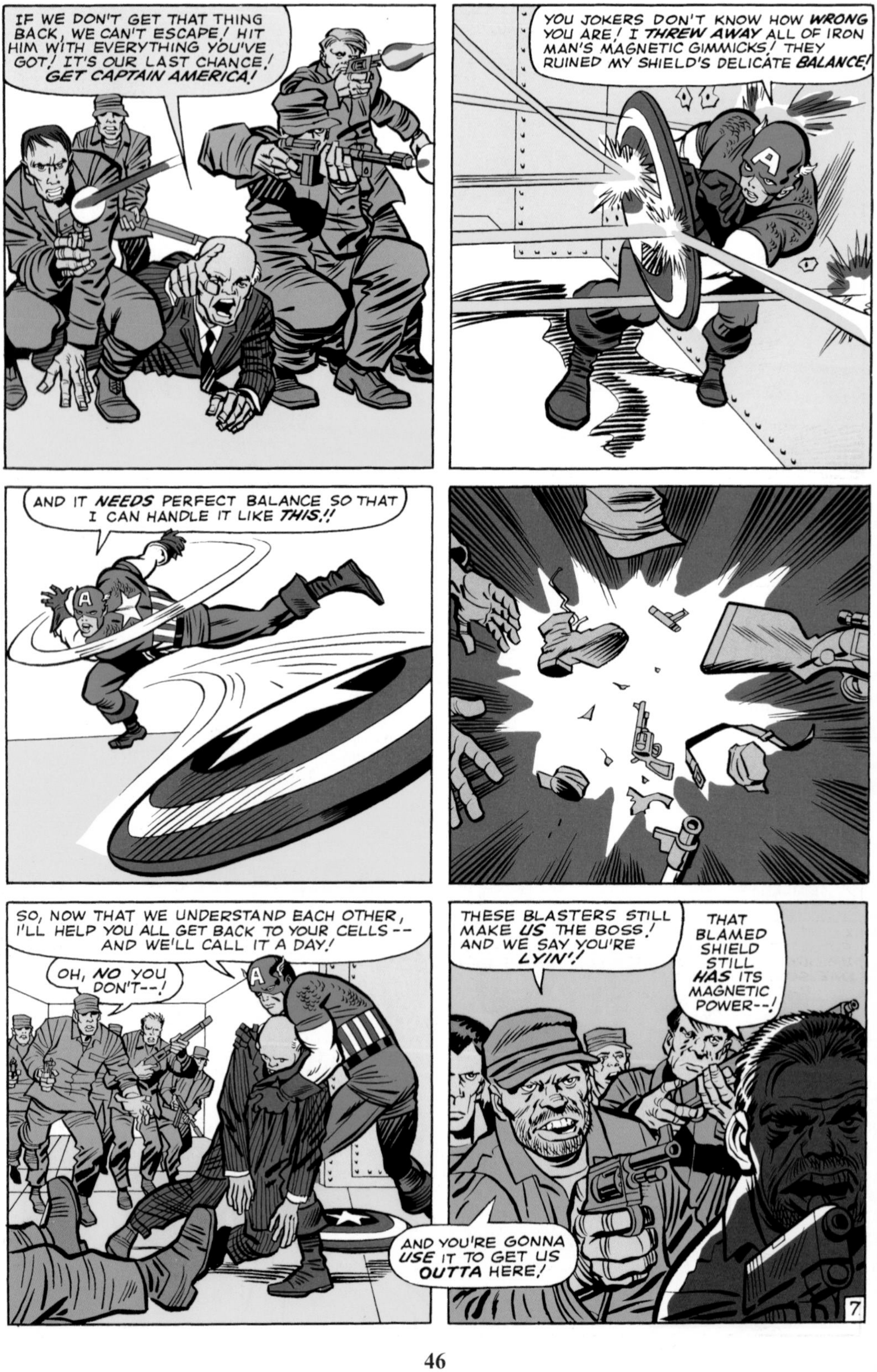
IF WE DON'T GET THAT THING BACK, WE CAN'T ESCAPE! HIT HIM WITH EVERYTHING YOU'VE GOT! IT'S OUR LAST CHANCE! GET CAPTAIN AMERICA!
YOU JOKERS DON'T KNOW HOW WRONG YOU ARE! I THREW AWAY ALL OF IRON MAN'S MAGNETIC GIMMICKS! THEY RUINED MY SHIELD'S DELICATE BALANCE!
AND IT NEEDS PERFECT BALANCE SO THAT I CAN HANDLE IT LIKE THIS!!
SO, NOW THAT WE UNDERSTAND EACH OTHER, I'LL HELP YOU ALL GET BACK TO YOUR CELLS -- AND WE'LL CALL IT A DAY!
OH, NO YOU DON'T--!
THESE BLASTERS STILL MAKE US THE BOSS! AND WE SAY YOU'RE LYIN'!
THAT BLAMED SHIELD STILL HAS ITS MAGNETIC POWER--!
AND YOU'RE GONNA USE IT TO GET US OUTTA HERE!
7

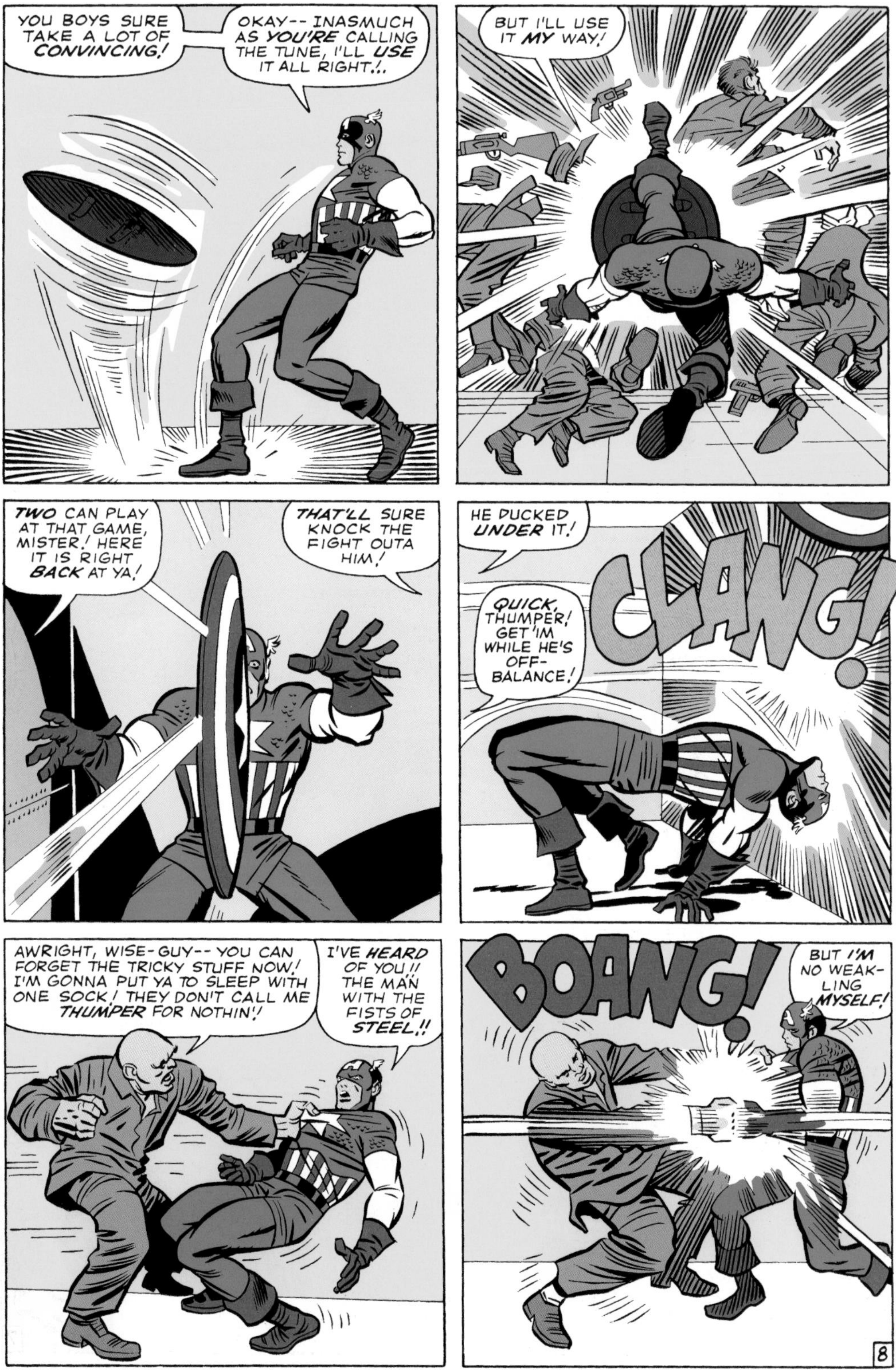

YOU BOYS SURE TAKE A LOT OF CONVINCING!
OKAY-- INASMUCH AS YOU'RE CALLING THE TUNE, I'LL USE IT ALL RIGHT!..
BUT I'LL USE IT MY WAY!
TWO CAN PLAY AT THAT GAME, MISTER! HERE IT IS RIGHT BACK AT YA!
THAT'LL SURE KNOCK THE FIGHT OUTA HIM!
HE DUCKED UNDER IT!
CLANG!
QUICK, THUMPER! GET 'IM WHILE HE'S OFF-BALANCE!
AWRIGHT, WISE-GUY-- YOU CAN FORGET THE TRICKY STUFF NOW! I'M GONNA PUT YA TO SLEEP WITH ONE SOCK! THEY DON'T CALL ME THUMPER FOR NOTHIN'!
I'VE HEARD OF YOU!! THE MAN WITH THE FISTS OF STEEL!!
BOANG!
BUT I'M NO WEAK-LING MYSELF!
8

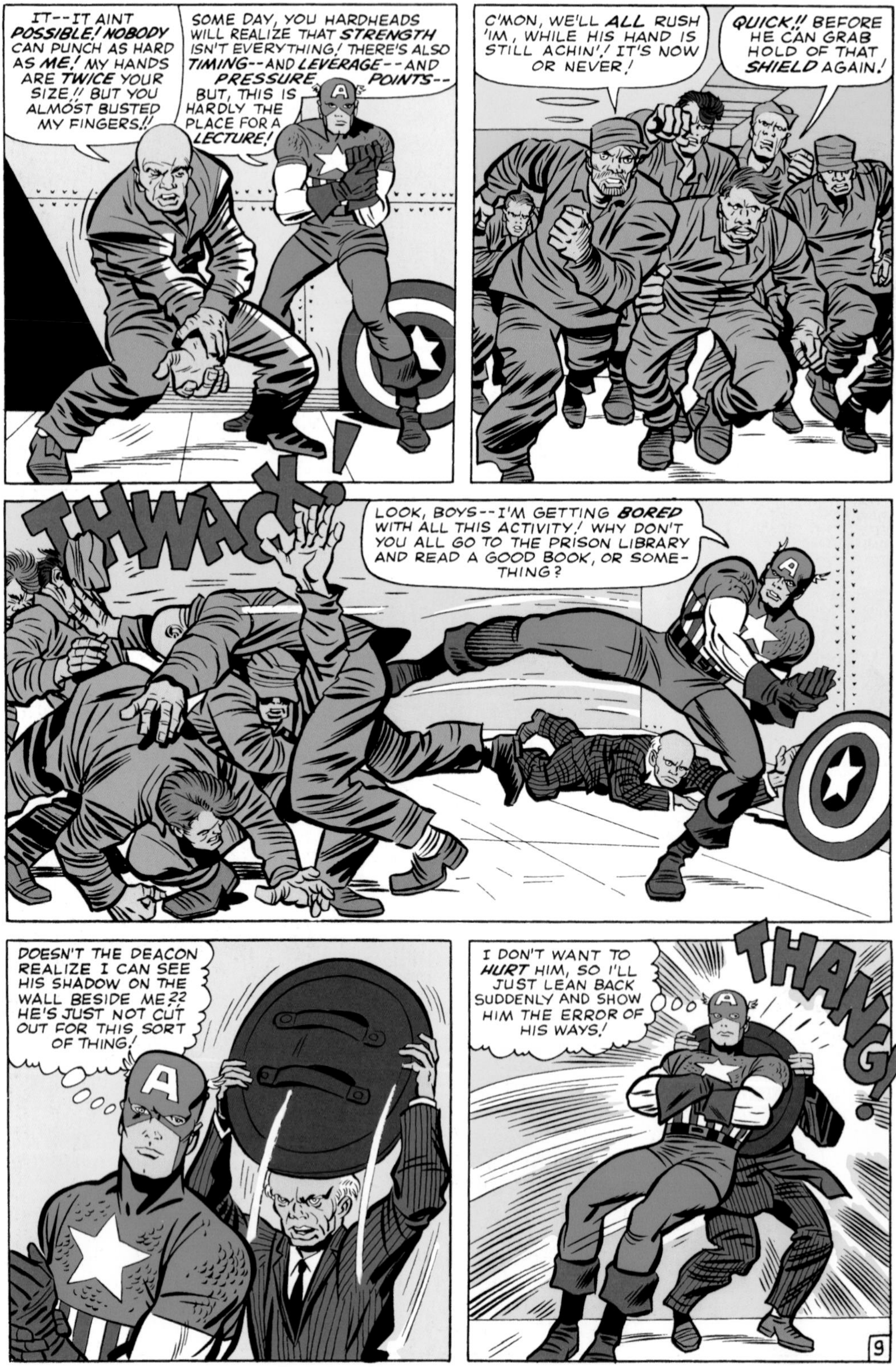
IT--IT AINT POSSIBLE! NOBODY CAN PUNCH AS HARD AS ME! MY HANDS ARE TWICE YOUR SIZE!! BUT YOU ALMOST BUSTED MY FINGERS!!
SOME DAY, YOU HARDHEADS WILL REALIZE THAT STRENGTH ISN'T EVERYTHING! THERE'S ALSO TIMING--AND LEVERAGE--AND PRESSURE POINTS-- BUT, THIS IS HARDLY THE PLACE FOR A LECTURE!
C'MON, WE'LL ALL RUSH 'IM, WHILE HIS HAND IS STILL ACHIN'! IT'S NOW OR NEVER!
QUICK!! BEFORE HE CAN GRAB HOLD OF THAT SHIELD AGAIN!
THWACK!
LOOK, BOYS--I'M GETTING BORED WITH ALL THIS ACTIVITY! WHY DON'T YOU ALL GO TO THE PRISON LIBRARY AND READ A GOOD BOOK, OR SOMETHING?
DOESN'T THE DEACON REALIZE I CAN SEE HIS SHADOW ON THE WALL BESIDE ME?? HE'S JUST NOT CUT OUT FOR THIS SORT OF THING!
I DON'T WANT TO HURT HIM, SO I'LL JUST LEAN BACK SUDDENLY AND SHOW HIM THE ERROR OF HIS WAYS!
THANG!
9

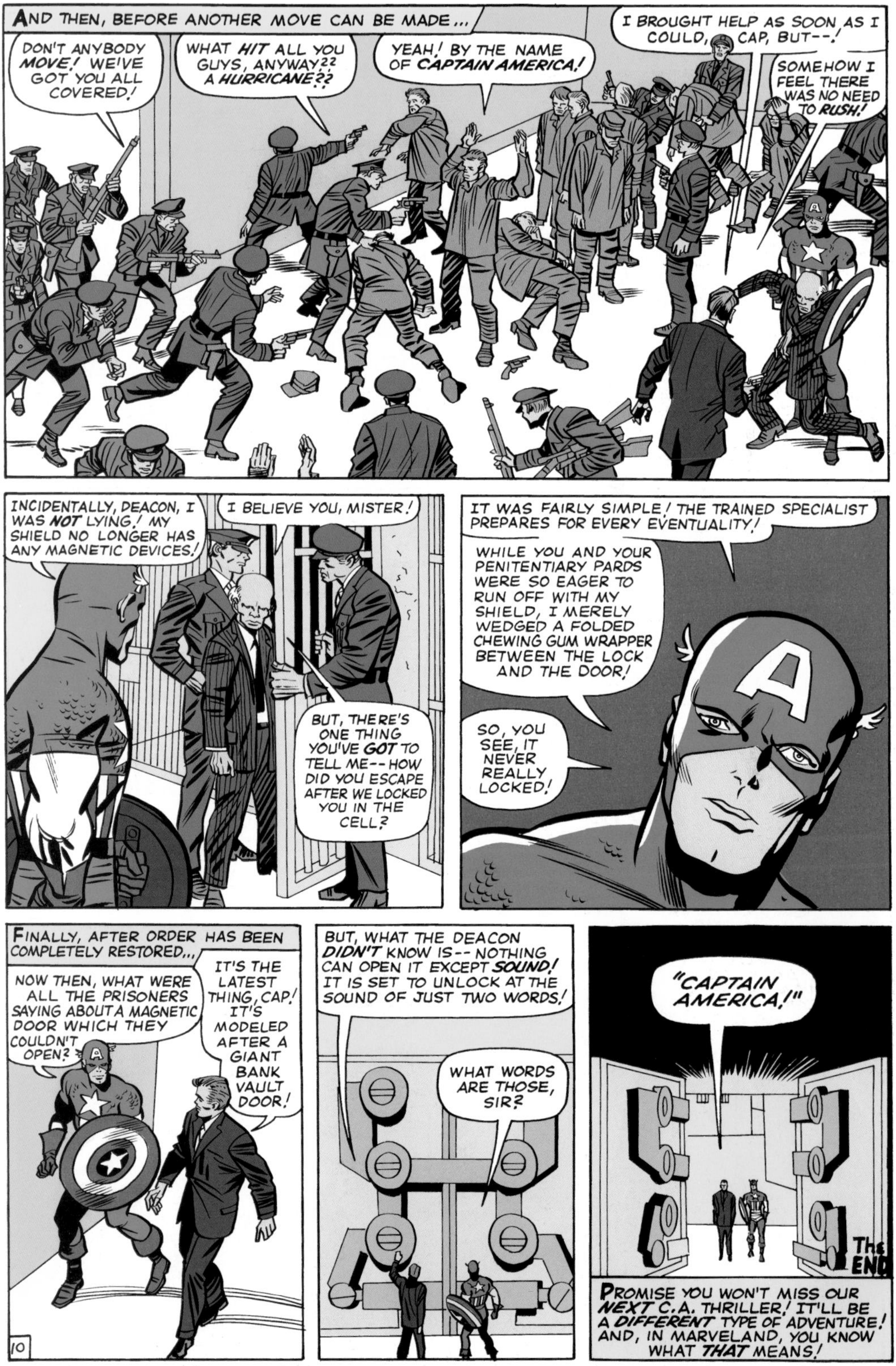
AND THEN, BEFORE ANOTHER MOVE CAN BE MADE...
DON'T ANYBODY MOVE! WE'VE GOT YOU ALL COVERED!
WHAT HIT ALL YOU GUYS, ANYWAY?? A HURRICANE??
YEAH! BY THE NAME OF CAPTAIN AMERICA!
I BROUGHT HELP AS SOON AS I COULD, CAP, BUT--!
SOMEHOW I FEEL THERE WAS NO NEED TO RUSH!
INCIDENTALLY, DEACON, I WAS NOT LYING! MY SHIELD NO LONGER HAS ANY MAGNETIC DEVICES!
I BELIEVE YOU, MISTER!
BUT, THERE'S ONE THING YOU'VE GOT TO TELL ME--HOW DID YOU ESCAPE AFTER WE LOCKED YOU IN THE CELL?
IT WAS FAIRLY SIMPLE! THE TRAINED SPECIALIST PREPARES FOR EVERY EVENTUALITY!
WHILE YOU AND YOUR PENITENTIARY PARDS WERE SO EAGER TO RUN OFF WITH MY SHIELD, I MERELY WEDGED A FOLDED CHEWING GUM WRAPPER BETWEEN THE LOCK AND THE DOOR!
SO, YOU SEE, IT NEVER REALLY LOCKED!
FINALLY, AFTER ORDER HAS BEEN COMPLETELY RESTORED...
NOW THEN, WHAT WERE ALL THE PRISONERS SAYING ABOUT A MAGNETIC DOOR WHICH THEY COULDN'T OPEN?
IT'S THE LATEST THING, CAP! IT'S MODELED AFTER A GIANT BANK VAULT DOOR!
10
BUT, WHAT THE DEACON DIDN'T KNOW IS-- NOTHING CAN OPEN IT EXCEPT SOUND! IT IS SET TO UNLOCK AT THE SOUND OF JUST TWO WORDS!
WHAT WORDS ARE THOSE, SIR?
"CAPTAIN AMERICA!"
The END
PROMISE YOU WON'T MISS OUR NEXT C.A. THRILLER! IT'LL BE A DIFFERENT TYPE OF ADVENTURE! AND, IN MARVELAND, YOU KNOW WHAT THAT MEANS!

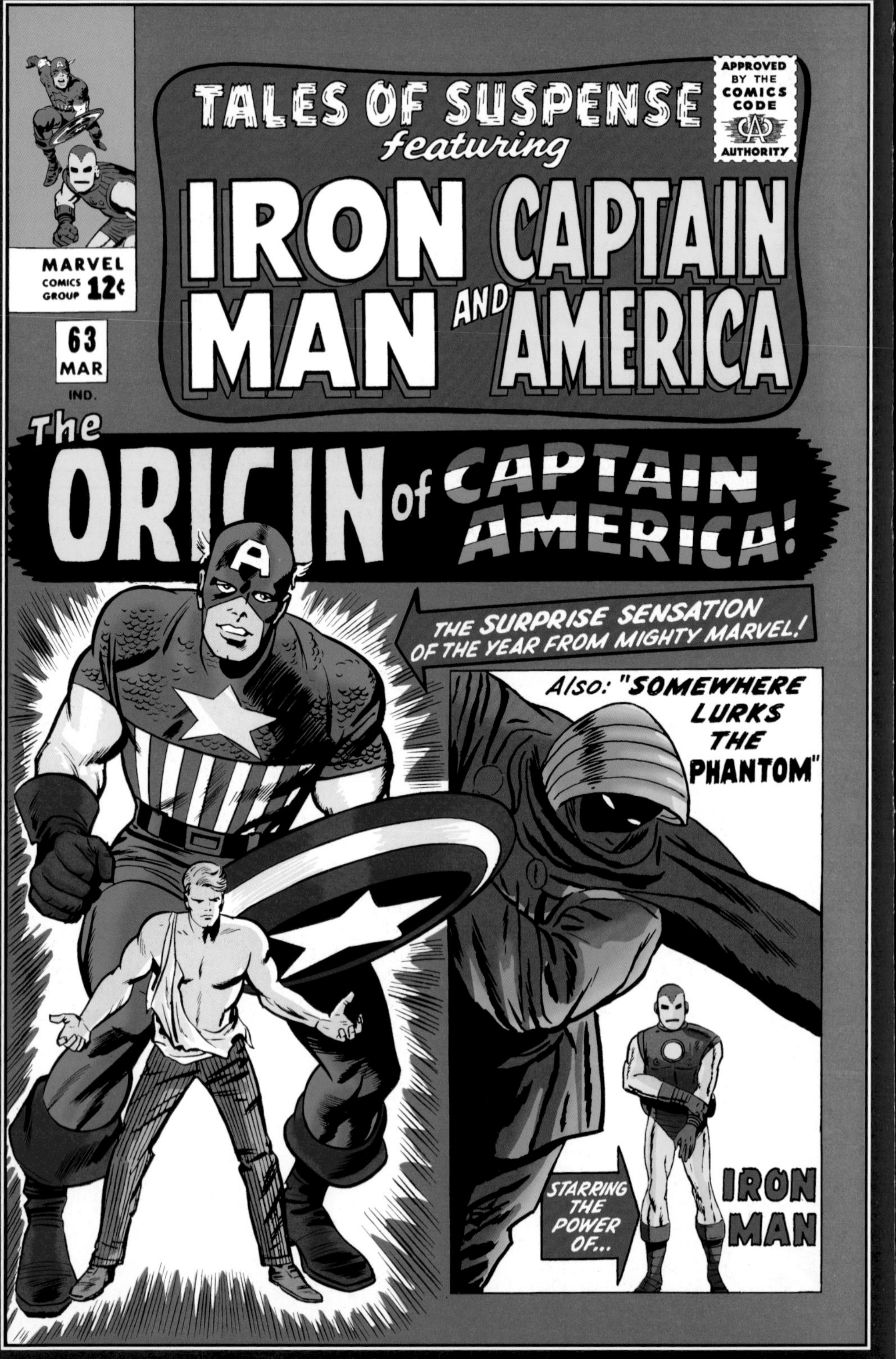

TALES OF SUSPENSE featuring
IRON MAN AND CAPTAIN AMERICA
APPROVED BY THE COMICS CODE AUTHORITY
MARVEL COMICS GROUP 12¢
63 MAR
IND.
The ORIGIN of CAPTAIN AMERICA!
THE SURPRISE SENSATION OF THE YEAR FROM MIGHTY MARVEL!
Also: "SOMEWHERE LURKS THE PHANTOM"
STARRING THE POWER OF...
IRON MAN

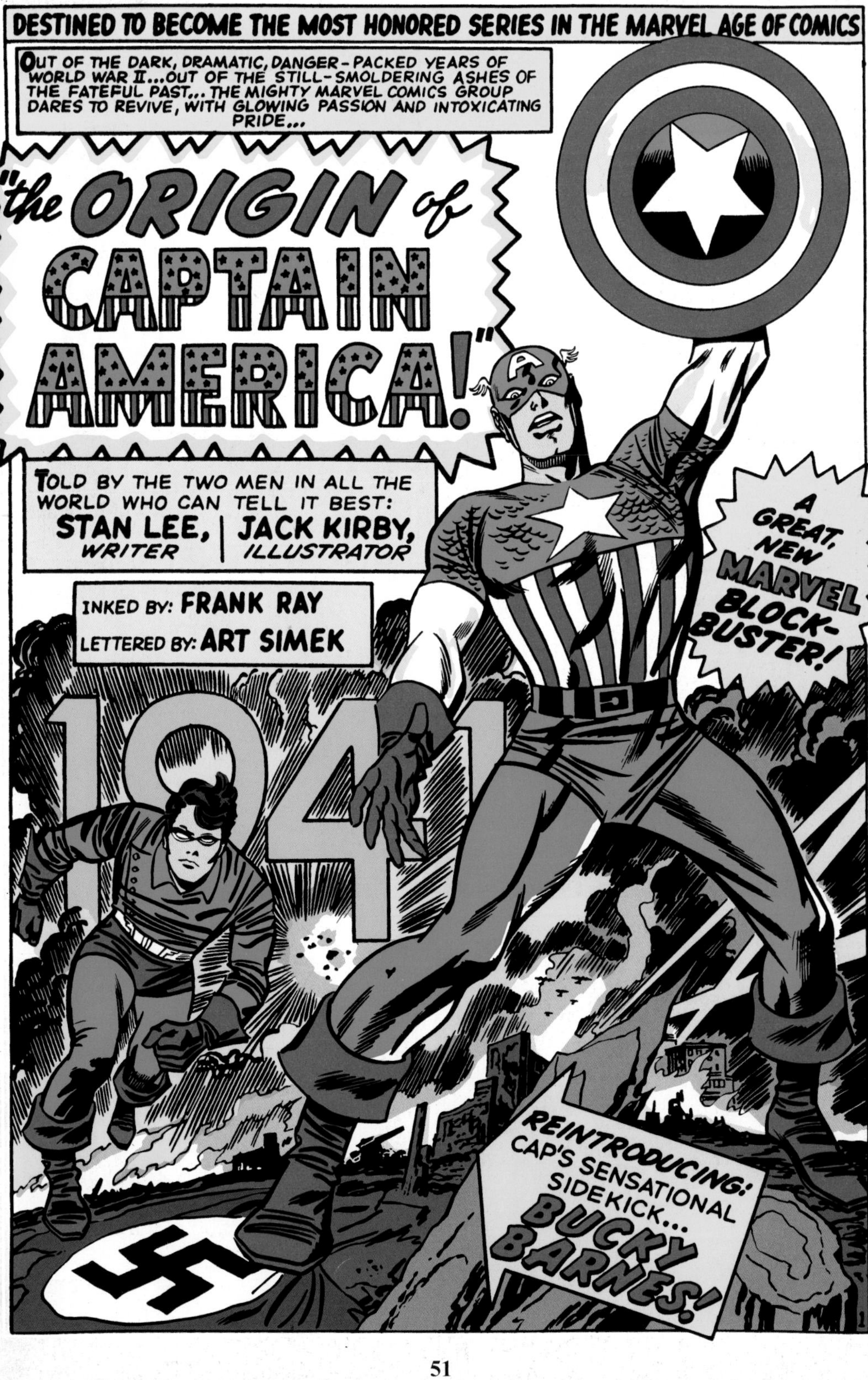

DESTINED TO BECOME THE MOST HONORED SERIES IN THE MARVEL AGE OF COMICS
OUT OF THE DARK, DRAMATIC, DANGER-PACKED YEARS OF WORLD WAR II...OUT OF THE STILL-SMOLDERING ASHES OF THE FATEFUL PAST... THE MIGHTY MARVEL COMICS GROUP DARES TO REVIVE, WITH GLOWING PASSION AND INTOXICATING PRIDE...
"the ORIGIN of CAPTAIN AMERICA!"
TOLD BY THE TWO MEN IN ALL THE WORLD WHO CAN TELL IT BEST:
STAN LEE, WRITER | JACK KIRBY, ILLUSTRATOR
INKED BY: FRANK RAY
LETTERED BY: ART SIMEK
A GREAT, NEW MARVEL BLOCK-BUSTER!
1941
REINTRODUCING: CAP'S SENSATIONAL SIDEKICK... BUCKY BARNES!

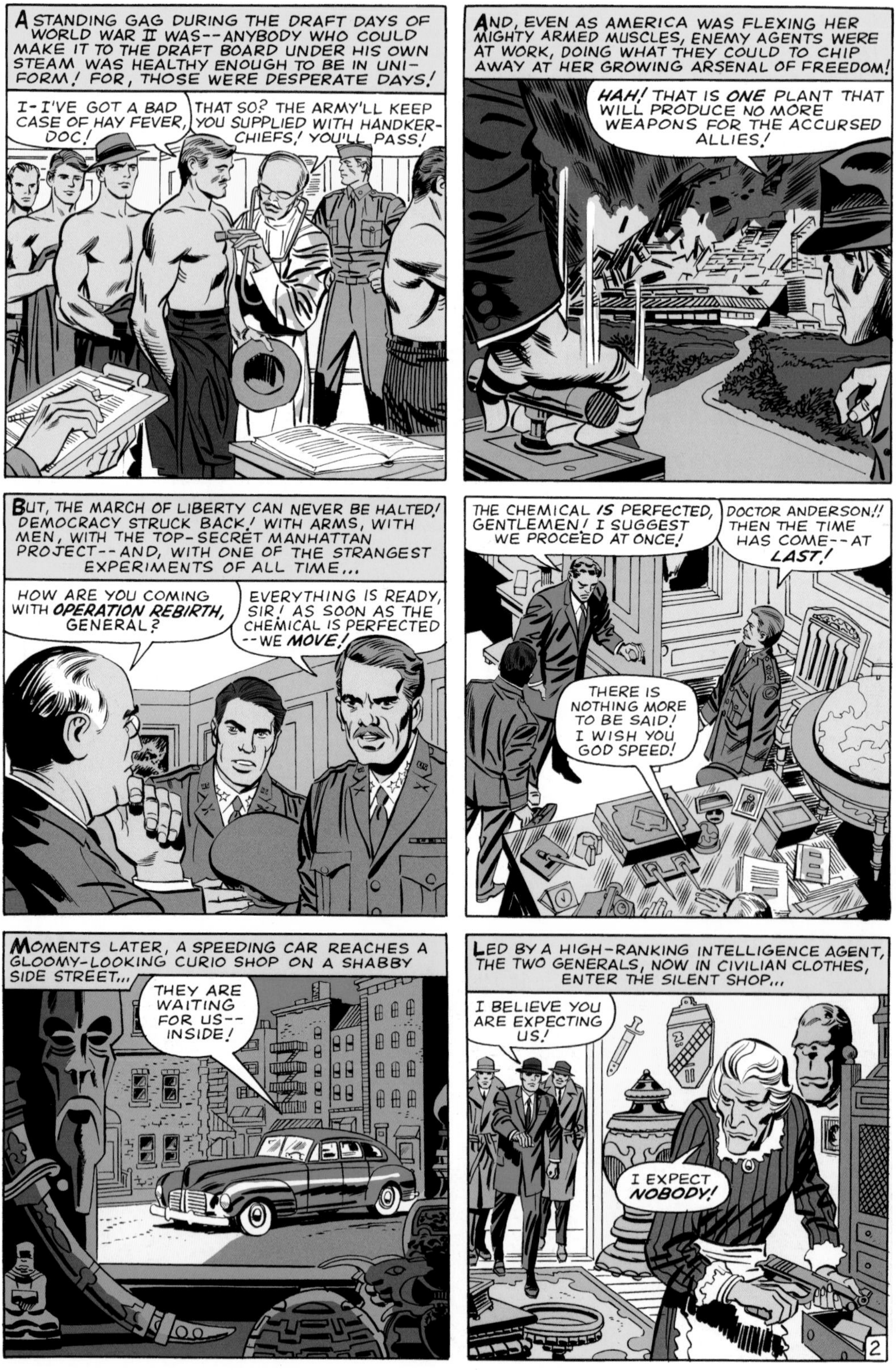
A STANDING GAG DURING THE DRAFT DAYS OF WORLD WAR II WAS--ANYBODY WHO COULD MAKE IT TO THE DRAFT BOARD UNDER HIS OWN STEAM WAS HEALTHY ENOUGH TO BE IN UNIFORM! FOR, THOSE WERE DESPERATE DAYS!
I-I'VE GOT A BAD CASE OF HAY FEVER, DOC!
THAT SO? THE ARMY'LL KEEP YOU SUPPLIED WITH HANDKERCHIEFS! YOU'LL PASS!
AND, EVEN AS AMERICA WAS FLEXING HER MIGHTY ARMED MUSCLES, ENEMY AGENTS WERE AT WORK, DOING WHAT THEY COULD TO CHIP AWAY AT HER GROWING ARSENAL OF FREEDOM!
HAH! THAT IS ONE PLANT THAT WILL PRODUCE NO MORE WEAPONS FOR THE ACCURSED ALLIES!
BUT, THE MARCH OF LIBERTY CAN NEVER BE HALTED! DEMOCRACY STRUCK BACK! WITH ARMS, WITH MEN, WITH THE TOP-SECRET MANHATTAN PROJECT--AND, WITH ONE OF THE STRANGEST EXPERIMENTS OF ALL TIME...
HOW ARE YOU COMING WITH OPERATION REBIRTH, GENERAL?
EVERYTHING IS READY, SIR! AS SOON AS THE CHEMICAL IS PERFECTED --WE MOVE!
THE CHEMICAL IS PERFECTED, GENTLEMEN! I SUGGEST WE PROCEED AT ONCE!
DOCTOR ANDERSON!! THEN THE TIME HAS COME--AT LAST!
THERE IS NOTHING MORE TO BE SAID! I WISH YOU GOD SPEED!
MOMENTS LATER, A SPEEDING CAR REACHES A GLOOMY-LOOKING CURIO SHOP ON A SHABBY SIDE STREET...
THEY ARE WAITING FOR US--INSIDE!
LED BY A HIGH-RANKING INTELLIGENCE AGENT, THE TWO GENERALS, NOW IN CIVILIAN CLOTHES, ENTER THE SILENT SHOP...
I BELIEVE YOU ARE EXPECTING US!
I EXPECT NOBODY!
2

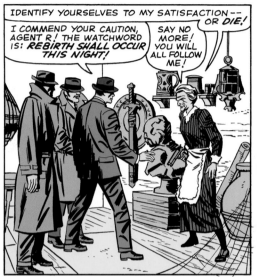

IDENTIFY YOURSELVES TO MY SATISFACTION-- OR *DIE!*

I COMMEND YOUR CAUTION, AGENT R! THE WATCHWORD IS: *REBIRTH SHALL OCCUR THIS NIGHT!*

SAY NO MORE! YOU WILL ALL FOLLOW ME!

IT'S HARD TO BELIEVE THAT THIS GLOOMY SHOP IS THE MOST IMPORTANT PIECE OF REAL ESTATE IN THE FREE WORLD TODAY!

SILENCE! THERE MUST BE NO UN-NECESSARY TALK! NOTHING MUST DISTRACT US FROM THE GREAT EXPERIMENT!

REACHING THE TOP FLOOR, THE SMALL PARTY WALKS THRU A HIDDEN DOORWAY, TO ENTER ONE OF THE MOST COMPLETELY EQUIPPED LABS IN THE WESTERN HEMISPHERE!

TAKE YOUR PLACES, GENTLEMEN! WE HAVE THIRTY SECONDS!

AT LAST I CAN DIVEST MYSELF OF THIS DISGUISE! THE DIE IS CAST! NOTHING CAN CHANGE THINGS NOW!

DO NOT BE SHOCKED, GENTLE-MEN! WHAT YOU ARE SOON ABOUT TO SEE WILL MAKE YOU FORGET ALL THESE MELODRAMATIC PRECAUTIONS!

BRING IN THE VOLUNTEER!

IT HAS TAKEN US *MONTHS* TO FIND THE PROPER 4F SPECIMEN WHOSE BODY WILL REACT PROPERLY TO OUR NEW TISSUE-BUILDING CHEMICAL!

HERE HE COMES NOW!

WITH OBVIOUS NERVOUSNESS, YET WITH A FIRM, FEARLESS TREAD, A THIN, SOMEWHAT SICKLY-LOOKING YOUTH ENTERS THE LAB--WALKING SLOWLY, SILENTLY, TOWARDS-- THE *UNKNOWN!*

STEP FORWARD, ROGERS!

3

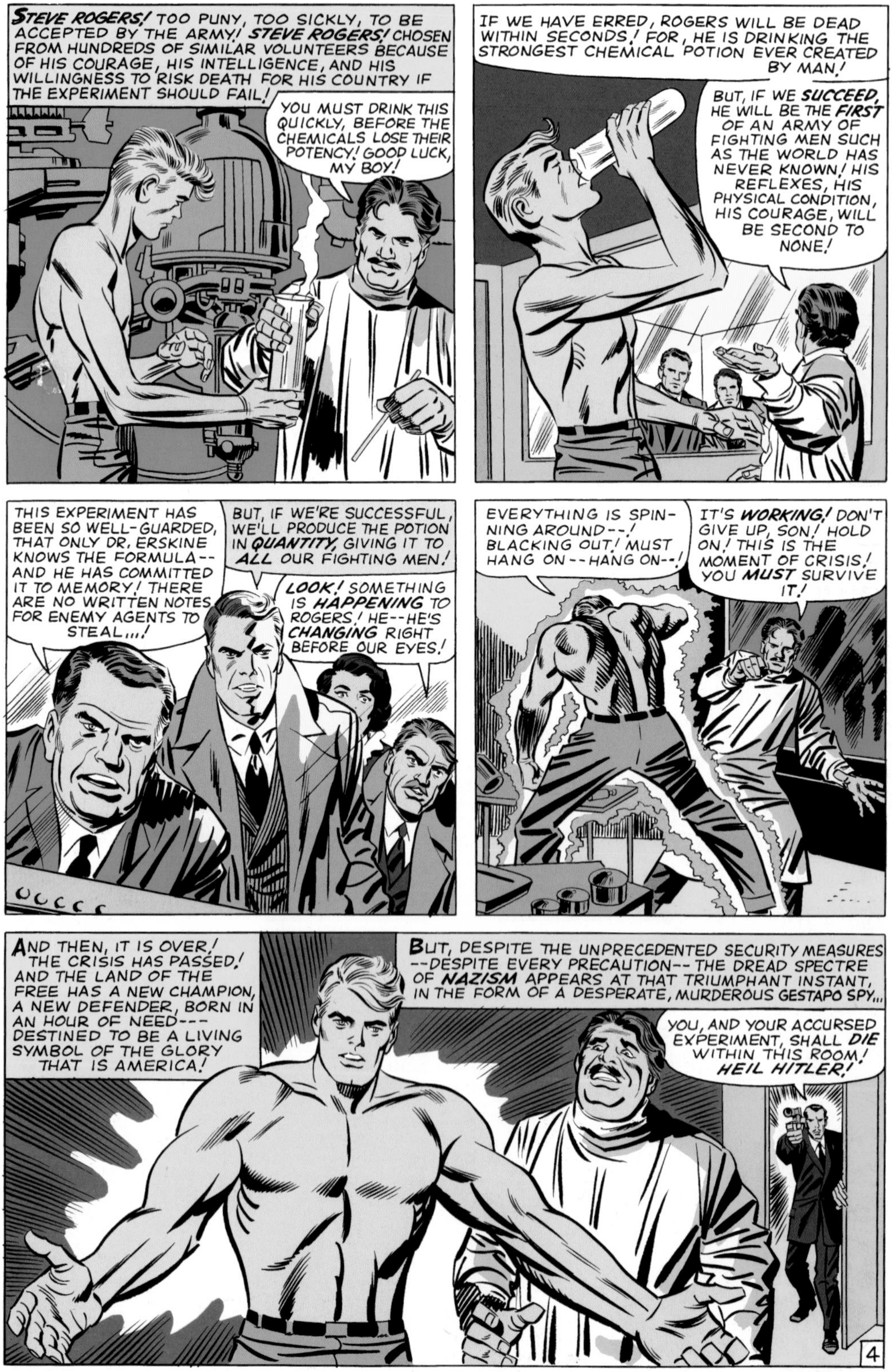
STEVE ROGERS! TOO PUNY, TOO SICKLY, TO BE ACCEPTED BY THE ARMY! STEVE ROGERS! CHOSEN FROM HUNDREDS OF SIMILAR VOLUNTEERS BECAUSE OF HIS COURAGE, HIS INTELLIGENCE, AND HIS WILLINGNESS TO RISK DEATH FOR HIS COUNTRY IF THE EXPERIMENT SHOULD FAIL!
YOU MUST DRINK THIS QUICKLY, BEFORE THE CHEMICALS LOSE THEIR POTENCY! GOOD LUCK, MY BOY!
IF WE HAVE ERRED, ROGERS WILL BE DEAD WITHIN SECONDS! FOR, HE IS DRINKING THE STRONGEST CHEMICAL POTION EVER CREATED BY MAN!
BUT, IF WE SUCCEED, HE WILL BE THE FIRST OF AN ARMY OF FIGHTING MEN SUCH AS THE WORLD HAS NEVER KNOWN! HIS REFLEXES, HIS PHYSICAL CONDITION, HIS COURAGE, WILL BE SECOND TO NONE!
THIS EXPERIMENT HAS BEEN SO WELL-GUARDED, THAT ONLY DR. ERSKINE KNOWS THE FORMULA--AND HE HAS COMMITTED IT TO MEMORY! THERE ARE NO WRITTEN NOTES FOR ENEMY AGENTS TO STEAL...!
BUT, IF WE'RE SUCCESSFUL, WE'LL PRODUCE THE POTION IN QUANTITY, GIVING IT TO ALL OUR FIGHTING MEN!
LOOK! SOMETHING IS HAPPENING TO ROGERS! HE--HE'S CHANGING RIGHT BEFORE OUR EYES!
EVERYTHING IS SPINNING AROUND--! BLACKING OUT! MUST HANG ON--HANG ON--!
IT'S WORKING! DON'T GIVE UP, SON! HOLD ON! THIS IS THE MOMENT OF CRISIS! YOU MUST SURVIVE IT!
AND THEN, IT IS OVER! THE CRISIS HAS PASSED! AND THE LAND OF THE FREE HAS A NEW CHAMPION, A NEW DEFENDER, BORN IN AN HOUR OF NEED---DESTINED TO BE A LIVING SYMBOL OF THE GLORY THAT IS AMERICA!
BUT, DESPITE THE UNPRECEDENTED SECURITY MEASURES--DESPITE EVERY PRECAUTION--THE DREAD SPECTRE OF NAZISM APPEARS AT THAT TRIUMPHANT INSTANT, IN THE FORM OF A DESPERATE, MURDEROUS GESTAPO SPY...
YOU, AND YOUR ACCURSED EXPERIMENT, SHALL DIE WITHIN THIS ROOM! HEIL HITLER!
4

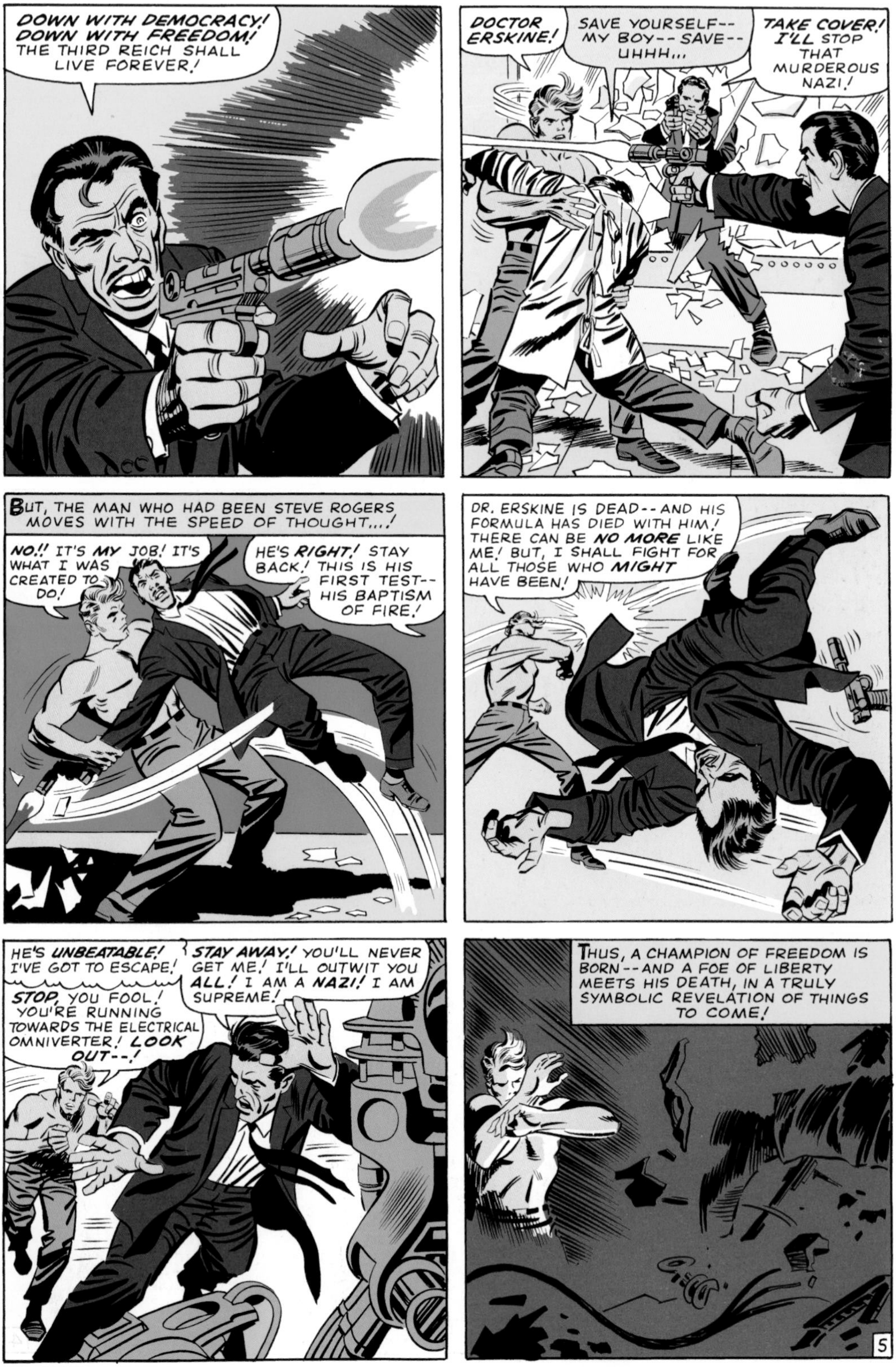
DOWN WITH DEMOCRACY! DOWN WITH FREEDOM! THE THIRD REICH SHALL LIVE FOREVER!
DOCTOR ERSKINE!
SAVE YOURSELF-- MY BOY-- SAVE-- UHHH...
TAKE COVER! I'LL STOP THAT MURDEROUS NAZI!
BUT, THE MAN WHO HAD BEEN STEVE ROGERS MOVES WITH THE SPEED OF THOUGHT...!
NO!! IT'S MY JOB! IT'S WHAT I WAS CREATED TO DO!
HE'S RIGHT! STAY BACK! THIS IS HIS FIRST TEST-- HIS BAPTISM OF FIRE!
DR. ERSKINE IS DEAD--AND HIS FORMULA HAS DIED WITH HIM! THERE CAN BE NO MORE LIKE ME! BUT, I SHALL FIGHT FOR ALL THOSE WHO MIGHT HAVE BEEN!
HE'S UNBEATABLE! I'VE GOT TO ESCAPE!
STAY AWAY! YOU'LL NEVER GET ME! I'LL OUTWIT YOU ALL! I AM A NAZI! I AM SUPREME!
STOP, YOU FOOL! YOU'RE RUNNING TOWARDS THE ELECTRICAL OMNIVERTER! LOOK OUT--!
THUS, A CHAMPION OF FREEDOM IS BORN--AND A FOE OF LIBERTY MEETS HIS DEATH, IN A TRULY SYMBOLIC REVELATION OF THINGS TO COME!
5

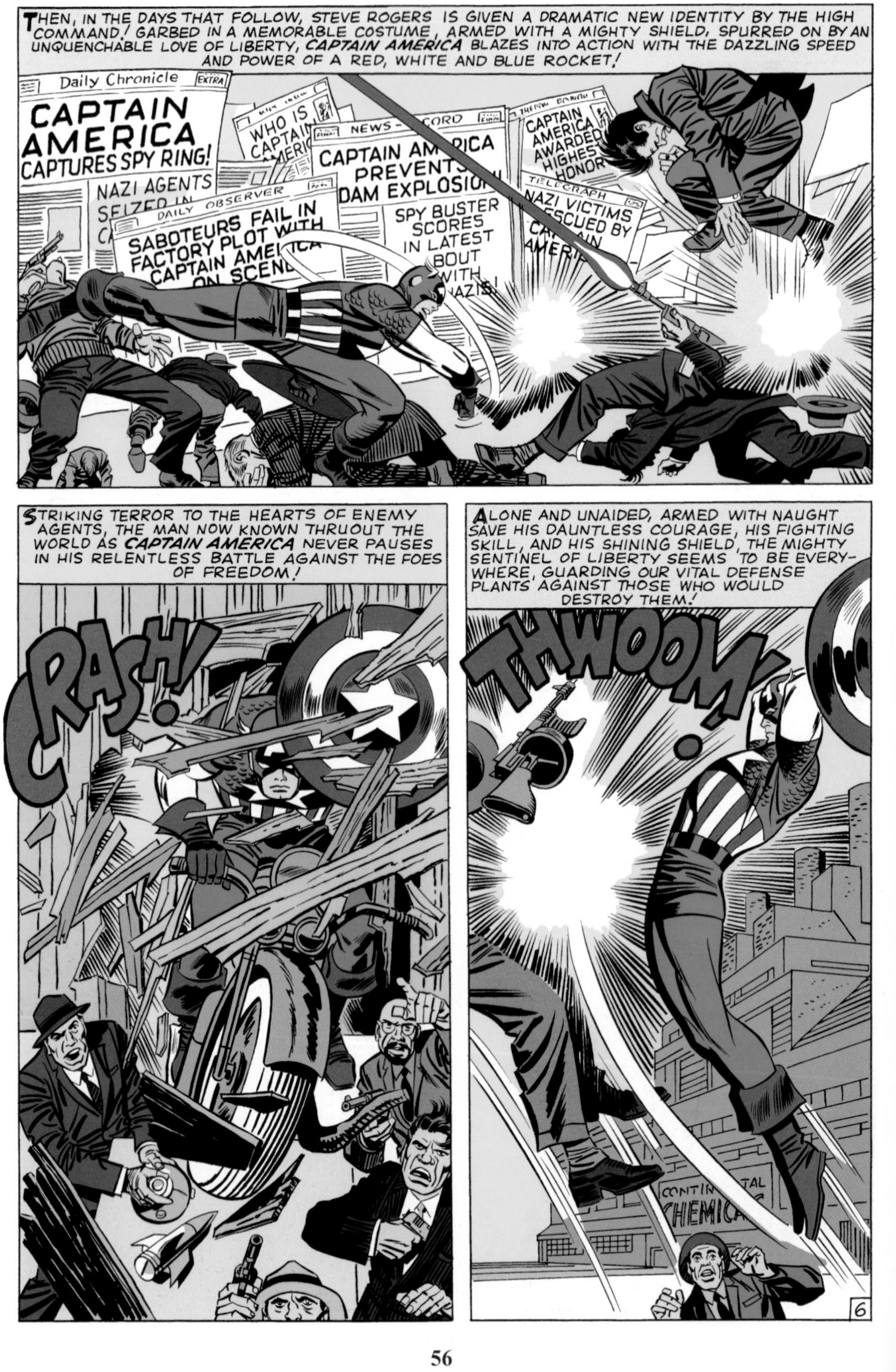
THEN, IN THE DAYS THAT FOLLOW, STEVE ROGERS IS GIVEN A DRAMATIC NEW IDENTITY BY THE HIGH COMMAND! GARBED IN A MEMORABLE COSTUME, ARMED WITH A MIGHTY SHIELD, SPURRED ON BY AN UNQUENCHABLE LOVE OF LIBERTY, CAPTAIN AMERICA BLAZES INTO ACTION WITH THE DAZZLING SPEED AND POWER OF A RED, WHITE AND BLUE ROCKET!
Daily Chronicle
EXTRA
CAPTAIN AMERICA CAPTURES SPY RING!
NAZI AGENTS
DAILY OBSERVER
SABOTEURS FAIL IN
TELEGRAPH
NAZI VICTIMS
SPY BUSTER SCORES IN LATEST BOUT
STRIKING TERROR TO THE HEARTS OF ENEMY AGENTS, THE MAN NOW KNOWN THRUOUT THE WORLD AS CAPTAIN AMERICA NEVER PAUSES IN HIS RELENTLESS BATTLE AGAINST THE FOES OF FREEDOM!
CRASH!
ALONE AND UNAIDED, ARMED WITH NAUGHT SAVE HIS DAUNTLESS COURAGE, HIS FIGHTING SKILL, AND HIS SHINING SHIELD, THE MIGHTY SENTINEL OF LIBERTY SEEMS TO BE EVERY-WHERE, GUARDING OUR VITAL DEFENSE PLANTS AGAINST THOSE WHO WOULD DESTROY THEM!
THWOOM!
6

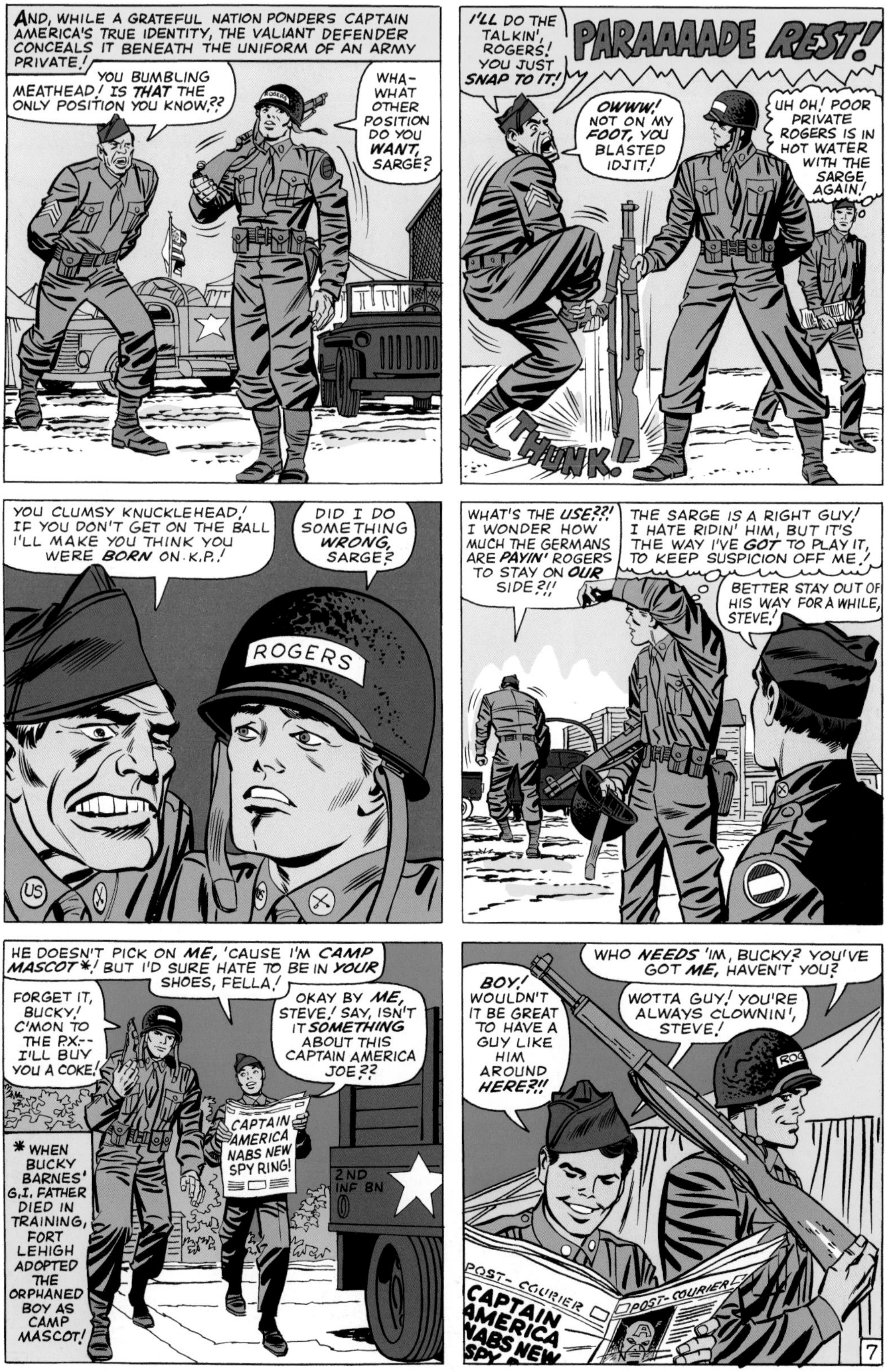
AND, WHILE A GRATEFUL NATION PONDERS CAPTAIN AMERICA'S TRUE IDENTITY, THE VALIANT DEFENDER CONCEALS IT BENEATH THE UNIFORM OF AN ARMY PRIVATE!
YOU BUMBLING MEATHEAD! IS THAT THE ONLY POSITION YOU KNOW??
WHA-WHAT OTHER POSITION DO YOU WANT, SARGE?
ROGERS
I'LL DO THE TALKIN', ROGERS! YOU JUST SNAP TO IT!
PARAAAADE REST!
OWWW! NOT ON MY FOOT, YOU BLASTED IDJIT!
UH OH! POOR PRIVATE ROGERS IS IN HOT WATER WITH THE SARGE AGAIN!
THUNK!
YOU CLUMSY KNUCKLEHEAD! IF YOU DON'T GET ON THE BALL I'LL MAKE YOU THINK YOU WERE BORN ON K.P.!
DID I DO SOMETHING WRONG, SARGE?
ROGERS
US
WHAT'S THE USE??! I WONDER HOW MUCH THE GERMANS ARE PAYIN' ROGERS TO STAY ON OUR SIDE?!!
THE SARGE IS A RIGHT GUY! I HATE RIDIN' HIM, BUT IT'S THE WAY I'VE GOT TO PLAY IT, TO KEEP SUSPICION OFF ME!
BETTER STAY OUT OF HIS WAY FOR A WHILE, STEVE!
HE DOESN'T PICK ON ME, 'CAUSE I'M CAMP MASCOT*! BUT I'D SURE HATE TO BE IN YOUR SHOES, FELLA!
FORGET IT, BUCKY! C'MON TO THE P.X.-- I'LL BUY YOU A COKE!
OKAY BY ME, STEVE! SAY, ISN'T IT SOMETHING ABOUT THIS CAPTAIN AMERICA JOE??
CAPTAIN AMERICA NABS NEW SPY RING!
2ND INF BN
* WHEN BUCKY BARNES' G.I. FATHER DIED IN TRAINING, FORT LEHIGH ADOPTED THE ORPHANED BOY AS CAMP MASCOT!
WHO NEEDS 'IM, BUCKY? YOU'VE GOT ME, HAVEN'T YOU?
BOY! WOULDN'T IT BE GREAT TO HAVE A GUY LIKE HIM AROUND HERE?!!
WOTTA GUY! YOU'RE ALWAYS CLOWNIN', STEVE!
ROG
POST-COURIER
POST-COURIER
CAPTAIN AMERICA NABS NEW SPY
7

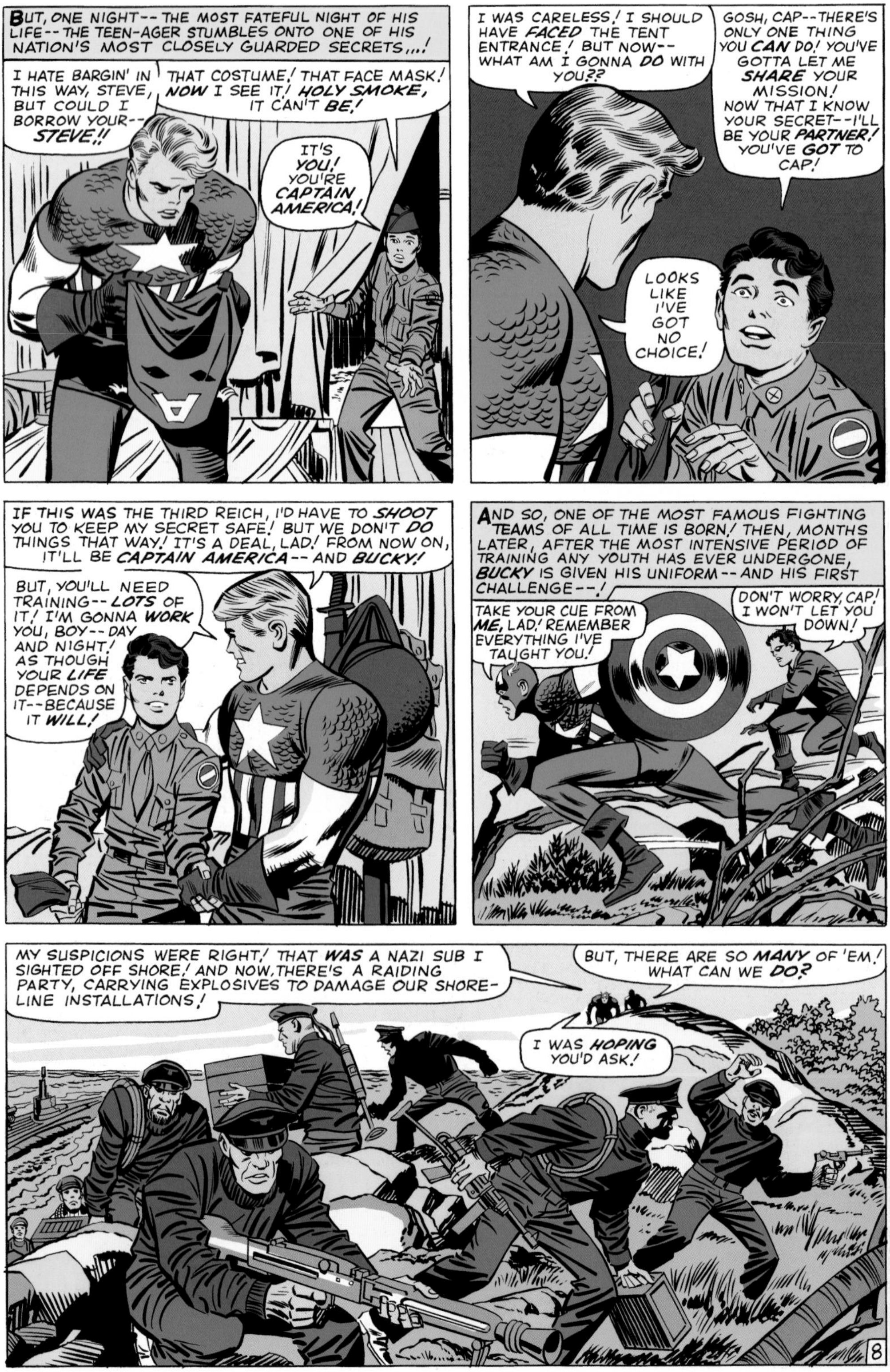
BUT, ONE NIGHT-- THE MOST FATEFUL NIGHT OF HIS LIFE-- THE TEEN-AGER STUMBLES ONTO ONE OF HIS NATION'S MOST CLOSELY GUARDED SECRETS...!
I HATE BARGIN' IN THIS WAY, STEVE, BUT COULD I BORROW YOUR-- STEVE!!
THAT COSTUME! THAT FACE MASK! NOW I SEE IT! HOLY SMOKE, IT CAN'T BE!
IT'S YOU! YOU'RE CAPTAIN AMERICA!
I WAS CARELESS! I SHOULD HAVE FACED THE TENT ENTRANCE! BUT NOW-- WHAT AM I GONNA DO WITH YOU??
GOSH, CAP--THERE'S ONLY ONE THING YOU CAN DO! YOU'VE GOTTA LET ME SHARE YOUR MISSION! NOW THAT I KNOW YOUR SECRET--I'LL BE YOUR PARTNER! YOU'VE GOT TO CAP!
LOOKS LIKE I'VE GOT NO CHOICE!
IF THIS WAS THE THIRD REICH, I'D HAVE TO SHOOT YOU TO KEEP MY SECRET SAFE! BUT WE DON'T DO THINGS THAT WAY! IT'S A DEAL, LAD! FROM NOW ON, IT'LL BE CAPTAIN AMERICA-- AND BUCKY!
BUT, YOU'LL NEED TRAINING-- LOTS OF IT! I'M GONNA WORK YOU, BOY-- DAY AND NIGHT! AS THOUGH YOUR LIFE DEPENDS ON IT--BECAUSE IT WILL!
AND SO, ONE OF THE MOST FAMOUS FIGHTING TEAMS OF ALL TIME IS BORN! THEN, MONTHS LATER, AFTER THE MOST INTENSIVE PERIOD OF TRAINING ANY YOUTH HAS EVER UNDERGONE, BUCKY IS GIVEN HIS UNIFORM -- AND HIS FIRST CHALLENGE--!
TAKE YOUR CUE FROM ME, LAD! REMEMBER EVERYTHING I'VE TAUGHT YOU!
DON'T WORRY, CAP! I WON'T LET YOU DOWN!
MY SUSPICIONS WERE RIGHT! THAT WAS A NAZI SUB I SIGHTED OFF SHORE! AND NOW, THERE'S A RAIDING PARTY, CARRYING EXPLOSIVES TO DAMAGE OUR SHORE-LINE INSTALLATIONS!
BUT, THERE ARE SO MANY OF 'EM! WHAT CAN WE DO?
I WAS HOPING YOU'D ASK!
8

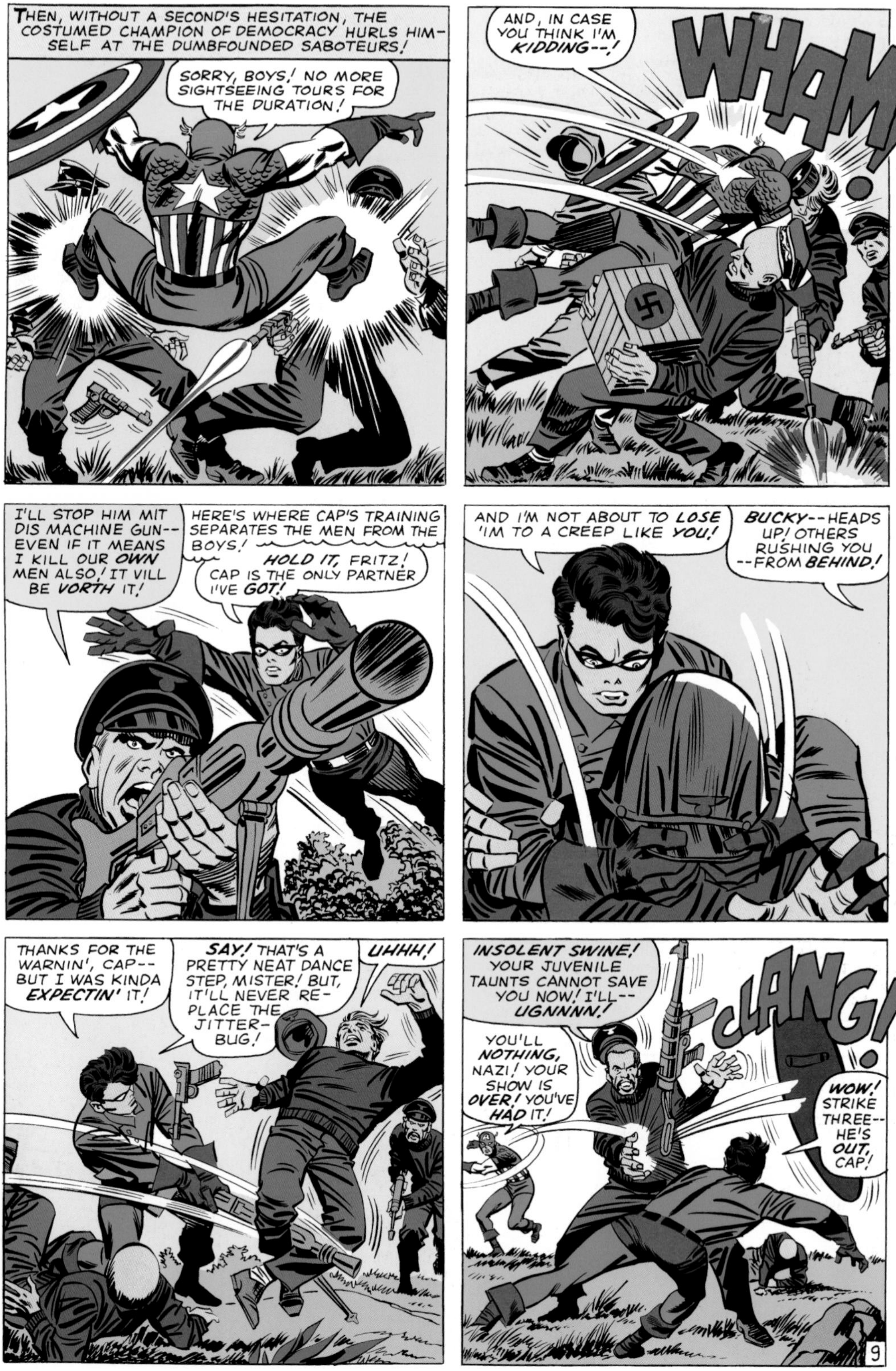
THEN, WITHOUT A SECOND'S HESITATION, THE COSTUMED CHAMPION OF DEMOCRACY HURLS HIMSELF AT THE DUMBFOUNDED SABOTEURS!
SORRY, BOYS! NO MORE SIGHTSEEING TOURS FOR THE DURATION!
AND, IN CASE YOU THINK I'M KIDDING--!
WHAM!
I'LL STOP HIM MIT DIS MACHINE GUN-- EVEN IF IT MEANS I KILL OUR OWN MEN ALSO! IT VILL BE VORTH IT!
HERE'S WHERE CAP'S TRAINING SEPARATES THE MEN FROM THE BOYS!
HOLD IT, FRITZ! CAP IS THE ONLY PARTNER I'VE GOT!
AND I'M NOT ABOUT TO LOSE 'IM TO A CREEP LIKE YOU!
BUCKY--HEADS UP! OTHERS RUSHING YOU --FROM BEHIND!
THANKS FOR THE WARNIN', CAP-- BUT I WAS KINDA EXPECTIN' IT!
SAY! THAT'S A PRETTY NEAT DANCE STEP, MISTER! BUT, IT'LL NEVER REPLACE THE JITTERBUG!
UHHH!
INSOLENT SWINE! YOUR JUVENILE TAUNTS CANNOT SAVE YOU NOW! I'LL-- UGNNNN!
CLANG!
YOU'LL NOTHING, NAZI! YOUR SHOW IS OVER! YOU'VE HAD IT!
WOW! STRIKE THREE-- HE'S OUT, CAP!
9

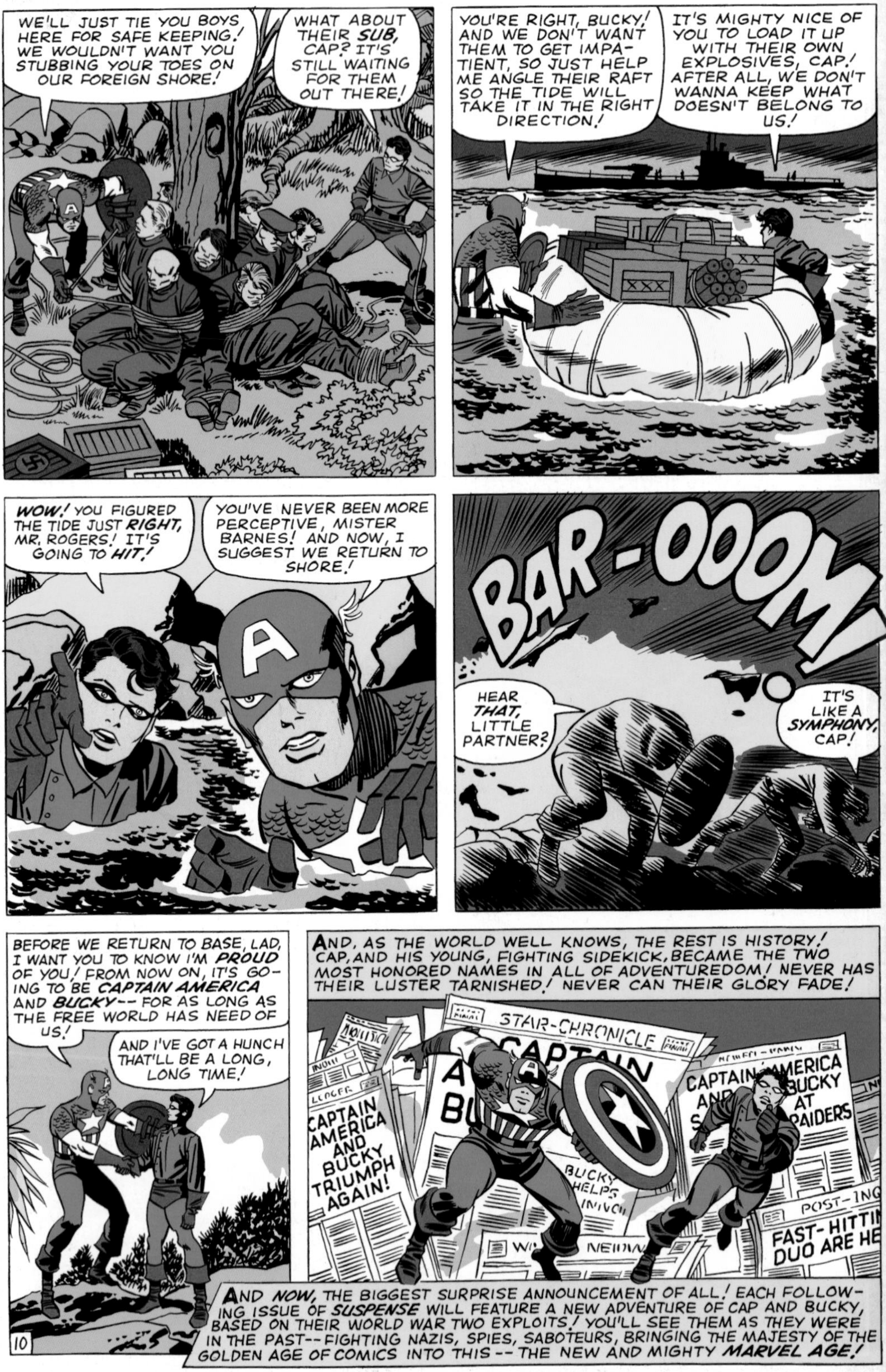
WE'LL JUST TIE YOU BOYS HERE FOR SAFE KEEPING! WE WOULDN'T WANT YOU STUBBING YOUR TOES ON OUR FOREIGN SHORE!
WHAT ABOUT THEIR SUB, CAP? IT'S STILL WAITING FOR THEM OUT THERE!
YOU'RE RIGHT, BUCKY! AND WE DON'T WANT THEM TO GET IMPATIENT, SO JUST HELP ME ANGLE THEIR RAFT SO THE TIDE WILL TAKE IT IN THE RIGHT DIRECTION!
IT'S MIGHTY NICE OF YOU TO LOAD IT UP WITH THEIR OWN EXPLOSIVES, CAP! AFTER ALL, WE DON'T WANNA KEEP WHAT DOESN'T BELONG TO US!
WOW! YOU FIGURED THE TIDE JUST RIGHT, MR. ROGERS! IT'S GOING TO HIT!
YOU'VE NEVER BEEN MORE PERCEPTIVE, MISTER BARNES! AND NOW, I SUGGEST WE RETURN TO SHORE!
BAR-OOOM!
HEAR THAT, LITTLE PARTNER?
IT'S LIKE A SYMPHONY, CAP!
BEFORE WE RETURN TO BASE, LAD, I WANT YOU TO KNOW I'M PROUD OF YOU! FROM NOW ON, IT'S GOING TO BE CAPTAIN AMERICA AND BUCKY-- FOR AS LONG AS THE FREE WORLD HAS NEED OF US!
AND I'VE GOT A HUNCH THAT'LL BE A LONG, LONG TIME!
10
AND, AS THE WORLD WELL KNOWS, THE REST IS HISTORY! CAP, AND HIS YOUNG, FIGHTING SIDEKICK, BECAME THE TWO MOST HONORED NAMES IN ALL OF ADVENTUREDOM! NEVER HAS THEIR LUSTER TARNISHED! NEVER CAN THEIR GLORY FADE!
STAR-CHRONICLE
CAPTAIN
CAPTAIN AMERICA AND BUCKY TRIUMPH AGAIN!
CAPTAIN AMERICA BUCKY AT RAIDERS
BUCKY HELPS
POST-ING
FAST-HITTIN DUO ARE HE
AND NOW, THE BIGGEST SURPRISE ANNOUNCEMENT OF ALL! EACH FOLLOWING ISSUE OF SUSPENSE WILL FEATURE A NEW ADVENTURE OF CAP AND BUCKY, BASED ON THEIR WORLD WAR TWO EXPLOITS! YOU'LL SEE THEM AS THEY WERE IN THE PAST-- FIGHTING NAZIS, SPIES, SABOTEURS, BRINGING THE MAJESTY OF THE GOLDEN AGE OF COMICS INTO THIS -- THE NEW AND MIGHTY MARVEL AGE!

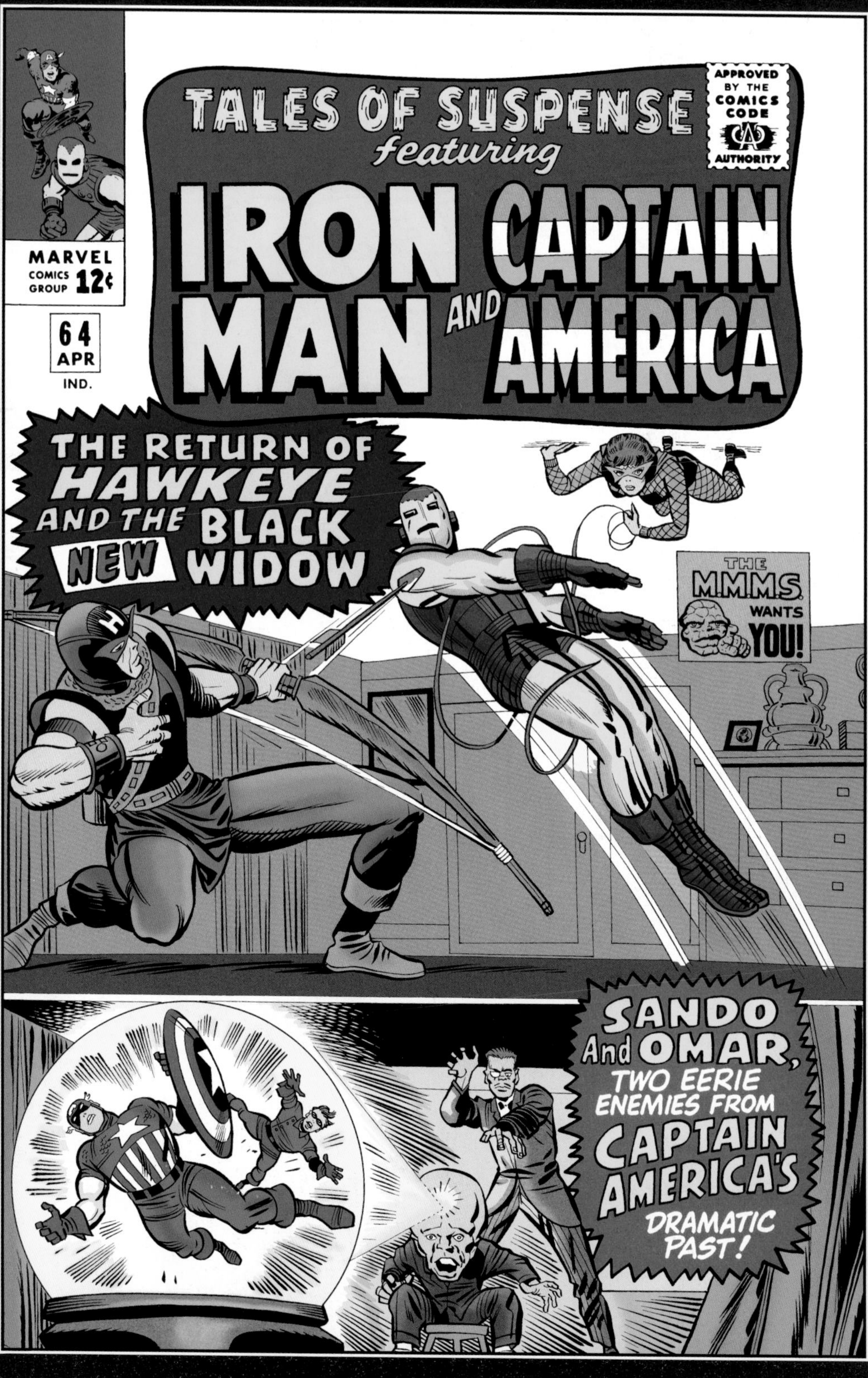
TALES OF SUSPENSE featuring
IRON MAN AND CAPTAIN AMERICA
APPROVED BY THE COMICS CODE AUTHORITY
MARVEL COMICS GROUP 12¢
64 APR
IND.
THE RETURN OF HAWKEYE AND THE NEW BLACK WIDOW
THE M.M.M.S. WANTS YOU!
SANDO And OMAR, TWO EERIE ENEMIES FROM CAPTAIN AMERICA'S DRAMATIC PAST!

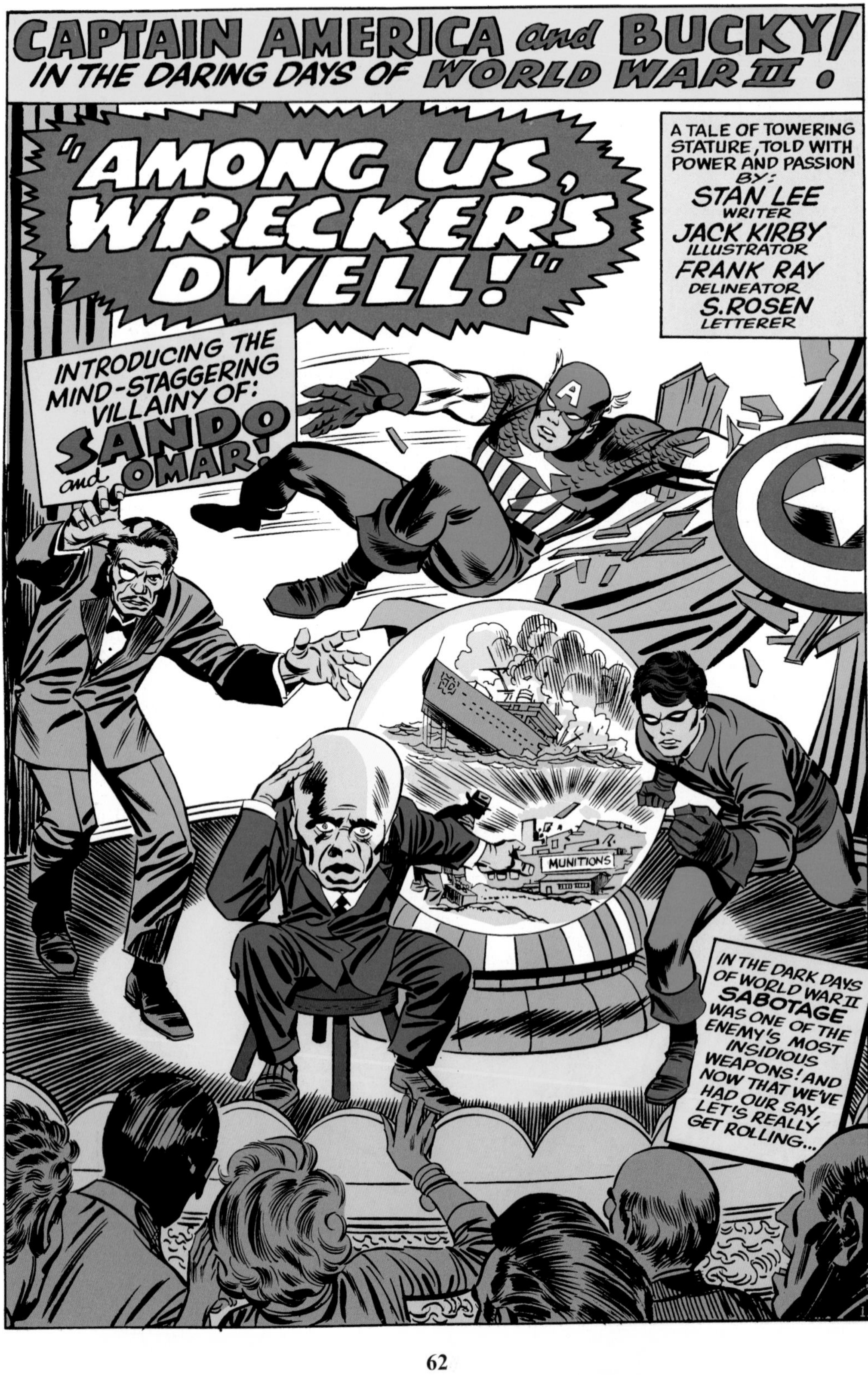
CAPTAIN AMERICA and BUCKY!
IN THE DARING DAYS OF WORLD WAR II!
"AMONG US, WRECKERS DWELL!"
A TALE OF TOWERING STATURE, TOLD WITH POWER AND PASSION BY:
STAN LEE WRITER
JACK KIRBY ILLUSTRATOR
FRANK RAY DELINEATOR
S. ROSEN LETTERER
INTRODUCING THE MIND-STAGGERING VILLAINY OF: SANDO and OMAR!
MUNITIONS
IN THE DARK DAYS OF WORLD WAR II SABOTAGE WAS ONE OF THE ENEMY'S MOST INSIDIOUS WEAPONS! AND NOW THAT WE'VE HAD OUR SAY, LET'S REALLY GET ROLLING...
1

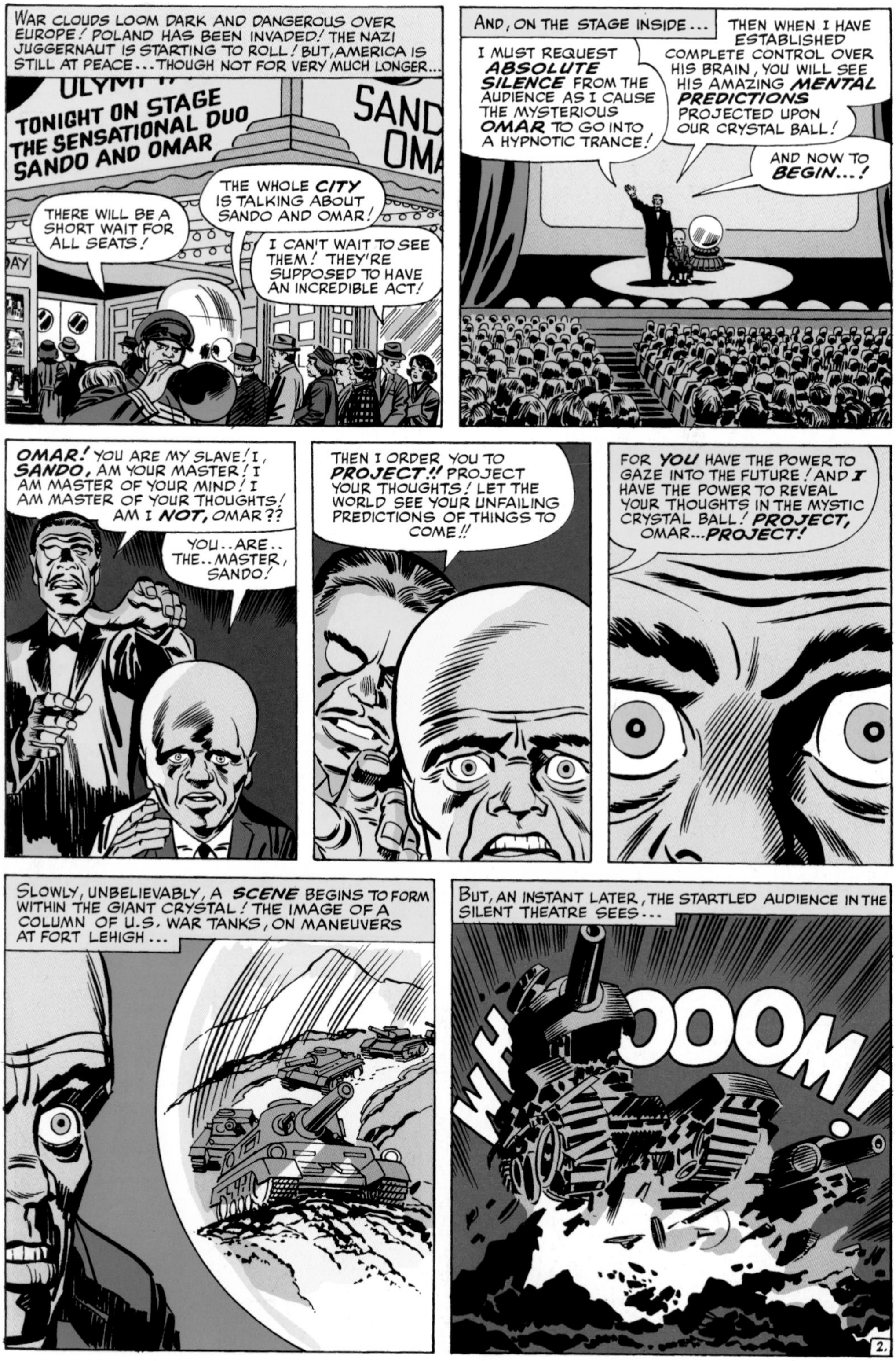
WAR CLOUDS LOOM DARK AND DANGEROUS OVER EUROPE! POLAND HAS BEEN INVADED! THE NAZI JUGGERNAUT IS STARTING TO ROLL! BUT, AMERICA IS STILL AT PEACE... THOUGH NOT FOR VERY MUCH LONGER...
TONIGHT ON STAGE THE SENSATIONAL DUO SANDO AND OMAR
THE WHOLE CITY IS TALKING ABOUT SANDO AND OMAR!
THERE WILL BE A SHORT WAIT FOR ALL SEATS!
I CAN'T WAIT TO SEE THEM! THEY'RE SUPPOSED TO HAVE AN INCREDIBLE ACT!
AND, ON THE STAGE INSIDE...
I MUST REQUEST ABSOLUTE SILENCE FROM THE AUDIENCE AS I CAUSE THE MYSTERIOUS OMAR TO GO INTO A HYPNOTIC TRANCE!
THEN WHEN I HAVE ESTABLISHED COMPLETE CONTROL OVER HIS BRAIN, YOU WILL SEE HIS AMAZING MENTAL PREDICTIONS PROJECTED UPON OUR CRYSTAL BALL!
AND NOW TO BEGIN...!
OMAR! YOU ARE MY SLAVE! I, SANDO, AM YOUR MASTER! I AM MASTER OF YOUR MIND! I AM MASTER OF YOUR THOUGHTS! AM I NOT, OMAR??
YOU..ARE.. THE..MASTER, SANDO!
THEN I ORDER YOU TO PROJECT!! PROJECT YOUR THOUGHTS! LET THE WORLD SEE YOUR UNFAILING PREDICTIONS OF THINGS TO COME!!
FOR YOU HAVE THE POWER TO GAZE INTO THE FUTURE! AND I HAVE THE POWER TO REVEAL YOUR THOUGHTS IN THE MYSTIC CRYSTAL BALL! PROJECT, OMAR...PROJECT!
SLOWLY, UNBELIEVABLY, A SCENE BEGINS TO FORM WITHIN THE GIANT CRYSTAL! THE IMAGE OF A COLUMN OF U.S. WAR TANKS, ON MANEUVERS AT FORT LEHIGH...
BUT, AN INSTANT LATER, THE STARTLED AUDIENCE IN THE SILENT THEATRE SEES...
WHOOOM!
2.

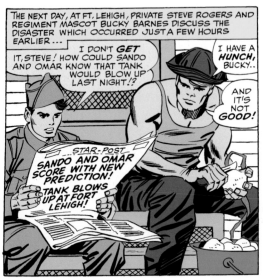

THE NEXT DAY, AT FT. LEHIGH, PRIVATE STEVE ROGERS AND REGIMENT MASCOT BUCKY BARNES DISCUSS THE DISASTER WHICH OCCURRED JUST A FEW HOURS EARLIER...

I DON'T *GET* IT, STEVE! HOW COULD SANDO AND OMAR KNOW THAT TANK WOULD BLOW UP LAST NIGHT!?

I HAVE A *HUNCH*, BUCKY...

AND IT'S NOT *GOOD*!

STAR-POST
SANDO AND OMAR SCORE WITH NEW PREDICTION!
TANK BLOWS UP AT FORT LEHIGH!

ROGERS! IZZAT ALL A YARDBIRD LIKE YOU HAS TO *DO* ?? YOU AIN'T GETTIN' PAID TO BE A *NEWS-CASTER!*

I PUTCHA ON K.P. TO PEEL THEM SPUDS, AND I WANT 'EM *PEELED!* STOP *BREATHIN'* WHEN I'M TALKIN' AT YA!

YES, SARGE! NO, SARGE! SURE, SARGE!

YOU'RE NOT ONLY THE BIGGEST GOLDBRICKIN' CLOWN IN THIS WHOLE DANGED REGIMENT, BUT...*WHEEEOOPS!!*

WHO LEFT THEM POTATOES ON THE BLASTED STEPS???

I GUESS *I* DID, SARGE!

THAT *SINKS* IT! YOU'RE A BIGGER MENACE THAN THE BLAMED *NAZIS!* YOU AIN'T EVEN FIT FOR K.P.!! WIPE THAT DUMB-LOOKIN' SMIRK OFFA YOUR KISSER! GET *OUTA* HERE BEFORE I *REALLY* LOSE MY TEMPER!

SURE, SARGE, IF YOU SAY SO!

AND SO, A FEW HOURS LATER...

I'LL BET YOU ARRANGED THE WHOLE THING SO YOU COULD COME TO SEE THE SHOW, STEVE!

BUCKY, WE'VE GOT TO DO SOMETHING ABOUT THAT SUSPICIOUS NATURE OF YOURS!

NOW PLAYING
ANDO
OMAR

3.

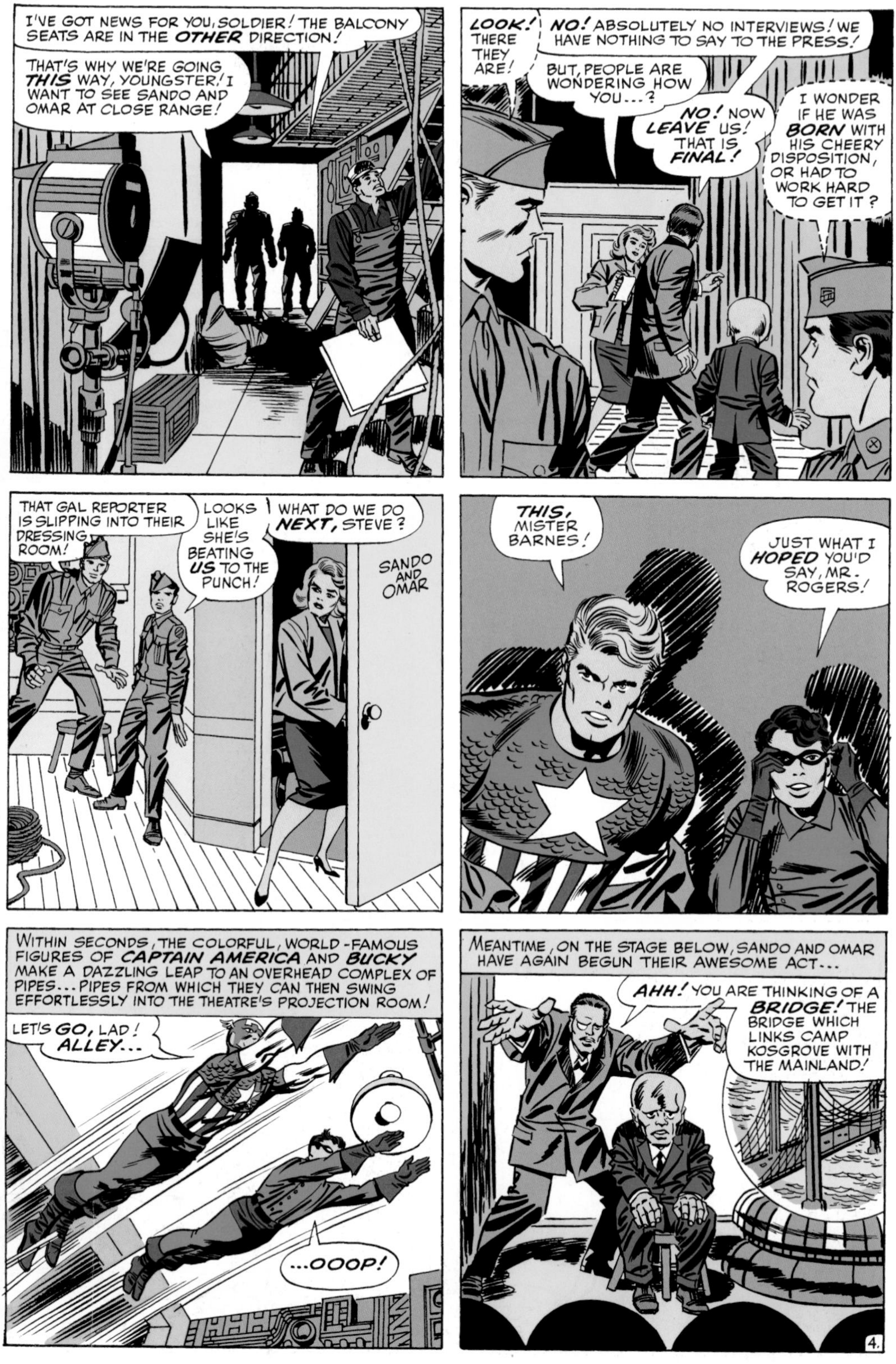
I'VE GOT NEWS FOR YOU, SOLDIER! THE BALCONY SEATS ARE IN THE OTHER DIRECTION!
THAT'S WHY WE'RE GOING THIS WAY, YOUNGSTER! I WANT TO SEE SANDO AND OMAR AT CLOSE RANGE!
LOOK! THERE THEY ARE!
NO! ABSOLUTELY NO INTERVIEWS! WE HAVE NOTHING TO SAY TO THE PRESS!
BUT, PEOPLE ARE WONDERING HOW YOU...?
NO! NOW LEAVE US! THAT IS FINAL!
I WONDER IF HE WAS BORN WITH HIS CHEERY DISPOSITION, OR HAD TO WORK HARD TO GET IT?
THAT GAL REPORTER IS SLIPPING INTO THEIR DRESSING ROOM!
LOOKS LIKE SHE'S BEATING US TO THE PUNCH!
WHAT DO WE DO NEXT, STEVE?
SANDO AND OMAR
THIS, MISTER BARNES!
JUST WHAT I HOPED YOU'D SAY, MR. ROGERS!
WITHIN SECONDS, THE COLORFUL, WORLD-FAMOUS FIGURES OF CAPTAIN AMERICA AND BUCKY MAKE A DAZZLING LEAP TO AN OVERHEAD COMPLEX OF PIPES... PIPES FROM WHICH THEY CAN THEN SWING EFFORTLESSLY INTO THE THEATRE'S PROJECTION ROOM!
LET'S GO, LAD! ALLEY...
...OOOP!
MEANTIME, ON THE STAGE BELOW, SANDO AND OMAR HAVE AGAIN BEGUN THEIR AWESOME ACT...
AHH! YOU ARE THINKING OF A BRIDGE! THE BRIDGE WHICH LINKS CAMP KOSGROVE WITH THE MAINLAND!
4.

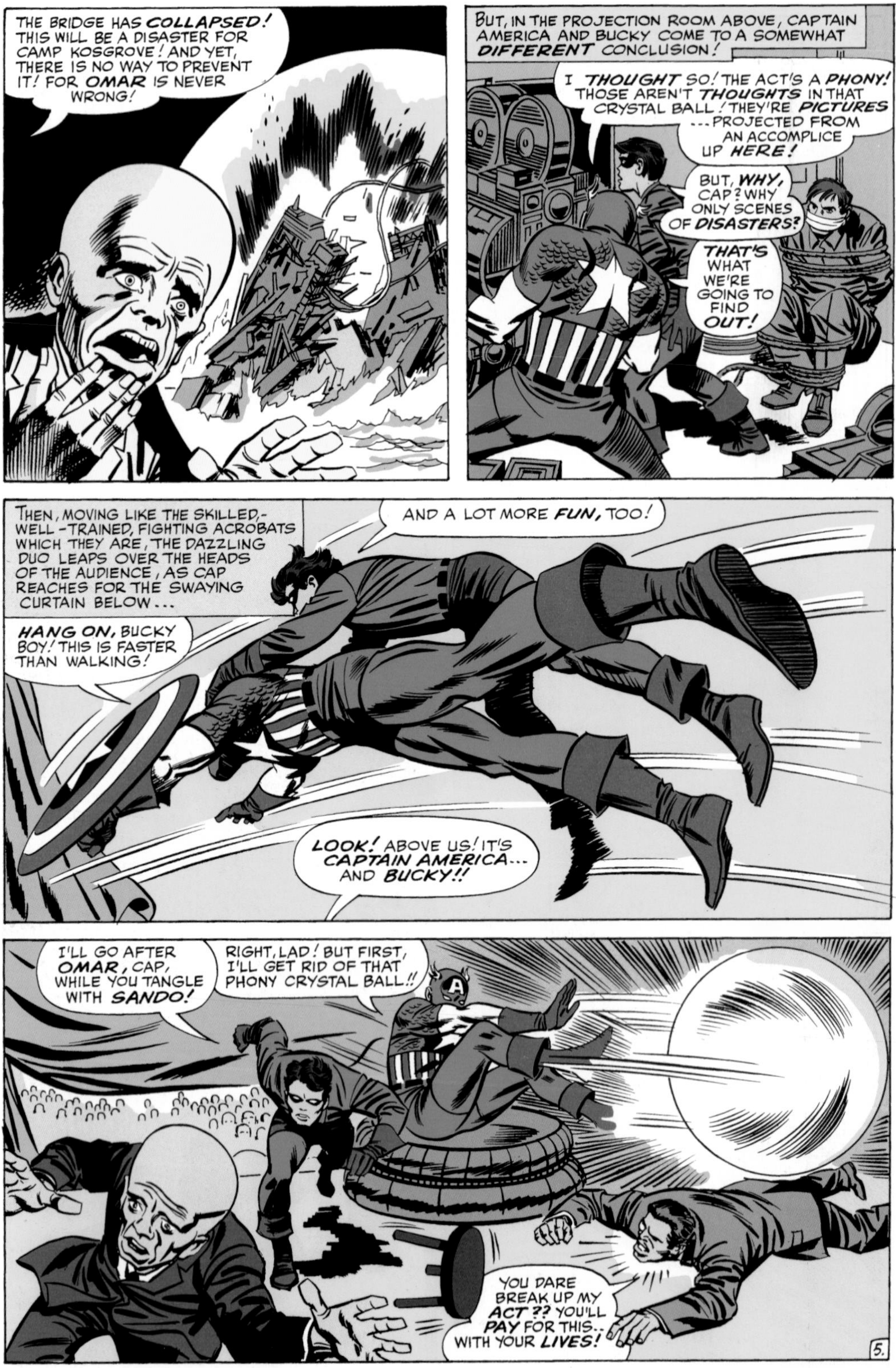
THE BRIDGE HAS COLLAPSED! THIS WILL BE A DISASTER FOR CAMP KOSGROVE! AND YET, THERE IS NO WAY TO PREVENT IT! FOR OMAR IS NEVER WRONG!
BUT, IN THE PROJECTION ROOM ABOVE, CAPTAIN AMERICA AND BUCKY COME TO A SOMEWHAT DIFFERENT CONCLUSION!
I THOUGHT SO! THE ACT'S A PHONY! THOSE AREN'T THOUGHTS IN THAT CRYSTAL BALL! THEY'RE PICTURES ...PROJECTED FROM AN ACCOMPLICE UP HERE!
BUT, WHY, CAP? WHY ONLY SCENES OF DISASTERS?
THAT'S WHAT WE'RE GOING TO FIND OUT!
THEN, MOVING LIKE THE SKILLED,- WELL-TRAINED, FIGHTING ACROBATS WHICH THEY ARE, THE DAZZLING DUO LEAPS OVER THE HEADS OF THE AUDIENCE, AS CAP REACHES FOR THE SWAYING CURTAIN BELOW...
AND A LOT MORE FUN, TOO!
HANG ON, BUCKY BOY! THIS IS FASTER THAN WALKING!
LOOK! ABOVE US! IT'S CAPTAIN AMERICA... AND BUCKY!!
I'LL GO AFTER OMAR, CAP, WHILE YOU TANGLE WITH SANDO!
RIGHT, LAD! BUT FIRST, I'LL GET RID OF THAT PHONY CRYSTAL BALL!!
YOU DARE BREAK UP MY ACT?? YOU'LL PAY FOR THIS.. WITH YOUR LIVES!
5.

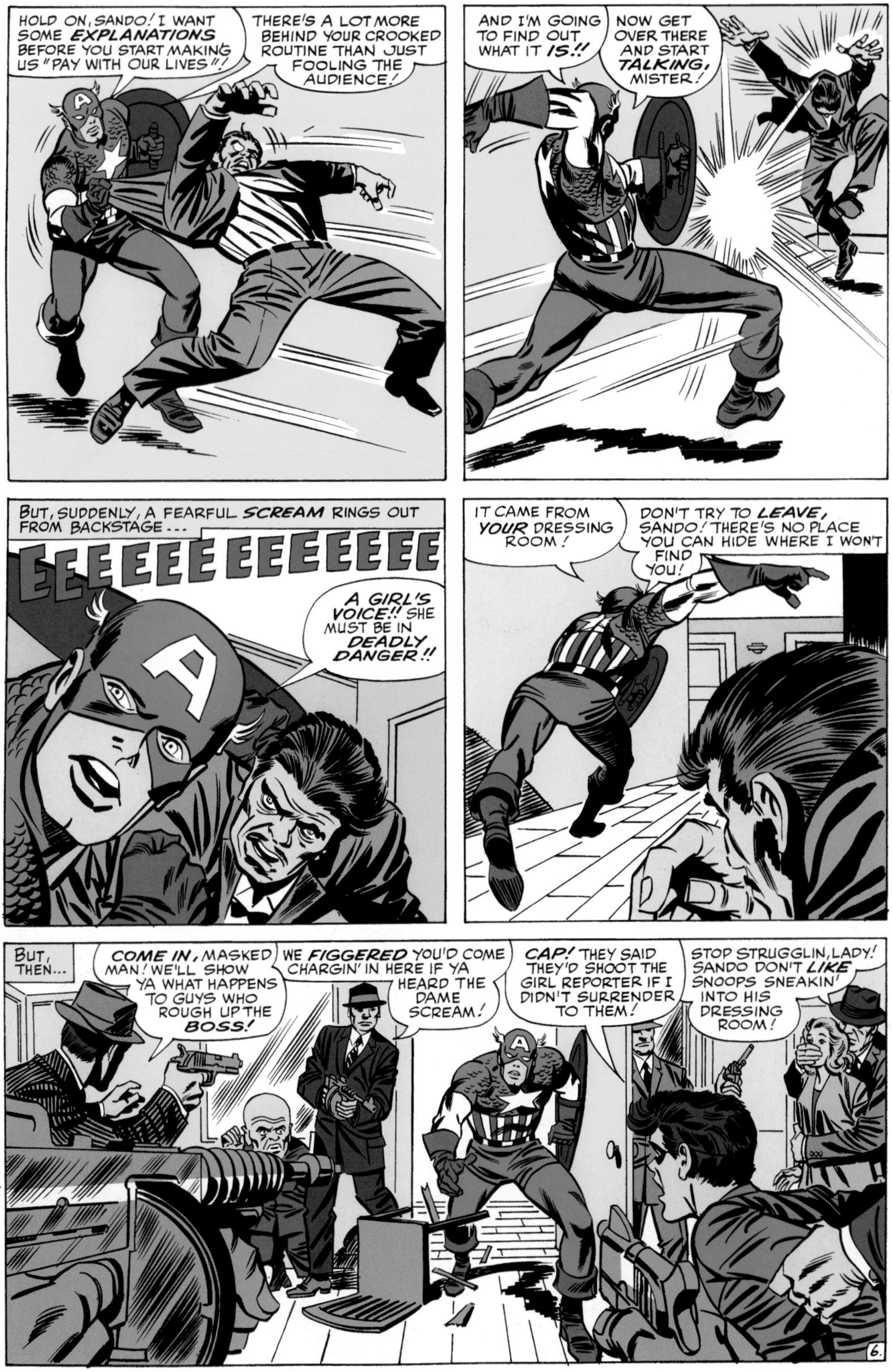

HOLD ON, SANDO! I WANT SOME EXPLANATIONS BEFORE YOU START MAKING US "PAY WITH OUR LIVES"!
THERE'S A LOT MORE BEHIND YOUR CROOKED ROUTINE THAN JUST FOOLING THE AUDIENCE!
AND I'M GOING TO FIND OUT WHAT IT IS!!
NOW GET OVER THERE AND START TALKING, MISTER!
BUT, SUDDENLY, A FEARFUL SCREAM RINGS OUT FROM BACKSTAGE...
EEEEEEEEEEEEE
A GIRL'S VOICE!! SHE MUST BE IN DEADLY DANGER!!
IT CAME FROM YOUR DRESSING ROOM!
DON'T TRY TO LEAVE, SANDO! THERE'S NO PLACE YOU CAN HIDE WHERE I WON'T FIND YOU!
BUT, THEN...
COME IN, MASKED MAN! WE'LL SHOW YA WHAT HAPPENS TO GUYS WHO ROUGH UP THE BOSS!
WE FIGGERED YOU'D COME CHARGIN' IN HERE IF YA HEARD THE DAME SCREAM!
CAP! THEY SAID THEY'D SHOOT THE GIRL REPORTER IF I DIDN'T SURRENDER TO THEM!
STOP STRUGGLIN, LADY! SANDO DON'T LIKE SNOOPS SNEAKIN' INTO HIS DRESSING ROOM!
6.

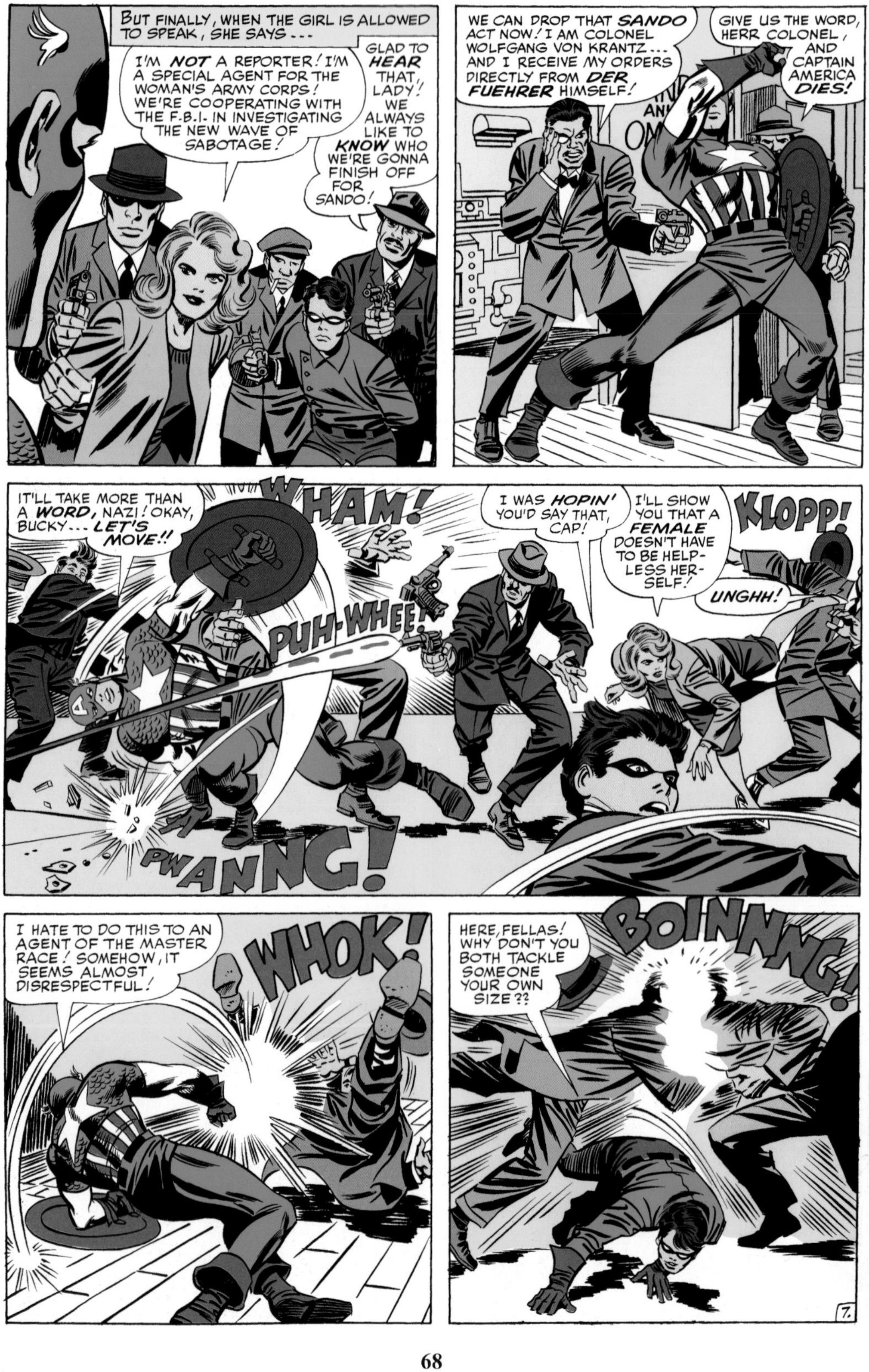

BUT FINALLY, WHEN THE GIRL IS ALLOWED TO SPEAK, SHE SAYS ...
I'M NOT A REPORTER! I'M A SPECIAL AGENT FOR THE WOMAN'S ARMY CORPS! WE'RE COOPERATING WITH THE F.B.I. IN INVESTIGATING THE NEW WAVE OF SABOTAGE!
GLAD TO HEAR THAT, LADY! WE ALWAYS LIKE TO KNOW WHO WE'RE GONNA FINISH OFF FOR SANDO!
WE CAN DROP THAT SANDO ACT NOW! I AM COLONEL WOLFGANG VON KRANTZ... AND I RECEIVE MY ORDERS DIRECTLY FROM DER FUEHRER HIMSELF!
GIVE US THE WORD, HERR COLONEL, AND CAPTAIN AMERICA DIES!
IT'LL TAKE MORE THAN A WORD, NAZI! OKAY, BUCKY... LET'S MOVE!!
WHAM!
PUH-WHEE!
PWANNG!
I WAS HOPIN' YOU'D SAY THAT, CAP!
I'LL SHOW YOU THAT A FEMALE DOESN'T HAVE TO BE HELP-LESS HER-SELF!
KLOPP!
UNGHH!
I HATE TO DO THIS TO AN AGENT OF THE MASTER RACE! SOMEHOW, IT SEEMS ALMOST DISRESPECTFUL!
WHOK!
HERE, FELLAS! WHY DON'T YOU BOTH TACKLE SOMEONE YOUR OWN SIZE??
BOINNNG!
7.

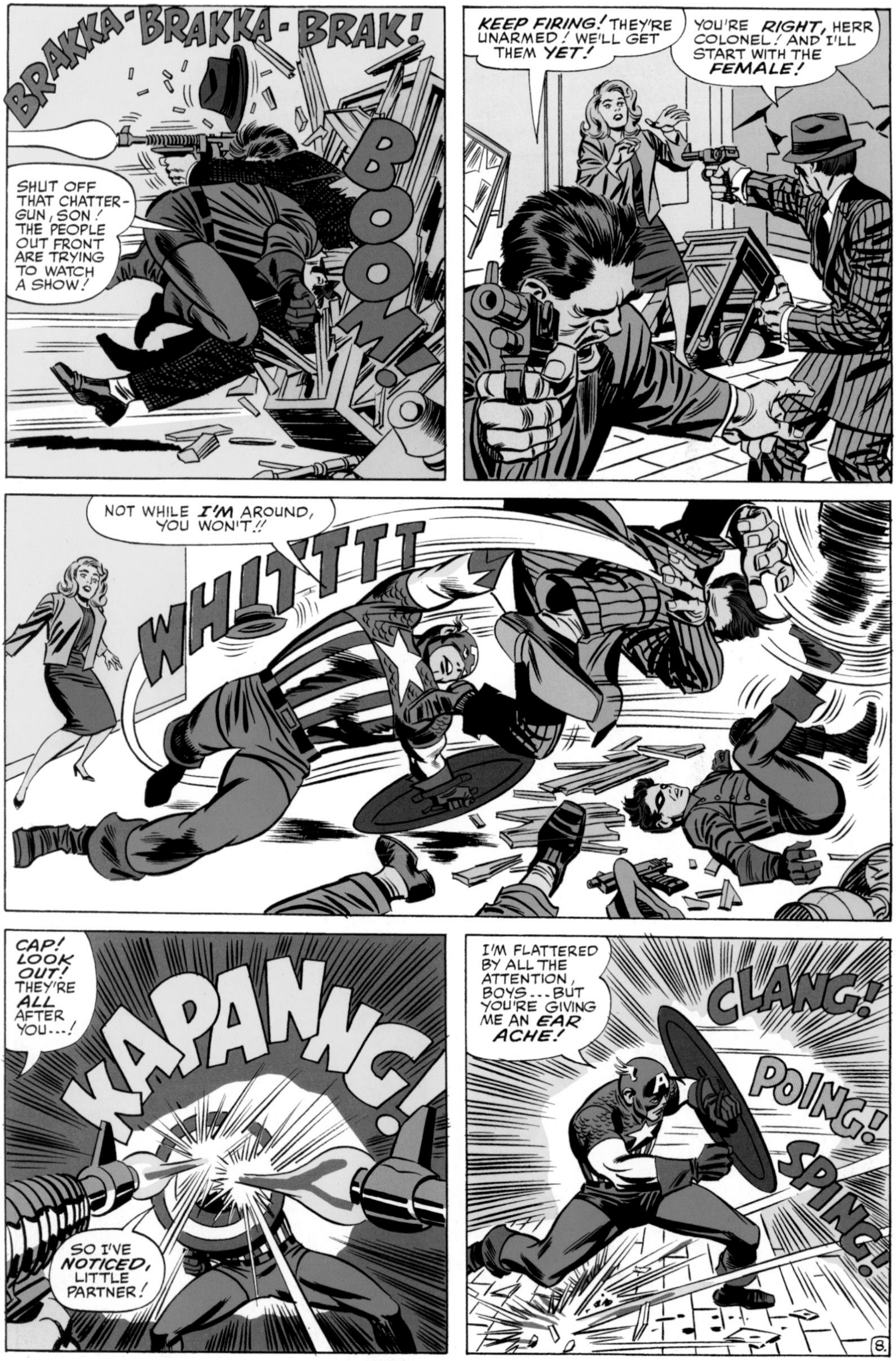

BRAKKA-BRAKKA-BRAK!
SHUT OFF THAT CHATTER-GUN, SON! THE PEOPLE OUT FRONT ARE TRYING TO WATCH A SHOW!
BOOM!
KEEP FIRING! THEY'RE UNARMED! WE'LL GET THEM YET!
YOU'RE RIGHT, HERR COLONEL! AND I'LL START WITH THE FEMALE!
NOT WHILE I'M AROUND, YOU WON'T!!
WHITTTT
CAP! LOOK OUT! THEY'RE ALL AFTER YOU...!
KAPANNG!
SO I'VE NOTICED, LITTLE PARTNER!
I'M FLATTERED BY ALL THE ATTENTION, BOYS... BUT YOU'RE GIVING ME AN EAR ACHE!
CLANG!
POING!
SPING!
8.

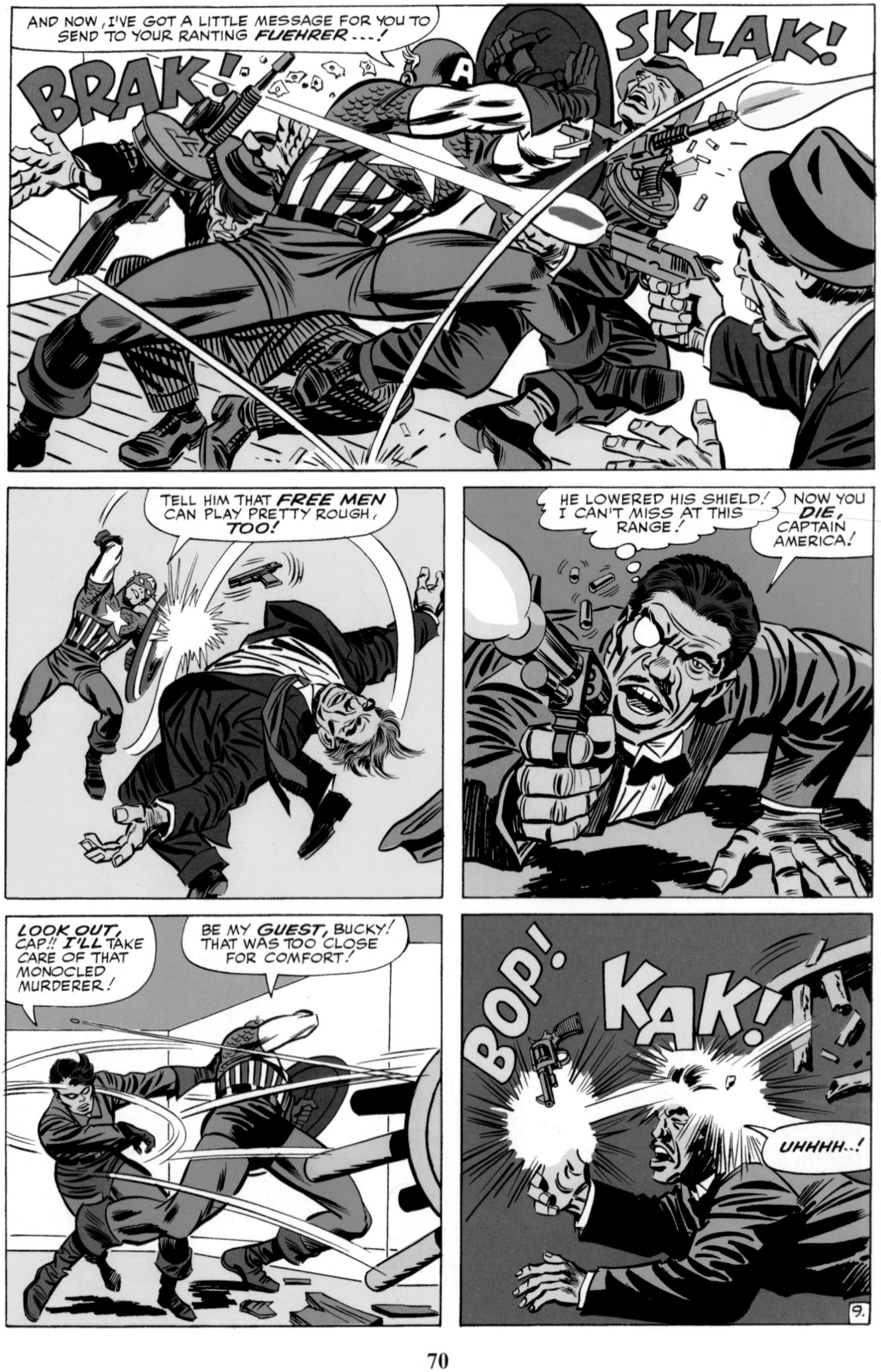

AND NOW, I'VE GOT A LITTLE MESSAGE FOR YOU TO SEND TO YOUR RANTING FUEHRER...!
SKLAK!
BRAK!
TELL HIM THAT FREE MEN CAN PLAY PRETTY ROUGH, TOO!
HE LOWERED HIS SHIELD! I CAN'T MISS AT THIS RANGE!
NOW YOU DIE, CAPTAIN AMERICA!
LOOK OUT, CAP!! I'LL TAKE CARE OF THAT MONOCLED MURDERER!
BE MY GUEST, BUCKY! THAT WAS TOO CLOSE FOR COMFORT!
BOP!
KAK!
UHHHH..!
9.

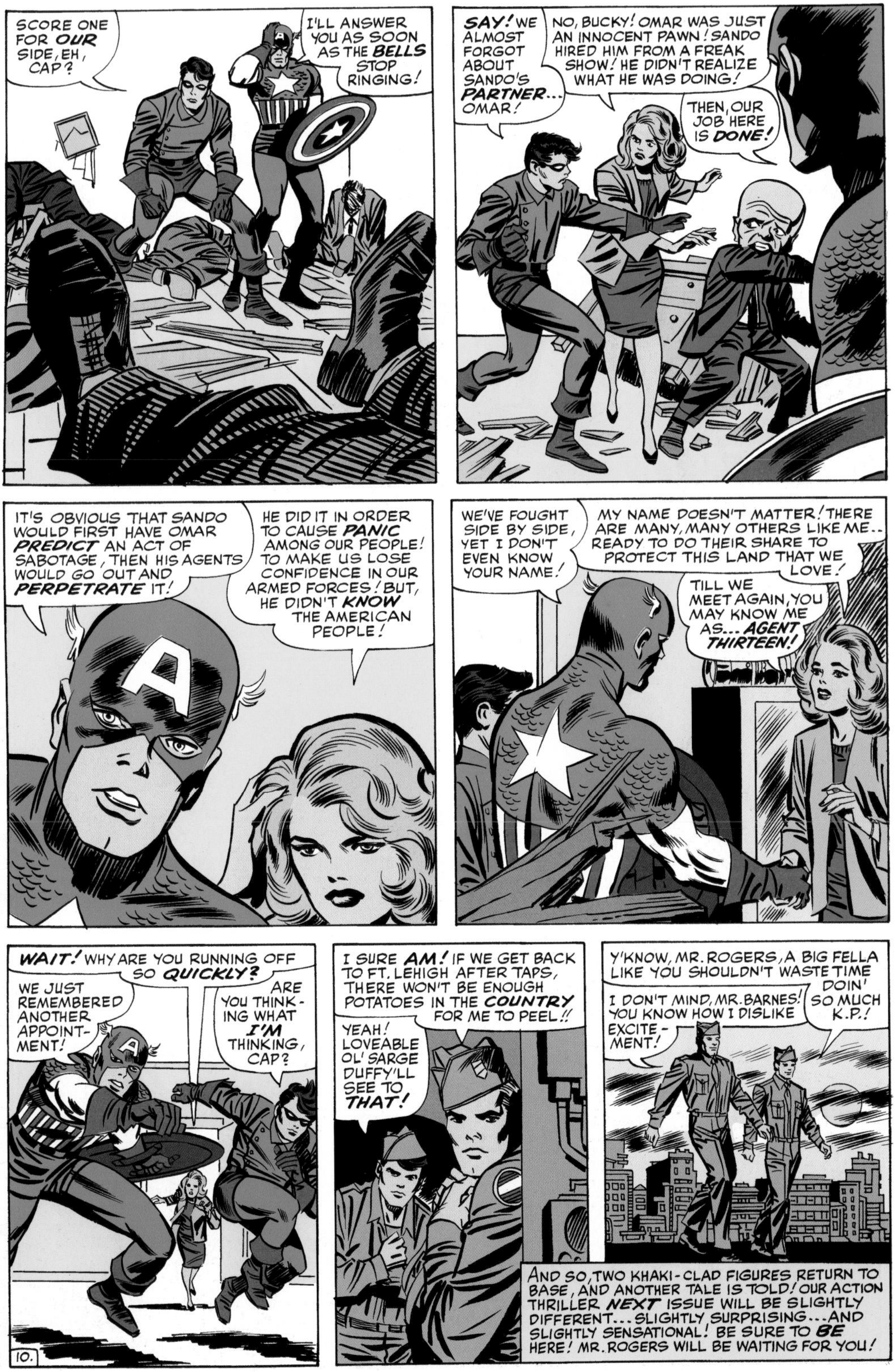
SCORE ONE FOR OUR SIDE, EH, CAP?
I'LL ANSWER YOU AS SOON AS THE BELLS STOP RINGING!
SAY! WE ALMOST FORGOT ABOUT SANDO'S PARTNER... OMAR!
NO, BUCKY! OMAR WAS JUST AN INNOCENT PAWN! SANDO HIRED HIM FROM A FREAK SHOW! HE DIDN'T REALIZE WHAT HE WAS DOING!
THEN, OUR JOB HERE IS DONE!
IT'S OBVIOUS THAT SANDO WOULD FIRST HAVE OMAR PREDICT AN ACT OF SABOTAGE, THEN HIS AGENTS WOULD GO OUT AND PERPETRATE IT!
HE DID IT IN ORDER TO CAUSE PANIC AMONG OUR PEOPLE! TO MAKE US LOSE CONFIDENCE IN OUR ARMED FORCES! BUT, HE DIDN'T KNOW THE AMERICAN PEOPLE!
WE'VE FOUGHT SIDE BY SIDE, YET I DON'T EVEN KNOW YOUR NAME!
MY NAME DOESN'T MATTER! THERE ARE MANY, MANY OTHERS LIKE ME.. READY TO DO THEIR SHARE TO PROTECT THIS LAND THAT WE LOVE!
TILL WE MEET AGAIN, YOU MAY KNOW ME AS... AGENT THIRTEEN!
WAIT! WHY ARE YOU RUNNING OFF SO QUICKLY?
WE JUST REMEMBERED ANOTHER APPOINTMENT!
ARE YOU THINKING WHAT I'M THINKING, CAP?
10.
I SURE AM! IF WE GET BACK TO FT. LEHIGH AFTER TAPS, THERE WON'T BE ENOUGH POTATOES IN THE COUNTRY FOR ME TO PEEL!!
YEAH! LOVEABLE OL' SARGE DUFFY'LL SEE TO THAT!
Y'KNOW, MR. ROGERS, A BIG FELLA LIKE YOU SHOULDN'T WASTE TIME DOIN' SO MUCH K.P.!
I DON'T MIND, MR. BARNES! YOU KNOW HOW I DISLIKE EXCITEMENT!
AND SO, TWO KHAKI-CLAD FIGURES RETURN TO BASE, AND ANOTHER TALE IS TOLD! OUR ACTION THRILLER NEXT ISSUE WILL BE SLIGHTLY DIFFERENT... SLIGHTLY SURPRISING... AND SLIGHTLY SENSATIONAL! BE SURE TO BE HERE! MR. ROGERS WILL BE WAITING FOR YOU!

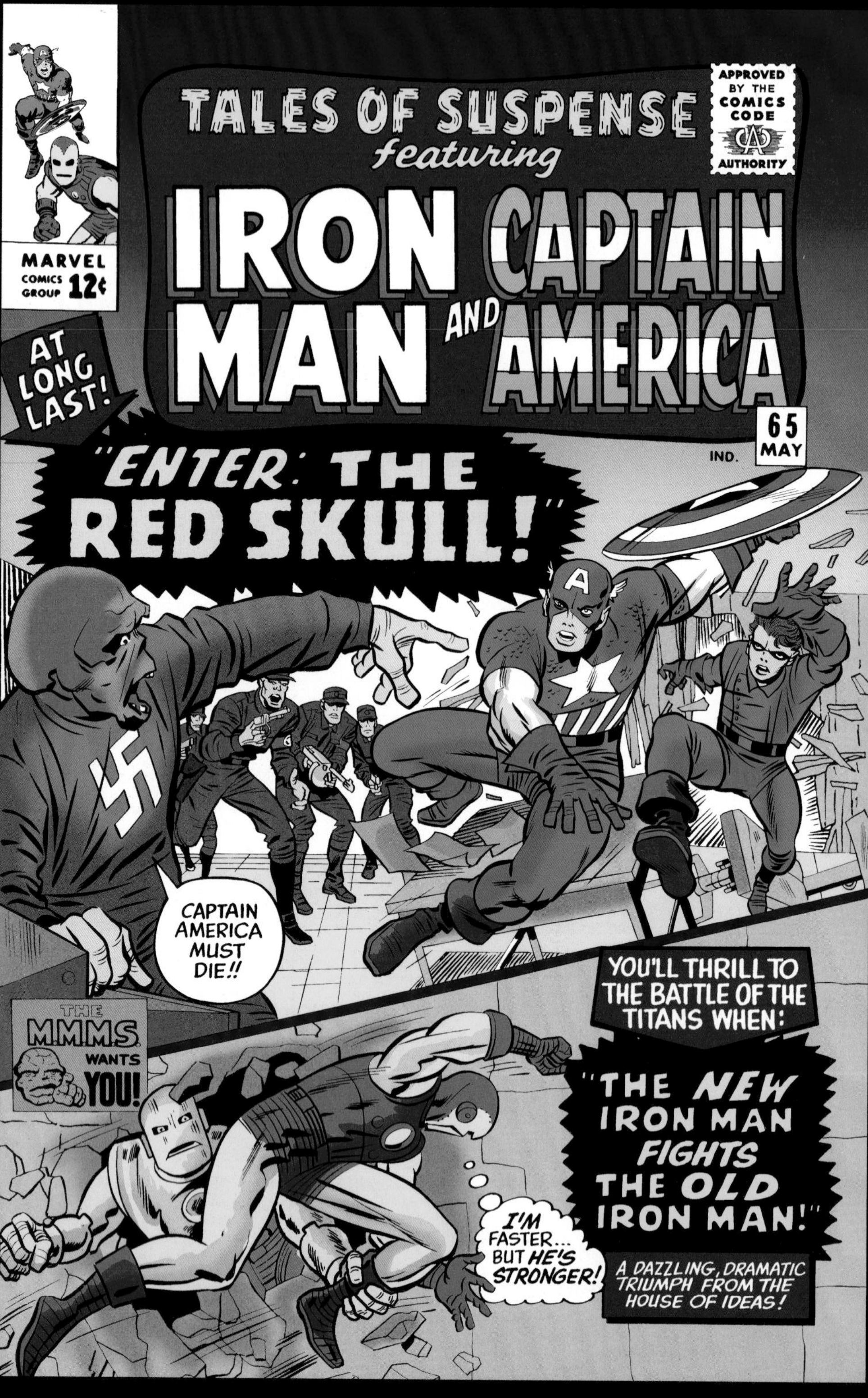
MARVEL COMICS GROUP 12¢
TALES OF SUSPENSE
featuring
IRON MAN AND CAPTAIN AMERICA
APPROVED BY THE COMICS CODE AUTHORITY
65 MAY
IND.
AT LONG LAST!
"ENTER: THE RED SKULL!"
CAPTAIN AMERICA MUST DIE!!
THE M.M.M.S. WANTS YOU!
YOU'LL THRILL TO THE BATTLE OF THE TITANS WHEN:
"THE NEW IRON MAN FIGHTS THE OLD IRON MAN!"
I'M FASTER... BUT HE'S STRONGER!
A DAZZLING, DRAMATIC TRIUMPH FROM THE HOUSE OF IDEAS!

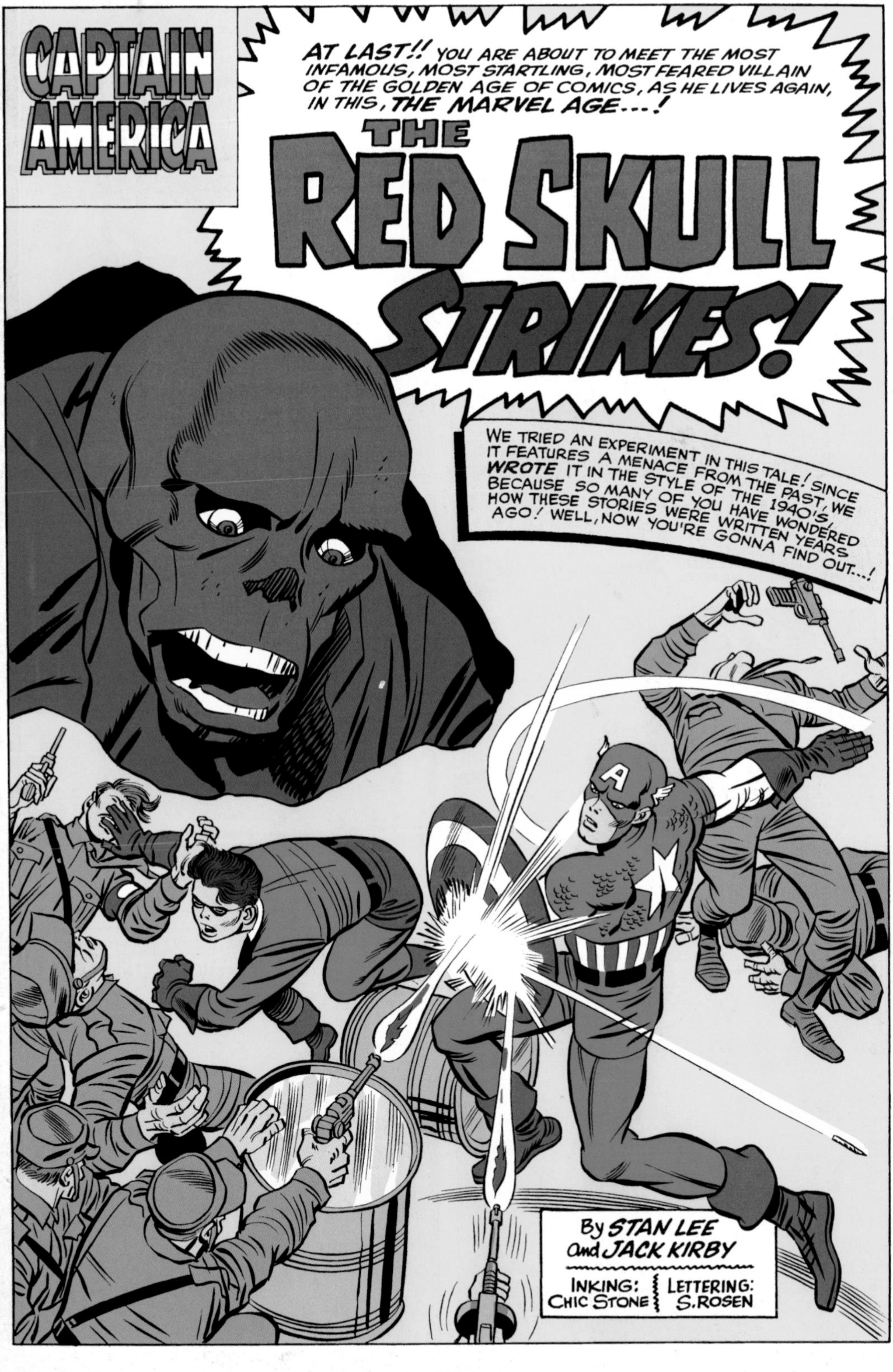
CAPTAIN AMERICA
AT LAST!! YOU ARE ABOUT TO MEET THE MOST INFAMOUS, MOST STARTLING, MOST FEARED VILLAIN OF THE GOLDEN AGE OF COMICS, AS HE LIVES AGAIN, IN THIS, THE MARVEL AGE...!
THE RED SKULL STRIKES!
WE TRIED AN EXPERIMENT IN THIS TALE! SINCE IT FEATURES A MENACE FROM THE PAST, WE WROTE IT IN THE STYLE OF THE 1940'S, BECAUSE SO MANY OF YOU HAVE WONDERED HOW THESE STORIES WERE WRITTEN YEARS AGO! WELL, NOW YOU'RE GONNA FIND OUT...!
By STAN LEE and JACK KIRBY
INKING: CHIC STONE
LETTERING: S.ROSEN

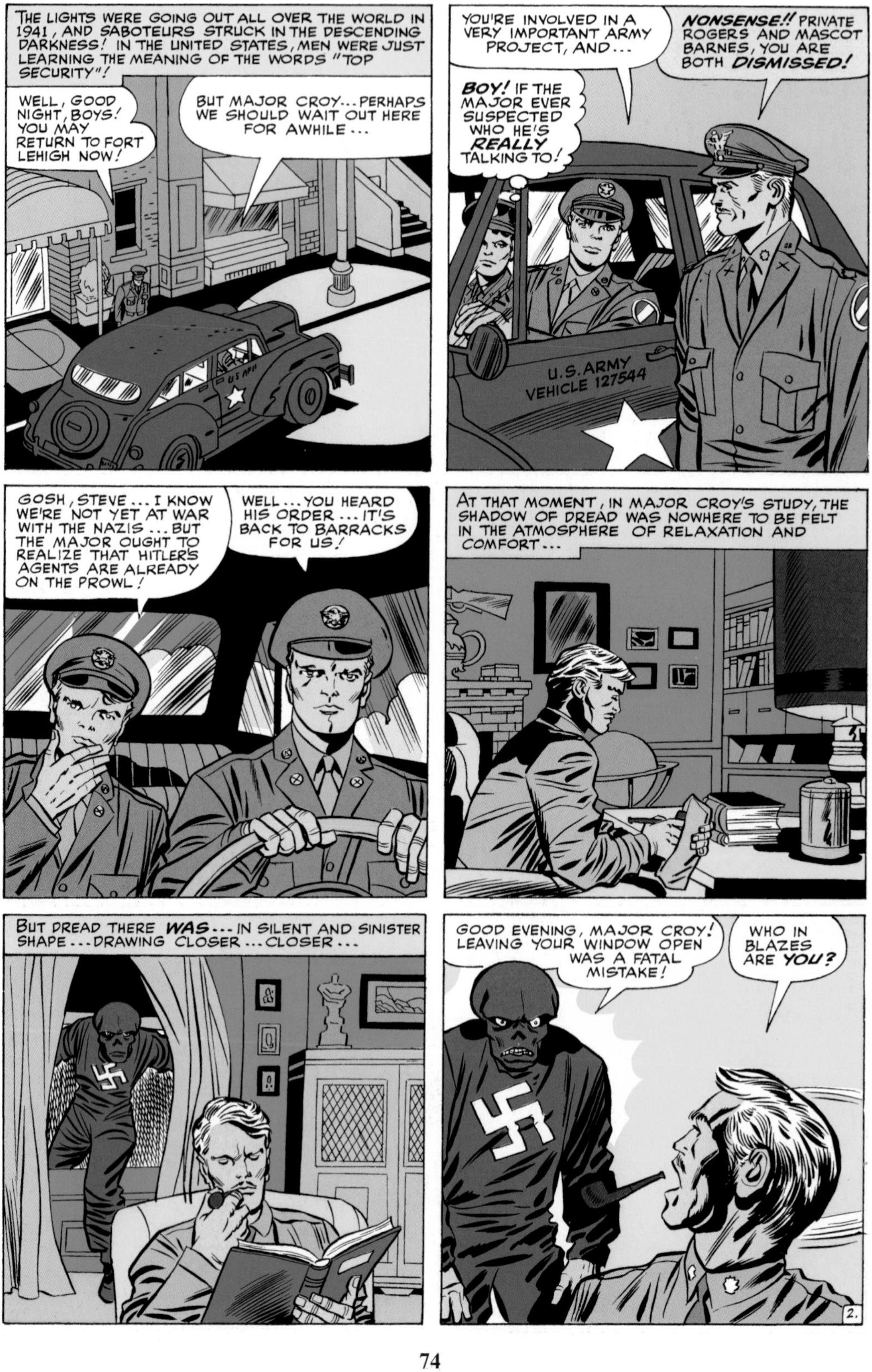
THE LIGHTS WERE GOING OUT ALL OVER THE WORLD IN 1941, AND SABOTEURS STRUCK IN THE DESCENDING DARKNESS! IN THE UNITED STATES, MEN WERE JUST LEARNING THE MEANING OF THE WORDS "TOP SECURITY"!
WELL, GOOD NIGHT, BOYS! YOU MAY RETURN TO FORT LEHIGH NOW!
BUT MAJOR CROY...PERHAPS WE SHOULD WAIT OUT HERE FOR AWHILE...
YOU'RE INVOLVED IN A VERY IMPORTANT ARMY PROJECT, AND...
NONSENSE!! PRIVATE ROGERS AND MASCOT BARNES, YOU ARE BOTH DISMISSED!
BOY! IF THE MAJOR EVER SUSPECTED WHO HE'S REALLY TALKING TO!
U.S. ARMY VEHICLE 127544
GOSH, STEVE...I KNOW WE'RE NOT YET AT WAR WITH THE NAZIS...BUT THE MAJOR OUGHT TO REALIZE THAT HITLER'S AGENTS ARE ALREADY ON THE PROWL!
WELL...YOU HEARD HIS ORDER...IT'S BACK TO BARRACKS FOR US!
AT THAT MOMENT, IN MAJOR CROY'S STUDY, THE SHADOW OF DREAD WAS NOWHERE TO BE FELT IN THE ATMOSPHERE OF RELAXATION AND COMFORT...
BUT DREAD THERE WAS...IN SILENT AND SINISTER SHAPE...DRAWING CLOSER...CLOSER...
GOOD EVENING, MAJOR CROY! LEAVING YOUR WINDOW OPEN WAS A FATAL MISTAKE!
WHO IN BLAZES ARE YOU?
2.

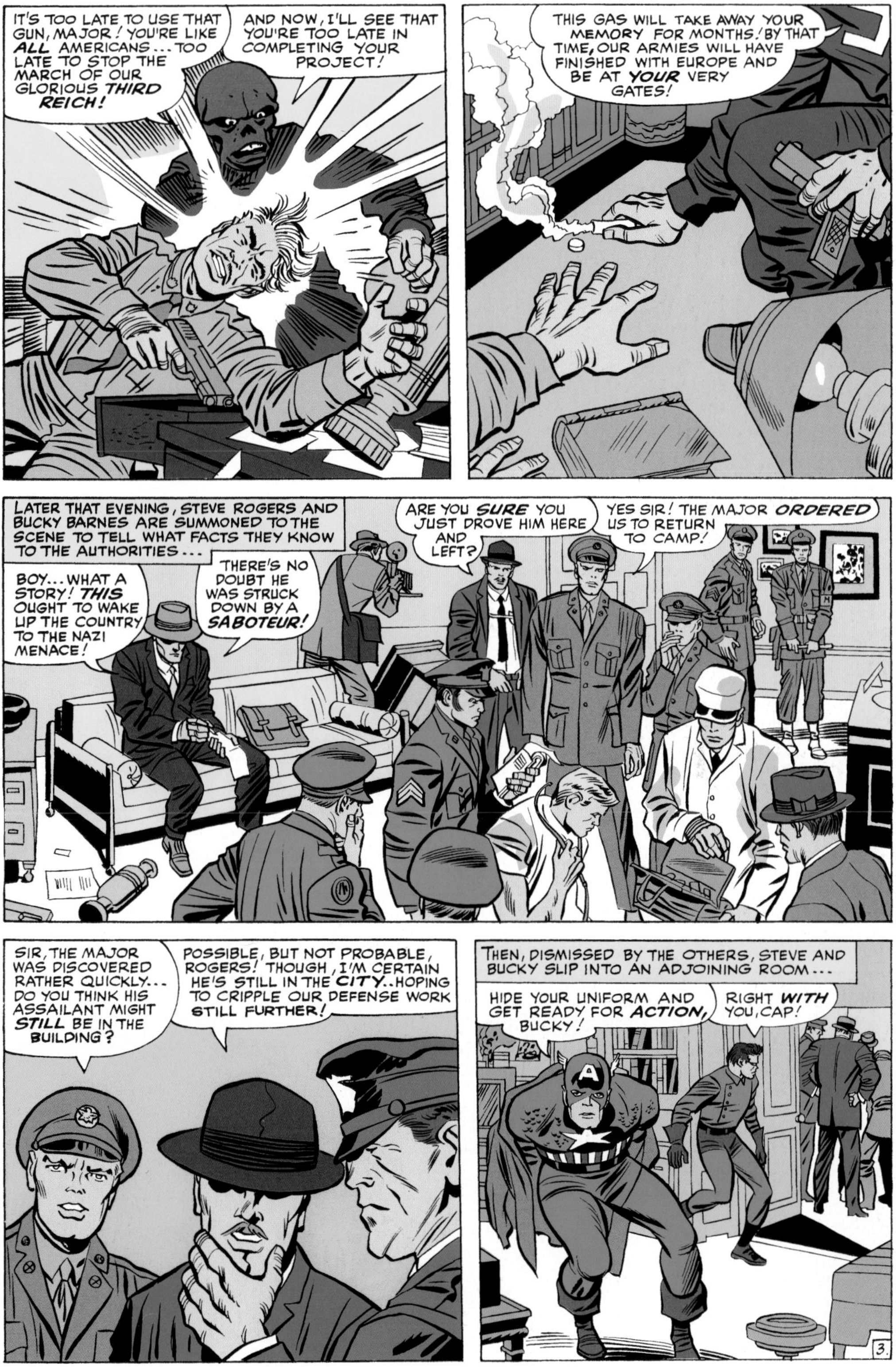
IT'S TOO LATE TO USE THAT GUN, MAJOR! YOU'RE LIKE ALL AMERICANS... TOO LATE TO STOP THE MARCH OF OUR GLORIOUS THIRD REICH!
AND NOW, I'LL SEE THAT YOU'RE TOO LATE IN COMPLETING YOUR PROJECT!
THIS GAS WILL TAKE AWAY YOUR MEMORY FOR MONTHS! BY THAT TIME, OUR ARMIES WILL HAVE FINISHED WITH EUROPE AND BE AT YOUR VERY GATES!
LATER THAT EVENING, STEVE ROGERS AND BUCKY BARNES ARE SUMMONED TO THE SCENE TO TELL WHAT FACTS THEY KNOW TO THE AUTHORITIES...
BOY... WHAT A STORY! THIS OUGHT TO WAKE UP THE COUNTRY TO THE NAZI MENACE!
THERE'S NO DOUBT HE WAS STRUCK DOWN BY A SABOTEUR!
ARE YOU SURE YOU JUST DROVE HIM HERE AND LEFT?
YES SIR! THE MAJOR ORDERED US TO RETURN TO CAMP!
SIR, THE MAJOR WAS DISCOVERED RATHER QUICKLY... DO YOU THINK HIS ASSAILANT MIGHT STILL BE IN THE BUILDING?
POSSIBLE, BUT NOT PROBABLE, ROGERS! THOUGH, I'M CERTAIN HE'S STILL IN THE CITY..HOPING TO CRIPPLE OUR DEFENSE WORK STILL FURTHER!
THEN, DISMISSED BY THE OTHERS, STEVE AND BUCKY SLIP INTO AN ADJOINING ROOM...
HIDE YOUR UNIFORM AND GET READY FOR ACTION, BUCKY!
RIGHT WITH YOU, CAP!
3.

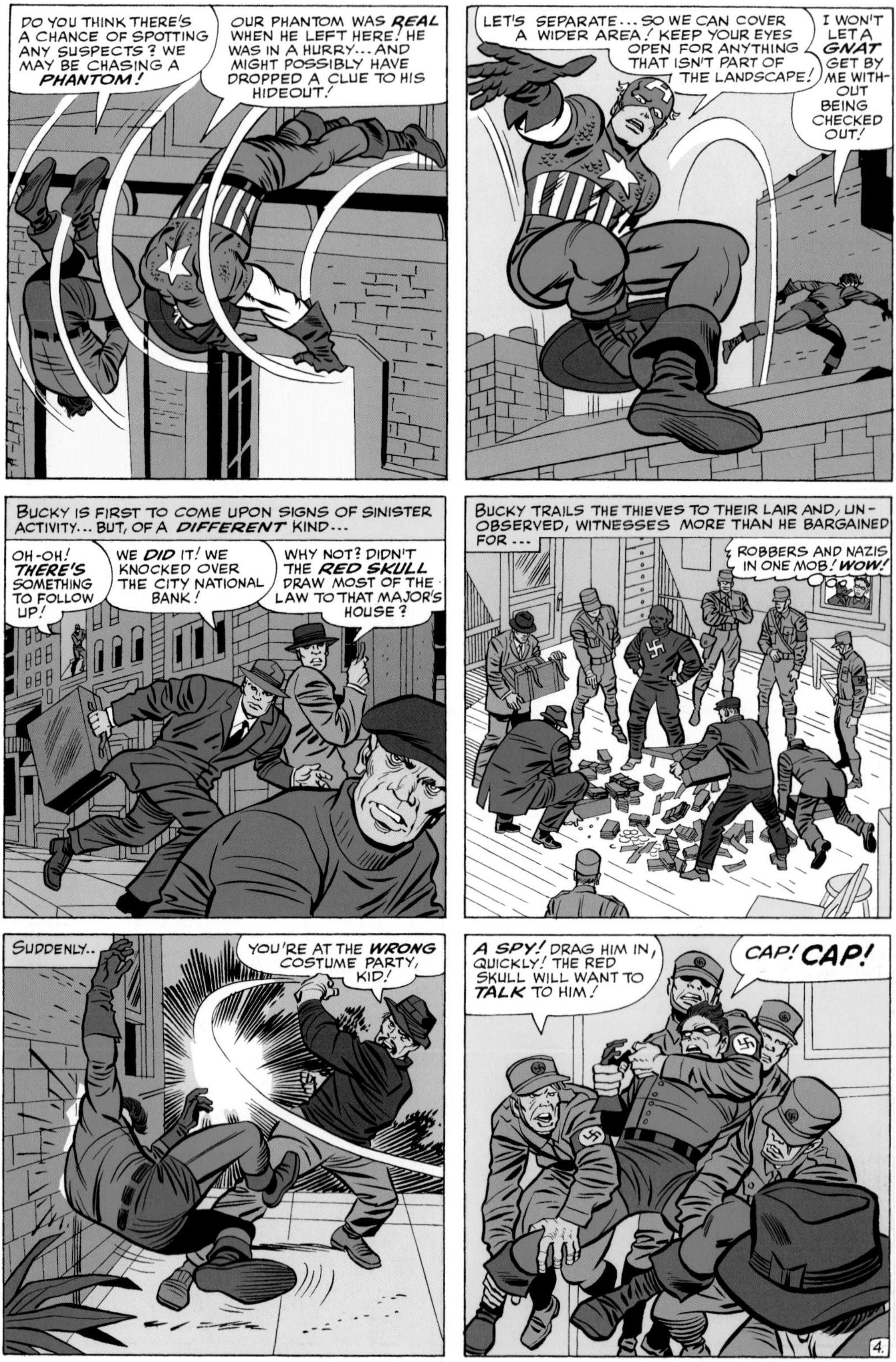
DO YOU THINK THERE'S A CHANCE OF SPOTTING ANY SUSPECTS? WE MAY BE CHASING A PHANTOM!
OUR PHANTOM WAS REAL WHEN HE LEFT HERE! HE WAS IN A HURRY... AND MIGHT POSSIBLY HAVE DROPPED A CLUE TO HIS HIDEOUT!
LET'S SEPARATE... SO WE CAN COVER A WIDER AREA! KEEP YOUR EYES OPEN FOR ANYTHING THAT ISN'T PART OF THE LANDSCAPE!
I WON'T LET A GNAT GET BY ME WITHOUT BEING CHECKED OUT!
BUCKY IS FIRST TO COME UPON SIGNS OF SINISTER ACTIVITY... BUT, OF A DIFFERENT KIND...
OH-OH! THERE'S SOMETHING TO FOLLOW UP!
WE DID IT! WE KNOCKED OVER THE CITY NATIONAL BANK!
WHY NOT? DIDN'T THE RED SKULL DRAW MOST OF THE LAW TO THAT MAJOR'S HOUSE?
BUCKY TRAILS THE THIEVES TO THEIR LAIR AND, UNOBSERVED, WITNESSES MORE THAN HE BARGAINED FOR...
ROBBERS AND NAZIS IN ONE MOB! WOW!
SUDDENLY..
YOU'RE AT THE WRONG COSTUME PARTY, KID!
A SPY! DRAG HIM IN, QUICKLY! THE RED SKULL WILL WANT TO TALK TO HIM!
CAP! CAP!
4.

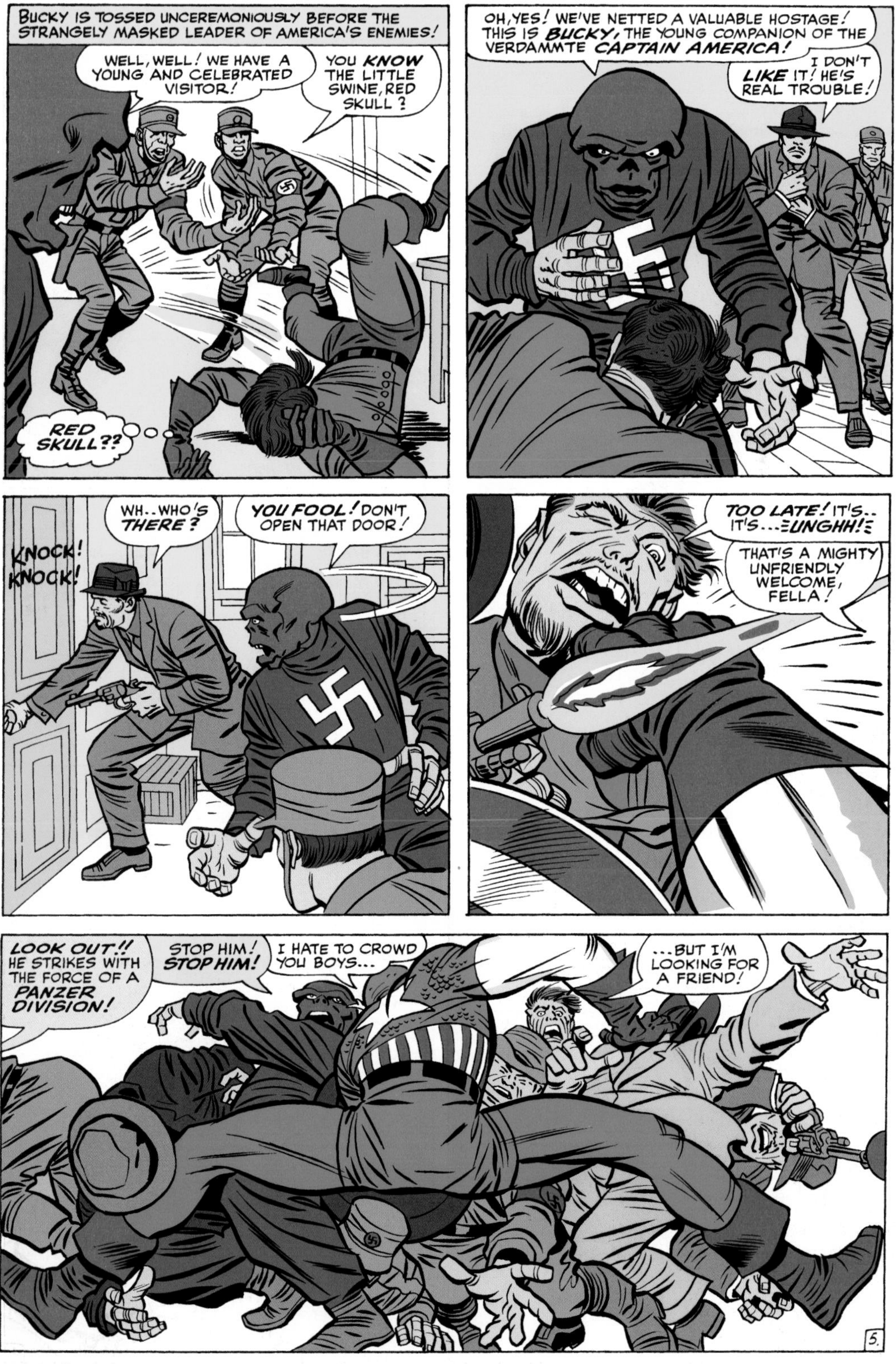
BUCKY IS TOSSED UNCEREMONIOUSLY BEFORE THE STRANGELY MASKED LEADER OF AMERICA'S ENEMIES!
WELL, WELL! WE HAVE A YOUNG AND CELEBRATED VISITOR!
YOU KNOW THE LITTLE SWINE, RED SKULL?
RED SKULL??
OH, YES! WE'VE NETTED A VALUABLE HOSTAGE! THIS IS BUCKY, THE YOUNG COMPANION OF THE VERDAMMTE CAPTAIN AMERICA!
I DON'T LIKE IT! HE'S REAL TROUBLE!
KNOCK! KNOCK!
WH..WHO'S THERE?
YOU FOOL! DON'T OPEN THAT DOOR!
TOO LATE! IT'S.. IT'S...UNGHH!
THAT'S A MIGHTY UNFRIENDLY WELCOME, FELLA!
LOOK OUT!! HE STRIKES WITH THE FORCE OF A PANZER DIVISION!
STOP HIM! STOP HIM!
I HATE TO CROWD YOU BOYS...
...BUT I'M LOOKING FOR A FRIEND!
5.

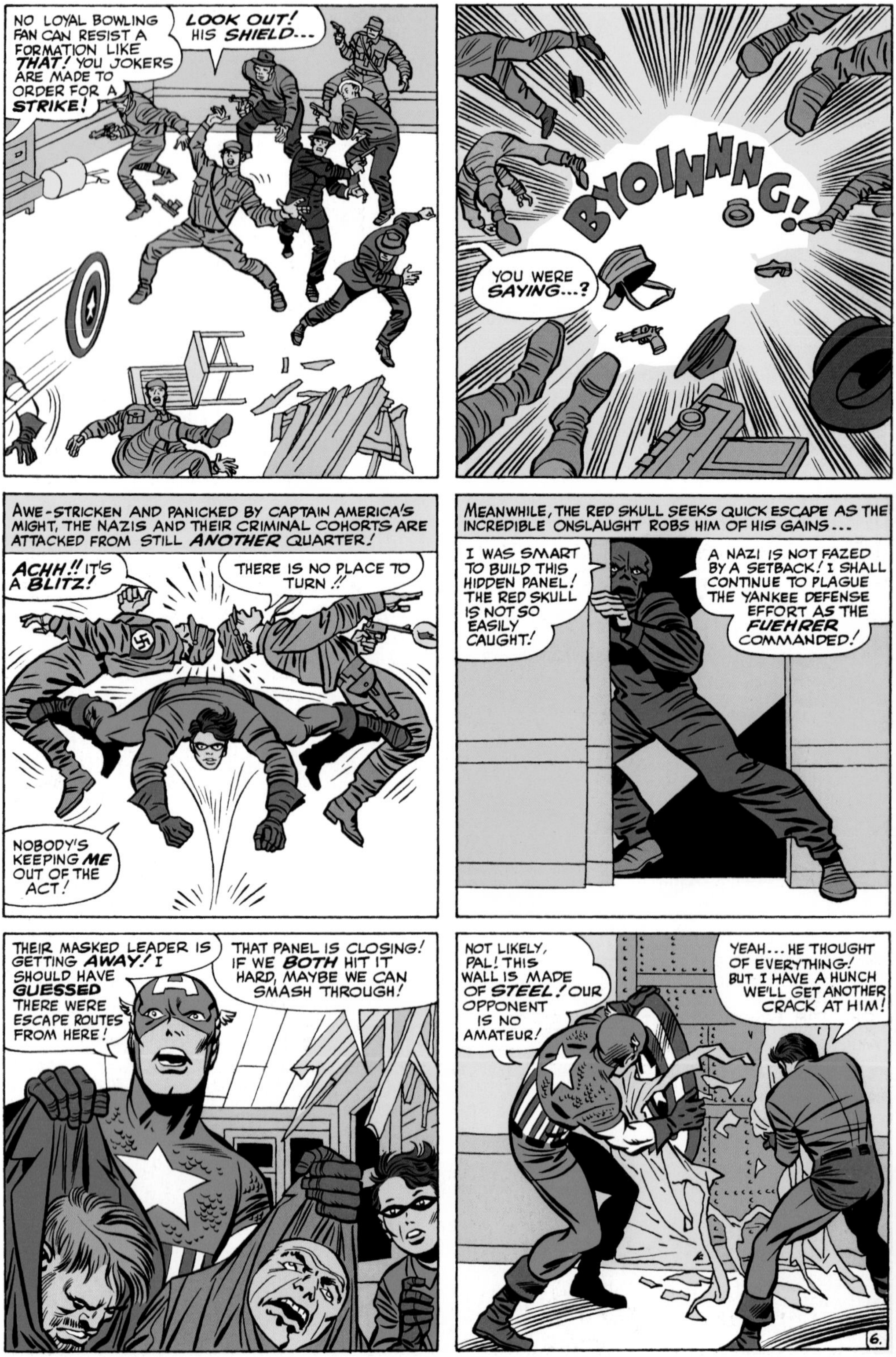
NO LOYAL BOWLING FAN CAN RESIST A FORMATION LIKE THAT! YOU JOKERS ARE MADE TO ORDER FOR A STRIKE!
LOOK OUT! HIS SHIELD...
BYOINNNG!
YOU WERE SAYING...?
AWE-STRICKEN AND PANICKED BY CAPTAIN AMERICA'S MIGHT, THE NAZIS AND THEIR CRIMINAL COHORTS ARE ATTACKED FROM STILL ANOTHER QUARTER!
ACHH!! IT'S A BLITZ!
THERE IS NO PLACE TO TURN!!
NOBODY'S KEEPING ME OUT OF THE ACT!
MEANWHILE, THE RED SKULL SEEKS QUICK ESCAPE AS THE INCREDIBLE ONSLAUGHT ROBS HIM OF HIS GAINS...
I WAS SMART TO BUILD THIS HIDDEN PANEL! THE RED SKULL IS NOT SO EASILY CAUGHT!
A NAZI IS NOT FAZED BY A SETBACK! I SHALL CONTINUE TO PLAGUE THE YANKEE DEFENSE EFFORT AS THE FUEHRER COMMANDED!
THEIR MASKED LEADER IS GETTING AWAY! I SHOULD HAVE GUESSED THERE WERE ESCAPE ROUTES FROM HERE!
THAT PANEL IS CLOSING! IF WE BOTH HIT IT HARD, MAYBE WE CAN SMASH THROUGH!
NOT LIKELY, PAL! THIS WALL IS MADE OF STEEL! OUR OPPONENT IS NO AMATEUR!
YEAH... HE THOUGHT OF EVERYTHING! BUT I HAVE A HUNCH WE'LL GET ANOTHER CRACK AT HIM!
6.

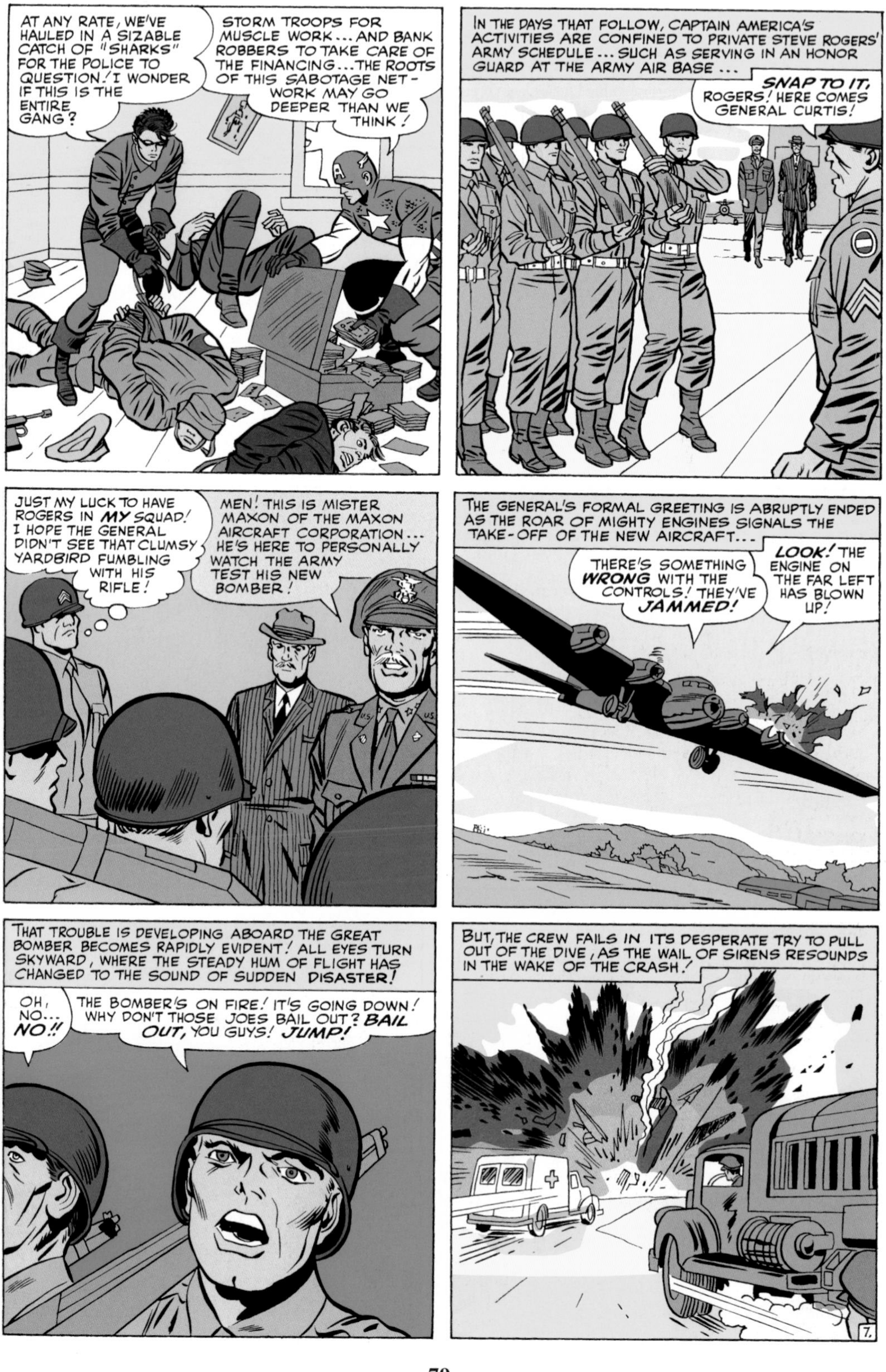
AT ANY RATE, WE'VE HAULED IN A SIZABLE CATCH OF "SHARKS" FOR THE POLICE TO QUESTION! I WONDER IF THIS IS THE ENTIRE GANG?
STORM TROOPS FOR MUSCLE WORK... AND BANK ROBBERS TO TAKE CARE OF THE FINANCING... THE ROOTS OF THIS SABOTAGE NET-WORK MAY GO DEEPER THAN WE THINK!
IN THE DAYS THAT FOLLOW, CAPTAIN AMERICA'S ACTIVITIES ARE CONFINED TO PRIVATE STEVE ROGERS' ARMY SCHEDULE... SUCH AS SERVING IN AN HONOR GUARD AT THE ARMY AIR BASE...
SNAP TO IT, ROGERS! HERE COMES GENERAL CURTIS!
JUST MY LUCK TO HAVE ROGERS IN MY SQUAD! I HOPE THE GENERAL DIDN'T SEE THAT CLUMSY YARDBIRD FUMBLING WITH HIS RIFLE!
MEN! THIS IS MISTER MAXON OF THE MAXON AIRCRAFT CORPORATION... HE'S HERE TO PERSONALLY WATCH THE ARMY TEST HIS NEW BOMBER!
THE GENERAL'S FORMAL GREETING IS ABRUPTLY ENDED AS THE ROAR OF MIGHTY ENGINES SIGNALS THE TAKE-OFF OF THE NEW AIRCRAFT...
THERE'S SOMETHING WRONG WITH THE CONTROLS! THEY'VE JAMMED!
LOOK! THE ENGINE ON THE FAR LEFT HAS BLOWN UP!
THAT TROUBLE IS DEVELOPING ABOARD THE GREAT BOMBER BECOMES RAPIDLY EVIDENT! ALL EYES TURN SKYWARD, WHERE THE STEADY HUM OF FLIGHT HAS CHANGED TO THE SOUND OF SUDDEN DISASTER!
OH, NO... NO!!
THE BOMBER'S ON FIRE! IT'S GOING DOWN! WHY DON'T THOSE JOES BAIL OUT? BAIL OUT, YOU GUYS! JUMP!
BUT, THE CREW FAILS IN ITS DESPERATE TRY TO PULL OUT OF THE DIVE, AS THE WAIL OF SIRENS RESOUNDS IN THE WAKE OF THE CRASH!
7.

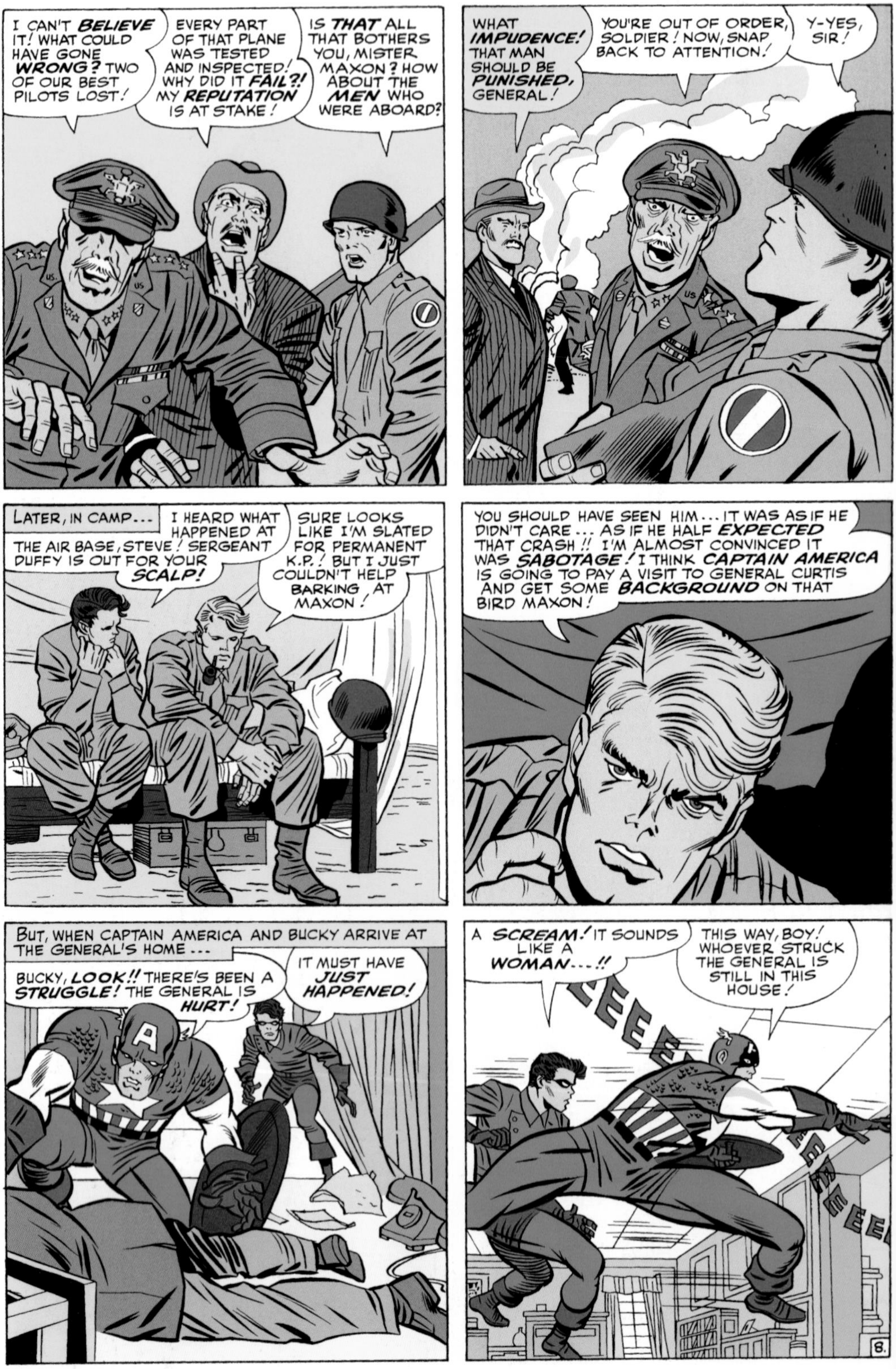
I CAN'T BELIEVE IT! WHAT COULD HAVE GONE WRONG? TWO OF OUR BEST PILOTS LOST!
EVERY PART OF THAT PLANE WAS TESTED AND INSPECTED! WHY DID IT FAIL?! MY REPUTATION IS AT STAKE!
IS THAT ALL THAT BOTHERS YOU, MISTER MAXON? HOW ABOUT THE MEN WHO WERE ABOARD?
WHAT IMPUDENCE! THAT MAN SHOULD BE PUNISHED, GENERAL!
YOU'RE OUT OF ORDER, SOLDIER! NOW, SNAP BACK TO ATTENTION!
Y-YES, SIR!
LATER, IN CAMP...
I HEARD WHAT HAPPENED AT THE AIR BASE, STEVE! SERGEANT DUFFY IS OUT FOR YOUR SCALP!
SURE LOOKS LIKE I'M SLATED FOR PERMANENT K.P.! BUT I JUST COULDN'T HELP BARKING AT MAXON!
YOU SHOULD HAVE SEEN HIM... IT WAS AS IF HE DIDN'T CARE... AS IF HE HALF EXPECTED THAT CRASH!! I'M ALMOST CONVINCED IT WAS SABOTAGE! I THINK CAPTAIN AMERICA IS GOING TO PAY A VISIT TO GENERAL CURTIS AND GET SOME BACKGROUND ON THAT BIRD MAXON!
BUT, WHEN CAPTAIN AMERICA AND BUCKY ARRIVE AT THE GENERAL'S HOME...
BUCKY, LOOK!! THERE'S BEEN A STRUGGLE! THE GENERAL IS HURT!
IT MUST HAVE JUST HAPPENED!
A SCREAM! IT SOUNDS LIKE A WOMAN...!!
THIS WAY, BOY! WHOEVER STRUCK THE GENERAL IS STILL IN THIS HOUSE!
8.

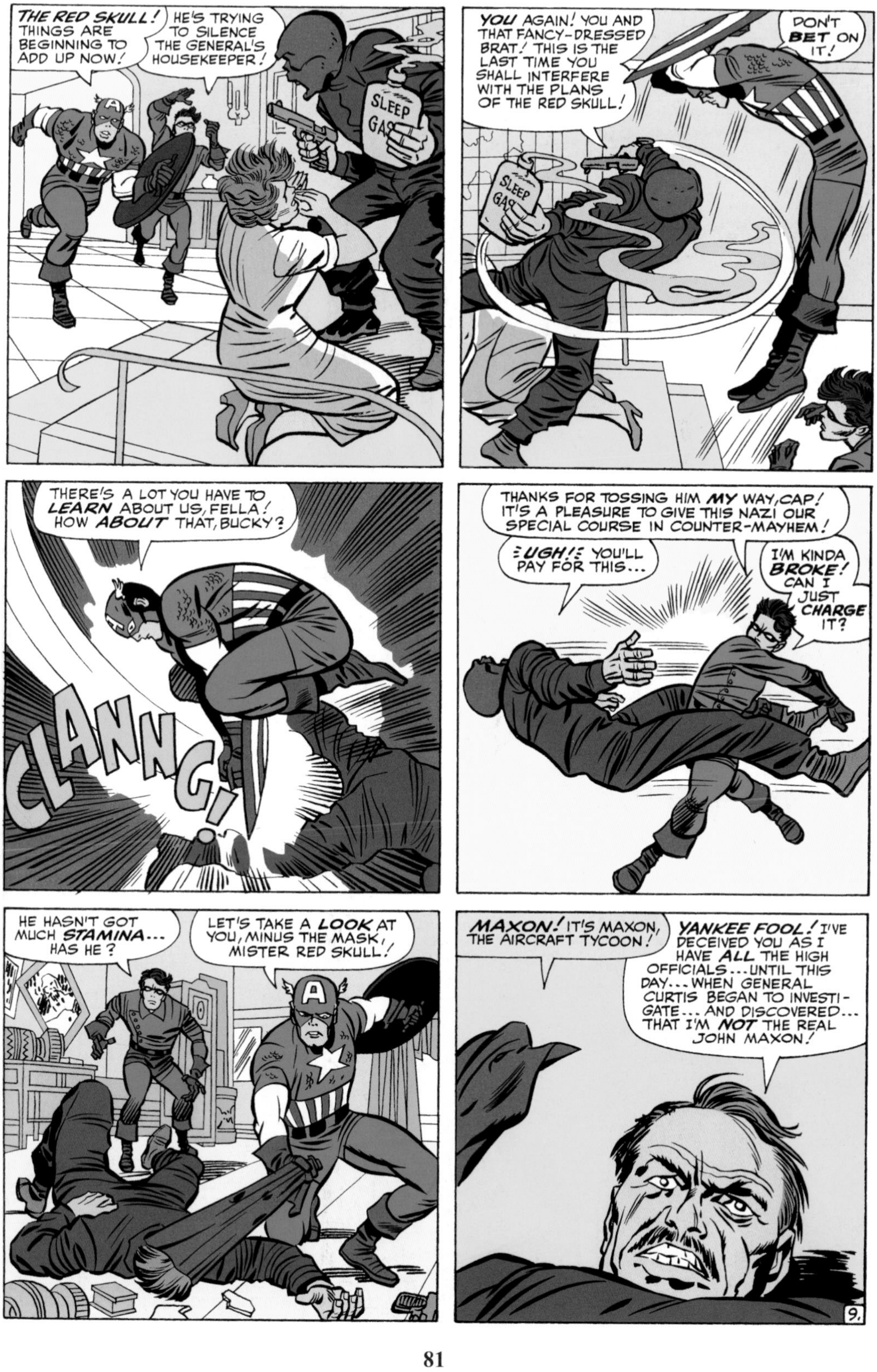
THE RED SKULL! THINGS ARE BEGINNING TO ADD UP NOW!
HE'S TRYING TO SILENCE THE GENERAL'S HOUSEKEEPER!
SLEEP GAS
YOU AGAIN! YOU AND THAT FANCY-DRESSED BRAT! THIS IS THE LAST TIME YOU SHALL INTERFERE WITH THE PLANS OF THE RED SKULL!
DON'T BET ON IT!
SLEEP GAS
THERE'S A LOT YOU HAVE TO LEARN ABOUT US, FELLA! HOW ABOUT THAT, BUCKY?
CLANNG!
THANKS FOR TOSSING HIM MY WAY, CAP! IT'S A PLEASURE TO GIVE THIS NAZI OUR SPECIAL COURSE IN COUNTER-MAYHEM!
UGH! YOU'LL PAY FOR THIS...
I'M KINDA BROKE! CAN I JUST CHARGE IT?
HE HASN'T GOT MUCH STAMINA... HAS HE?
LET'S TAKE A LOOK AT YOU, MINUS THE MASK, MISTER RED SKULL!
MAXON! IT'S MAXON, THE AIRCRAFT TYCOON!
YANKEE FOOL! I'VE DECEIVED YOU AS I HAVE ALL THE HIGH OFFICIALS... UNTIL THIS DAY... WHEN GENERAL CURTIS BEGAN TO INVESTI-GATE... AND DISCOVERED... THAT I'M NOT THE REAL JOHN MAXON!
9.

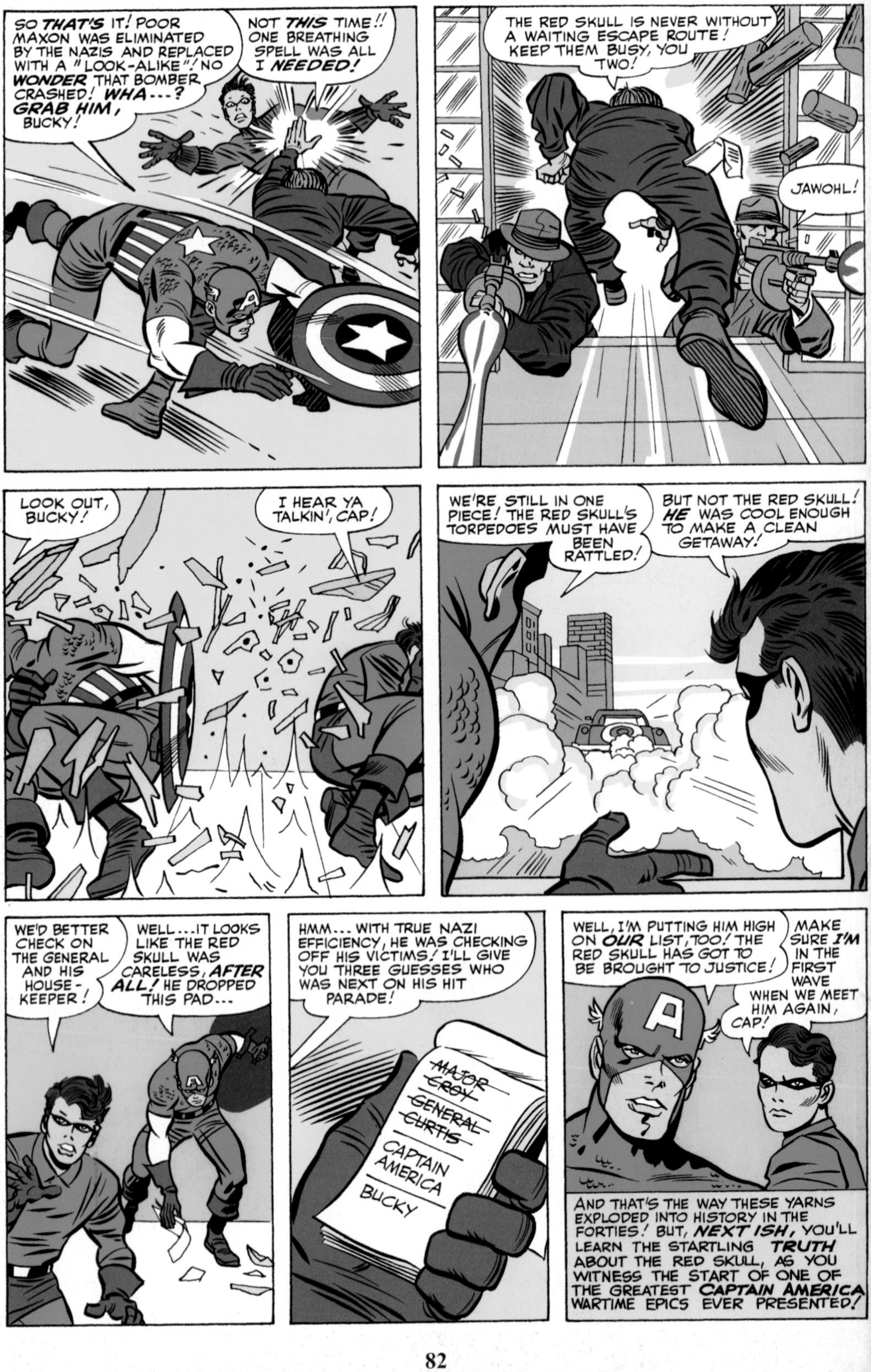
SO THAT'S IT! POOR MAXON WAS ELIMINATED BY THE NAZIS AND REPLACED WITH A "LOOK-ALIKE"! NO WONDER THAT BOMBER CRASHED! WHA---? GRAB HIM, BUCKY!
NOT THIS TIME!! ONE BREATHING SPELL WAS ALL I NEEDED!
THE RED SKULL IS NEVER WITHOUT A WAITING ESCAPE ROUTE! KEEP THEM BUSY, YOU TWO!
JAWOHL!
LOOK OUT, BUCKY!
I HEAR YA TALKIN', CAP!
WE'RE STILL IN ONE PIECE! THE RED SKULL'S TORPEDOES MUST HAVE BEEN RATTLED!
BUT NOT THE RED SKULL! HE WAS COOL ENOUGH TO MAKE A CLEAN GETAWAY!
WE'D BETTER CHECK ON THE GENERAL AND HIS HOUSE-KEEPER!
WELL...IT LOOKS LIKE THE RED SKULL WAS CARELESS, AFTER ALL! HE DROPPED THIS PAD...
HMM... WITH TRUE NAZI EFFICIENCY, HE WAS CHECKING OFF HIS VICTIMS! I'LL GIVE YOU THREE GUESSES WHO WAS NEXT ON HIS HIT PARADE!
MAJOR CROY
GENERAL CURTIS
CAPTAIN AMERICA
BUCKY
WELL, I'M PUTTING HIM HIGH ON OUR LIST, TOO! THE RED SKULL HAS GOT TO BE BROUGHT TO JUSTICE!
MAKE SURE I'M IN THE FIRST WAVE WHEN WE MEET HIM AGAIN, CAP!
AND THAT'S THE WAY THESE YARNS EXPLODED INTO HISTORY IN THE FORTIES! BUT, NEXT ISH, YOU'LL LEARN THE STARTLING TRUTH ABOUT THE RED SKULL, AS YOU WITNESS THE START OF ONE OF THE GREATEST CAPTAIN AMERICA WARTIME EPICS EVER PRESENTED!

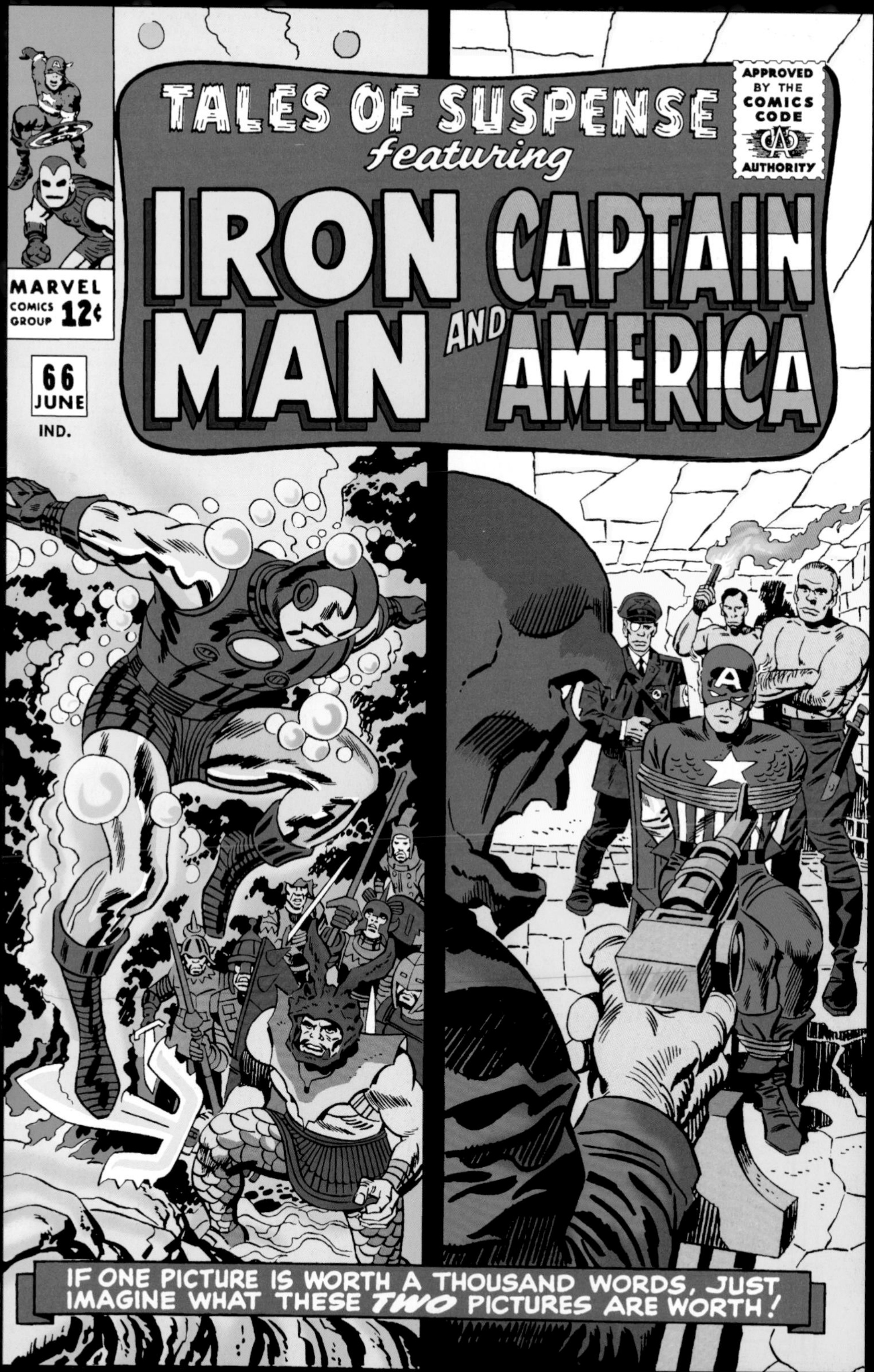
TALES OF SUSPENSE
featuring
IRON MAN AND CAPTAIN AMERICA
APPROVED BY THE COMICS CODE AUTHORITY
MARVEL COMICS GROUP 12¢
66 JUNE
IND.
IF ONE PICTURE IS WORTH A THOUSAND WORDS, JUST IMAGINE WHAT THESE TWO PICTURES ARE WORTH!

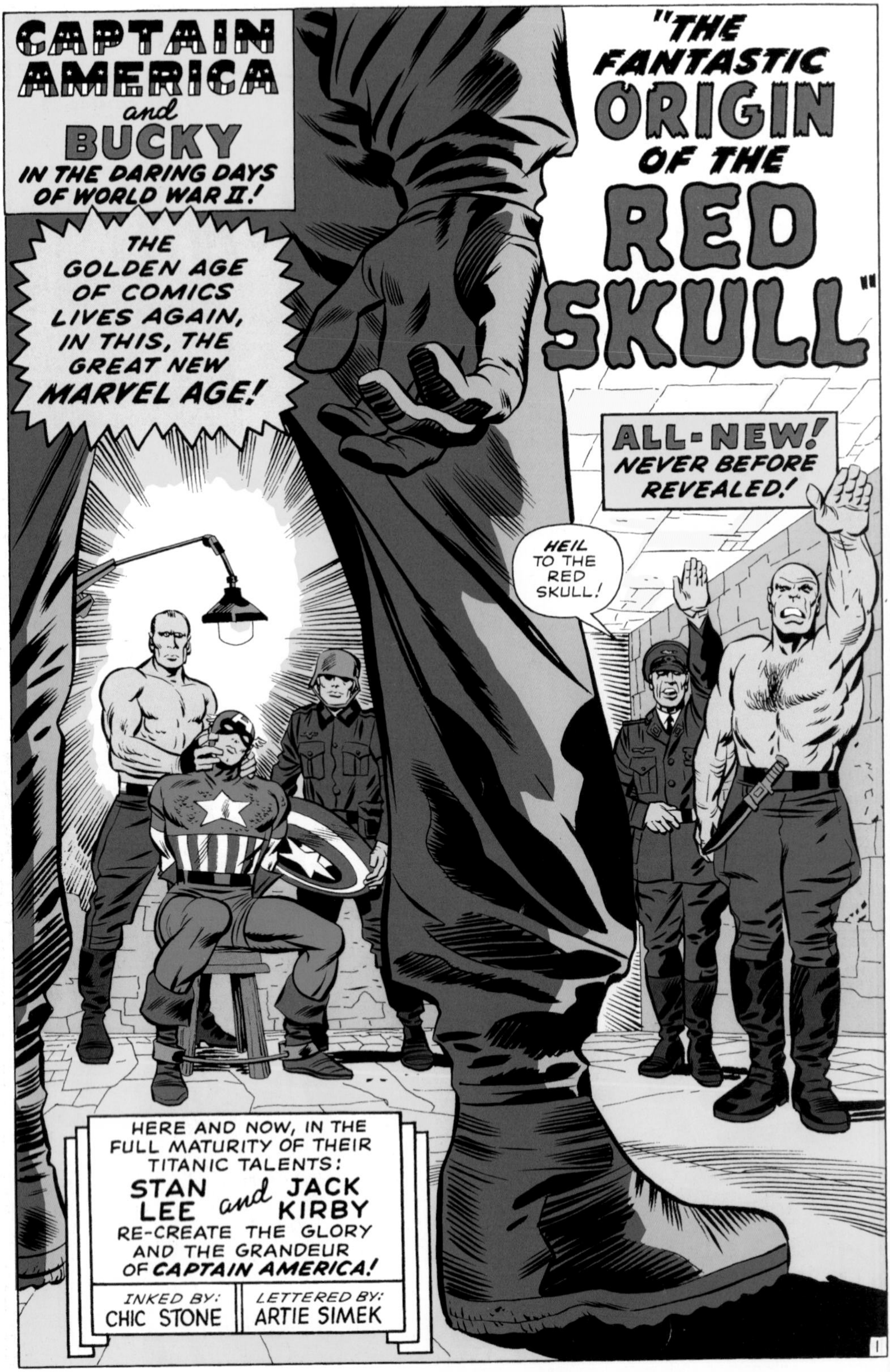
CAPTAIN AMERICA and BUCKY IN THE DARING DAYS OF WORLD WAR II!
"THE FANTASTIC ORIGIN OF THE RED SKULL"
THE GOLDEN AGE OF COMICS LIVES AGAIN, IN THIS, THE GREAT NEW MARVEL AGE!
ALL-NEW! NEVER BEFORE REVEALED!
HEIL TO THE RED SKULL!
HERE AND NOW, IN THE FULL MATURITY OF THEIR TITANIC TALENTS: STAN LEE and JACK KIRBY RE-CREATE THE GLORY AND THE GRANDEUR OF CAPTAIN AMERICA!
INKED BY: CHIC STONE
LETTERED BY: ARTIE SIMEK
1

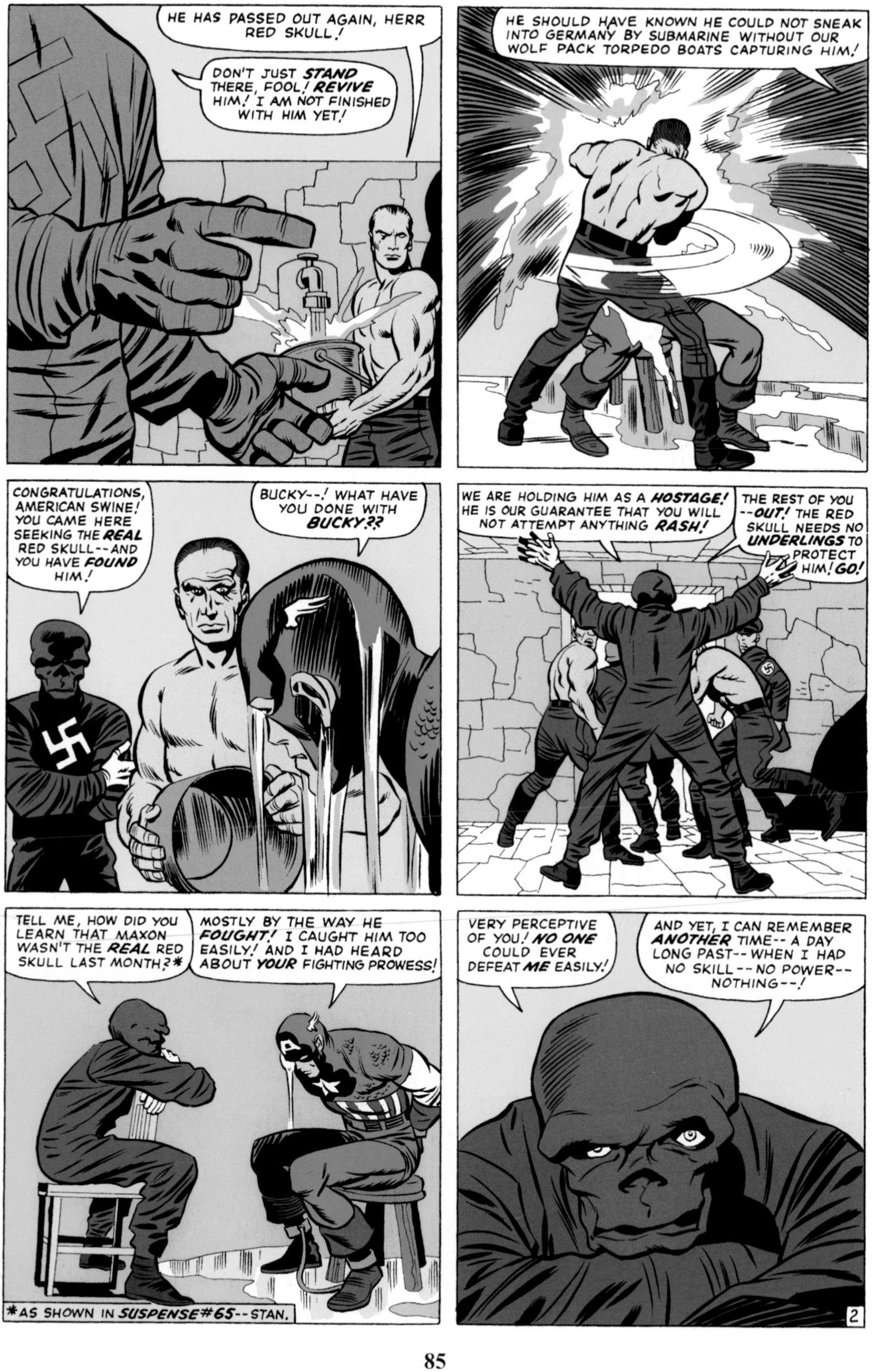
HE HAS PASSED OUT AGAIN, HERR RED SKULL!
DON'T JUST STAND THERE, FOOL! REVIVE HIM! I AM NOT FINISHED WITH HIM YET!
HE SHOULD HAVE KNOWN HE COULD NOT SNEAK INTO GERMANY BY SUBMARINE WITHOUT OUR WOLF PACK TORPEDO BOATS CAPTURING HIM!
CONGRATULATIONS, AMERICAN SWINE! YOU CAME HERE SEEKING THE REAL RED SKULL--AND YOU HAVE FOUND HIM!
BUCKY--! WHAT HAVE YOU DONE WITH BUCKY??
WE ARE HOLDING HIM AS A HOSTAGE! HE IS OUR GUARANTEE THAT YOU WILL NOT ATTEMPT ANYTHING RASH!
THE REST OF YOU --OUT! THE RED SKULL NEEDS NO UNDERLINGS TO PROTECT HIM! GO!
TELL ME, HOW DID YOU LEARN THAT MAXON WASN'T THE REAL RED SKULL LAST MONTH?*
MOSTLY BY THE WAY HE FOUGHT! I CAUGHT HIM TOO EASILY! AND I HAD HEARD ABOUT YOUR FIGHTING PROWESS!
*AS SHOWN IN SUSPENSE #65--STAN.
VERY PERCEPTIVE OF YOU! NO ONE COULD EVER DEFEAT ME EASILY!
AND YET, I CAN REMEMBER ANOTHER TIME-- A DAY LONG PAST--WHEN I HAD NO SKILL--NO POWER--NOTHING--!
2

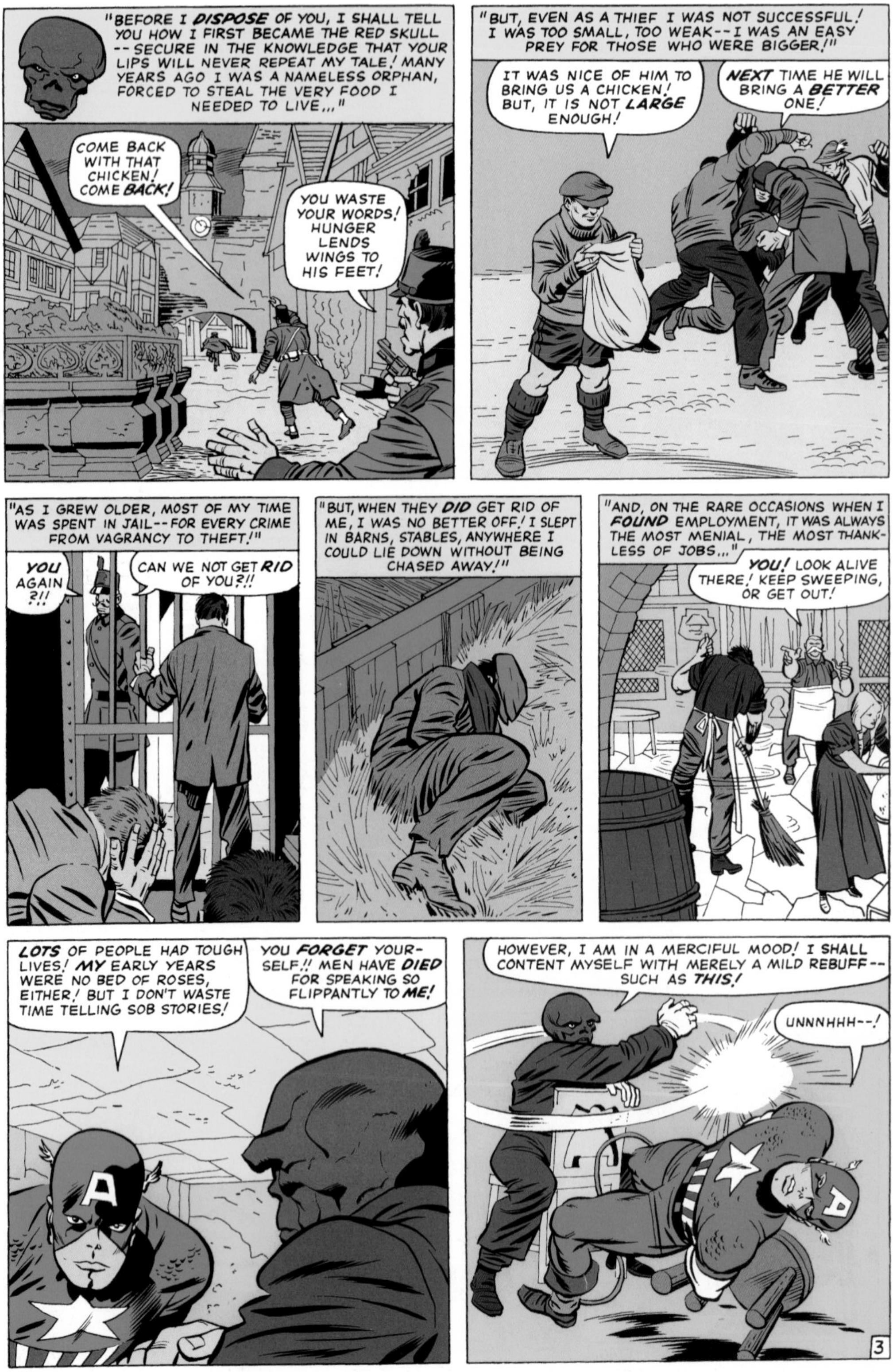
"BEFORE I DISPOSE OF YOU, I SHALL TELL YOU HOW I FIRST BECAME THE RED SKULL -- SECURE IN THE KNOWLEDGE THAT YOUR LIPS WILL NEVER REPEAT MY TALE! MANY YEARS AGO I WAS A NAMELESS ORPHAN, FORCED TO STEAL THE VERY FOOD I NEEDED TO LIVE..."
COME BACK WITH THAT CHICKEN! COME BACK!
YOU WASTE YOUR WORDS! HUNGER LENDS WINGS TO HIS FEET!
"BUT, EVEN AS A THIEF I WAS NOT SUCCESSFUL! I WAS TOO SMALL, TOO WEAK-- I WAS AN EASY PREY FOR THOSE WHO WERE BIGGER!"
IT WAS NICE OF HIM TO BRING US A CHICKEN! BUT, IT IS NOT LARGE ENOUGH!
NEXT TIME HE WILL BRING A BETTER ONE!
"AS I GREW OLDER, MOST OF MY TIME WAS SPENT IN JAIL-- FOR EVERY CRIME FROM VAGRANCY TO THEFT!"
YOU AGAIN ?!!
CAN WE NOT GET RID OF YOU?!!
"BUT, WHEN THEY DID GET RID OF ME, I WAS NO BETTER OFF! I SLEPT IN BARNS, STABLES, ANYWHERE I COULD LIE DOWN WITHOUT BEING CHASED AWAY!"
"AND, ON THE RARE OCCASIONS WHEN I FOUND EMPLOYMENT, IT WAS ALWAYS THE MOST MENIAL, THE MOST THANKLESS OF JOBS..."
YOU! LOOK ALIVE THERE! KEEP SWEEPING, OR GET OUT!
LOTS OF PEOPLE HAD TOUGH LIVES! MY EARLY YEARS WERE NO BED OF ROSES, EITHER! BUT I DON'T WASTE TIME TELLING SOB STORIES!
YOU FORGET YOURSELF!! MEN HAVE DIED FOR SPEAKING SO FLIPPANTLY TO ME!
HOWEVER, I AM IN A MERCIFUL MOOD! I SHALL CONTENT MYSELF WITH MERELY A MILD REBUFF -- SUCH AS THIS!
UNNNHHH--!
3

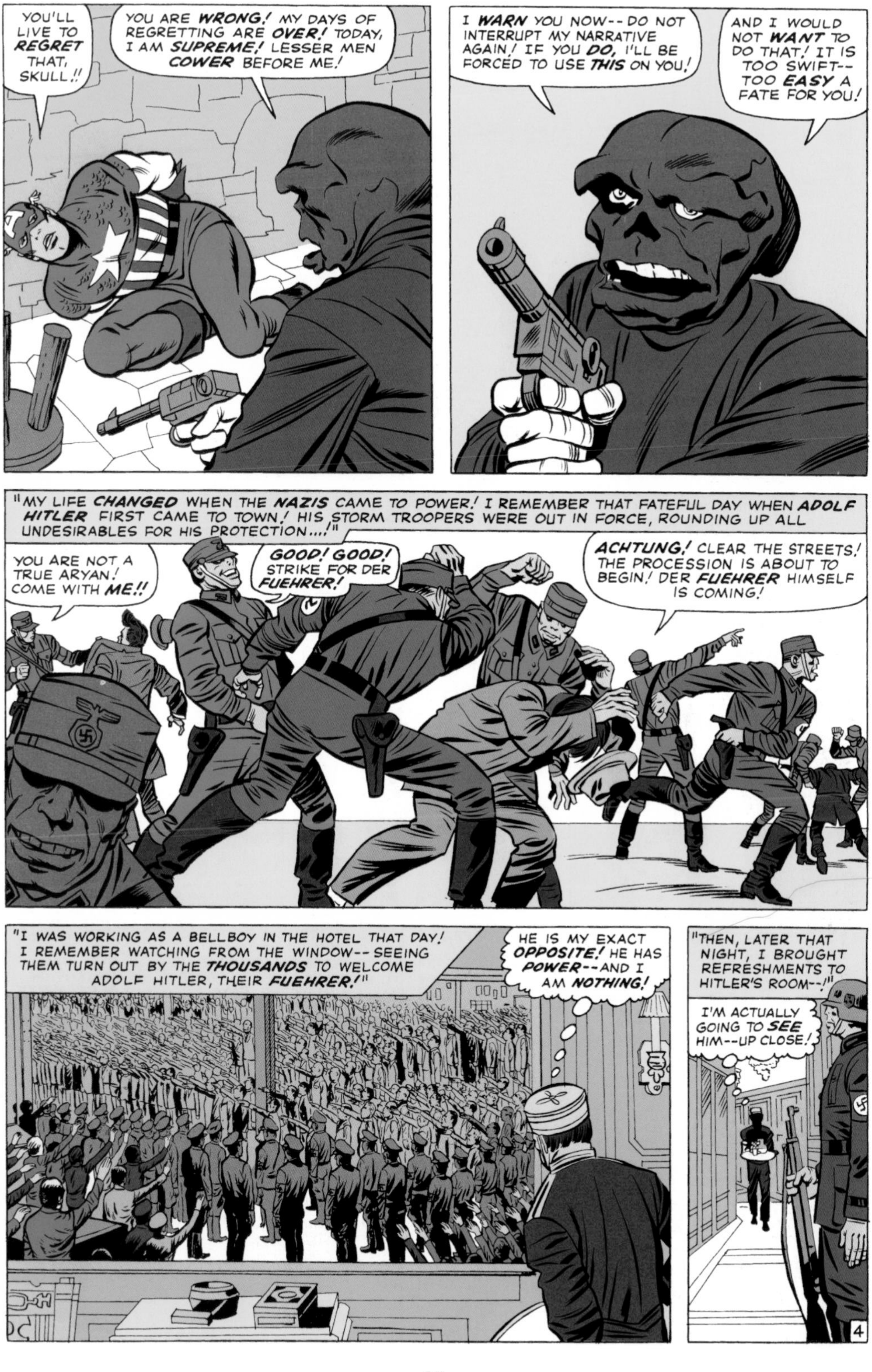
YOU'LL LIVE TO REGRET THAT, SKULL!!
YOU ARE WRONG! MY DAYS OF REGRETTING ARE OVER! TODAY, I AM SUPREME! LESSER MEN COWER BEFORE ME!
I WARN YOU NOW--DO NOT INTERRUPT MY NARRATIVE AGAIN! IF YOU DO, I'LL BE FORCED TO USE THIS ON YOU!
AND I WOULD NOT WANT TO DO THAT! IT IS TOO SWIFT--TOO EASY A FATE FOR YOU!
"MY LIFE CHANGED WHEN THE NAZIS CAME TO POWER! I REMEMBER THAT FATEFUL DAY WHEN ADOLF HITLER FIRST CAME TO TOWN! HIS STORM TROOPERS WERE OUT IN FORCE, ROUNDING UP ALL UNDESIRABLES FOR HIS PROTECTION...!"
YOU ARE NOT A TRUE ARYAN! COME WITH ME!!
GOOD! GOOD! STRIKE FOR DER FUEHRER!
ACHTUNG! CLEAR THE STREETS! THE PROCESSION IS ABOUT TO BEGIN! DER FUEHRER HIMSELF IS COMING!
"I WAS WORKING AS A BELLBOY IN THE HOTEL THAT DAY! I REMEMBER WATCHING FROM THE WINDOW--SEEING THEM TURN OUT BY THE THOUSANDS TO WELCOME ADOLF HITLER, THEIR FUEHRER!"
HE IS MY EXACT OPPOSITE! HE HAS POWER--AND I AM NOTHING!
"THEN, LATER THAT NIGHT, I BROUGHT REFRESHMENTS TO HITLER'S ROOM--!"
I'M ACTUALLY GOING TO SEE HIM--UP CLOSE!
4

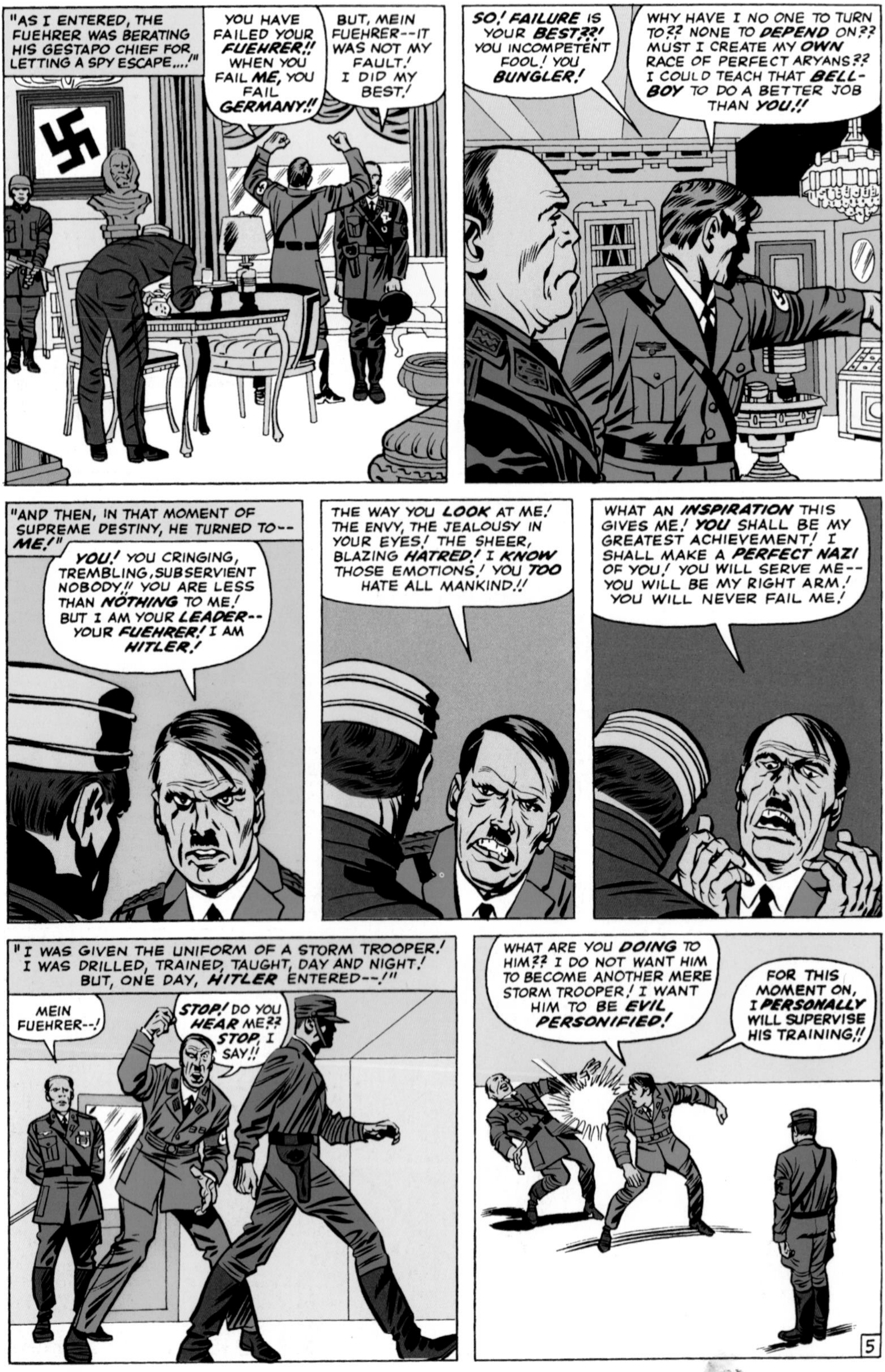
"AS I ENTERED, THE FUEHRER WAS BERATING HIS GESTAPO CHIEF FOR LETTING A SPY ESCAPE....!"
YOU HAVE FAILED YOUR FUEHRER!! WHEN YOU FAIL ME, YOU FAIL GERMANY!!
BUT, MEIN FUEHRER--IT WAS NOT MY FAULT! I DID MY BEST!
SO! FAILURE IS YOUR BEST??! YOU INCOMPETENT FOOL! YOU BUNGLER!
WHY HAVE I NO ONE TO TURN TO?? NONE TO DEPEND ON?? MUST I CREATE MY OWN RACE OF PERFECT ARYANS?? I COULD TEACH THAT BELL-BOY TO DO A BETTER JOB THAN YOU!!
"AND THEN, IN THAT MOMENT OF SUPREME DESTINY, HE TURNED TO--ME!"
YOU! YOU CRINGING, TREMBLING, SUBSERVIENT NOBODY!! YOU ARE LESS THAN NOTHING TO ME! BUT I AM YOUR LEADER--YOUR FUEHRER! I AM HITLER!
THE WAY YOU LOOK AT ME! THE ENVY, THE JEALOUSY IN YOUR EYES! THE SHEER, BLAZING HATRED! I KNOW THOSE EMOTIONS! YOU TOO HATE ALL MANKIND!!
WHAT AN INSPIRATION THIS GIVES ME! YOU SHALL BE MY GREATEST ACHIEVEMENT! I SHALL MAKE A PERFECT NAZI OF YOU! YOU WILL SERVE ME--YOU WILL BE MY RIGHT ARM! YOU WILL NEVER FAIL ME!
"I WAS GIVEN THE UNIFORM OF A STORM TROOPER! I WAS DRILLED, TRAINED, TAUGHT, DAY AND NIGHT! BUT, ONE DAY, HITLER ENTERED--!"
MEIN FUEHRER--!
STOP! DO YOU HEAR ME?? STOP, I SAY!!
WHAT ARE YOU DOING TO HIM?? I DO NOT WANT HIM TO BECOME ANOTHER MERE STORM TROOPER! I WANT HIM TO BE EVIL PERSONIFIED!
FOR THIS MOMENT ON, I PERSONALLY WILL SUPERVISE HIS TRAINING!!
5

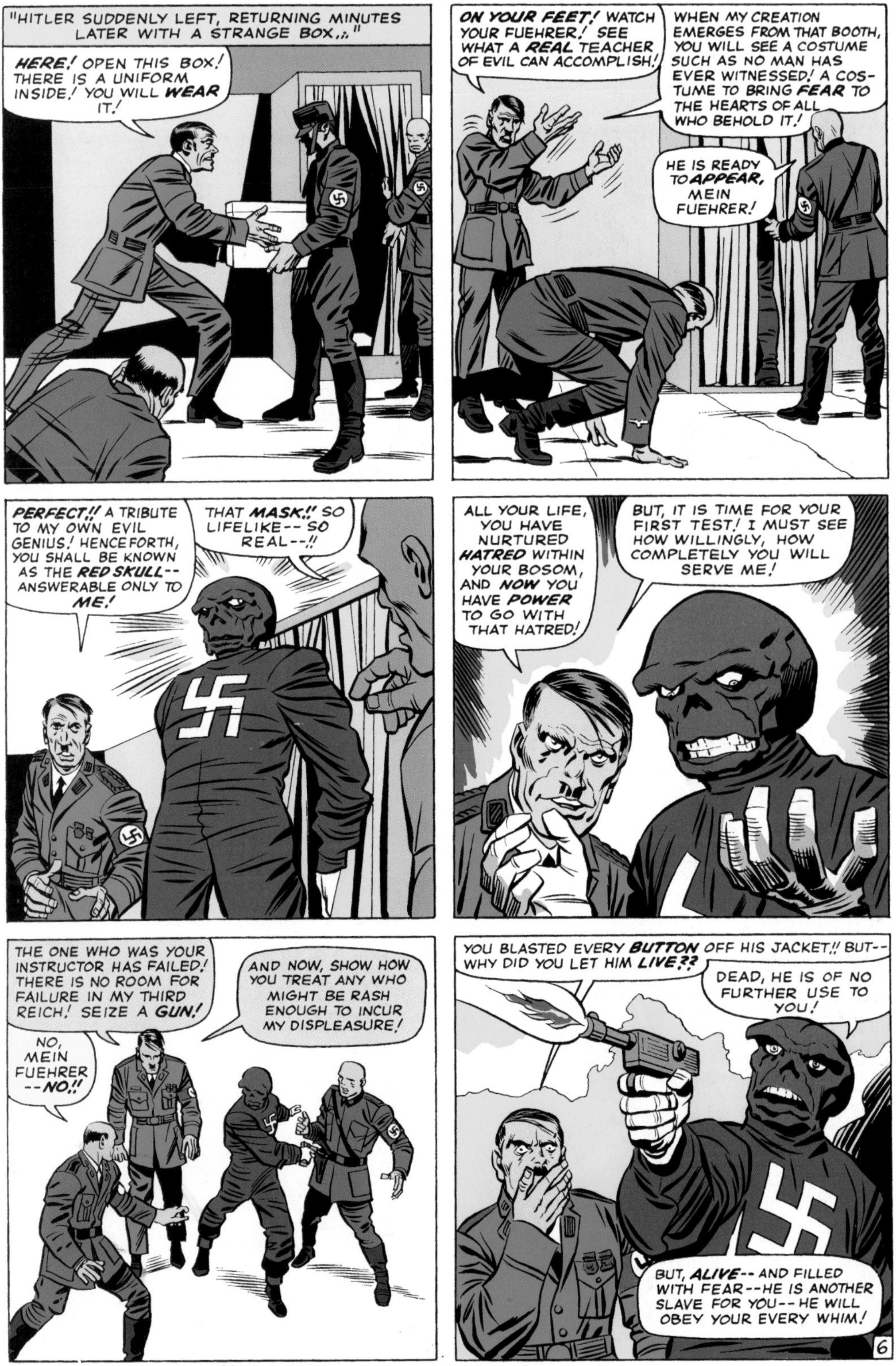

"HITLER SUDDENLY LEFT, RETURNING MINUTES LATER WITH A STRANGE BOX...."
HERE! OPEN THIS BOX! THERE IS A UNIFORM INSIDE! YOU WILL WEAR IT!
ON YOUR FEET! WATCH YOUR FUEHRER! SEE WHAT A REAL TEACHER OF EVIL CAN ACCOMPLISH!
WHEN MY CREATION EMERGES FROM THAT BOOTH, YOU WILL SEE A COSTUME SUCH AS NO MAN HAS EVER WITNESSED! A COSTUME TO BRING FEAR TO THE HEARTS OF ALL WHO BEHOLD IT!
HE IS READY TO APPEAR, MEIN FUEHRER!
PERFECT!! A TRIBUTE TO MY OWN EVIL GENIUS! HENCEFORTH, YOU SHALL BE KNOWN AS THE RED SKULL-- ANSWERABLE ONLY TO ME!
THAT MASK!" SO LIFELIKE-- SO REAL--!!
ALL YOUR LIFE, YOU HAVE NURTURED HATRED WITHIN YOUR BOSOM, AND NOW YOU HAVE POWER TO GO WITH THAT HATRED!
BUT, IT IS TIME FOR YOUR FIRST TEST! I MUST SEE HOW WILLINGLY, HOW COMPLETELY YOU WILL SERVE ME!
THE ONE WHO WAS YOUR INSTRUCTOR HAS FAILED! THERE IS NO ROOM FOR FAILURE IN MY THIRD REICH! SEIZE A GUN!
AND NOW, SHOW HOW YOU TREAT ANY WHO MIGHT BE RASH ENOUGH TO INCUR MY DISPLEASURE!
NO, MEIN FUEHRER --NO!!
YOU BLASTED EVERY BUTTON OFF HIS JACKET!! BUT-- WHY DID YOU LET HIM LIVE??
DEAD, HE IS OF NO FURTHER USE TO YOU!
BUT, ALIVE-- AND FILLED WITH FEAR--HE IS ANOTHER SLAVE FOR YOU-- HE WILL OBEY YOUR EVERY WHIM!
6

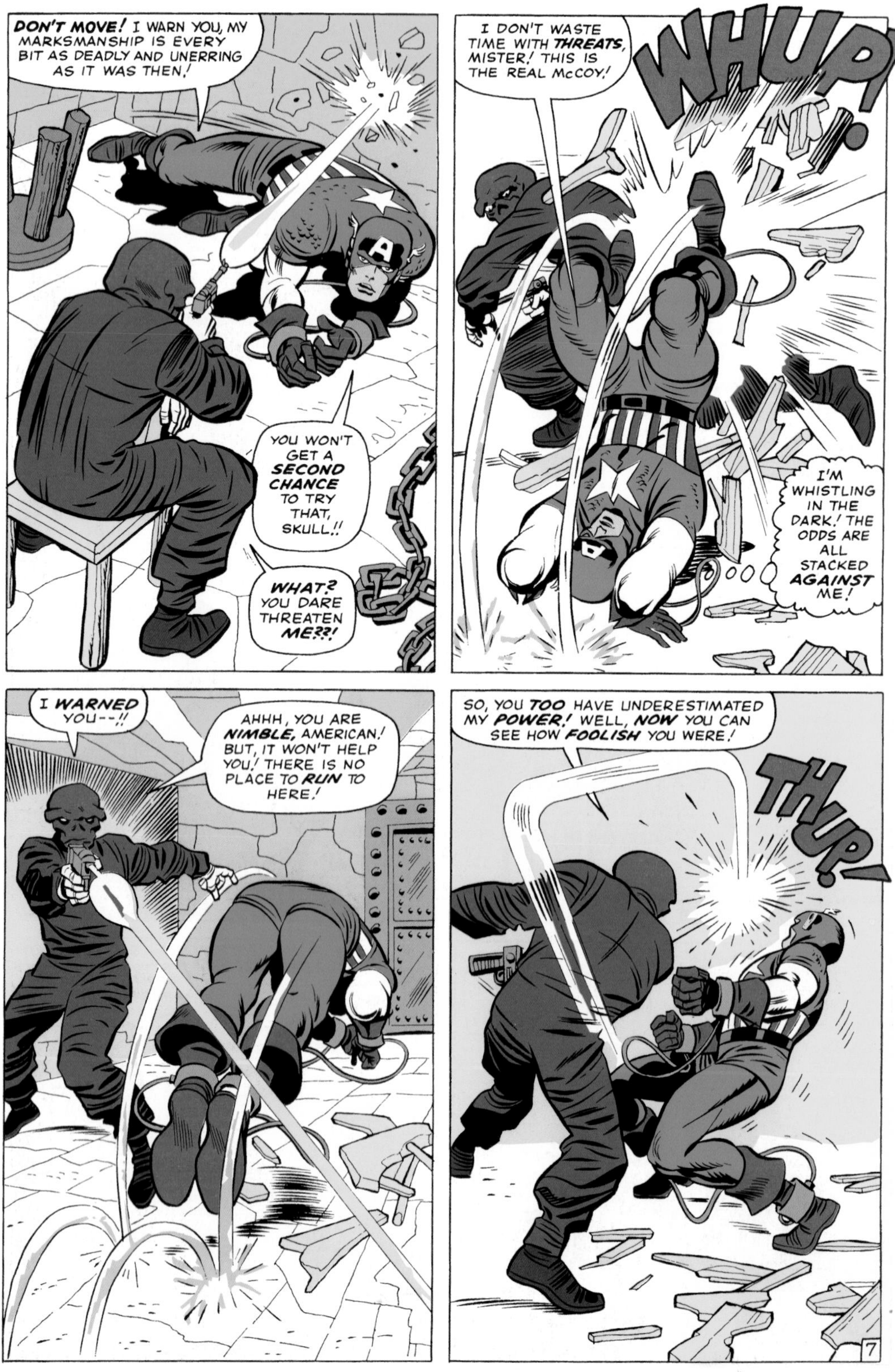
DON'T MOVE! I WARN YOU, MY MARKSMANSHIP IS EVERY BIT AS DEADLY AND UNERRING AS IT WAS THEN!
YOU WON'T GET A SECOND CHANCE TO TRY THAT, SKULL!!
WHAT? YOU DARE THREATEN ME??!
I DON'T WASTE TIME WITH THREATS, MISTER! THIS IS THE REAL McCOY!
WHUP!
I'M WHISTLING IN THE DARK! THE ODDS ARE ALL STACKED AGAINST ME!
I WARNED YOU--!!
AHHH, YOU ARE NIMBLE, AMERICAN! BUT, IT WON'T HELP YOU! THERE IS NO PLACE TO RUN TO HERE!
SO, YOU TOO HAVE UNDERESTIMATED MY POWER! WELL, NOW YOU CAN SEE HOW FOOLISH YOU WERE!
THUP!
7

AND NOW, IF I MAY FINISH MY NARRATIVE WITHOUT ANY FURTHER INTERRUPTION!

LET US AGAIN RETURN TO THE EARLY DAYS OF THE WAR--!

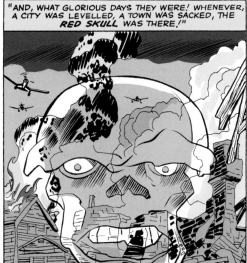

"AND, WHAT GLORIOUS DAYS THEY WERE! WHENEVER, A CITY WAS LEVELLED, A TOWN WAS SACKED, THE *RED SKULL* WAS THERE!"

"WHENEVER THERE WAS INJUSTICE, TYRANNY, RUTHLESSNESS, THE *RED SKULL* WAS THERE, LEADING THE ATTACK UPON THE WEAK AND THE HELPLESS!"

KEEP FIRING! LET THE WORLD KNOW THAT THE RED SKULL STOPS AT *NOTHING!*

"YES, I SERVED THE FUEHRER WELL -- IN MY OWN FASHION!"

NO, *NO!* YOU CANNOT TAKE MY SON! HE HAS DONE NOTHING! HE IS LOYAL TO THE FUEHRER!

BAH! IT IS HIS LOYALTY TO *ME* THAT COUNTS!! TAKE HIM *AWAY!*

"THANKS TO MY CLEVERNESS, MANY OF HITLER'S MOST TRUSTED ADVISERS BEGAN TO MYSTERIOUSLY *VANISH--!*"

8

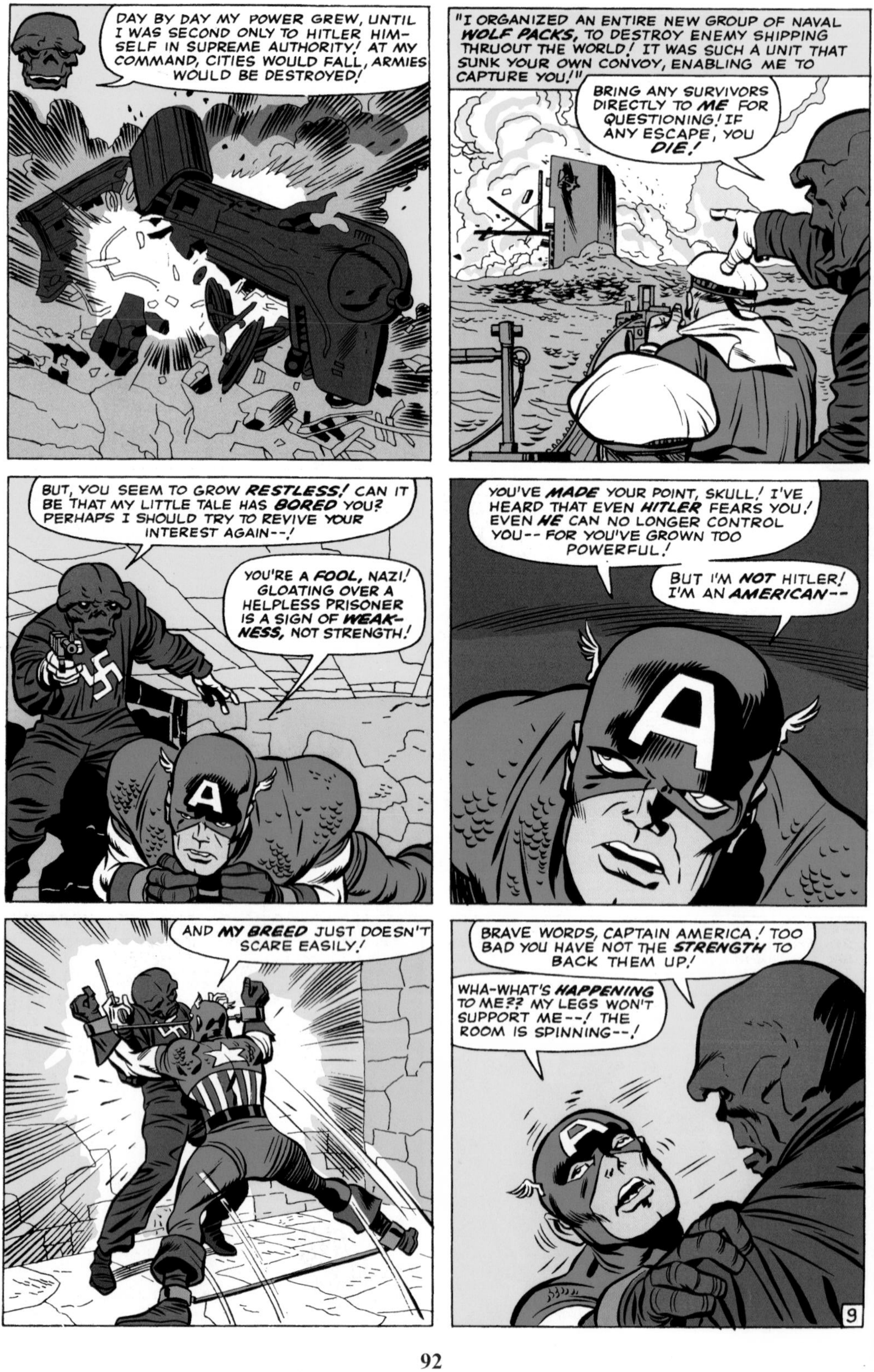
DAY BY DAY MY POWER GREW, UNTIL I WAS SECOND ONLY TO HITLER HIMSELF IN SUPREME AUTHORITY! AT MY COMMAND, CITIES WOULD FALL, ARMIES WOULD BE DESTROYED!
"I ORGANIZED AN ENTIRE NEW GROUP OF NAVAL WOLF PACKS, TO DESTROY ENEMY SHIPPING THRUOUT THE WORLD! IT WAS SUCH A UNIT THAT SUNK YOUR OWN CONVOY, ENABLING ME TO CAPTURE YOU!"
BRING ANY SURVIVORS DIRECTLY TO ME FOR QUESTIONING! IF ANY ESCAPE, YOU DIE!
BUT, YOU SEEM TO GROW RESTLESS! CAN IT BE THAT MY LITTLE TALE HAS BORED YOU? PERHAPS I SHOULD TRY TO REVIVE YOUR INTEREST AGAIN--!
YOU'RE A FOOL, NAZI! GLOATING OVER A HELPLESS PRISONER IS A SIGN OF WEAKNESS, NOT STRENGTH!
YOU'VE MADE YOUR POINT, SKULL! I'VE HEARD THAT EVEN HITLER FEARS YOU! EVEN HE CAN NO LONGER CONTROL YOU-- FOR YOU'VE GROWN TOO POWERFUL!
BUT I'M NOT HITLER! I'M AN AMERICAN--
AND MY BREED JUST DOESN'T SCARE EASILY!
BRAVE WORDS, CAPTAIN AMERICA! TOO BAD YOU HAVE NOT THE STRENGTH TO BACK THEM UP!
WHA-WHAT'S HAPPENING TO ME?? MY LEGS WON'T SUPPORT ME--! THE ROOM IS SPINNING--!
9

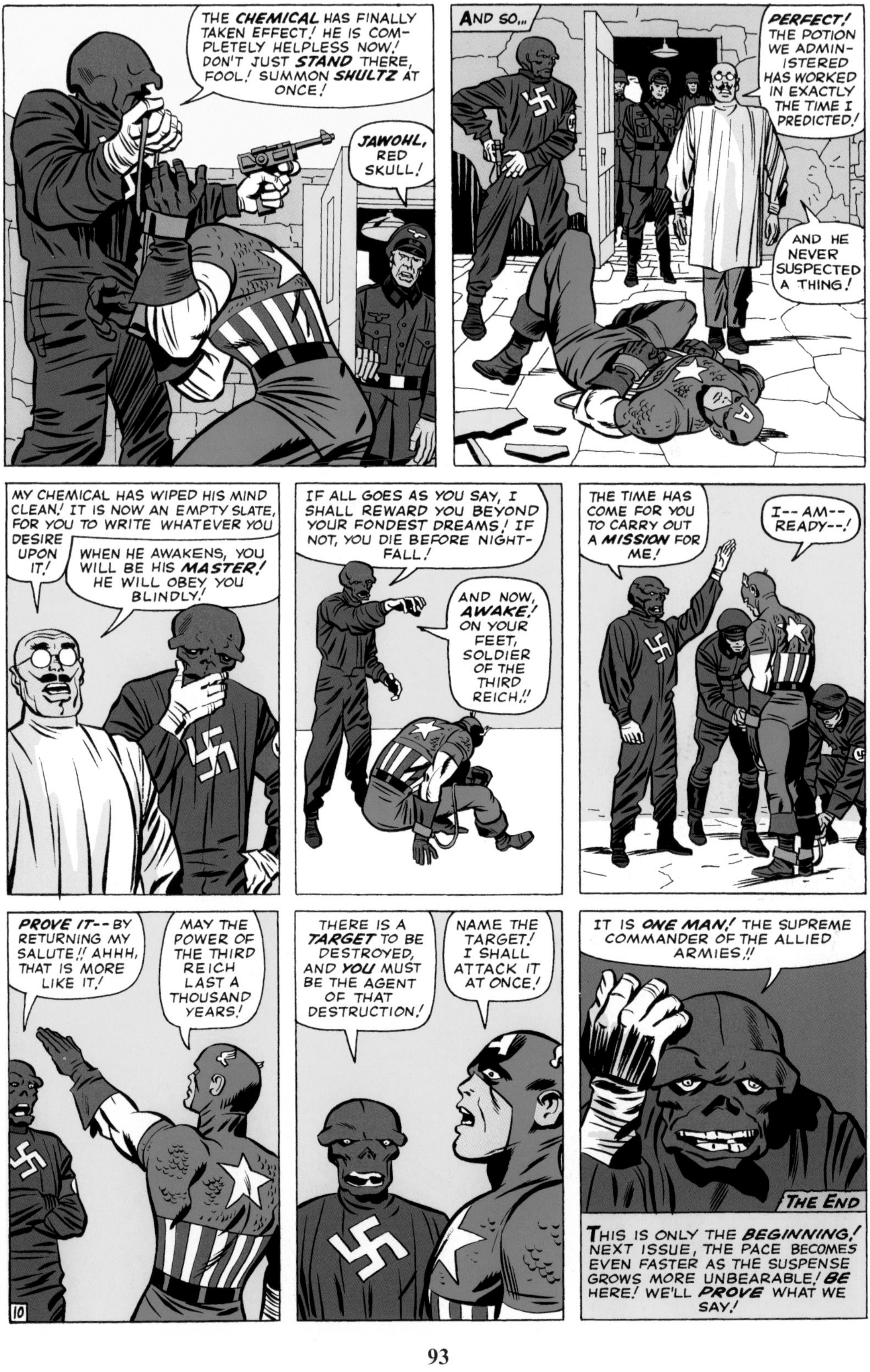
THE CHEMICAL HAS FINALLY TAKEN EFFECT! HE IS COMPLETELY HELPLESS NOW! DON'T JUST STAND THERE, FOOL! SUMMON SHULTZ AT ONCE!
JAWOHL, RED SKULL!
AND SO...
PERFECT! THE POTION WE ADMINISTERED HAS WORKED IN EXACTLY THE TIME I PREDICTED!
AND HE NEVER SUSPECTED A THING!
MY CHEMICAL HAS WIPED HIS MIND CLEAN! IT IS NOW AN EMPTY SLATE, FOR YOU TO WRITE WHATEVER YOU DESIRE UPON IT!
WHEN HE AWAKENS, YOU WILL BE HIS MASTER! HE WILL OBEY YOU BLINDLY!
IF ALL GOES AS YOU SAY, I SHALL REWARD YOU BEYOND YOUR FONDEST DREAMS! IF NOT, YOU DIE BEFORE NIGHTFALL!
AND NOW, AWAKE! ON YOUR FEET, SOLDIER OF THE THIRD REICH!!
THE TIME HAS COME FOR YOU TO CARRY OUT A MISSION FOR ME!
I-- AM-- READY--!
PROVE IT-- BY RETURNING MY SALUTE!! AHHH, THAT IS MORE LIKE IT!
MAY THE POWER OF THE THIRD REICH LAST A THOUSAND YEARS!
10
THERE IS A TARGET TO BE DESTROYED, AND YOU MUST BE THE AGENT OF THAT DESTRUCTION!
NAME THE TARGET! I SHALL ATTACK IT AT ONCE!
IT IS ONE MAN! THE SUPREME COMMANDER OF THE ALLIED ARMIES!!
THE END
THIS IS ONLY THE BEGINNING! NEXT ISSUE, THE PACE BECOMES EVEN FASTER AS THE SUSPENSE GROWS MORE UNBEARABLE! BE HERE! WE'LL PROVE WHAT WE SAY!

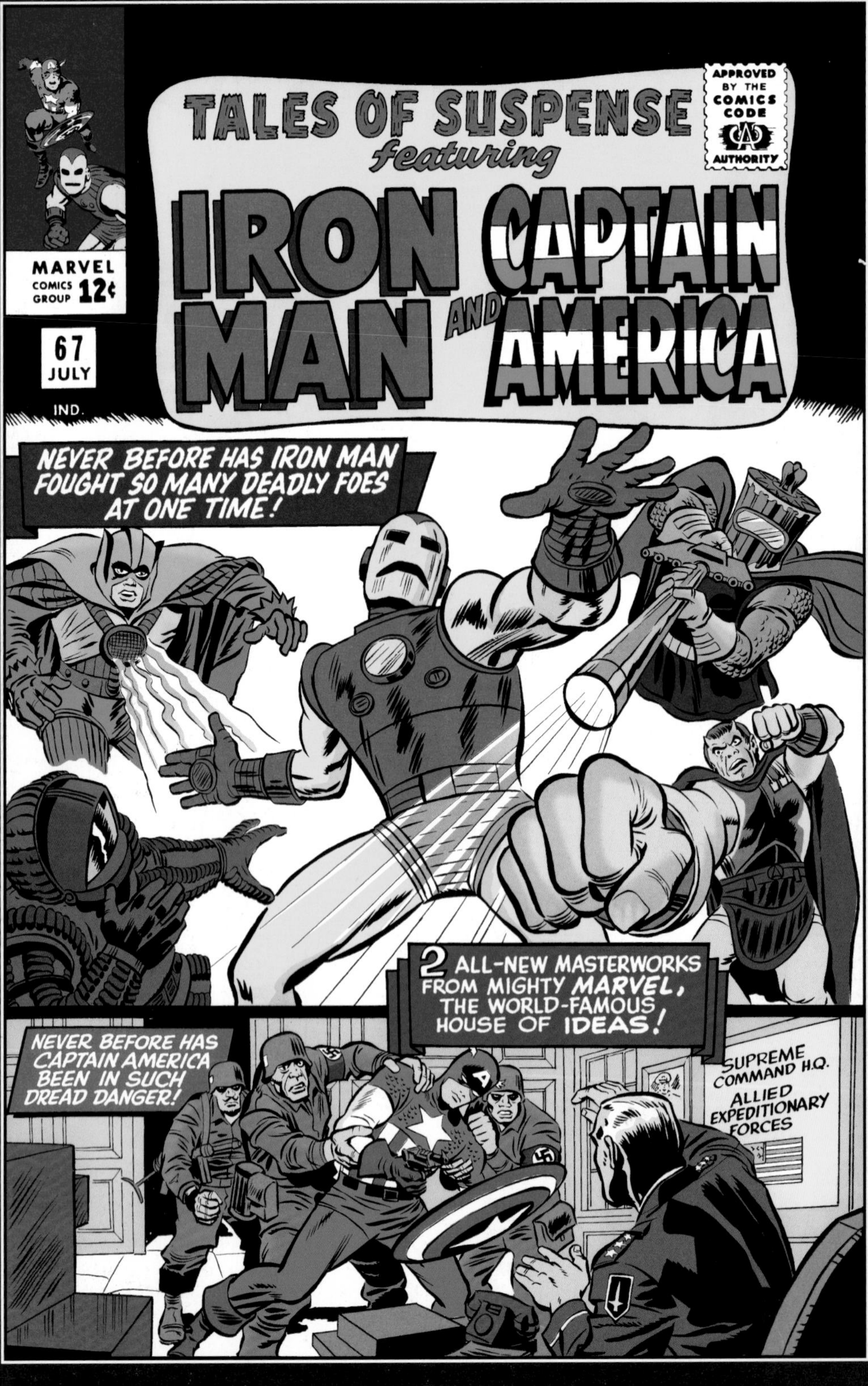

TALES OF SUSPENSE
featuring
IRON MAN AND CAPTAIN AMERICA
APPROVED BY THE COMICS CODE AUTHORITY
MARVEL COMICS GROUP 12¢
67 JULY
IND.
NEVER BEFORE HAS IRON MAN FOUGHT SO MANY DEADLY FOES AT ONE TIME!
2 ALL-NEW MASTERWORKS FROM MIGHTY MARVEL, THE WORLD-FAMOUS HOUSE OF IDEAS!
NEVER BEFORE HAS CAPTAIN AMERICA BEEN IN SUCH DREAD DANGER!
SUPREME COMMAND H.Q.
ALLIED EXPEDITIONARY FORCES

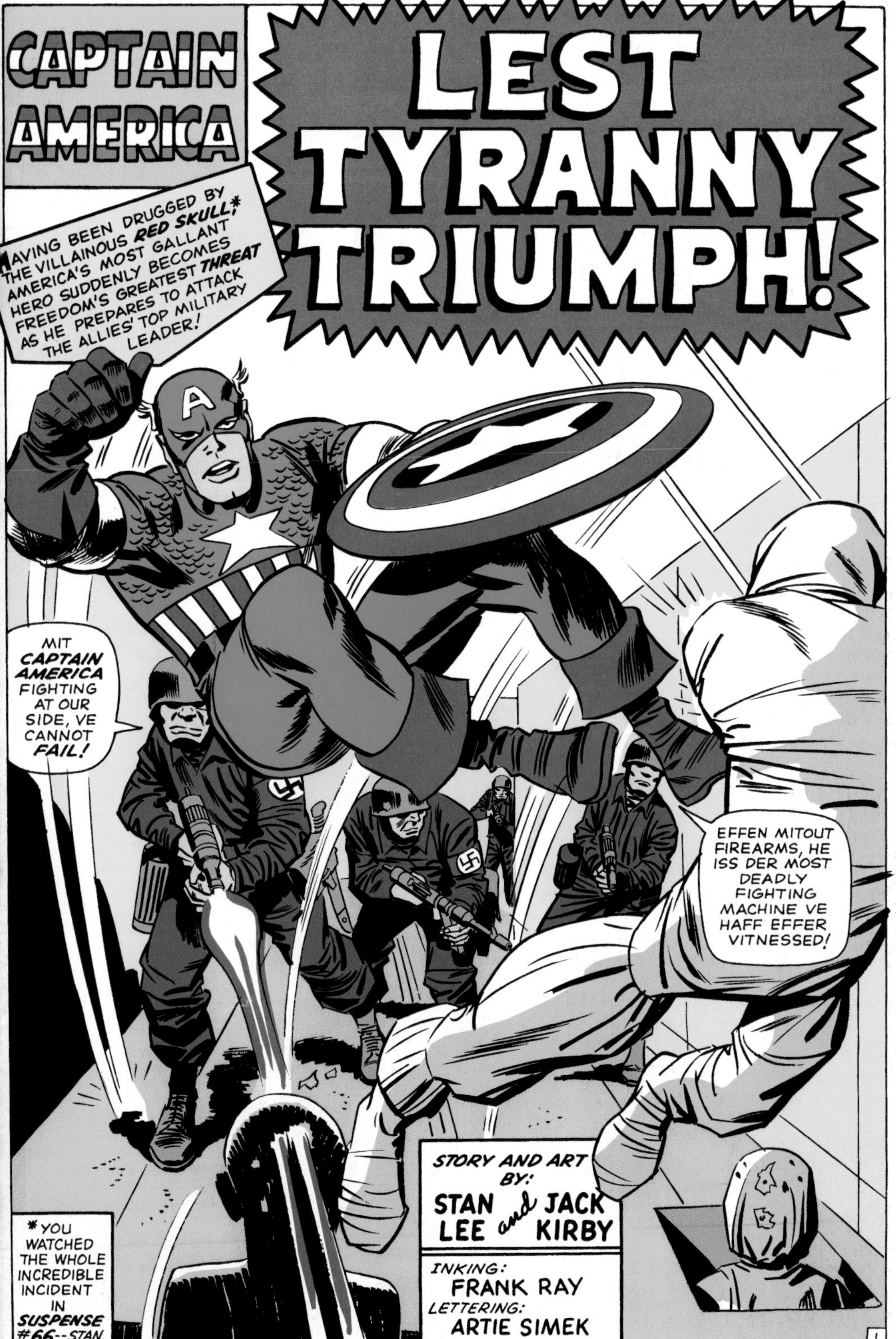
CAPTAIN AMERICA
LEST TYRANNY TRIUMPH!
HAVING BEEN DRUGGED BY THE VILLAINOUS RED SKULL,* AMERICA'S MOST GALLANT HERO SUDDENLY BECOMES FREEDOM'S GREATEST THREAT AS HE PREPARES TO ATTACK THE ALLIES' TOP MILITARY LEADER!
MIT CAPTAIN AMERICA FIGHTING AT OUR SIDE, VE CANNOT FAIL!
EFFEN MITOUT FIREARMS, HE ISS DER MOST DEADLY FIGHTING MACHINE VE HAFF EFFER VITNESSED!
STORY AND ART BY: STAN LEE and JACK KIRBY
INKING: FRANK RAY
LETTERING: ARTIE SIMEK
*YOU WATCHED THE WHOLE INCREDIBLE INCIDENT IN SUSPENSE #66--STAN.
1

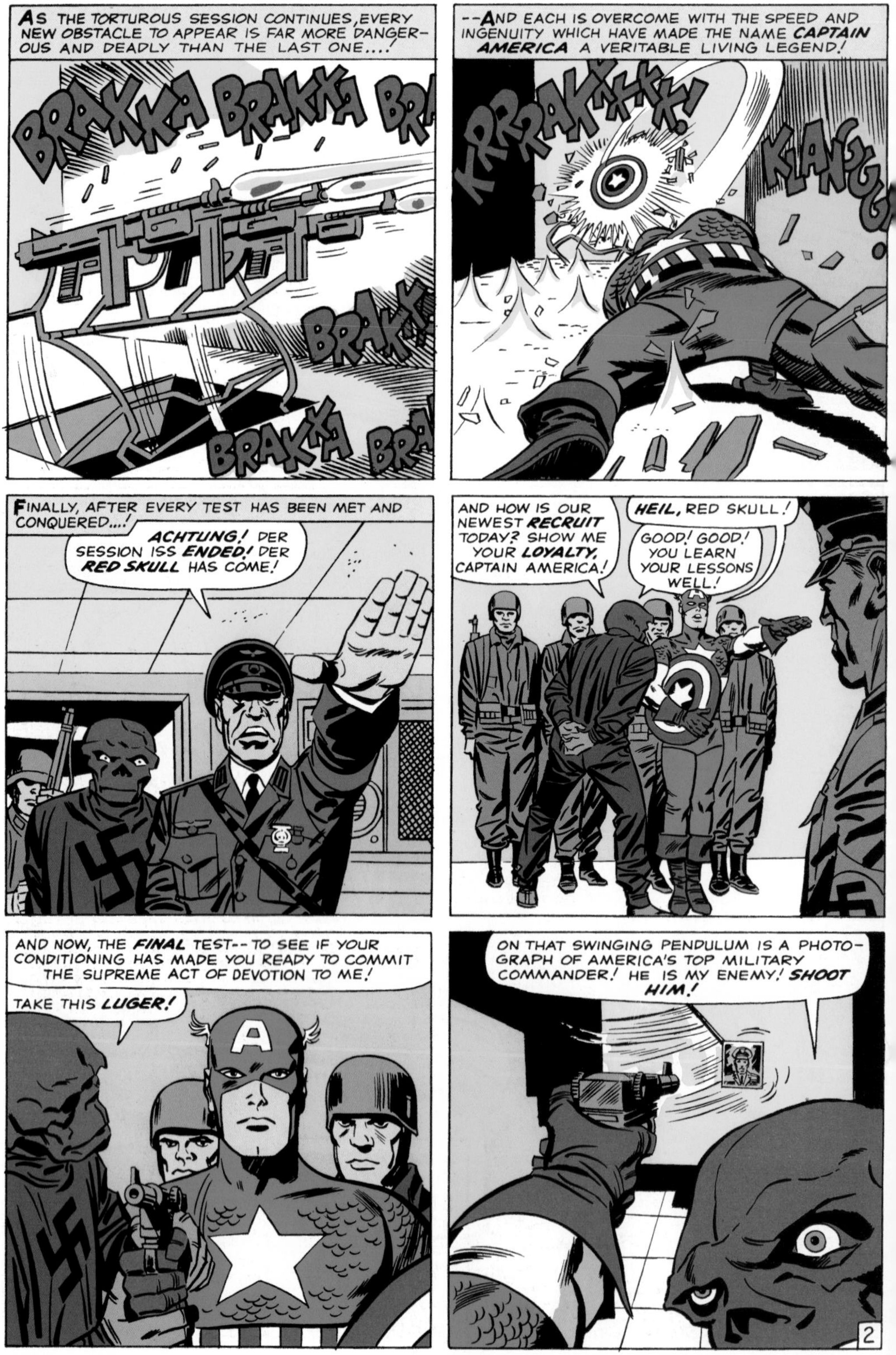
AS THE TORTUROUS SESSION CONTINUES, EVERY NEW OBSTACLE TO APPEAR IS FAR MORE DANGEROUS AND DEADLY THAN THE LAST ONE....!
BRAKKA BRAKKA BRA
BRAKK
BRAKKA BRA
--AND EACH IS OVERCOME WITH THE SPEED AND INGENUITY WHICH HAVE MADE THE NAME CAPTAIN AMERICA A VERITABLE LIVING LEGEND!
KRRRAKKKKK!
KLANGGG!
FINALLY, AFTER EVERY TEST HAS BEEN MET AND CONQUERED...!
ACHTUNG! DER SESSION ISS ENDED! DER RED SKULL HAS COME!
AND HOW IS OUR NEWEST RECRUIT TODAY? SHOW ME YOUR LOYALTY, CAPTAIN AMERICA!
HEIL, RED SKULL!
GOOD! GOOD! YOU LEARN YOUR LESSONS WELL!
AND NOW, THE FINAL TEST-- TO SEE IF YOUR CONDITIONING HAS MADE YOU READY TO COMMIT THE SUPREME ACT OF DEVOTION TO ME!
TAKE THIS LUGER!
ON THAT SWINGING PENDULUM IS A PHOTOGRAPH OF AMERICA'S TOP MILITARY COMMANDER! HE IS MY ENEMY! SHOOT HIM!
2

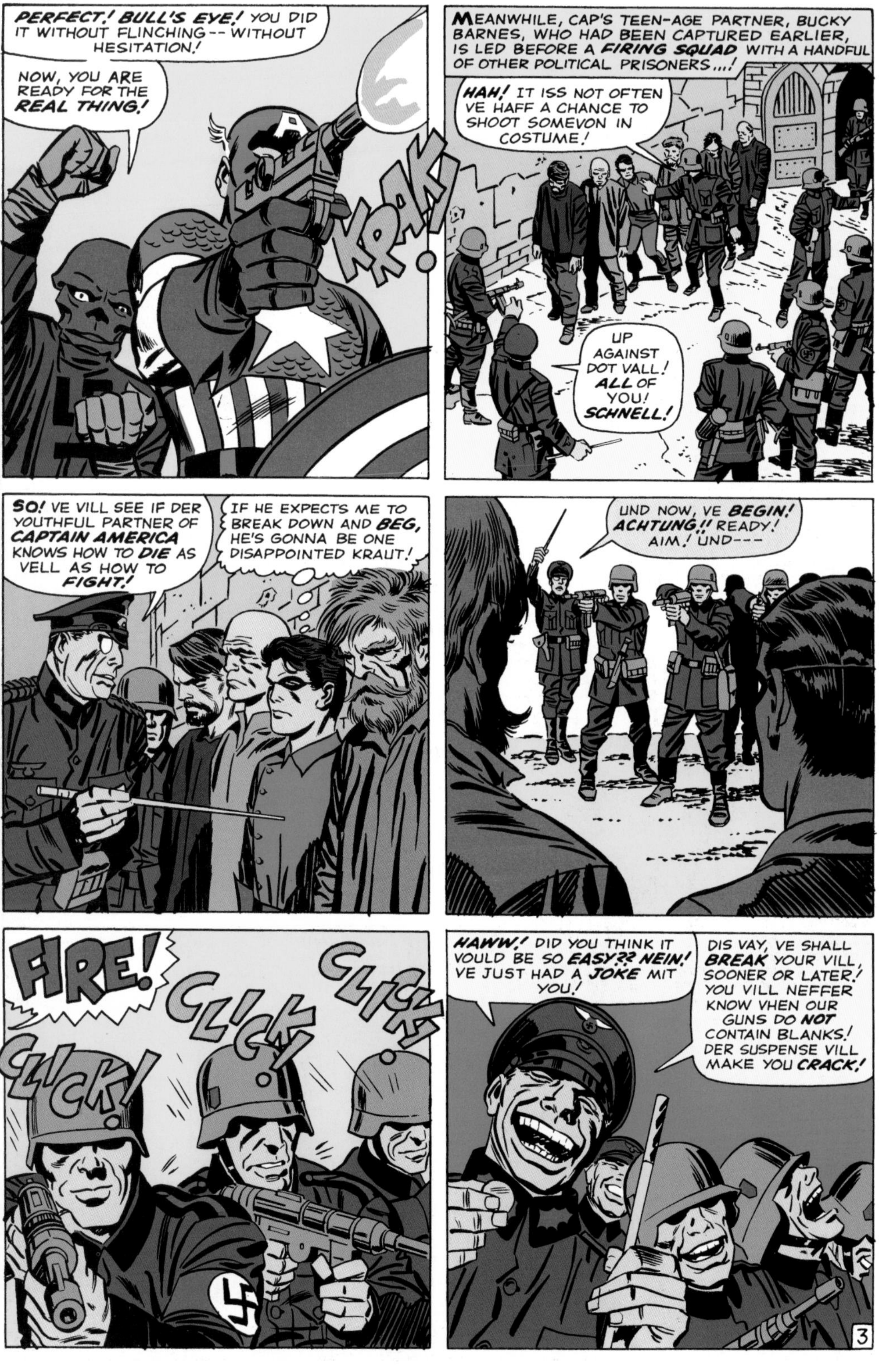
PERFECT! BULL'S EYE! YOU DID IT WITHOUT FLINCHING -- WITHOUT HESITATION!
NOW, YOU ARE READY FOR THE REAL THING!
KRAK!
MEANWHILE, CAP'S TEEN-AGE PARTNER, BUCKY BARNES, WHO HAD BEEN CAPTURED EARLIER, IS LED BEFORE A FIRING SQUAD WITH A HANDFUL OF OTHER POLITICAL PRISONERS...!
HAH! IT ISS NOT OFTEN VE HAFF A CHANCE TO SHOOT SOMEVON IN COSTUME!
UP AGAINST DOT VALL! ALL OF YOU! SCHNELL!
SO! VE VILL SEE IF DER YOUTHFUL PARTNER OF CAPTAIN AMERICA KNOWS HOW TO DIE AS VELL AS HOW TO FIGHT!
IF HE EXPECTS ME TO BREAK DOWN AND BEG, HE'S GONNA BE ONE DISAPPOINTED KRAUT!
UND NOW, VE BEGIN! ACHTUNG!! READY! AIM! UND---
FIRE!
CLICK!
CLICK!
CLICK!
HAWW! DID YOU THINK IT VOULD BE SO EASY?? NEIN! VE JUST HAD A JOKE MIT YOU!
DIS VAY, VE SHALL BREAK YOUR VILL, SOONER OR LATER! YOU VILL NEFFER KNOW VHEN OUR GUNS DO NOT CONTAIN BLANKS! DER SUSPENSE VILL MAKE YOU CRACK!
3

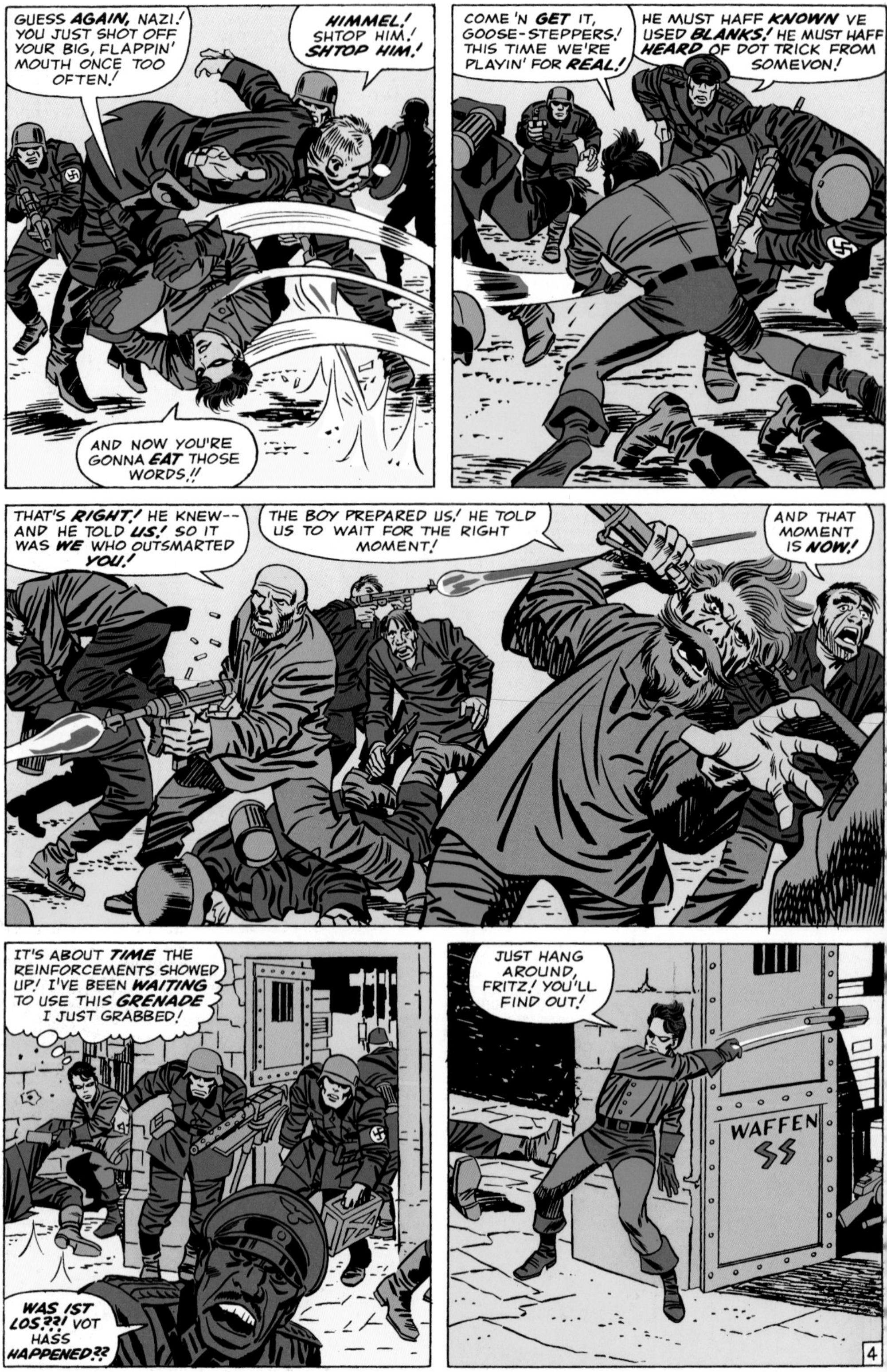
GUESS AGAIN, NAZI! YOU JUST SHOT OFF YOUR BIG, FLAPPIN' MOUTH ONCE TOO OFTEN!
HIMMEL! SHTOP HIM! SHTOP HIM!
AND NOW YOU'RE GONNA EAT THOSE WORDS!!
COME 'N GET IT, GOOSE-STEPPERS! THIS TIME WE'RE PLAYIN' FOR REAL!
HE MUST HAFF KNOWN VE USED BLANKS! HE MUST HAFF HEARD OF DOT TRICK FROM SOMEVON!
THAT'S RIGHT! HE KNEW-- AND HE TOLD US! SO IT WAS WE WHO OUTSMARTED YOU!
THE BOY PREPARED US! HE TOLD US TO WAIT FOR THE RIGHT MOMENT!
AND THAT MOMENT IS NOW!
IT'S ABOUT TIME THE REINFORCEMENTS SHOWED UP! I'VE BEEN WAITING TO USE THIS GRENADE I JUST GRABBED!
WAS IST LOS??! VOT HASS HAPPENED??
JUST HANG AROUND, FRITZ! YOU'LL FIND OUT!
WAFFEN SS
4

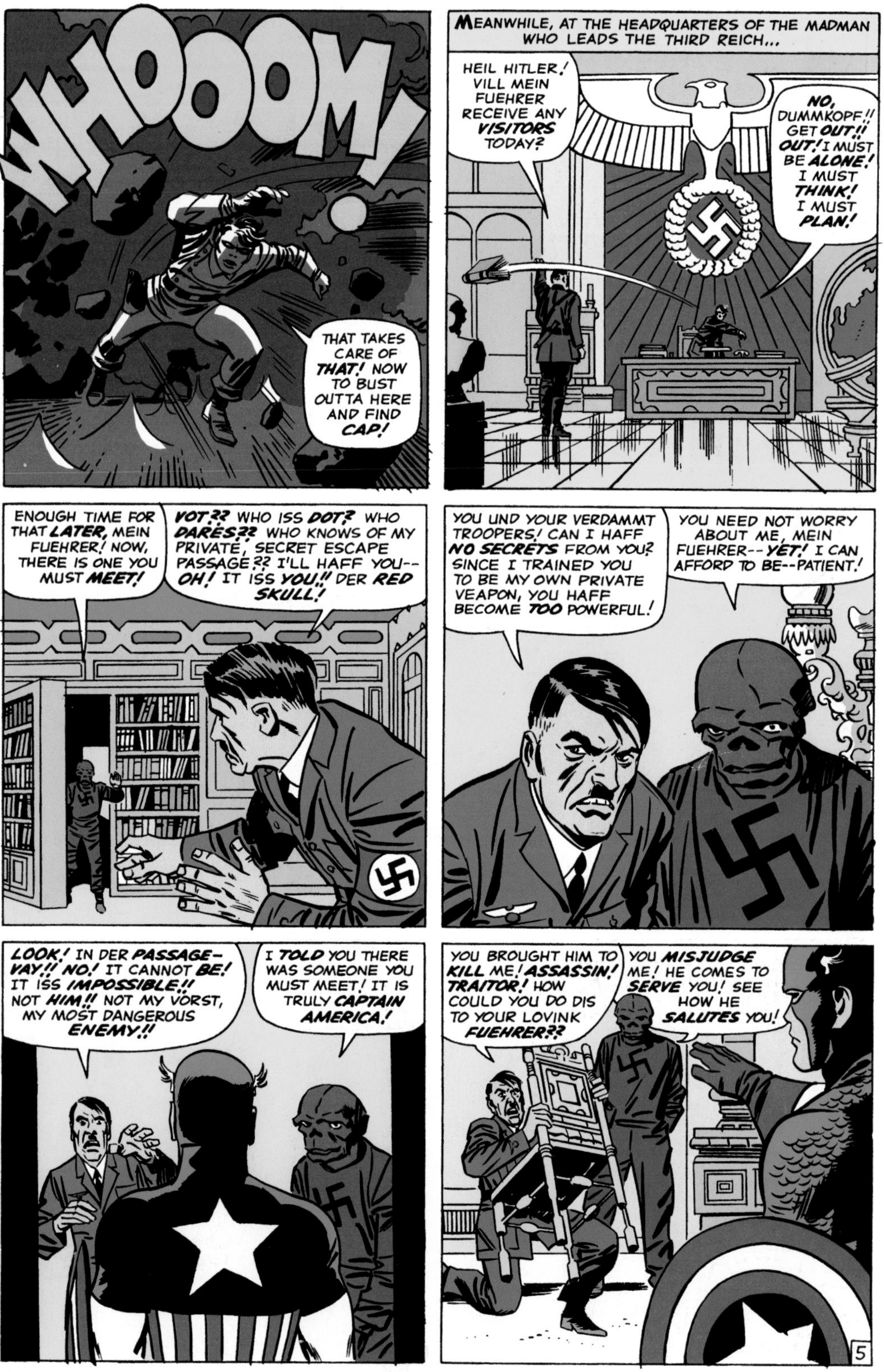
WHOOOM!
THAT TAKES CARE OF THAT! NOW TO BUST OUTTA HERE AND FIND CAP!
MEANWHILE, AT THE HEADQUARTERS OF THE MADMAN WHO LEADS THE THIRD REICH...
HEIL HITLER! VILL MEIN FUEHRER RECEIVE ANY VISITORS TODAY?
NO, DUMMKOPF!! GET OUT!! OUT! I MUST BE ALONE! I MUST THINK! I MUST PLAN!
ENOUGH TIME FOR THAT LATER, MEIN FUEHRER! NOW, THERE IS ONE YOU MUST MEET!
VOT?? WHO ISS DOT? WHO DARES?? WHO KNOWS OF MY PRIVATE, SECRET ESCAPE PASSAGE?? I'LL HAFF YOU-- OH! IT ISS YOU!! DER RED SKULL!
YOU UND YOUR VERDAMMT TROOPERS! CAN I HAFF NO SECRETS FROM YOU? SINCE I TRAINED YOU TO BE MY OWN PRIVATE VEAPON, YOU HAFF BECOME TOO POWERFUL!
YOU NEED NOT WORRY ABOUT ME, MEIN FUEHRER-- YET! I CAN AFFORD TO BE--PATIENT!
LOOK! IN DER PASSAGE-VAY!! NO! IT CANNOT BE! IT ISS IMPOSSIBLE!! NOT HIM!! NOT MY VORST, MY MOST DANGEROUS ENEMY!!
I TOLD YOU THERE WAS SOMEONE YOU MUST MEET! IT IS TRULY CAPTAIN AMERICA!
YOU BROUGHT HIM TO KILL ME! ASSASSIN! TRAITOR! HOW COULD YOU DO DIS TO YOUR LOVINK FUEHRER??
YOU MISJUDGE ME! HE COMES TO SERVE YOU! SEE HOW HE SALUTES YOU!
5

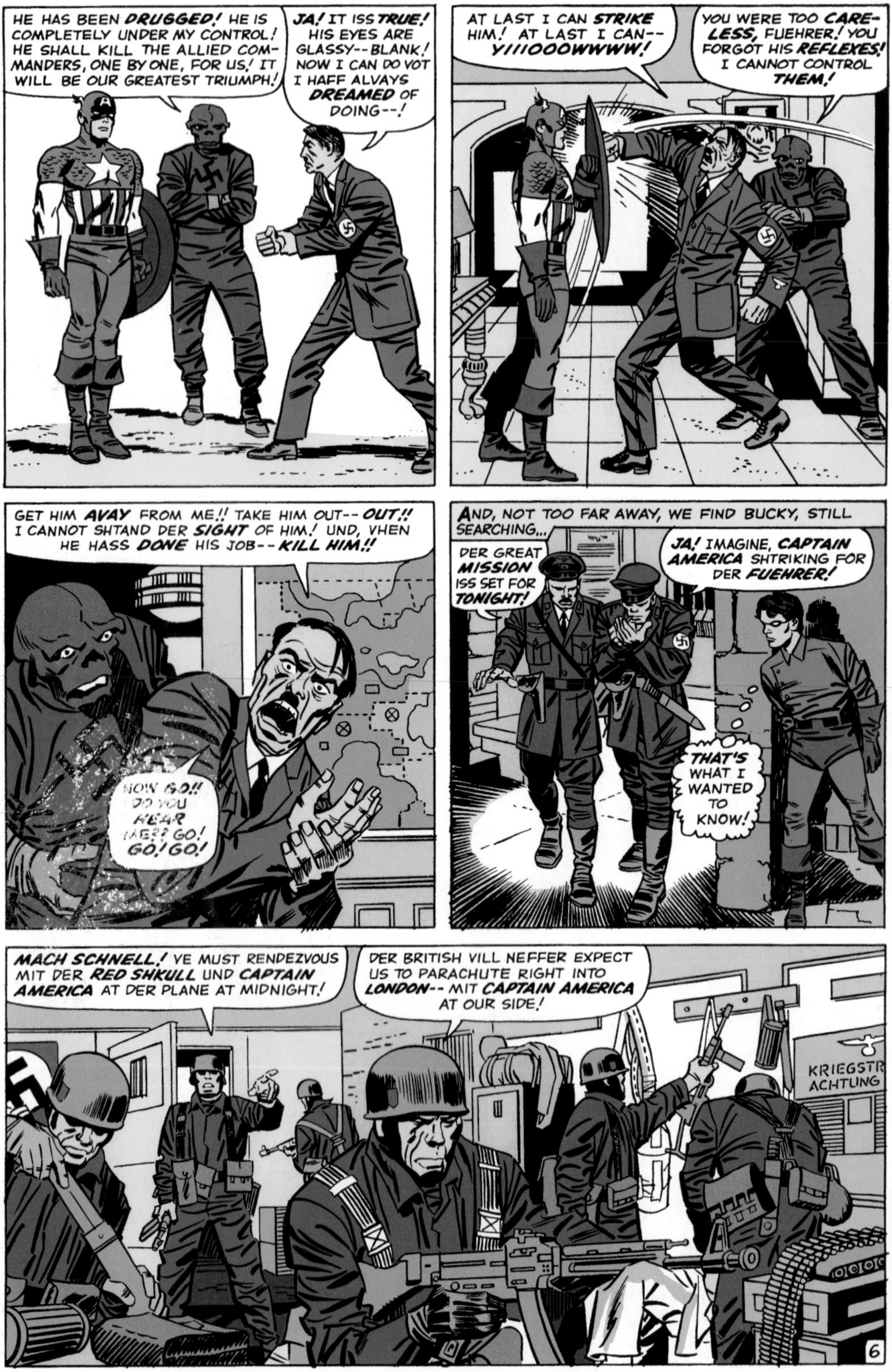
HE HAS BEEN DRUGGED! HE IS COMPLETELY UNDER MY CONTROL! HE SHALL KILL THE ALLIED COMMANDERS, ONE BY ONE, FOR US! IT WILL BE OUR GREATEST TRIUMPH!
JA! IT ISS TRUE! HIS EYES ARE GLASSY--BLANK! NOW I CAN DO VOT I HAFF ALVAYS DREAMED OF DOING--!
AT LAST I CAN STRIKE HIM! AT LAST I CAN-- YIIIOOOWWWW!
YOU WERE TOO CARELESS, FUEHRER! YOU FORGOT HIS REFLEXES! I CANNOT CONTROL THEM!
GET HIM AVAY FROM ME!! TAKE HIM OUT-- OUT!! I CANNOT SHTAND DER SIGHT OF HIM! UND, VHEN HE HASS DONE HIS JOB-- KILL HIM!!
NOW GO!! DO YOU HEAR ME?? GO! GO! GO!
AND, NOT TOO FAR AWAY, WE FIND BUCKY, STILL SEARCHING...
DER GREAT MISSION ISS SET FOR TONIGHT!
JA! IMAGINE, CAPTAIN AMERICA SHTRIKING FOR DER FUEHRER!
THAT'S WHAT I WANTED TO KNOW!
MACH SCHNELL! VE MUST RENDEZVOUS MIT DER RED SHKULL UND CAPTAIN AMERICA AT DER PLANE AT MIDNIGHT!
DER BRITISH VILL NEFFER EXPECT US TO PARACHUTE RIGHT INTO LONDON-- MIT CAPTAIN AMERICA AT OUR SIDE!
KRIEGSTR
ACHTUNG
6

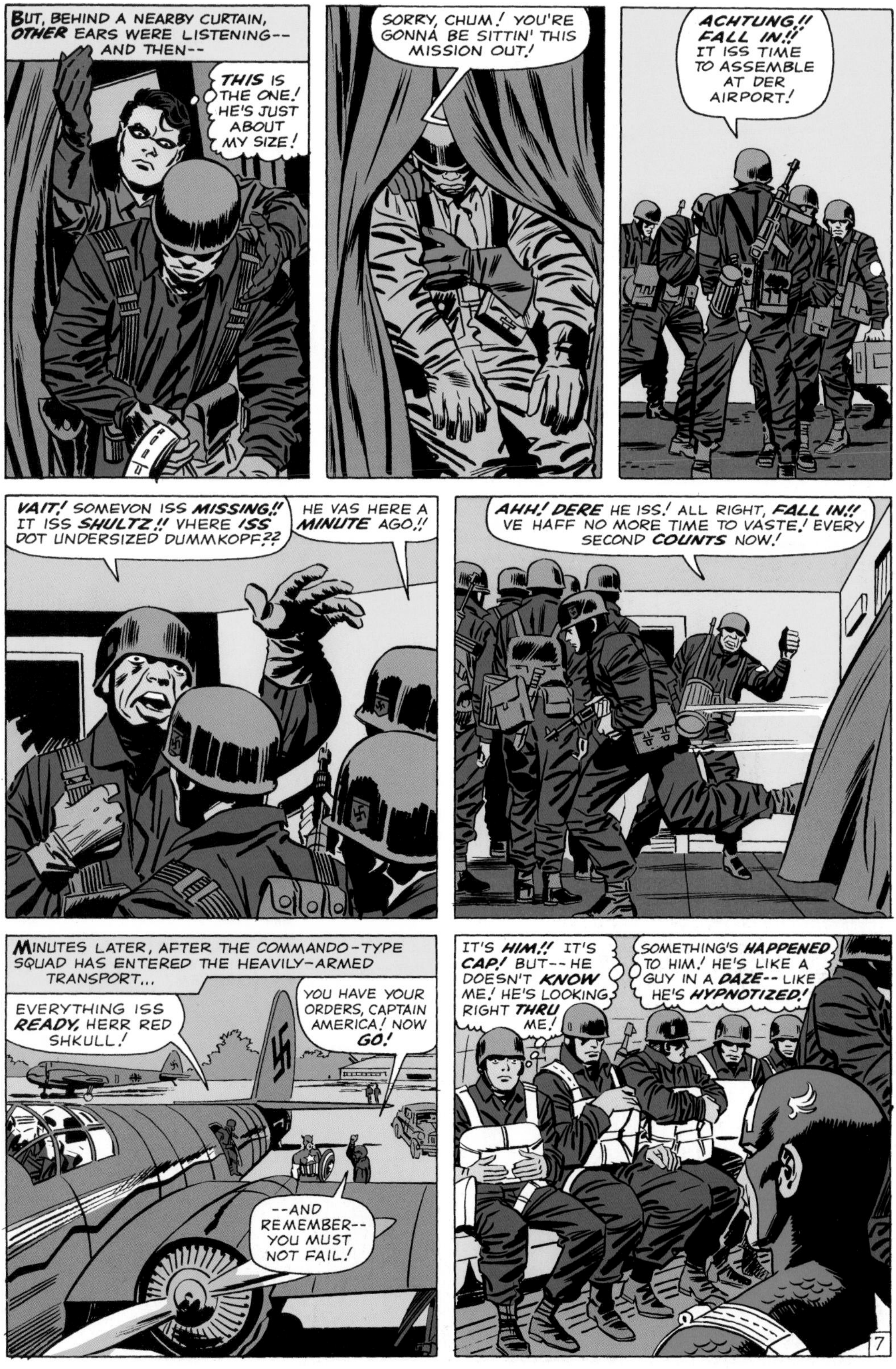

BUT, BEHIND A NEARBY CURTAIN, OTHER EARS WERE LISTENING-- AND THEN--
THIS IS THE ONE! HE'S JUST ABOUT MY SIZE!
SORRY, CHUM! YOU'RE GONNA BE SITTIN' THIS MISSION OUT!
ACHTUNG!! FALL IN!! IT ISS TIME TO ASSEMBLE AT DER AIRPORT!
VAIT! SOMEVON ISS MISSING!! IT ISS SHULTZ!! VHERE ISS DOT UNDERSIZED DUMMKOPF??
HE VAS HERE A MINUTE AGO!!
AHH! DERE HE ISS! ALL RIGHT, FALL IN!! VE HAFF NO MORE TIME TO VASTE! EVERY SECOND COUNTS NOW!
MINUTES LATER, AFTER THE COMMANDO-TYPE SQUAD HAS ENTERED THE HEAVILY-ARMED TRANSPORT...
EVERYTHING ISS READY, HERR RED SHKULL!
YOU HAVE YOUR ORDERS, CAPTAIN AMERICA! NOW GO!
--AND REMEMBER-- YOU MUST NOT FAIL!
IT'S HIM!! IT'S CAP! BUT--HE DOESN'T KNOW ME! HE'S LOOKING RIGHT THRU ME!
SOMETHING'S HAPPENED TO HIM! HE'S LIKE A GUY IN A DAZE-- LIKE HE'S HYPNOTIZED!
7

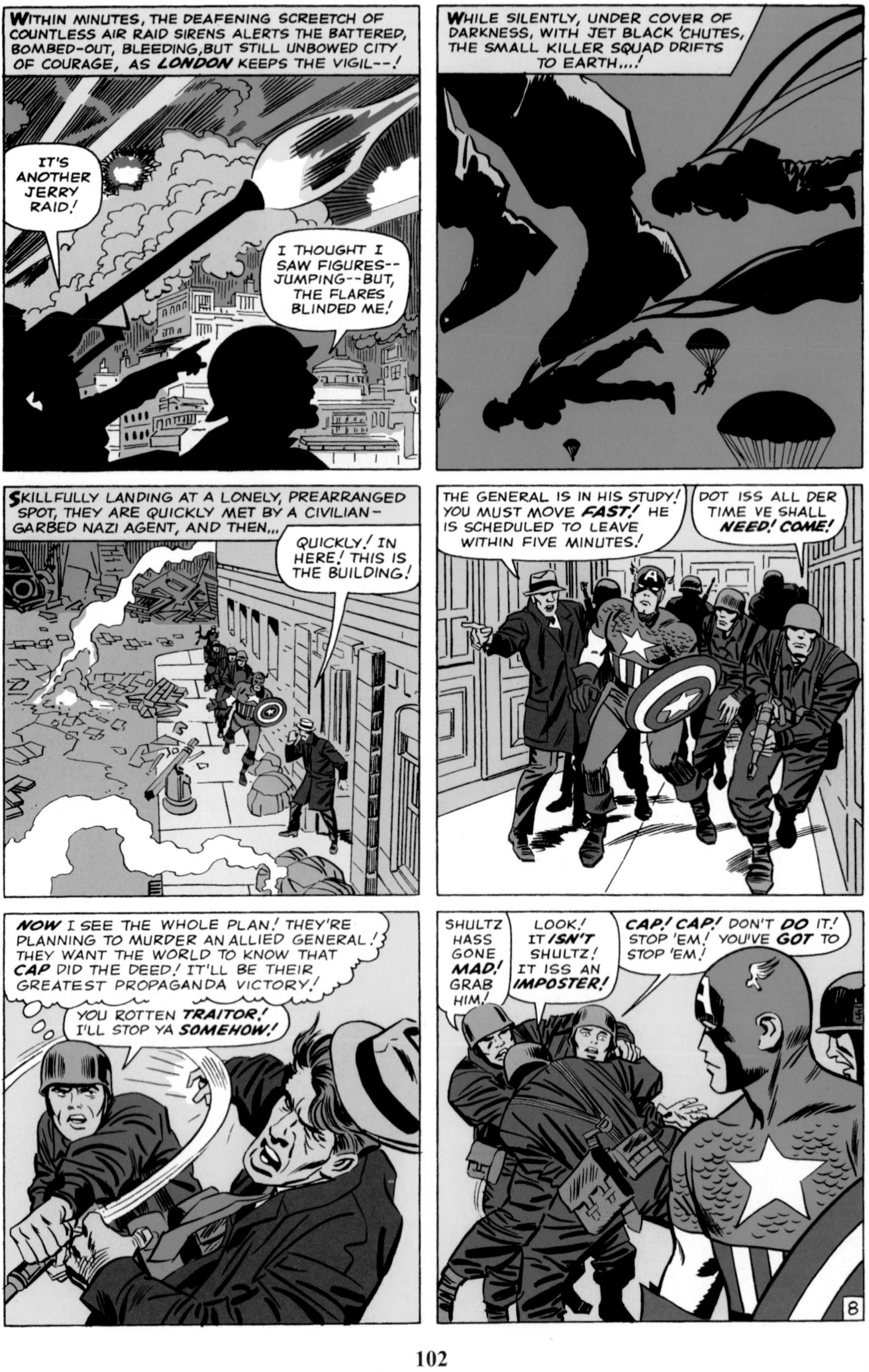
WITHIN MINUTES, THE DEAFENING SCREETCH OF COUNTLESS AIR RAID SIRENS ALERTS THE BATTERED, BOMBED-OUT, BLEEDING, BUT STILL UNBOWED CITY OF COURAGE, AS LONDON KEEPS THE VIGIL--!
IT'S ANOTHER JERRY RAID!
I THOUGHT I SAW FIGURES--JUMPING--BUT, THE FLARES BLINDED ME!
WHILE SILENTLY, UNDER COVER OF DARKNESS, WITH JET BLACK 'CHUTES, THE SMALL KILLER SQUAD DRIFTS TO EARTH...!
SKILLFULLY LANDING AT A LONELY, PREARRANGED SPOT, THEY ARE QUICKLY MET BY A CIVILIAN-GARBED NAZI AGENT, AND THEN...
QUICKLY! IN HERE! THIS IS THE BUILDING!
THE GENERAL IS IN HIS STUDY! YOU MUST MOVE FAST! HE IS SCHEDULED TO LEAVE WITHIN FIVE MINUTES!
DOT ISS ALL DER TIME VE SHALL NEED! COME!
NOW I SEE THE WHOLE PLAN! THEY'RE PLANNING TO MURDER AN ALLIED GENERAL! THEY WANT THE WORLD TO KNOW THAT CAP DID THE DEED! IT'LL BE THEIR GREATEST PROPAGANDA VICTORY!
YOU ROTTEN TRAITOR! I'LL STOP YA SOMEHOW!
SHULTZ HASS GONE MAD! GRAB HIM!
LOOK! IT ISN'T SHULTZ! IT ISS AN IMPOSTER!
CAP! CAP! DON'T DO IT! STOP 'EM! YOU'VE GOT TO STOP 'EM!
8

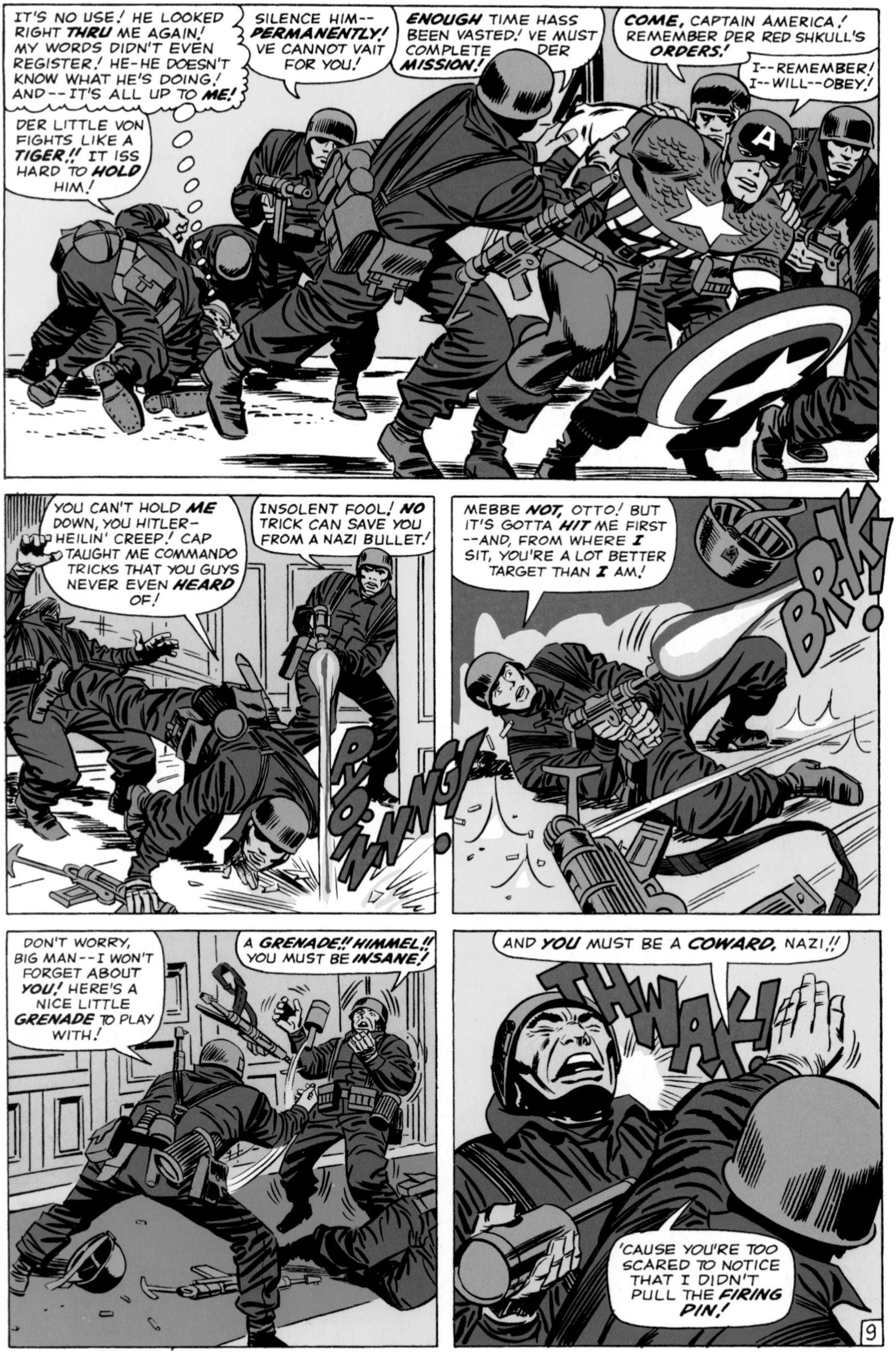

IT'S NO USE! HE LOOKED RIGHT THRU ME AGAIN! MY WORDS DIDN'T EVEN REGISTER! HE-HE DOESN'T KNOW WHAT HE'S DOING! AND--IT'S ALL UP TO ME!
DER LITTLE VON FIGHTS LIKE A TIGER!! IT ISS HARD TO HOLD HIM!
SILENCE HIM--PERMANENTLY! VE CANNOT VAIT FOR YOU!
ENOUGH TIME HASS BEEN VASTED! VE MUST COMPLETE DER MISSION!
COME, CAPTAIN AMERICA! REMEMBER DER RED SHKULL'S ORDERS!
I--REMEMBER! I--WILL--OBEY!
YOU CAN'T HOLD ME DOWN, YOU HITLER-HEILIN' CREEP! CAP TAUGHT ME COMMANDO TRICKS THAT YOU GUYS NEVER EVEN HEARD OF!
INSOLENT FOOL! NO TRICK CAN SAVE YOU FROM A NAZI BULLET!
RYOINNNG!
MEBBE NOT, OTTO! BUT IT'S GOTTA HIT ME FIRST --AND, FROM WHERE I SIT, YOU'RE A LOT BETTER TARGET THAN I AM!
BRAK!
DON'T WORRY, BIG MAN--I WON'T FORGET ABOUT YOU! HERE'S A NICE LITTLE GRENADE TO PLAY WITH!
A GRENADE!! HIMMEL!! YOU MUST BE INSANE!
AND YOU MUST BE A COWARD, NAZI!!
THWAK!
'CAUSE YOU'RE TOO SCARED TO NOTICE THAT I DIDN'T PULL THE FIRING PIN!
9

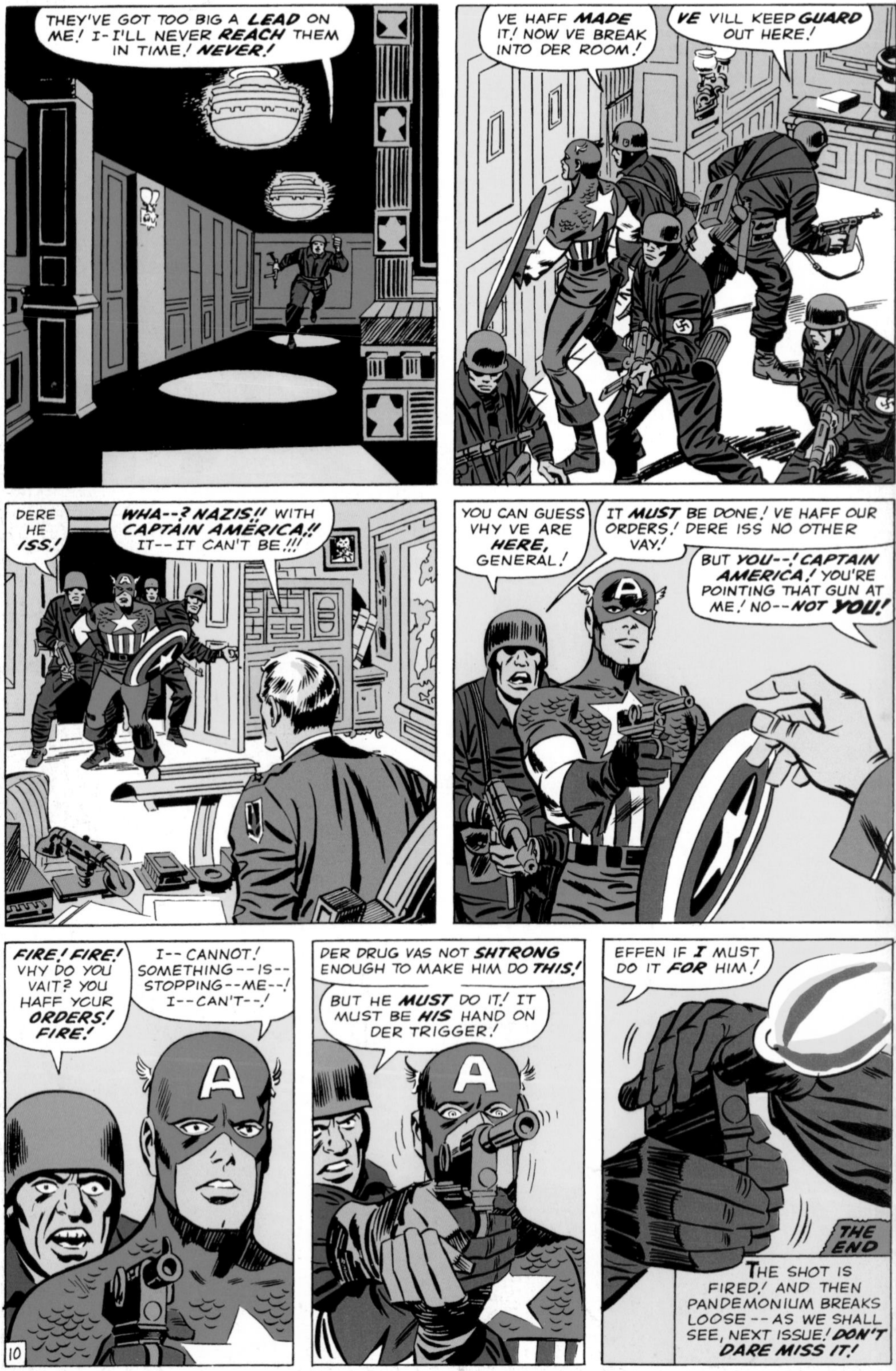

THEY'VE GOT TOO BIG A LEAD ON ME! I-I'LL NEVER REACH THEM IN TIME! NEVER!
VE HAFF MADE IT! NOW VE BREAK INTO DER ROOM!
VE VILL KEEP GUARD OUT HERE!
DERE HE ISS!
WHA--? NAZIS!! WITH CAPTAIN AMERICA!! IT-- IT CAN'T BE!!!
YOU CAN GUESS VHY VE ARE HERE, GENERAL!
IT MUST BE DONE! VE HAFF OUR ORDERS! DERE ISS NO OTHER VAY!
BUT YOU--! CAPTAIN AMERICA! YOU'RE POINTING THAT GUN AT ME! NO--NOT YOU!
FIRE! FIRE! VHY DO YOU VAIT? YOU HAFF YOUR ORDERS! FIRE!
I-- CANNOT! SOMETHING--IS--STOPPING--ME--! I--CAN'T--!
10
DER DRUG VAS NOT SHTRONG ENOUGH TO MAKE HIM DO THIS!
BUT HE MUST DO IT! IT MUST BE HIS HAND ON DER TRIGGER!
EFFEN IF I MUST DO IT FOR HIM!
THE END
THE SHOT IS FIRED! AND THEN PANDEMONIUM BREAKS LOOSE -- AS WE SHALL SEE, NEXT ISSUE! DON'T DARE MISS IT!

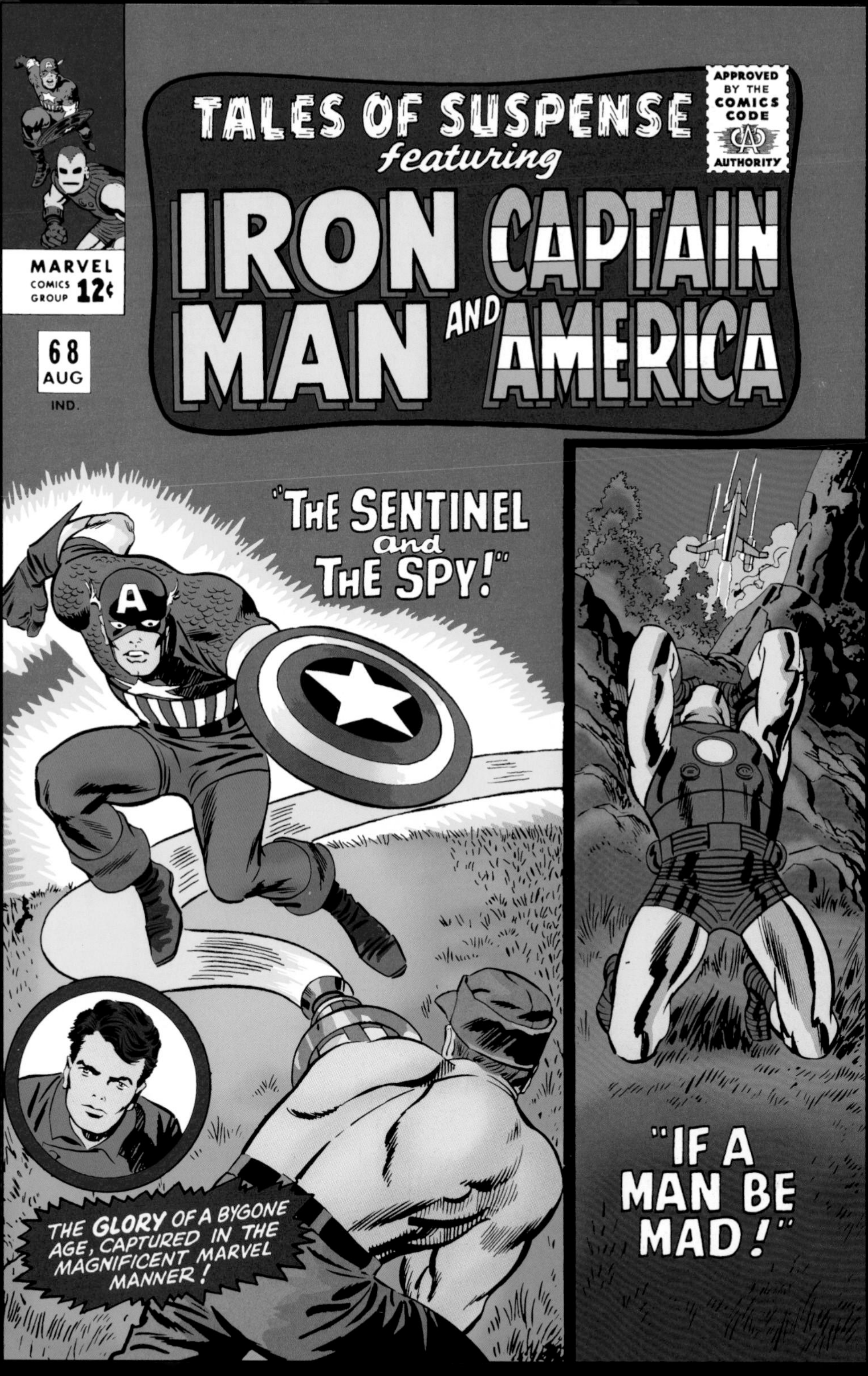

TALES OF SUSPENSE
featuring
IRON MAN AND CAPTAIN AMERICA
APPROVED BY THE COMICS CODE AUTHORITY
MARVEL COMICS GROUP 12¢
68 AUG
IND.
"THE SENTINEL and THE SPY!"
THE GLORY OF A BYGONE AGE, CAPTURED IN THE MAGNIFICENT MARVEL MANNER!
"IF A MAN BE MAD!"

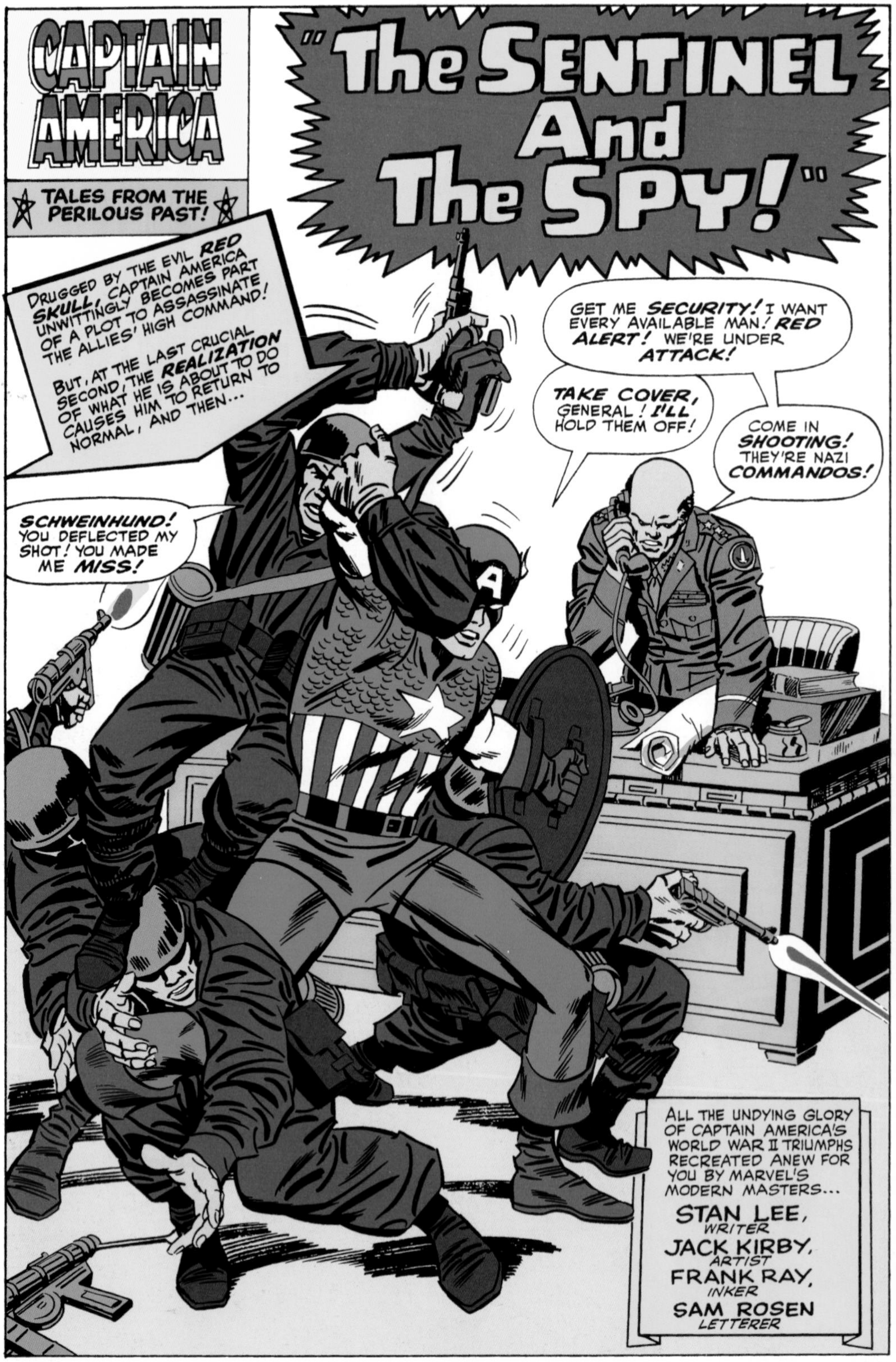
CAPTAIN AMERICA
TALES FROM THE PERILOUS PAST!
"The SENTINEL And The SPY!"
DRUGGED BY THE EVIL RED SKULL, CAPTAIN AMERICA UNWITTINGLY BECOMES PART OF A PLOT TO ASSASSINATE THE ALLIES' HIGH COMMAND!
BUT, AT THE LAST CRUCIAL SECOND, THE REALIZATION OF WHAT HE IS ABOUT TO DO CAUSES HIM TO RETURN TO NORMAL, AND THEN...
GET ME SECURITY! I WANT EVERY AVAILABLE MAN! RED ALERT! WE'RE UNDER ATTACK!
TAKE COVER, GENERAL! I'LL HOLD THEM OFF!
COME IN SHOOTING! THEY'RE NAZI COMMANDOS!
SCHWEINHUND! YOU DEFLECTED MY SHOT! YOU MADE ME MISS!
ALL THE UNDYING GLORY OF CAPTAIN AMERICA'S WORLD WAR II TRIUMPHS RECREATED ANEW FOR YOU BY MARVEL'S MODERN MASTERS...
STAN LEE, WRITER
JACK KIRBY, ARTIST
FRANK RAY, INKER
SAM ROSEN LETTERER

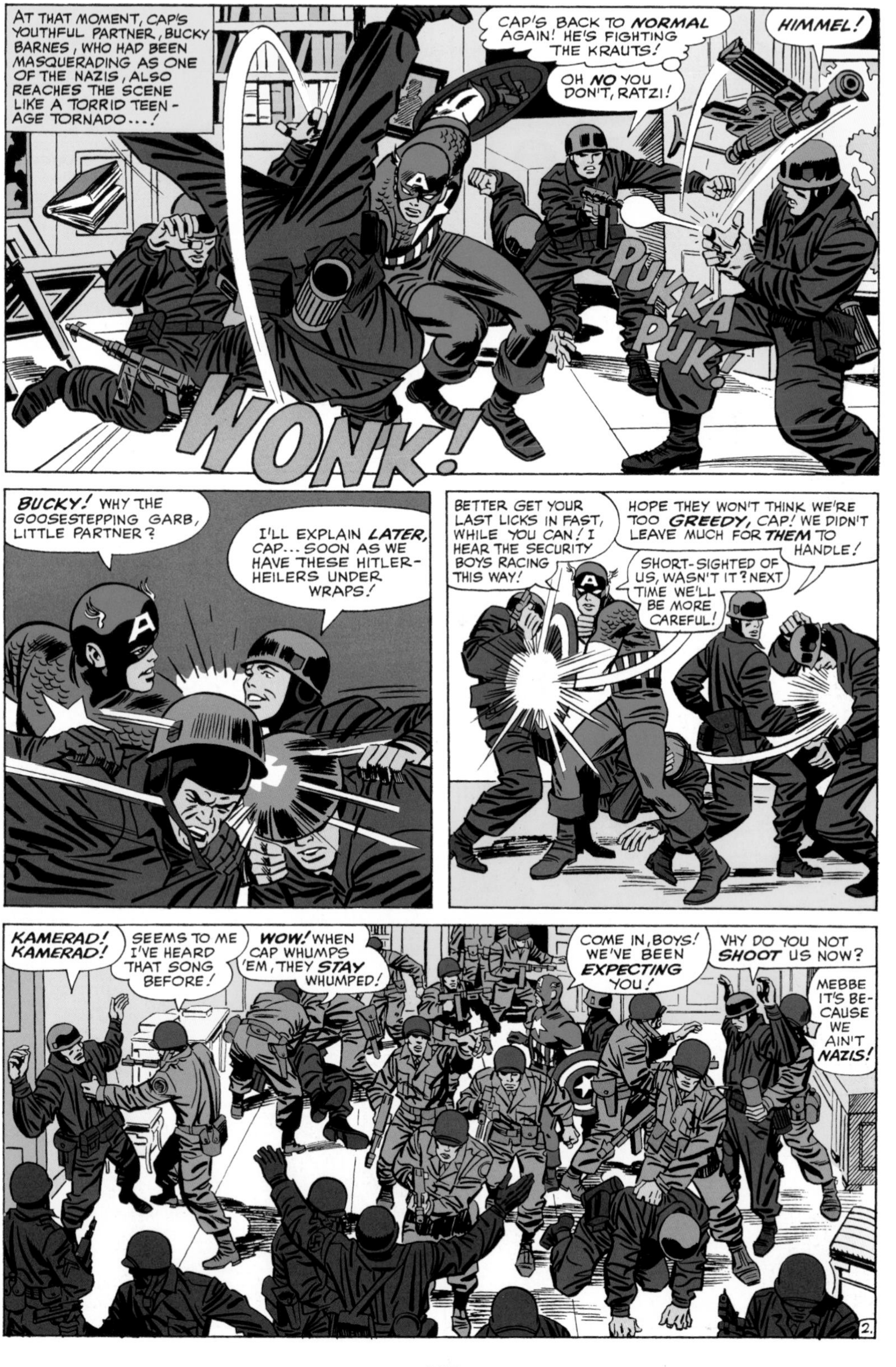

AT THAT MOMENT, CAP'S YOUTHFUL PARTNER, BUCKY BARNES, WHO HAD BEEN MASQUERADING AS ONE OF THE NAZIS, ALSO REACHES THE SCENE LIKE A TORRID TEEN-AGE TORNADO...!
CAP'S BACK TO NORMAL AGAIN! HE'S FIGHTING THE KRAUTS!
OH NO YOU DON'T, RATZI!
HIMMEL!
PUKKA PUKKA PUK!
WONK!
BUCKY! WHY THE GOOSESTEPPING GARB, LITTLE PARTNER?
I'LL EXPLAIN LATER, CAP... SOON AS WE HAVE THESE HITLER-HEILERS UNDER WRAPS!
BETTER GET YOUR LAST LICKS IN FAST, WHILE YOU CAN! I HEAR THE SECURITY BOYS RACING THIS WAY!
HOPE THEY WON'T THINK WE'RE TOO GREEDY, CAP! WE DIDN'T LEAVE MUCH FOR THEM TO HANDLE!
SHORT-SIGHTED OF US, WASN'T IT? NEXT TIME WE'LL BE MORE CAREFUL!
KAMERAD! KAMERAD!
SEEMS TO ME I'VE HEARD THAT SONG BEFORE!
WOW! WHEN CAP WHUMPS 'EM, THEY STAY WHUMPED!
COME IN, BOYS! WE'VE BEEN EXPECTING YOU!
VHY DO YOU NOT SHOOT US NOW?
MEBBE IT'S BE-CAUSE WE AIN'T NAZIS!
2.

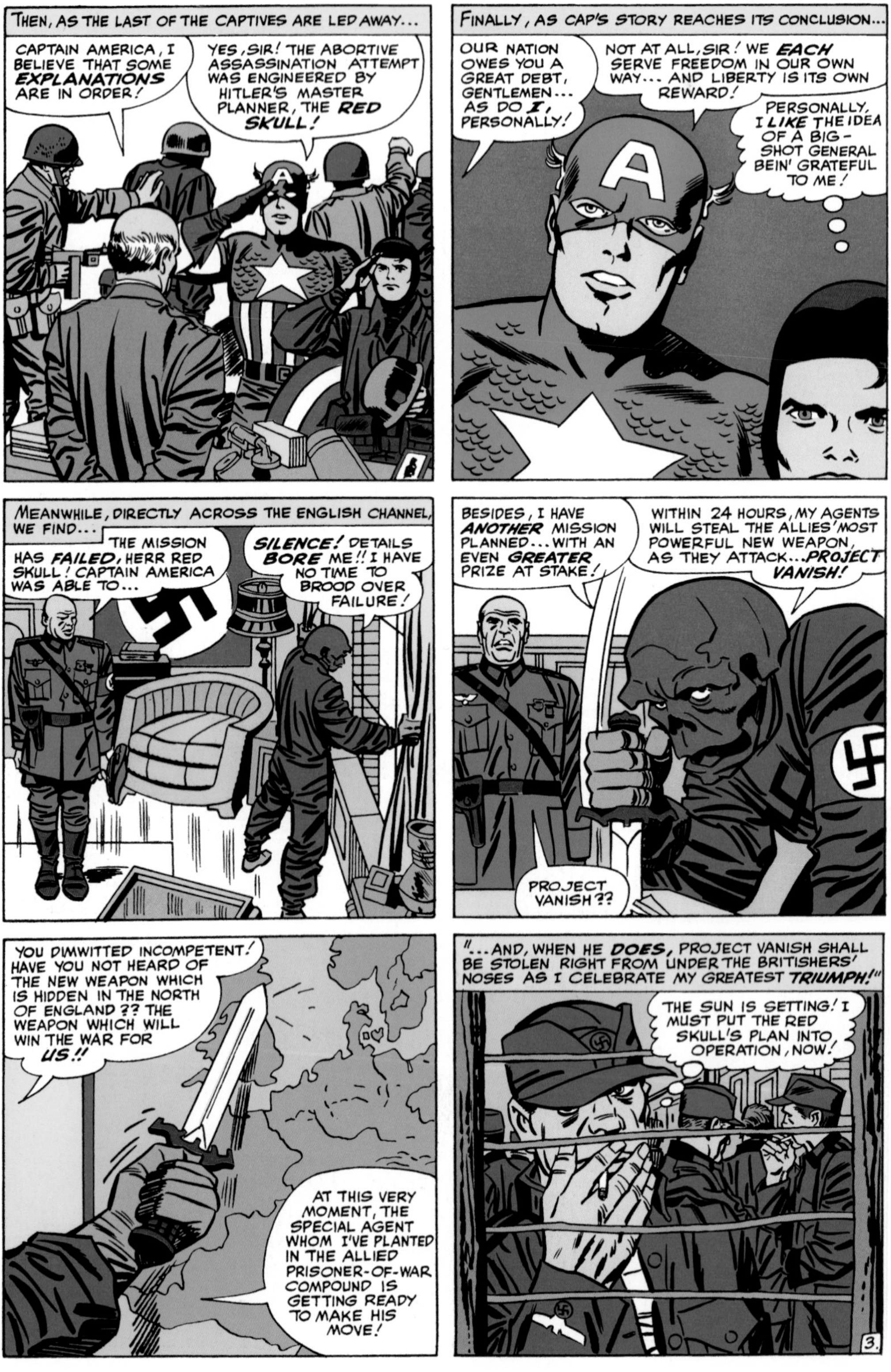
THEN, AS THE LAST OF THE CAPTIVES ARE LED AWAY...
CAPTAIN AMERICA, I BELIEVE THAT SOME EXPLANATIONS ARE IN ORDER!
YES, SIR! THE ABORTIVE ASSASSINATION ATTEMPT WAS ENGINEERED BY HITLER'S MASTER PLANNER, THE RED SKULL!
FINALLY, AS CAP'S STORY REACHES ITS CONCLUSION...
OUR NATION OWES YOU A GREAT DEBT, GENTLEMEN... AS DO I, PERSONALLY!
NOT AT ALL, SIR! WE EACH SERVE FREEDOM IN OUR OWN WAY... AND LIBERTY IS ITS OWN REWARD!
PERSONALLY, I LIKE THE IDEA OF A BIG-SHOT GENERAL BEIN' GRATEFUL TO ME!
MEANWHILE, DIRECTLY ACROSS THE ENGLISH CHANNEL, WE FIND...
THE MISSION HAS FAILED, HERR RED SKULL! CAPTAIN AMERICA WAS ABLE TO...
SILENCE! DETAILS BORE ME!! I HAVE NO TIME TO BROOD OVER FAILURE!
BESIDES, I HAVE ANOTHER MISSION PLANNED... WITH AN EVEN GREATER PRIZE AT STAKE!
WITHIN 24 HOURS, MY AGENTS WILL STEAL THE ALLIES' MOST POWERFUL NEW WEAPON, AS THEY ATTACK... PROJECT VANISH!
PROJECT VANISH??
YOU DIMWITTED INCOMPETENT! HAVE YOU NOT HEARD OF THE NEW WEAPON WHICH IS HIDDEN IN THE NORTH OF ENGLAND?? THE WEAPON WHICH WILL WIN THE WAR FOR US!!
AT THIS VERY MOMENT, THE SPECIAL AGENT WHOM I'VE PLANTED IN THE ALLIED PRISONER-OF-WAR COMPOUND IS GETTING READY TO MAKE HIS MOVE!
"...AND, WHEN HE DOES, PROJECT VANISH SHALL BE STOLEN RIGHT FROM UNDER THE BRITISHERS' NOSES AS I CELEBRATE MY GREATEST TRIUMPH!"
THE SUN IS SETTING! I MUST PUT THE RED SKULL'S PLAN INTO OPERATION, NOW!
3.

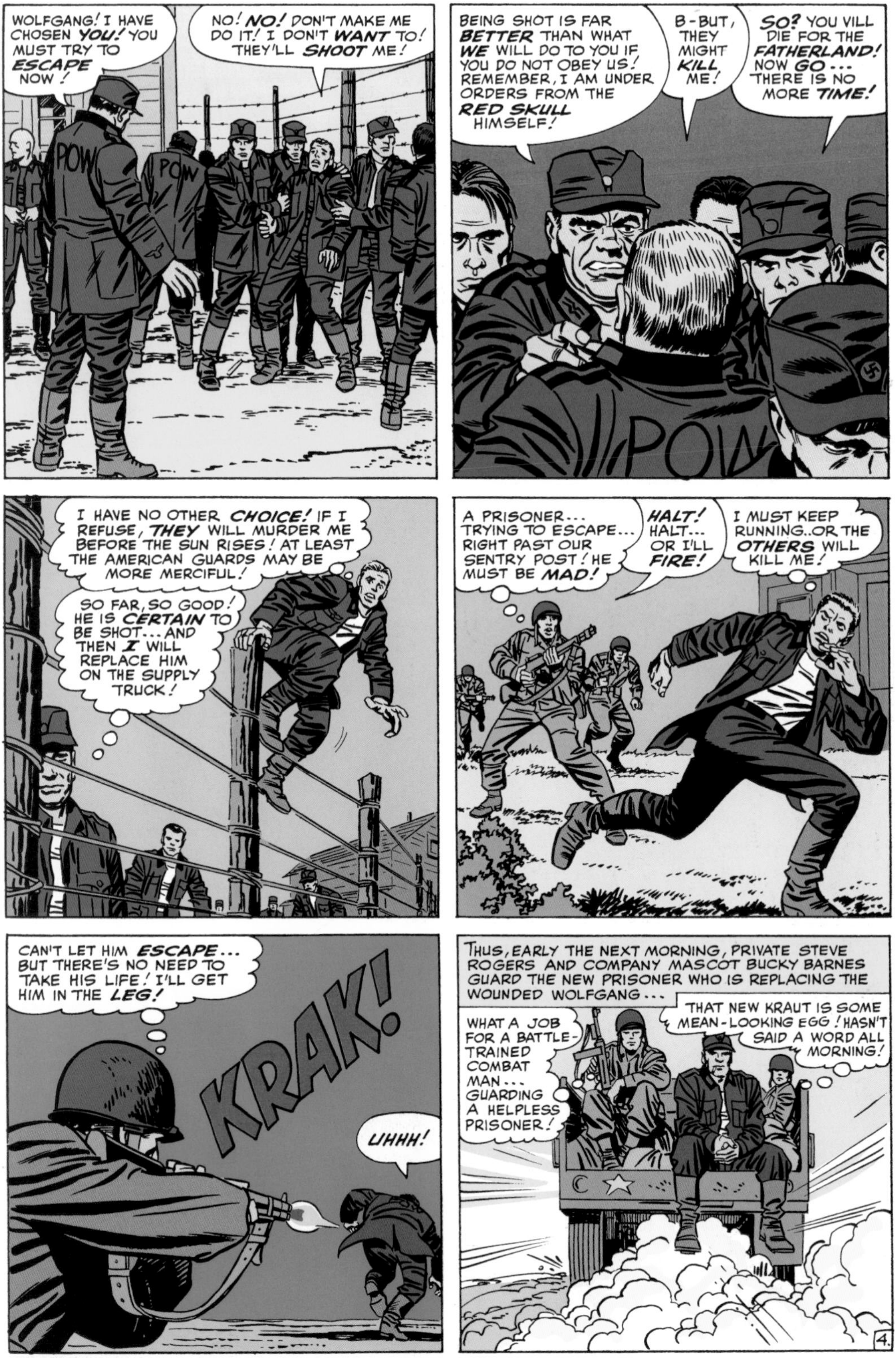
WOLFGANG! I HAVE CHOSEN YOU! YOU MUST TRY TO ESCAPE NOW!
NO! NO! DON'T MAKE ME DO IT! I DON'T WANT TO! THEY'LL SHOOT ME!
BEING SHOT IS FAR BETTER THAN WHAT WE WILL DO TO YOU IF YOU DO NOT OBEY US! REMEMBER, I AM UNDER ORDERS FROM THE RED SKULL HIMSELF!
B-BUT, THEY MIGHT KILL ME!
SO? YOU VILL DIE FOR THE FATHERLAND! NOW GO... THERE IS NO MORE TIME!
I HAVE NO OTHER CHOICE! IF I REFUSE, THEY WILL MURDER ME BEFORE THE SUN RISES! AT LEAST THE AMERICAN GUARDS MAY BE MORE MERCIFUL!
SO FAR, SO GOOD! HE IS CERTAIN TO BE SHOT... AND THEN I WILL REPLACE HIM ON THE SUPPLY TRUCK!
A PRISONER... TRYING TO ESCAPE... RIGHT PAST OUR SENTRY POST! HE MUST BE MAD!
HALT! HALT... OR I'LL FIRE!
I MUST KEEP RUNNING..OR THE OTHERS WILL KILL ME!
CAN'T LET HIM ESCAPE... BUT THERE'S NO NEED TO TAKE HIS LIFE! I'LL GET HIM IN THE LEG!
KRAK!
UHHH!
THUS, EARLY THE NEXT MORNING, PRIVATE STEVE ROGERS AND COMPANY MASCOT BUCKY BARNES GUARD THE NEW PRISONER WHO IS REPLACING THE WOUNDED WOLFGANG...
WHAT A JOB FOR A BATTLE-TRAINED COMBAT MAN... GUARDING A HELPLESS PRISONER!
THAT NEW KRAUT IS SOME MEAN-LOOKING EGG! HASN'T SAID A WORD ALL MORNING!
4.

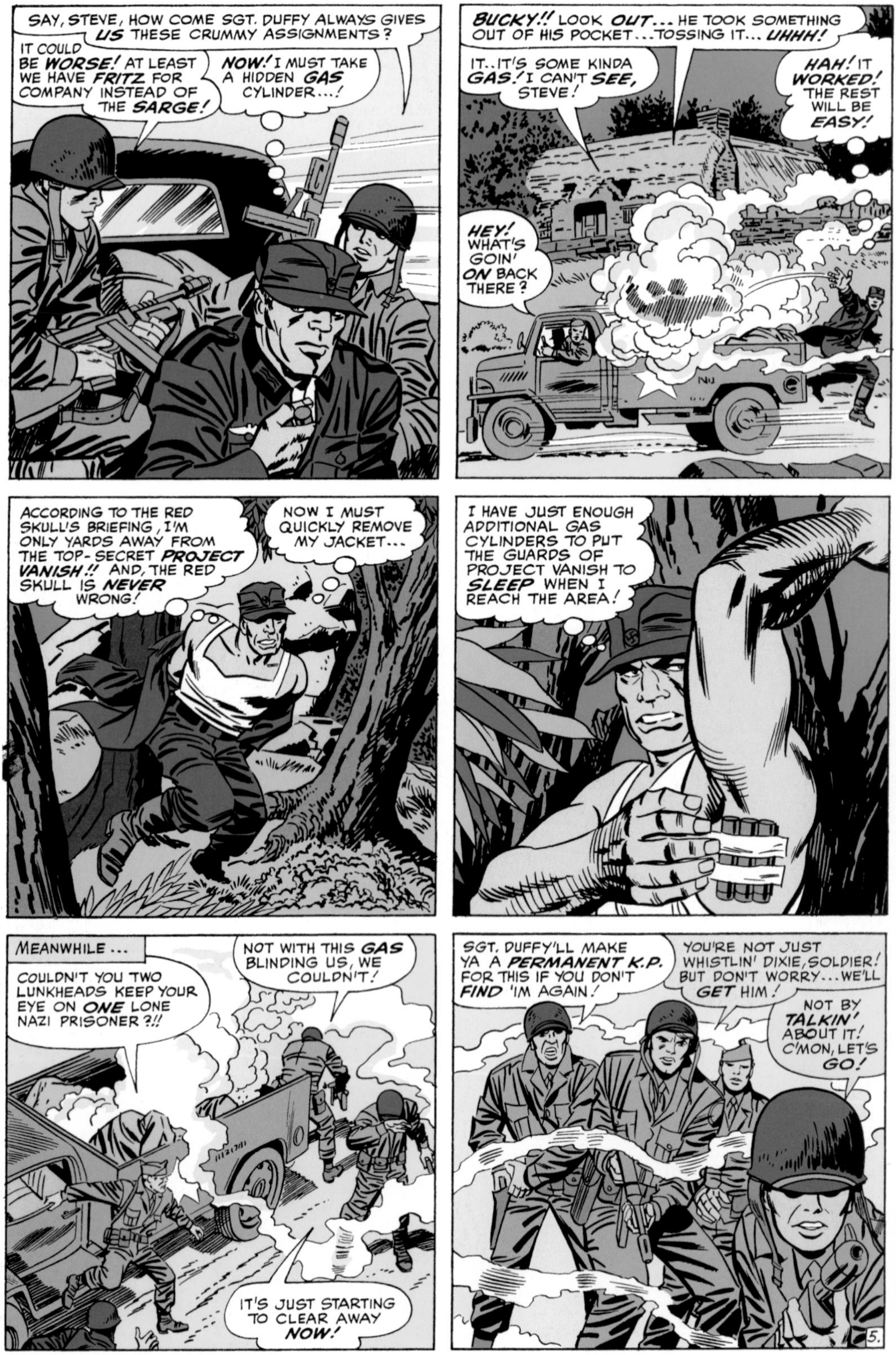
SAY, STEVE, HOW COME SGT. DUFFY ALWAYS GIVES US THESE CRUMMY ASSIGNMENTS?
IT COULD BE WORSE! AT LEAST WE HAVE FRITZ FOR COMPANY INSTEAD OF THE SARGE!
NOW! I MUST TAKE A HIDDEN GAS CYLINDER...!
BUCKY!! LOOK OUT... HE TOOK SOMETHING OUT OF HIS POCKET...TOSSING IT... UHHH!
IT..IT'S SOME KINDA GAS! I CAN'T SEE, STEVE!
HAH! IT WORKED! THE REST WILL BE EASY!
HEY! WHAT'S GOIN' ON BACK THERE?
ACCORDING TO THE RED SKULL'S BRIEFING, I'M ONLY YARDS AWAY FROM THE TOP-SECRET PROJECT VANISH!! AND, THE RED SKULL IS NEVER WRONG!
NOW I MUST QUICKLY REMOVE MY JACKET...
I HAVE JUST ENOUGH ADDITIONAL GAS CYLINDERS TO PUT THE GUARDS OF PROJECT VANISH TO SLEEP WHEN I REACH THE AREA!
MEANWHILE...
COULDN'T YOU TWO LUNKHEADS KEEP YOUR EYE ON ONE LONE NAZI PRISONER?!!
NOT WITH THIS GAS BLINDING US, WE COULDN'T!
IT'S JUST STARTING TO CLEAR AWAY NOW!
SGT. DUFFY'LL MAKE YA A PERMANENT K.P. FOR THIS IF YOU DON'T FIND 'IM AGAIN!
YOU'RE NOT JUST WHISTLIN' DIXIE, SOLDIER! BUT DON'T WORRY...WE'LL GET HIM!
NOT BY TALKIN' ABOUT IT! C'MON, LET'S GO!
5.

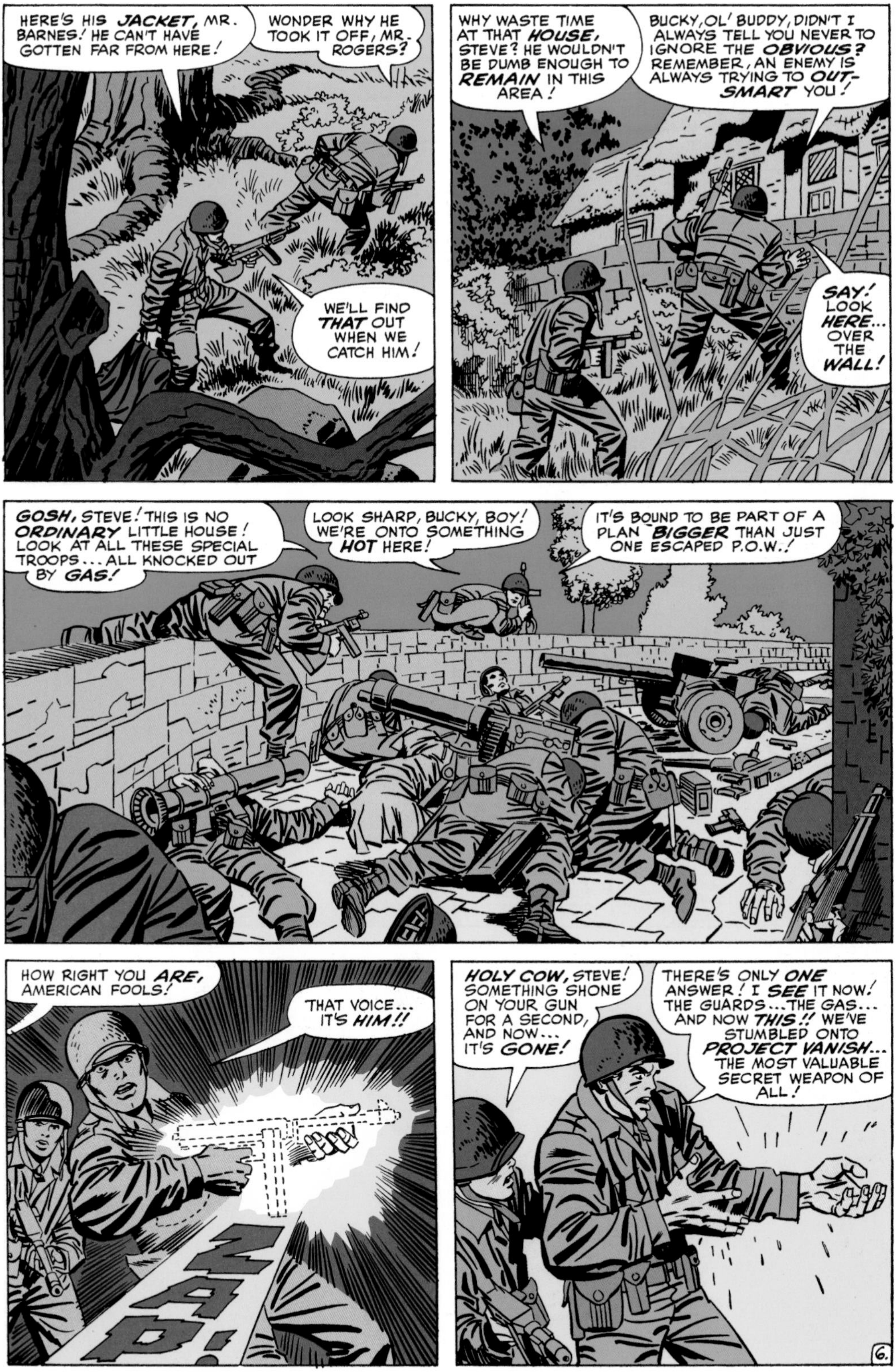
HERE'S HIS JACKET, MR. BARNES! HE CAN'T HAVE GOTTEN FAR FROM HERE!
WONDER WHY HE TOOK IT OFF, MR. ROGERS?
WE'LL FIND THAT OUT WHEN WE CATCH HIM!
WHY WASTE TIME AT THAT HOUSE, STEVE? HE WOULDN'T BE DUMB ENOUGH TO REMAIN IN THIS AREA!
BUCKY, OL' BUDDY, DIDN'T I ALWAYS TELL YOU NEVER TO IGNORE THE OBVIOUS? REMEMBER, AN ENEMY IS ALWAYS TRYING TO OUT-SMART YOU!
SAY! LOOK HERE... OVER THE WALL!
GOSH, STEVE! THIS IS NO ORDINARY LITTLE HOUSE! LOOK AT ALL THESE SPECIAL TROOPS... ALL KNOCKED OUT BY GAS!
LOOK SHARP, BUCKY, BOY! WE'RE ONTO SOMETHING HOT HERE!
IT'S BOUND TO BE PART OF A PLAN BIGGER THAN JUST ONE ESCAPED P.O.W.!
HOW RIGHT YOU ARE, AMERICAN FOOLS!
THAT VOICE... IT'S HIM!!
ZAP!
HOLY COW, STEVE! SOMETHING SHONE ON YOUR GUN FOR A SECOND, AND NOW... IT'S GONE!
THERE'S ONLY ONE ANSWER! I SEE IT NOW! THE GUARDS... THE GAS... AND NOW THIS!! WE'VE STUMBLED ONTO PROJECT VANISH... THE MOST VALUABLE SECRET WEAPON OF ALL!
6.

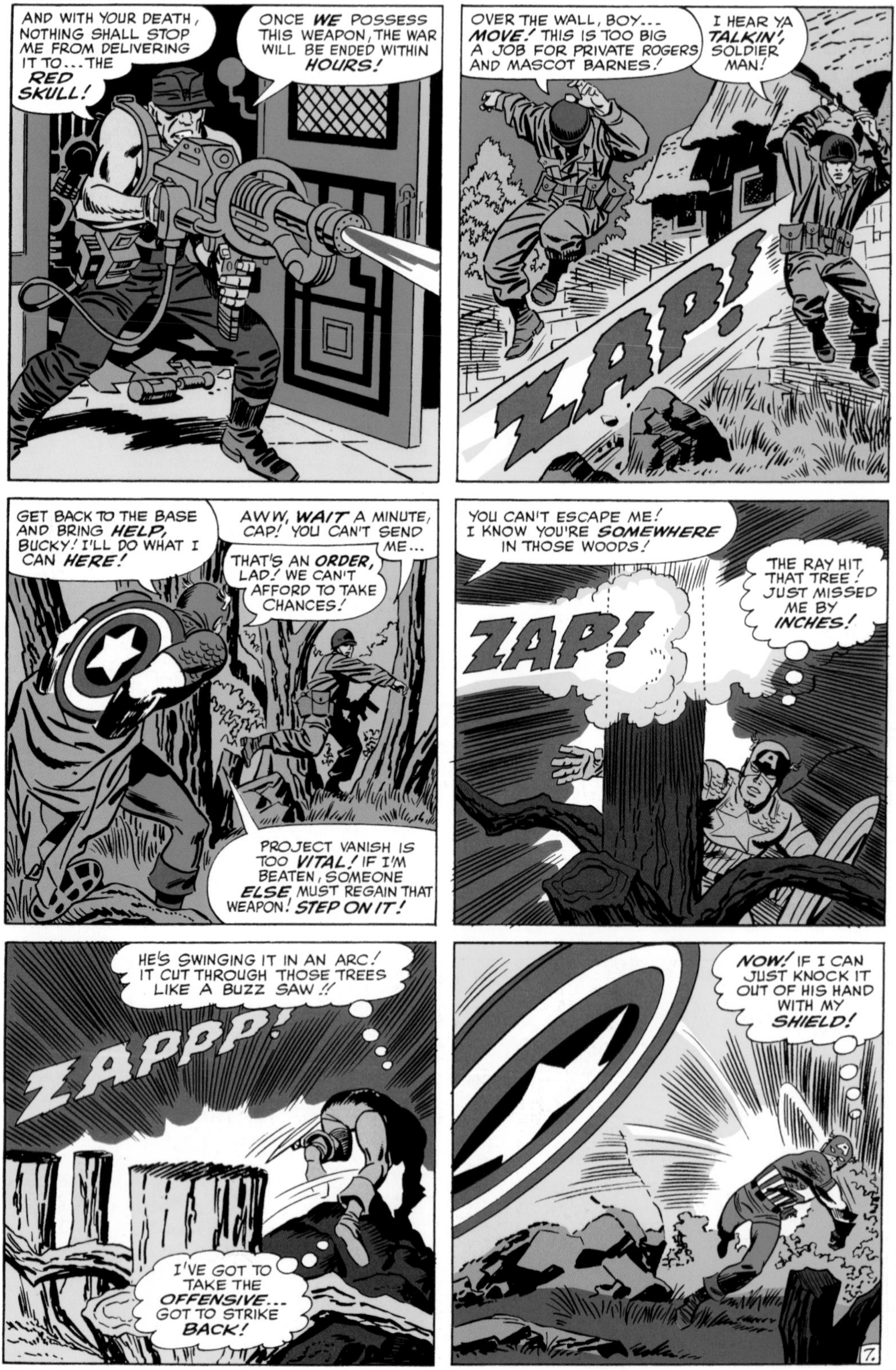

AND WITH YOUR DEATH, NOTHING SHALL STOP ME FROM DELIVERING IT TO... THE RED SKULL!
ONCE WE POSSESS THIS WEAPON, THE WAR WILL BE ENDED WITHIN HOURS!
OVER THE WALL, BOY... MOVE! THIS IS TOO BIG A JOB FOR PRIVATE ROGERS AND MASCOT BARNES!
I HEAR YA TALKIN', SOLDIER MAN!
ZAP!
GET BACK TO THE BASE AND BRING HELP, BUCKY! I'LL DO WHAT I CAN HERE!
AWW, WAIT A MINUTE, CAP! YOU CAN'T SEND ME...
THAT'S AN ORDER, LAD! WE CAN'T AFFORD TO TAKE CHANCES!
PROJECT VANISH IS TOO VITAL! IF I'M BEATEN, SOMEONE ELSE MUST REGAIN THAT WEAPON! STEP ON IT!
YOU CAN'T ESCAPE ME! I KNOW YOU'RE SOMEWHERE IN THOSE WOODS!
ZAP!
THE RAY HIT THAT TREE! JUST MISSED ME BY INCHES!
HE'S SWINGING IT IN AN ARC! IT CUT THROUGH THOSE TREES LIKE A BUZZ SAW!!
ZAPPPP!
I'VE GOT TO TAKE THE OFFENSIVE... GOT TO STRIKE BACK!
NOW! IF I CAN JUST KNOCK IT OUT OF HIS HAND WITH MY SHIELD!
7.

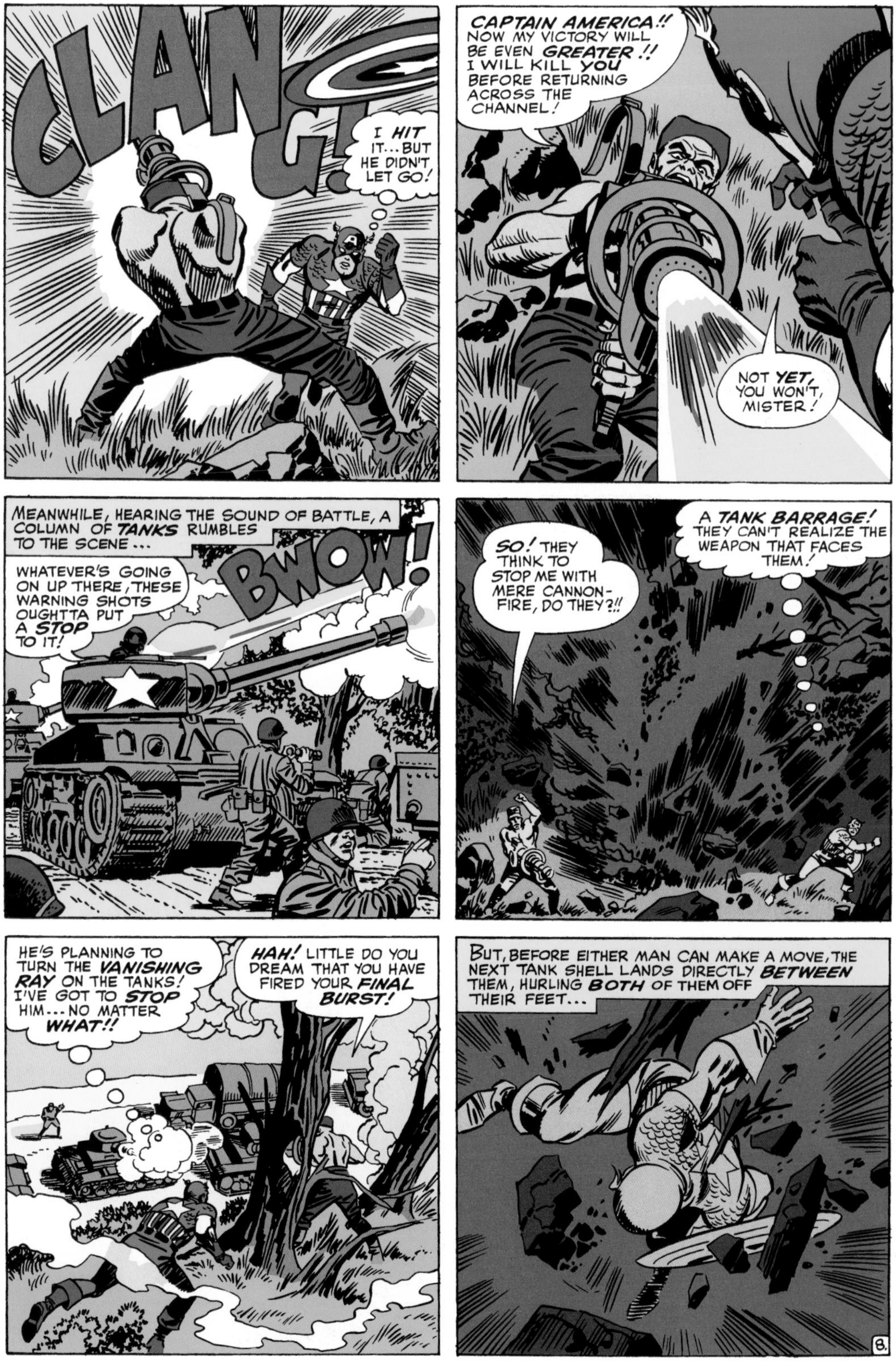
CLANG!
I HIT IT... BUT HE DIDN'T LET GO!
CAPTAIN AMERICA!! NOW MY VICTORY WILL BE EVEN GREATER!! I WILL KILL YOU BEFORE RETURNING ACROSS THE CHANNEL!
NOT YET, YOU WON'T, MISTER!
MEANWHILE, HEARING THE SOUND OF BATTLE, A COLUMN OF TANKS RUMBLES TO THE SCENE...
WHATEVER'S GOING ON UP THERE, THESE WARNING SHOTS OUGHTTA PUT A STOP TO IT!
BWOW!
SO! THEY THINK TO STOP ME WITH MERE CANNON-FIRE, DO THEY?!!
A TANK BARRAGE! THEY CAN'T REALIZE THE WEAPON THAT FACES THEM!
HE'S PLANNING TO TURN THE VANISHING RAY ON THE TANKS! I'VE GOT TO STOP HIM... NO MATTER WHAT!!
HAH! LITTLE DO YOU DREAM THAT YOU HAVE FIRED YOUR FINAL BURST!
BUT, BEFORE EITHER MAN CAN MAKE A MOVE, THE NEXT TANK SHELL LANDS DIRECTLY BETWEEN THEM, HURLING BOTH OF THEM OFF THEIR FEET...
8.

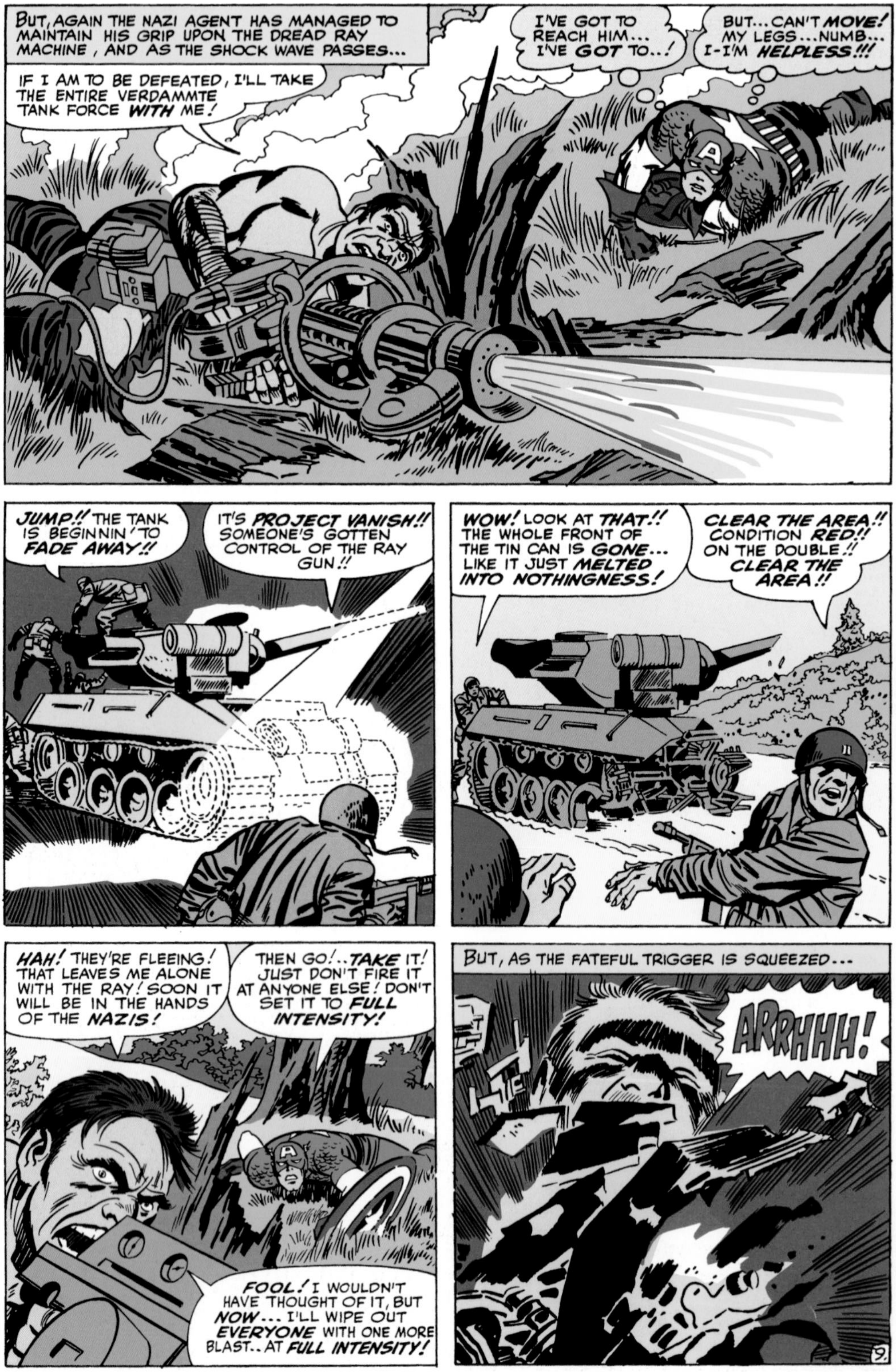
BUT, AGAIN THE NAZI AGENT HAS MANAGED TO MAINTAIN HIS GRIP UPON THE DREAD RAY MACHINE, AND AS THE SHOCK WAVE PASSES...
IF I AM TO BE DEFEATED, I'LL TAKE THE ENTIRE VERDAMMTE TANK FORCE WITH ME!
I'VE GOT TO REACH HIM... I'VE GOT TO..!
BUT...CAN'T MOVE! MY LEGS...NUMB... I-I'M HELPLESS!!!
JUMP!! THE TANK IS BEGINNIN' TO FADE AWAY!!
IT'S PROJECT VANISH!! SOMEONE'S GOTTEN CONTROL OF THE RAY GUN!!
WOW! LOOK AT THAT!! THE WHOLE FRONT OF THE TIN CAN IS GONE... LIKE IT JUST MELTED INTO NOTHINGNESS!
CLEAR THE AREA!! CONDITION RED!! ON THE DOUBLE!! CLEAR THE AREA!!
HAH! THEY'RE FLEEING! THAT LEAVES ME ALONE WITH THE RAY! SOON IT WILL BE IN THE HANDS OF THE NAZIS!
THEN GO!..TAKE IT! JUST DON'T FIRE IT AT ANYONE ELSE! DON'T SET IT TO FULL INTENSITY!
FOOL! I WOULDN'T HAVE THOUGHT OF IT, BUT NOW... I'LL WIPE OUT EVERYONE WITH ONE MORE BLAST.. AT FULL INTENSITY!
BUT, AS THE FATEFUL TRIGGER IS SQUEEZED...
ARRHHH!
9

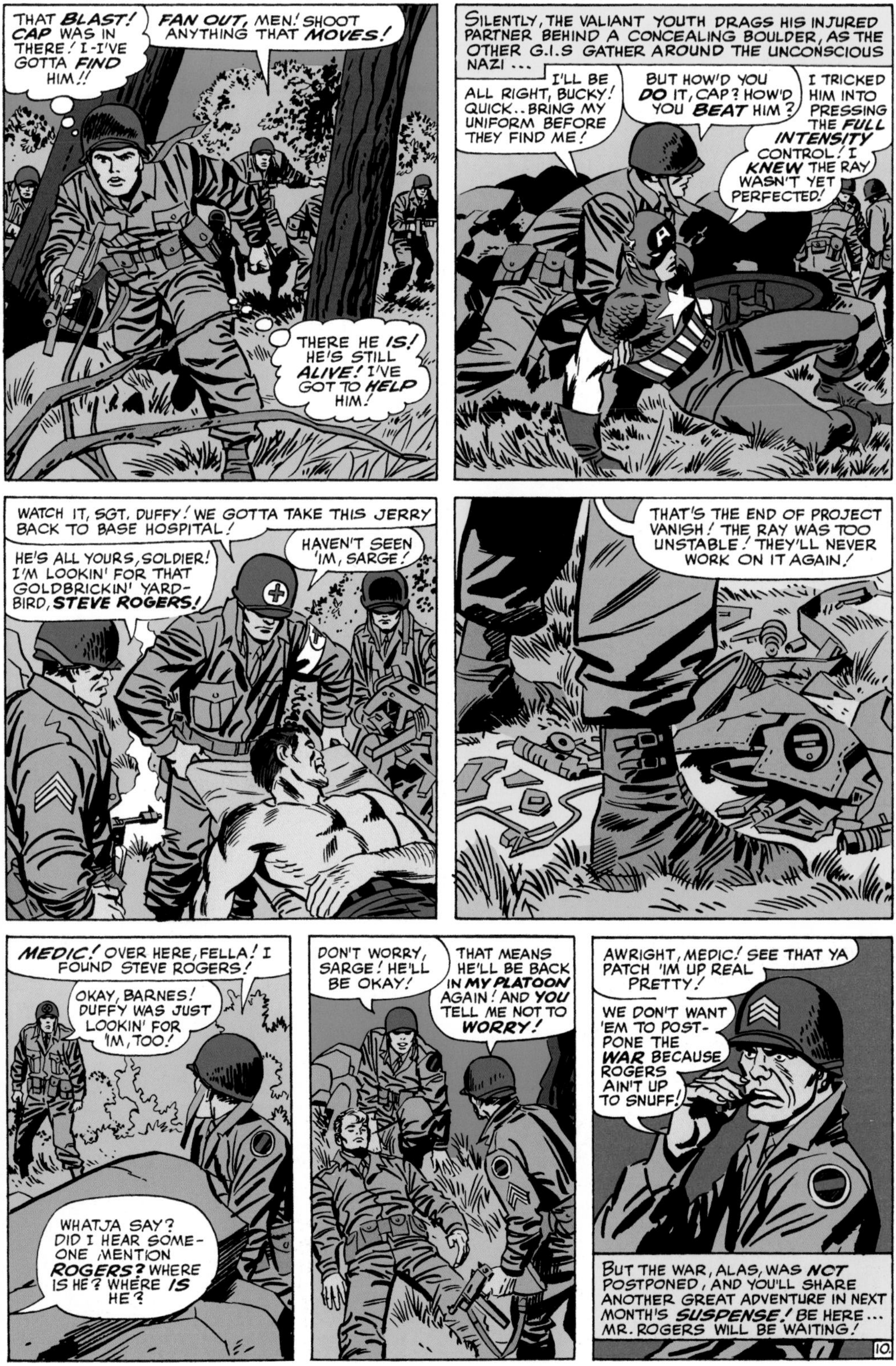

THAT BLAST! CAP WAS IN THERE! I-I'VE GOTTA FIND HIM!!
FAN OUT, MEN! SHOOT ANYTHING THAT MOVES!
THERE HE IS! HE'S STILL ALIVE! I'VE GOT TO HELP HIM!
SILENTLY, THE VALIANT YOUTH DRAGS HIS INJURED PARTNER BEHIND A CONCEALING BOULDER, AS THE OTHER G.I.S GATHER AROUND THE UNCONSCIOUS NAZI...
I'LL BE ALL RIGHT, BUCKY! QUICK.. BRING MY UNIFORM BEFORE THEY FIND ME!
BUT HOW'D YOU DO IT, CAP? HOW'D YOU BEAT HIM?
I TRICKED HIM INTO PRESSING THE FULL INTENSITY CONTROL! I KNEW THE RAY WASN'T YET PERFECTED!
WATCH IT, SGT. DUFFY! WE GOTTA TAKE THIS JERRY BACK TO BASE HOSPITAL!
HE'S ALL YOURS, SOLDIER! I'M LOOKIN' FOR THAT GOLDBRICKIN' YARD-BIRD, STEVE ROGERS!
HAVEN'T SEEN 'IM, SARGE!
THAT'S THE END OF PROJECT VANISH! THE RAY WAS TOO UNSTABLE! THEY'LL NEVER WORK ON IT AGAIN!
MEDIC! OVER HERE, FELLA! I FOUND STEVE ROGERS!
OKAY, BARNES! DUFFY WAS JUST LOOKIN' FOR 'IM, TOO!
WHATJA SAY? DID I HEAR SOME-ONE MENTION ROGERS? WHERE IS HE? WHERE IS HE?
DON'T WORRY, SARGE! HE'LL BE OKAY!
THAT MEANS HE'LL BE BACK IN MY PLATOON AGAIN! AND YOU TELL ME NOT TO WORRY!
AWRIGHT, MEDIC! SEE THAT YA PATCH 'IM UP REAL PRETTY!
WE DON'T WANT 'EM TO POST-PONE THE WAR BECAUSE ROGERS AIN'T UP TO SNUFF!
BUT THE WAR, ALAS, WAS NOT POSTPONED, AND YOU'LL SHARE ANOTHER GREAT ADVENTURE IN NEXT MONTH'S SUSPENSE! BE HERE... MR. ROGERS WILL BE WAITING!
10.

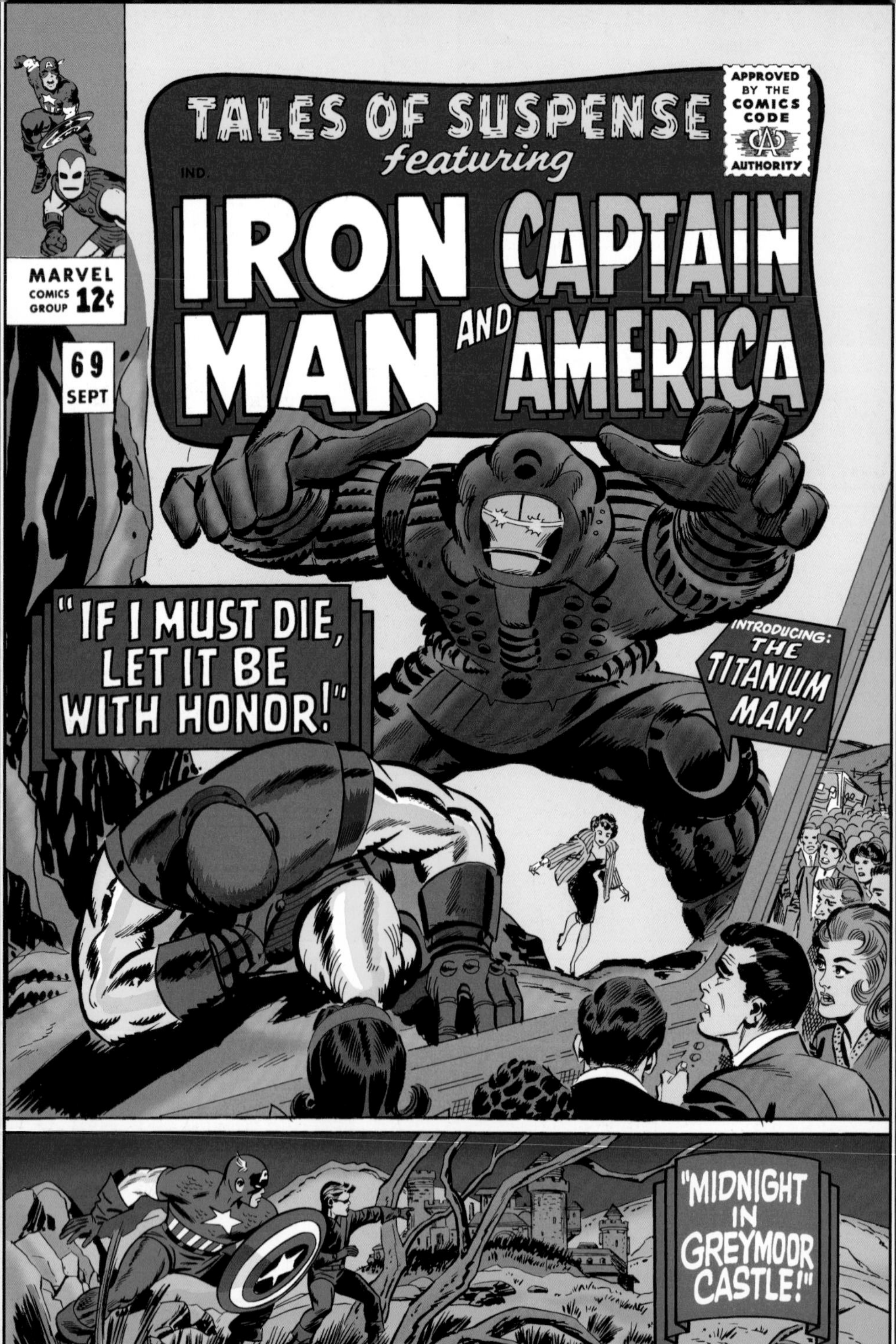
TALES OF SUSPENSE
featuring
IRON MAN AND CAPTAIN AMERICA
APPROVED BY THE COMICS CODE AUTHORITY
MARVEL COMICS GROUP 12¢
69 SEPT
IND.
"IF I MUST DIE, LET IT BE WITH HONOR!"
INTRODUCING: THE TITANIUM MAN!
"MIDNIGHT IN GREYMOOR CASTLE!"

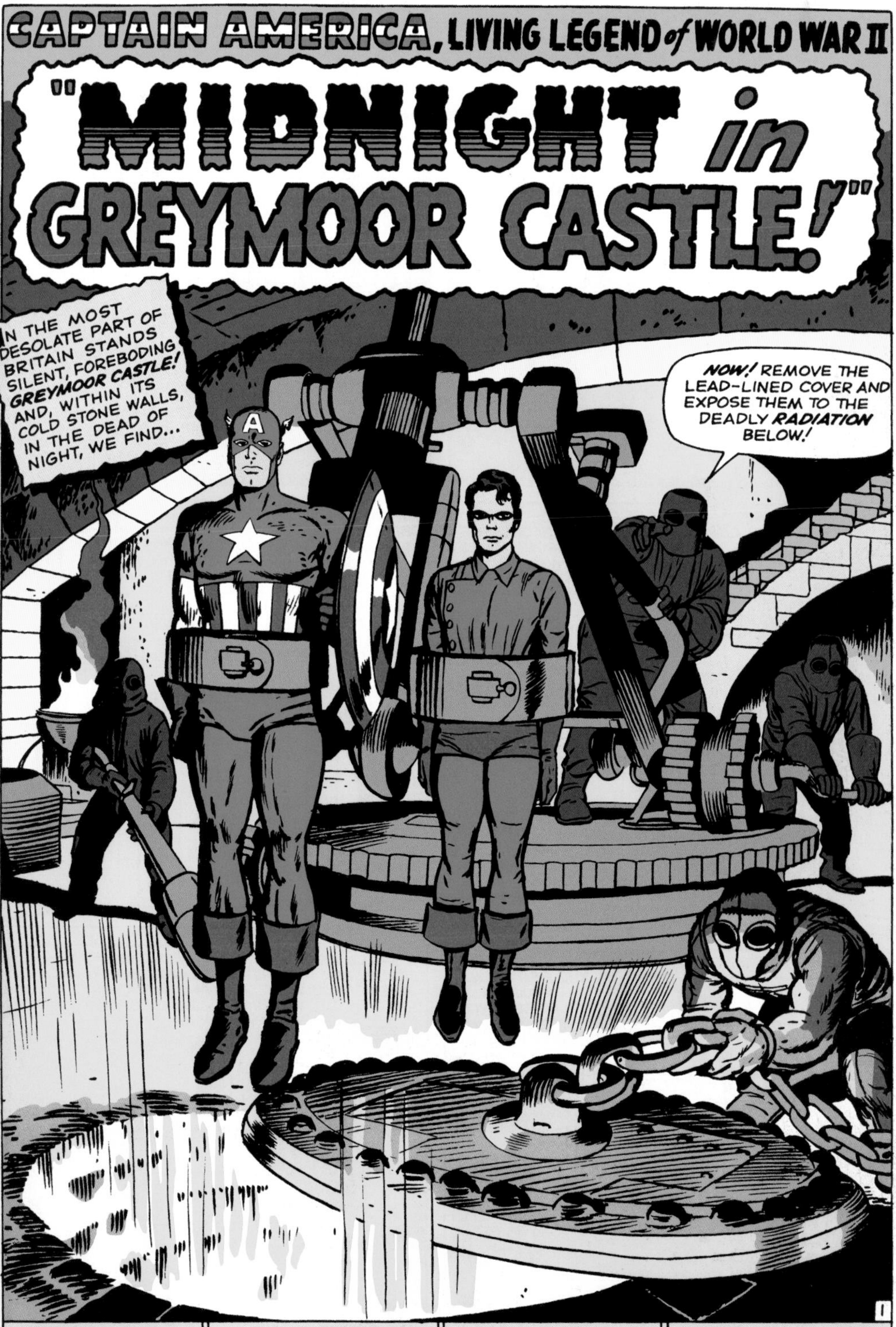
CAPTAIN AMERICA, LIVING LEGEND of WORLD WAR II
"MIDNIGHT in GREYMOOR CASTLE!"
IN THE MOST DESOLATE PART OF BRITAIN STANDS SILENT, FOREBODING GREYMOOR CASTLE! AND, WITHIN ITS COLD STONE WALLS, IN THE DEAD OF NIGHT, WE FIND...
NOW! REMOVE THE LEAD-LINED COVER AND EXPOSE THEM TO THE DEADLY RADIATION BELOW!
1
SCRIPT BY: FRIENDLY STAN LEE
LAYOUTS BY: FROLICKSOME JACK KIRBY
RENDERING BY: FRIVOLOUS DICK AYERS
LETTERING BY: FEARLESS ARTIE SIMEK

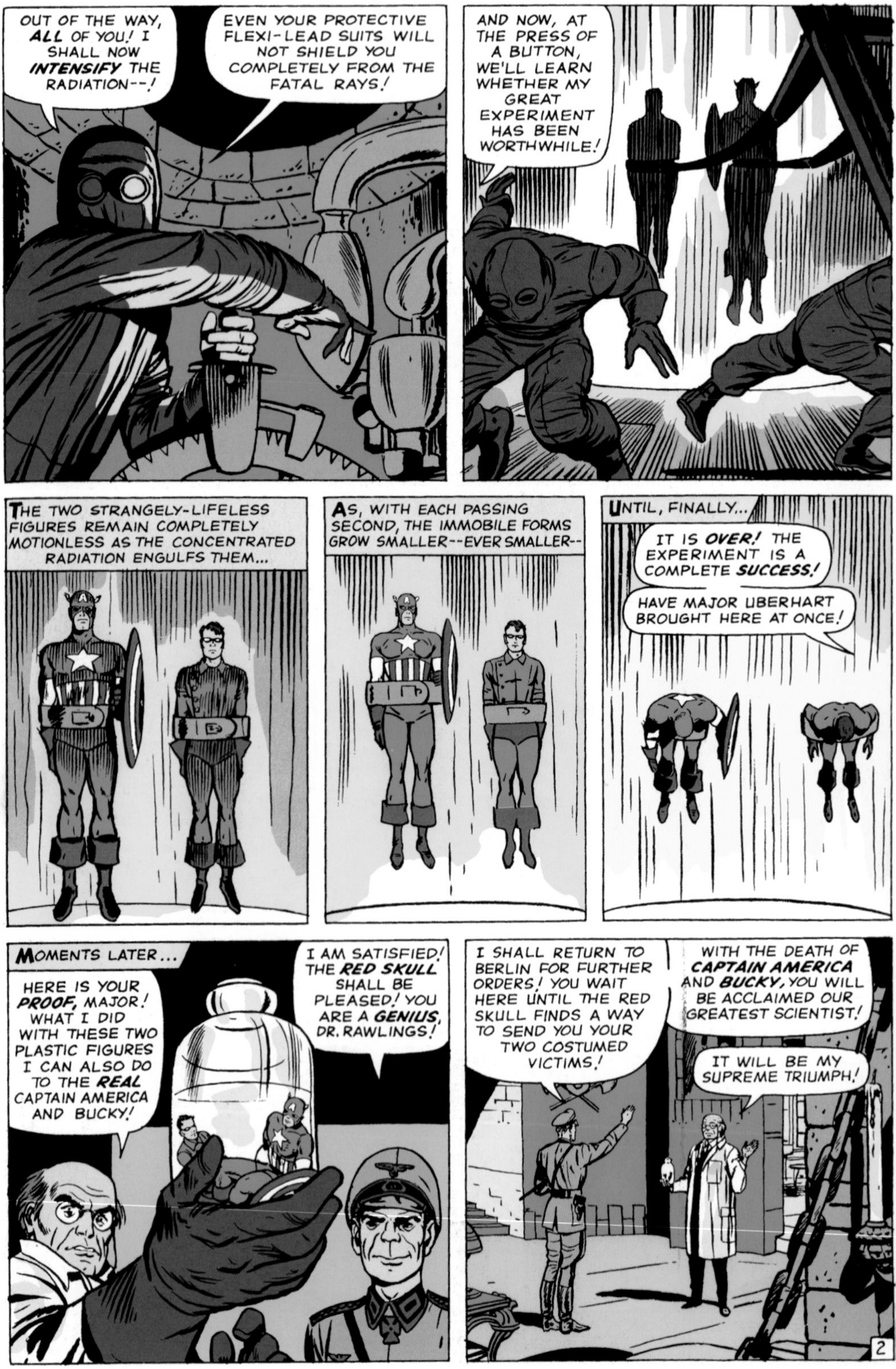
OUT OF THE WAY, ALL OF YOU! I SHALL NOW INTENSIFY THE RADIATION--!
EVEN YOUR PROTECTIVE FLEXI-LEAD SUITS WILL NOT SHIELD YOU COMPLETELY FROM THE FATAL RAYS!
AND NOW, AT THE PRESS OF A BUTTON, WE'LL LEARN WHETHER MY GREAT EXPERIMENT HAS BEEN WORTHWHILE!
THE TWO STRANGELY-LIFELESS FIGURES REMAIN COMPLETELY MOTIONLESS AS THE CONCENTRATED RADIATION ENGULFS THEM...
AS, WITH EACH PASSING SECOND, THE IMMOBILE FORMS GROW SMALLER--EVER SMALLER--
UNTIL, FINALLY...
IT IS OVER! THE EXPERIMENT IS A COMPLETE SUCCESS!
HAVE MAJOR UBERHART BROUGHT HERE AT ONCE!
MOMENTS LATER...
HERE IS YOUR PROOF, MAJOR! WHAT I DID WITH THESE TWO PLASTIC FIGURES I CAN ALSO DO TO THE REAL CAPTAIN AMERICA AND BUCKY!
I AM SATISFIED! THE RED SKULL SHALL BE PLEASED! YOU ARE A GENIUS, DR. RAWLINGS!
I SHALL RETURN TO BERLIN FOR FURTHER ORDERS! YOU WAIT HERE UNTIL THE RED SKULL FINDS A WAY TO SEND YOU YOUR TWO COSTUMED VICTIMS!
WITH THE DEATH OF CAPTAIN AMERICA AND BUCKY, YOU WILL BE ACCLAIMED OUR GREATEST SCIENTIST!
IT WILL BE MY SUPREME TRIUMPH!
2

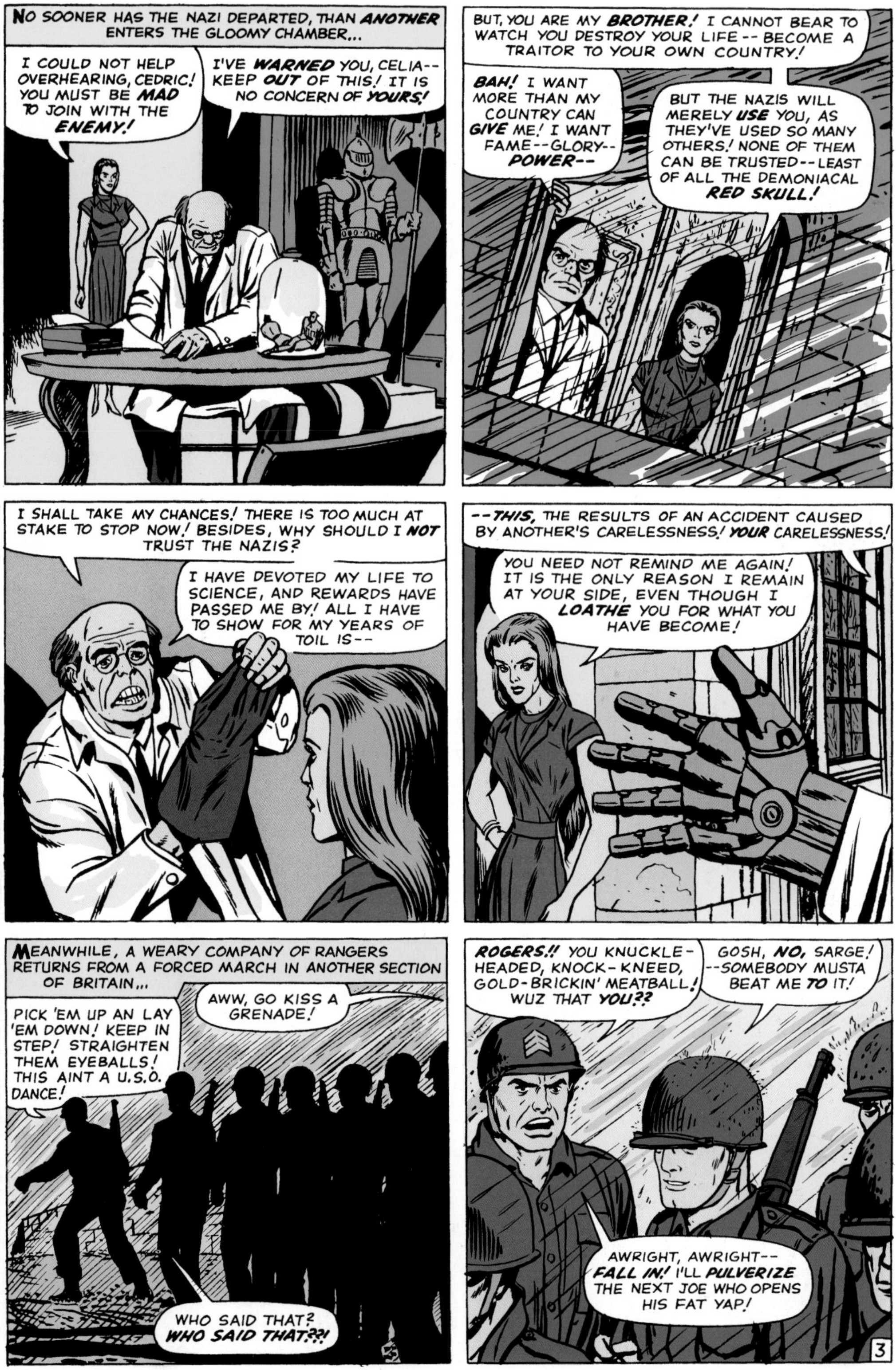

NO SOONER HAS THE NAZI DEPARTED, THAN ANOTHER ENTERS THE GLOOMY CHAMBER...
I COULD NOT HELP OVERHEARING, CEDRIC! YOU MUST BE MAD TO JOIN WITH THE ENEMY!
I'VE WARNED YOU, CELIA-- KEEP OUT OF THIS! IT IS NO CONCERN OF YOURS!
BUT, YOU ARE MY BROTHER! I CANNOT BEAR TO WATCH YOU DESTROY YOUR LIFE -- BECOME A TRAITOR TO YOUR OWN COUNTRY!
BAH! I WANT MORE THAN MY COUNTRY CAN GIVE ME! I WANT FAME--GLORY-- POWER--
BUT THE NAZIS WILL MERELY USE YOU, AS THEY'VE USED SO MANY OTHERS! NONE OF THEM CAN BE TRUSTED--LEAST OF ALL THE DEMONIACAL RED SKULL!
I SHALL TAKE MY CHANCES! THERE IS TOO MUCH AT STAKE TO STOP NOW! BESIDES, WHY SHOULD I NOT TRUST THE NAZIS?
I HAVE DEVOTED MY LIFE TO SCIENCE, AND REWARDS HAVE PASSED ME BY! ALL I HAVE TO SHOW FOR MY YEARS OF TOIL IS--
--THIS, THE RESULTS OF AN ACCIDENT CAUSED BY ANOTHER'S CARELESSNESS! YOUR CARELESSNESS!
YOU NEED NOT REMIND ME AGAIN! IT IS THE ONLY REASON I REMAIN AT YOUR SIDE, EVEN THOUGH I LOATHE YOU FOR WHAT YOU HAVE BECOME!
MEANWHILE, A WEARY COMPANY OF RANGERS RETURNS FROM A FORCED MARCH IN ANOTHER SECTION OF BRITAIN...
PICK 'EM UP AN LAY 'EM DOWN! KEEP IN STEP! STRAIGHTEN THEM EYEBALLS! THIS AINT A U.S.O. DANCE!
AWW, GO KISS A GRENADE!
WHO SAID THAT? WHO SAID THAT??!
ROGERS!! YOU KNUCKLE-HEADED, KNOCK-KNEED, GOLD-BRICKIN' MEATBALL! WUZ THAT YOU??
GOSH, NO, SARGE! --SOMEBODY MUSTA BEAT ME TO IT!
AWRIGHT, AWRIGHT-- FALL IN! I'LL PULVERIZE THE NEXT JOE WHO OPENS HIS FAT YAP!
3

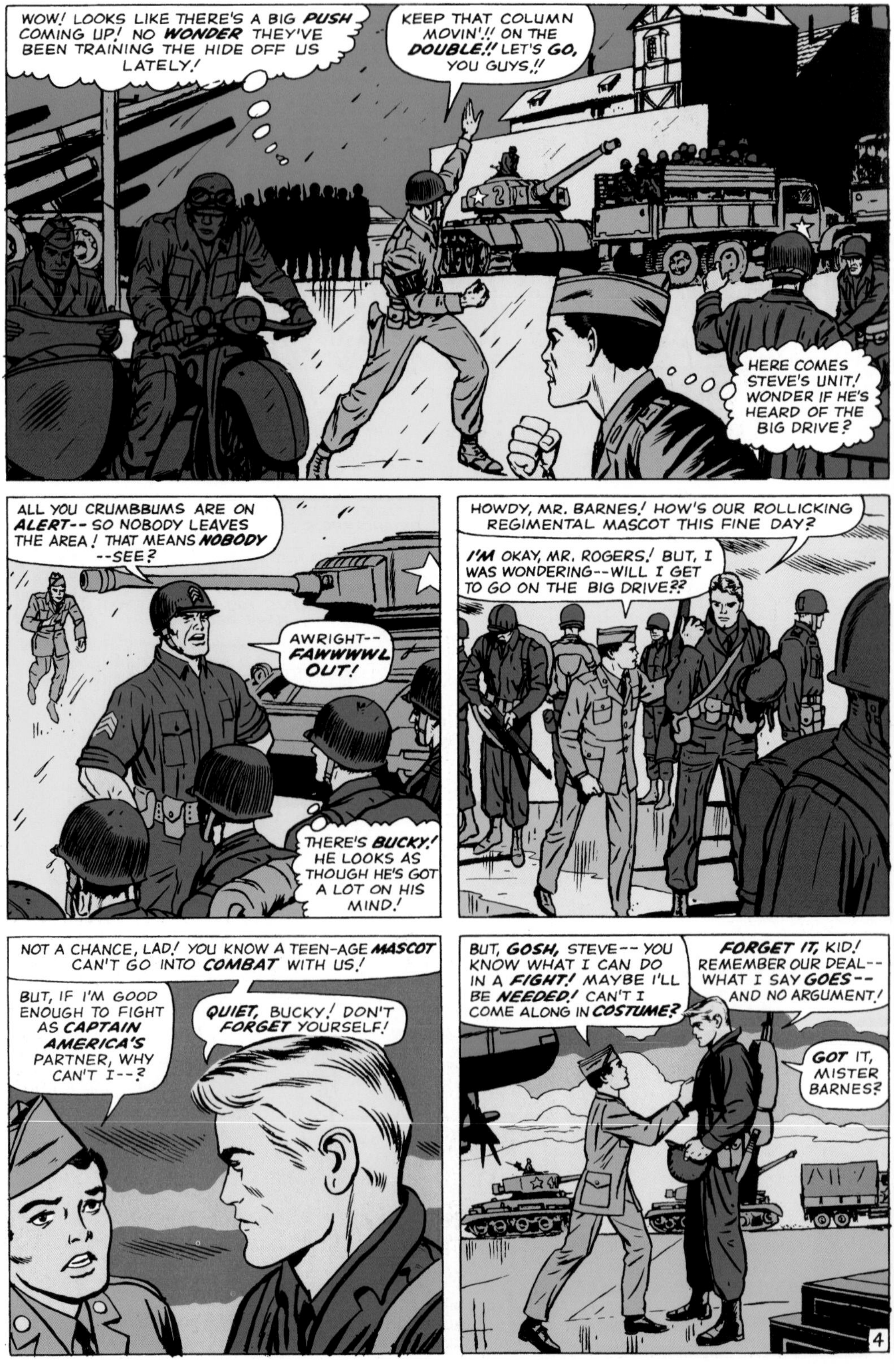
WOW! LOOKS LIKE THERE'S A BIG PUSH COMING UP! NO WONDER THEY'VE BEEN TRAINING THE HIDE OFF US LATELY!
KEEP THAT COLUMN MOVIN'!! ON THE DOUBLE!! LET'S GO, YOU GUYS!!
HERE COMES STEVE'S UNIT! WONDER IF HE'S HEARD OF THE BIG DRIVE?
ALL YOU CRUMBBUMS ARE ON ALERT-- SO NOBODY LEAVES THE AREA! THAT MEANS NOBODY --SEE?
AWRIGHT-- FAWWWWL OUT!
THERE'S BUCKY! HE LOOKS AS THOUGH HE'S GOT A LOT ON HIS MIND!
HOWDY, MR. BARNES! HOW'S OUR ROLLICKING REGIMENTAL MASCOT THIS FINE DAY?
I'M OKAY, MR. ROGERS! BUT, I WAS WONDERING--WILL I GET TO GO ON THE BIG DRIVE??
NOT A CHANCE, LAD! YOU KNOW A TEEN-AGE MASCOT CAN'T GO INTO COMBAT WITH US!
BUT, IF I'M GOOD ENOUGH TO FIGHT AS CAPTAIN AMERICA'S PARTNER, WHY CAN'T I--?
QUIET, BUCKY! DON'T FORGET YOURSELF!
BUT, GOSH, STEVE-- YOU KNOW WHAT I CAN DO IN A FIGHT! MAYBE I'LL BE NEEDED! CAN'T I COME ALONG IN COSTUME?
FORGET IT, KID! REMEMBER OUR DEAL-- WHAT I SAY GOES-- AND NO ARGUMENT!
GOT IT, MISTER BARNES?
4

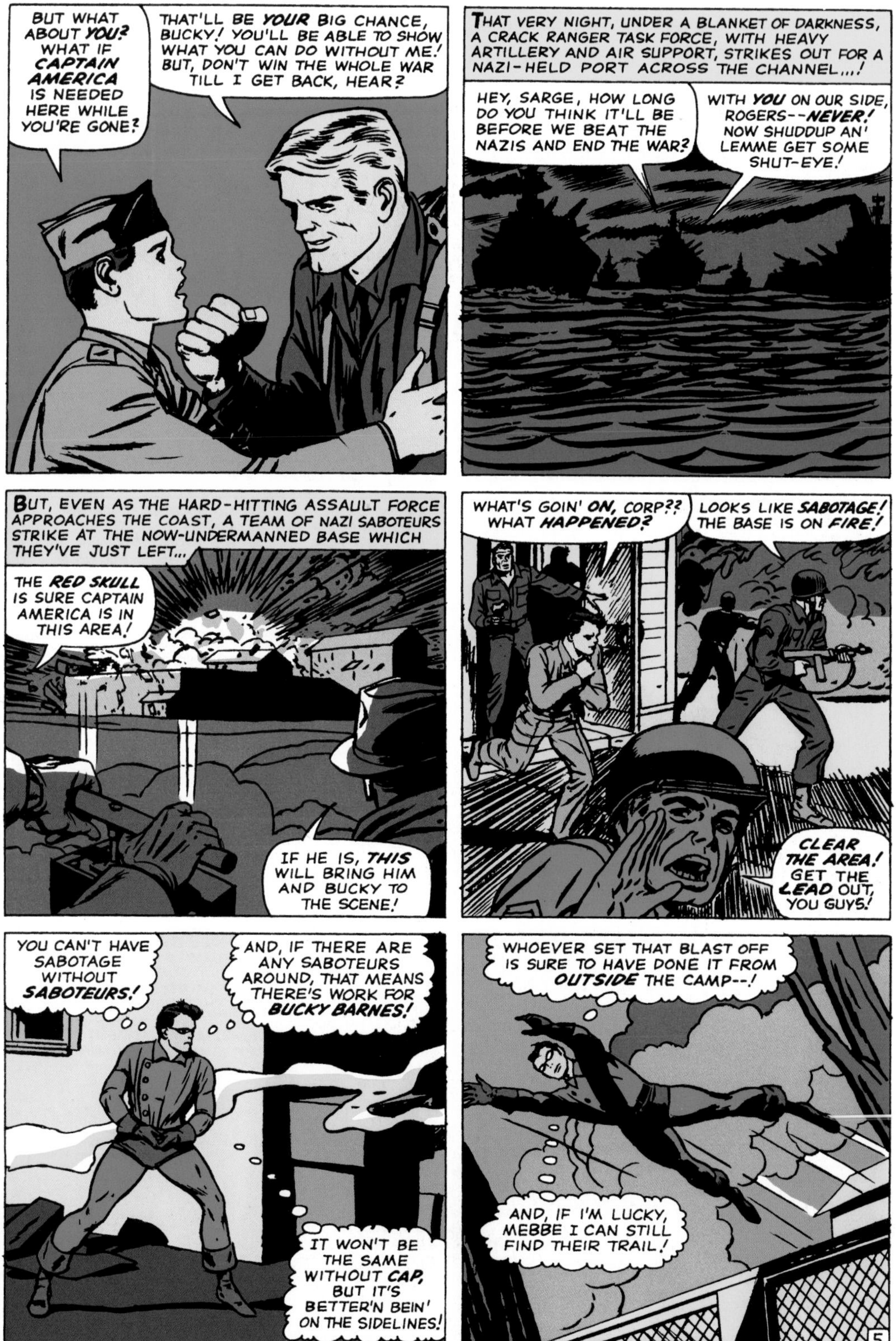
BUT WHAT ABOUT YOU? WHAT IF CAPTAIN AMERICA IS NEEDED HERE WHILE YOU'RE GONE?
THAT'LL BE YOUR BIG CHANCE, BUCKY! YOU'LL BE ABLE TO SHOW WHAT YOU CAN DO WITHOUT ME! BUT, DON'T WIN THE WHOLE WAR TILL I GET BACK, HEAR?
THAT VERY NIGHT, UNDER A BLANKET OF DARKNESS, A CRACK RANGER TASK FORCE, WITH HEAVY ARTILLERY AND AIR SUPPORT, STRIKES OUT FOR A NAZI-HELD PORT ACROSS THE CHANNEL...!
HEY, SARGE, HOW LONG DO YOU THINK IT'LL BE BEFORE WE BEAT THE NAZIS AND END THE WAR?
WITH YOU ON OUR SIDE, ROGERS--NEVER! NOW SHUDDUP AN' LEMME GET SOME SHUT-EYE!
BUT, EVEN AS THE HARD-HITTING ASSAULT FORCE APPROACHES THE COAST, A TEAM OF NAZI SABOTEURS STRIKE AT THE NOW-UNDERMANNED BASE WHICH THEY'VE JUST LEFT...
THE RED SKULL IS SURE CAPTAIN AMERICA IS IN THIS AREA!
IF HE IS, THIS WILL BRING HIM AND BUCKY TO THE SCENE!
WHAT'S GOIN' ON, CORP?? WHAT HAPPENED?
LOOKS LIKE SABOTAGE! THE BASE IS ON FIRE!
CLEAR THE AREA! GET THE LEAD OUT, YOU GUYS!
YOU CAN'T HAVE SABOTAGE WITHOUT SABOTEURS!
AND, IF THERE ARE ANY SABOTEURS AROUND, THAT MEANS THERE'S WORK FOR BUCKY BARNES!
IT WON'T BE THE SAME WITHOUT CAP, BUT IT'S BETTER'N BEIN' ON THE SIDELINES!
WHOEVER SET THAT BLAST OFF IS SURE TO HAVE DONE IT FROM OUTSIDE THE CAMP--!
AND, IF I'M LUCKY, MEBBE I CAN STILL FIND THEIR TRAIL!
5

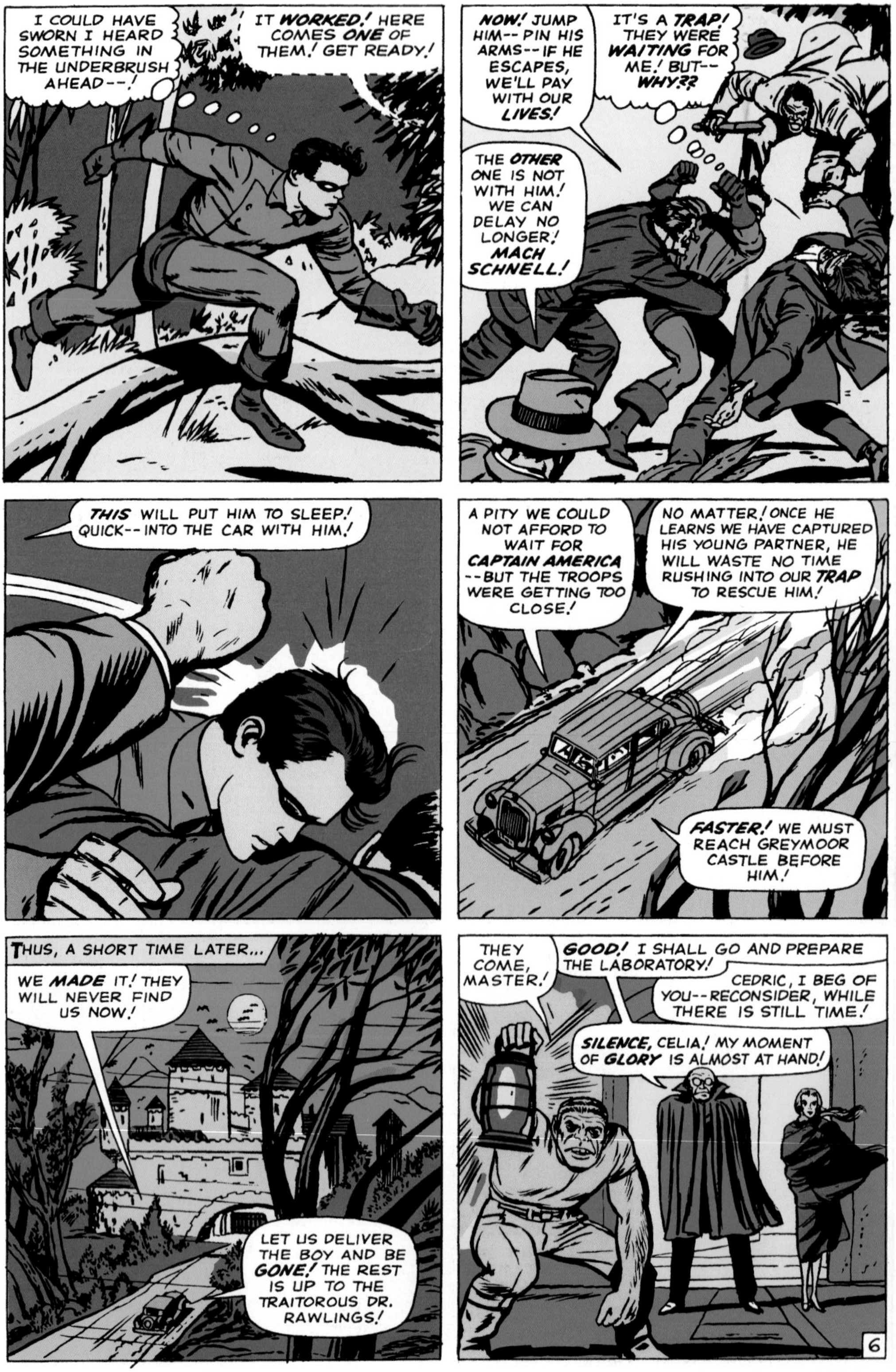
I COULD HAVE SWORN I HEARD SOMETHING IN THE UNDERBRUSH AHEAD--!
IT WORKED! HERE COMES ONE OF THEM! GET READY!
NOW! JUMP HIM-- PIN HIS ARMS-- IF HE ESCAPES, WE'LL PAY WITH OUR LIVES!
IT'S A TRAP! THEY WERE WAITING FOR ME! BUT-- WHY??
THE OTHER ONE IS NOT WITH HIM! WE CAN DELAY NO LONGER! MACH SCHNELL!
THIS WILL PUT HIM TO SLEEP! QUICK-- INTO THE CAR WITH HIM!
A PITY WE COULD NOT AFFORD TO WAIT FOR CAPTAIN AMERICA --BUT THE TROOPS WERE GETTING TOO CLOSE!
NO MATTER! ONCE HE LEARNS WE HAVE CAPTURED HIS YOUNG PARTNER, HE WILL WASTE NO TIME RUSHING INTO OUR TRAP TO RESCUE HIM!
FASTER! WE MUST REACH GREYMOOR CASTLE BEFORE HIM!
THUS, A SHORT TIME LATER...
WE MADE IT! THEY WILL NEVER FIND US NOW!
LET US DELIVER THE BOY AND BE GONE! THE REST IS UP TO THE TRAITOROUS DR. RAWLINGS!
THEY COME, MASTER!
GOOD! I SHALL GO AND PREPARE THE LABORATORY!
CEDRIC, I BEG OF YOU--RECONSIDER, WHILE THERE IS STILL TIME!
SILENCE, CELIA! MY MOMENT OF GLORY IS ALMOST AT HAND!
6

MEANWHILE, AT A COASTAL TOWN OF NAZI-OCCUPIED FRANCE...

WE'VE GOT TO COMPLETE OUR MISSION BEFORE THE MAIN NAZI FORCE CAN REACH US! SO *MOVE!*

WE'RE OUTNUMBERED, BUT THE ELEMENT OF *SURPRISE* IS IN OUR FAVOR!

LIFT EM', YOU GUYS! OUR JOB IS TO HIT GESTAPO HEADQUARTERS-- KNOCK OUT THEIR RECORDS AND COMMUNICATIONS --AND THEN HEAD HOME!

SO LET'S *GO!*

CRASH!

HIMMEL! RANGERS!

STOP THEM!

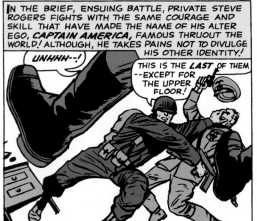

IN THE BRIEF, ENSUING BATTLE, PRIVATE STEVE ROGERS FIGHTS WITH THE SAME COURAGE AND SKILL THAT HAVE MADE THE NAME OF HIS ALTER EGO, *CAPTAIN AMERICA,* FAMOUS THRUOUT THE WORLD! ALTHOUGH, HE TAKES PAINS NOT TO DIVULGE HIS OTHER IDENTITY!

UNHHH--!

THIS IS THE *LAST* OF THEM --EXCEPT FOR THE UPPER FLOOR!

WHILE THE OTHERS FINISH MOPPING UP DOWNSTAIRS, I'LL JUST CHECK OUT THE TOP OF THIS LANDING!

I COULD SWEAR I HEAR A *RADIO TRANSMITTER* OPERATING!

7

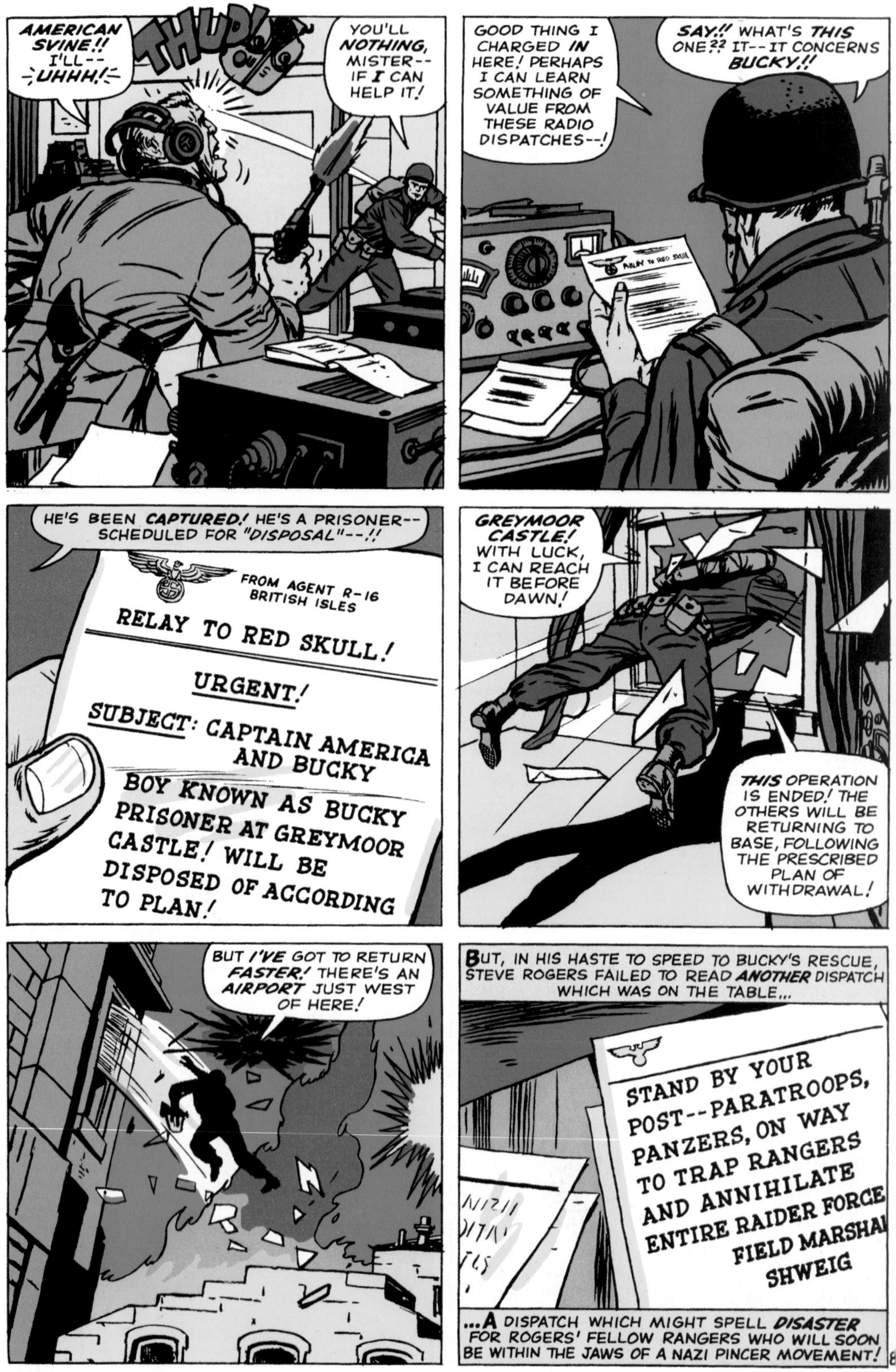

AMERICAN SVINE!! I'LL-- UHHH!
THUD!
YOU'LL NOTHING, MISTER-- IF I CAN HELP IT!
GOOD THING I CHARGED IN HERE! PERHAPS I CAN LEARN SOMETHING OF VALUE FROM THESE RADIO DISPATCHES--!
SAY!! WHAT'S THIS ONE?? IT--IT CONCERNS BUCKY!!
HE'S BEEN CAPTURED! HE'S A PRISONER-- SCHEDULED FOR "DISPOSAL"--!!
FROM AGENT R-16 BRITISH ISLES
RELAY TO RED SKULL!
URGENT!
SUBJECT: CAPTAIN AMERICA AND BUCKY
BOY KNOWN AS BUCKY PRISONER AT GREYMOOR CASTLE! WILL BE DISPOSED OF ACCORDING TO PLAN!
GREYMOOR CASTLE! WITH LUCK, I CAN REACH IT BEFORE DAWN!
THIS OPERATION IS ENDED! THE OTHERS WILL BE RETURNING TO BASE, FOLLOWING THE PRESCRIBED PLAN OF WITHDRAWAL!
BUT I'VE GOT TO RETURN FASTER! THERE'S AN AIRPORT JUST WEST OF HERE!
BUT, IN HIS HASTE TO SPEED TO BUCKY'S RESCUE, STEVE ROGERS FAILED TO READ ANOTHER DISPATCH WHICH WAS ON THE TABLE...
STAND BY YOUR POST--PARATROOPS, PANZERS, ON WAY TO TRAP RANGERS AND ANNIHILATE ENTIRE RAIDER FORCE
FIELD MARSHA
SHWEIG
...A DISPATCH WHICH MIGHT SPELL DISASTER FOR ROGERS' FELLOW RANGERS WHO WILL SOON BE WITHIN THE JAWS OF A NAZI PINCER MOVEMENT!

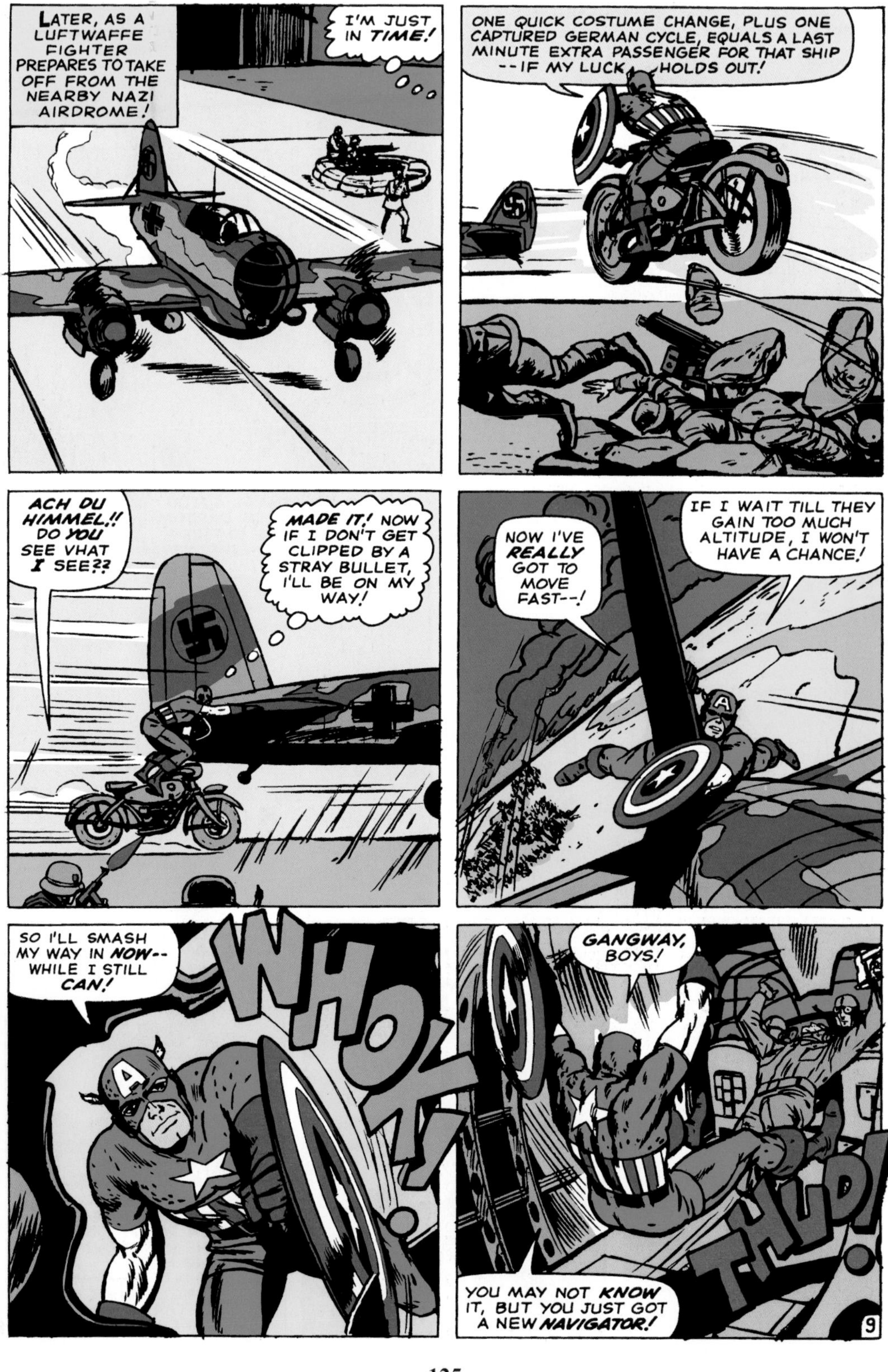

LATER, AS A LUFTWAFFE FIGHTER PREPARES TO TAKE OFF FROM THE NEARBY NAZI AIRDROME!
I'M JUST IN TIME!
ONE QUICK COSTUME CHANGE, PLUS ONE CAPTURED GERMAN CYCLE, EQUALS A LAST MINUTE EXTRA PASSENGER FOR THAT SHIP --IF MY LUCK HOLDS OUT!
ACH DU HIMMEL!! DO YOU SEE VHAT I SEE??
MADE IT! NOW IF I DON'T GET CLIPPED BY A STRAY BULLET, I'LL BE ON MY WAY!
NOW I'VE REALLY GOT TO MOVE FAST--!
IF I WAIT TILL THEY GAIN TOO MUCH ALTITUDE, I WON'T HAVE A CHANCE!
SO I'LL SMASH MY WAY IN NOW-- WHILE I STILL CAN!
WHOK!
GANGWAY, BOYS!
THUD!
YOU MAY NOT KNOW IT, BUT YOU JUST GOT A NEW NAVIGATOR!
9

WHILE, BACK AT GREYMOOR CASTLE...

CEDRIC, EVEN IF YOU CARE NOTHING FOR YOURSELF, OR ME-- THINK OF YOUR COUNTRY! YOU'RE BETRAYING US ALL!

QUITE THE CONTRARY! THE NAZIS ARE SURE TO WIN-- AND, WHEN THEY DO, I'LL BE A HERO!

NOW BE SILENT! THIS IS THE MOMENT I'VE BEEN WAITING FOR! I MUST PREPARE THE SUBJECT BY BATHING HIM WITH Z-RAYS--!

ALL OF YOU, TAKE YOUR POSITIONS! YOU KNOW WHAT TO DO!

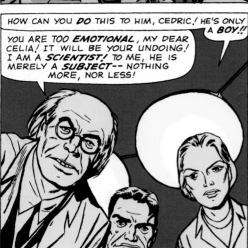

HOW CAN YOU DO THIS TO HIM, CEDRIC! HE'S ONLY A BOY!!

YOU ARE TOO EMOTIONAL, MY DEAR CELIA! IT WILL BE YOUR UNDOING! I AM A SCIENTIST! TO ME, HE IS MERELY A SUBJECT-- NOTHING MORE, NOR LESS!

NOW, NOTHING REMAINS BUT TO AWAIT THE ARRIVAL OF CAPTAIN AMERICA! ONCE HE ENTERS MY TRAP, THE GREAT EXPERIMENT SHALL BEGIN!

AND, EVEN AS CEDRIC RAWLINGS SPEAKS...

I'VE GOT TO COME IN LOW-- TO DODGE THE RADAR--!

I'LL LAND AS SOON AS POSSIBLE AND HEAD FOR GREYMOOR CASTLE! I'VE GOT TO SAVE BUCKY--!

--NO MATTER WHAT THEY THROW AGAINST ME!!

THE END

PERHAPS, AT THIS MOMENT, IT IS BEST THAT CAPTAIN AMERICA DOESN'T REALIZE THAT THE RANGER UNIT WHOM HE HAS JUST LEFT IS ALSO IN DEADLY DANGER-- BUT, MORE OF THAT NEXT ISSUE AS THRILL FOLLOWS THRILL!!

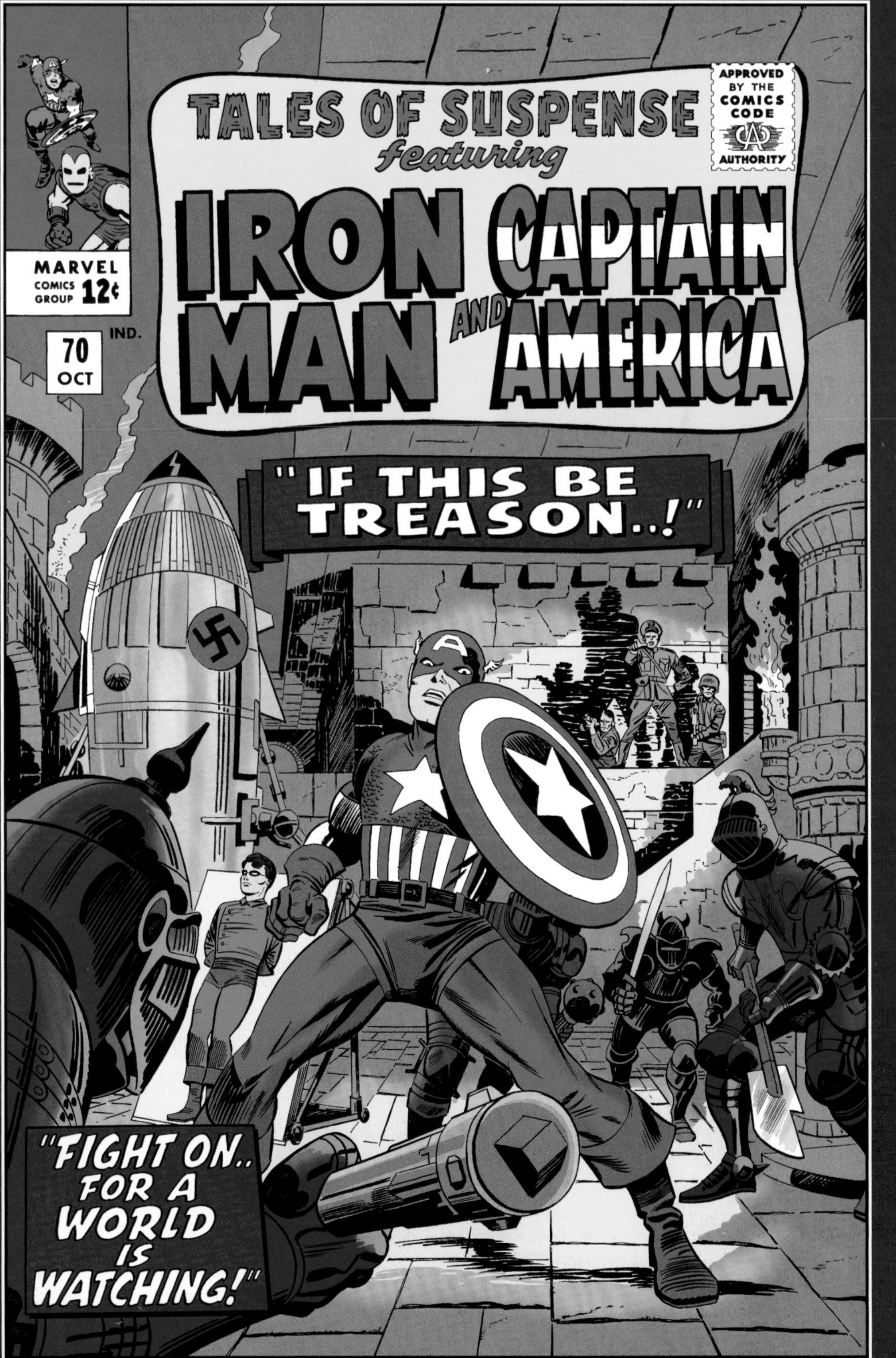
TALES OF SUSPENSE
featuring
IRON MAN AND CAPTAIN AMERICA
APPROVED BY THE COMICS CODE AUTHORITY
MARVEL COMICS GROUP 12¢
IND.
70 OCT
"IF THIS BE TREASON..!"
"FIGHT ON.. FOR A WORLD IS WATCHING!"

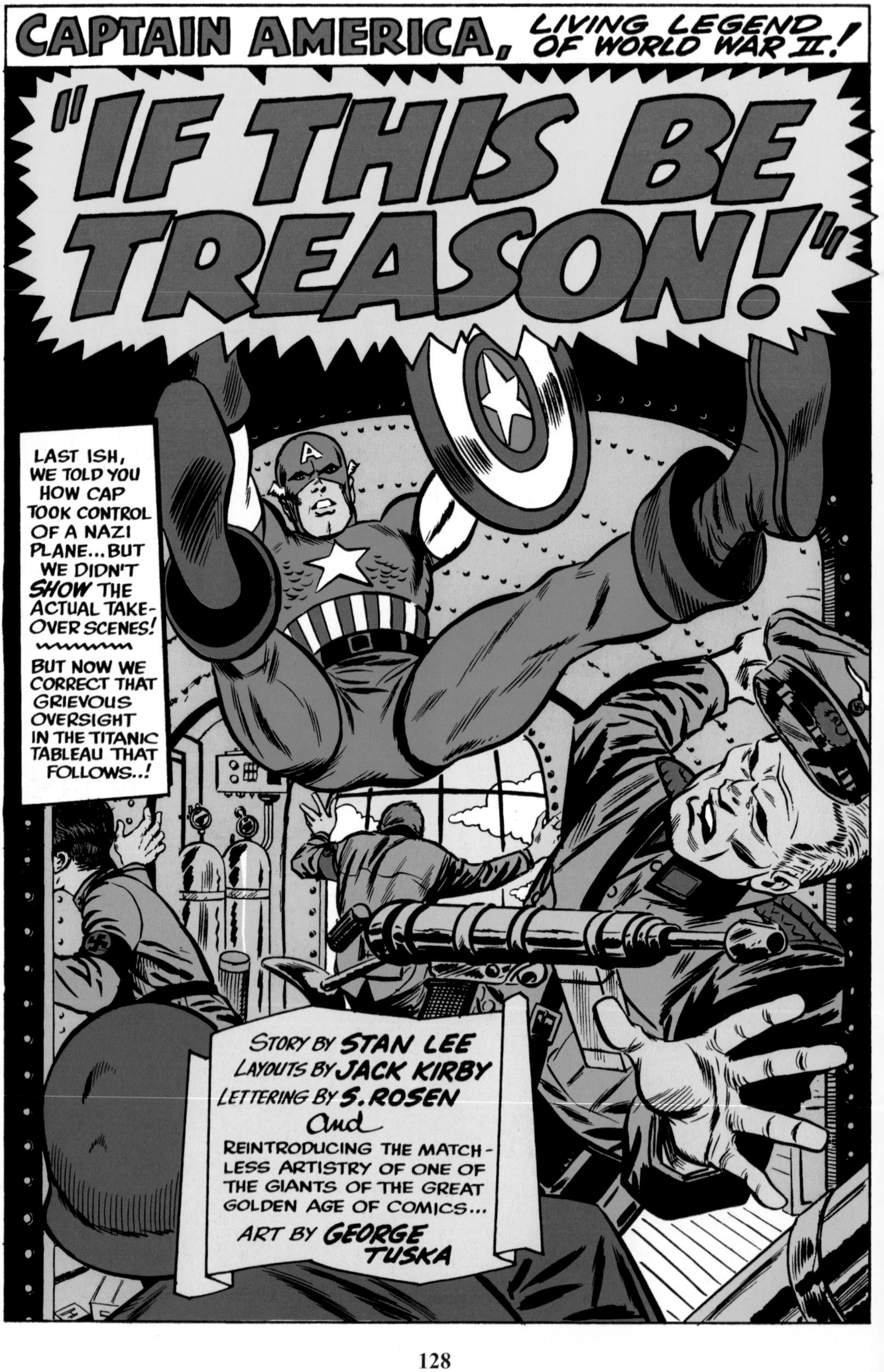
CAPTAIN AMERICA, LIVING LEGEND OF WORLD WAR II!
"IF THIS BE TREASON!"
LAST ISH, WE TOLD YOU HOW CAP TOOK CONTROL OF A NAZI PLANE... BUT WE DIDN'T SHOW THE ACTUAL TAKE-OVER SCENES!
BUT NOW WE CORRECT THAT GRIEVOUS OVERSIGHT IN THE TITANIC TABLEAU THAT FOLLOWS..!
STORY BY STAN LEE
LAYOUTS BY JACK KIRBY
LETTERING BY S. ROSEN
and
REINTRODUCING THE MATCHLESS ARTISTRY OF ONE OF THE GIANTS OF THE GREAT GOLDEN AGE OF COMICS...
ART BY GEORGE TUSKA

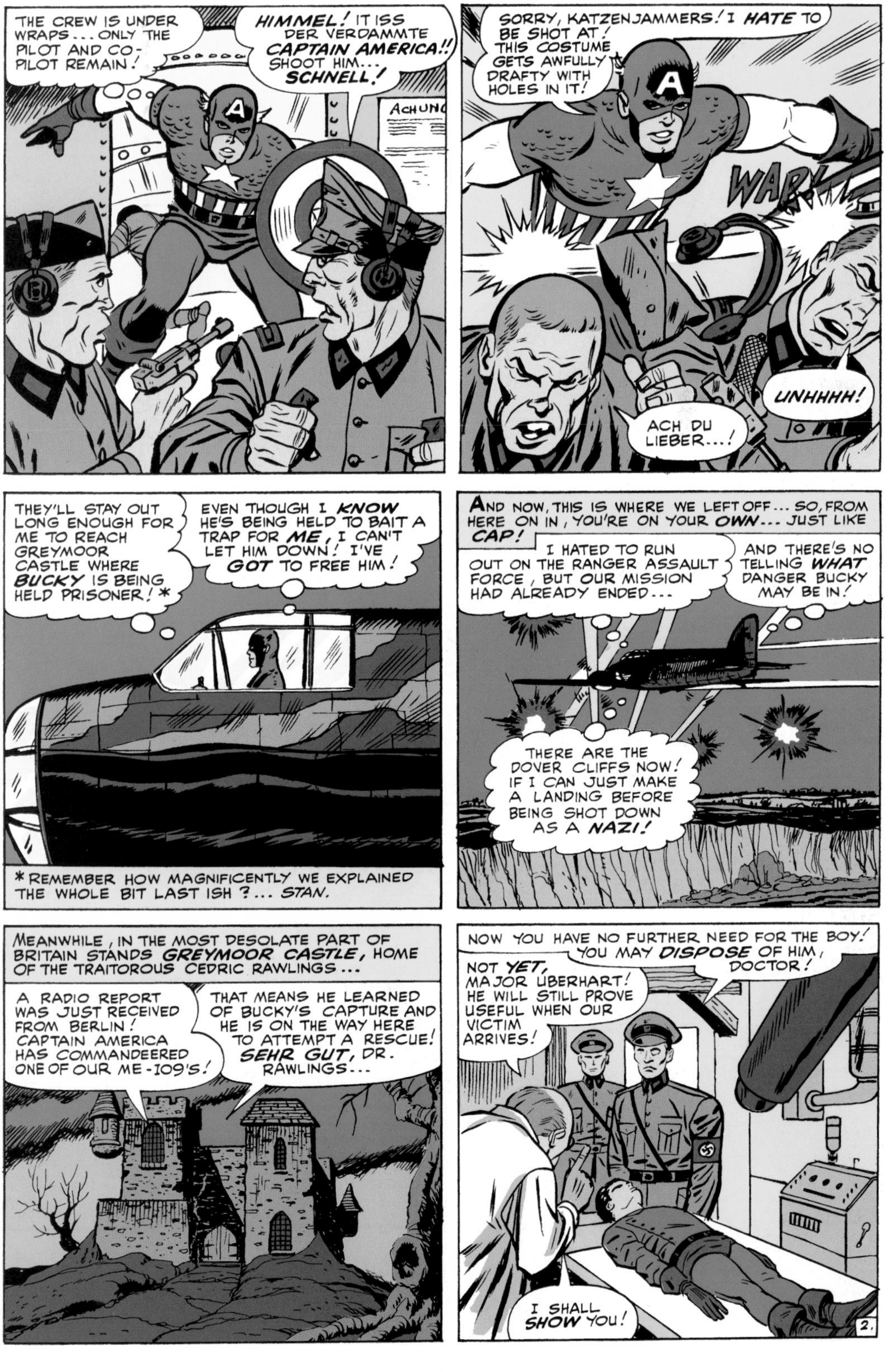
THE CREW IS UNDER WRAPS... ONLY THE PILOT AND CO-PILOT REMAIN!
HIMMEL! IT ISS DER VERDAMMTE CAPTAIN AMERICA!! SHOOT HIM... SCHNELL!
ACHUNG
SORRY, KATZENJAMMERS! I HATE TO BE SHOT AT! THIS COSTUME GETS AWFULLY DRAFTY WITH HOLES IN IT!
WAP!
UNHHHH!
ACH DU LIEBER...!
THEY'LL STAY OUT LONG ENOUGH FOR ME TO REACH GREYMOOR CASTLE WHERE BUCKY IS BEING HELD PRISONER! *
EVEN THOUGH I KNOW HE'S BEING HELD TO BAIT A TRAP FOR ME, I CAN'T LET HIM DOWN! I'VE GOT TO FREE HIM!
* REMEMBER HOW MAGNIFICENTLY WE EXPLAINED THE WHOLE BIT LAST ISH?... STAN.
AND NOW, THIS IS WHERE WE LEFT OFF... SO, FROM HERE ON IN, YOU'RE ON YOUR OWN... JUST LIKE CAP!
I HATED TO RUN OUT ON THE RANGER ASSAULT FORCE, BUT OUR MISSION HAD ALREADY ENDED...
AND THERE'S NO TELLING WHAT DANGER BUCKY MAY BE IN!
THERE ARE THE DOVER CLIFFS NOW! IF I CAN JUST MAKE A LANDING BEFORE BEING SHOT DOWN AS A NAZI!
MEANWHILE, IN THE MOST DESOLATE PART OF BRITAIN STANDS GREYMOOR CASTLE, HOME OF THE TRAITOROUS CEDRIC RAWLINGS...
A RADIO REPORT WAS JUST RECEIVED FROM BERLIN! CAPTAIN AMERICA HAS COMMANDEERED ONE OF OUR ME-109'S!
THAT MEANS HE LEARNED OF BUCKY'S CAPTURE AND HE IS ON THE WAY HERE TO ATTEMPT A RESCUE! SEHR GUT, DR. RAWLINGS...
NOW YOU HAVE NO FURTHER NEED FOR THE BOY! YOU MAY DISPOSE OF HIM, DOCTOR!
NOT YET, MAJOR UBERHART! HE WILL STILL PROVE USEFUL WHEN OUR VICTIM ARRIVES!
I SHALL SHOW YOU!
2.

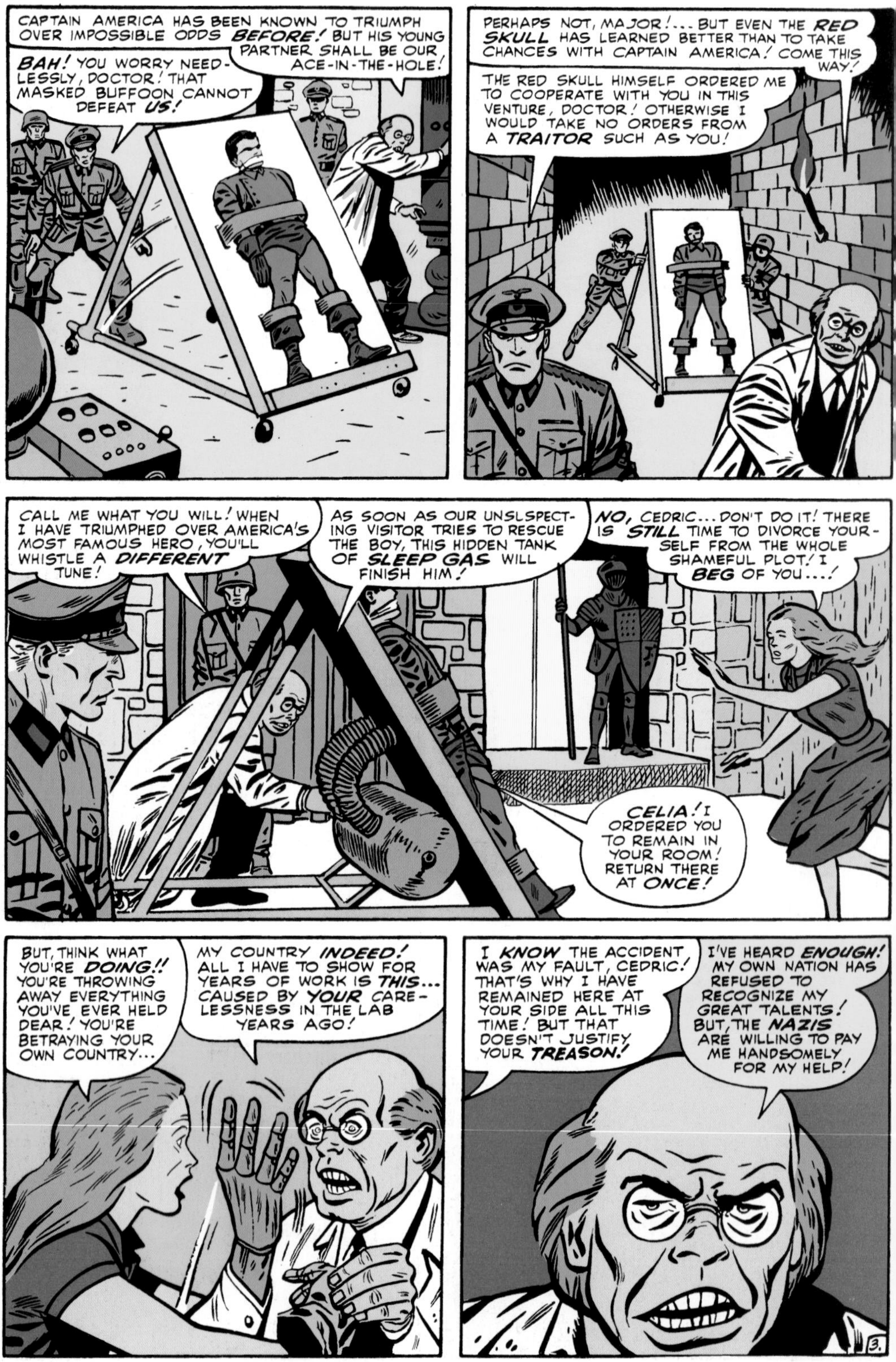
CAPTAIN AMERICA HAS BEEN KNOWN TO TRIUMPH OVER IMPOSSIBLE ODDS BEFORE! BUT HIS YOUNG PARTNER SHALL BE OUR ACE-IN-THE-HOLE!
BAH! YOU WORRY NEEDLESSLY, DOCTOR! THAT MASKED BUFFOON CANNOT DEFEAT US!
PERHAPS NOT, MAJOR!... BUT EVEN THE RED SKULL HAS LEARNED BETTER THAN TO TAKE CHANCES WITH CAPTAIN AMERICA! COME THIS WAY!
THE RED SKULL HIMSELF ORDERED ME TO COOPERATE WITH YOU IN THIS VENTURE, DOCTOR! OTHERWISE I WOULD TAKE NO ORDERS FROM A TRAITOR SUCH AS YOU!
CALL ME WHAT YOU WILL! WHEN I HAVE TRIUMPHED OVER AMERICA'S MOST FAMOUS HERO, YOU'LL WHISTLE A DIFFERENT TUNE!
AS SOON AS OUR UNSLSPECTING VISITOR TRIES TO RESCUE THE BOY, THIS HIDDEN TANK OF SLEEP GAS WILL FINISH HIM!
NO, CEDRIC... DON'T DO IT! THERE IS STILL TIME TO DIVORCE YOURSELF FROM THE WHOLE SHAMEFUL PLOT! I BEG OF YOU...!
CELIA! I ORDERED YOU TO REMAIN IN YOUR ROOM! RETURN THERE AT ONCE!
BUT, THINK WHAT YOU'RE DOING!! YOU'RE THROWING AWAY EVERYTHING YOU'VE EVER HELD DEAR! YOU'RE BETRAYING YOUR OWN COUNTRY...
MY COUNTRY INDEED! ALL I HAVE TO SHOW FOR YEARS OF WORK IS THIS... CAUSED BY YOUR CARELESSNESS IN THE LAB YEARS AGO!
I KNOW THE ACCIDENT WAS MY FAULT, CEDRIC! THAT'S WHY I HAVE REMAINED HERE AT YOUR SIDE ALL THIS TIME! BUT THAT DOESN'T JUSTIFY YOUR TREASON!
I'VE HEARD ENOUGH! MY OWN NATION HAS REFUSED TO RECOGNIZE MY GREAT TALENTS! BUT, THE NAZIS ARE WILLING TO PAY ME HANDSOMELY FOR MY HELP!
3.

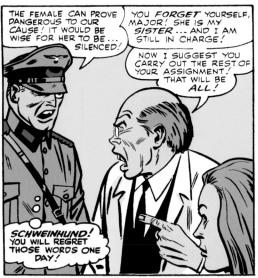

THE FEMALE CAN PROVE DANGEROUS TO OUR CAUSE! IT WOULD BE WISE FOR HER TO BE... SILENCED!

YOU *FORGET* YOURSELF, MAJOR! SHE IS MY *SISTER*... AND I AM STILL IN CHARGE!

NOW I SUGGEST YOU CARRY OUT THE REST OF YOUR ASSIGNMENT! THAT WILL BE *ALL!*

SCHWEINHUND! YOU WILL REGRET THOSE WORDS ONE DAY!

MINUTES LATER, MAJOR UBERHART BROADCASTS A RADIO MESSAGE OVER A SPECIAL FREQUENCY...

ACHTUNG, CAPTAIN AMERICA..!

IF YOU WISH TO SEE THE ONE YOU CALL *BUCKY* ALIVE AGAIN, YOU WILL FLY THE PLANE YOU HAVE SEIZED TO GREYMOOR CASTLE WITHIN THE HOUR!

SO! I SHALL NOW BROADCAST THE EXACT COORDINATES TO YOU..!

QUICKLY, MAJOR... BEFORE BRITISH INTELLIGENCE DISCOVERS OUR WAVE-LENGTH!

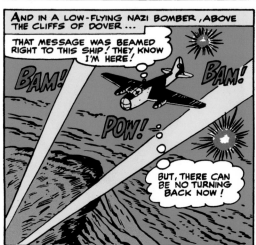

AND IN A LOW-FLYING NAZI BOMBER, ABOVE THE CLIFFS OF DOVER...

THAT MESSAGE WAS BEAMED RIGHT TO THIS SHIP! THEY KNOW I'M HERE!

BAM! BAM! POW!

BUT, THERE CAN BE NO TURNING BACK NOW!

AND THEN, SUDDENLY...

BRITISH *NIGHT FIGHTERS,...* ATTACKING ME! NO TIME TO EXPLAIN! I'VE GOT TO OUT-MANEUVER THEM!

WITH THE SKILL AND DARING WHICH HAVE MADE HIS NAME A HOUSEHOLD WORD THROUGHOUT THE WORLD, CAPTAIN AMERICA HEDGE-HOPS, SKIMS OVER ROOFTOPS... BETWEEN BARRAGE BALLOONS ...UNDER BRIDGES... UNTIL AT LAST...

I'VE *LOST* THEM! NOW, I'VE JUST ENOUGH FUEL LEFT TO REACH GREYMOOR CASTLE!

THUS, FOLLOWING THE COORDINATES HE HAD BEEN GIVEN BY THE NAZI, CAP BRINGS HIS PLANE DOWN ON A MAKESHIFT FIELD, HEWN BETWEEN A TANGLED FOREST OF GNARLED, ANCIENT TREES...

I *MADE* IT! BUT THE MOST DANGEROUS PART STILL LIES AHEAD!

THEY KNOW WHAT TO EXPECT...WHILE *I* DON'T!

4.

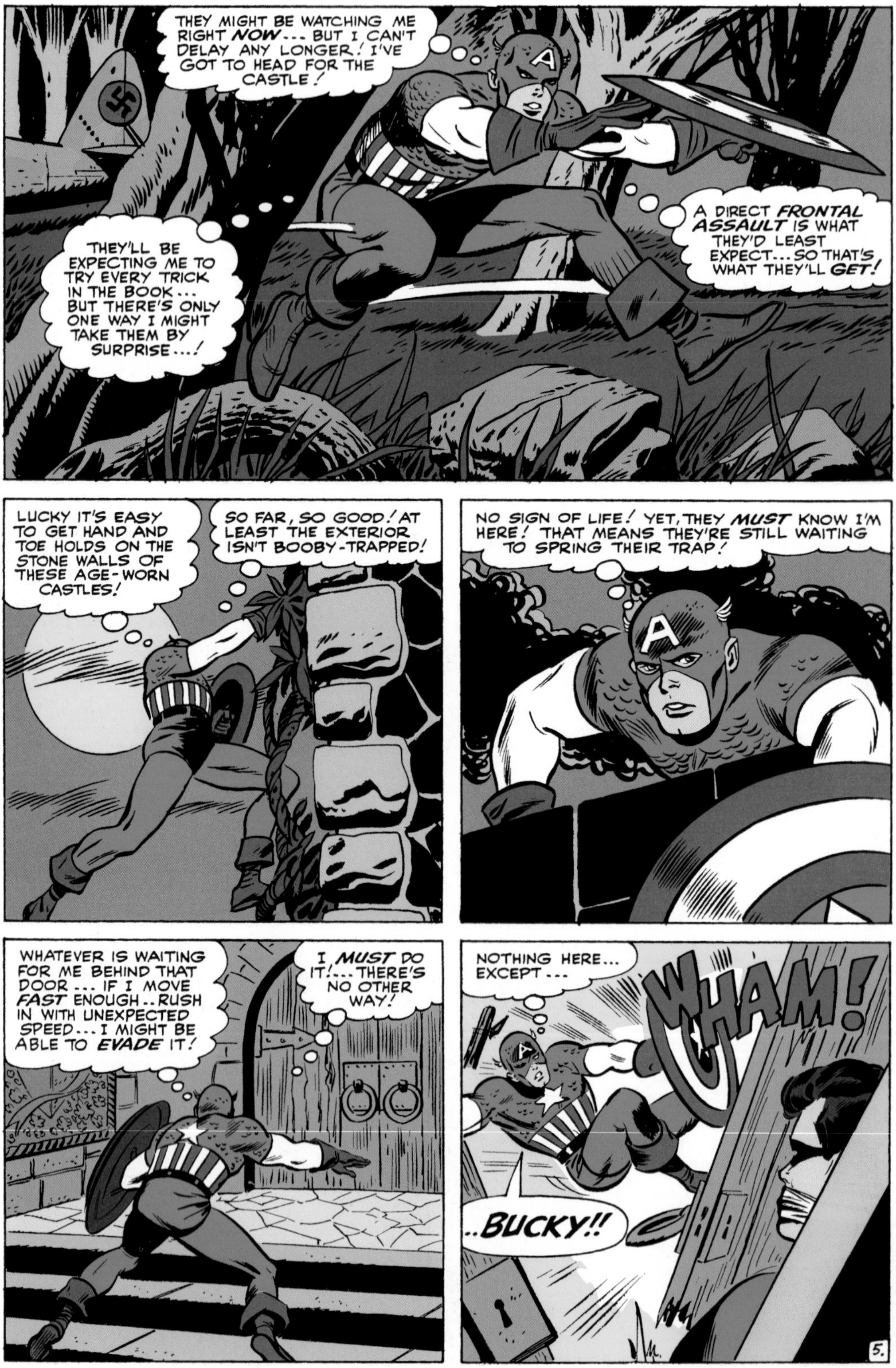
THEY MIGHT BE WATCHING ME RIGHT NOW... BUT I CAN'T DELAY ANY LONGER! I'VE GOT TO HEAD FOR THE CASTLE!
THEY'LL BE EXPECTING ME TO TRY EVERY TRICK IN THE BOOK... BUT THERE'S ONLY ONE WAY I MIGHT TAKE THEM BY SURPRISE...!
A DIRECT FRONTAL ASSAULT IS WHAT THEY'D LEAST EXPECT... SO THAT'S WHAT THEY'LL GET!
LUCKY IT'S EASY TO GET HAND AND TOE HOLDS ON THE STONE WALLS OF THESE AGE-WORN CASTLES!
SO FAR, SO GOOD! AT LEAST THE EXTERIOR ISN'T BOOBY-TRAPPED!
NO SIGN OF LIFE! YET, THEY MUST KNOW I'M HERE! THAT MEANS THEY'RE STILL WAITING TO SPRING THEIR TRAP!
WHATEVER IS WAITING FOR ME BEHIND THAT DOOR... IF I MOVE FAST ENOUGH.. RUSH IN WITH UNEXPECTED SPEED... I MIGHT BE ABLE TO EVADE IT!
I MUST DO IT!... THERE'S NO OTHER WAY!
NOTHING HERE... EXCEPT...
WHAM!
..BUCKY!!
5.

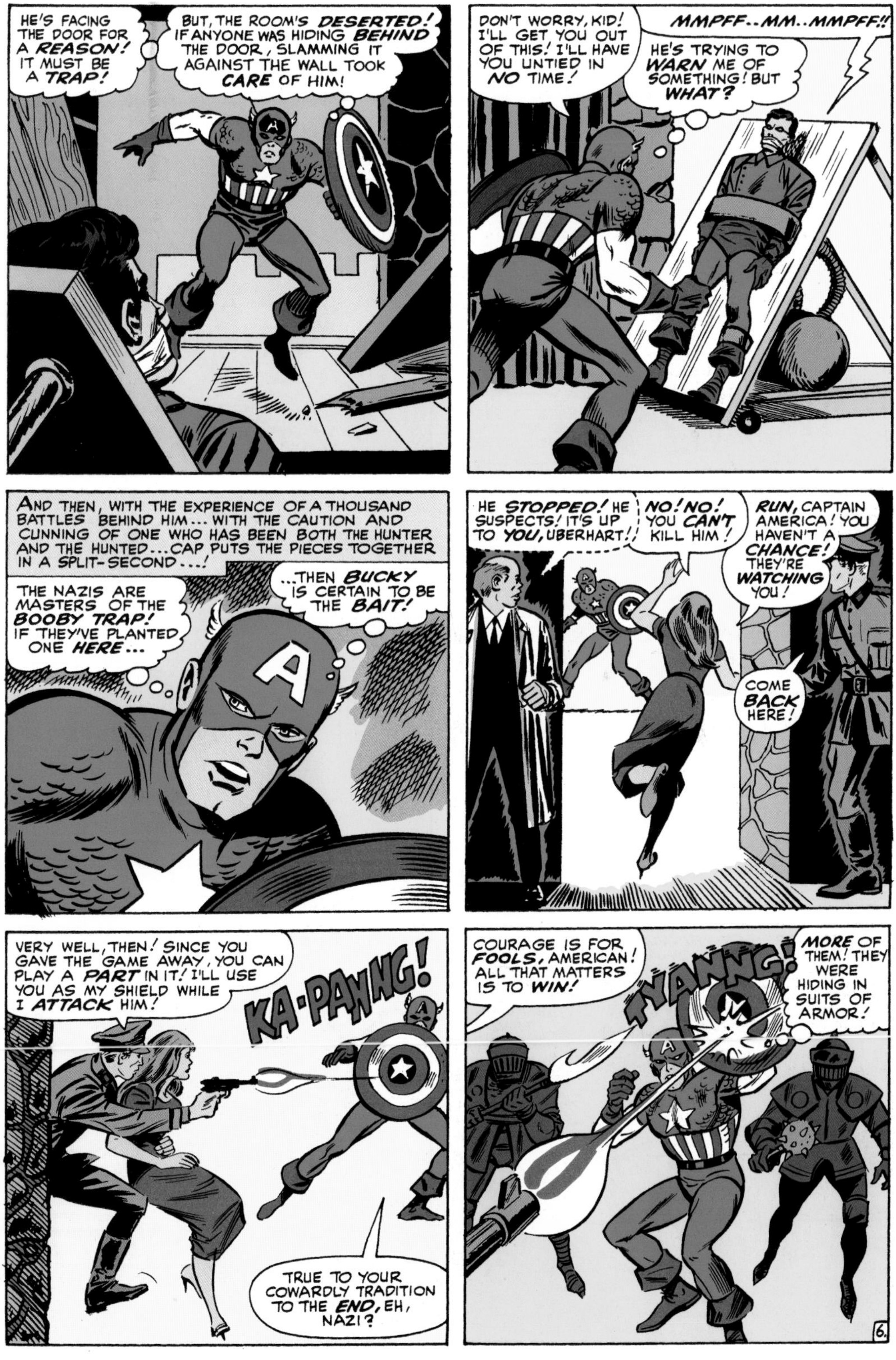
HE'S FACING THE DOOR FOR A REASON! IT MUST BE A TRAP!
BUT, THE ROOM'S DESERTED! IF ANYONE WAS HIDING BEHIND THE DOOR, SLAMMING IT AGAINST THE WALL TOOK CARE OF HIM!
DON'T WORRY, KID! I'LL GET YOU OUT OF THIS! I'LL HAVE YOU UNTIED IN NO TIME!
MMPFF..MM..MMPFF!!
HE'S TRYING TO WARN ME OF SOMETHING! BUT WHAT?
AND THEN, WITH THE EXPERIENCE OF A THOUSAND BATTLES BEHIND HIM... WITH THE CAUTION AND CUNNING OF ONE WHO HAS BEEN BOTH THE HUNTER AND THE HUNTED... CAP PUTS THE PIECES TOGETHER IN A SPLIT-SECOND...!
THE NAZIS ARE MASTERS OF THE BOOBY TRAP! IF THEY'VE PLANTED ONE HERE...
...THEN BUCKY IS CERTAIN TO BE THE BAIT!
HE STOPPED! HE SUSPECTS! IT'S UP TO YOU, UBERHART!
NO! NO! YOU CAN'T KILL HIM!
RUN, CAPTAIN AMERICA! YOU HAVEN'T A CHANCE! THEY'RE WATCHING YOU!
COME BACK HERE!
VERY WELL, THEN! SINCE YOU GAVE THE GAME AWAY, YOU CAN PLAY A PART IN IT! I'LL USE YOU AS MY SHIELD WHILE I ATTACK HIM!
KA-PANNG!
TRUE TO YOUR COWARDLY TRADITION TO THE END, EH, NAZI?
COURAGE IS FOR FOOLS, AMERICAN! ALL THAT MATTERS IS TO WIN!
TYANNG!
MORE OF THEM! THEY WERE HIDING IN SUITS OF ARMOR!
6.

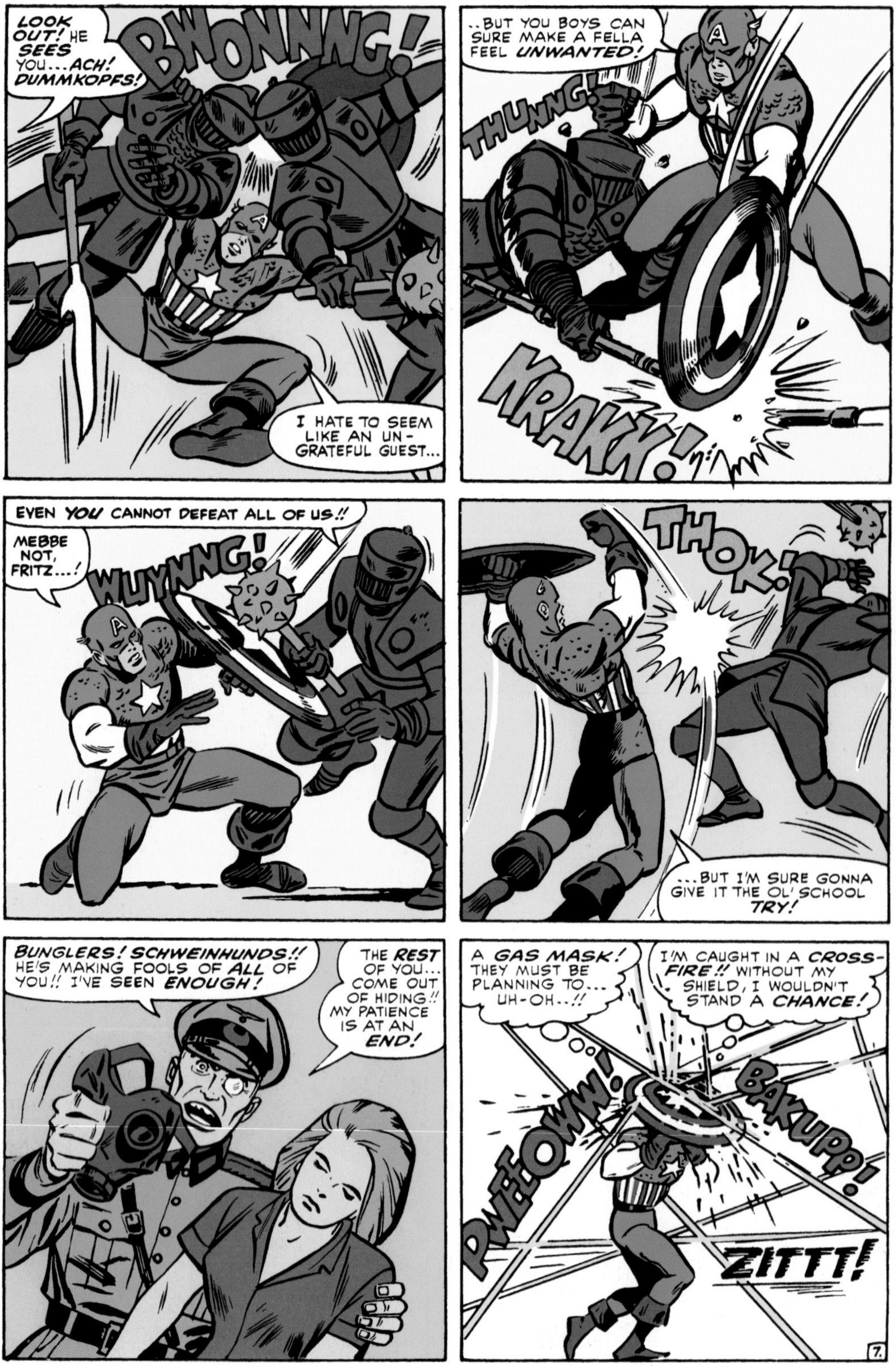
LOOK OUT! HE SEES YOU...ACH! DUMMKOPFS!
BWONNNG!
I HATE TO SEEM LIKE AN UN-GRATEFUL GUEST...
..BUT YOU BOYS CAN SURE MAKE A FELLA FEEL UNWANTED!
THUNNG!
KRAKK!
EVEN YOU CANNOT DEFEAT ALL OF US!!
MEBBE NOT, FRITZ...!
WUYNNG!
THOK!
...BUT I'M SURE GONNA GIVE IT THE OL' SCHOOL TRY!
BUNGLERS! SCHWEINHUNDS!! HE'S MAKING FOOLS OF ALL OF YOU!! I'VE SEEN ENOUGH!
THE REST OF YOU... COME OUT OF HIDING!! MY PATIENCE IS AT AN END!
A GAS MASK! THEY MUST BE PLANNING TO... UH-OH..!!
I'M CAUGHT IN A CROSS-FIRE!! WITHOUT MY SHIELD, I WOULDN'T STAND A CHANCE!
PWEEOWW!
BAKUPP!
ZITTT!
7.

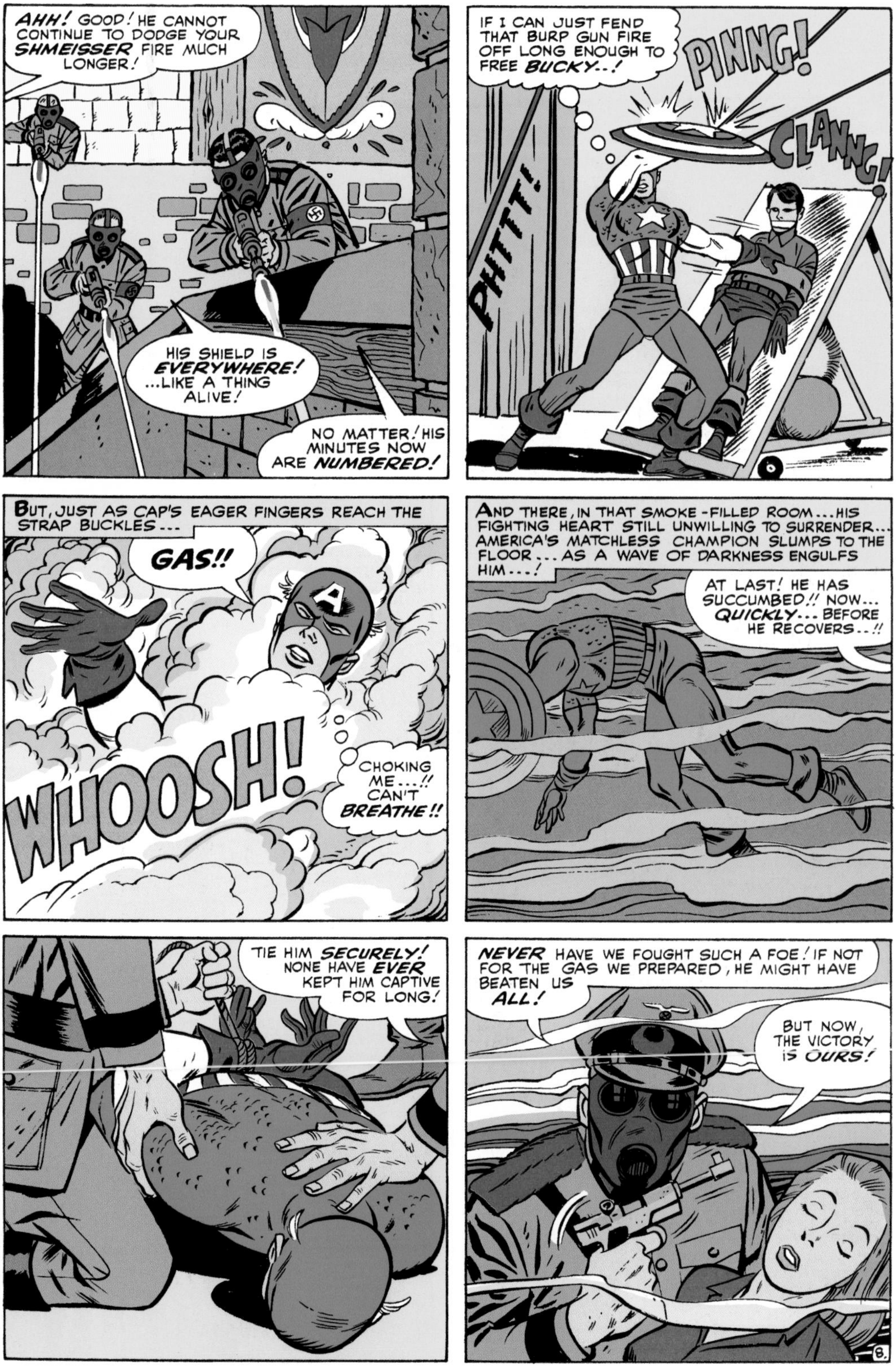
AHH! GOOD! HE CANNOT CONTINUE TO DODGE YOUR SHMEISSER FIRE MUCH LONGER!
HIS SHIELD IS EVERYWHERE! ...LIKE A THING ALIVE!
NO MATTER! HIS MINUTES NOW ARE NUMBERED!
IF I CAN JUST FEND THAT BURP GUN FIRE OFF LONG ENOUGH TO FREE BUCKY..!
PINNG!
CLANNG!
PHTTTT!
BUT, JUST AS CAP'S EAGER FINGERS REACH THE STRAP BUCKLES...
GAS!!
WHOOSH!
CHOKING ME...!! CAN'T BREATHE!!
AND THERE, IN THAT SMOKE-FILLED ROOM...HIS FIGHTING HEART STILL UNWILLING TO SURRENDER... AMERICA'S MATCHLESS CHAMPION SLUMPS TO THE FLOOR... AS A WAVE OF DARKNESS ENGULFS HIM...!
AT LAST! HE HAS SUCCUMBED!! NOW... QUICKLY... BEFORE HE RECOVERS..!!
TIE HIM SECURELY! NONE HAVE EVER KEPT HIM CAPTIVE FOR LONG!
NEVER HAVE WE FOUGHT SUCH A FOE! IF NOT FOR THE GAS WE PREPARED, HE MIGHT HAVE BEATEN US ALL!
BUT NOW, THE VICTORY IS OURS!
8.

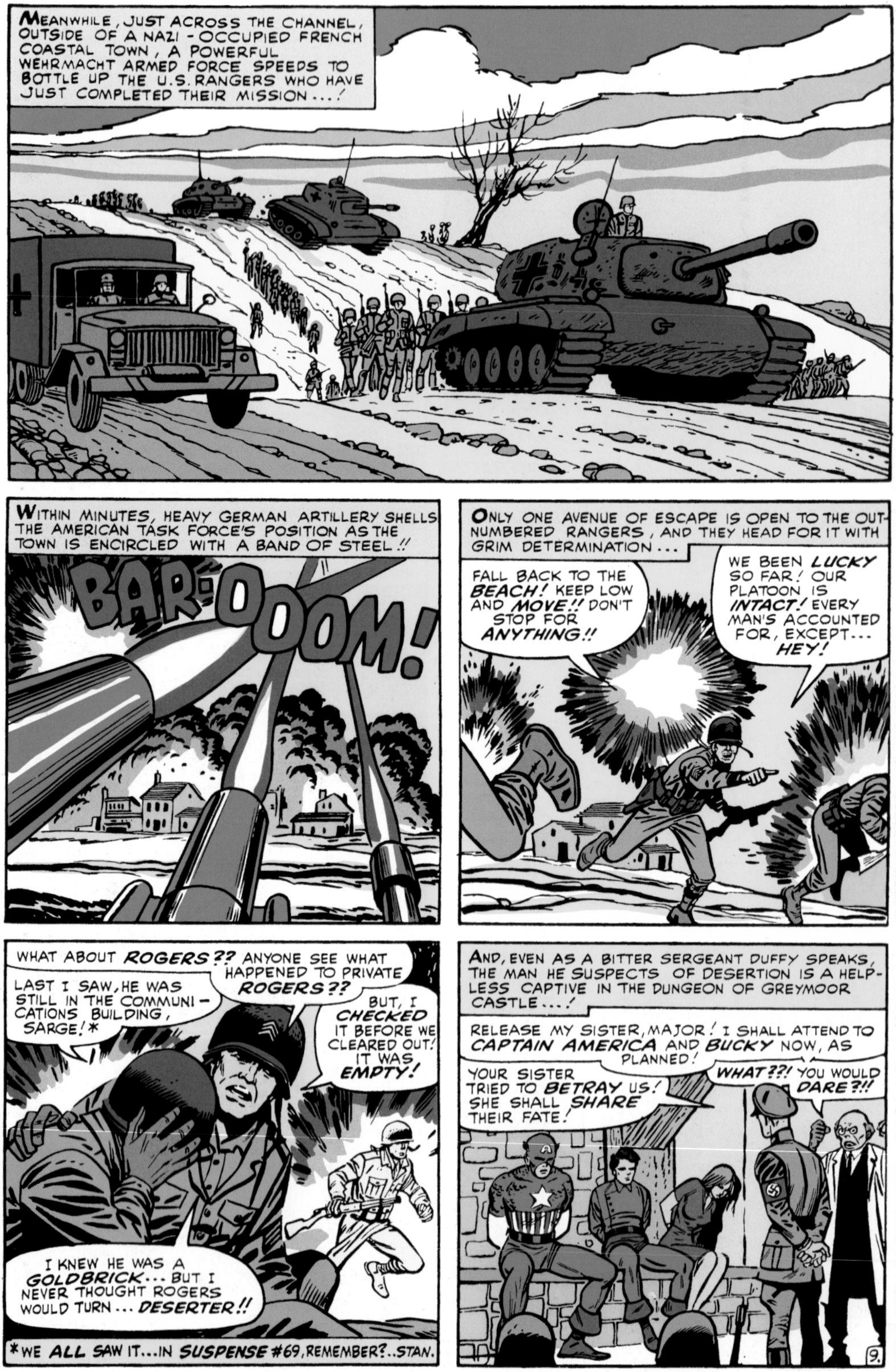
MEANWHILE, JUST ACROSS THE CHANNEL, OUTSIDE OF A NAZI - OCCUPIED FRENCH COASTAL TOWN, A POWERFUL WEHRMACHT ARMED FORCE SPEEDS TO BOTTLE UP THE U.S. RANGERS WHO HAVE JUST COMPLETED THEIR MISSION...!
WITHIN MINUTES, HEAVY GERMAN ARTILLERY SHELLS THE AMERICAN TASK FORCE'S POSITION AS THE TOWN IS ENCIRCLED WITH A BAND OF STEEL!!
BAR-OOOM!
ONLY ONE AVENUE OF ESCAPE IS OPEN TO THE OUT-NUMBERED RANGERS, AND THEY HEAD FOR IT WITH GRIM DETERMINATION...
FALL BACK TO THE BEACH! KEEP LOW AND MOVE!! DON'T STOP FOR ANYTHING!!
WE BEEN LUCKY SO FAR! OUR PLATOON IS INTACT! EVERY MAN'S ACCOUNTED FOR, EXCEPT--- HEY!
WHAT ABOUT ROGERS?? ANYONE SEE WHAT HAPPENED TO PRIVATE ROGERS??
LAST I SAW, HE WAS STILL IN THE COMMUNI-CATIONS BUILDING, SARGE!*
BUT, I CHECKED IT BEFORE WE CLEARED OUT! IT WAS EMPTY!
I KNEW HE WAS A GOLDBRICK... BUT I NEVER THOUGHT ROGERS WOULD TURN... DESERTER!!
*WE ALL SAW IT...IN SUSPENSE #69, REMEMBER?..STAN.
AND, EVEN AS A BITTER SERGEANT DUFFY SPEAKS, THE MAN HE SUSPECTS OF DESERTION IS A HELP-LESS CAPTIVE IN THE DUNGEON OF GREYMOOR CASTLE...!
RELEASE MY SISTER, MAJOR! I SHALL ATTEND TO CAPTAIN AMERICA AND BUCKY NOW, AS PLANNED!
YOUR SISTER TRIED TO BETRAY US! SHE SHALL SHARE THEIR FATE!
WHAT??! YOU WOULD DARE?!!
9.

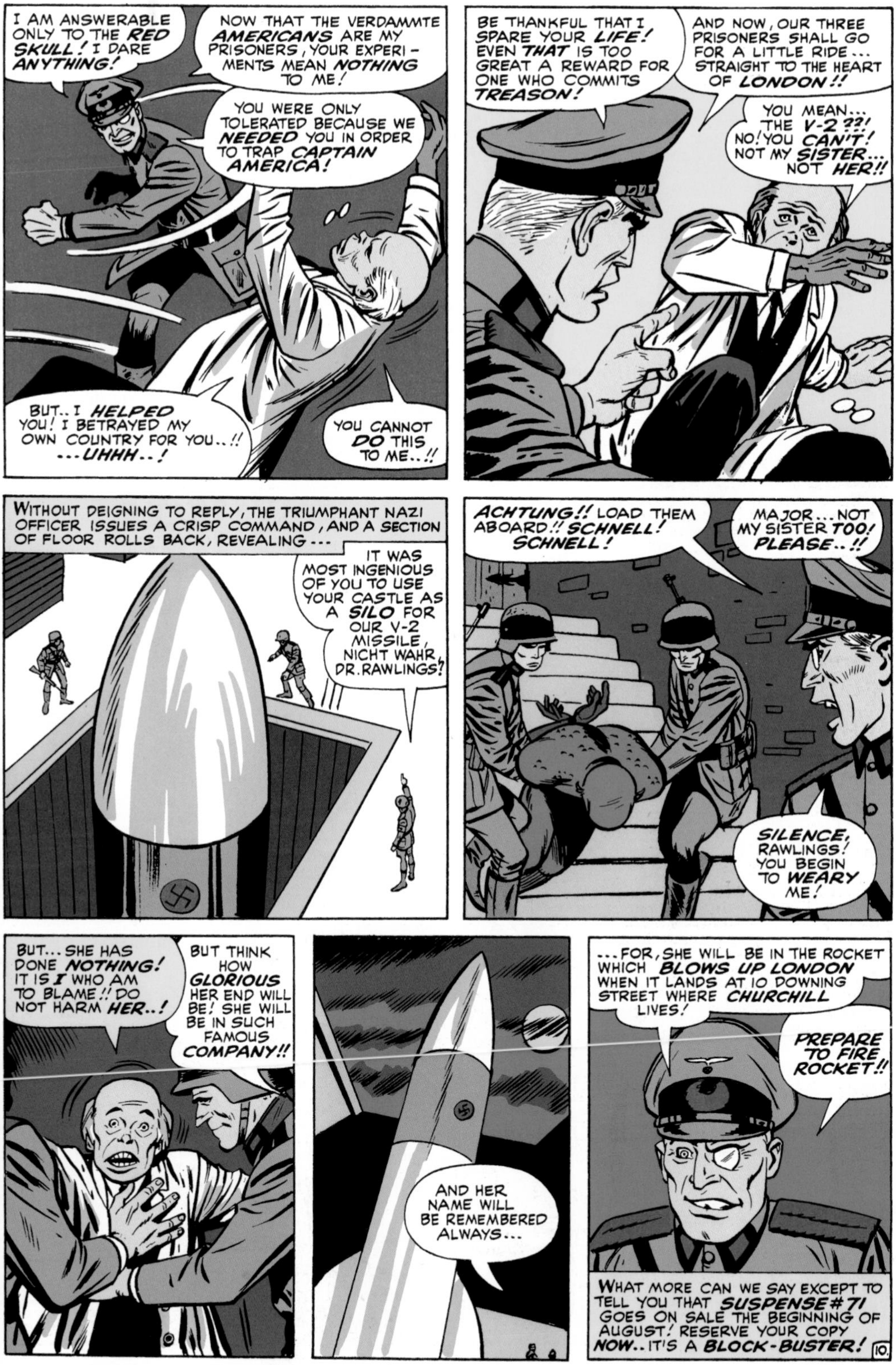
I AM ANSWERABLE ONLY TO THE RED SKULL! I DARE ANYTHING!
NOW THAT THE VERDAMMTE AMERICANS ARE MY PRISONERS, YOUR EXPERIMENTS MEAN NOTHING TO ME!
YOU WERE ONLY TOLERATED BECAUSE WE NEEDED YOU IN ORDER TO TRAP CAPTAIN AMERICA!
BUT.. I HELPED YOU! I BETRAYED MY OWN COUNTRY FOR YOU..!! ...UHHH..!
YOU CANNOT DO THIS TO ME..!!
BE THANKFUL THAT I SPARE YOUR LIFE! EVEN THAT IS TOO GREAT A REWARD FOR ONE WHO COMMITS TREASON!
AND NOW, OUR THREE PRISONERS SHALL GO FOR A LITTLE RIDE... STRAIGHT TO THE HEART OF LONDON!!
YOU MEAN... THE V-2 ??! NO! YOU CAN'T! NOT MY SISTER... NOT HER!!
WITHOUT DEIGNING TO REPLY, THE TRIUMPHANT NAZI OFFICER ISSUES A CRISP COMMAND, AND A SECTION OF FLOOR ROLLS BACK, REVEALING ---
IT WAS MOST INGENIOUS OF YOU TO USE YOUR CASTLE AS A SILO FOR OUR V-2 MISSILE, NICHT WAHR, DR. RAWLINGS?
ACHTUNG!! LOAD THEM ABOARD!! SCHNELL! SCHNELL!
MAJOR... NOT MY SISTER TOO! PLEASE..!!
SILENCE, RAWLINGS! YOU BEGIN TO WEARY ME!
BUT... SHE HAS DONE NOTHING! IT IS I WHO AM TO BLAME!! DO NOT HARM HER..!
BUT THINK HOW GLORIOUS HER END WILL BE! SHE WILL BE IN SUCH FAMOUS COMPANY!!
AND HER NAME WILL BE REMEMBERED ALWAYS...
...FOR, SHE WILL BE IN THE ROCKET WHICH BLOWS UP LONDON WHEN IT LANDS AT 10 DOWNING STREET WHERE CHURCHILL LIVES!
PREPARE TO FIRE ROCKET!!
WHAT MORE CAN WE SAY EXCEPT TO TELL YOU THAT SUSPENSE #71 GOES ON SALE THE BEGINNING OF AUGUST! RESERVE YOUR COPY NOW.. IT'S A BLOCK-BUSTER!
10.

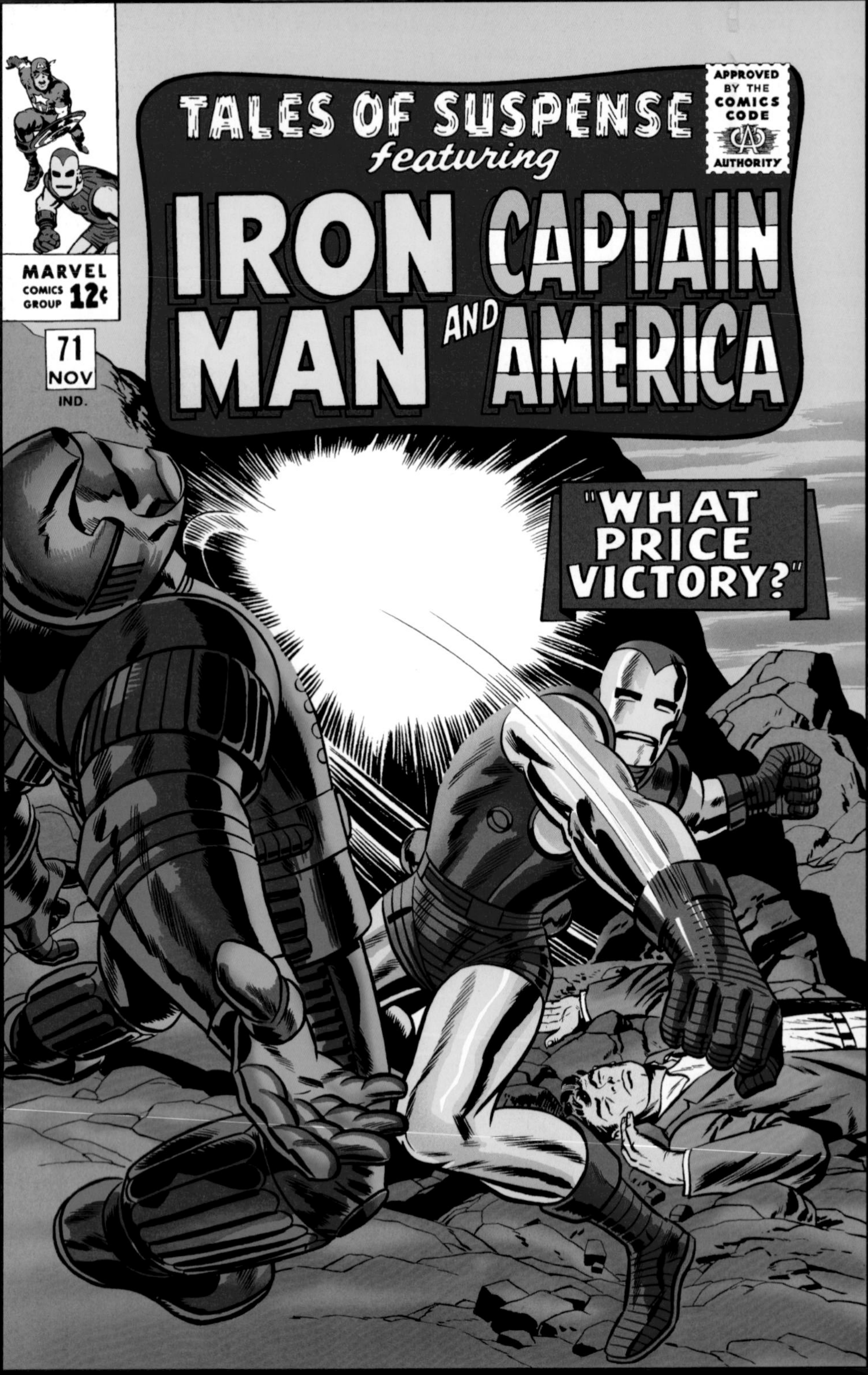
TALES OF SUSPENSE
featuring
IRON MAN AND CAPTAIN AMERICA
APPROVED BY THE COMICS CODE AUTHORITY
MARVEL COMICS GROUP 12¢
71 NOV
IND.
"WHAT PRICE VICTORY?"

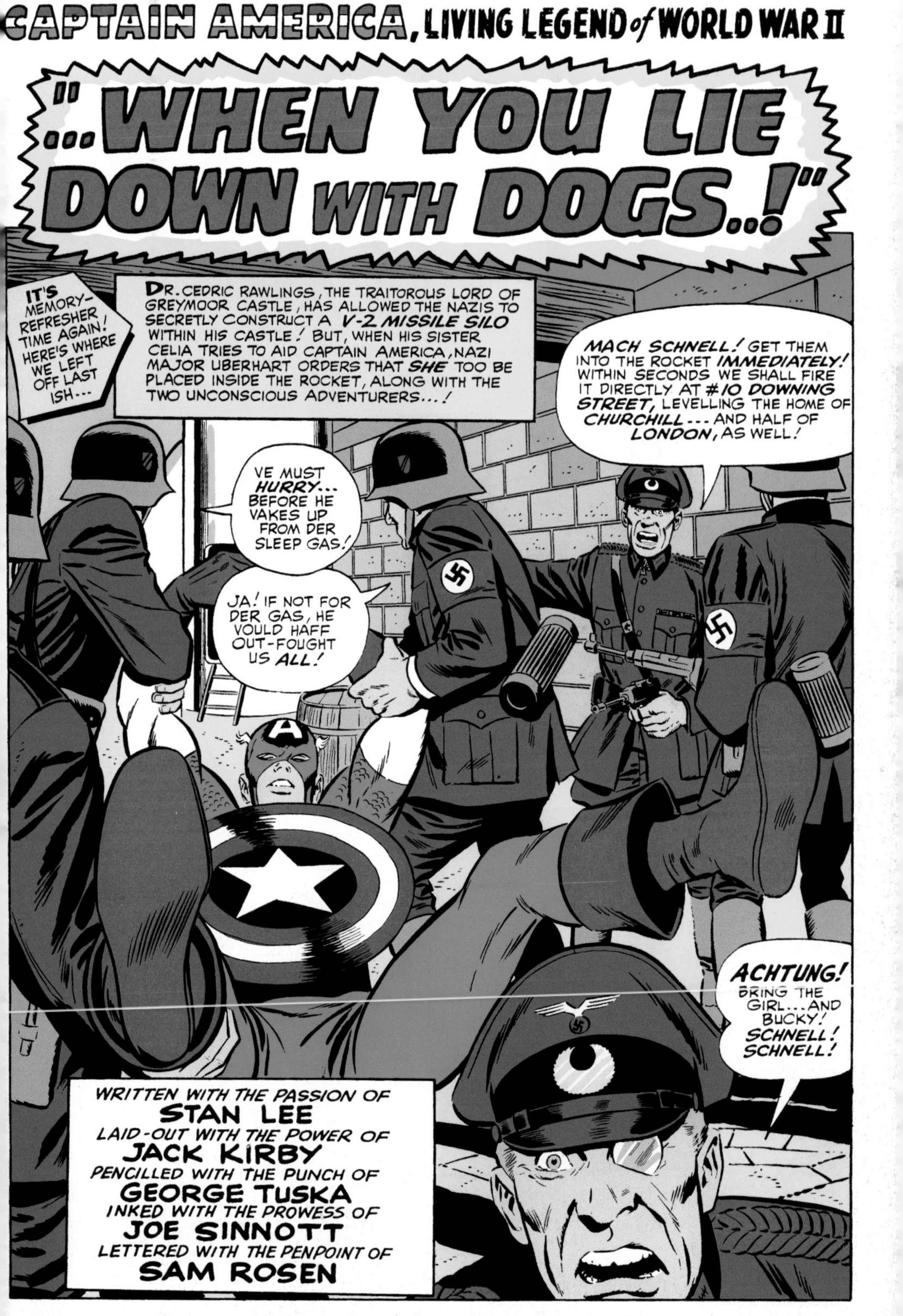

CAPTAIN AMERICA, LIVING LEGEND of WORLD WAR II
"...WHEN YOU LIE DOWN WITH DOGS..!"
IT'S MEMORY-REFRESHER TIME AGAIN! HERE'S WHERE WE LEFT OFF LAST ISH---
DR. CEDRIC RAWLINGS, THE TRAITOROUS LORD OF GREYMOOR CASTLE, HAS ALLOWED THE NAZIS TO SECRETLY CONSTRUCT A V-2 MISSILE SILO WITHIN HIS CASTLE! BUT, WHEN HIS SISTER CELIA TRIES TO AID CAPTAIN AMERICA, NAZI MAJOR UBERHART ORDERS THAT SHE TOO BE PLACED INSIDE THE ROCKET, ALONG WITH THE TWO UNCONSCIOUS ADVENTURERS...!
MACH SCHNELL! GET THEM INTO THE ROCKET IMMEDIATELY! WITHIN SECONDS WE SHALL FIRE IT DIRECTLY AT #10 DOWNING STREET, LEVELLING THE HOME OF CHURCHILL... AND HALF OF LONDON, AS WELL!
VE MUST HURRY... BEFORE HE VAKES UP FROM DER SLEEP GAS!
JA! IF NOT FOR DER GAS, HE VOULD HAFF OUT-FOUGHT US ALL!
ACHTUNG! BRING THE GIRL... AND BUCKY! SCHNELL! SCHNELL!
WRITTEN WITH THE PASSION OF STAN LEE
LAID-OUT WITH THE POWER OF JACK KIRBY
PENCILLED WITH THE PUNCH OF GEORGE TUSKA
INKED WITH THE PROWESS OF JOE SINNOTT
LETTERED WITH THE PENPOINT OF SAM ROSEN

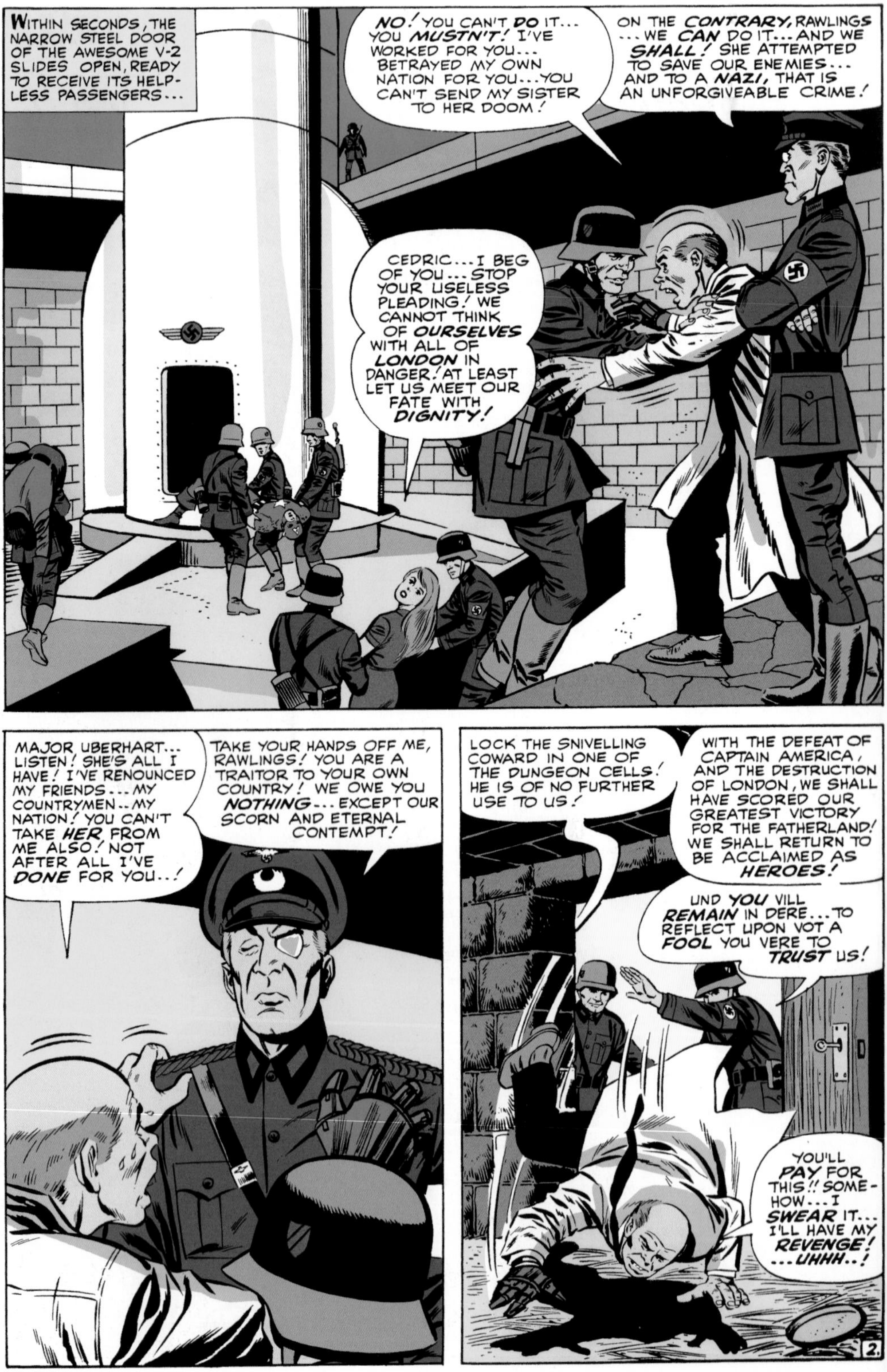
WITHIN SECONDS, THE NARROW STEEL DOOR OF THE AWESOME V-2 SLIDES OPEN, READY TO RECEIVE ITS HELP-LESS PASSENGERS...
NO! YOU CAN'T DO IT... YOU MUSTN'T! I'VE WORKED FOR YOU... BETRAYED MY OWN NATION FOR YOU...YOU CAN'T SEND MY SISTER TO HER DOOM!
ON THE CONTRARY, RAWLINGS ...WE CAN DO IT...AND WE SHALL! SHE ATTEMPTED TO SAVE OUR ENEMIES... AND TO A NAZI, THAT IS AN UNFORGIVEABLE CRIME!
CEDRIC...I BEG OF YOU... STOP YOUR USELESS PLEADING! WE CANNOT THINK OF OURSELVES WITH ALL OF LONDON IN DANGER! AT LEAST LET US MEET OUR FATE WITH DIGNITY!
MAJOR UBERHART... LISTEN! SHE'S ALL I HAVE! I'VE RENOUNCED MY FRIENDS...MY COUNTRYMEN...MY NATION! YOU CAN'T TAKE HER FROM ME ALSO! NOT AFTER ALL I'VE DONE FOR YOU...!
TAKE YOUR HANDS OFF ME, RAWLINGS! YOU ARE A TRAITOR TO YOUR OWN COUNTRY! WE OWE YOU NOTHING... EXCEPT OUR SCORN AND ETERNAL CONTEMPT!
LOCK THE SNIVELLING COWARD IN ONE OF THE DUNGEON CELLS! HE IS OF NO FURTHER USE TO US!
WITH THE DEFEAT OF CAPTAIN AMERICA, AND THE DESTRUCTION OF LONDON, WE SHALL HAVE SCORED OUR GREATEST VICTORY FOR THE FATHERLAND! WE SHALL RETURN TO BE ACCLAIMED AS HEROES!
UND YOU VILL REMAIN IN DERE... TO REFLECT UPON VOT A FOOL YOU VERE TO TRUST US!
YOU'LL PAY FOR THIS!! SOME-HOW... I SWEAR IT... I'LL HAVE MY REVENGE! ...UHHH..!
2.

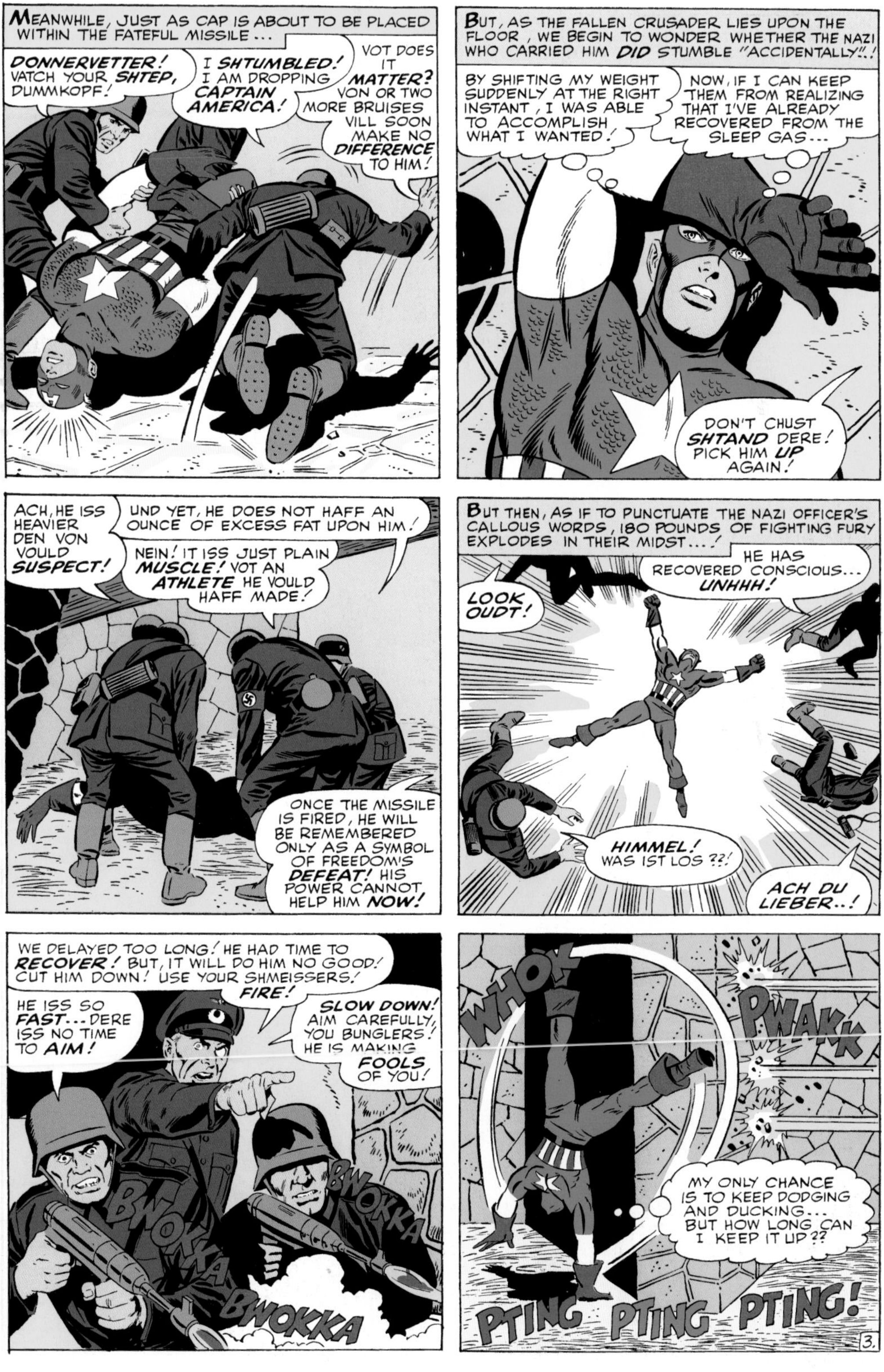

MEANWHILE, JUST AS CAP IS ABOUT TO BE PLACED WITHIN THE FATEFUL MISSILE...
DONNERVETTER! VATCH YOUR SHTEP, DUMMKOPF!
I SHTUMBLED! I AM DROPPING CAPTAIN AMERICA!
VOT DOES IT MATTER? VON OR TWO MORE BRUISES VILL SOON MAKE NO DIFFERENCE TO HIM!
BUT, AS THE FALLEN CRUSADER LIES UPON THE FLOOR, WE BEGIN TO WONDER WHETHER THE NAZI WHO CARRIED HIM DID STUMBLE "ACCIDENTALLY"!!
BY SHIFTING MY WEIGHT SUDDENLY AT THE RIGHT INSTANT, I WAS ABLE TO ACCOMPLISH WHAT I WANTED!
NOW, IF I CAN KEEP THEM FROM REALIZING THAT I'VE ALREADY RECOVERED FROM THE SLEEP GAS...
DON'T CHUST SHTAND DERE! PICK HIM UP AGAIN!
ACH, HE ISS HEAVIER DEN VON VOULD SUSPECT!
UND YET, HE DOES NOT HAFF AN OUNCE OF EXCESS FAT UPON HIM!
NEIN! IT ISS JUST PLAIN MUSCLE! VOT AN ATHLETE HE VOULD HAFF MADE!
ONCE THE MISSILE IS FIRED, HE WILL BE REMEMBERED ONLY AS A SYMBOL OF FREEDOM'S DEFEAT! HIS POWER CANNOT HELP HIM NOW!
BUT THEN, AS IF TO PUNCTUATE THE NAZI OFFICER'S CALLOUS WORDS, 180 POUNDS OF FIGHTING FURY EXPLODES IN THEIR MIDST...!
LOOK OUDT!
HE HAS RECOVERED CONSCIOUS... UNHHH!
HIMMEL! WAS IST LOS ??!
ACH DU LIEBER..!
WE DELAYED TOO LONG! HE HAD TIME TO RECOVER! BUT, IT WILL DO HIM NO GOOD! CUT HIM DOWN! USE YOUR SHMEISSERS! FIRE!
HE ISS SO FAST... DERE ISS NO TIME TO AIM!
SLOW DOWN! AIM CAREFULLY, YOU BUNGLERS! HE IS MAKING FOOLS OF YOU!
BWOKKA
BWOKKA
BWOKKA
BWOKKA
WHOK
PWAKK
MY ONLY CHANCE IS TO KEEP DODGING AND DUCKING... BUT HOW LONG CAN I KEEP IT UP??
PTING PTING PTING!
3.

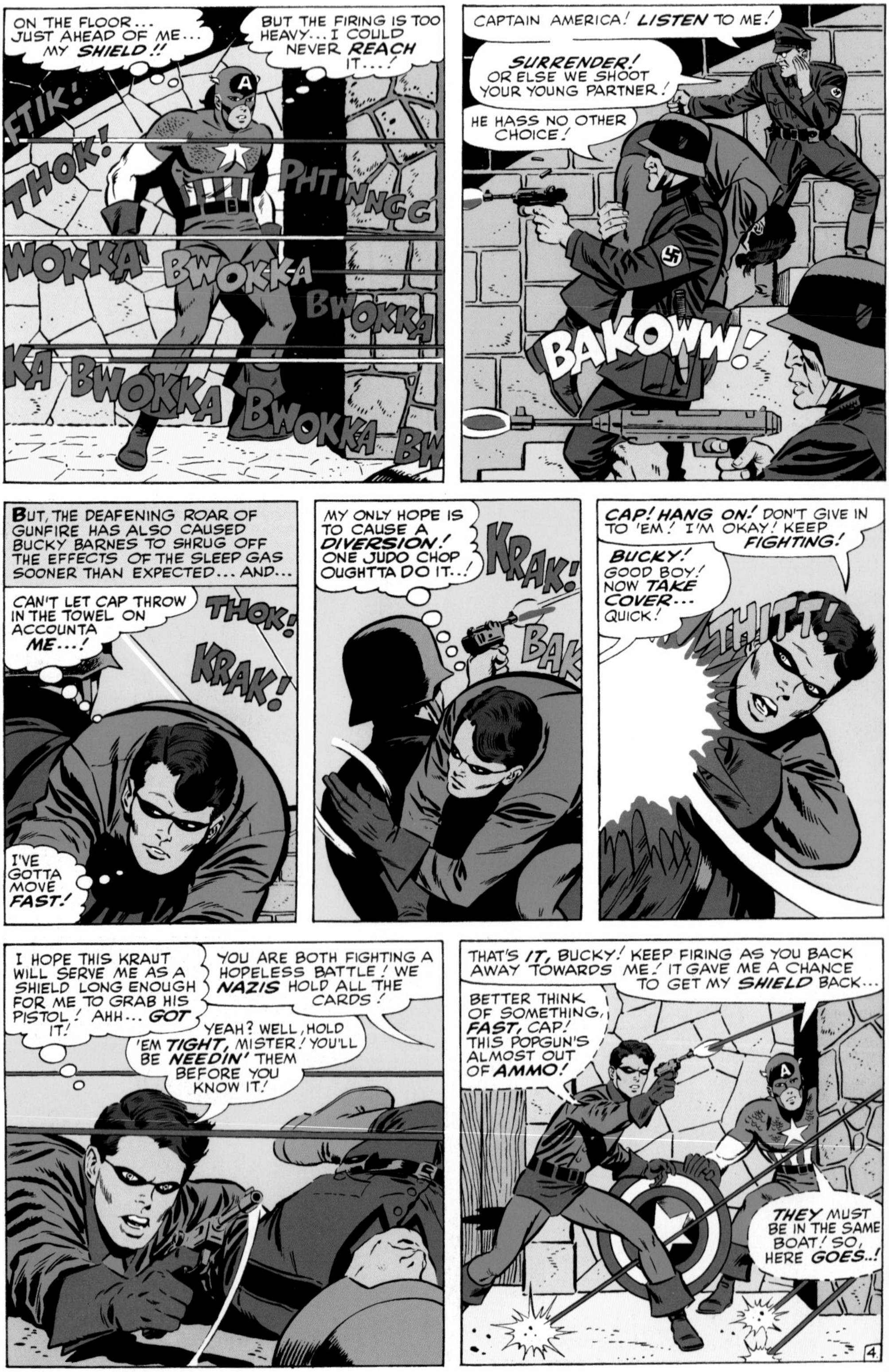

ON THE FLOOR... JUST AHEAD OF ME... MY SHIELD!!
BUT THE FIRING IS TOO HEAVY... I COULD NEVER REACH IT...!
FTIK!
THOK!
PHTINNGG
WOKKA BWOKKA BWOKKA
KA BWOKKA BWOKKA BW
CAPTAIN AMERICA! LISTEN TO ME!
SURRENDER! OR ELSE WE SHOOT YOUR YOUNG PARTNER!
HE HASS NO OTHER CHOICE!
BAKOWW!
BUT, THE DEAFENING ROAR OF GUNFIRE HAS ALSO CAUSED BUCKY BARNES TO SHRUG OFF THE EFFECTS OF THE SLEEP GAS SOONER THAN EXPECTED... AND...
CAN'T LET CAP THROW IN THE TOWEL ON ACCOUNTA ME...!
THOK!
KRAK!
I'VE GOTTA MOVE FAST!
MY ONLY HOPE IS TO CAUSE A DIVERSION! ONE JUDO CHOP OUGHTTA DO IT...!
KRAK!
BAK
CAP! HANG ON! DON'T GIVE IN TO 'EM! I'M OKAY! KEEP FIGHTING!
BUCKY! GOOD BOY! NOW TAKE COVER... QUICK!
THITT!
I HOPE THIS KRAUT WILL SERVE ME AS A SHIELD LONG ENOUGH FOR ME TO GRAB HIS PISTOL! AHH... GOT IT!
YOU ARE BOTH FIGHTING A HOPELESS BATTLE! WE NAZIS HOLD ALL THE CARDS!
YEAH? WELL, HOLD 'EM TIGHT, MISTER! YOU'LL BE NEEDIN' THEM BEFORE YOU KNOW IT!
THAT'S IT, BUCKY! KEEP FIRING AS YOU BACK AWAY TOWARDS ME! IT GAVE ME A CHANCE TO GET MY SHIELD BACK...
BETTER THINK OF SOMETHING, FAST, CAP! THIS POPGUN'S ALMOST OUT OF AMMO!
THEY MUST BE IN THE SAME BOAT! SO, HERE GOES..!
4

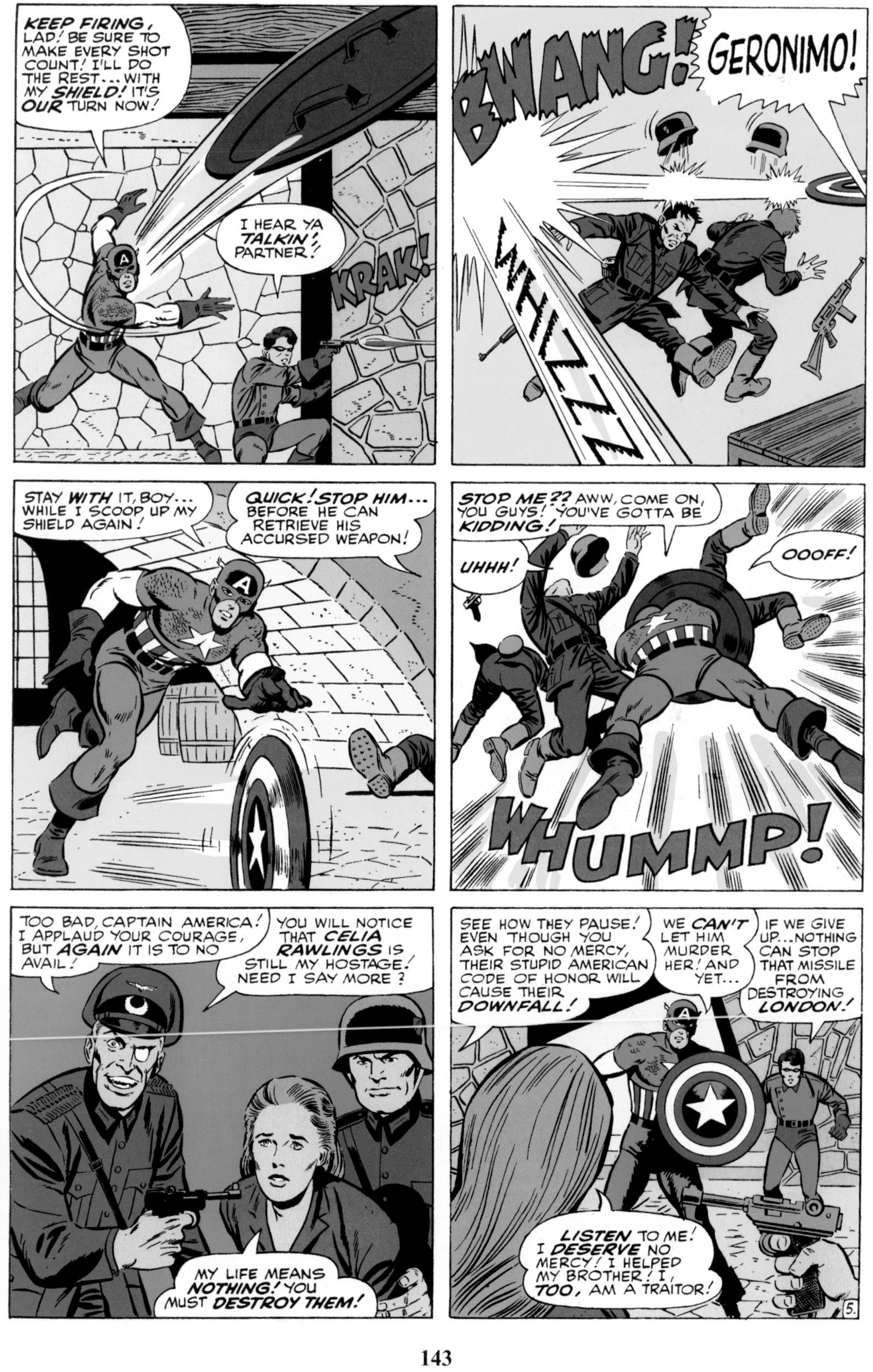
KEEP FIRING, LAD! BE SURE TO MAKE EVERY SHOT COUNT! I'LL DO THE REST... WITH MY SHIELD! IT'S OUR TURN NOW!
I HEAR YA TALKIN'! PARTNER!
KRAK!
BWANG!
GERONIMO!
WHIZZZ
STAY WITH IT, BOY... WHILE I SCOOP UP MY SHIELD AGAIN!
QUICK! STOP HIM... BEFORE HE CAN RETRIEVE HIS ACCURSED WEAPON!
STOP ME?? AWW, COME ON, YOU GUYS! YOU'VE GOTTA BE KIDDING!
UHHH!
OOOFF!
WHUMMP!
TOO BAD, CAPTAIN AMERICA! I APPLAUD YOUR COURAGE, BUT AGAIN IT IS TO NO AVAIL!
YOU WILL NOTICE THAT CELIA RAWLINGS IS STILL MY HOSTAGE! NEED I SAY MORE ?
MY LIFE MEANS NOTHING! YOU MUST DESTROY THEM!
SEE HOW THEY PAUSE! EVEN THOUGH YOU ASK FOR NO MERCY, THEIR STUPID AMERICAN CODE OF HONOR WILL CAUSE THEIR DOWNFALL!
WE CAN'T LET HIM MURDER HER! AND YET...
IF WE GIVE UP...NOTHING CAN STOP THAT MISSILE FROM DESTROYING LONDON!
LISTEN TO ME! I DESERVE NO MERCY! I HELPED MY BROTHER! I, TOO, AM A TRAITOR!
5.

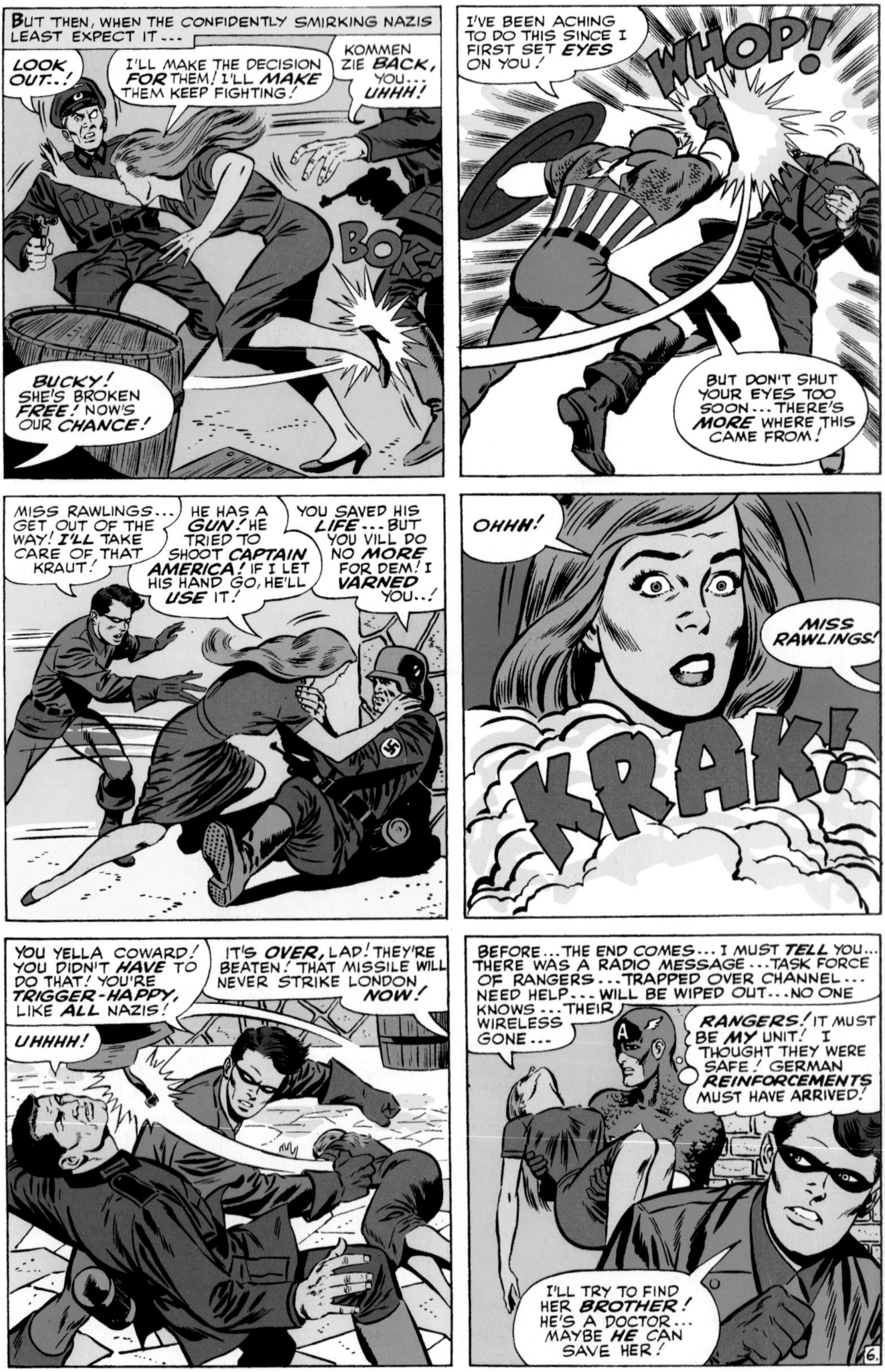

BUT THEN, WHEN THE CONFIDENTLY SMIRKING NAZIS LEAST EXPECT IT...
LOOK OUT..!
I'LL MAKE THE DECISION FOR THEM! I'LL MAKE THEM KEEP FIGHTING!
KOMMEN ZIE BACK, YOU... UHHH!
BOK!
BUCKY! SHE'S BROKEN FREE! NOW'S OUR CHANCE!
I'VE BEEN ACHING TO DO THIS SINCE I FIRST SET EYES ON YOU!
WHOP!
BUT DON'T SHUT YOUR EYES TOO SOON... THERE'S MORE WHERE THIS CAME FROM!
MISS RAWLINGS... GET OUT OF THE WAY! I'LL TAKE CARE OF THAT KRAUT!
HE HAS A GUN! HE TRIED TO SHOOT CAPTAIN AMERICA! IF I LET HIS HAND GO, HE'LL USE IT!
YOU SAVED HIS LIFE... BUT YOU VILL DO NO MORE FOR DEM! I VARNED YOU..!
OHHH!
MISS RAWLINGS!
KRAK!
YOU YELLA COWARD! YOU DIDN'T HAVE TO DO THAT! YOU'RE TRIGGER-HAPPY, LIKE ALL NAZIS!
IT'S OVER, LAD! THEY'RE BEATEN! THAT MISSILE WILL NEVER STRIKE LONDON NOW!
UHHHH!
BEFORE... THE END COMES... I MUST TELL YOU... THERE WAS A RADIO MESSAGE... TASK FORCE OF RANGERS... TRAPPED OVER CHANNEL... NEED HELP... WILL BE WIPED OUT... NO ONE KNOWS... THEIR WIRELESS GONE...
RANGERS! IT MUST BE MY UNIT! I THOUGHT THEY WERE SAFE! GERMAN REINFORCEMENTS MUST HAVE ARRIVED!
I'LL TRY TO FIND HER BROTHER! HE'S A DOCTOR... MAYBE HE CAN SAVE HER!
6.

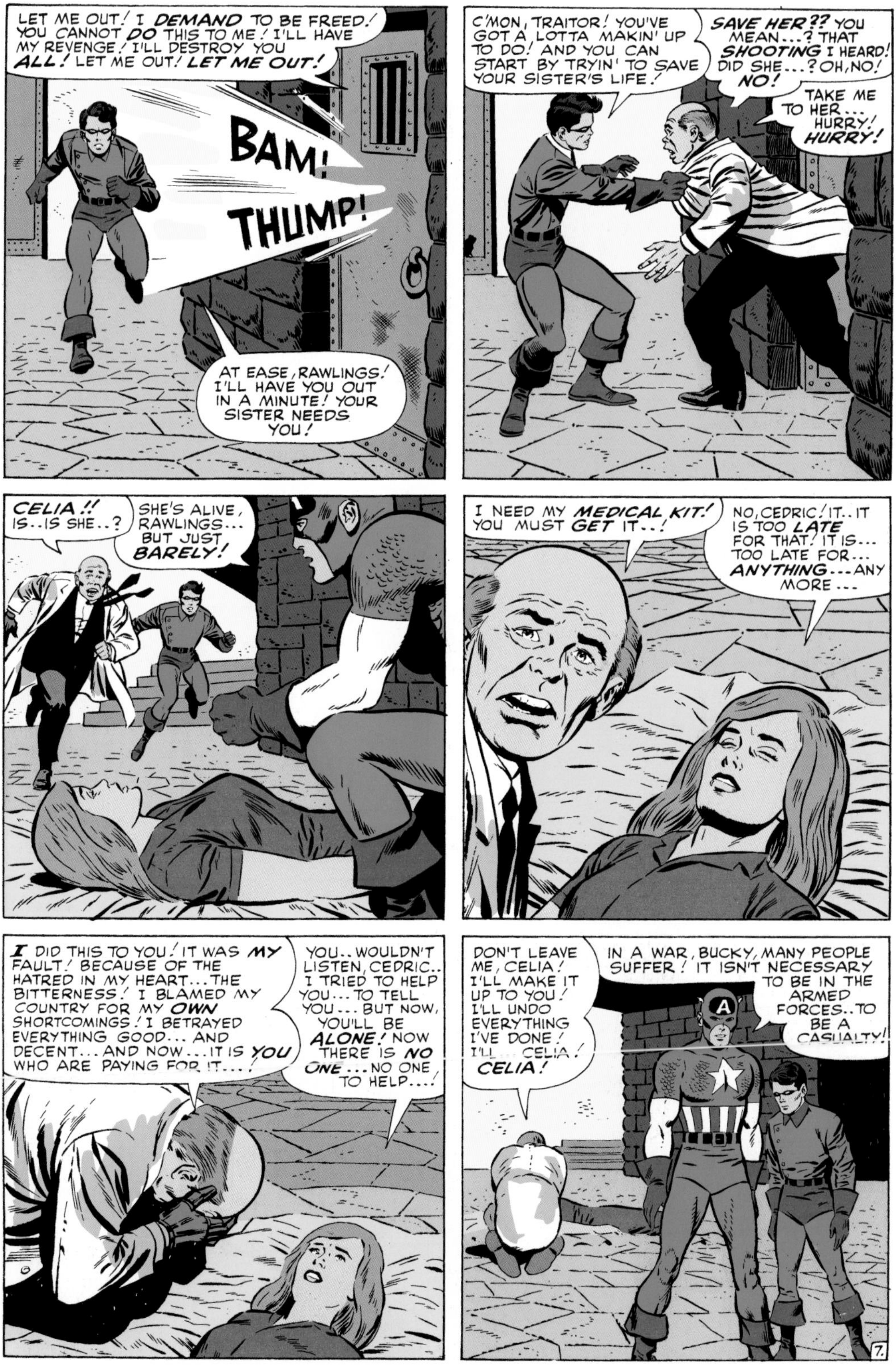
LET ME OUT! I DEMAND TO BE FREED! YOU CANNOT DO THIS TO ME! I'LL HAVE MY REVENGE! I'LL DESTROY YOU ALL! LET ME OUT! LET ME OUT!
BAM!
THUMP!
AT EASE, RAWLINGS! I'LL HAVE YOU OUT IN A MINUTE! YOUR SISTER NEEDS YOU!
C'MON, TRAITOR! YOU'VE GOT A LOTTA MAKIN' UP TO DO! AND YOU CAN START BY TRYIN' TO SAVE YOUR SISTER'S LIFE!
SAVE HER?? YOU MEAN...? THAT SHOOTING I HEARD! DID SHE...? OH, NO! NO!
TAKE ME TO HER... HURRY! HURRY!
CELIA!! IS..IS SHE..?
SHE'S ALIVE, RAWLINGS... BUT JUST BARELY!
I NEED MY MEDICAL KIT! YOU MUST GET IT..!
NO, CEDRIC! IT.. IT IS TOO LATE FOR THAT! IT IS... TOO LATE FOR... ANYTHING... ANY MORE...
I DID THIS TO YOU! IT WAS MY FAULT! BECAUSE OF THE HATRED IN MY HEART... THE BITTERNESS! I BLAMED MY COUNTRY FOR MY OWN SHORTCOMINGS! I BETRAYED EVERYTHING GOOD... AND DECENT... AND NOW... IT IS YOU WHO ARE PAYING FOR IT...!
YOU.. WOULDN'T LISTEN, CEDRIC.. I TRIED TO HELP YOU... TO TELL YOU... BUT NOW, YOU'LL BE ALONE! NOW THERE IS NO ONE... NO ONE TO HELP...!
DON'T LEAVE ME, CELIA! I'LL MAKE IT UP TO YOU! I'LL UNDO EVERYTHING I'VE DONE! I'LL... CELIA! CELIA!
IN A WAR, BUCKY, MANY PEOPLE SUFFER! IT ISN'T NECESSARY TO BE IN THE ARMED FORCES.. TO BE A CASUALTY!
7.

SECONDS LATER ...

THIS IS THE *LAST* OF 'EM, CAP! THEY'LL BE NICE AND SNUG IN HERE TILL THE M.P.S ARRIVE TO CLAIM THEM!

BUT THERE'S *ANOTHER* MATTER TO ATTEND TO NOW, BUCKY! THE RANGER UNIT I SLIPPED AWAY FROM, IN ORDER TO REACH GREY-MOOR CASTLE, IS IN *TROUBLE!**

NAZI REINFORCEMENTS HAVE THEM TRAPPED ACROSS THE CHANNEL! I KNOW OUR BATTLE STRATEGY ... OUR TROOPS WILL HAVE HEADED FOR THE COAST ... THEY'RE PROBABLY HOLDING OFF THE ENEMY RIGHT NOW, WITH THEIR BACKS TO THE SEA!

UNLESS I CAN FIND SOME WAY TO *SAVE* THEM, I'LL LIVE WITH THE KNOWLEDGE THAT I *DESERTED* THEM .. WHEN I WAS NEEDED MOST!

* AS EVERY READER OF *SUSPENSE* #*69* KNOWS BY NOW! ---STAN.

BUT, YOU THOUGHT THE MISSION WAS OVER! YOU THOUGHT THEY WERE *SAFE!* AND ... YOU WERE NEEDED *HERE!* IT WASN'T *YOUR* FAULT, CAP!

THAT DOESN'T MATTER! ALL THAT COUNTS IS *RESCUING* THEM ... AND THERE'S ONLY *ONE* WAY TO DO IT ... IN *TIME!*

THEN, AFTER CAP HAS QUICKLY EXPLAINED HIS DARING PLAN ...

RAWLINGS IS THE ONLY ONE WHO CAN PULL IT OFF! BUT, *WILL* HE?

OF *COURSE* I WILL DO IT!

SOMEHOW, I THINK THAT HE *WILL!*

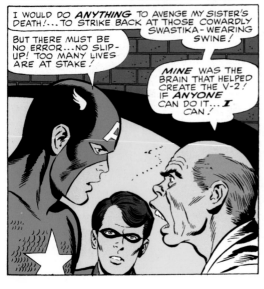

I WOULD DO *ANYTHING* TO AVENGE MY SISTER'S DEATH! ... TO STRIKE BACK AT THOSE COWARDLY SWASTIKA-WEARING SWINE!

BUT THERE MUST BE NO ERROR ... NO SLIP-UP! TOO MANY LIVES ARE AT STAKE!

MINE WAS THE BRAIN THAT HELPED CREATE THE V-2! IF *ANYONE* CAN DO IT ... *I* CAN!

THEN WE'VE NO MORE TIME TO WASTE! THE NAZIS PLANNED TO USE THAT MISSILE ... AND NOW, IT *WILL* BE USED!

AND *MINE* WILL BE THE HAND TO GUIDE IT ... I SHALL NOT FAIL!

8.

FOLLOW ME! THE GUIDANCE CONTROL ROOM IS DOWN THESE STEPS!

I'LL HAVE TO COMPUTE THE TRAJECTORY TO WITHIN A HAIRS-BREADTH OF OUR OBJECTIVE!

RIGHT! THE SLIGHTEST ERROR COULD BE FATAL TO OUR OWN MEN!

THEN, AFTER MOMENTS OF TENSE COMPUTATIONS...

HOLD IT! I WANT TO DOUBLE CHECK YOUR CALCULATIONS!

YOU? WHAT DO YOU KNOW OF SUCH TECHNICAL THINGS? IF THERE'S ANYTHING CAP DOESN'T KNOW ABOUT, I'D LIKE TO SEE IT!

ALL RIGHT, RAWLINGS! THE ROCKET'S ATTITUDE SEEMS TO BE CORRECT! I'M SATISFIED! NOW IT'S UP TO YOU....!

YOU WILL NOT BE DISAPPOINTED! I WANT TO STRIKE BACK AT THE NAZIS EVEN MORE THAN YOU DO!

STAND BY FOR COUNT-DOWN... TEN.. NINE... EIGHT...

WHOOM!

ZERO!

BUT, NO SOONER HAS THE V-2 ROCKET BEEN LAUNCHED, THAN A SECOND DEAFENING EXPLOSION ROCKS THE UNDERGROUND CONTROL ROOM ---

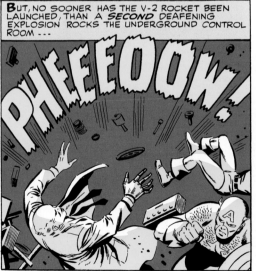

PHEEEOOW!!

I DID IT!! HA HA!! I SET THOSE EXPLOSIVES WHICH IGNITED THE STORED ROCKET FUEL!

THE SHOCK WAS TOO MUCH FOR RAWLINGS... HE'S GONE MAD!

CAP! THE WHOLE CASTLE IS CRUMBLING!! WE'VE GOT TO GET OUT!

9.

147

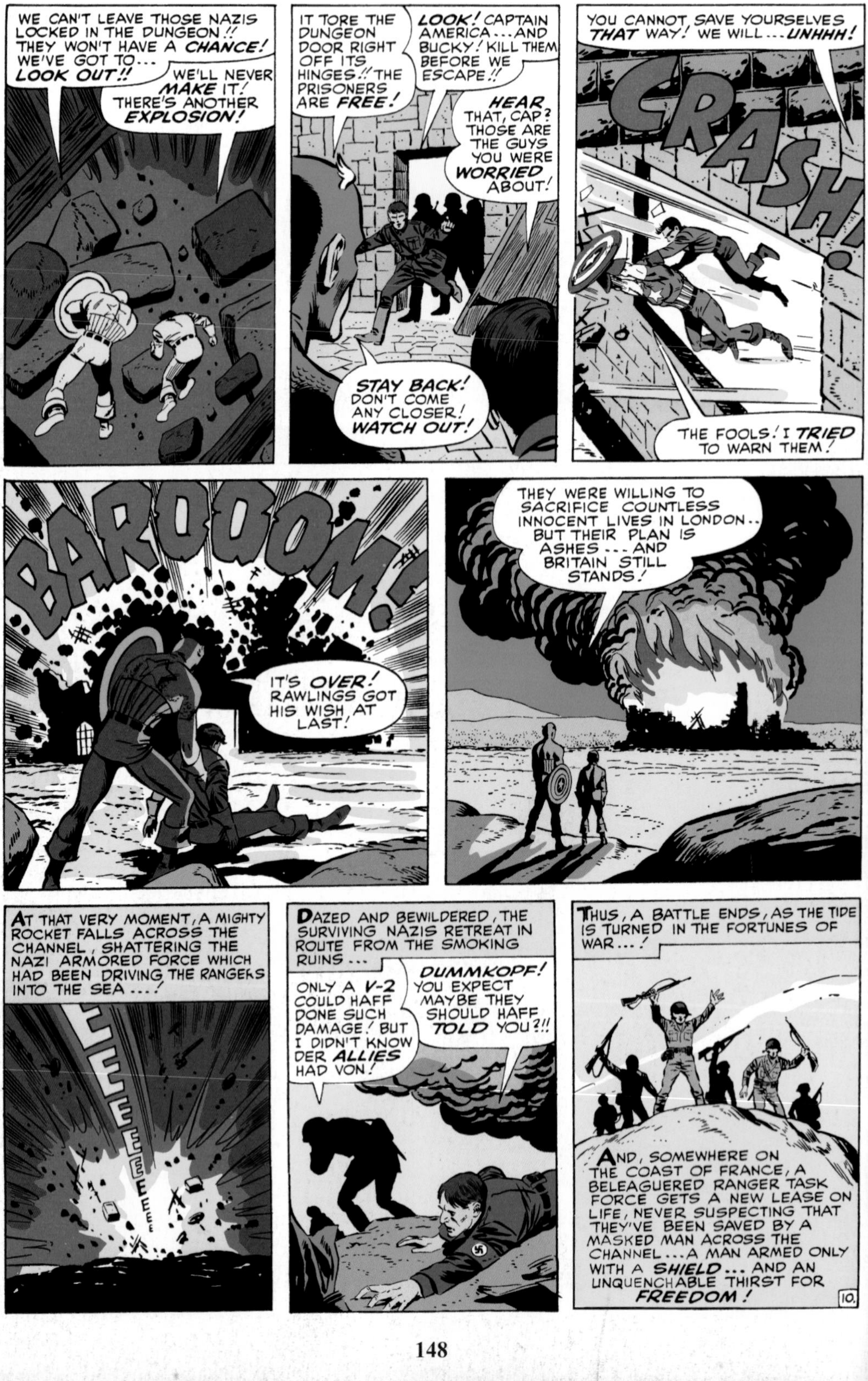

WE CAN'T LEAVE THOSE NAZIS LOCKED IN THE DUNGEON!! THEY WON'T HAVE A CHANCE! WE'VE GOT TO... LOOK OUT!!
WE'LL NEVER MAKE IT! THERE'S ANOTHER EXPLOSION!
IT TORE THE DUNGEON DOOR RIGHT OFF ITS HINGES!! THE PRISONERS ARE FREE!
LOOK! CAPTAIN AMERICA... AND BUCKY! KILL THEM BEFORE WE ESCAPE!!
HEAR THAT, CAP? THOSE ARE THE GUYS YOU WERE WORRIED ABOUT!
STAY BACK! DON'T COME ANY CLOSER! WATCH OUT!
YOU CANNOT SAVE YOURSELVES THAT WAY! WE WILL... UNHHH!
CRASH!
THE FOOLS! I TRIED TO WARN THEM!
BAROOOM!
IT'S OVER! RAWLINGS GOT HIS WISH AT LAST!
THEY WERE WILLING TO SACRIFICE COUNTLESS INNOCENT LIVES IN LONDON.. BUT THEIR PLAN IS ASHES... AND BRITAIN STILL STANDS!
AT THAT VERY MOMENT, A MIGHTY ROCKET FALLS ACROSS THE CHANNEL, SHATTERING THE NAZI ARMORED FORCE WHICH HAD BEEN DRIVING THE RANGERS INTO THE SEA...!
EEEEEEEEEEEEE
DAZED AND BEWILDERED, THE SURVIVING NAZIS RETREAT IN ROUTE FROM THE SMOKING RUINS...
ONLY A V-2 COULD HAFF DONE SUCH DAMAGE! BUT I DIDN'T KNOW DER ALLIES HAD VON!
DUMMKOPF! YOU EXPECT MAYBE THEY SHOULD HAFF TOLD YOU?!!
THUS, A BATTLE ENDS, AS THE TIDE IS TURNED IN THE FORTUNES OF WAR...!
AND, SOMEWHERE ON THE COAST OF FRANCE, A BELEAGUERED RANGER TASK FORCE GETS A NEW LEASE ON LIFE, NEVER SUSPECTING THAT THEY'VE BEEN SAVED BY A MASKED MAN ACROSS THE CHANNEL... A MAN ARMED ONLY WITH A SHIELD... AND AN UNQUENCHABLE THIRST FOR FREEDOM!
10.

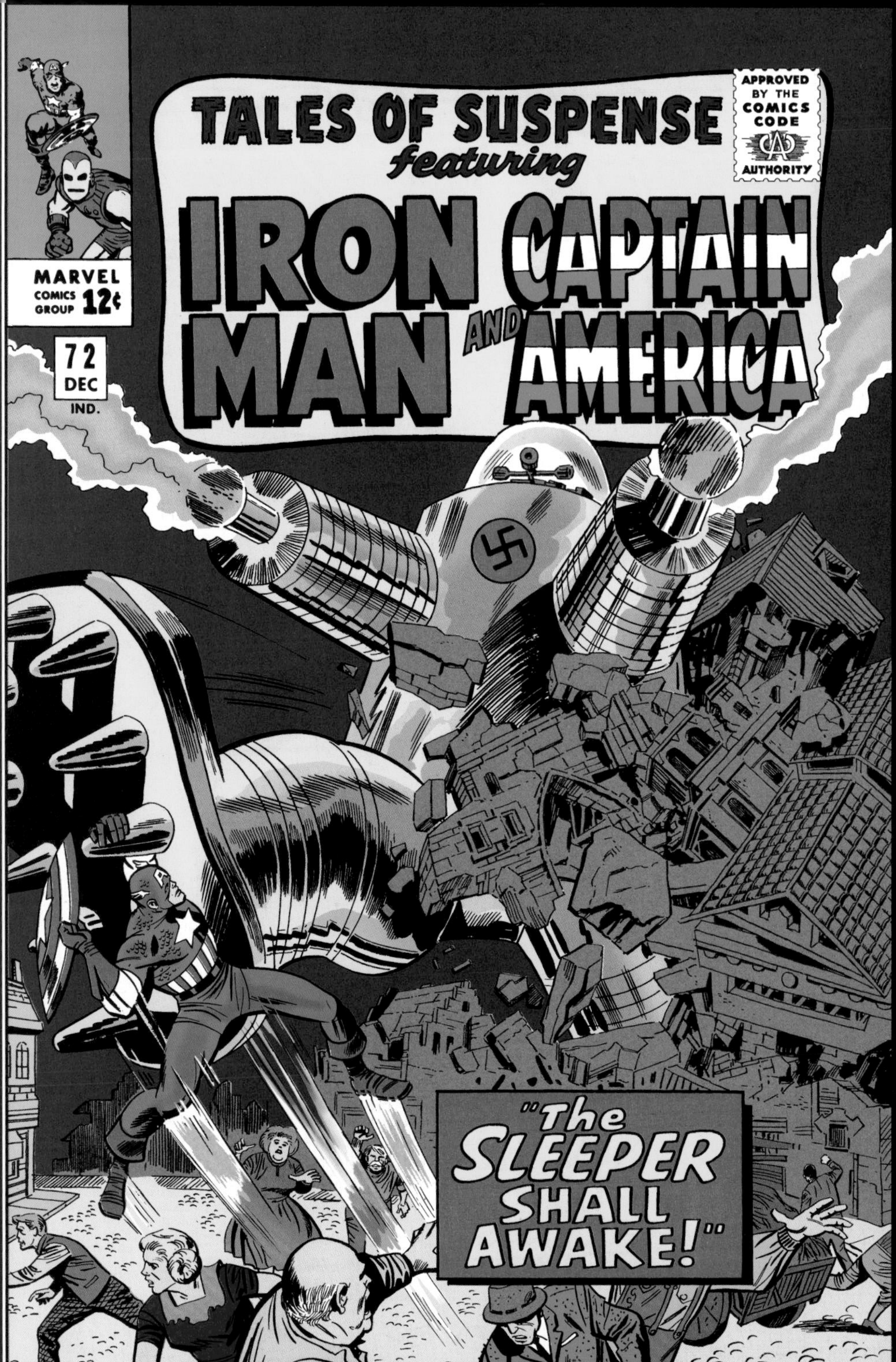

TALES OF SUSPENSE featuring
IRON MAN AND CAPTAIN AMERICA
APPROVED BY THE COMICS CODE AUTHORITY
MARVEL COMICS GROUP 12¢
72 DEC
IND.
"The SLEEPER SHALL AWAKE!"

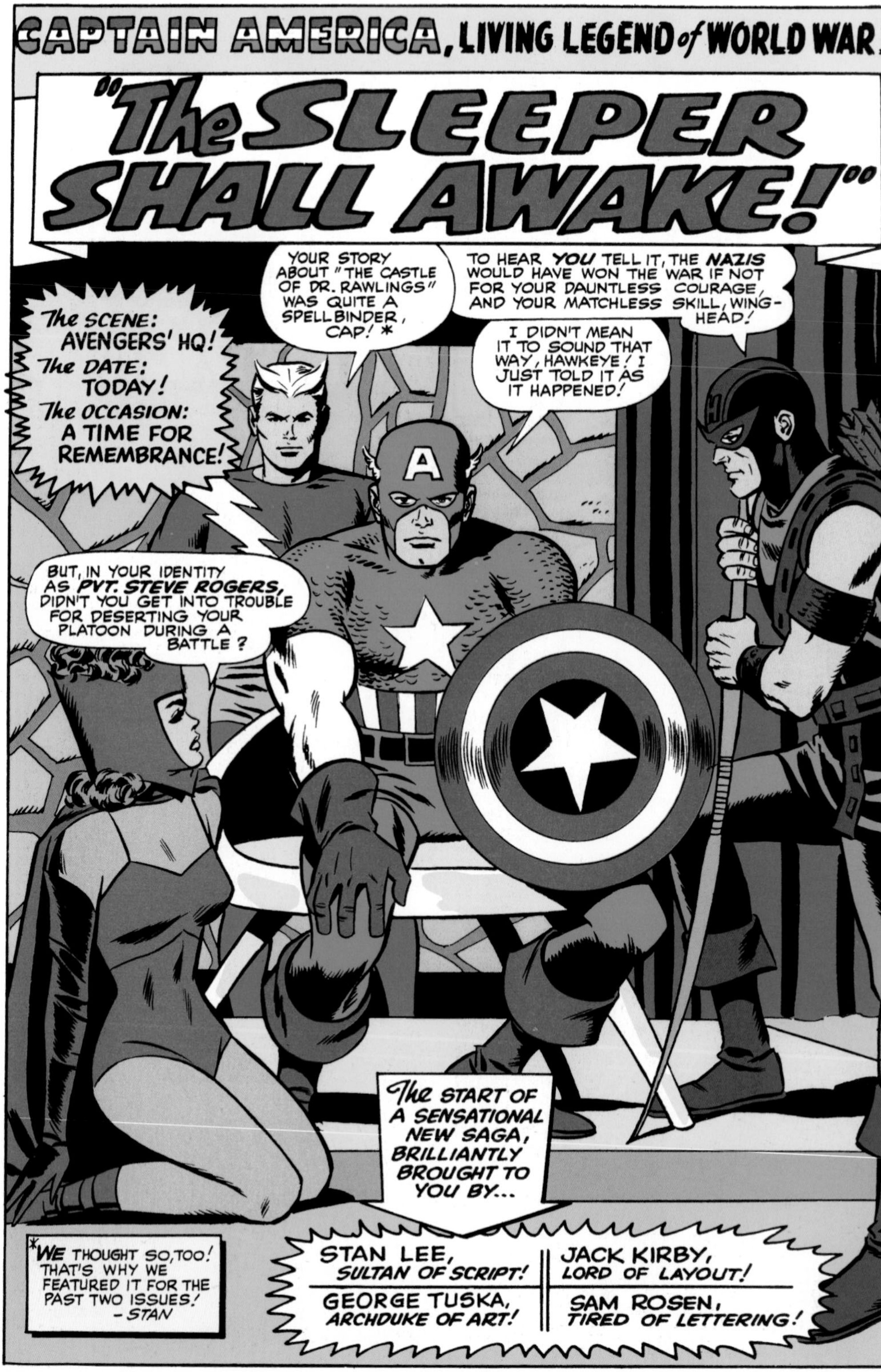

CAPTAIN AMERICA, LIVING LEGEND of WORLD WAR II
"The SLEEPER SHALL AWAKE!"
The SCENE: AVENGERS' HQ! The DATE: TODAY! The OCCASION: A TIME FOR REMEMBRANCE!
YOUR STORY ABOUT "THE CASTLE OF DR. RAWLINGS" WAS QUITE A SPELLBINDER, CAP! *
TO HEAR YOU TELL IT, THE NAZIS WOULD HAVE WON THE WAR IF NOT FOR YOUR DAUNTLESS COURAGE, AND YOUR MATCHLESS SKILL, WING-HEAD!
I DIDN'T MEAN IT TO SOUND THAT WAY, HAWKEYE! I JUST TOLD IT AS IT HAPPENED!
BUT, IN YOUR IDENTITY AS PVT. STEVE ROGERS, DIDN'T YOU GET INTO TROUBLE FOR DESERTING YOUR PLATOON DURING A BATTLE?
The START OF A SENSATIONAL NEW SAGA, BRILLIANTLY BROUGHT TO YOU BY...
*WE THOUGHT SO, TOO! THAT'S WHY WE FEATURED IT FOR THE PAST TWO ISSUES! - STAN
STAN LEE, SULTAN OF SCRIPT!
JACK KIRBY, LORD OF LAYOUT!
GEORGE TUSKA, ARCHDUKE OF ART!
SAM ROSEN, TIRED OF LETTERING!

REMEMBER, WANDA, THE HIGHEST ECHELON OF ARMY INTELLIGENCE *KNEW* THAT CAPTAIN AMERICA AND PVT. ROGERS WERE ONE AND THE SAME...

...SO THEY COOKED UP A STORY TO COVER FOR ME! THEY TESTIFIED THAT I HAD LEFT MY PLATOON IN ORDER TO SUMMON CAPTAIN AMERICA TO DESTROY THE NAZIS' V-BOMB!

PIETRO AND I WERE JUST *YOUNGSTERS* DURING THOSE DRAMATIC YEARS, STEVE!

AND, IN A WAY, THERE WAS FAR MORE TRUTH THAN FICTION TO THAT EXPLANATION! WHAT EVER HAPPENED TO THAT KID, *BUCKY*, THAT YOU MENTIONED? WHAT'S HE DOIN' *TODAY*?

BUCKY WAS...LOST..ON A MISSION, LATER IN THE WAR! HE DIED AS BRAVELY AS HE HAD LIVED..!

TOO BAD! THE WAY YOU DESCRIBE HIM, HE MIGHTA MADE A REAL SWINGIN' *AVENGER!*

I THINK STEVE WOULD PREFER NOT TO DISCUSS BUCKY ANY MORE, HAWKEYE!

WHY THE *HAMLET* ACT, WANDA? IT HAPPENED MORE THAN 20 YEARS AGO! HE OUGHTTA BE *OVER* IT BY NOW!

HE'LL *NEVER* BE OVER IT! I HAVE HEARD THAT HE BLAMES *HIMSELF* FOR HIS YOUNG PARTNER'S FATE! AND SUCH A MAN CAN *NEVER* FORGIVE HIMSELF!

SO! EVEN *HE* ISN'T PERFECT! WELL, WADDAYA KNOW?

LATER, IN THE GUEST ROOM WHICH HE OCCUPIES ON THE TOP FLOOR OF ANTHONY STARK'S LUXURIOUS MANSION...

WHAT SUPREME IRONY! *CAPTAIN AMERICA*, THE IDOL OF MILLIONS...THE MAN WHO SAVED COUNTLESS LIVES DURING THE TRAGIC WAR YEARS...UNABLE TO SAVE THE LIFE OF HIS OWN PARTNER!

IF ONLY I HADN'T TAKEN BUCKY WITH ME ON THAT FINAL MISSION...

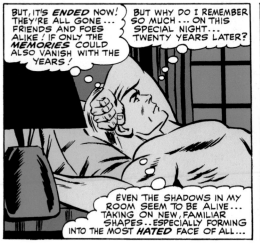

BUT, IT'S *ENDED* NOW! THEY'RE ALL GONE... FRIENDS AND FOES ALIKE! IF ONLY THE *MEMORIES* COULD ALSO VANISH WITH THE YEARS!

BUT WHY DO I REMEMBER SO MUCH... ON THIS SPECIAL NIGHT... TWENTY YEARS LATER?

EVEN THE SHADOWS IN MY ROOM SEEM TO BE ALIVE... TAKING ON NEW, FAMILIAR SHAPES..ESPECIALLY FORMING INTO THE MOST *HATED* FACE OF ALL...

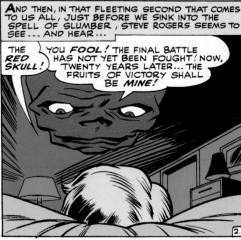

AND THEN, IN THAT FLEETING SECOND THAT COMES TO US ALL, JUST BEFORE WE SINK INTO THE SPELL OF SLUMBER, STEVE ROGERS SEEMS TO SEE....AND HEAR...

THE *RED SKULL!*

YOU *FOOL!* THE FINAL BATTLE HAS NOT YET BEEN FOUGHT! NOW, TWENTY YEARS LATER... THE FRUITS OF VICTORY SHALL BE *MINE!*

2.

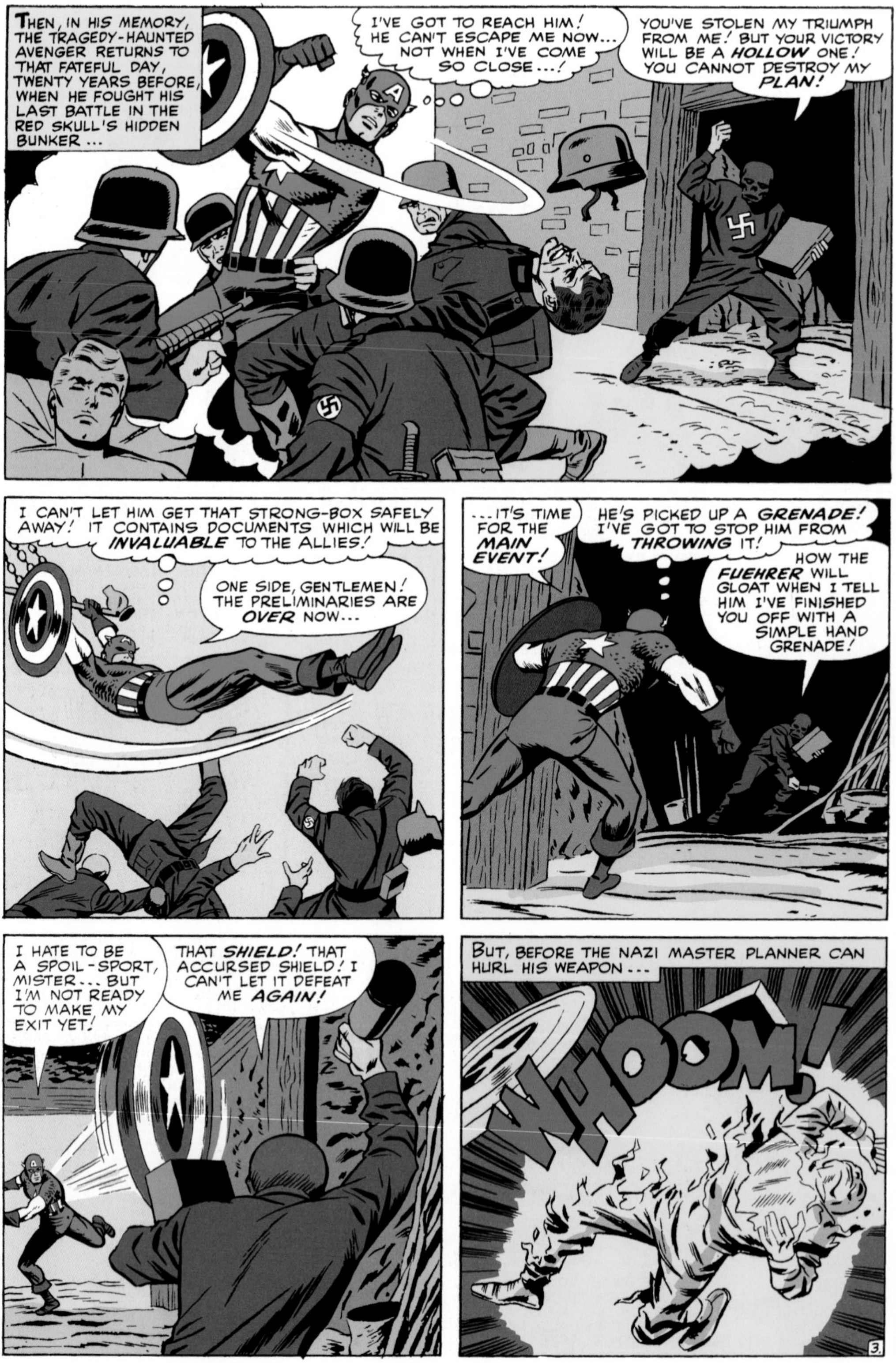
THEN, IN HIS MEMORY, THE TRAGEDY-HAUNTED AVENGER RETURNS TO THAT FATEFUL DAY, TWENTY YEARS BEFORE, WHEN HE FOUGHT HIS LAST BATTLE IN THE RED SKULL'S HIDDEN BUNKER...
I'VE GOT TO REACH HIM! HE CAN'T ESCAPE ME NOW... NOT WHEN I'VE COME SO CLOSE...!
YOU'VE STOLEN MY TRIUMPH FROM ME! BUT YOUR VICTORY WILL BE A *HOLLOW* ONE! YOU CANNOT DESTROY MY *PLAN!*
I CAN'T LET HIM GET THAT STRONG-BOX SAFELY AWAY! IT CONTAINS DOCUMENTS WHICH WILL BE *INVALUABLE* TO THE ALLIES!
ONE SIDE, GENTLEMEN! THE PRELIMINARIES ARE *OVER* NOW...
...IT'S TIME FOR THE *MAIN EVENT!*
HE'S PICKED UP A *GRENADE!* I'VE GOT TO STOP HIM FROM *THROWING* IT!
HOW THE *FUEHRER* WILL GLOAT WHEN I TELL HIM I'VE FINISHED YOU OFF WITH A SIMPLE HAND GRENADE!
I HATE TO BE A SPOIL-SPORT, MISTER... BUT I'M NOT READY TO MAKE MY EXIT YET!
THAT *SHIELD!* THAT ACCURSED SHIELD! I CAN'T LET IT DEFEAT ME *AGAIN!*
BUT, BEFORE THE NAZI MASTER PLANNER CAN HURL HIS WEAPON...
WHOOM!
3.

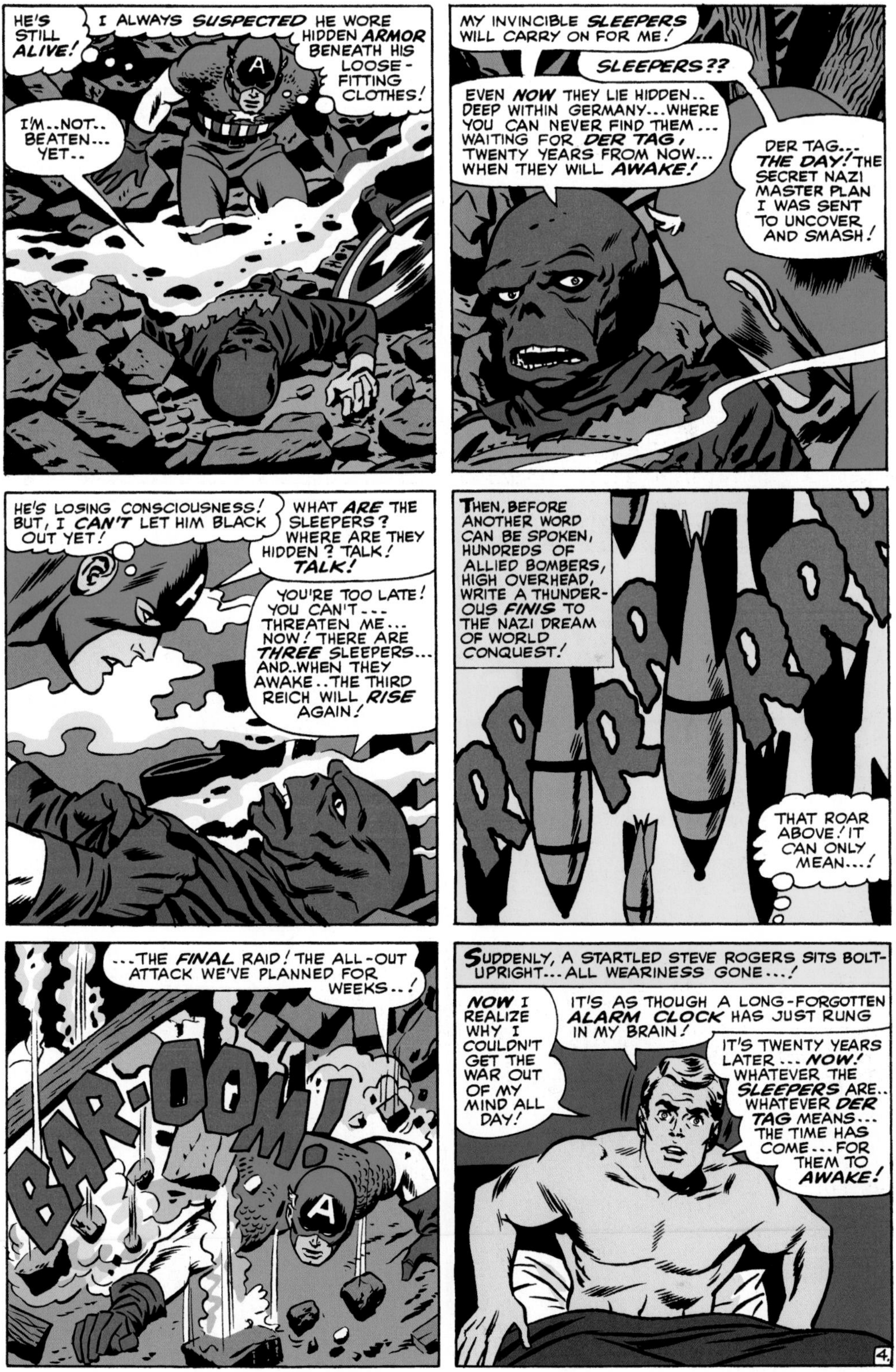

HE'S STILL ALIVE!
I ALWAYS SUSPECTED HE WORE HIDDEN ARMOR BENEATH HIS LOOSE-FITTING CLOTHES!
I'M..NOT.. BEATEN... YET..
MY INVINCIBLE SLEEPERS WILL CARRY ON FOR ME!
SLEEPERS??
EVEN NOW THEY LIE HIDDEN.. DEEP WITHIN GERMANY...WHERE YOU CAN NEVER FIND THEM... WAITING FOR DER TAG, TWENTY YEARS FROM NOW... WHEN THEY WILL AWAKE!
DER TAG... THE DAY! THE SECRET NAZI MASTER PLAN I WAS SENT TO UNCOVER AND SMASH!
HE'S LOSING CONSCIOUSNESS! BUT, I CAN'T LET HIM BLACK OUT YET!
WHAT ARE THE SLEEPERS? WHERE ARE THEY HIDDEN? TALK! TALK!
YOU'RE TOO LATE! YOU CAN'T--- THREATEN ME... NOW! THERE ARE THREE SLEEPERS... AND..WHEN THEY AWAKE..THE THIRD REICH WILL RISE AGAIN!
THEN, BEFORE ANOTHER WORD CAN BE SPOKEN, HUNDREDS OF ALLIED BOMBERS, HIGH OVERHEAD, WRITE A THUNDEROUS FINIS TO THE NAZI DREAM OF WORLD CONQUEST!
RRRRRR
THAT ROAR ABOVE! IT CAN ONLY MEAN...!
...THE FINAL RAID! THE ALL-OUT ATTACK WE'VE PLANNED FOR WEEKS..!
BAR-OOM!
SUDDENLY, A STARTLED STEVE ROGERS SITS BOLT-UPRIGHT...ALL WEARINESS GONE...!
NOW I REALIZE WHY I COULDN'T GET THE WAR OUT OF MY MIND ALL DAY!
IT'S AS THOUGH A LONG-FORGOTTEN ALARM CLOCK HAS JUST RUNG IN MY BRAIN!
IT'S TWENTY YEARS LATER... NOW! WHATEVER THE SLEEPERS ARE.. WHATEVER DER TAG MEANS... THE TIME HAS COME... FOR THEM TO AWAKE!
4.

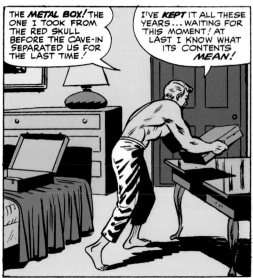

THE **METAL BOX!** THE ONE I TOOK FROM THE RED SKULL BEFORE THE CAVE-IN SEPARATED US FOR THE LAST TIME!

I'VE **KEPT** IT ALL THESE YEARS... WAITING FOR THIS MOMENT! AT LAST I KNOW WHAT ITS CONTENTS **MEAN!**

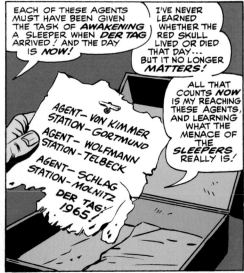

EACH OF THESE AGENTS MUST HAVE BEEN GIVEN THE TASK OF **AWAKENING** A SLEEPER WHEN **DER TAG** ARRIVED! AND THE DAY IS **NOW!**

I'VE NEVER LEARNED WHETHER THE RED SKULL LIVED OR DIED THAT DAY... BUT IT NO LONGER **MATTERS!**

ALL THAT COUNTS **NOW** IS MY REACHING THESE AGENTS, AND LEARNING WHAT THE MENACE OF THE **SLEEPERS** REALLY IS!

AGENT— VON KIMMER
STATION— GORTMUND
AGENT— WOLFMANN
STATION— TELBECK
AGENT— SCHLAG
STATION— MOLNITZ
DER TAG!
1965!

SOMETIME LATER, ON A STORMY, WINDSWEPT NIGHT IN A SMALL, ISOLATED BAVARIAN VILLAGE...

WHY WOULD **HERR VON KIMMER** HAVE SENT FOR US ON SUCH A NIGHT?

IT IS NOT MUCH FURTHER! LET US BE SILENT! HE WILL BE WRATHFUL TO LEARN THAT WE QUESTION HIS COMMAND!

IT IS NOT FOR US TO QUESTION THE **BURGO-MASTER!** WHEN HE ORDERS, WE OBEY!

HERR VON KIMMER, WE HAVE COME, AS YOU ORDERED!

KNOCK!

KNOCK!

MEIN HERR! YOUR UNIFORM! IT IS THE UNIFORM OF.. OF...

SILENCE! I STAND BEFORE YOU AS I STOOD TWENTY YEARS AGO, WHEN LESSER MEN TREMBLED AT THE SIGHT OF ME!

THE TIME HAS **COME!** TONIGHT THE THIRD REICH SHALL **LIVE** AGAIN!

5.

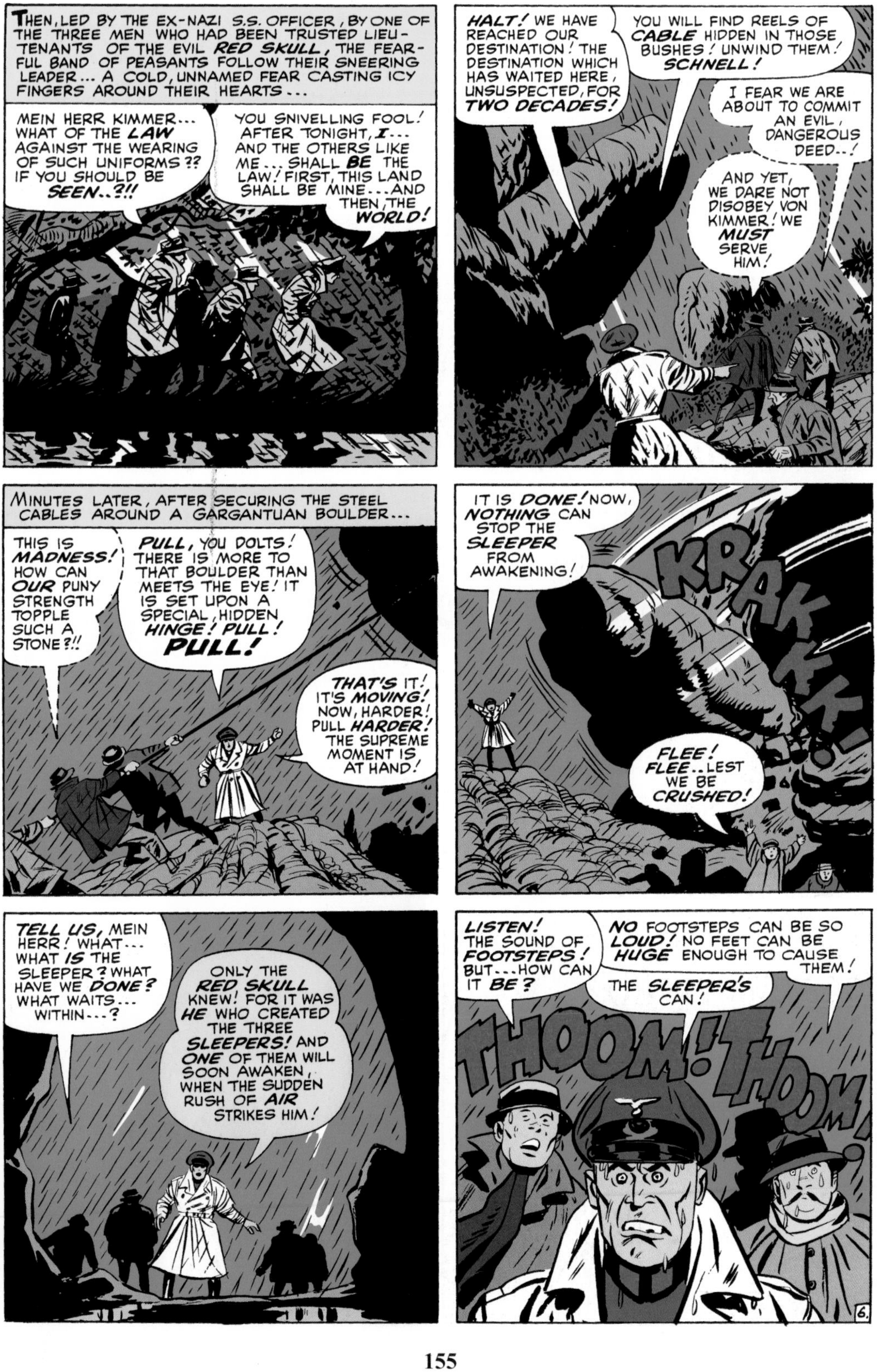
THEN, LED BY THE EX-NAZI S.S. OFFICER, BY ONE OF THE THREE MEN WHO HAD BEEN TRUSTED LIEUTENANTS OF THE EVIL RED SKULL, THE FEARFUL BAND OF PEASANTS FOLLOW THEIR SNEERING LEADER... A COLD, UNNAMED FEAR CASTING ICY FINGERS AROUND THEIR HEARTS...
MEIN HERR KIMMER... WHAT OF THE LAW AGAINST THE WEARING OF SUCH UNIFORMS?? IF YOU SHOULD BE SEEN..?!!
YOU SNIVELLING FOOL! AFTER TONIGHT, I... AND THE OTHERS LIKE ME... SHALL BE THE LAW! FIRST, THIS LAND SHALL BE MINE... AND THEN, THE WORLD!
HALT! WE HAVE REACHED OUR DESTINATION! THE DESTINATION WHICH HAS WAITED HERE, UNSUSPECTED, FOR TWO DECADES!
YOU WILL FIND REELS OF CABLE HIDDEN IN THOSE BUSHES! UNWIND THEM! SCHNELL!
I FEAR WE ARE ABOUT TO COMMIT AN EVIL, DANGEROUS DEED..!
AND YET, WE DARE NOT DISOBEY VON KIMMER! WE MUST SERVE HIM!
MINUTES LATER, AFTER SECURING THE STEEL CABLES AROUND A GARGANTUAN BOULDER...
THIS IS MADNESS! HOW CAN OUR PUNY STRENGTH TOPPLE SUCH A STONE?!!
PULL, YOU DOLTS! THERE IS MORE TO THAT BOULDER THAN MEETS THE EYE! IT IS SET UPON A SPECIAL, HIDDEN HINGE! PULL! PULL!
THAT'S IT! IT'S MOVING! NOW, HARDER! PULL HARDER! THE SUPREME MOMENT IS AT HAND!
IT IS DONE! NOW, NOTHING CAN STOP THE SLEEPER FROM AWAKENING!
KRAKKKK!
FLEE! FLEE.. LEST WE BE CRUSHED!
TELL US, MEIN HERR! WHAT... WHAT IS THE SLEEPER? WHAT HAVE WE DONE? WHAT WAITS... WITHIN...?
ONLY THE RED SKULL KNEW! FOR IT WAS HE WHO CREATED THE THREE SLEEPERS! AND ONE OF THEM WILL SOON AWAKEN, WHEN THE SUDDEN RUSH OF AIR STRIKES HIM!
LISTEN! THE SOUND OF FOOTSTEPS! BUT... HOW CAN IT BE?
NO FOOTSTEPS CAN BE SO LOUD! NO FEET CAN BE HUGE ENOUGH TO CAUSE THEM!
THE SLEEPER'S CAN!
THOOM! THOOM!
6.

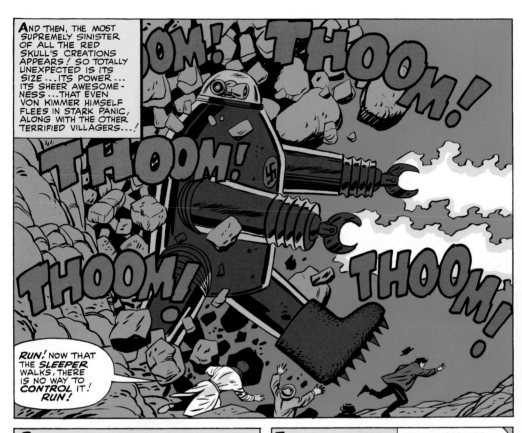

AND THEN, THE MOST SUPREMELY SINISTER OF ALL THE RED SKULL'S CREATIONS APPEARS! SO TOTALLY UNEXPECTED IS ITS SIZE...ITS POWER... ITS SHEER AWESOMENESS...THAT EVEN VON KIMMER HIMSELF FLEES IN STARK PANIC, ALONG WITH THE OTHER TERRIFIED VILLAGERS...!

THOOM! THOOM! THOOM! THOOM! THOOM!

RUN! NOW THAT THE SLEEPER WALKS, THERE IS NO WAY TO CONTROL IT! RUN!

BUT, AT THAT VERY MOMENT, MANY THOUSANDS OF FEET ABOVE THE HEART OF BAVARIA, A POWERFUL, RED-WHITE-AND-BLUE-CLAD FIGURE HITS THE SILK WITH THE SKILL AND EASE BORN OF A THOUSAND COMBAT MISSIONS...

THIS IS THE AREA MENTIONED WITH THE FIRST NAME ON THE RED SKULL'S LIST!

MAN, IT'S LIKE OLD TIMES, SEEING THAT GENT GO INTO ACTION AGAIN!

WHOEVER, OR WHATEVER THE SLEEPER MAY BE, I HOPE I'M NOT TOO LATE FOR DER TAG!

THEN, MINUTES LATER... PEOPLE HEADING AWAY FROM TOWN... WITH ALL THEIR BELONGINGS... LIKE REFUGEES! THEY LOOK BEWILDERED... FRIGHTENED... ON THE VERGE OF PANIC!

BUT, WHAT CAN THEY BE FLEEING FROM? IS IT WHAT I FEAR IT IS??

7.

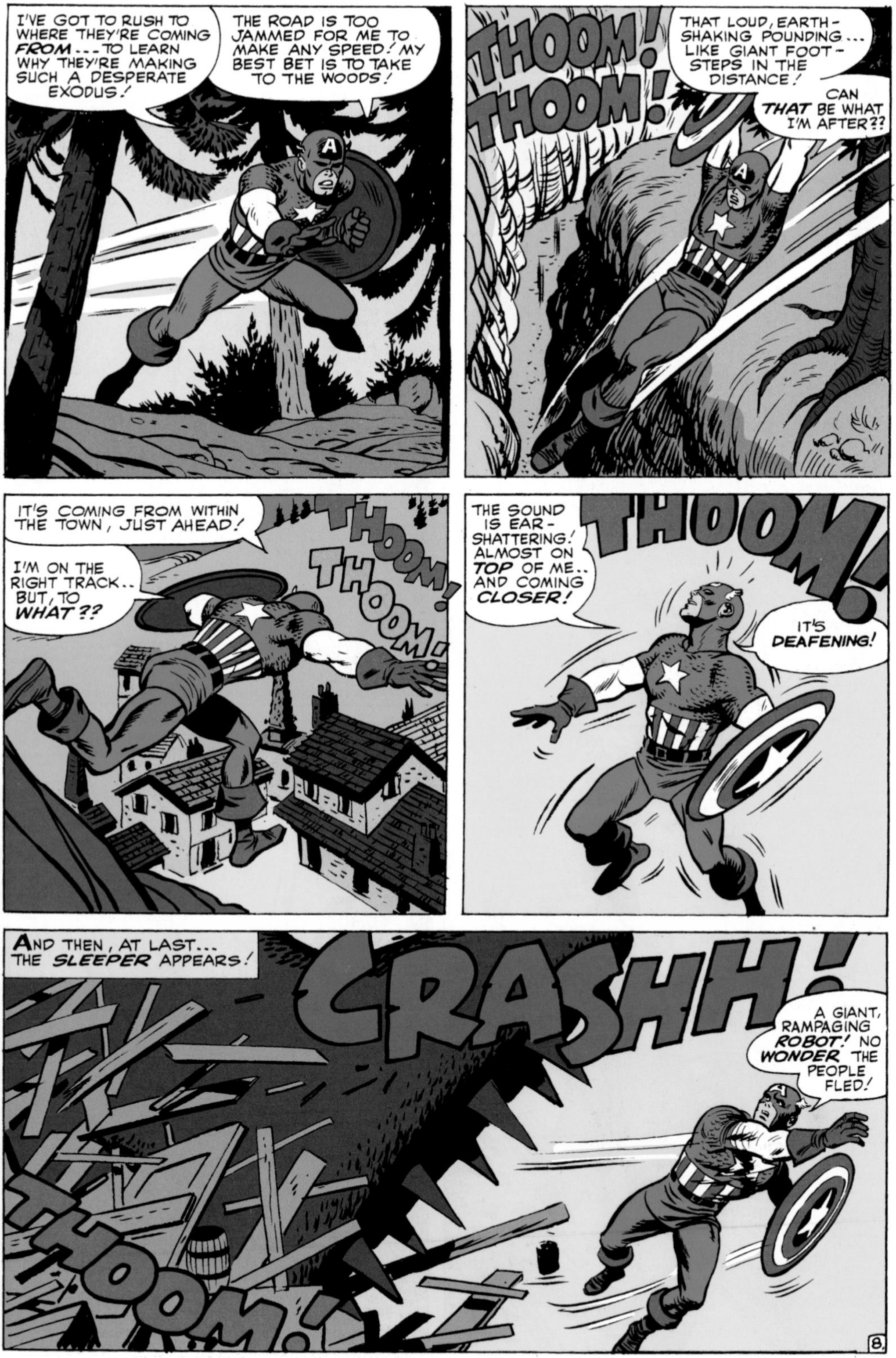
I'VE GOT TO RUSH TO WHERE THEY'RE COMING FROM... TO LEARN WHY THEY'RE MAKING SUCH A DESPERATE EXODUS!
THE ROAD IS TOO JAMMED FOR ME TO MAKE ANY SPEED! MY BEST BET IS TO TAKE TO THE WOODS!
THOOM! THOOM!
THAT LOUD, EARTH-SHAKING POUNDING... LIKE GIANT FOOT-STEPS IN THE DISTANCE!
CAN THAT BE WHAT I'M AFTER??
IT'S COMING FROM WITHIN THE TOWN, JUST AHEAD!
I'M ON THE RIGHT TRACK.. BUT, TO WHAT??
THOOM! THOOM!
THE SOUND IS EAR-SHATTERING! ALMOST ON TOP OF ME.. AND COMING CLOSER!
THOOM!!
IT'S DEAFENING!
AND THEN, AT LAST... THE SLEEPER APPEARS!
CRASHH!
A GIANT, RAMPAGING ROBOT! NO WONDER THE PEOPLE FLED!
THOOM!
8

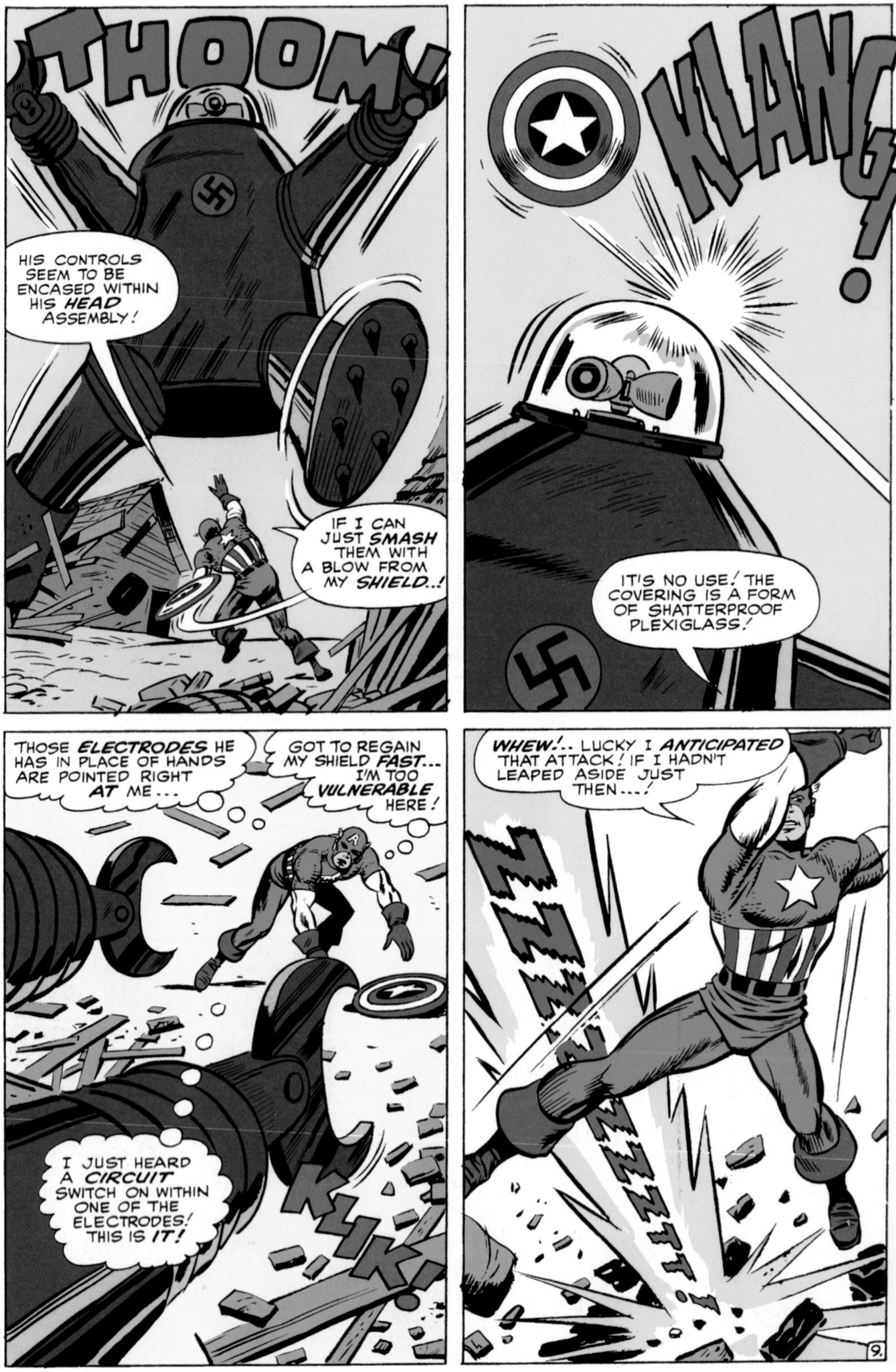
THOOM!
HIS CONTROLS SEEM TO BE ENCASED WITHIN HIS HEAD ASSEMBLY!
IF I CAN JUST SMASH THEM WITH A BLOW FROM MY SHIELD..!
KLANG!
IT'S NO USE! THE COVERING IS A FORM OF SHATTERPROOF PLEXIGLASS!
THOSE ELECTRODES HE HAS IN PLACE OF HANDS ARE POINTED RIGHT AT ME...
GOT TO REGAIN MY SHIELD FAST... I'M TOO VULNERABLE HERE!
I JUST HEARD A CIRCUIT SWITCH ON WITHIN ONE OF THE ELECTRODES! THIS IS IT!
KLIK!
WHEW!.. LUCKY I ANTICIPATED THAT ATTACK! IF I HADN'T LEAPED ASIDE JUST THEN...!
ZZZZZZZZZZZTTTT
9.

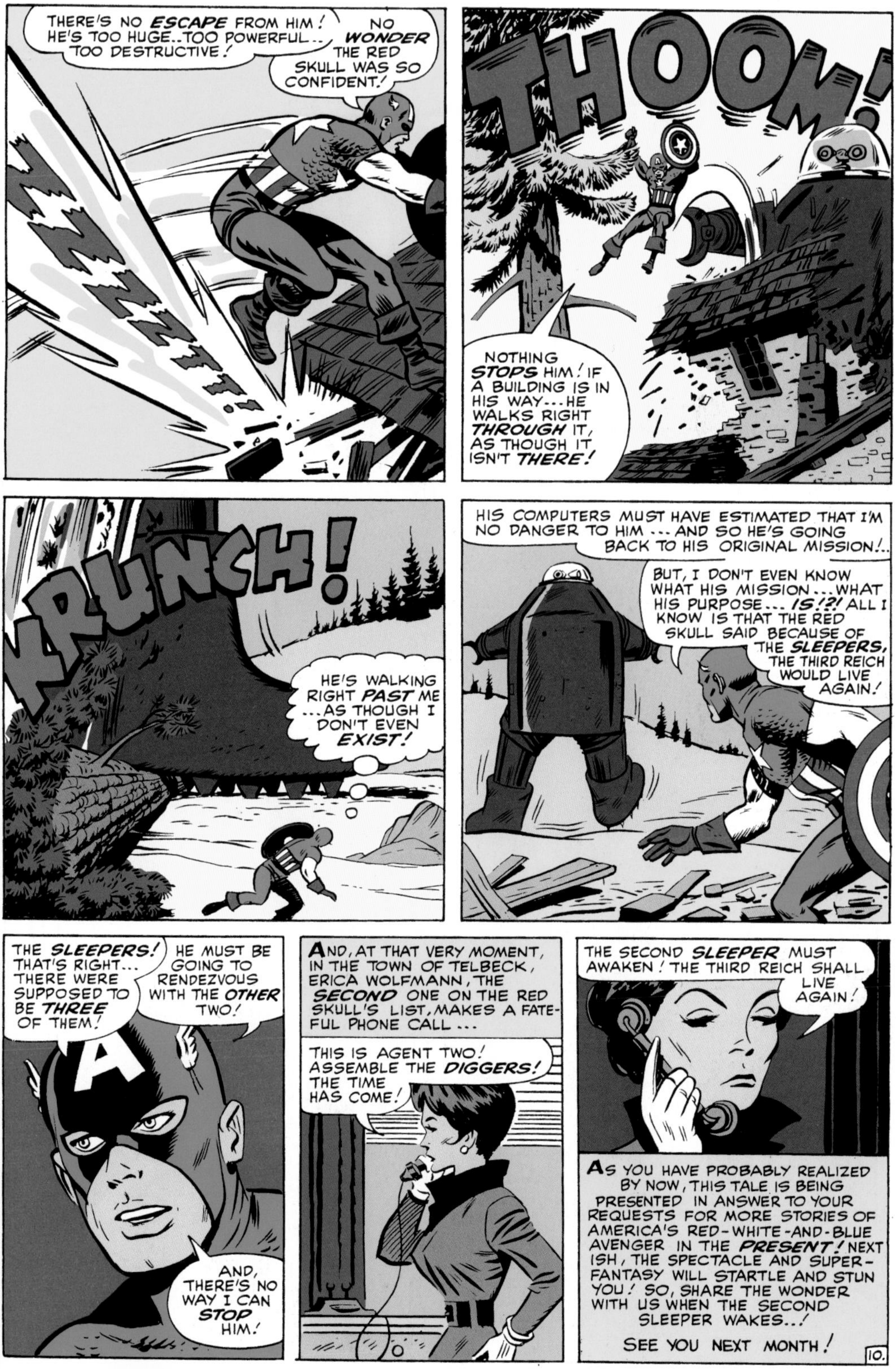

THERE'S NO ESCAPE FROM HIM! HE'S TOO HUGE..TOO POWERFUL.. TOO DESTRUCTIVE!
NO WONDER THE RED SKULL WAS SO CONFIDENT!
THOOM!
NOTHING STOPS HIM! IF A BUILDING IS IN HIS WAY---HE WALKS RIGHT THROUGH IT, AS THOUGH IT ISN'T THERE!
KRUNCH!
HE'S WALKING RIGHT PAST ME ...AS THOUGH I DON'T EVEN EXIST!
HIS COMPUTERS MUST HAVE ESTIMATED THAT I'M NO DANGER TO HIM --- AND SO HE'S GOING BACK TO HIS ORIGINAL MISSION!..
BUT, I DON'T EVEN KNOW WHAT HIS MISSION ...WHAT HIS PURPOSE... IS!?! ALL I KNOW IS THAT THE RED SKULL SAID BECAUSE OF THE SLEEPERS, THE THIRD REICH WOULD LIVE AGAIN!
THE SLEEPERS! THAT'S RIGHT... THERE WERE SUPPOSED TO BE THREE OF THEM!
HE MUST BE GOING TO RENDEZVOUS WITH THE OTHER TWO!
AND, THERE'S NO WAY I CAN STOP HIM!
AND, AT THAT VERY MOMENT, IN THE TOWN OF TELBECK, ERICA WOLFMANN, THE SECOND ONE ON THE RED SKULL'S LIST, MAKES A FATEFUL PHONE CALL ...
THIS IS AGENT TWO! ASSEMBLE THE DIGGERS! THE TIME HAS COME!
THE SECOND SLEEPER MUST AWAKEN! THE THIRD REICH SHALL LIVE AGAIN!
AS YOU HAVE PROBABLY REALIZED BY NOW, THIS TALE IS BEING PRESENTED IN ANSWER TO YOUR REQUESTS FOR MORE STORIES OF AMERICA'S RED-WHITE-AND-BLUE AVENGER IN THE PRESENT! NEXT ISH, THE SPECTACLE AND SUPER-FANTASY WILL STARTLE AND STUN YOU! SO, SHARE THE WONDER WITH US WHEN THE SECOND SLEEPER WAKES..!
SEE YOU NEXT MONTH!
10.

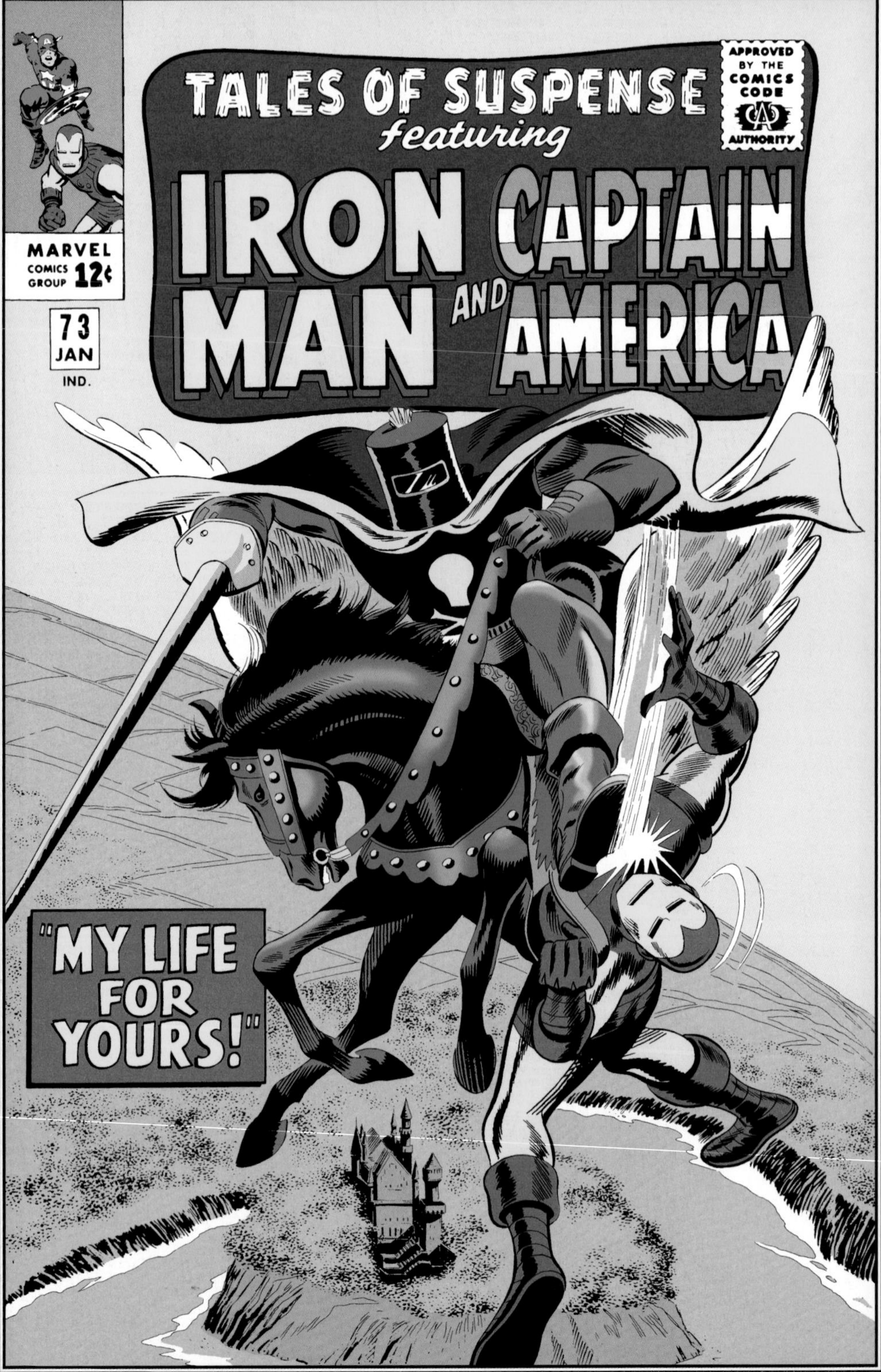
APPROVED BY THE COMICS CODE AUTHORITY
TALES OF SUSPENSE
featuring
IRON MAN AND CAPTAIN AMERICA
MARVEL COMICS GROUP 12¢
73 JAN
IND.
"MY LIFE FOR YOURS!"

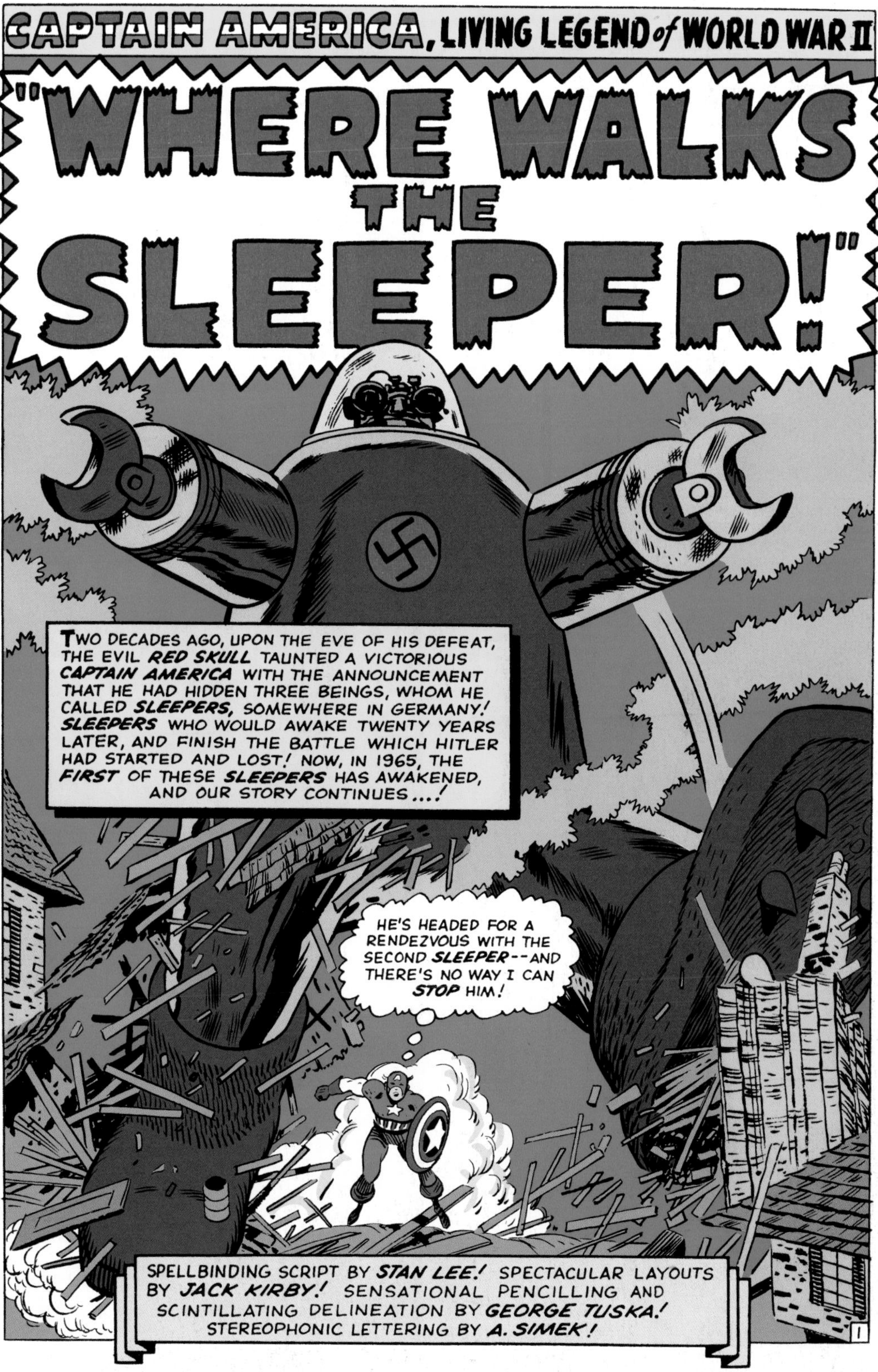
CAPTAIN AMERICA, LIVING LEGEND of WORLD WAR II
"WHERE WALKS THE SLEEPER!"
TWO DECADES AGO, UPON THE EVE OF HIS DEFEAT, THE EVIL RED SKULL TAUNTED A VICTORIOUS CAPTAIN AMERICA WITH THE ANNOUNCEMENT THAT HE HAD HIDDEN THREE BEINGS, WHOM HE CALLED SLEEPERS, SOMEWHERE IN GERMANY! SLEEPERS WHO WOULD AWAKE TWENTY YEARS LATER, AND FINISH THE BATTLE WHICH HITLER HAD STARTED AND LOST! NOW, IN 1965, THE FIRST OF THESE SLEEPERS HAS AWAKENED, AND OUR STORY CONTINUES...!
HE'S HEADED FOR A RENDEZVOUS WITH THE SECOND SLEEPER--AND THERE'S NO WAY I CAN STOP HIM!
SPELLBINDING SCRIPT BY STAN LEE! SPECTACULAR LAYOUTS BY JACK KIRBY! SENSATIONAL PENCILLING AND SCINTILLATING DELINEATION BY GEORGE TUSKA! STEREOPHONIC LETTERING BY A. SIMEK!
1

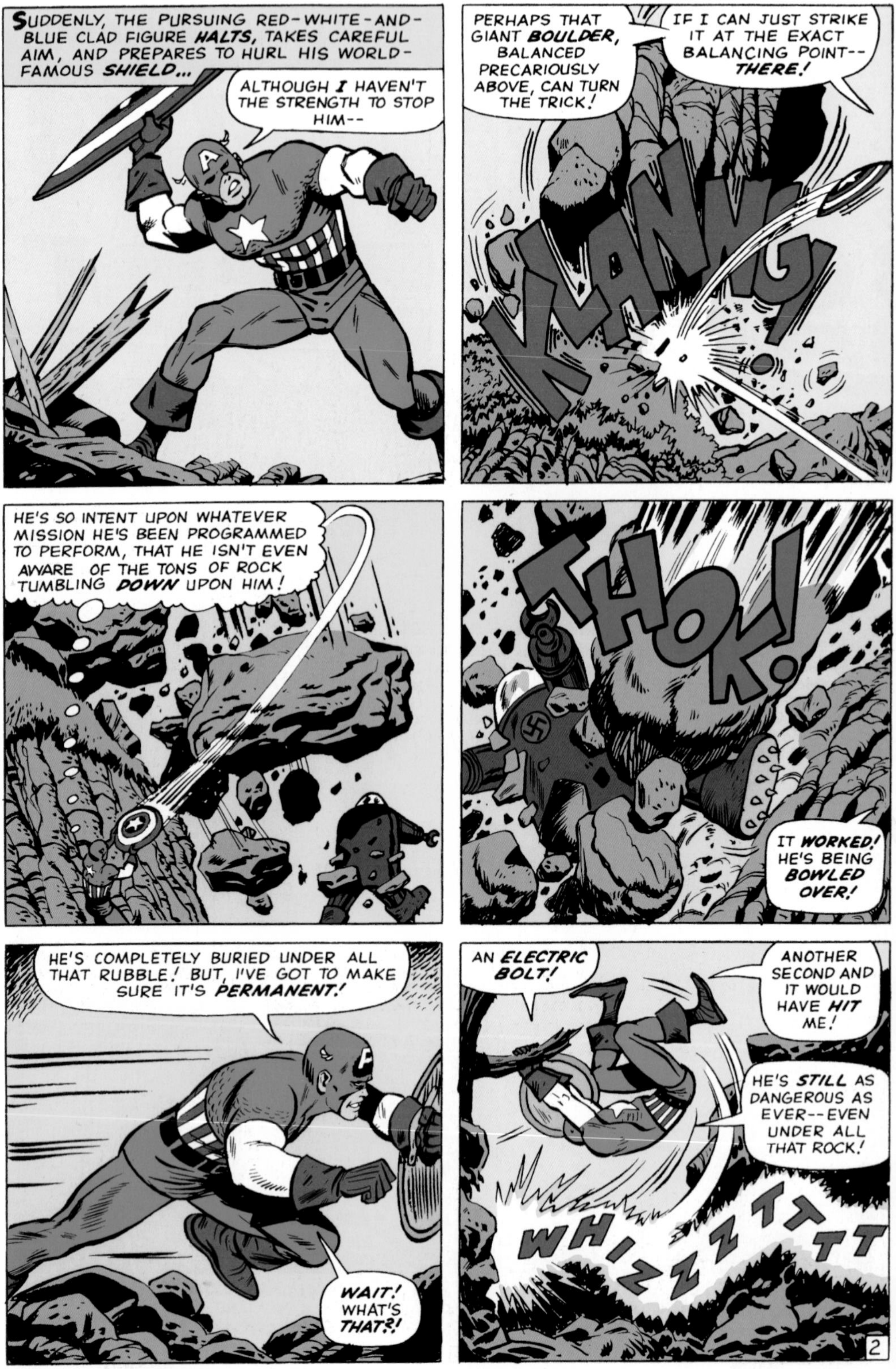
SUDDENLY, THE PURSUING RED-WHITE-AND-BLUE CLAD FIGURE HALTS, TAKES CAREFUL AIM, AND PREPARES TO HURL HIS WORLD-FAMOUS SHIELD...
ALTHOUGH I HAVEN'T THE STRENGTH TO STOP HIM--
PERHAPS THAT GIANT BOULDER, BALANCED PRECARIOUSLY ABOVE, CAN TURN THE TRICK!
IF I CAN JUST STRIKE IT AT THE EXACT BALANCING POINT-- THERE!
KLANNG!
HE'S SO INTENT UPON WHATEVER MISSION HE'S BEEN PROGRAMMED TO PERFORM, THAT HE ISN'T EVEN AWARE OF THE TONS OF ROCK TUMBLING DOWN UPON HIM!
THOK!
IT WORKED! HE'S BEING BOWLED OVER!
HE'S COMPLETELY BURIED UNDER ALL THAT RUBBLE! BUT, I'VE GOT TO MAKE SURE IT'S PERMANENT!
WAIT! WHAT'S THAT?!
AN ELECTRIC BOLT!
ANOTHER SECOND AND IT WOULD HAVE HIT ME!
HE'S STILL AS DANGEROUS AS EVER--EVEN UNDER ALL THAT ROCK!
WHIZZZTTTT
2

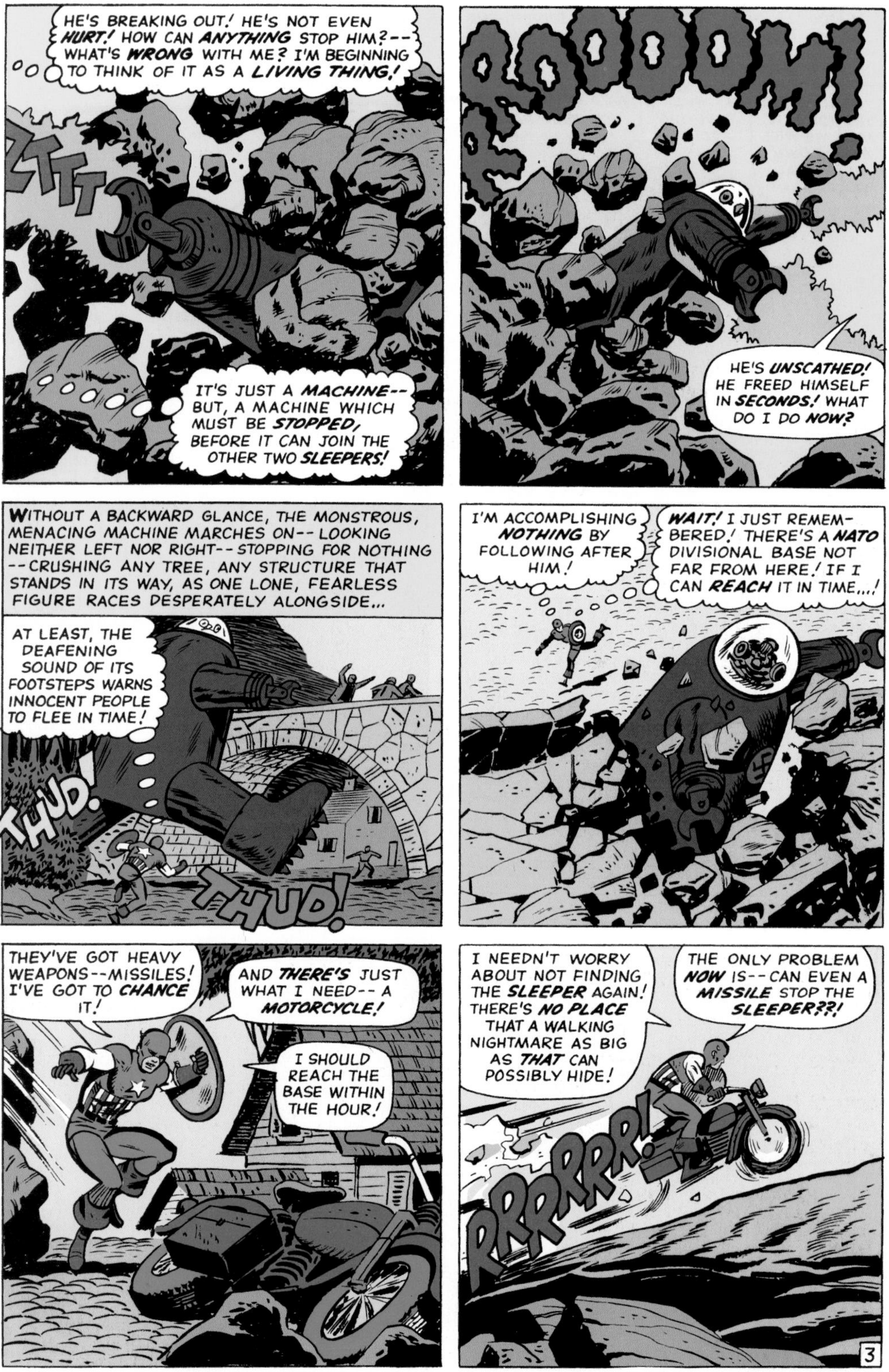
HE'S BREAKING OUT! HE'S NOT EVEN HURT! HOW CAN ANYTHING STOP HIM?-- WHAT'S WRONG WITH ME? I'M BEGINNING TO THINK OF IT AS A LIVING THING!
ZTTTT
IT'S JUST A MACHINE-- BUT, A MACHINE WHICH MUST BE STOPPED, BEFORE IT CAN JOIN THE OTHER TWO SLEEPERS!
RROOOOM!
HE'S UNSCATHED! HE FREED HIMSELF IN SECONDS! WHAT DO I DO NOW?
WITHOUT A BACKWARD GLANCE, THE MONSTROUS, MENACING MACHINE MARCHES ON-- LOOKING NEITHER LEFT NOR RIGHT-- STOPPING FOR NOTHING --CRUSHING ANY TREE, ANY STRUCTURE THAT STANDS IN ITS WAY, AS ONE LONE, FEARLESS FIGURE RACES DESPERATELY ALONGSIDE...
AT LEAST, THE DEAFENING SOUND OF ITS FOOTSTEPS WARNS INNOCENT PEOPLE TO FLEE IN TIME!
THUD!
THUD!
I'M ACCOMPLISHING NOTHING BY FOLLOWING AFTER HIM!
WAIT! I JUST REMEMBERED! THERE'S A NATO DIVISIONAL BASE NOT FAR FROM HERE! IF I CAN REACH IT IN TIME...!
THEY'VE GOT HEAVY WEAPONS--MISSILES! I'VE GOT TO CHANCE IT!
AND THERE'S JUST WHAT I NEED-- A MOTORCYCLE!
I SHOULD REACH THE BASE WITHIN THE HOUR!
I NEEDN'T WORRY ABOUT NOT FINDING THE SLEEPER AGAIN! THERE'S NO PLACE THAT A WALKING NIGHTMARE AS BIG AS THAT CAN POSSIBLY HIDE!
THE ONLY PROBLEM NOW IS-- CAN EVEN A MISSILE STOP THE SLEEPER??!
RRRRRRR!
3

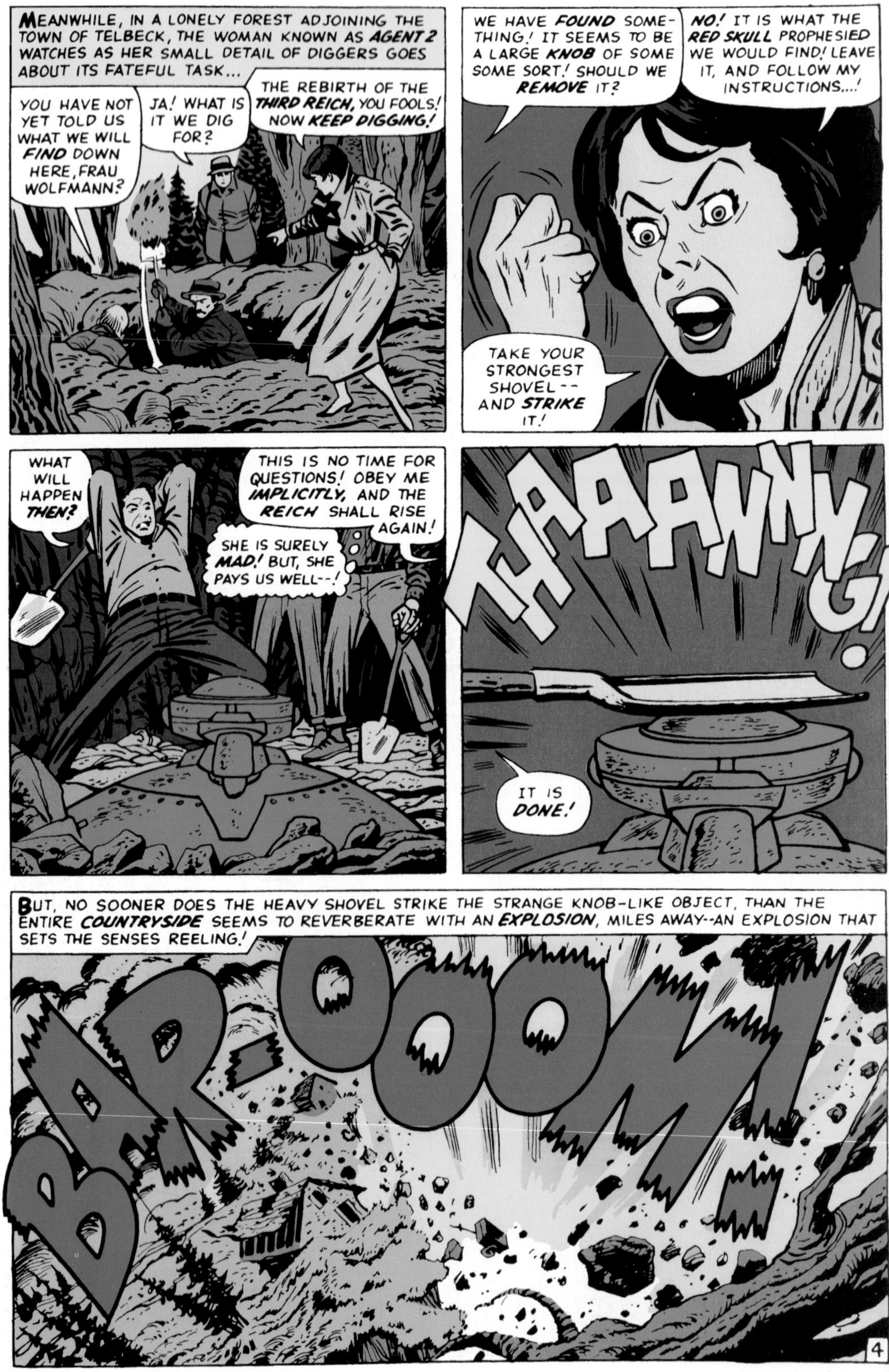
MEANWHILE, IN A LONELY FOREST ADJOINING THE TOWN OF TELBECK, THE WOMAN KNOWN AS AGENT 2 WATCHES AS HER SMALL DETAIL OF DIGGERS GOES ABOUT ITS FATEFUL TASK...
YOU HAVE NOT YET TOLD US WHAT WE WILL FIND DOWN HERE, FRAU WOLFMANN?
JA! WHAT IS IT WE DIG FOR?
THE REBIRTH OF THE THIRD REICH, YOU FOOLS! NOW KEEP DIGGING!
WE HAVE FOUND SOMETHING! IT SEEMS TO BE A LARGE KNOB OF SOME SOME SORT! SHOULD WE REMOVE IT?
NO! IT IS WHAT THE RED SKULL PROPHESIED WE WOULD FIND! LEAVE IT, AND FOLLOW MY INSTRUCTIONS...!
TAKE YOUR STRONGEST SHOVEL -- AND STRIKE IT!
WHAT WILL HAPPEN THEN?
THIS IS NO TIME FOR QUESTIONS! OBEY ME IMPLICITLY, AND THE REICH SHALL RISE AGAIN!
SHE IS SURELY MAD! BUT, SHE PAYS US WELL--!
THAAANNNG!
IT IS DONE!
BUT, NO SOONER DOES THE HEAVY SHOVEL STRIKE THE STRANGE KNOB-LIKE OBJECT, THAN THE ENTIRE COUNTRYSIDE SEEMS TO REVERBERATE WITH AN EXPLOSION, MILES AWAY--AN EXPLOSION THAT SETS THE SENSES REELING!
BAR-OOOM!
4

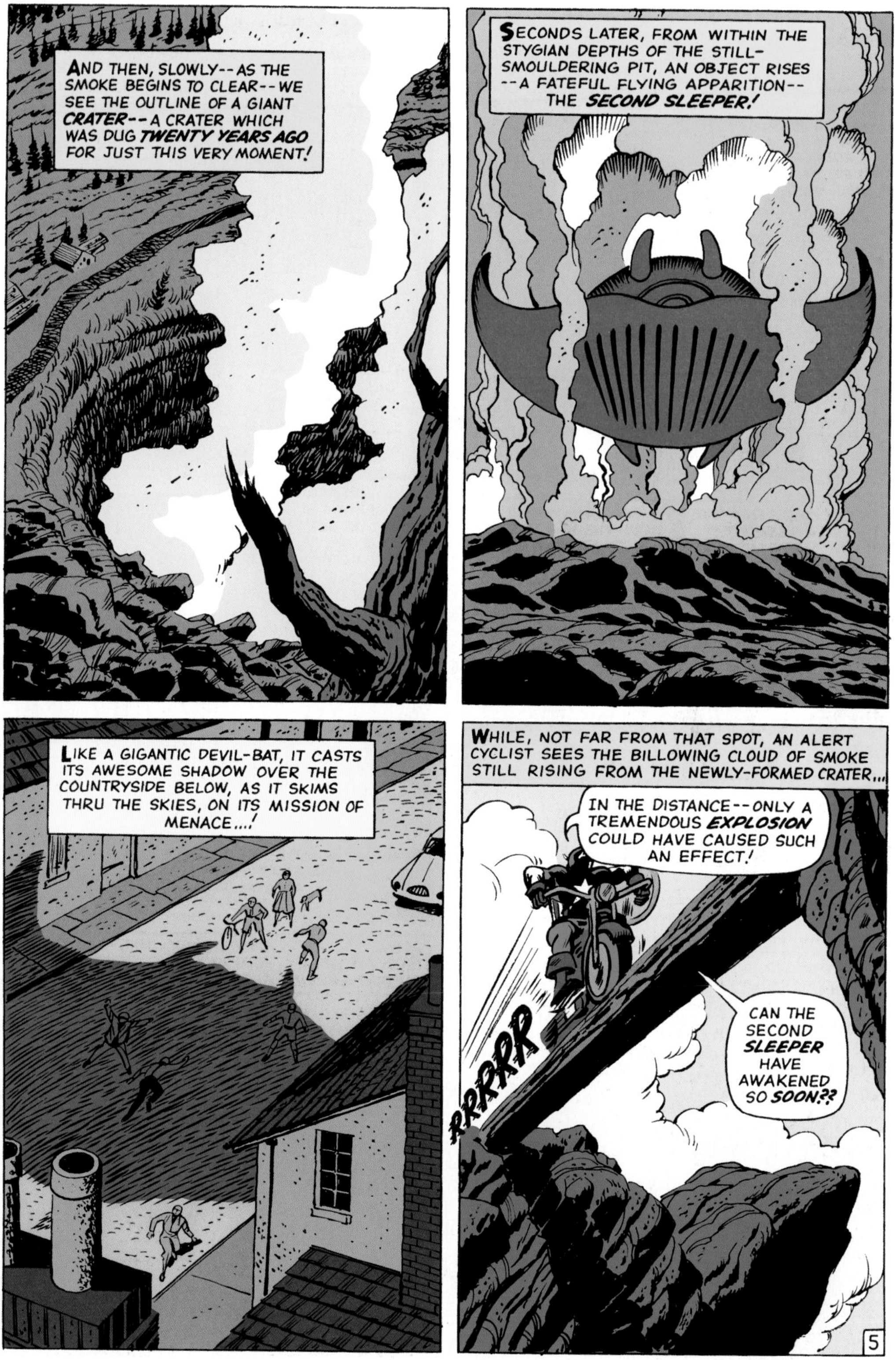
AND THEN, SLOWLY--AS THE SMOKE BEGINS TO CLEAR--WE SEE THE OUTLINE OF A GIANT CRATER--A CRATER WHICH WAS DUG TWENTY YEARS AGO FOR JUST THIS VERY MOMENT!
SECONDS LATER, FROM WITHIN THE STYGIAN DEPTHS OF THE STILL-SMOULDERING PIT, AN OBJECT RISES --A FATEFUL FLYING APPARITION-- THE SECOND SLEEPER!
LIKE A GIGANTIC DEVIL-BAT, IT CASTS ITS AWESOME SHADOW OVER THE COUNTRYSIDE BELOW, AS IT SKIMS THRU THE SKIES, ON ITS MISSION OF MENACE...!
WHILE, NOT FAR FROM THAT SPOT, AN ALERT CYCLIST SEES THE BILLOWING CLOUD OF SMOKE STILL RISING FROM THE NEWLY-FORMED CRATER...
IN THE DISTANCE--ONLY A TREMENDOUS EXPLOSION COULD HAVE CAUSED SUCH AN EFFECT!
RRRRRR
CAN THE SECOND SLEEPER HAVE AWAKENED SO SOON??
5

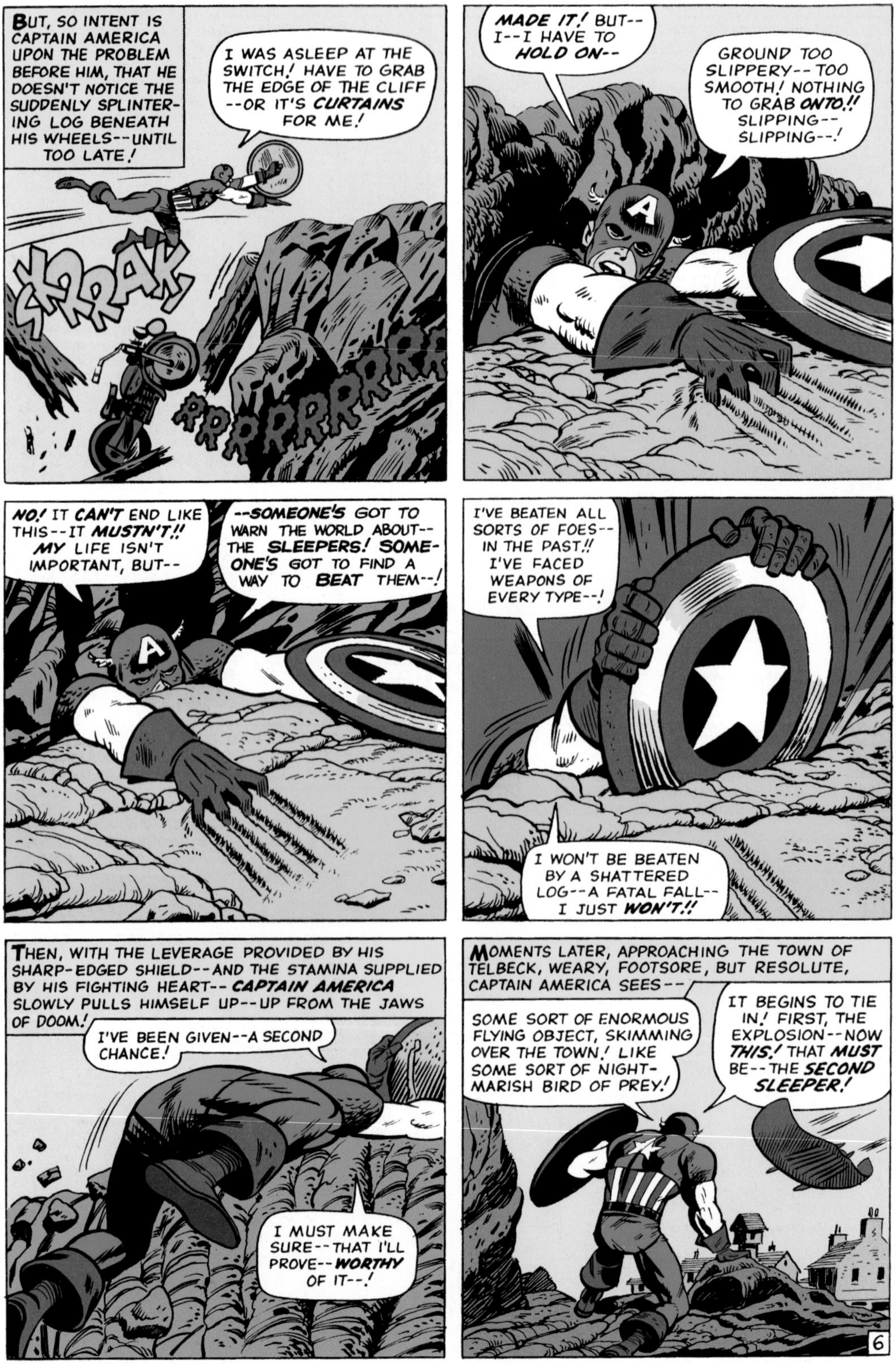
BUT, SO INTENT IS CAPTAIN AMERICA UPON THE PROBLEM BEFORE HIM, THAT HE DOESN'T NOTICE THE SUDDENLY SPLINTERING LOG BENEATH HIS WHEELS--UNTIL TOO LATE!
I WAS ASLEEP AT THE SWITCH! HAVE TO GRAB THE EDGE OF THE CLIFF --OR IT'S CURTAINS FOR ME!
SKRRAK
RRRRRRRRR
MADE IT! BUT-- I--I HAVE TO HOLD ON--
GROUND TOO SLIPPERY--TOO SMOOTH! NOTHING TO GRAB ONTO!! SLIPPING-- SLIPPING--!
NO! IT CAN'T END LIKE THIS--IT MUSTN'T!! MY LIFE ISN'T IMPORTANT, BUT--
--SOMEONE'S GOT TO WARN THE WORLD ABOUT-- THE SLEEPERS! SOMEONE'S GOT TO FIND A WAY TO BEAT THEM--!
I'VE BEATEN ALL SORTS OF FOES-- IN THE PAST!! I'VE FACED WEAPONS OF EVERY TYPE--!
I WON'T BE BEATEN BY A SHATTERED LOG--A FATAL FALL-- I JUST WON'T!!
THEN, WITH THE LEVERAGE PROVIDED BY HIS SHARP-EDGED SHIELD--AND THE STAMINA SUPPLIED BY HIS FIGHTING HEART-- CAPTAIN AMERICA SLOWLY PULLS HIMSELF UP--UP FROM THE JAWS OF DOOM!
I'VE BEEN GIVEN--A SECOND CHANCE!
I MUST MAKE SURE--THAT I'LL PROVE--WORTHY OF IT--!
MOMENTS LATER, APPROACHING THE TOWN OF TELBECK, WEARY, FOOTSORE, BUT RESOLUTE, CAPTAIN AMERICA SEES--
SOME SORT OF ENORMOUS FLYING OBJECT, SKIMMING OVER THE TOWN! LIKE SOME SORT OF NIGHTMARISH BIRD OF PREY!
IT BEGINS TO TIE IN! FIRST, THE EXPLOSION--NOW THIS! THAT MUST BE--THE SECOND SLEEPER!
6

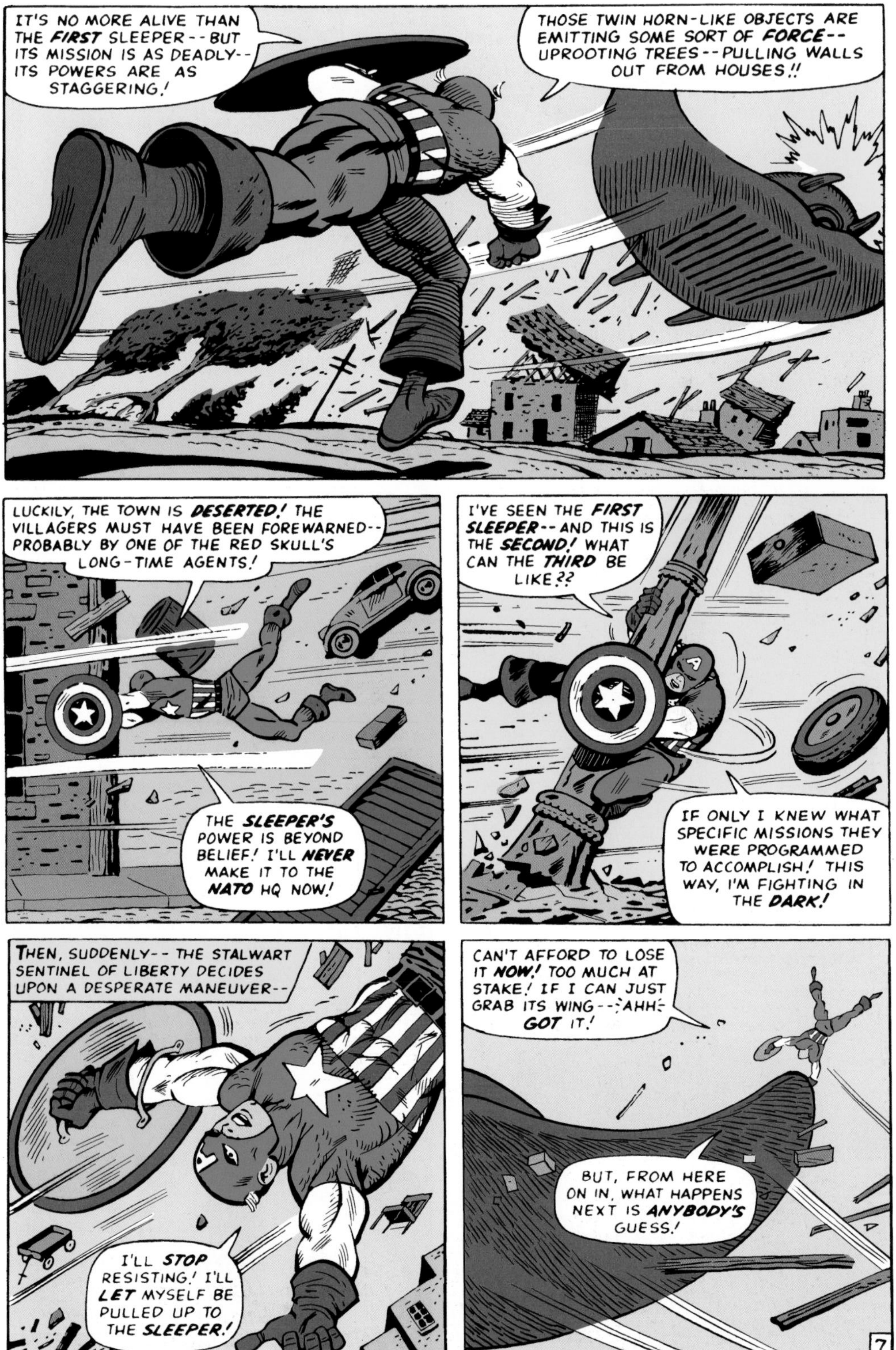
IT'S NO MORE ALIVE THAN THE FIRST SLEEPER--BUT ITS MISSION IS AS DEADLY--ITS POWERS ARE AS STAGGERING!
THOSE TWIN HORN-LIKE OBJECTS ARE EMITTING SOME SORT OF FORCE--UPROOTING TREES--PULLING WALLS OUT FROM HOUSES!!
LUCKILY, THE TOWN IS DESERTED! THE VILLAGERS MUST HAVE BEEN FOREWARNED--PROBABLY BY ONE OF THE RED SKULL'S LONG-TIME AGENTS!
THE SLEEPER'S POWER IS BEYOND BELIEF! I'LL NEVER MAKE IT TO THE NATO HQ NOW!
I'VE SEEN THE FIRST SLEEPER--AND THIS IS THE SECOND! WHAT CAN THE THIRD BE LIKE??
IF ONLY I KNEW WHAT SPECIFIC MISSIONS THEY WERE PROGRAMMED TO ACCOMPLISH! THIS WAY, I'M FIGHTING IN THE DARK!
THEN, SUDDENLY--THE STALWART SENTINEL OF LIBERTY DECIDES UPON A DESPERATE MANEUVER--
I'LL STOP RESISTING! I'LL LET MYSELF BE PULLED UP TO THE SLEEPER!
CAN'T AFFORD TO LOSE IT NOW! TOO MUCH AT STAKE! IF I CAN JUST GRAB ITS WING--AHH--GOT IT!
BUT, FROM HERE ON IN, WHAT HAPPENS NEXT IS ANYBODY'S GUESS!
7

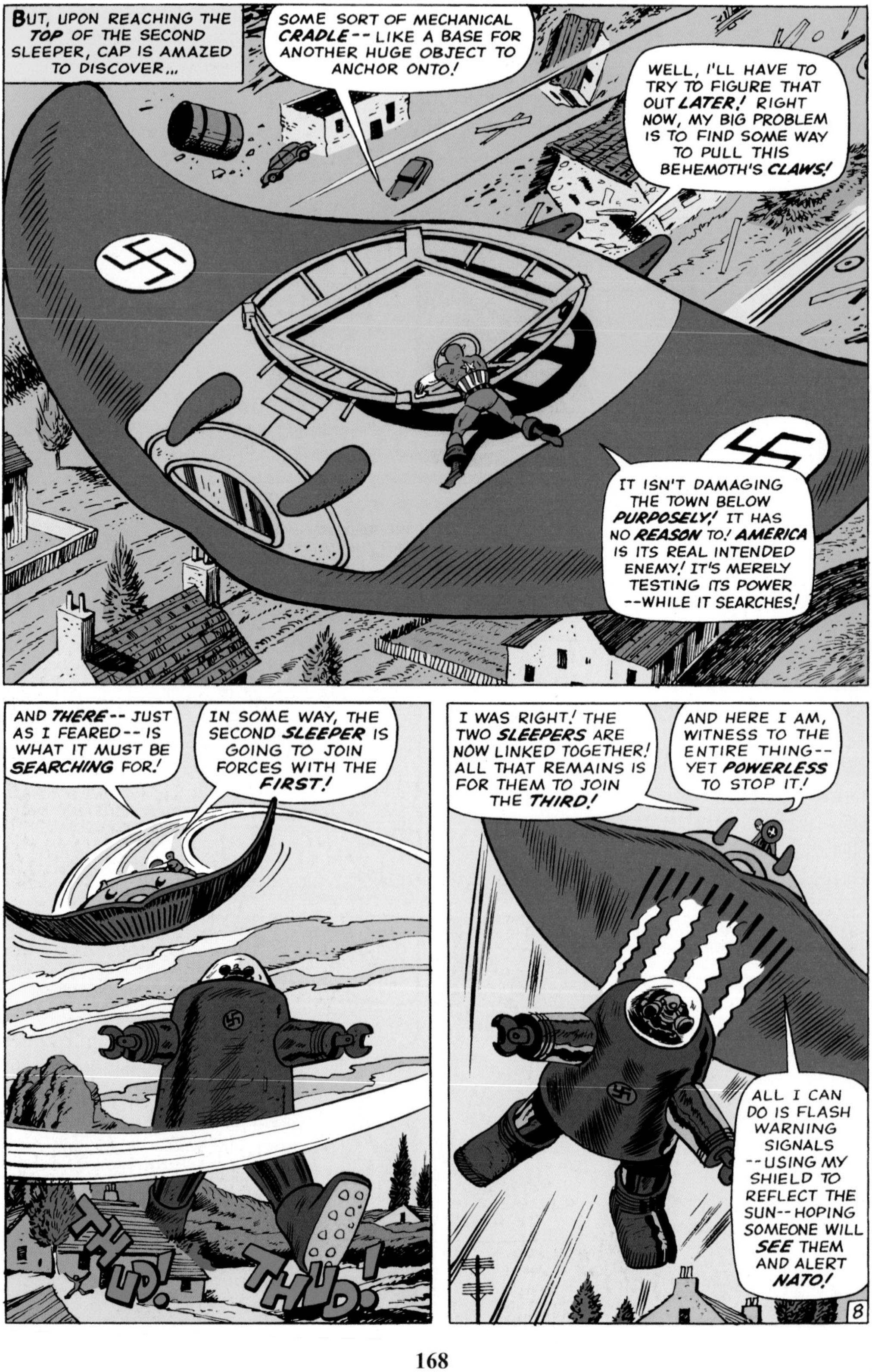

BUT, UPON REACHING THE TOP OF THE SECOND SLEEPER, CAP IS AMAZED TO DISCOVER...
SOME SORT OF MECHANICAL CRADLE-- LIKE A BASE FOR ANOTHER HUGE OBJECT TO ANCHOR ONTO!
WELL, I'LL HAVE TO TRY TO FIGURE THAT OUT LATER! RIGHT NOW, MY BIG PROBLEM IS TO FIND SOME WAY TO PULL THIS BEHEMOTH'S CLAWS!
IT ISN'T DAMAGING THE TOWN BELOW PURPOSELY! IT HAS NO REASON TO! AMERICA IS ITS REAL INTENDED ENEMY! IT'S MERELY TESTING ITS POWER --WHILE IT SEARCHES!
AND THERE-- JUST AS I FEARED-- IS WHAT IT MUST BE SEARCHING FOR!
IN SOME WAY, THE SECOND SLEEPER IS GOING TO JOIN FORCES WITH THE FIRST!
THUD! THUD!
I WAS RIGHT! THE TWO SLEEPERS ARE NOW LINKED TOGETHER! ALL THAT REMAINS IS FOR THEM TO JOIN THE THIRD!
AND HERE I AM, WITNESS TO THE ENTIRE THING-- YET POWERLESS TO STOP IT!
ALL I CAN DO IS FLASH WARNING SIGNALS --USING MY SHIELD TO REFLECT THE SUN-- HOPING SOMEONE WILL SEE THEM AND ALERT NATO!
8

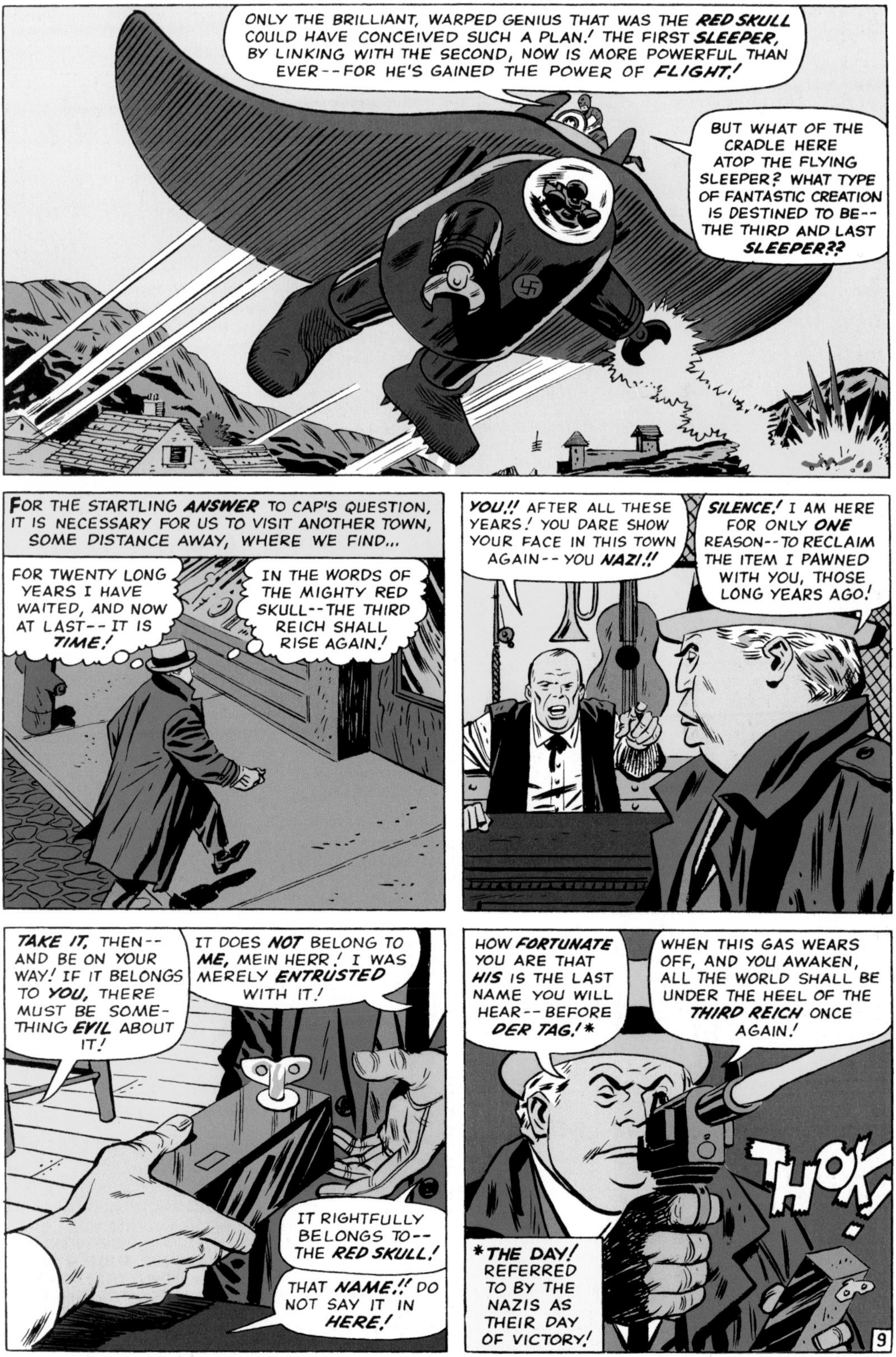
ONLY THE BRILLIANT, WARPED GENIUS THAT WAS THE RED SKULL COULD HAVE CONCEIVED SUCH A PLAN! THE FIRST SLEEPER, BY LINKING WITH THE SECOND, NOW IS MORE POWERFUL THAN EVER--FOR HE'S GAINED THE POWER OF FLIGHT!
BUT WHAT OF THE CRADLE HERE ATOP THE FLYING SLEEPER? WHAT TYPE OF FANTASTIC CREATION IS DESTINED TO BE--THE THIRD AND LAST SLEEPER??
FOR THE STARTLING ANSWER TO CAP'S QUESTION, IT IS NECESSARY FOR US TO VISIT ANOTHER TOWN, SOME DISTANCE AWAY, WHERE WE FIND...
FOR TWENTY LONG YEARS I HAVE WAITED, AND NOW AT LAST--IT IS TIME!
IN THE WORDS OF THE MIGHTY RED SKULL--THE THIRD REICH SHALL RISE AGAIN!
YOU!! AFTER ALL THESE YEARS! YOU DARE SHOW YOUR FACE IN THIS TOWN AGAIN--YOU NAZI!!
SILENCE! I AM HERE FOR ONLY ONE REASON--TO RECLAIM THE ITEM I PAWNED WITH YOU, THOSE LONG YEARS AGO!
TAKE IT, THEN--AND BE ON YOUR WAY! IF IT BELONGS TO YOU, THERE MUST BE SOMETHING EVIL ABOUT IT!
IT DOES NOT BELONG TO ME, MEIN HERR! I WAS MERELY ENTRUSTED WITH IT!
IT RIGHTFULLY BELONGS TO--THE RED SKULL!
THAT NAME!! DO NOT SAY IT IN HERE!
HOW FORTUNATE YOU ARE THAT HIS IS THE LAST NAME YOU WILL HEAR--BEFORE DER TAG!*
WHEN THIS GAS WEARS OFF, AND YOU AWAKEN, ALL THE WORLD SHALL BE UNDER THE HEEL OF THE THIRD REICH ONCE AGAIN!
THOK!
*THE DAY! REFERRED TO BY THE NAZIS AS THEIR DAY OF VICTORY!
9

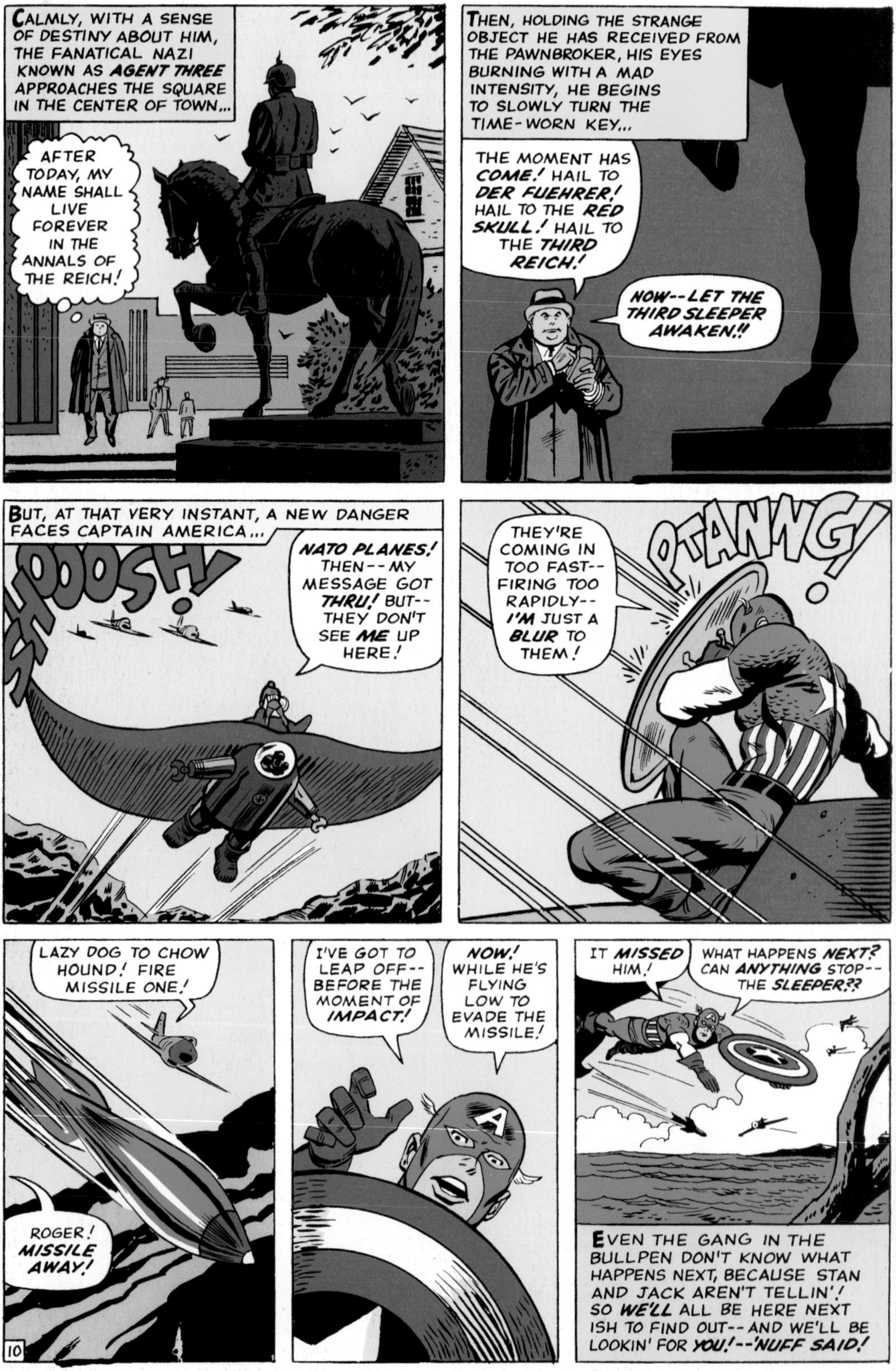

CALMLY, WITH A SENSE OF DESTINY ABOUT HIM, THE FANATICAL NAZI KNOWN AS AGENT THREE APPROACHES THE SQUARE IN THE CENTER OF TOWN...
AFTER TODAY, MY NAME SHALL LIVE FOREVER IN THE ANNALS OF THE REICH!
THEN, HOLDING THE STRANGE OBJECT HE HAS RECEIVED FROM THE PAWNBROKER, HIS EYES BURNING WITH A MAD INTENSITY, HE BEGINS TO SLOWLY TURN THE TIME-WORN KEY...
THE MOMENT HAS COME! HAIL TO DER FUEHRER! HAIL TO THE RED SKULL! HAIL TO THE THIRD REICH!
NOW--LET THE THIRD SLEEPER AWAKEN!!
BUT, AT THAT VERY INSTANT, A NEW DANGER FACES CAPTAIN AMERICA...
SHOOOSH!
NATO PLANES! THEN--MY MESSAGE GOT THRU! BUT--THEY DON'T SEE ME UP HERE!
PTANNG!
THEY'RE COMING IN TOO FAST--FIRING TOO RAPIDLY--I'M JUST A BLUR TO THEM!
LAZY DOG TO CHOW HOUND! FIRE MISSILE ONE!
ROGER! MISSILE AWAY!
10
I'VE GOT TO LEAP OFF--BEFORE THE MOMENT OF IMPACT!
NOW! WHILE HE'S FLYING LOW TO EVADE THE MISSILE!
IT MISSED HIM!
WHAT HAPPENS NEXT? CAN ANYTHING STOP--THE SLEEPER??
EVEN THE GANG IN THE BULLPEN DON'T KNOW WHAT HAPPENS NEXT, BECAUSE STAN AND JACK AREN'T TELLIN'! SO WE'LL ALL BE HERE NEXT ISH TO FIND OUT--AND WE'LL BE LOOKIN' FOR YOU!--'NUFF SAID!

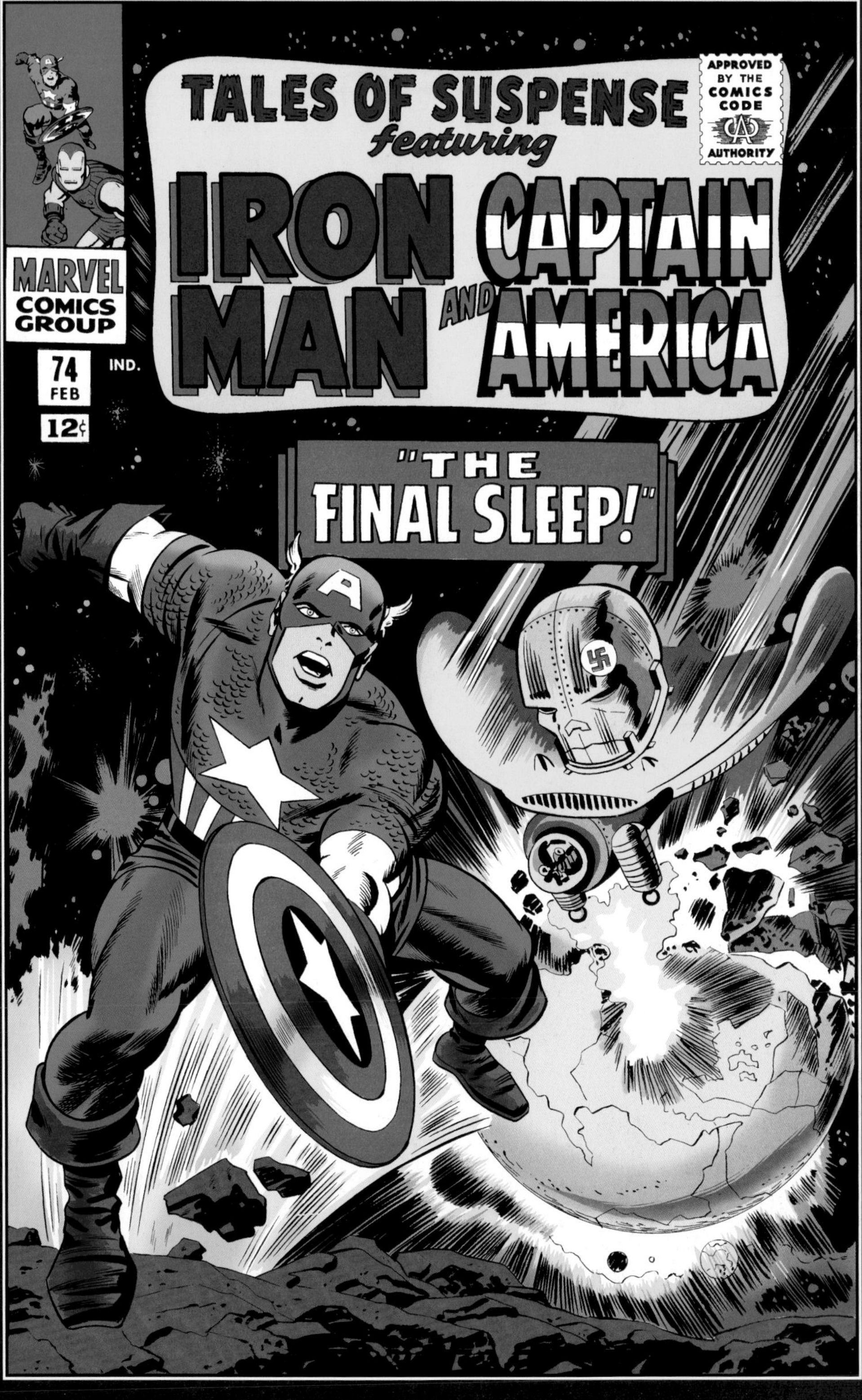
MARVEL
COMICS
GROUP
74
FEB
12¢
IND.
TALES OF SUSPENSE
featuring
IRON MAN
AND
CAPTAIN AMERICA
APPROVED
BY THE
COMICS
CODE
AUTHORITY
"THE
FINAL SLEEP!"

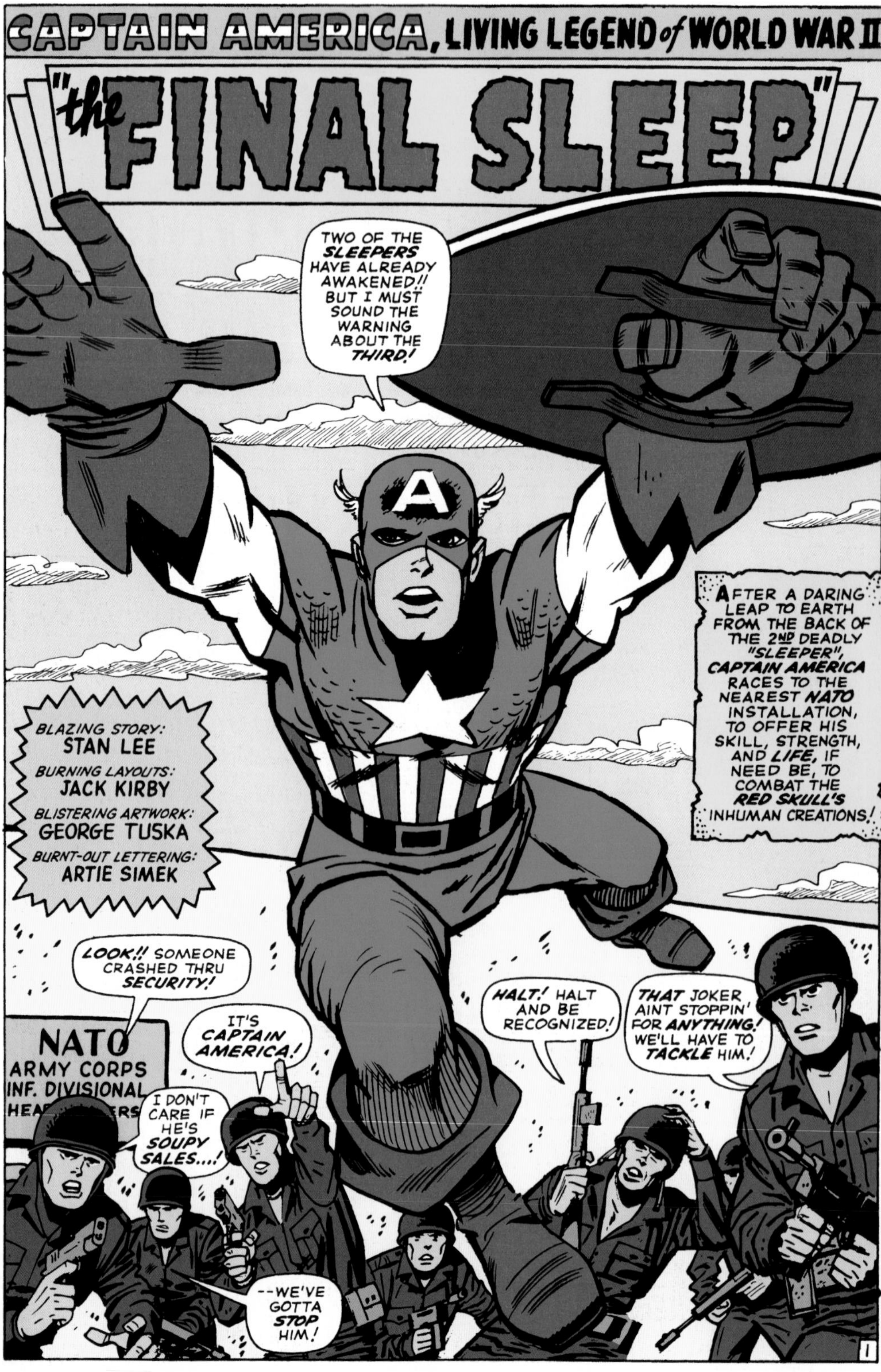
CAPTAIN AMERICA, LIVING LEGEND of WORLD WAR II
"the FINAL SLEEP"
TWO OF THE SLEEPERS HAVE ALREADY AWAKENED!! BUT I MUST SOUND THE WARNING ABOUT THE THIRD!
AFTER A DARING LEAP TO EARTH FROM THE BACK OF THE 2ND DEADLY "SLEEPER", CAPTAIN AMERICA RACES TO THE NEAREST NATO INSTALLATION, TO OFFER HIS SKILL, STRENGTH, AND LIFE, IF NEED BE, TO COMBAT THE RED SKULL'S INHUMAN CREATIONS!
BLAZING STORY: STAN LEE
BURNING LAYOUTS: JACK KIRBY
BLISTERING ARTWORK: GEORGE TUSKA
BURNT-OUT LETTERING: ARTIE SIMEK
LOOK!! SOMEONE CRASHED THRU SECURITY!
NATO ARMY CORPS INF. DIVISIONAL
IT'S CAPTAIN AMERICA!
I DON'T CARE IF HE'S SOUPY SALES...!
--WE'VE GOTTA STOP HIM!
HALT! HALT AND BE RECOGNIZED!
THAT JOKER AINT STOPPIN' FOR ANYTHING! WE'LL HAVE TO TACKLE HIM!
1

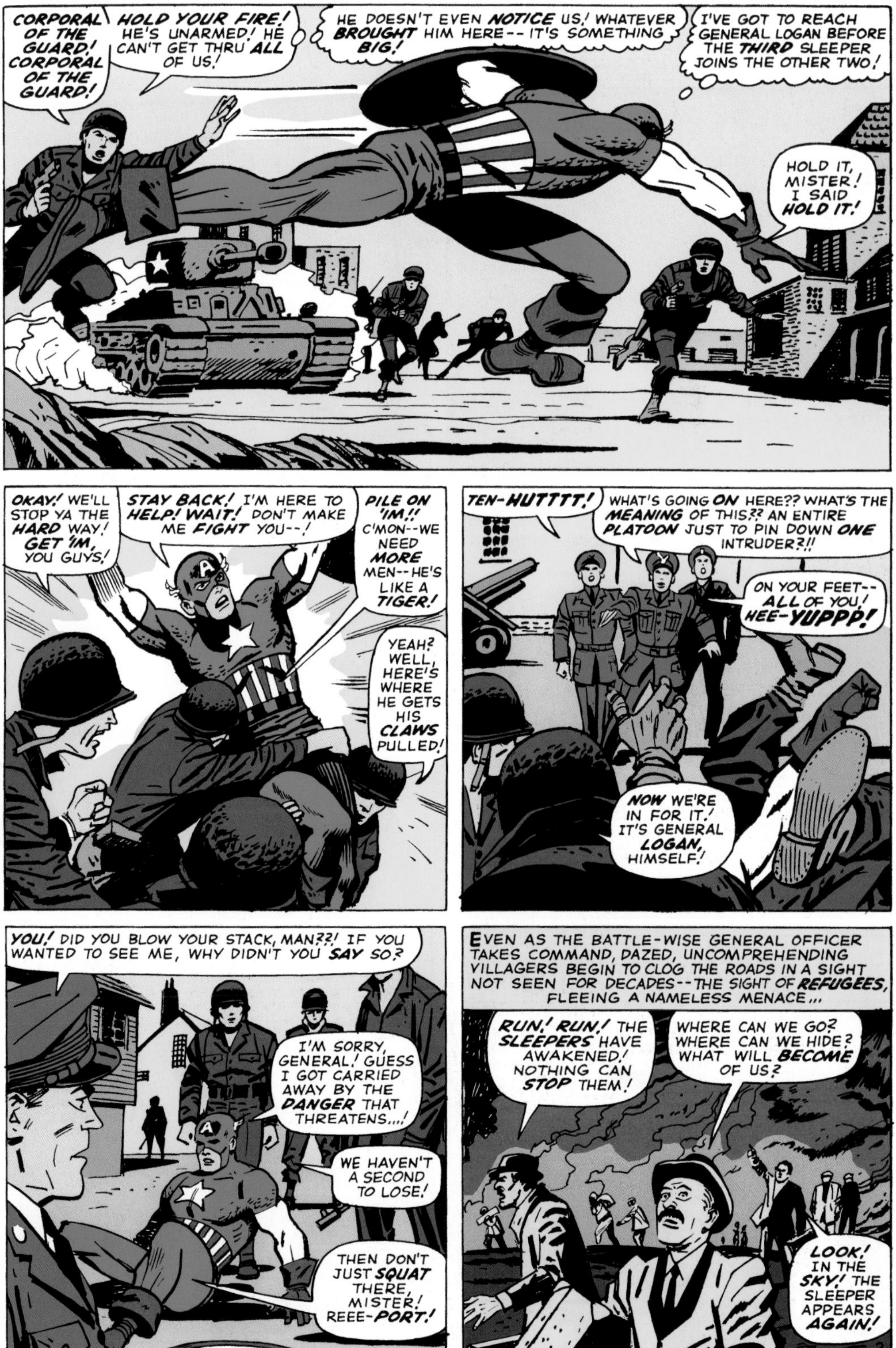
CORPORAL OF THE GUARD! CORPORAL OF THE GUARD!
HOLD YOUR FIRE! HE'S UNARMED! HE CAN'T GET THRU ALL OF US!
HE DOESN'T EVEN NOTICE US! WHATEVER BROUGHT HIM HERE-- IT'S SOMETHING BIG!
I'VE GOT TO REACH GENERAL LOGAN BEFORE THE THIRD SLEEPER JOINS THE OTHER TWO!
HOLD IT, MISTER! I SAID HOLD IT!
OKAY! WE'LL STOP YA THE HARD WAY! GET 'IM, YOU GUYS!
STAY BACK! I'M HERE TO HELP! WAIT! DON'T MAKE ME FIGHT YOU--!
PILE ON 'IM!! C'MON--WE NEED MORE MEN--HE'S LIKE A TIGER!
YEAH? WELL, HERE'S WHERE HE GETS HIS CLAWS PULLED!
TEN-HUTTTT!
WHAT'S GOING ON HERE?? WHAT'S THE MEANING OF THIS?? AN ENTIRE PLATOON JUST TO PIN DOWN ONE INTRUDER?!!
ON YOUR FEET-- ALL OF YOU! HEE-YUPPP!
NOW WE'RE IN FOR IT! IT'S GENERAL LOGAN, HIMSELF!
YOU! DID YOU BLOW YOUR STACK, MAN??! IF YOU WANTED TO SEE ME, WHY DIDN'T YOU SAY SO?
I'M SORRY, GENERAL! GUESS I GOT CARRIED AWAY BY THE DANGER THAT THREATENS...!
WE HAVEN'T A SECOND TO LOSE!
THEN DON'T JUST SQUAT THERE, MISTER! REEE-PORT!
EVEN AS THE BATTLE-WISE GENERAL OFFICER TAKES COMMAND, DAZED, UNCOMPREHENDING VILLAGERS BEGIN TO CLOG THE ROADS IN A SIGHT NOT SEEN FOR DECADES--THE SIGHT OF REFUGEES, FLEEING A NAMELESS MENACE...
RUN! RUN! THE SLEEPERS HAVE AWAKENED! NOTHING CAN STOP THEM!
WHERE CAN WE GO? WHERE CAN WE HIDE? WHAT WILL BECOME OF US?
LOOK! IN THE SKY! THE SLEEPER APPEARS AGAIN!
2.

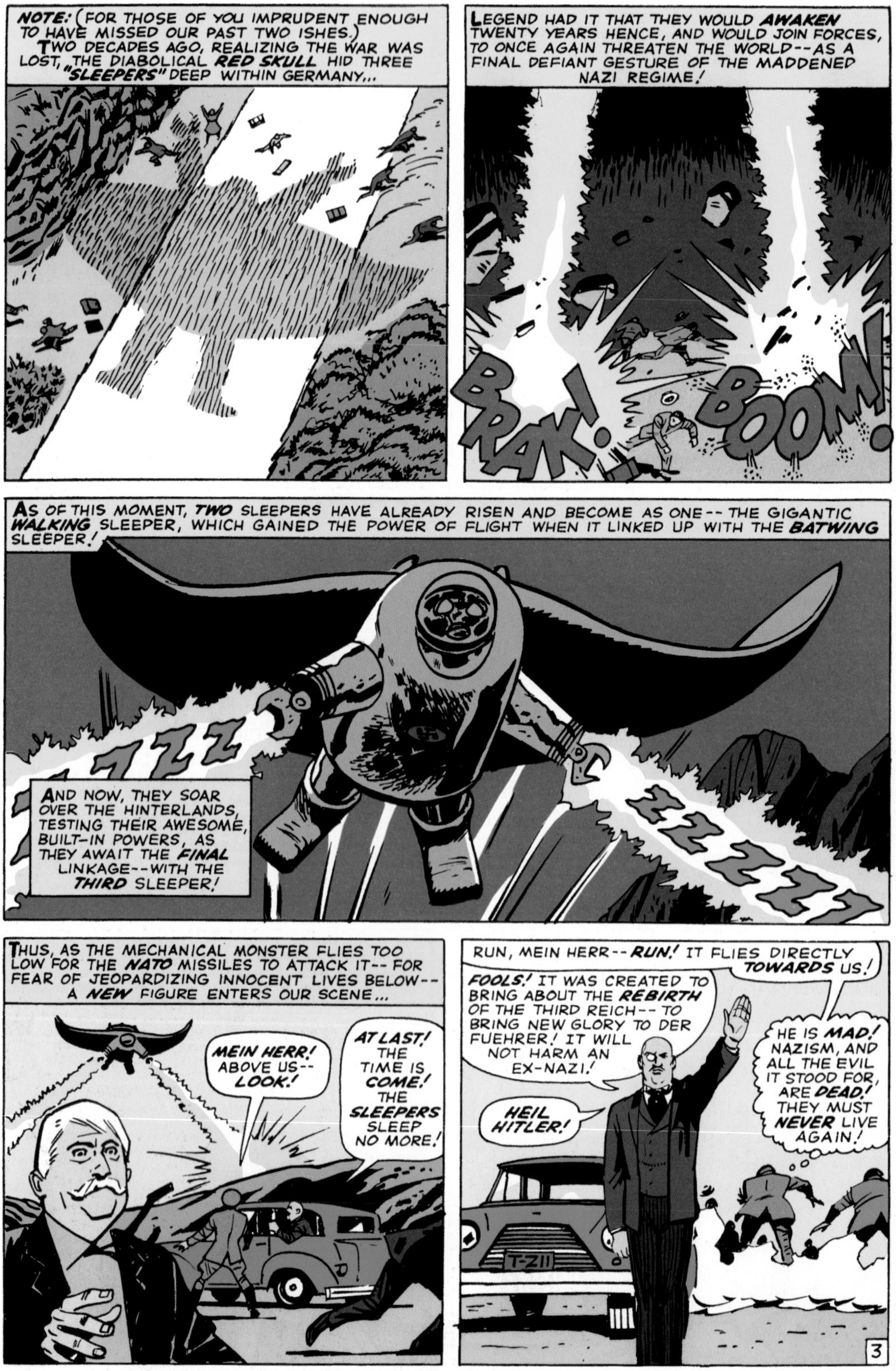
NOTE: (FOR THOSE OF YOU IMPRUDENT ENOUGH TO HAVE MISSED OUR PAST TWO ISHES.)
TWO DECADES AGO, REALIZING THE WAR WAS LOST, THE DIABOLICAL RED SKULL HID THREE "SLEEPERS" DEEP WITHIN GERMANY...
LEGEND HAD IT THAT THEY WOULD AWAKEN TWENTY YEARS HENCE, AND WOULD JOIN FORCES, TO ONCE AGAIN THREATEN THE WORLD--AS A FINAL DEFIANT GESTURE OF THE MADDENED NAZI REGIME!
BRAK!
BOOM!
AS OF THIS MOMENT, TWO SLEEPERS HAVE ALREADY RISEN AND BECOME AS ONE-- THE GIGANTIC WALKING SLEEPER, WHICH GAINED THE POWER OF FLIGHT WHEN IT LINKED UP WITH THE BATWING SLEEPER!
AND NOW, THEY SOAR OVER THE HINTERLANDS, TESTING THEIR AWESOME, BUILT-IN POWERS, AS THEY AWAIT THE FINAL LINKAGE--WITH THE THIRD SLEEPER!
THUS, AS THE MECHANICAL MONSTER FLIES TOO LOW FOR THE NATO MISSILES TO ATTACK IT-- FOR FEAR OF JEOPARDIZING INNOCENT LIVES BELOW-- A NEW FIGURE ENTERS OUR SCENE...
MEIN HERR! ABOVE US-- LOOK!
AT LAST! THE TIME IS COME! THE SLEEPERS SLEEP NO MORE!
RUN, MEIN HERR--RUN! IT FLIES DIRECTLY TOWARDS US!
FOOLS! IT WAS CREATED TO BRING ABOUT THE REBIRTH OF THE THIRD REICH-- TO BRING NEW GLORY TO DER FUEHRER! IT WILL NOT HARM AN EX-NAZI!
HEIL HITLER!
HE IS MAD! NAZISM, AND ALL THE EVIL IT STOOD FOR, ARE DEAD! THEY MUST NEVER LIVE AGAIN!
T-Z11
3

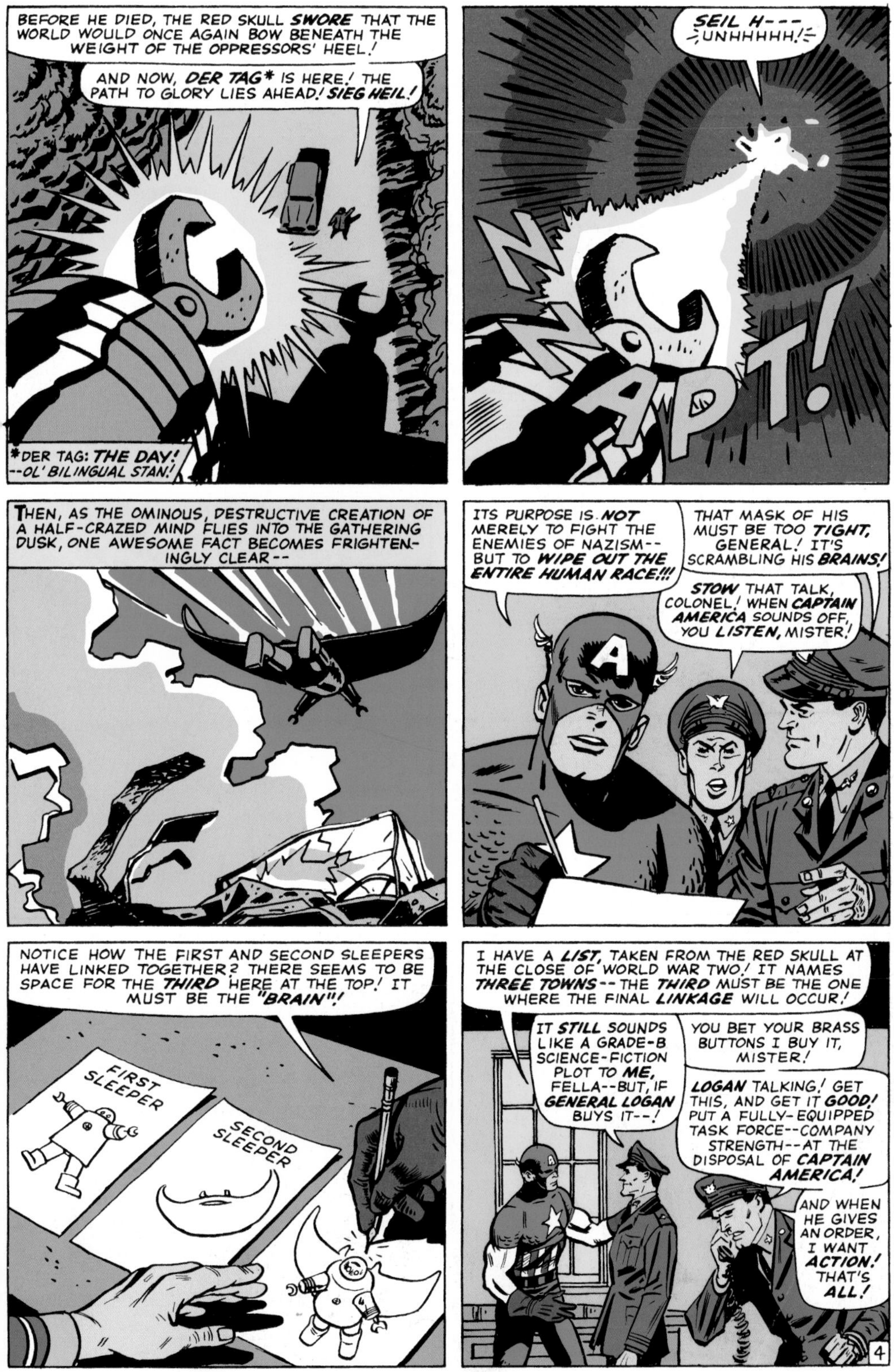
BEFORE HE DIED, THE RED SKULL SWORE THAT THE WORLD WOULD ONCE AGAIN BOW BENEATH THE WEIGHT OF THE OPPRESSORS' HEEL!
AND NOW, DER TAG* IS HERE! THE PATH TO GLORY LIES AHEAD! SIEG HEIL!
*DER TAG: THE DAY! --OL' BILINGUAL STAN!
SEIL H--- UNHHHHH!
ZNAPT!
THEN, AS THE OMINOUS, DESTRUCTIVE CREATION OF A HALF-CRAZED MIND FLIES INTO THE GATHERING DUSK, ONE AWESOME FACT BECOMES FRIGHTENINGLY CLEAR--
ITS PURPOSE IS NOT MERELY TO FIGHT THE ENEMIES OF NAZISM--BUT TO WIPE OUT THE ENTIRE HUMAN RACE!!!
THAT MASK OF HIS MUST BE TOO TIGHT, GENERAL! IT'S SCRAMBLING HIS BRAINS!
STOW THAT TALK, COLONEL! WHEN CAPTAIN AMERICA SOUNDS OFF, YOU LISTEN, MISTER!
NOTICE HOW THE FIRST AND SECOND SLEEPERS HAVE LINKED TOGETHER? THERE SEEMS TO BE SPACE FOR THE THIRD HERE AT THE TOP! IT MUST BE THE "BRAIN"!
FIRST SLEEPER
SECOND SLEEPER
I HAVE A LIST, TAKEN FROM THE RED SKULL AT THE CLOSE OF WORLD WAR TWO! IT NAMES THREE TOWNS--THE THIRD MUST BE THE ONE WHERE THE FINAL LINKAGE WILL OCCUR!
IT STILL SOUNDS LIKE A GRADE-B SCIENCE-FICTION PLOT TO ME, FELLA--BUT, IF GENERAL LOGAN BUYS IT--!
YOU BET YOUR BRASS BUTTONS I BUY IT, MISTER!
LOGAN TALKING! GET THIS, AND GET IT GOOD! PUT A FULLY-EQUIPPED TASK FORCE--COMPANY STRENGTH--AT THE DISPOSAL OF CAPTAIN AMERICA!
AND WHEN HE GIVES AN ORDER, I WANT ACTION! THAT'S ALL!
4

THEN, SATISFIED THAT THE RED-WHITE-AND-BLUE AVENGER HAS ALL THE FIREPOWER HE NEEDS, THE PEPPERY GENERAL TAKES PERSONAL COMMAND OF HIS MOST POTENT ARMORED DIVISION, AS HE RINGS THE AREA WITH A CORDON OF FIGHTING MEN AND MACHINES,...!

LEADER ONE TO RAT PACK! PUSSYCAT DEAD AHEAD! THIS IS *IT!*

WHAT'S ALL THIS SCUTTLEBUTT ABOUT US SEARCHIN' FOR THREE *SLEEPERS?* IS IT SOME KINDA *GAG*, OR SOMETHIN'?

IF IT *IS*, OL' LOGAN WILL DO *ANYTHING* FOR A LAUGH! I AINT SEEN SO MUCH MUSCLE ASSEMBLED AT ONE TIME SINCE *D-DAY.!!*

NOTING THAT THE SLEEPER IS NOW FLYING HIGH ENOUGH FOR EFFECTIVE MISSILE ACTION, GENERAL LOGAN'S FIGHTER JETS ATTACK ON SIGHT,...!

BUT, THE FANTASTIC SLEEPER'S *FORCE RAYS* PROVE TO BE TOO FORMIDABLE A DEFENSE FOR THE SPEEDY JETS,...

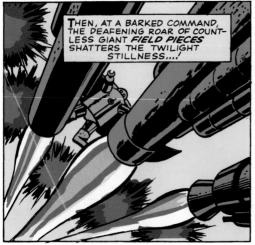

THEN, AT A BARKED COMMAND, THE DEAFENING ROAR OF COUNT-LESS GIANT *FIELD PIECES* SHATTERS THE TWILIGHT STILLNESS....!

BUT, ONCE AGAIN, THE SLEEPER'S FORCE RAYS TURN THE TIDE, ENABLING HIM TO ESCAPE WITH IMPUNITY--!

5

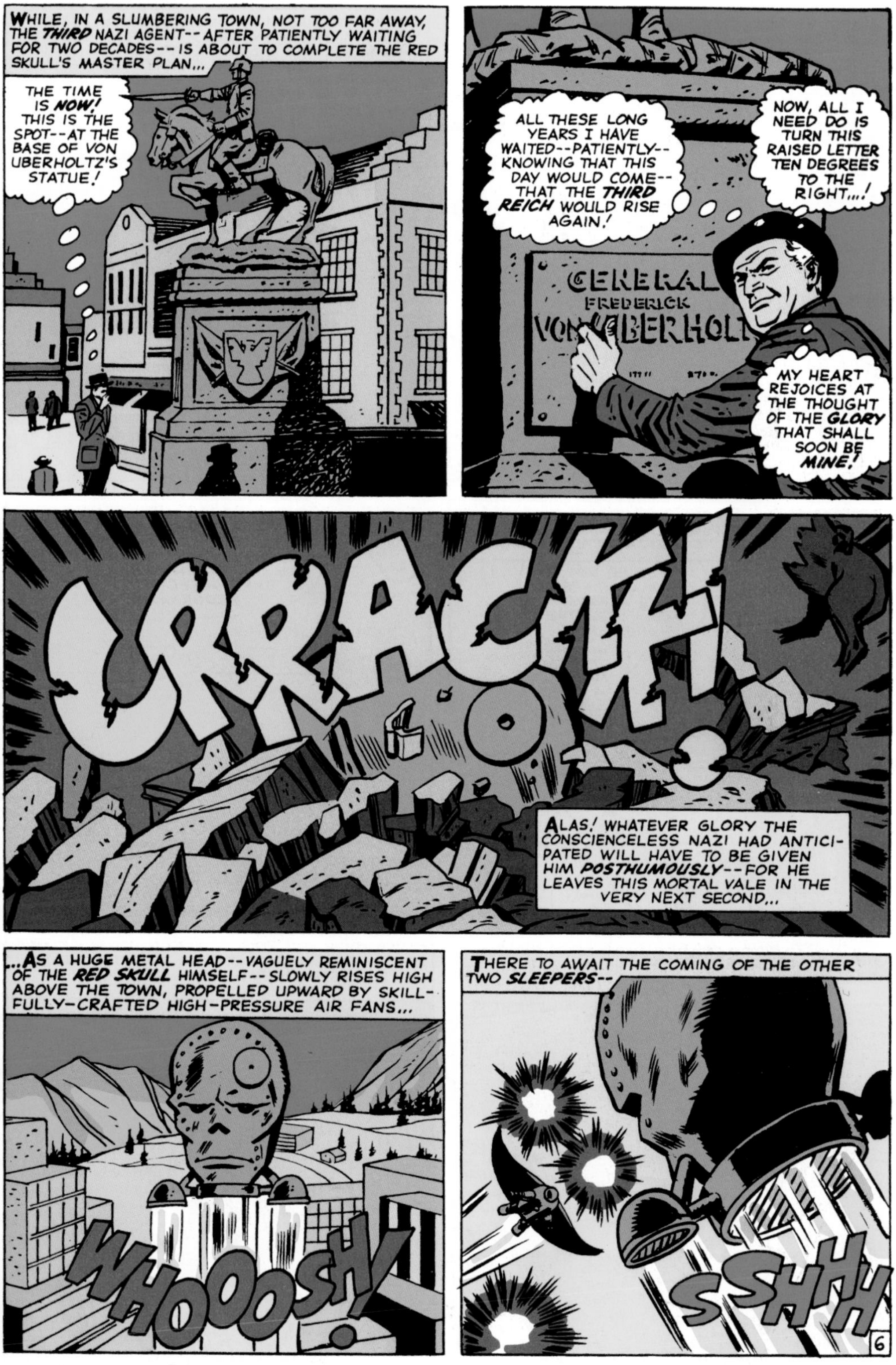

WHILE, IN A SLUMBERING TOWN, NOT TOO FAR AWAY, THE THIRD NAZI AGENT--AFTER PATIENTLY WAITING FOR TWO DECADES--IS ABOUT TO COMPLETE THE RED SKULL'S MASTER PLAN...
THE TIME IS NOW! THIS IS THE SPOT--AT THE BASE OF VON UBERHOLTZ'S STATUE!
ALL THESE LONG YEARS I HAVE WAITED--PATIENTLY--KNOWING THAT THIS DAY WOULD COME--THAT THE THIRD REICH WOULD RISE AGAIN!
NOW, ALL I NEED DO IS TURN THIS RAISED LETTER TEN DEGREES TO THE RIGHT...!
GENERAL FREDERICK VON UBERHOLT
MY HEART REJOICES AT THE THOUGHT OF THE GLORY THAT SHALL SOON BE MINE!
CRRACK!
ALAS! WHATEVER GLORY THE CONSCIENCELESS NAZI HAD ANTICIPATED WILL HAVE TO BE GIVEN HIM POSTHUMOUSLY--FOR HE LEAVES THIS MORTAL VALE IN THE VERY NEXT SECOND...
...AS A HUGE METAL HEAD--VAGUELY REMINISCENT OF THE RED SKULL HIMSELF--SLOWLY RISES HIGH ABOVE THE TOWN, PROPELLED UPWARD BY SKILLFULLY-CRAFTED HIGH-PRESSURE AIR FANS...
WHOOOSH!
THERE TO AWAIT THE COMING OF THE OTHER TWO SLEEPERS--
SSHHH
6

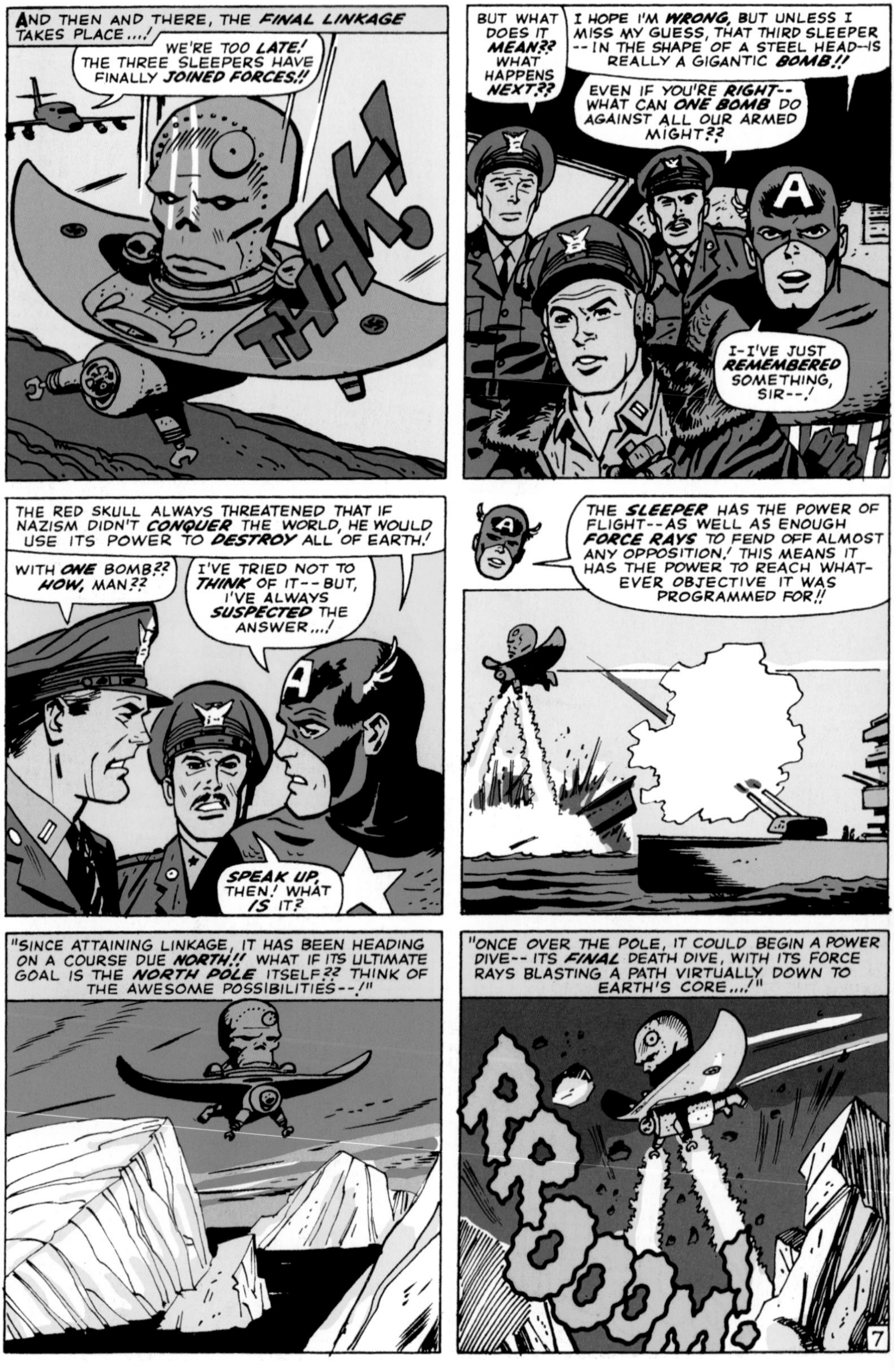
AND THEN AND THERE, THE FINAL LINKAGE TAKES PLACE...!
WE'RE TOO LATE! THE THREE SLEEPERS HAVE FINALLY JOINED FORCES!!
THAK!
BUT WHAT DOES IT MEAN?? WHAT HAPPENS NEXT??
I HOPE I'M WRONG, BUT UNLESS I MISS MY GUESS, THAT THIRD SLEEPER -- IN THE SHAPE OF A STEEL HEAD--IS REALLY A GIGANTIC BOMB!!
EVEN IF YOU'RE RIGHT-- WHAT CAN ONE BOMB DO AGAINST ALL OUR ARMED MIGHT??
I-I'VE JUST REMEMBERED SOMETHING, SIR--!
THE RED SKULL ALWAYS THREATENED THAT IF NAZISM DIDN'T CONQUER THE WORLD, HE WOULD USE ITS POWER TO DESTROY ALL OF EARTH!
WITH ONE BOMB?? HOW, MAN??
I'VE TRIED NOT TO THINK OF IT--BUT, I'VE ALWAYS SUSPECTED THE ANSWER...!
SPEAK UP, THEN! WHAT IS IT?
THE SLEEPER HAS THE POWER OF FLIGHT--AS WELL AS ENOUGH FORCE RAYS TO FEND OFF ALMOST ANY OPPOSITION! THIS MEANS IT HAS THE POWER TO REACH WHATEVER OBJECTIVE IT WAS PROGRAMMED FOR!!
"SINCE ATTAINING LINKAGE, IT HAS BEEN HEADING ON A COURSE DUE NORTH!! WHAT IF ITS ULTIMATE GOAL IS THE NORTH POLE ITSELF?? THINK OF THE AWESOME POSSIBILITIES--!"
"ONCE OVER THE POLE, IT COULD BEGIN A POWER DIVE-- ITS FINAL DEATH DIVE, WITH ITS FORCE RAYS BLASTING A PATH VIRTUALLY DOWN TO EARTH'S CORE...!"
BA-ROOOM!
7

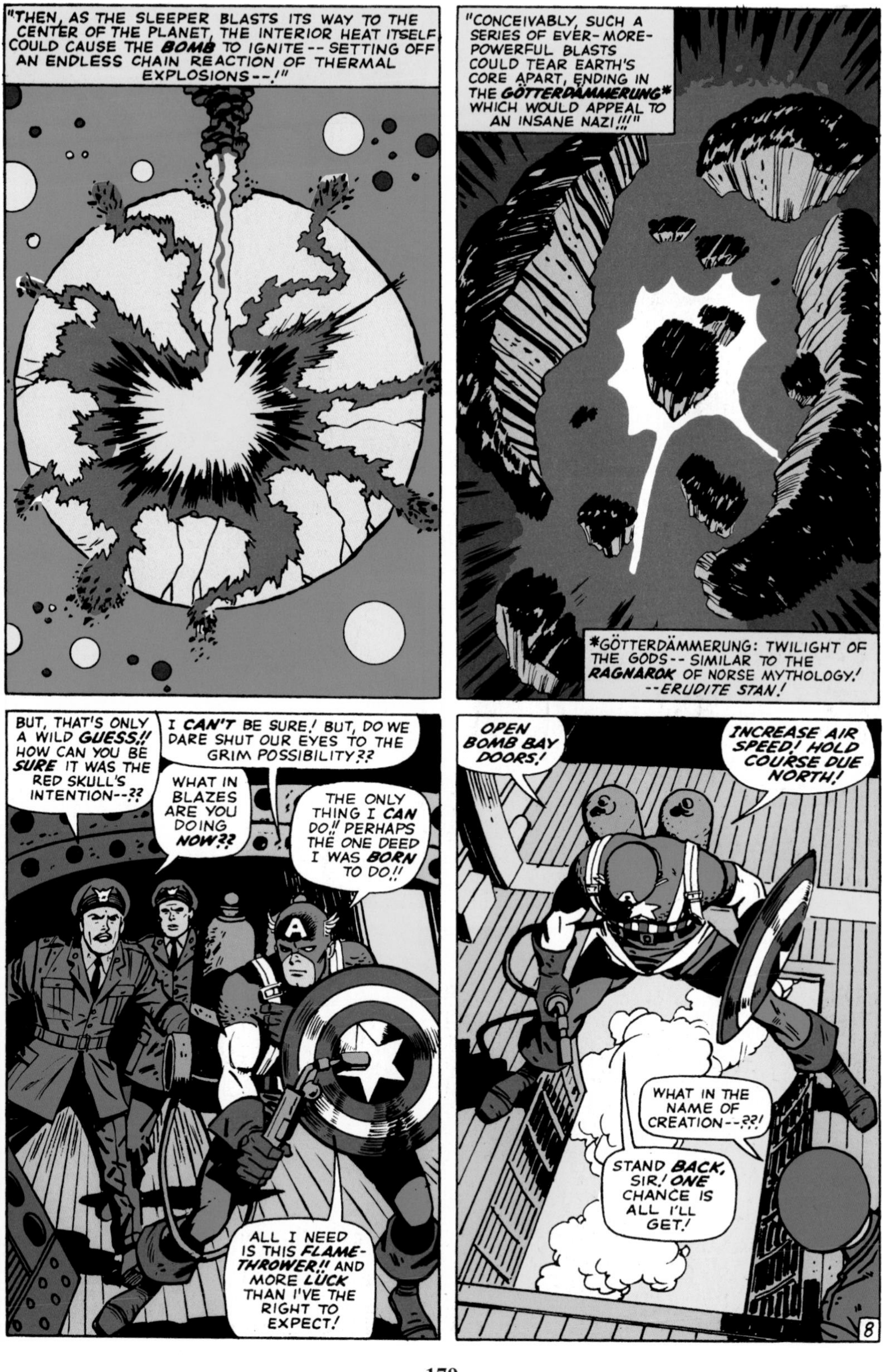
"THEN, AS THE SLEEPER BLASTS ITS WAY TO THE CENTER OF THE PLANET, THE INTERIOR HEAT ITSELF COULD CAUSE THE BOMB TO IGNITE -- SETTING OFF AN ENDLESS CHAIN REACTION OF THERMAL EXPLOSIONS--!"
"CONCEIVABLY, SUCH A SERIES OF EVER-MORE-POWERFUL BLASTS COULD TEAR EARTH'S CORE APART, ENDING IN THE GÖTTERDÄMMERUNG* WHICH WOULD APPEAL TO AN INSANE NAZI!!!"
*GÖTTERDÄMMERUNG: TWILIGHT OF THE GODS-- SIMILAR TO THE RAGNAROK OF NORSE MYTHOLOGY! --ERUDITE STAN!
BUT, THAT'S ONLY A WILD GUESS!! HOW CAN YOU BE SURE IT WAS THE RED SKULL'S INTENTION--??
I CAN'T BE SURE! BUT, DO WE DARE SHUT OUR EYES TO THE GRIM POSSIBILITY??
WHAT IN BLAZES ARE YOU DOING NOW??
THE ONLY THING I CAN DO!! PERHAPS THE ONE DEED I WAS BORN TO DO!!
ALL I NEED IS THIS FLAME-THROWER!! AND MORE LUCK THAN I'VE THE RIGHT TO EXPECT!
OPEN BOMB BAY DOORS!
INCREASE AIR SPEED! HOLD COURSE DUE NORTH!
WHAT IN THE NAME OF CREATION--??!
STAND BACK, SIR! ONE CHANCE IS ALL I'LL GET!
8

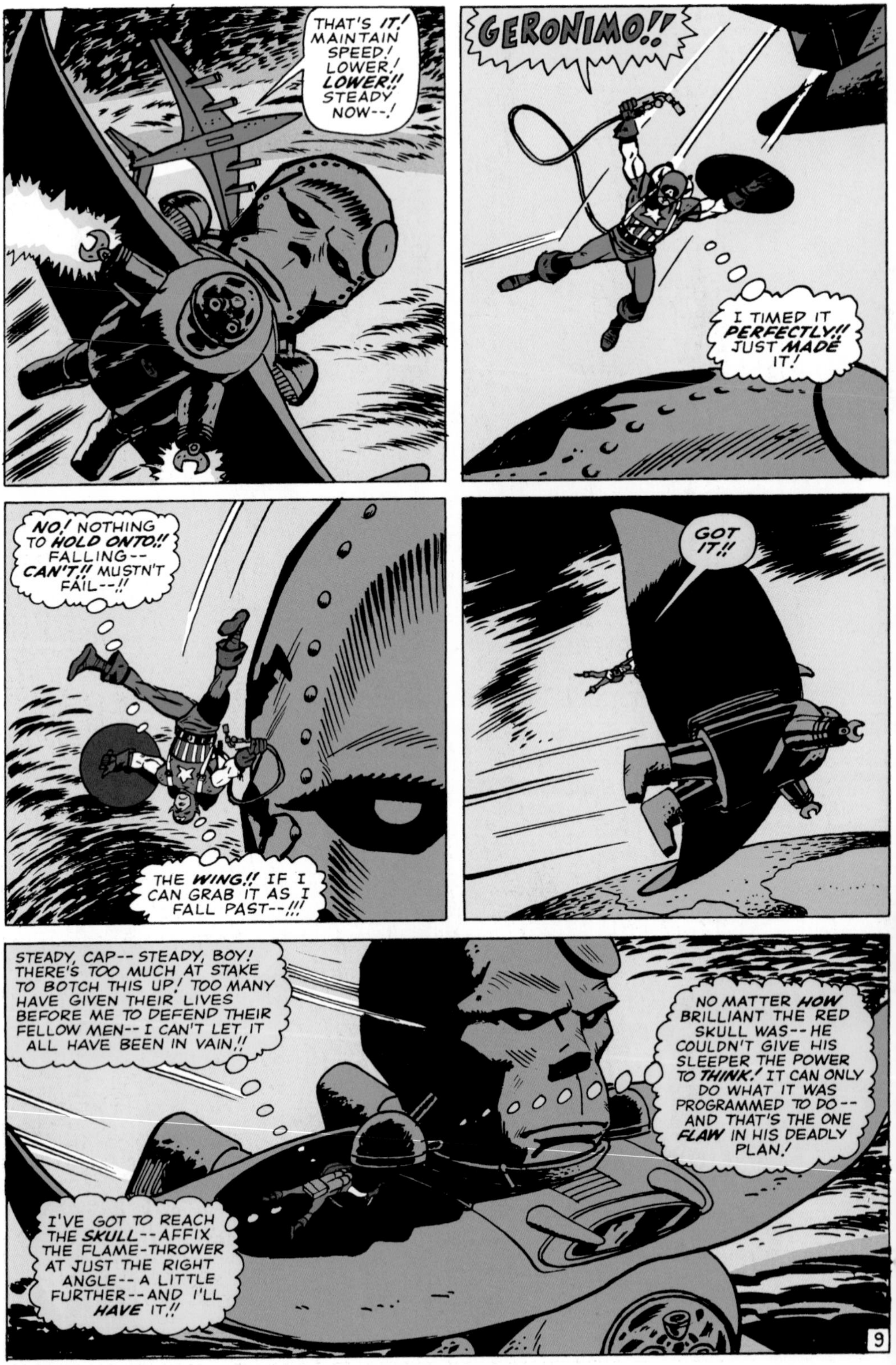

THAT'S IT! MAINTAIN SPEED! LOWER! LOWER!! STEADY NOW--!
GERONIMO!!
I TIMED IT PERFECTLY!! JUST MADE IT!
NO! NOTHING TO HOLD ONTO!! FALLING-- CAN'T!! MUSTN'T FAIL--!!
THE WING!! IF I CAN GRAB IT AS I FALL PAST--!!!
GOT IT!!
STEADY, CAP-- STEADY, BOY! THERE'S TOO MUCH AT STAKE TO BOTCH THIS UP! TOO MANY HAVE GIVEN THEIR LIVES BEFORE ME TO DEFEND THEIR FELLOW MEN-- I CAN'T LET IT ALL HAVE BEEN IN VAIN!!
NO MATTER HOW BRILLIANT THE RED SKULL WAS-- HE COULDN'T GIVE HIS SLEEPER THE POWER TO THINK! IT CAN ONLY DO WHAT IT WAS PROGRAMMED TO DO-- AND THAT'S THE ONE FLAW IN HIS DEADLY PLAN!
I'VE GOT TO REACH THE SKULL-- AFFIX THE FLAME-THROWER AT JUST THE RIGHT ANGLE-- A LITTLE FURTHER-- AND I'LL HAVE IT!!
9

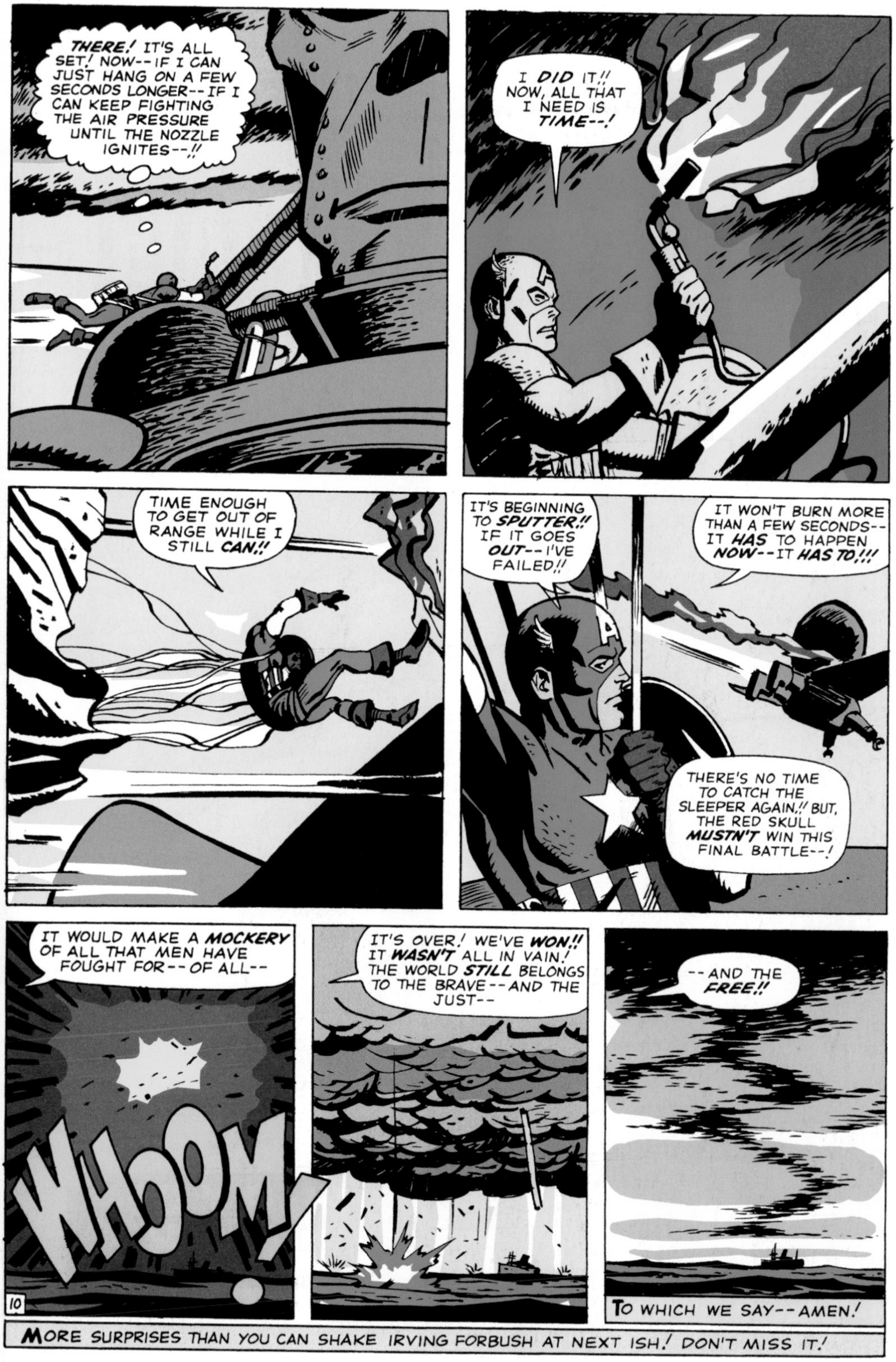
THERE! IT'S ALL SET! NOW-- IF I CAN JUST HANG ON A FEW SECONDS LONGER-- IF I CAN KEEP FIGHTING THE AIR PRESSURE UNTIL THE NOZZLE IGNITES--!!
I DID IT!! NOW, ALL THAT I NEED IS TIME--!
TIME ENOUGH TO GET OUT OF RANGE WHILE I STILL CAN!!
IT'S BEGINNING TO SPUTTER!! IF IT GOES OUT-- I'VE FAILED!!
IT WON'T BURN MORE THAN A FEW SECONDS-- IT HAS TO HAPPEN NOW-- IT HAS TO!!!
THERE'S NO TIME TO CATCH THE SLEEPER AGAIN!! BUT, THE RED SKULL MUSTN'T WIN THIS FINAL BATTLE--!
IT WOULD MAKE A MOCKERY OF ALL THAT MEN HAVE FOUGHT FOR-- OF ALL--
WHOOM!
10
IT'S OVER! WE'VE WON!! IT WASN'T ALL IN VAIN! THE WORLD STILL BELONGS TO THE BRAVE-- AND THE JUST--
--AND THE FREE!!
TO WHICH WE SAY--AMEN!
MORE SURPRISES THAN YOU CAN SHAKE IRVING FORBUSH AT NEXT ISH! DON'T MISS IT!

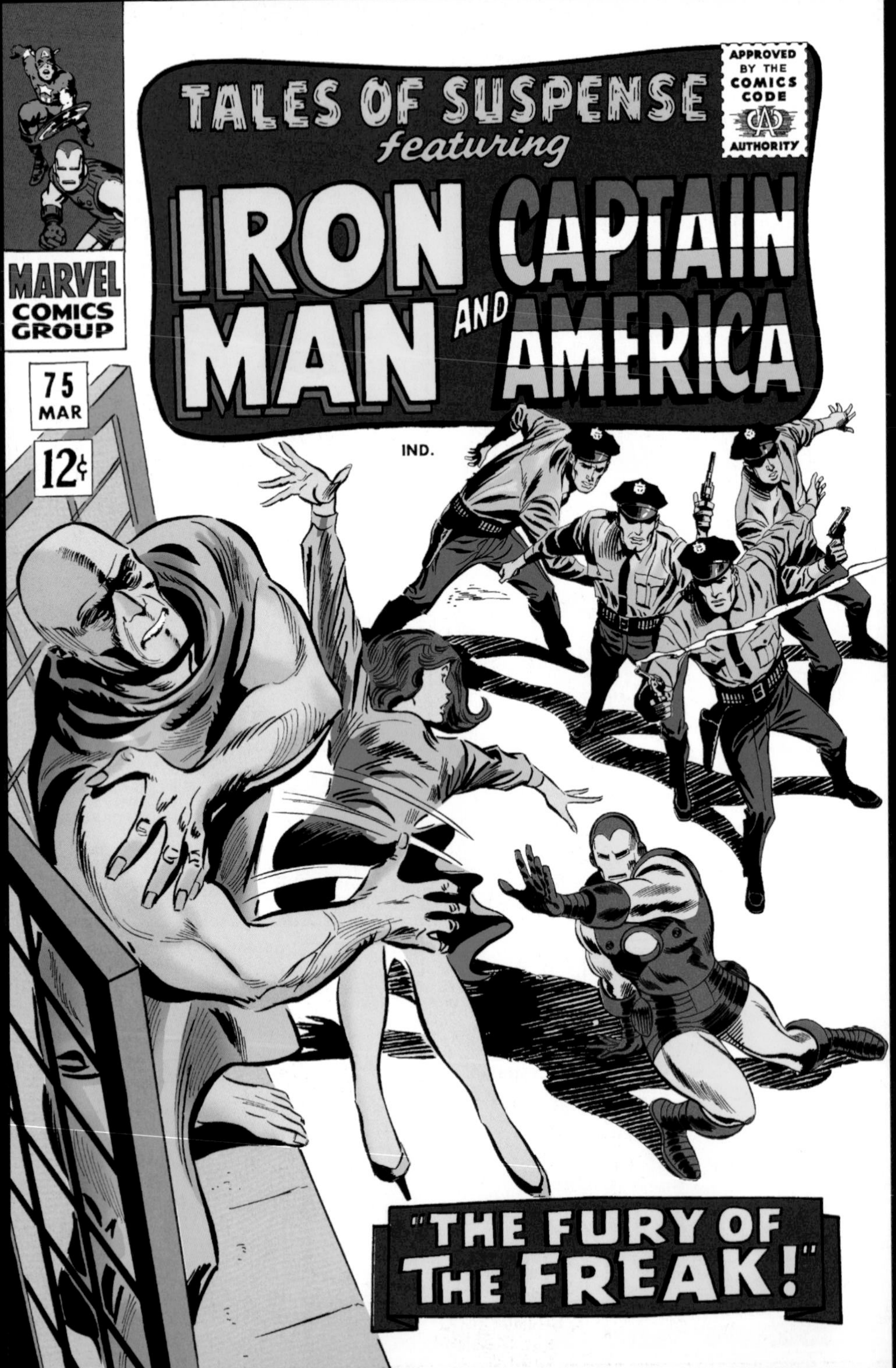

TALES OF SUSPENSE
featuring
IRON MAN AND CAPTAIN AMERICA
APPROVED BY THE COMICS CODE AUTHORITY
MARVEL COMICS GROUP
75 MAR
12¢
IND.
"THE FURY OF THE FREAK!"

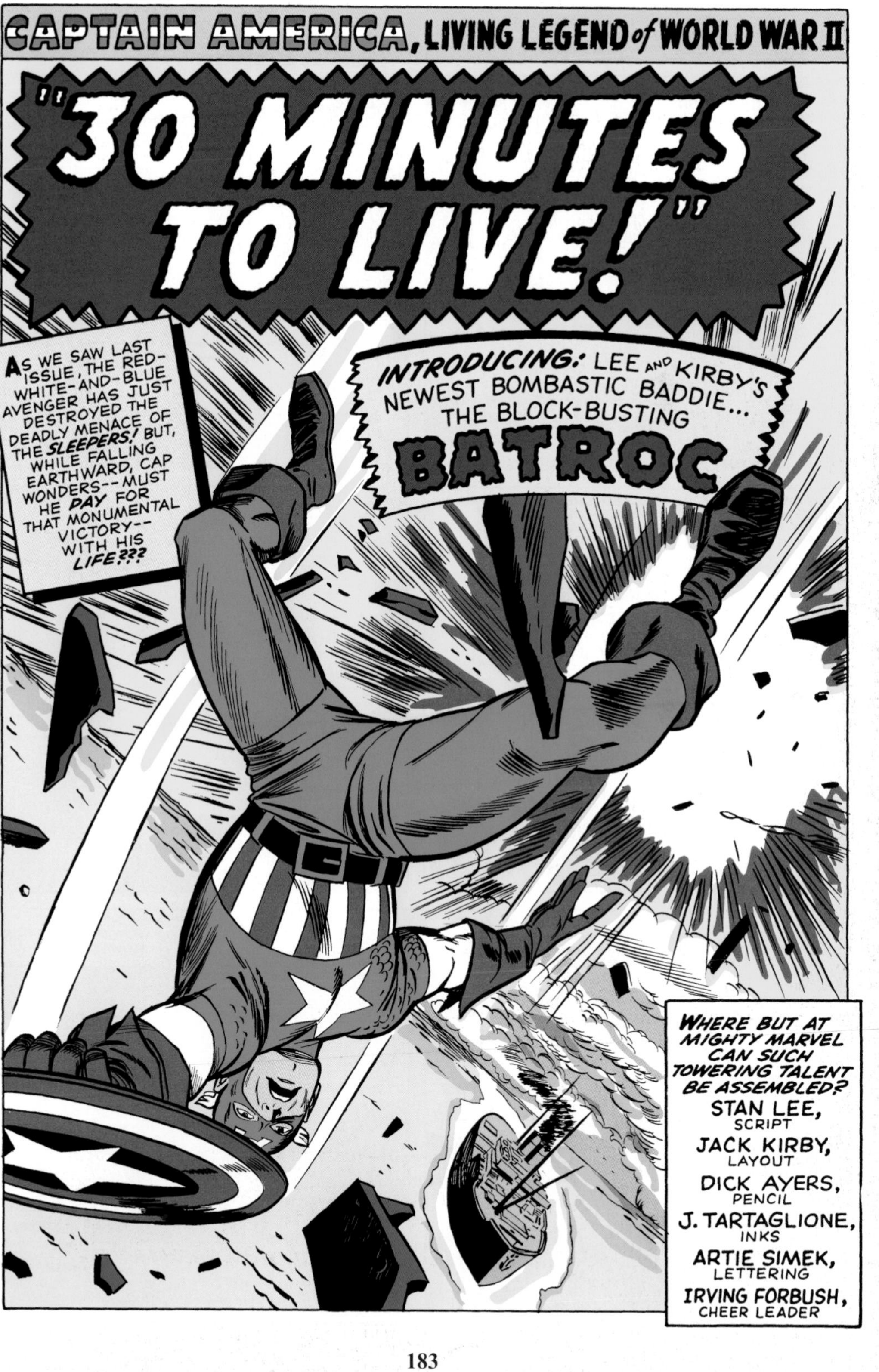
CAPTAIN AMERICA, LIVING LEGEND of WORLD WAR II
"30 MINUTES TO LIVE!"
AS WE SAW LAST ISSUE, THE RED-WHITE-AND-BLUE AVENGER HAS JUST DESTROYED THE DEADLY MENACE OF THE SLEEPERS! BUT, WHILE FALLING EARTHWARD, CAP WONDERS--MUST HE PAY FOR THAT MONUMENTAL VICTORY--WITH HIS LIFE???
INTRODUCING: LEE AND KIRBY'S NEWEST BOMBASTIC BADDIE... THE BLOCK-BUSTING BATROC
WHERE BUT AT MIGHTY MARVEL CAN SUCH TOWERING TALENT BE ASSEMBLED?
STAN LEE, SCRIPT
JACK KIRBY, LAYOUT
DICK AYERS, PENCIL
J. TARTAGLIONE, INKS
ARTIE SIMEK, LETTERING
IRVING FORBUSH, CHEER LEADER

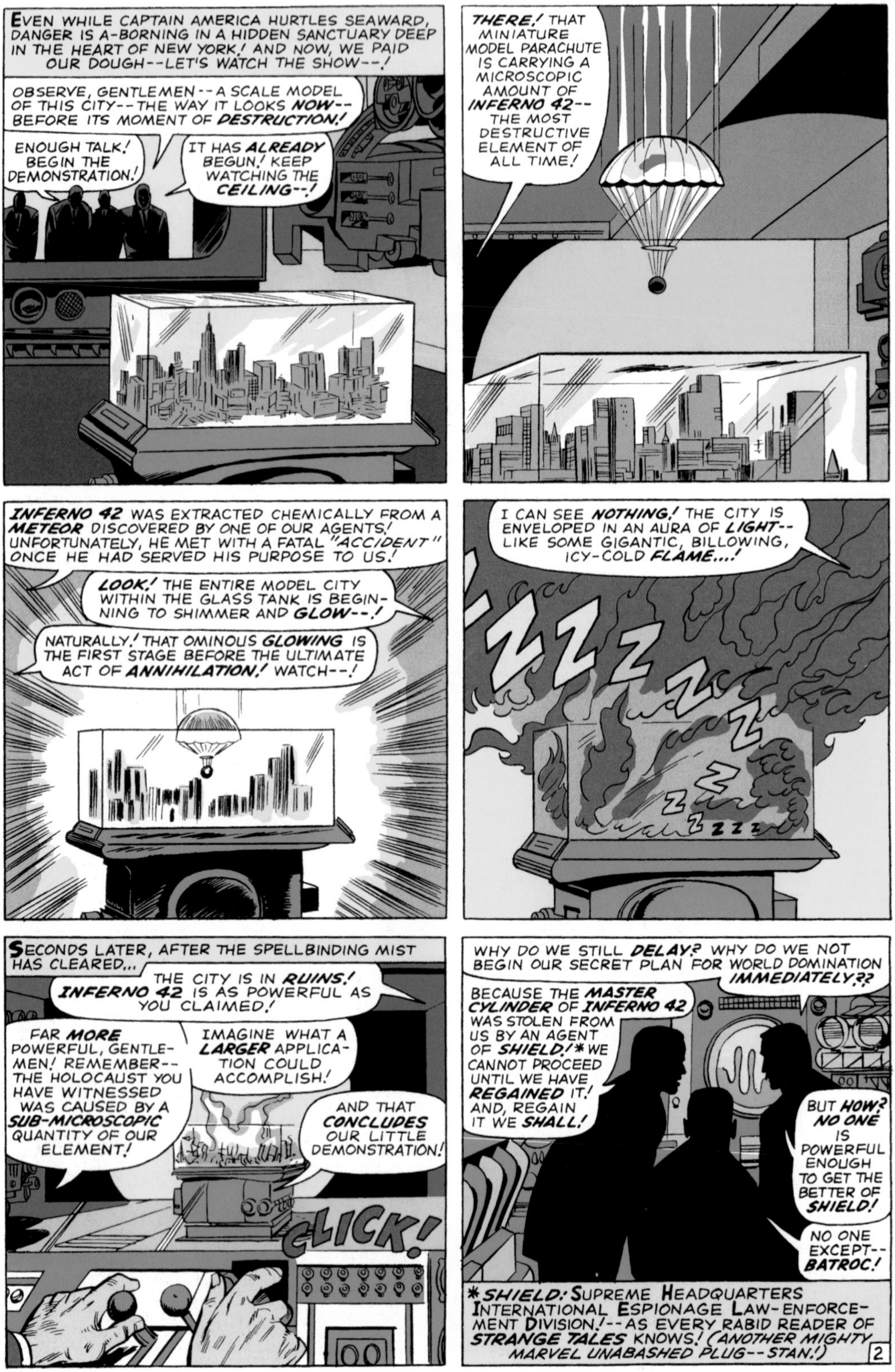

EVEN WHILE CAPTAIN AMERICA HURTLES SEAWARD, DANGER IS A-BORNING IN A HIDDEN SANCTUARY DEEP IN THE HEART OF NEW YORK! AND NOW, WE PAID OUR DOUGH--LET'S WATCH THE SHOW--!
OBSERVE, GENTLEMEN--A SCALE MODEL OF THIS CITY--THE WAY IT LOOKS NOW--BEFORE ITS MOMENT OF DESTRUCTION!
ENOUGH TALK! BEGIN THE DEMONSTRATION!
IT HAS ALREADY BEGUN! KEEP WATCHING THE CEILING--!
THERE! THAT MINIATURE MODEL PARACHUTE IS CARRYING A MICROSCOPIC AMOUNT OF INFERNO 42--THE MOST DESTRUCTIVE ELEMENT OF ALL TIME!
INFERNO 42 WAS EXTRACTED CHEMICALLY FROM A METEOR DISCOVERED BY ONE OF OUR AGENTS! UNFORTUNATELY, HE MET WITH A FATAL "ACCIDENT" ONCE HE HAD SERVED HIS PURPOSE TO US!
LOOK! THE ENTIRE MODEL CITY WITHIN THE GLASS TANK IS BEGINNING TO SHIMMER AND GLOW--!
NATURALLY! THAT OMINOUS GLOWING IS THE FIRST STAGE BEFORE THE ULTIMATE ACT OF ANNIHILATION! WATCH--!
I CAN SEE NOTHING! THE CITY IS ENVELOPED IN AN AURA OF LIGHT--LIKE SOME GIGANTIC, BILLOWING, ICY-COLD FLAME...!
ZZZZZZZZZZZZ
SECONDS LATER, AFTER THE SPELLBINDING MIST HAS CLEARED...
THE CITY IS IN RUINS! INFERNO 42 IS AS POWERFUL AS YOU CLAIMED!
FAR MORE POWERFUL, GENTLEMEN! REMEMBER--THE HOLOCAUST YOU HAVE WITNESSED WAS CAUSED BY A SUB-MICROSCOPIC QUANTITY OF OUR ELEMENT!
IMAGINE WHAT A LARGER APPLICATION COULD ACCOMPLISH!
AND THAT CONCLUDES OUR LITTLE DEMONSTRATION!
CLICK!
WHY DO WE STILL DELAY? WHY DO WE NOT BEGIN OUR SECRET PLAN FOR WORLD DOMINATION IMMEDIATELY??
BECAUSE THE MASTER CYLINDER OF INFERNO 42 WAS STOLEN FROM US BY AN AGENT OF SHIELD!* WE CANNOT PROCEED UNTIL WE HAVE REGAINED IT! AND, REGAIN IT WE SHALL!
BUT HOW? NO ONE IS POWERFUL ENOUGH TO GET THE BETTER OF SHIELD!
NO ONE EXCEPT--BATROC!
*SHIELD: SUPREME HEADQUARTERS INTERNATIONAL ESPIONAGE LAW-ENFORCEMENT DIVISION!--AS EVERY RABID READER OF STRANGE TALES KNOWS! (ANOTHER MIGHTY MARVEL UNABASHED PLUG--STAN!)
2

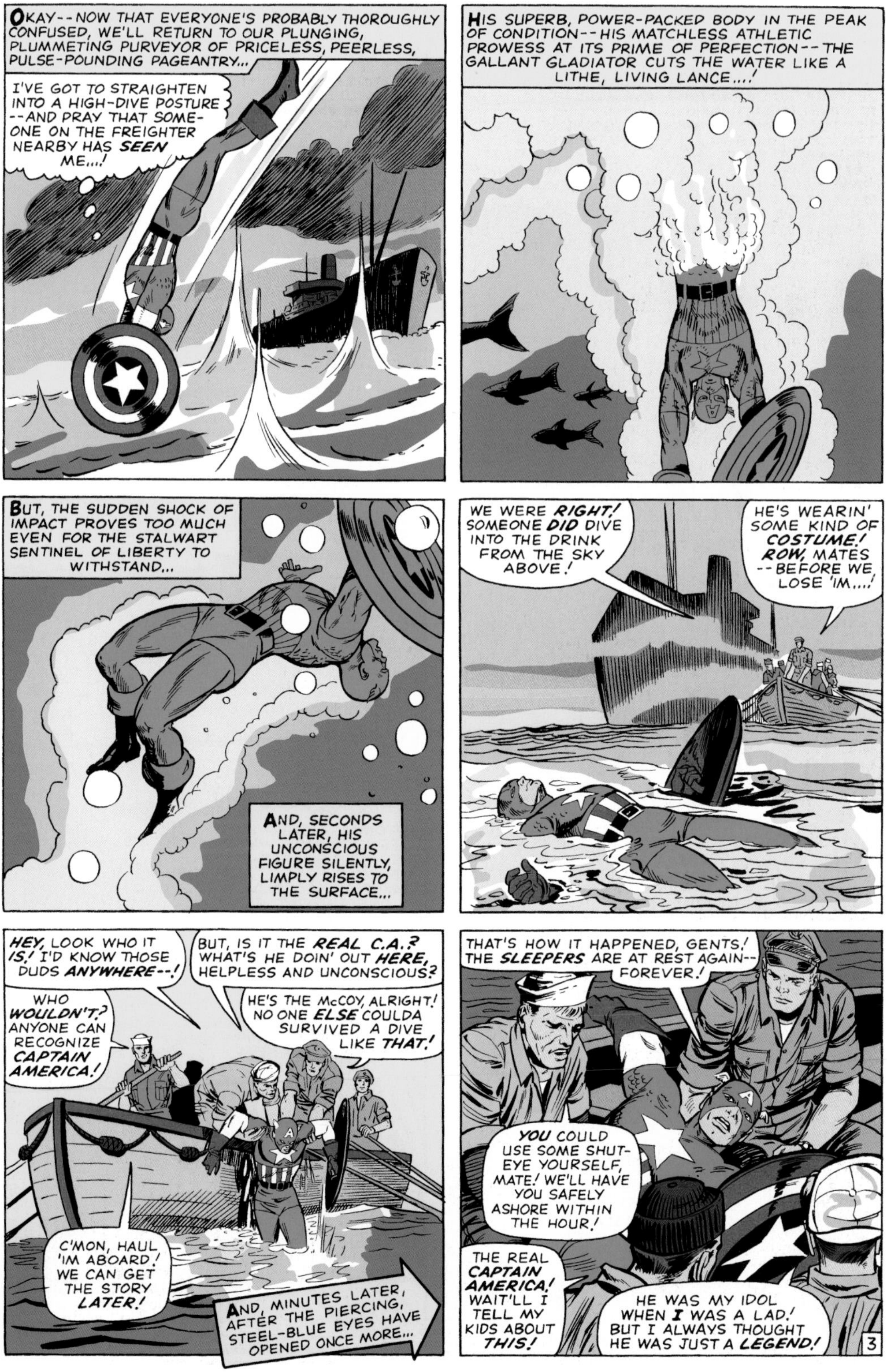
OKAY--NOW THAT EVERYONE'S PROBABLY THOROUGHLY CONFUSED, WE'LL RETURN TO OUR PLUNGING, PLUMMETING PURVEYOR OF PRICELESS, PEERLESS, PULSE-POUNDING PAGEANTRY...
I'VE GOT TO STRAIGHTEN INTO A HIGH-DIVE POSTURE --AND PRAY THAT SOMEONE ON THE FREIGHTER NEARBY HAS SEEN ME...!
HIS SUPERB, POWER-PACKED BODY IN THE PEAK OF CONDITION--HIS MATCHLESS ATHLETIC PROWESS AT ITS PRIME OF PERFECTION--THE GALLANT GLADIATOR CUTS THE WATER LIKE A LITHE, LIVING LANCE....!
BUT, THE SUDDEN SHOCK OF IMPACT PROVES TOO MUCH EVEN FOR THE STALWART SENTINEL OF LIBERTY TO WITHSTAND...
AND, SECONDS LATER, HIS UNCONSCIOUS FIGURE SILENTLY, LIMPLY RISES TO THE SURFACE...
WE WERE RIGHT! SOMEONE DID DIVE INTO THE DRINK FROM THE SKY ABOVE!
HE'S WEARIN' SOME KIND OF COSTUME! ROW, MATES --BEFORE WE LOSE 'IM....!
HEY, LOOK WHO IT IS! I'D KNOW THOSE DUDS ANYWHERE--!
BUT, IS IT THE REAL C.A.? WHAT'S HE DOIN' OUT HERE, HELPLESS AND UNCONSCIOUS?
WHO WOULDN'T? ANYONE CAN RECOGNIZE CAPTAIN AMERICA!
HE'S THE McCOY, ALRIGHT! NO ONE ELSE COULDA SURVIVED A DIVE LIKE THAT!
C'MON, HAUL 'IM ABOARD! WE CAN GET THE STORY LATER!
AND, MINUTES LATER, AFTER THE PIERCING, STEEL-BLUE EYES HAVE OPENED ONCE MORE...
THAT'S HOW IT HAPPENED, GENTS! THE SLEEPERS ARE AT REST AGAIN--FOREVER!
YOU COULD USE SOME SHUT-EYE YOURSELF, MATE! WE'LL HAVE YOU SAFELY ASHORE WITHIN THE HOUR!
THE REAL CAPTAIN AMERICA! WAIT'LL I TELL MY KIDS ABOUT THIS!
HE WAS MY IDOL WHEN I WAS A LAD! BUT I ALWAYS THOUGHT HE WAS JUST A LEGEND!
3

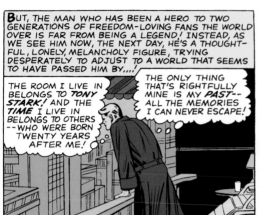

BUT, THE MAN WHO HAS BEEN A HERO TO TWO GENERATIONS OF FREEDOM-LOVING FANS THE WORLD OVER IS FAR FROM BEING A LEGEND! INSTEAD, AS WE SEE HIM NOW, THE NEXT DAY, HE'S A THOUGHTFUL, LONELY, MELANCHOLY FIGURE, TRYING DESPERATELY TO ADJUST TO A WORLD THAT SEEMS TO HAVE PASSED HIM BY....!

THE ROOM I LIVE IN BELONGS TO *TONY STARK!* AND THE *TIME* I LIVE IN BELONGS TO OTHERS --WHO WERE BORN TWENTY YEARS AFTER ME!

THE ONLY THING THAT'S RIGHTFULLY MINE IS MY *PAST*-- ALL THE MEMORIES I CAN NEVER ESCAPE!

BUT, MEMORY IS SUCH AN *ELUSIVE* THING! SO MANY IMAGES HAVE BEEN BLURRED BY THE PASSAGE OF TIME-- THE TWO DECADES I SPENT IN *SUSPENDED ANIMATION!* *

YET, SOME MEMORIES CAN *NEVER* DIE! THEY WILL LIVE FOREVER IN MY BRAIN-- NO MATTER HOW MANY YEARS PASS BY-- THEY'LL REMAIN-- TO HAUNT ME--!

*AS EXQUISITELY EXPLAINED IN *AVENGERS #4*, THE REASON STEVE ROGERS HAS MAINTAINED HIS YOUTH IS THAT HE WAS FROZEN ALIVE FOR YEARS AFTER WORLD WAR II--STAN.

CAN I EVER FORGET *BUCKY BARNES*, THE TEEN-AGER WHO WAS LIKE A BROTHER TO ME? HE SHARED MY BATTLES, MY DANGERS, MY TRIUMPHS!

BUT, THOUGH WE SAVED COUNTLESS LIVES IN THE PAST, HIS *OWN* WAS SACRIFICED IN THE NAME OF FREEDOM!

AND, WHAT HAS BECOME OF *SGT. DUFFY*, THE WONDERFUL, WILD NONCOM WHO SWORE THAT *STEVE ROGERS* WAS THE MOST FOULED-UP G.I. OF ALL TIME!

IF ONLY I COULD HAVE SEEN HIS FACE WHEN HE LEARNED--IF EVER HE *DID*-- THAT ROGERS AND *CAPTAIN AMERICA* WERE ONE AND THE SAME!

BUT, THERE WAS ONE *OTHER!* OUR LIVES TOUCHED FOR ONLY A SHORT TIME--BUT I'VE NEVER FORGOTTEN HER! I CAN STILL REMEMBER OUR FINAL DATE--WHEN SHE WHISPERED TO ME, THRU TREMBLING LIPS...

I'LL WAIT TILL YOU RETURN, STEVE! NO MATTER HOW LONG-- NO MATTER WHAT HAPPENS--I'LL WAIT FOR YOU, MY DARLING....!

BUT, THAT WAS AN ETERNITY AGO-- IN THE DEAD PAST-- THE FORGOTTEN PAST-- THE PAST WHICH WILL LIVE WITH ME FOREVER!

TODAY, IT'S ALL BEHIND ME! THIS IS A *NEW* WORLD --A NEW AGE! AN AGE OF ATOMIC POWER, SPACE EXPLORATION, SOCIAL UPHEAVAL--YET, AN AGE OVER WHICH THE THREAT OF *WAR* HANGS HEAVY ONCE AGAIN!

AND, SO LONG AS *DANGER* BECKONS, THERE IS STILL A NEED FOR AN OLD RELIC LIKE *CAPTAIN AMERICA!* A NEED THAT MUST BE *MET!*

4

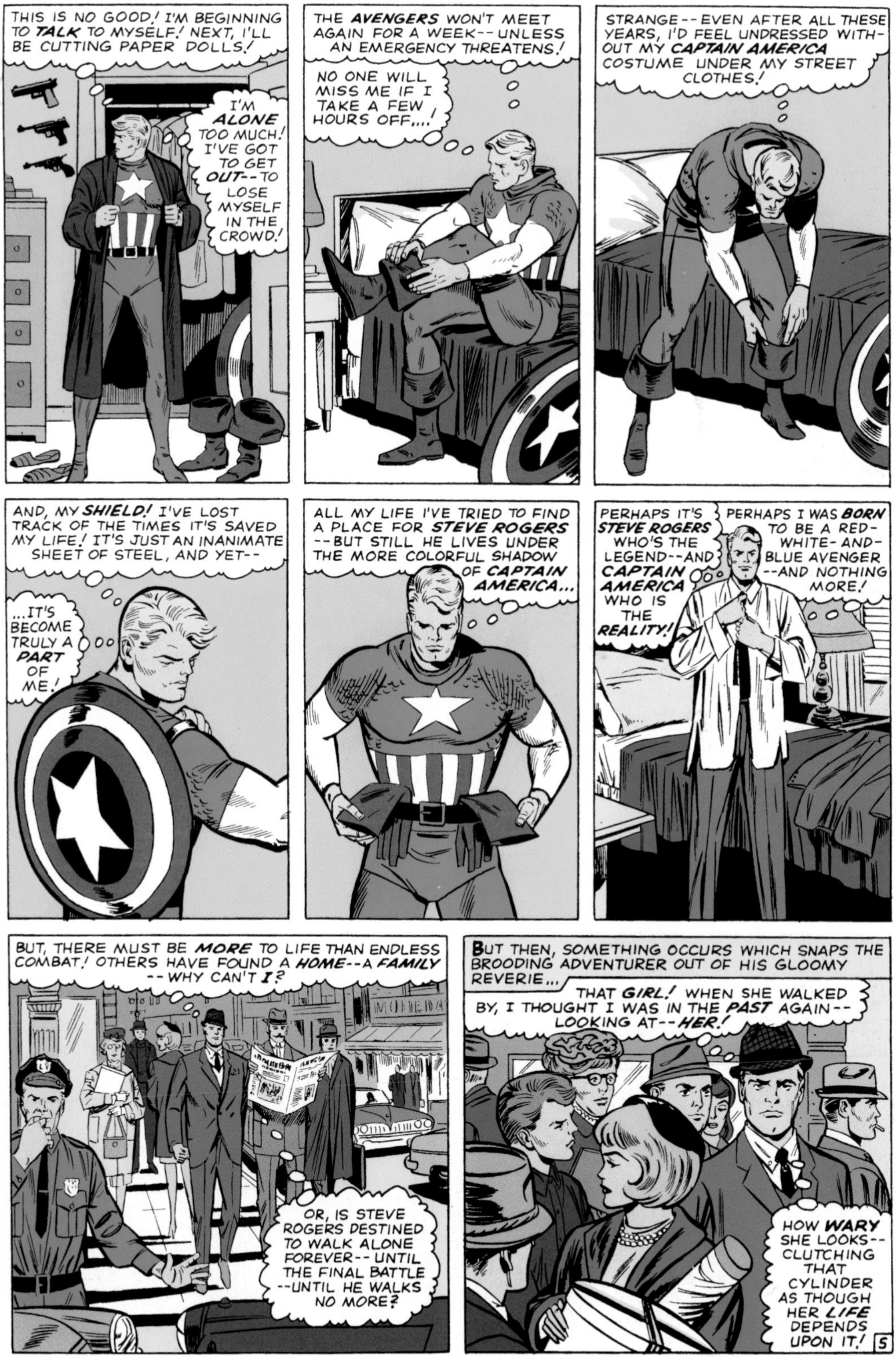
THIS IS NO GOOD! I'M BEGINNING TO TALK TO MYSELF! NEXT, I'LL BE CUTTING PAPER DOLLS!
I'M ALONE TOO MUCH! I'VE GOT TO GET OUT--TO LOSE MYSELF IN THE CROWD!
THE AVENGERS WON'T MEET AGAIN FOR A WEEK--UNLESS AN EMERGENCY THREATENS!
NO ONE WILL MISS ME IF I TAKE A FEW HOURS OFF...!
STRANGE--EVEN AFTER ALL THESE YEARS, I'D FEEL UNDRESSED WITHOUT MY CAPTAIN AMERICA COSTUME UNDER MY STREET CLOTHES!
AND, MY SHIELD! I'VE LOST TRACK OF THE TIMES IT'S SAVED MY LIFE! IT'S JUST AN INANIMATE SHEET OF STEEL, AND YET--
...IT'S BECOME TRULY A PART OF ME!
ALL MY LIFE I'VE TRIED TO FIND A PLACE FOR STEVE ROGERS--BUT STILL HE LIVES UNDER THE MORE COLORFUL SHADOW OF CAPTAIN AMERICA...
PERHAPS IT'S STEVE ROGERS WHO'S THE LEGEND--AND CAPTAIN AMERICA WHO IS THE REALITY!
PERHAPS I WAS BORN TO BE A RED-WHITE-AND-BLUE AVENGER--AND NOTHING MORE!
BUT, THERE MUST BE MORE TO LIFE THAN ENDLESS COMBAT! OTHERS HAVE FOUND A HOME--A FAMILY--WHY CAN'T I?
OR, IS STEVE ROGERS DESTINED TO WALK ALONE FOREVER--UNTIL THE FINAL BATTLE--UNTIL HE WALKS NO MORE?
BUT THEN, SOMETHING OCCURS WHICH SNAPS THE BROODING ADVENTURER OUT OF HIS GLOOMY REVERIE...
THAT GIRL! WHEN SHE WALKED BY, I THOUGHT I WAS IN THE PAST AGAIN--LOOKING AT--HER!
HOW WARY SHE LOOKS--CLUTCHING THAT CYLINDER AS THOUGH HER LIFE DEPENDS UPON IT!
5

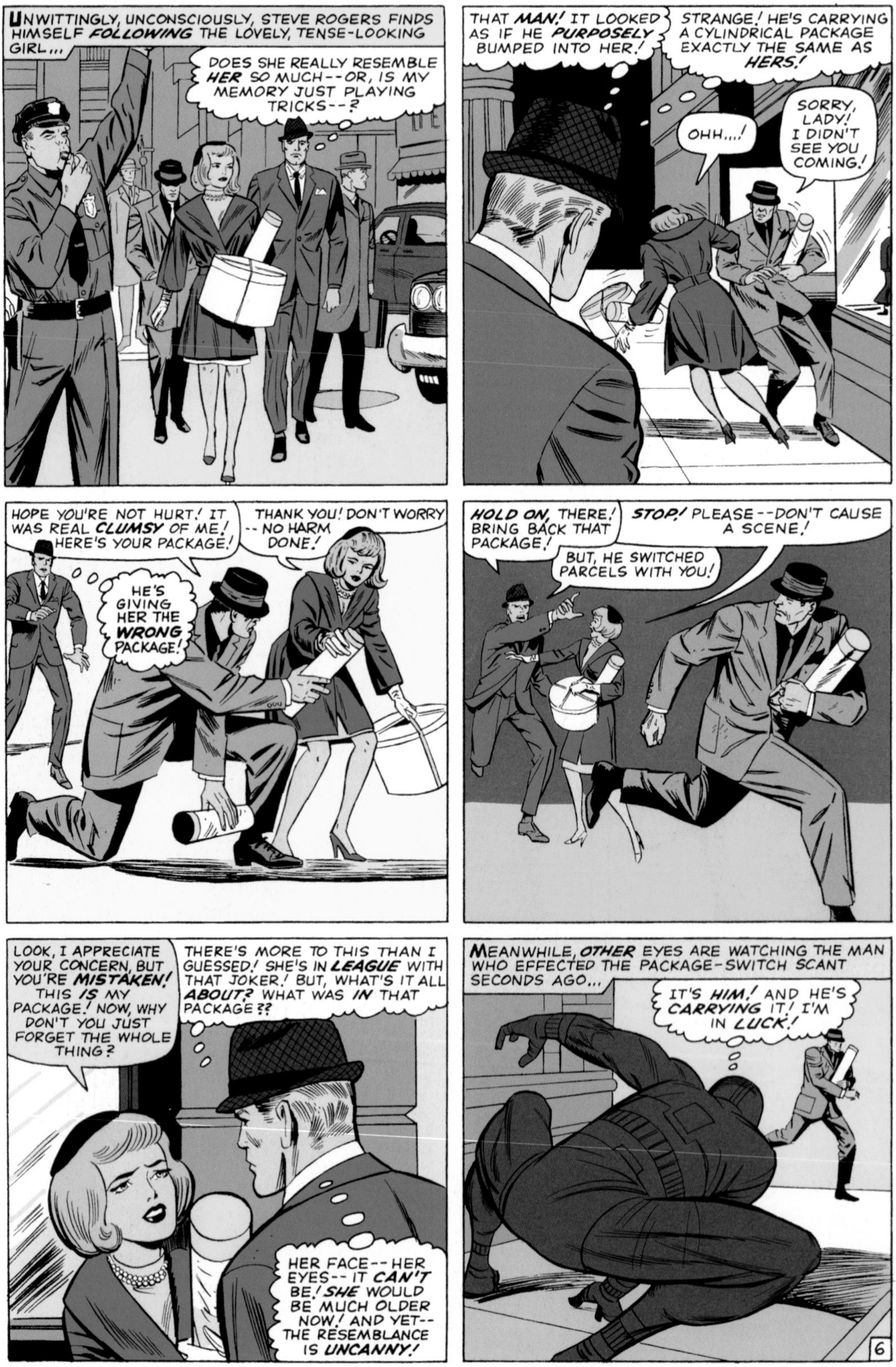
UNWITTINGLY, UNCONSCIOUSLY, STEVE ROGERS FINDS HIMSELF FOLLOWING THE LOVELY, TENSE-LOOKING GIRL...
DOES SHE REALLY RESEMBLE HER SO MUCH--OR, IS MY MEMORY JUST PLAYING TRICKS--?
THAT MAN! IT LOOKED AS IF HE PURPOSELY BUMPED INTO HER!
STRANGE! HE'S CARRYING A CYLINDRICAL PACKAGE EXACTLY THE SAME AS HERS!
OHH...!
SORRY, LADY! I DIDN'T SEE YOU COMING!
HOPE YOU'RE NOT HURT! IT WAS REAL CLUMSY OF ME! HERE'S YOUR PACKAGE!
THANK YOU! DON'T WORRY -- NO HARM DONE!
HE'S GIVING HER THE WRONG PACKAGE!
HOLD ON, THERE! BRING BACK THAT PACKAGE!
STOP! PLEASE--DON'T CAUSE A SCENE!
BUT, HE SWITCHED PARCELS WITH YOU!
LOOK, I APPRECIATE YOUR CONCERN, BUT YOU'RE MISTAKEN! THIS IS MY PACKAGE! NOW, WHY DON'T YOU JUST FORGET THE WHOLE THING?
THERE'S MORE TO THIS THAN I GUESSED! SHE'S IN LEAGUE WITH THAT JOKER! BUT, WHAT'S IT ALL ABOUT? WHAT WAS IN THAT PACKAGE??
HER FACE--HER EYES-- IT CAN'T BE! SHE WOULD BE MUCH OLDER NOW! AND YET-- THE RESEMBLANCE IS UNCANNY!
MEANWHILE, OTHER EYES ARE WATCHING THE MAN WHO EFFECTED THE PACKAGE-SWITCH SCANT SECONDS AGO...
IT'S HIM! AND HE'S CARRYING IT! I'M IN LUCK!
6

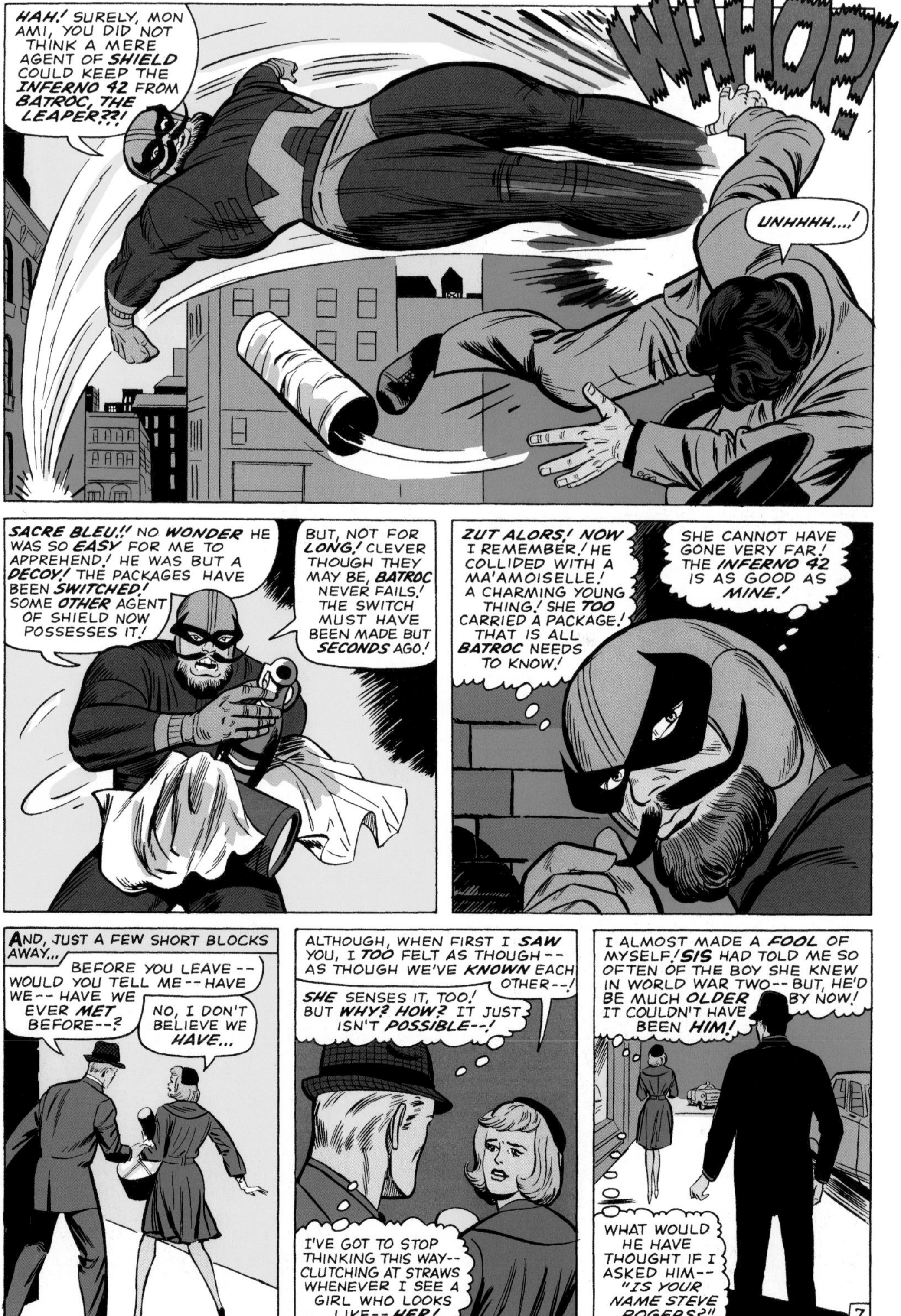
HAH! SURELY, MON AMI, YOU DID NOT THINK A MERE AGENT OF SHIELD COULD KEEP THE INFERNO 42 FROM BATROC, THE LEAPER??!
WHHOP!
UNHHHH...!
SACRE BLEU!! NO WONDER HE WAS SO EASY FOR ME TO APPREHEND! HE WAS BUT A DECOY! THE PACKAGES HAVE BEEN SWITCHED! SOME OTHER AGENT OF SHIELD NOW POSSESSES IT!
BUT, NOT FOR LONG! CLEVER THOUGH THEY MAY BE, BATROC NEVER FAILS! THE SWITCH MUST HAVE BEEN MADE BUT SECONDS AGO!
ZUT ALORS! NOW I REMEMBER! HE COLLIDED WITH A MA'AMOISELLE! A CHARMING YOUNG THING! SHE TOO CARRIED A PACKAGE! THAT IS ALL BATROC NEEDS TO KNOW!
SHE CANNOT HAVE GONE VERY FAR! THE INFERNO 42 IS AS GOOD AS MINE!
AND, JUST A FEW SHORT BLOCKS AWAY...
BEFORE YOU LEAVE -- WOULD YOU TELL ME -- HAVE WE -- HAVE WE EVER MET BEFORE--?
NO, I DON'T BELIEVE WE HAVE...
ALTHOUGH, WHEN FIRST I SAW YOU, I TOO FELT AS THOUGH -- AS THOUGH WE'VE KNOWN EACH OTHER--!
SHE SENSES IT, TOO! BUT WHY? HOW? IT JUST ISN'T POSSIBLE--!
I'VE GOT TO STOP THINKING THIS WAY-- CLUTCHING AT STRAWS WHENEVER I SEE A GIRL WHO LOOKS LIKE-- HER!
I ALMOST MADE A FOOL OF MYSELF! SIS HAD TOLD ME SO OFTEN OF THE BOY SHE KNEW IN WORLD WAR TWO-- BUT, HE'D BE MUCH OLDER BY NOW! IT COULDN'T HAVE BEEN HIM!
WHAT WOULD HE HAVE THOUGHT IF I ASKED HIM-- "IS YOUR NAME STEVE ROGERS?"
7

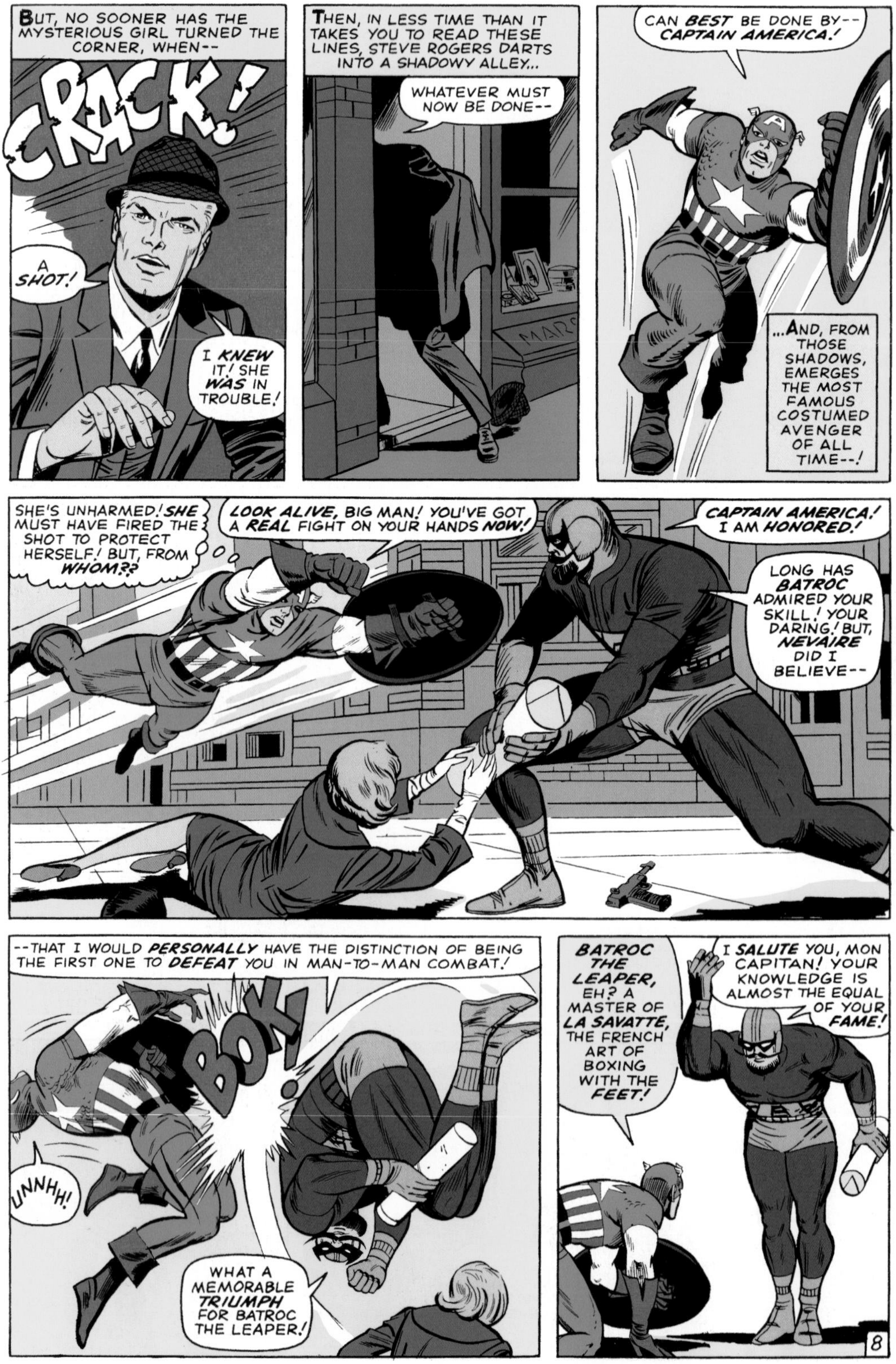
BUT, NO SOONER HAS THE MYSTERIOUS GIRL TURNED THE CORNER, WHEN--
CRACK!
A SHOT!
I KNEW IT! SHE WAS IN TROUBLE!
THEN, IN LESS TIME THAN IT TAKES YOU TO READ THESE LINES, STEVE ROGERS DARTS INTO A SHADOWY ALLEY...
WHATEVER MUST NOW BE DONE--
CAN BEST BE DONE BY-- CAPTAIN AMERICA!
...AND, FROM THOSE SHADOWS, EMERGES THE MOST FAMOUS COSTUMED AVENGER OF ALL TIME--!
SHE'S UNHARMED! SHE MUST HAVE FIRED THE SHOT TO PROTECT HERSELF! BUT, FROM WHOM??
LOOK ALIVE, BIG MAN! YOU'VE GOT A REAL FIGHT ON YOUR HANDS NOW!
CAPTAIN AMERICA! I AM HONORED!
LONG HAS BATROC ADMIRED YOUR SKILL! YOUR DARING! BUT, NEVAIRE DID I BELIEVE--
--THAT I WOULD PERSONALLY HAVE THE DISTINCTION OF BEING THE FIRST ONE TO DEFEAT YOU IN MAN-TO-MAN COMBAT!
BOK!
UNNHH!
WHAT A MEMORABLE TRIUMPH FOR BATROC THE LEAPER!
BATROC THE LEAPER, EH? A MASTER OF LA SAVATTE, THE FRENCH ART OF BOXING WITH THE FEET!
I SALUTE YOU, MON CAPITAN! YOUR KNOWLEDGE IS ALMOST THE EQUAL OF YOUR FAME!
8

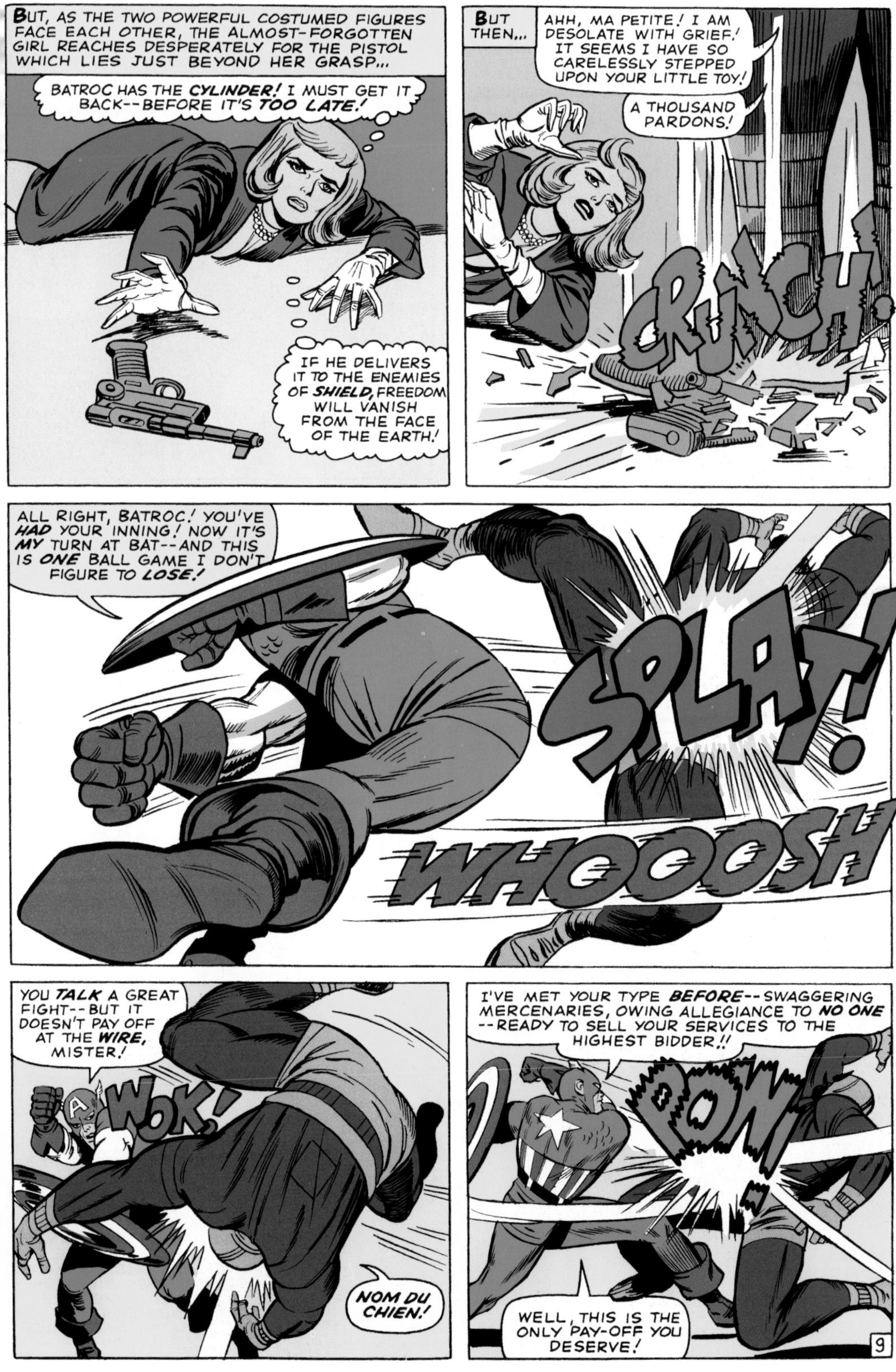
BUT, AS THE TWO POWERFUL COSTUMED FIGURES FACE EACH OTHER, THE ALMOST-FORGOTTEN GIRL REACHES DESPERATELY FOR THE PISTOL WHICH LIES JUST BEYOND HER GRASP...
BATROC HAS THE CYLINDER! I MUST GET IT BACK--BEFORE IT'S TOO LATE!
IF HE DELIVERS IT TO THE ENEMIES OF SHIELD, FREEDOM WILL VANISH FROM THE FACE OF THE EARTH!
BUT THEN...
AHH, MA PETITE! I AM DESOLATE WITH GRIEF! IT SEEMS I HAVE SO CARELESSLY STEPPED UPON YOUR LITTLE TOY!
A THOUSAND PARDONS!
CRUNCH!
ALL RIGHT, BATROC! YOU'VE HAD YOUR INNING! NOW IT'S MY TURN AT BAT--AND THIS IS ONE BALL GAME I DON'T FIGURE TO LOSE!
SPLAT!
WHOOOSH
YOU TALK A GREAT FIGHT--BUT IT DOESN'T PAY OFF AT THE WIRE, MISTER!
WOK!
NOM DU CHIEN!
I'VE MET YOUR TYPE BEFORE--SWAGGERING MERCENARIES, OWING ALLEGIANCE TO NO ONE--READY TO SELL YOUR SERVICES TO THE HIGHEST BIDDER!!
POW!
WELL, THIS IS THE ONLY PAY-OFF YOU DESERVE!
9

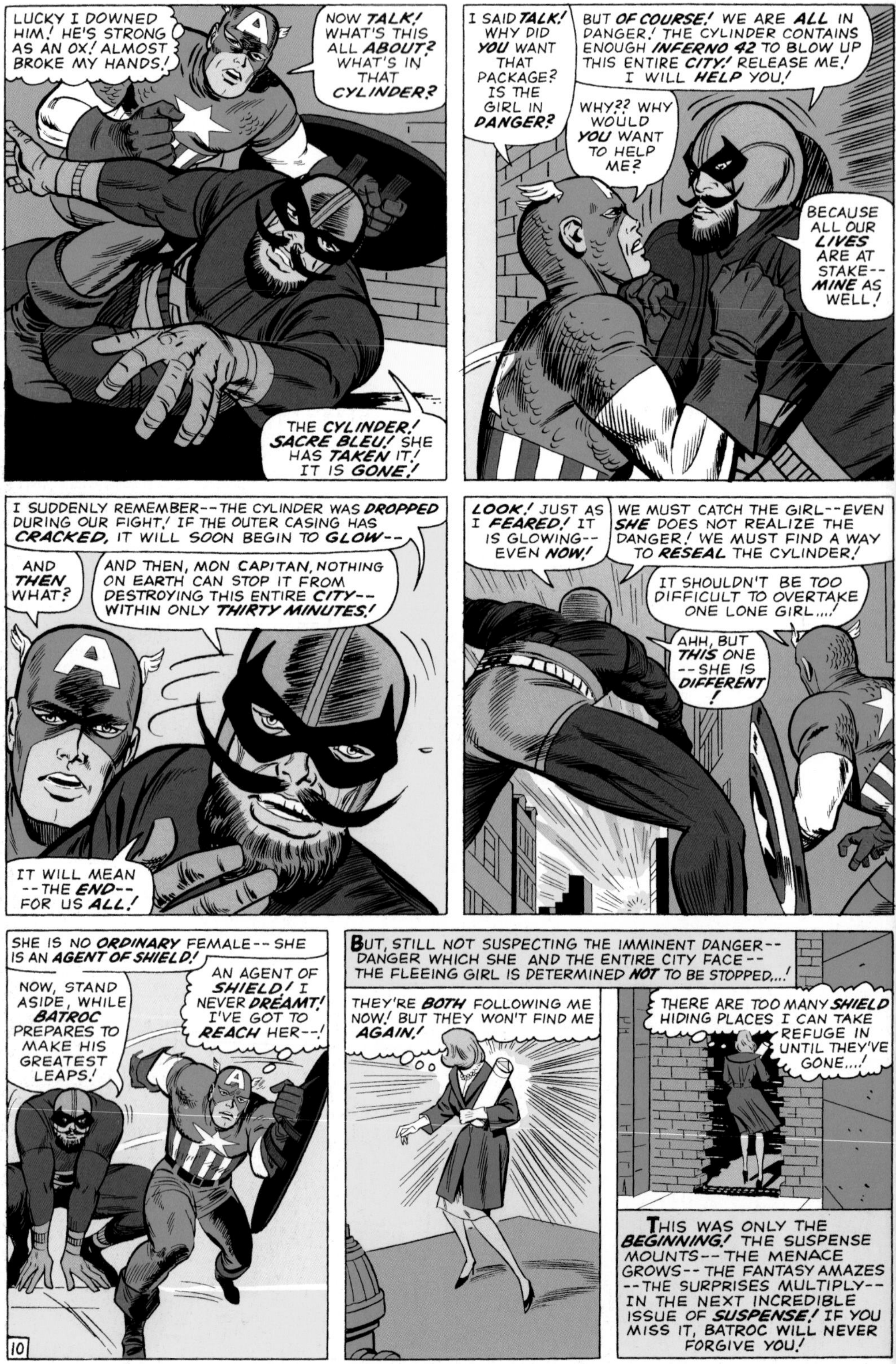
LUCKY I DOWNED HIM! HE'S STRONG AS AN OX! ALMOST BROKE MY HANDS!
NOW TALK! WHAT'S THIS ALL ABOUT? WHAT'S IN THAT CYLINDER?
THE CYLINDER! SACRE BLEU! SHE HAS TAKEN IT! IT IS GONE!
I SAID TALK! WHY DID YOU WANT THAT PACKAGE? IS THE GIRL IN DANGER?
BUT OF COURSE! WE ARE ALL IN DANGER! THE CYLINDER CONTAINS ENOUGH INFERNO 42 TO BLOW UP THIS ENTIRE CITY! RELEASE ME! I WILL HELP YOU!
WHY?? WHY WOULD YOU WANT TO HELP ME?
BECAUSE ALL OUR LIVES ARE AT STAKE-- MINE AS WELL!
I SUDDENLY REMEMBER--THE CYLINDER WAS DROPPED DURING OUR FIGHT! IF THE OUTER CASING HAS CRACKED, IT WILL SOON BEGIN TO GLOW--
AND THEN WHAT?
AND THEN, MON CAPITAN, NOTHING ON EARTH CAN STOP IT FROM DESTROYING THIS ENTIRE CITY-- WITHIN ONLY THIRTY MINUTES!
IT WILL MEAN --THE END-- FOR US ALL!
LOOK! JUST AS I FEARED! IT IS GLOWING-- EVEN NOW!
WE MUST CATCH THE GIRL--EVEN SHE DOES NOT REALIZE THE DANGER! WE MUST FIND A WAY TO RESEAL THE CYLINDER!
IT SHOULDN'T BE TOO DIFFICULT TO OVERTAKE ONE LONE GIRL....!
AHH, BUT THIS ONE --SHE IS DIFFERENT!
SHE IS NO ORDINARY FEMALE--SHE IS AN AGENT OF SHIELD!
NOW, STAND ASIDE, WHILE BATROC PREPARES TO MAKE HIS GREATEST LEAPS!
AN AGENT OF SHIELD! I NEVER DREAMT! I'VE GOT TO REACH HER--!
10
BUT, STILL NOT SUSPECTING THE IMMINENT DANGER-- DANGER WHICH SHE AND THE ENTIRE CITY FACE-- THE FLEEING GIRL IS DETERMINED NOT TO BE STOPPED...!
THEY'RE BOTH FOLLOWING ME NOW! BUT THEY WON'T FIND ME AGAIN!
THERE ARE TOO MANY SHIELD HIDING PLACES I CAN TAKE REFUGE IN UNTIL THEY'VE GONE...!
THIS WAS ONLY THE BEGINNING! THE SUSPENSE MOUNTS--THE MENACE GROWS--THE FANTASY AMAZES --THE SURPRISES MULTIPLY-- IN THE NEXT INCREDIBLE ISSUE OF SUSPENSE! IF YOU MISS IT, BATROC WILL NEVER FORGIVE YOU!

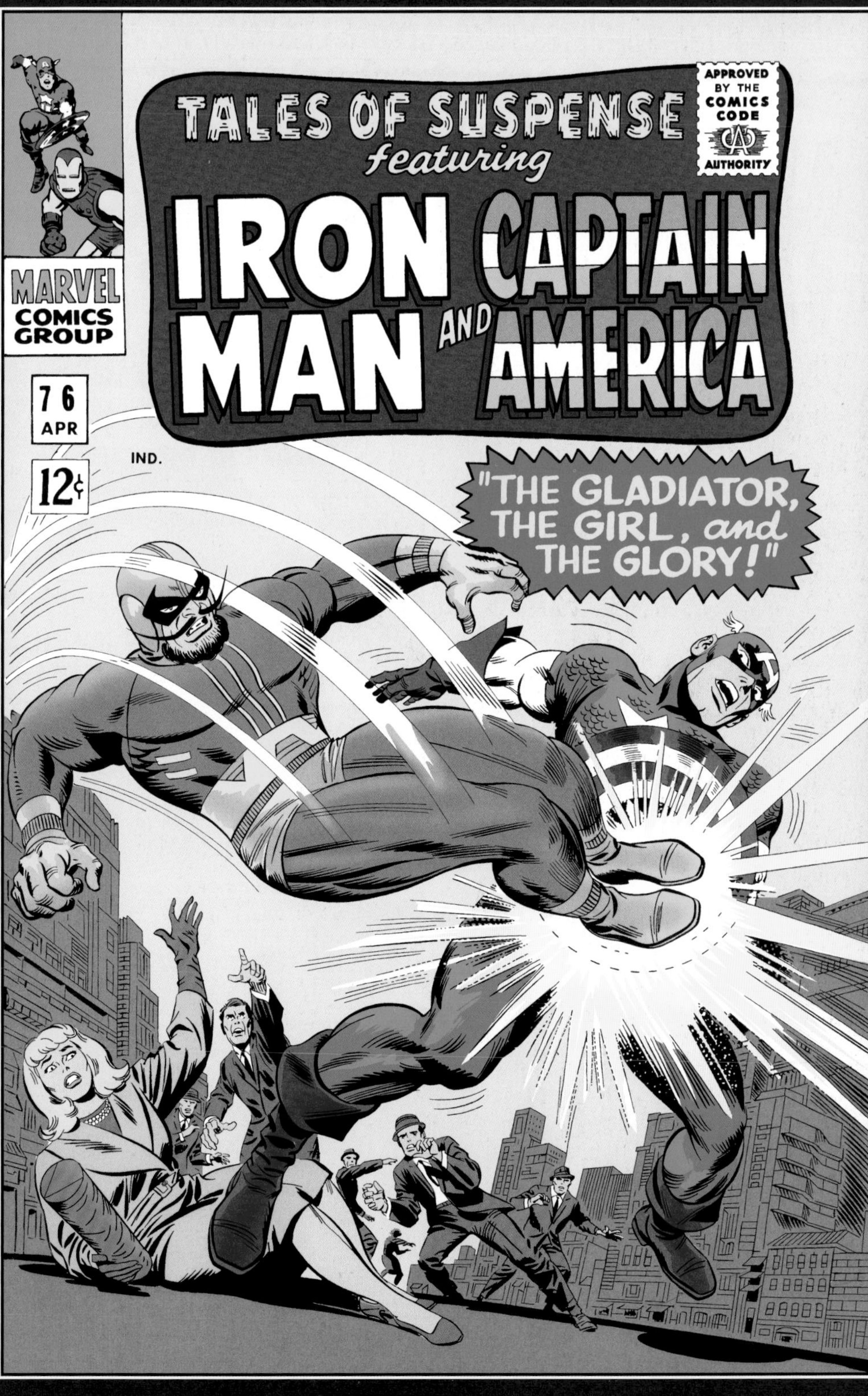
TALES OF SUSPENSE
featuring
IRON MAN AND CAPTAIN AMERICA
APPROVED BY THE COMICS CODE AUTHORITY
MARVEL COMICS GROUP
76 APR
IND.
12¢
"THE GLADIATOR, THE GIRL, and THE GLORY!"

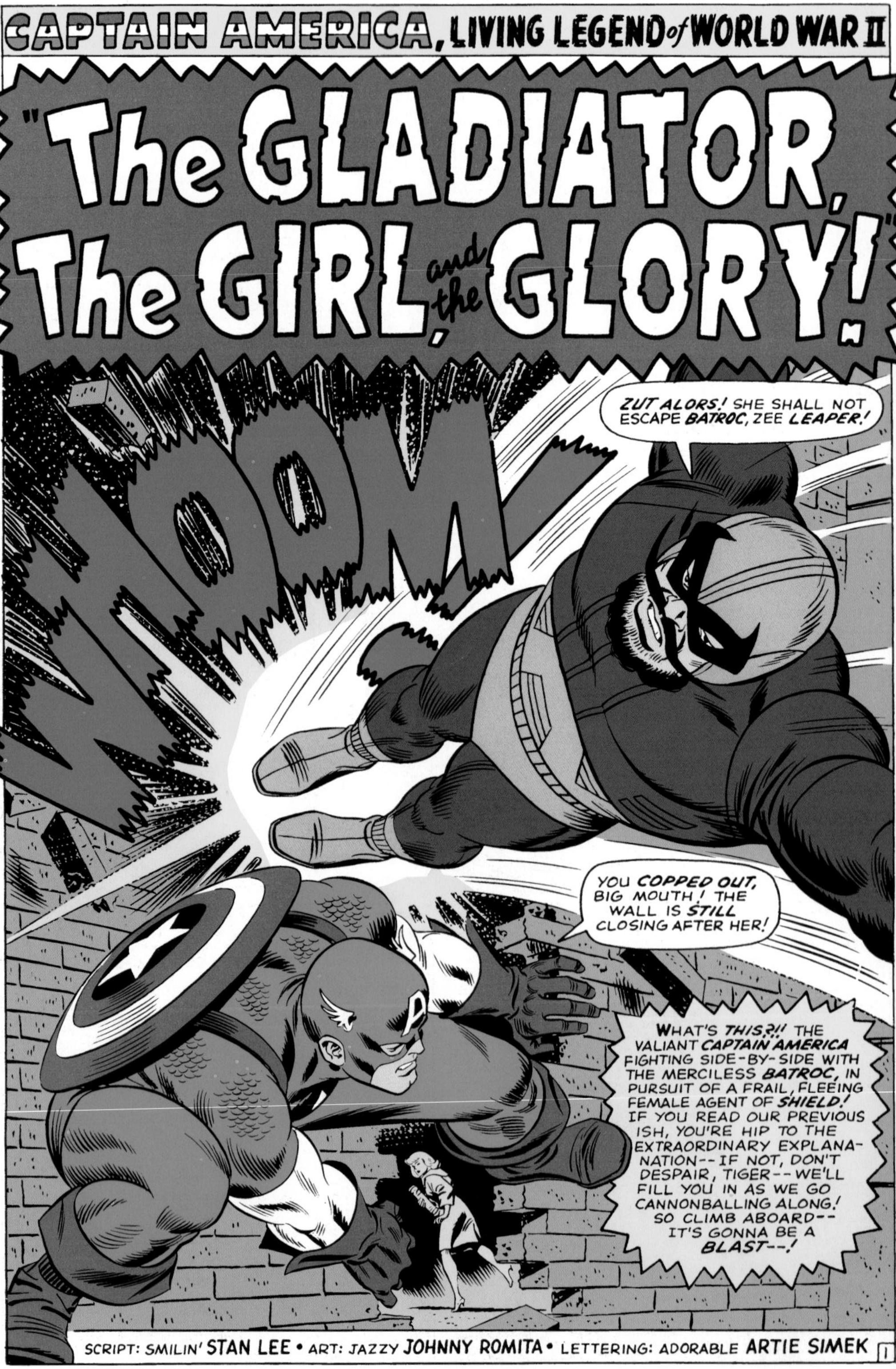
CAPTAIN AMERICA, LIVING LEGEND of WORLD WAR II
"The GLADIATOR, The GIRL, and the GLORY!"
WHOOM!
ZUT ALORS! SHE SHALL NOT ESCAPE BATROC, ZEE LEAPER!
YOU COPPED OUT, BIG MOUTH! THE WALL IS STILL CLOSING AFTER HER!
WHAT'S THIS?!! THE VALIANT CAPTAIN AMERICA FIGHTING SIDE-BY-SIDE WITH THE MERCILESS BATROC, IN PURSUIT OF A FRAIL, FLEEING FEMALE AGENT OF SHIELD! IF YOU READ OUR PREVIOUS ISH, YOU'RE HIP TO THE EXTRAORDINARY EXPLANA-NATION--IF NOT, DON'T DESPAIR, TIGER--WE'LL FILL YOU IN AS WE GO CANNONBALLING ALONG! SO CLIMB ABOARD-- IT'S GONNA BE A BLAST--!
SCRIPT: SMILIN' STAN LEE • ART: JAZZY JOHNNY ROMITA • LETTERING: ADORABLE ARTIE SIMEK
1

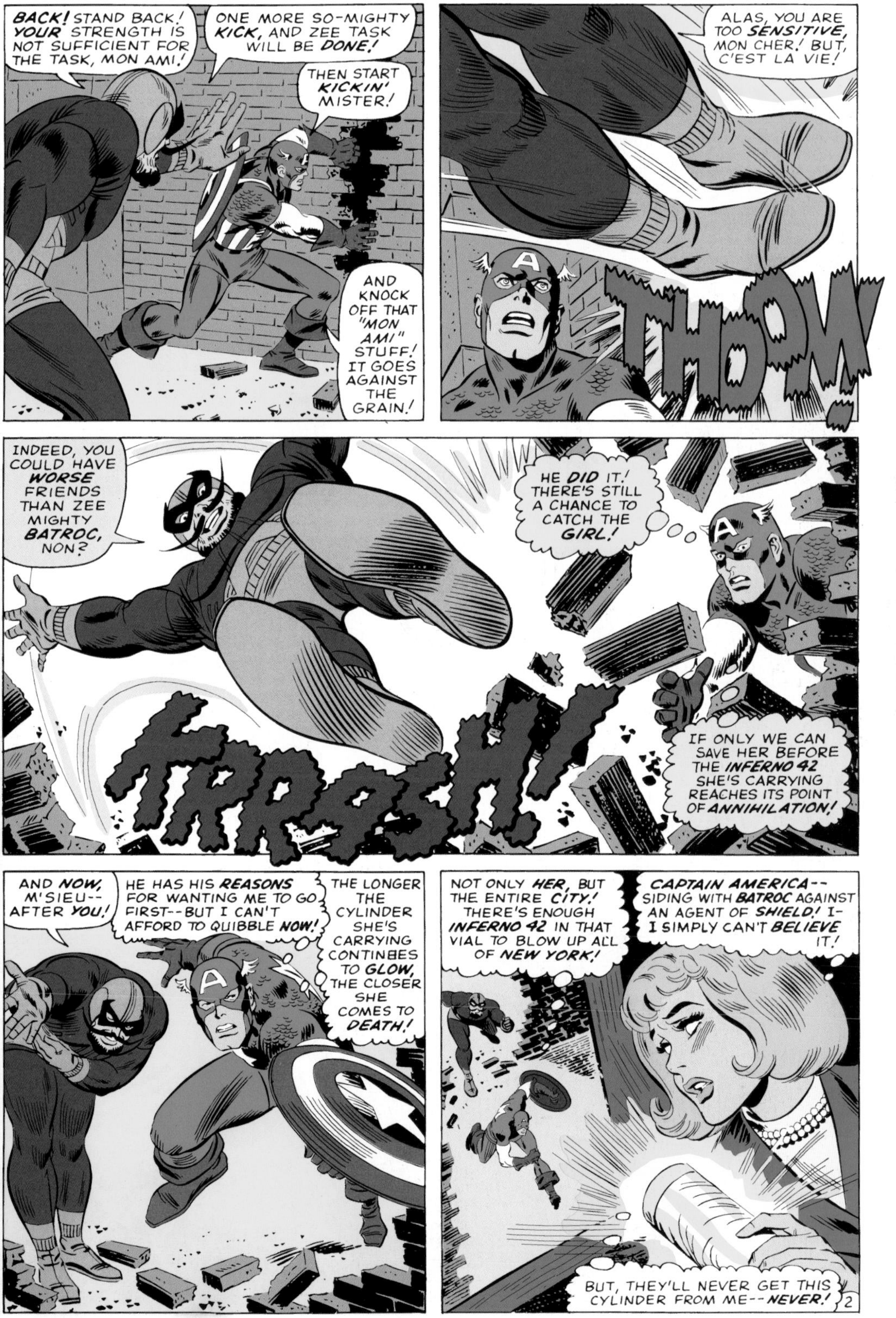
BACK! STAND BACK! YOUR STRENGTH IS NOT SUFFICIENT FOR THE TASK, MON AMI!
ONE MORE SO-MIGHTY KICK, AND ZEE TASK WILL BE DONE!
THEN START KICKIN' MISTER!
AND KNOCK OFF THAT "MON AMI" STUFF! IT GOES AGAINST THE GRAIN!
ALAS, YOU ARE TOO SENSITIVE, MON CHER! BUT, C'EST LA VIE!
THOOM!
INDEED, YOU COULD HAVE WORSE FRIENDS THAN ZEE MIGHTY BATROC, NON?
HE DID IT! THERE'S STILL A CHANCE TO CATCH THE GIRL!
TRRASH!!
IF ONLY WE CAN SAVE HER BEFORE THE INFERNO 42 SHE'S CARRYING REACHES ITS POINT OF ANNIHILATION!
AND NOW, M'SIEU-- AFTER YOU!
HE HAS HIS REASONS FOR WANTING ME TO GO FIRST--BUT I CAN'T AFFORD TO QUIBBLE NOW!
THE LONGER THE CYLINDER SHE'S CARRYING CONTINUES TO GLOW, THE CLOSER SHE COMES TO DEATH!
NOT ONLY HER, BUT THE ENTIRE CITY! THERE'S ENOUGH INFERNO 42 IN THAT VIAL TO BLOW UP ALL OF NEW YORK!
CAPTAIN AMERICA-- SIDING WITH BATROC AGAINST AN AGENT OF SHIELD! I-I SIMPLY CAN'T BELIEVE IT!
BUT, THEY'LL NEVER GET THIS CYLINDER FROM ME--NEVER!
2

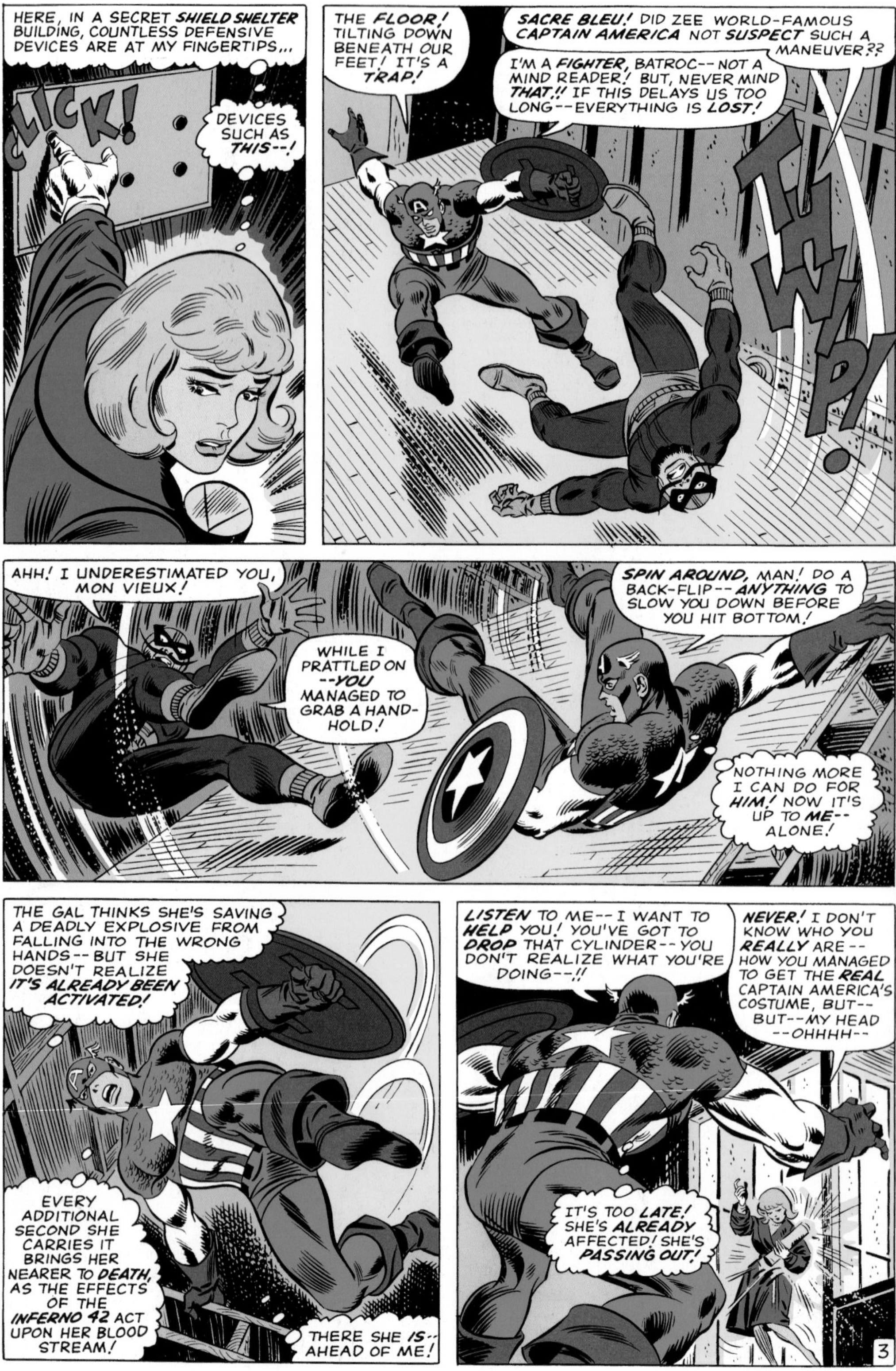
HERE, IN A SECRET SHIELD SHELTER BUILDING, COUNTLESS DEFENSIVE DEVICES ARE AT MY FINGERTIPS,..
CLICK!
DEVICES SUCH AS THIS--!
THE FLOOR! TILTING DOWN BENEATH OUR FEET! IT'S A TRAP!
SACRE BLEU! DID ZEE WORLD-FAMOUS CAPTAIN AMERICA NOT SUSPECT SUCH A MANEUVER??
I'M A FIGHTER, BATROC-- NOT A MIND READER! BUT, NEVER MIND THAT!! IF THIS DELAYS US TOO LONG--EVERYTHING IS LOST!
THWIP!
AHH! I UNDERESTIMATED YOU, MON VIEUX!
WHILE I PRATTLED ON --YOU MANAGED TO GRAB A HAND-HOLD!
SPIN AROUND, MAN! DO A BACK-FLIP--ANYTHING TO SLOW YOU DOWN BEFORE YOU HIT BOTTOM!
NOTHING MORE I CAN DO FOR HIM! NOW IT'S UP TO ME-- ALONE!
THE GAL THINKS SHE'S SAVING A DEADLY EXPLOSIVE FROM FALLING INTO THE WRONG HANDS--BUT SHE DOESN'T REALIZE IT'S ALREADY BEEN ACTIVATED!
EVERY ADDITIONAL SECOND SHE CARRIES IT BRINGS HER NEARER TO DEATH, AS THE EFFECTS OF THE INFERNO 42 ACT UPON HER BLOOD STREAM!
THERE SHE IS-- AHEAD OF ME!
LISTEN TO ME-- I WANT TO HELP YOU! YOU'VE GOT TO DROP THAT CYLINDER--YOU DON'T REALIZE WHAT YOU'RE DOING--!!
NEVER! I DON'T KNOW WHO YOU REALLY ARE-- HOW YOU MANAGED TO GET THE REAL CAPTAIN AMERICA'S COSTUME, BUT-- BUT--MY HEAD --OHHHH--
IT'S TOO LATE! SHE'S ALREADY AFFECTED! SHE'S PASSING OUT!
3

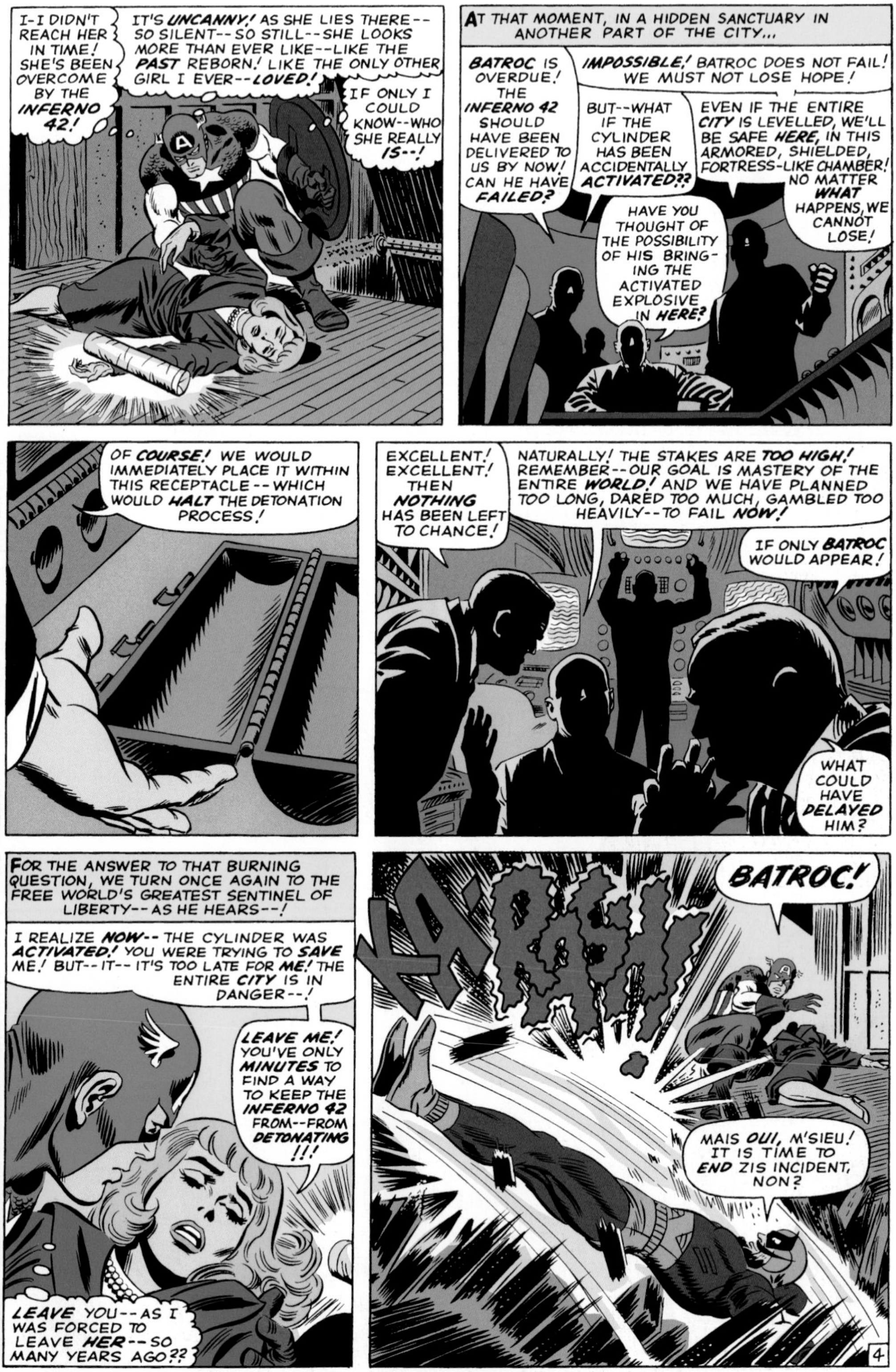
I-I DIDN'T REACH HER IN TIME! SHE'S BEEN OVERCOME BY THE INFERNO 42!
IT'S UNCANNY! AS SHE LIES THERE-- SO SILENT--SO STILL--SHE LOOKS MORE THAN EVER LIKE--LIKE THE PAST REBORN! LIKE THE ONLY OTHER GIRL I EVER--LOVED!
IF ONLY I COULD KNOW--WHO SHE REALLY IS--!
AT THAT MOMENT, IN A HIDDEN SANCTUARY IN ANOTHER PART OF THE CITY...
BATROC IS OVERDUE! THE INFERNO 42 SHOULD HAVE BEEN DELIVERED TO US BY NOW! CAN HE HAVE FAILED?
IMPOSSIBLE! BATROC DOES NOT FAIL! WE MUST NOT LOSE HOPE!
BUT--WHAT IF THE CYLINDER HAS BEEN ACCIDENTALLY ACTIVATED??
EVEN IF THE ENTIRE CITY IS LEVELLED, WE'LL BE SAFE HERE, IN THIS ARMORED, SHIELDED, FORTRESS-LIKE CHAMBER! NO MATTER WHAT HAPPENS, WE CANNOT LOSE!
HAVE YOU THOUGHT OF THE POSSIBILITY OF HIS BRINGING THE ACTIVATED EXPLOSIVE IN HERE?
OF COURSE! WE WOULD IMMEDIATELY PLACE IT WITHIN THIS RECEPTACLE--WHICH WOULD HALT THE DETONATION PROCESS!
EXCELLENT! EXCELLENT! THEN NOTHING HAS BEEN LEFT TO CHANCE!
NATURALLY! THE STAKES ARE TOO HIGH! REMEMBER--OUR GOAL IS MASTERY OF THE ENTIRE WORLD! AND WE HAVE PLANNED TOO LONG, DARED TOO MUCH, GAMBLED TOO HEAVILY--TO FAIL NOW!
IF ONLY BATROC WOULD APPEAR!
WHAT COULD HAVE DELAYED HIM?
FOR THE ANSWER TO THAT BURNING QUESTION, WE TURN ONCE AGAIN TO THE FREE WORLD'S GREATEST SENTINEL OF LIBERTY--AS HE HEARS--!
I REALIZE NOW--THE CYLINDER WAS ACTIVATED! YOU WERE TRYING TO SAVE ME! BUT--IT--IT'S TOO LATE FOR ME! THE ENTIRE CITY IS IN DANGER--!
LEAVE ME! YOU'VE ONLY MINUTES TO FIND A WAY TO KEEP THE INFERNO 42 FROM--FROM DETONATING!!!
LEAVE YOU--AS I WAS FORCED TO LEAVE HER--SO MANY YEARS AGO??
KA-RASH!
BATROC!
MAIS OUI, M'SIEU! IT IS TIME TO END ZIS INCIDENT, NON?
4

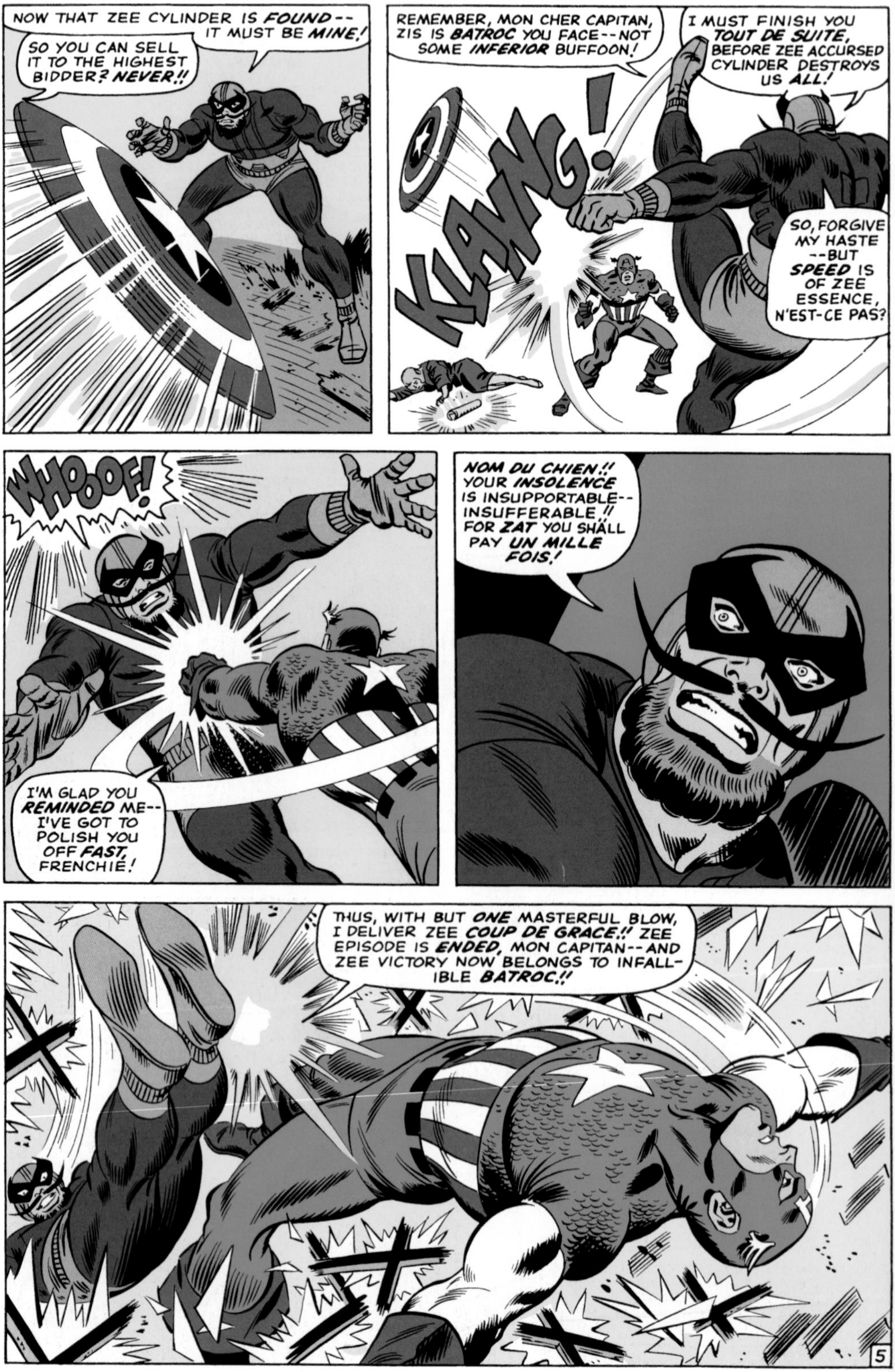
NOW THAT ZEE CYLINDER IS FOUND-- IT MUST BE MINE!
SO YOU CAN SELL IT TO THE HIGHEST BIDDER? NEVER!!
REMEMBER, MON CHER CAPITAN, ZIS IS BATROC YOU FACE--NOT SOME INFERIOR BUFFOON!
I MUST FINISH YOU TOUT DE SUITE, BEFORE ZEE ACCURSED CYLINDER DESTROYS US ALL!
KLANNG!
SO, FORGIVE MY HASTE --BUT SPEED IS OF ZEE ESSENCE, N'EST-CE PAS?
WHOOOF!
I'M GLAD YOU REMINDED ME-- I'VE GOT TO POLISH YOU OFF FAST, FRENCHIE!
NOM DU CHIEN!! YOUR INSOLENCE IS INSUPPORTABLE-- INSUFFERABLE!! FOR ZAT YOU SHALL PAY UN MILLE FOIS!
THUS, WITH BUT ONE MASTERFUL BLOW, I DELIVER ZEE COUP DE GRACE!! ZEE EPISODE IS ENDED, MON CAPITAN--AND ZEE VICTORY NOW BELONGS TO INFALL-IBLE BATROC!!
5

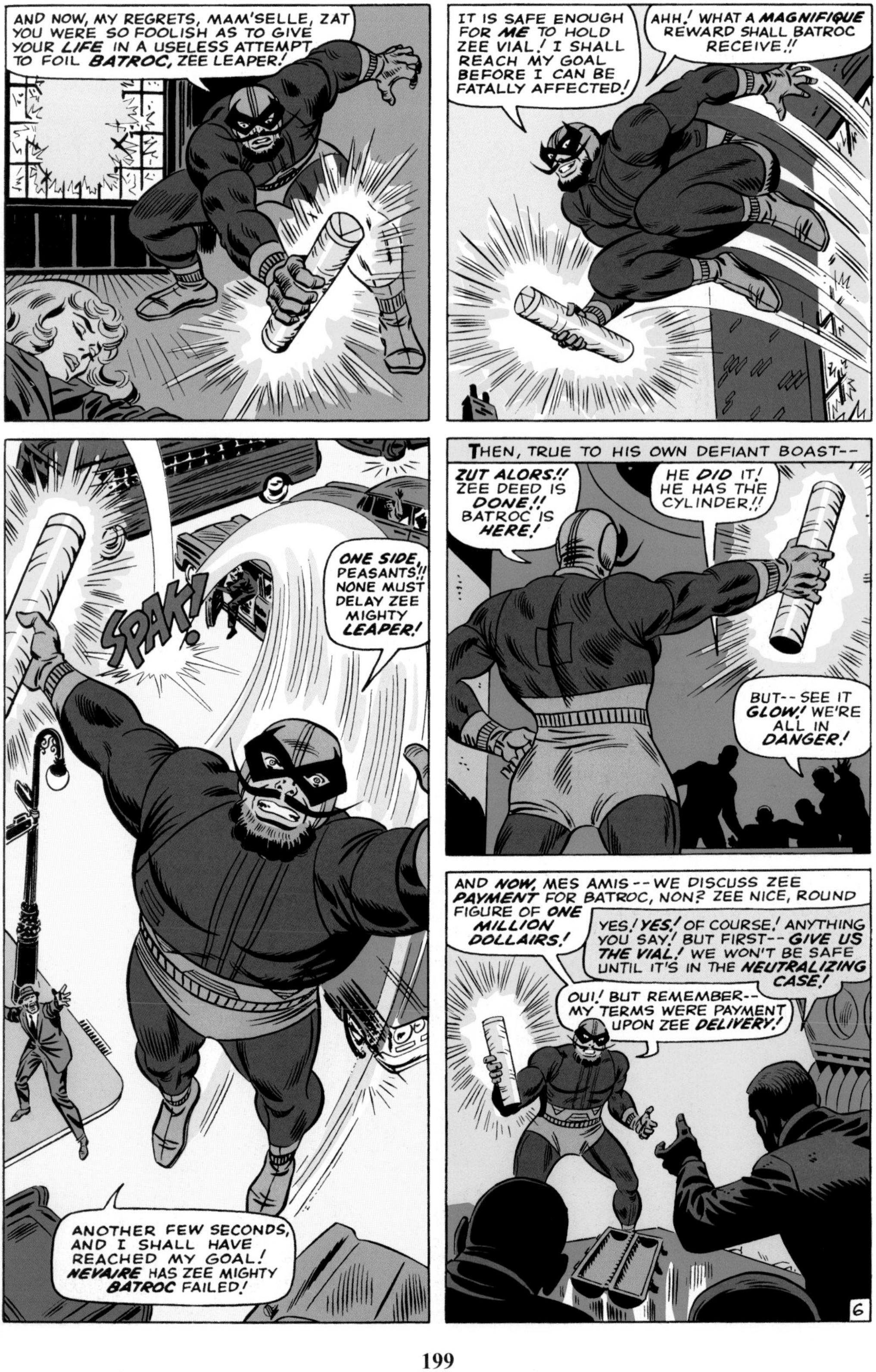
AND NOW, MY REGRETS, MAM'SELLE, ZAT YOU WERE SO FOOLISH AS TO GIVE YOUR LIFE IN A USELESS ATTEMPT TO FOIL BATROC, ZEE LEAPER!
IT IS SAFE ENOUGH FOR ME TO HOLD ZEE VIAL! I SHALL REACH MY GOAL BEFORE I CAN BE FATALLY AFFECTED!
AHH! WHAT A MAGNIFIQUE REWARD SHALL BATROC RECEIVE!!
SPAK!
ONE SIDE, PEASANTS!! NONE MUST DELAY ZEE MIGHTY LEAPER!
ANOTHER FEW SECONDS, AND I SHALL HAVE REACHED MY GOAL! NEVAIRE HAS ZEE MIGHTY BATROC FAILED!
THEN, TRUE TO HIS OWN DEFIANT BOAST--
ZUT ALORS!! ZEE DEED IS DONE!! BATROC IS HERE!
HE DID IT! HE HAS THE CYLINDER!!
BUT-- SEE IT GLOW! WE'RE ALL IN DANGER!
AND NOW, MES AMIS -- WE DISCUSS ZEE PAYMENT FOR BATROC, NON? ZEE NICE, ROUND FIGURE OF ONE MILLION DOLLAIRS!
YES! YES! OF COURSE! ANYTHING YOU SAY! BUT FIRST-- GIVE US THE VIAL! WE WON'T BE SAFE UNTIL IT'S IN THE NEUTRALIZING CASE!
OUI! BUT REMEMBER-- MY TERMS WERE PAYMENT UPON ZEE DELIVERY!
6

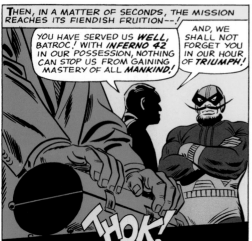

THEN, IN A MATTER OF SECONDS, THE MISSION REACHES ITS FIENDISH FRUITION--!

YOU HAVE SERVED US *WELL*, BATROC! WITH *INFERNO 42* IN OUR POSSESSION, NOTHING CAN STOP US FROM GAINING MASTERY OF ALL *MANKIND!*

AND, WE SHALL NOT FORGET YOU IN OUR HOUR OF *TRIUMPH!*

THOK!

I CARE NOT FOR YOUR REMEMBRANCE --NOR FOR YOUR FLOWERY PHRASES, MES AMIS!

BATROC NOW CLAIMS HIS *PAYMENT*--AND ZEE *PATIENCE* OF ZEE MIGHTY LEAPER GROWS *SHORTER* WITH EACH PASSING MOMENT!

FOOL! YOU DARE TO ANTAGONIZE US-- TO SPEAK TO US *THUS*---OVER A PALTRY MILLION DOLLARS?!! IF YOU BUT KNEW WHO WE REALLY *ARE!*

WE PLAY FOR THE HIGHEST STAKES ON EARTH! WE HAVE *BILLIONS* AT OUR DISPOSAL!

THE MILLION WE SHALL GIVE YOU IS A *PITTANCE* COMPARED TO WHAT YOU MAY EARN IF YOU CONTINUE TO SERVE US! FOR *NONE* CAN EVER RESIGN!

DON'T BOTHER *ANSWERING*, BATROC! IT'S AN *ACADEMIC* POINT, ANYWAY! YOU'RE NOT GONNA BE ABLE TO *SPEND* ANY OF THAT PAYMENT, NO MATTER WHAT! *I'LL* SEE TO THAT!

AND NOW, GENTLEMEN--I'LL TAKE THAT CYLINDER, IF YOU PLEASE! OR, EVEN IF YOU *DON'T!*

CAPTAIN AMERICA!! BUT-- IT IS *IMPOSSIBLE!!* I CRUSHED HIM LIKE A *BUG!*

BATROC! YOU BLUNDERING *FOOL!* AND YOU CALL YOURSELF *INFALLIBLE!*

DON'T BE TOO HARD ON THE LEAPER! HE DESERVES AN "A" FOR EFFORT! HE DIDN'T GUESS THAT I WAS PLAYING POSSUM, SO HE'D LEAD ME BACK TO *YOU!*

DON'T JUST *STAND* THERE, YOU FRENCH FEATHERBRAIN!! IF YOU WANT THAT MILLION, THIS IS WHERE YOU'LL *EARN* IT! *CAPTAIN AMERICA MUST DIE!*

MAIS CERTAINMENT!! HE HAS BECOME TOO MUCH ZEE *NUISANCE*, ZAT ONE! NO ONE MAKES ZEE FOOL OF *BATROC*, AND LIVES TO BOAST OF IT!

7

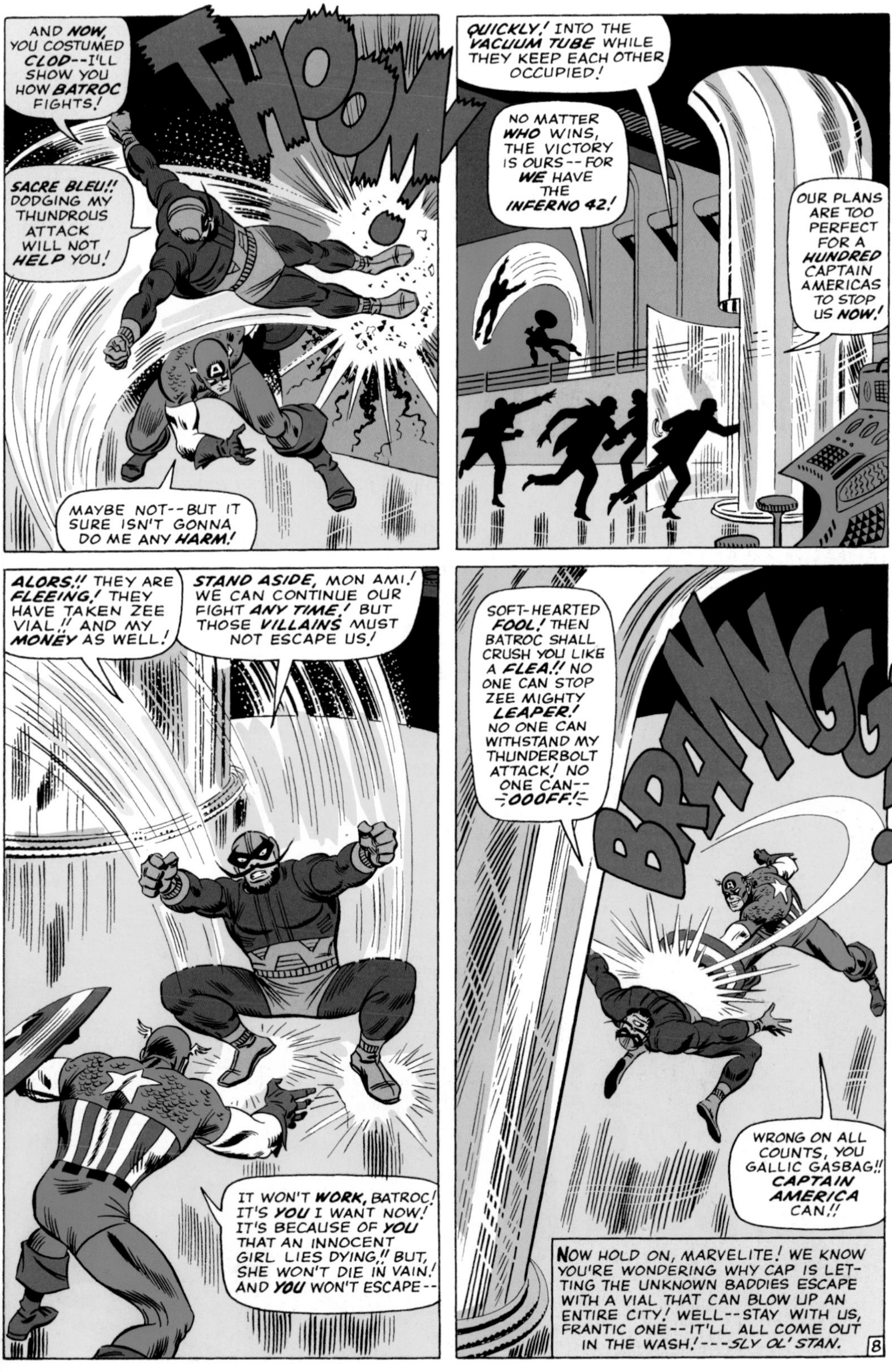
AND NOW, YOU COSTUMED CLOD--I'LL SHOW YOU HOW BATROC FIGHTS!
THOOM
SACRE BLEU!! DODGING MY THUNDROUS ATTACK WILL NOT HELP YOU!
MAYBE NOT--BUT IT SURE ISN'T GONNA DO ME ANY HARM!
QUICKLY! INTO THE VACUUM TUBE WHILE THEY KEEP EACH OTHER OCCUPIED!
NO MATTER WHO WINS, THE VICTORY IS OURS--FOR WE HAVE THE INFERNO 42!
OUR PLANS ARE TOO PERFECT FOR A HUNDRED CAPTAIN AMERICAS TO STOP US NOW!
ALORS!! THEY ARE FLEEING! THEY HAVE TAKEN ZEE VIAL!! AND MY MONEY AS WELL!
STAND ASIDE, MON AMI! WE CAN CONTINUE OUR FIGHT ANY TIME! BUT THOSE VILLAINS MUST NOT ESCAPE US!
IT WON'T WORK, BATROC! IT'S YOU I WANT NOW! IT'S BECAUSE OF YOU THAT AN INNOCENT GIRL LIES DYING!! BUT, SHE WON'T DIE IN VAIN! AND YOU WON'T ESCAPE--
SOFT-HEARTED FOOL! THEN BATROC SHALL CRUSH YOU LIKE A FLEA!! NO ONE CAN STOP ZEE MIGHTY LEAPER! NO ONE CAN WITHSTAND MY THUNDERBOLT ATTACK! NO ONE CAN-- OOOFF!
BRANNGG!
WRONG ON ALL COUNTS, YOU GALLIC GASBAG!! CAPTAIN AMERICA CAN!!
NOW HOLD ON, MARVELITE! WE KNOW YOU'RE WONDERING WHY CAP IS LETTING THE UNKNOWN BADDIES ESCAPE WITH A VIAL THAT CAN BLOW UP AN ENTIRE CITY! WELL--STAY WITH US, FRANTIC ONE--IT'LL ALL COME OUT IN THE WASH!---SLY OL' STAN.
8

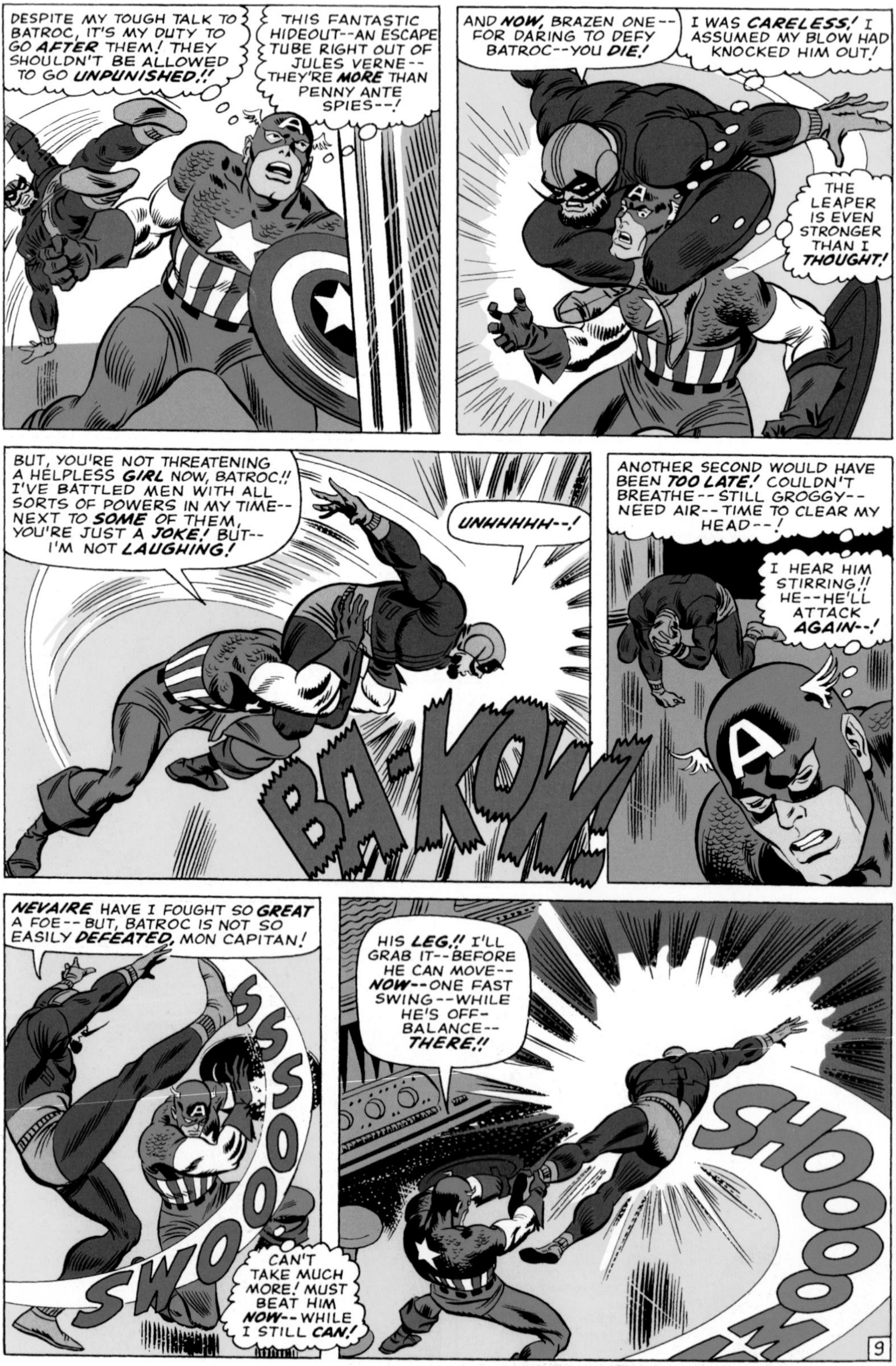
DESPITE MY TOUGH TALK TO BATROC, IT'S MY DUTY TO GO AFTER THEM! THEY SHOULDN'T BE ALLOWED TO GO UNPUNISHED!!
THIS FANTASTIC HIDEOUT--AN ESCAPE TUBE RIGHT OUT OF JULES VERNE--THEY'RE MORE THAN PENNY ANTE SPIES--!
AND NOW, BRAZEN ONE--FOR DARING TO DEFY BATROC--YOU DIE!
I WAS CARELESS! I ASSUMED MY BLOW HAD KNOCKED HIM OUT!
THE LEAPER IS EVEN STRONGER THAN I THOUGHT!
BUT, YOU'RE NOT THREATENING A HELPLESS GIRL NOW, BATROC!! I'VE BATTLED MEN WITH ALL SORTS OF POWERS IN MY TIME--NEXT TO SOME OF THEM, YOU'RE JUST A JOKE! BUT--I'M NOT LAUGHING!
UNHHHHH--!
BA-KOW
ANOTHER SECOND WOULD HAVE BEEN TOO LATE! COULDN'T BREATHE--STILL GROGGY--NEED AIR--TIME TO CLEAR MY HEAD--!
I HEAR HIM STIRRING!! HE--HE'LL ATTACK AGAIN--!
NEVAIRE HAVE I FOUGHT SO GREAT A FOE--BUT, BATROC IS NOT SO EASILY DEFEATED, MON CAPITAN!
SSSOOOOSWOOO
CAN'T TAKE MUCH MORE! MUST BEAT HIM NOW--WHILE I STILL CAN!
HIS LEG!! I'LL GRAB IT--BEFORE HE CAN MOVE--NOW--ONE FAST SWING--WHILE HE'S OFF-BALANCE--THERE!!
SHOOOOM
9

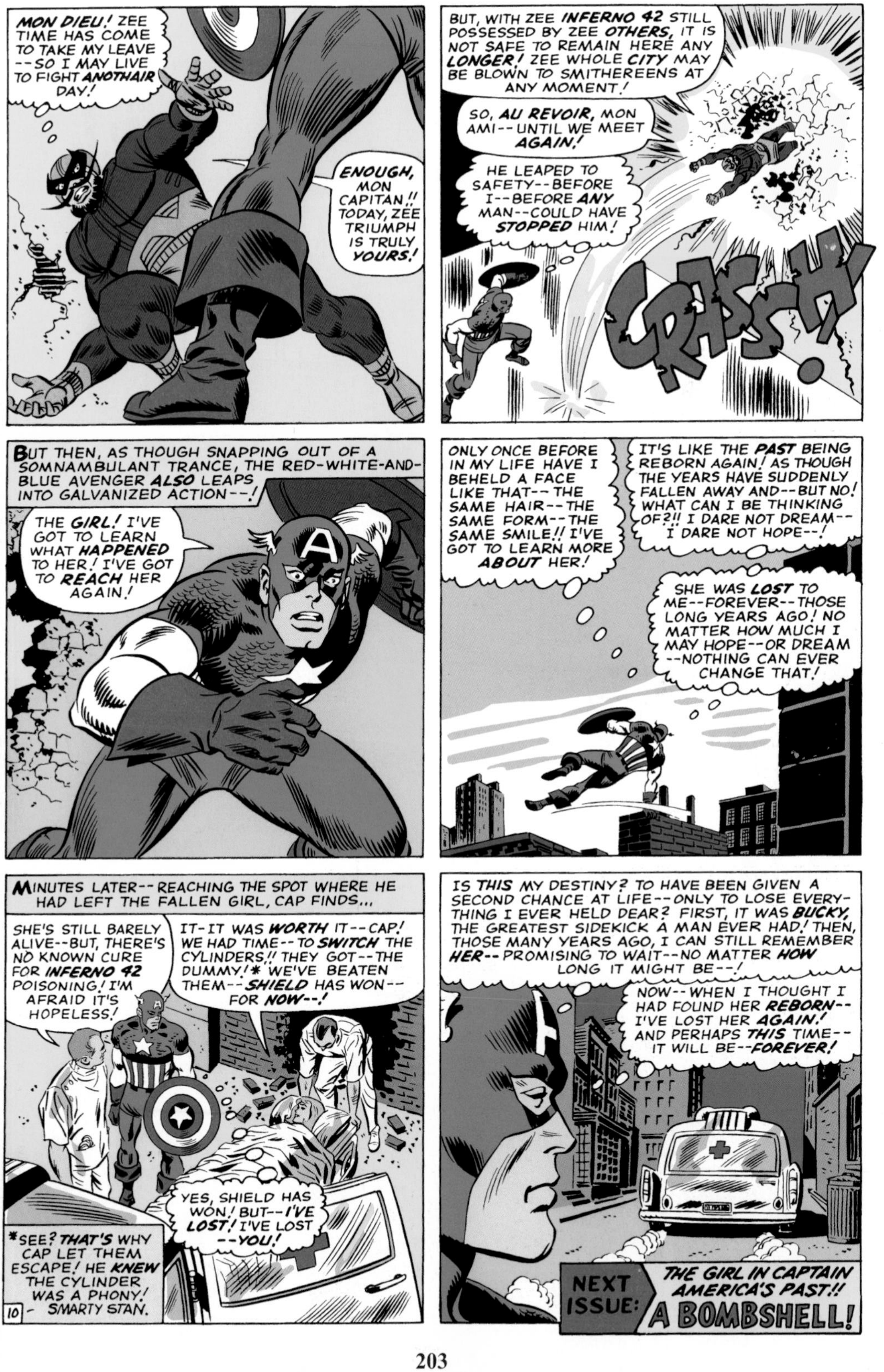
MON DIEU! ZEE TIME HAS COME TO TAKE MY LEAVE --SO I MAY LIVE TO FIGHT ANOTHAIR DAY!
ENOUGH, MON CAPITAN!! TODAY, ZEE TRIUMPH IS TRULY YOURS!
BUT, WITH ZEE INFERNO 42 STILL POSSESSED BY ZEE OTHERS, IT IS NOT SAFE TO REMAIN HERE ANY LONGER! ZEE WHOLE CITY MAY BE BLOWN TO SMITHEREENS AT ANY MOMENT!
SO, AU REVOIR, MON AMI--UNTIL WE MEET AGAIN!
HE LEAPED TO SAFETY--BEFORE I--BEFORE ANY MAN--COULD HAVE STOPPED HIM!
CRASSH!
BUT THEN, AS THOUGH SNAPPING OUT OF A SOMNAMBULANT TRANCE, THE RED-WHITE-AND-BLUE AVENGER ALSO LEAPS INTO GALVANIZED ACTION--!
THE GIRL! I'VE GOT TO LEARN WHAT HAPPENED TO HER! I'VE GOT TO REACH HER AGAIN!
ONLY ONCE BEFORE IN MY LIFE HAVE I BEHELD A FACE LIKE THAT--THE SAME HAIR--THE SAME FORM--THE SAME SMILE!! I'VE GOT TO LEARN MORE ABOUT HER!
IT'S LIKE THE PAST BEING REBORN AGAIN! AS THOUGH THE YEARS HAVE SUDDENLY FALLEN AWAY AND--BUT NO! WHAT CAN I BE THINKING OF?!! I DARE NOT DREAM--I DARE NOT HOPE--!
SHE WAS LOST TO ME--FOREVER--THOSE LONG YEARS AGO! NO MATTER HOW MUCH I MAY HOPE--OR DREAM--NOTHING CAN EVER CHANGE THAT!
MINUTES LATER--REACHING THE SPOT WHERE HE HAD LEFT THE FALLEN GIRL, CAP FINDS...
SHE'S STILL BARELY ALIVE--BUT, THERE'S NO KNOWN CURE FOR INFERNO 42 POISONING! I'M AFRAID IT'S HOPELESS!
IT-IT WAS WORTH IT--CAP! WE HAD TIME--TO SWITCH THE CYLINDERS!! THEY GOT--THE DUMMY!* WE'VE BEATEN THEM--SHIELD HAS WON--FOR NOW--!
YES, SHIELD HAS WON! BUT--I'VE LOST! I'VE LOST--YOU!
*SEE? THAT'S WHY CAP LET THEM ESCAPE! HE KNEW THE CYLINDER WAS A PHONY! --SMARTY STAN.
10
IS THIS MY DESTINY? TO HAVE BEEN GIVEN A SECOND CHANCE AT LIFE--ONLY TO LOSE EVERYTHING I EVER HELD DEAR? FIRST, IT WAS BUCKY, THE GREATEST SIDEKICK A MAN EVER HAD! THEN, THOSE MANY YEARS AGO, I CAN STILL REMEMBER HER--PROMISING TO WAIT--NO MATTER HOW LONG IT MIGHT BE--!
NOW--WHEN I THOUGHT I HAD FOUND HER REBORN--I'VE LOST HER AGAIN! AND PERHAPS THIS TIME--IT WILL BE--FOREVER!
NEXT ISSUE: THE GIRL IN CAPTAIN AMERICA'S PAST!! A BOMBSHELL!

TALES OF SUSPENSE
featuring
IRON MAN AND CAPTAIN AMERICA
APPROVED BY THE COMICS CODE AUTHORITY
MARVEL COMICS GROUP
77 MAY
12¢
IND.
"ULTIMO LIVES!"

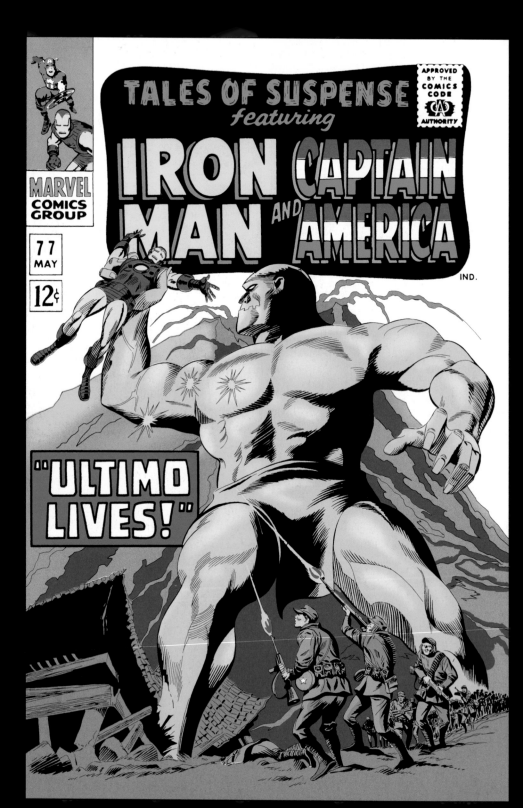

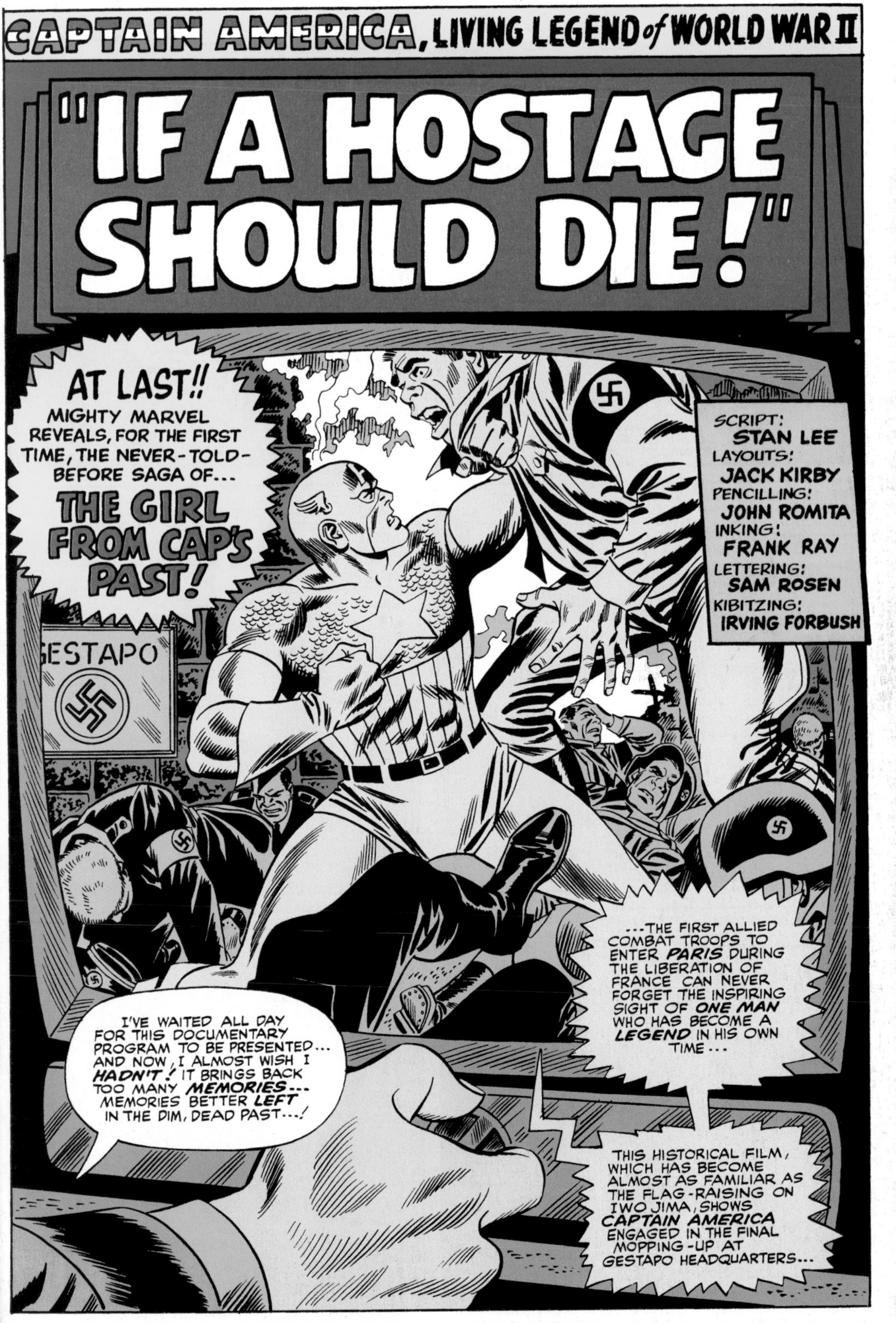
CAPTAIN AMERICA, LIVING LEGEND of WORLD WAR II
"IF A HOSTAGE SHOULD DIE!"
AT LAST!! MIGHTY MARVEL REVEALS, FOR THE FIRST TIME, THE NEVER-TOLD-BEFORE SAGA OF... THE GIRL FROM CAP'S PAST!
SCRIPT: STAN LEE LAYOUTS: JACK KIRBY PENCILLING: JOHN ROMITA INKING: FRANK RAY LETTERING: SAM ROSEN KIBITZING: IRVING FORBUSH
GESTAPO
...THE FIRST ALLIED COMBAT TROOPS TO ENTER PARIS DURING THE LIBERATION OF FRANCE CAN NEVER FORGET THE INSPIRING SIGHT OF ONE MAN WHO HAS BECOME A LEGEND IN HIS OWN TIME...
I'VE WAITED ALL DAY FOR THIS DOCUMENTARY PROGRAM TO BE PRESENTED... AND NOW, I ALMOST WISH I HADN'T! IT BRINGS BACK TOO MANY MEMORIES... MEMORIES BETTER LEFT IN THE DIM, DEAD PAST...!
THIS HISTORICAL FILM, WHICH HAS BECOME ALMOST AS FAMILIAR AS THE FLAG-RAISING ON IWO JIMA, SHOWS CAPTAIN AMERICA ENGAGED IN THE FINAL MOPPING-UP AT GESTAPO HEADQUARTERS...

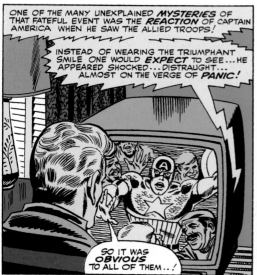

ONE OF THE MANY UNEXPLAINED *MYSTERIES* OF THAT FATEFUL EVENT WAS THE *REACTION* OF CAPTAIN AMERICA WHEN HE SAW THE ALLIED TROOPS!

INSTEAD OF WEARING THE TRIUMPHANT SMILE ONE WOULD *EXPECT* TO SEE...HE APPEARED SHOCKED...DISTRAUGHT... ALMOST ON THE VERGE OF *PANIC!*

SO IT WAS *OBVIOUS* TO ALL OF THEM...!

FINALLY, AMERICA'S MOST GALLANT SENTINEL OF LIBERTY FREED HIMSELF FROM THE CHEERING G.I.'s WHO HAD HAPPILY LIFTED HIM UPON THEIR SHOULDERS ...AND WITHIN BRIEF MOMENTS, HE HAD LOST HIM- SELF IN THE CROWD!

BUT, IT WASN'T SOON *ENOUGH!* I WAS STILL *TOO LATE!*

...TOO LATE EVER TO SEE *HER* AGAIN!

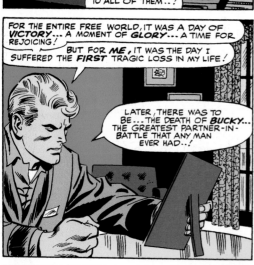

FOR THE ENTIRE FREE WORLD, IT WAS A DAY OF *VICTORY*...A MOMENT OF *GLORY*...A TIME FOR REJOICING!

BUT FOR *ME*, IT WAS THE DAY I SUFFERED THE *FIRST* TRAGIC LOSS IN MY LIFE!

LATER, THERE WAS TO BE...THE DEATH OF *BUCKY*... THE GREATEST PARTNER-IN- BATTLE THAT ANY MAN EVER HAD...!

BUT THAT DAY, AT THE LAST FEW MOMENTS OF FIGHTING...WHEN THE VICTORY HAD FINALLY BEEN WON...I LOST *HER*...FOREVER!

I NEVER KNEW FOR CERTAIN WHETHER SHE HAD BEEN *KILLED*--OR IF-- BUT, IT'S BEEN MORE THAN *TWENTY YEARS* SINCE THEN...

...IF SHE WERE STILL ALIVE, SURELY SHE'D HAVE *FOUND* ME BY NOW!

I NEVER *TOLD* THEM...THAT IT WAS BECAUSE OF *YOU* I WAS SO DESPERATE ON THAT FATAL DAY!

I WANTED TO *FIND* YOU...TO TEAR ALL OF *PARIS* APART UNTIL WE WERE TOGETHER AGAIN...BUT, IT WAS *TOO LATE*, MY DARLING...I HAD *LOST* YOU...FOREVER!

THAT LIGHTNING AND THUNDER...IT'S LIKE THE ANGRY ROAR OF THE *PAST*...TRYING TO CAPTURE ME AGAIN!

IF ONLY I *COULD* RETURN TO THAT DAY...IF ONLY I *COULD* GO BACK...AND HAVE A SECOND CHANCE..!

206

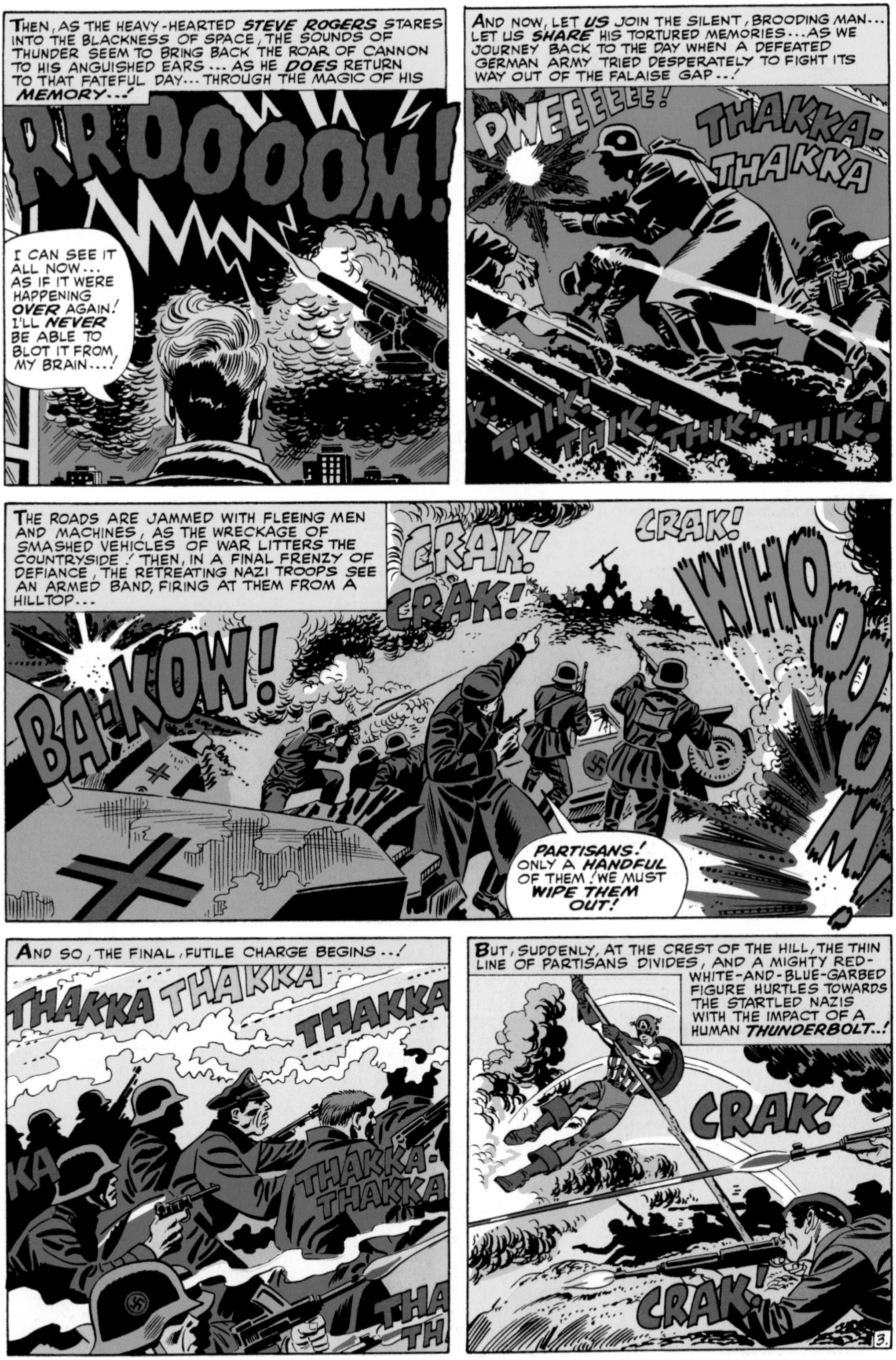
THEN, AS THE HEAVY-HEARTED STEVE ROGERS STARES INTO THE BLACKNESS OF SPACE, THE SOUNDS OF THUNDER SEEM TO BRING BACK THE ROAR OF CANNON TO HIS ANGUISHED EARS... AS HE DOES RETURN TO THAT FATEFUL DAY... THROUGH THE MAGIC OF HIS MEMORY...!
RROOOOM!
I CAN SEE IT ALL NOW... AS IF IT WERE HAPPENING OVER AGAIN! I'LL NEVER BE ABLE TO BLOT IT FROM MY BRAIN...!
AND NOW, LET US JOIN THE SILENT, BROODING MAN... LET US SHARE HIS TORTURED MEMORIES... AS WE JOURNEY BACK TO THE DAY WHEN A DEFEATED GERMAN ARMY TRIED DESPERATELY TO FIGHT ITS WAY OUT OF THE FALAISE GAP...!
PWEEEEEE!
THAKKA-THAKKA
THIK! THIK! THIK! THIK!
THE ROADS ARE JAMMED WITH FLEEING MEN AND MACHINES, AS THE WRECKAGE OF SMASHED VEHICLES OF WAR LITTERS THE COUNTRYSIDE! THEN, IN A FINAL FRENZY OF DEFIANCE, THE RETREATING NAZI TROOPS SEE AN ARMED BAND, FIRING AT THEM FROM A HILLTOP...
CRAK! CRAK!
CRAK!
BA-KOW!
WHOOOOM!
PARTISANS! ONLY A HANDFUL OF THEM! WE MUST WIPE THEM OUT!
AND SO, THE FINAL, FUTILE CHARGE BEGINS...!
THAKKA THAKKA
THAKKA
THAKKA-THAKKA
BUT, SUDDENLY, AT THE CREST OF THE HILL, THE THIN LINE OF PARTISANS DIVIDES, AND A MIGHTY RED-WHITE-AND-BLUE-GARBED FIGURE HURTLES TOWARDS THE STARTLED NAZIS WITH THE IMPACT OF A HUMAN THUNDERBOLT..!
CRAK!
CRAK!
3.

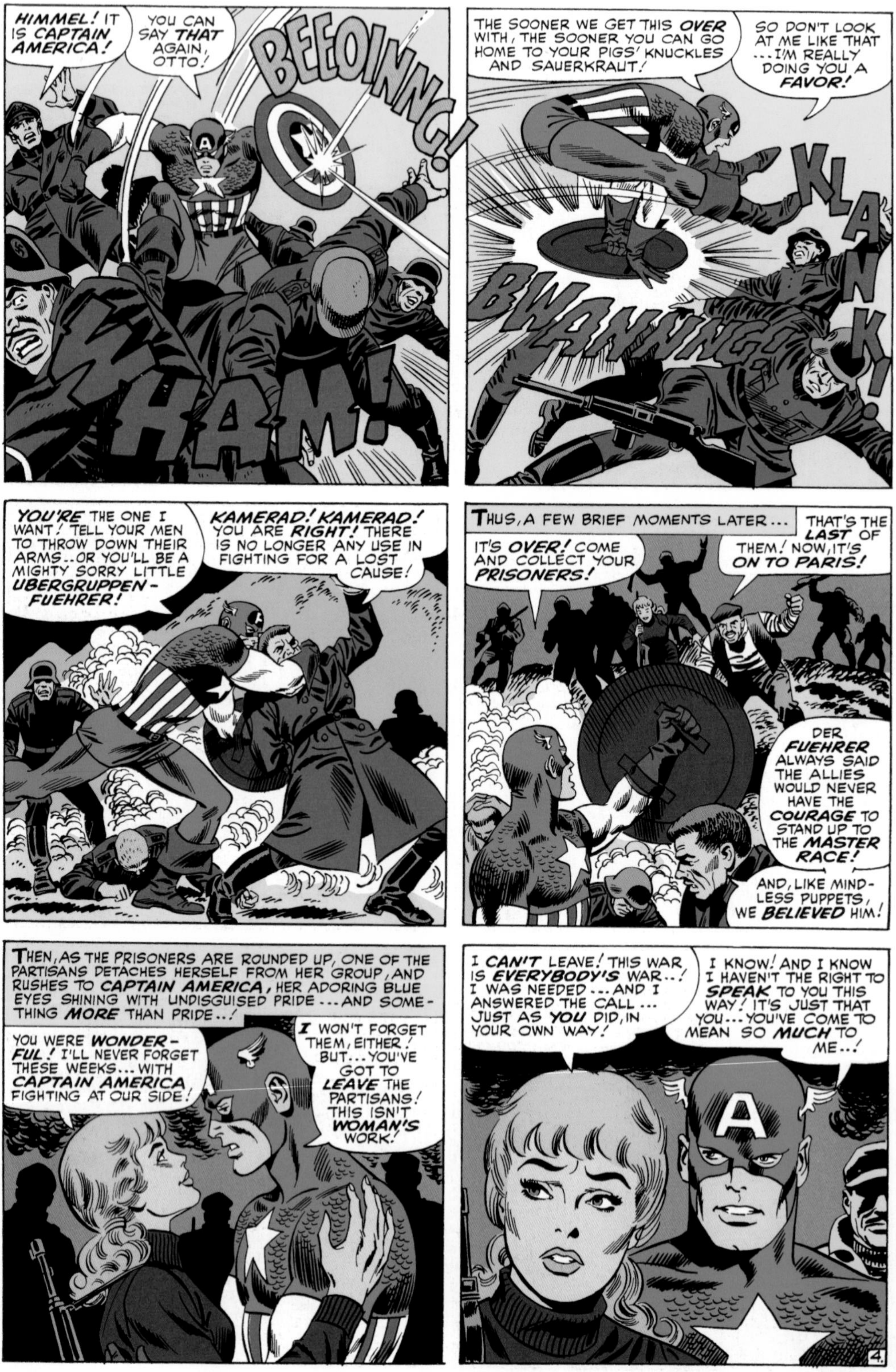
HIMMEL! IT IS CAPTAIN AMERICA!
YOU CAN SAY THAT AGAIN, OTTO!
BEEOINNG!
WHAM!
THE SOONER WE GET THIS OVER WITH, THE SOONER YOU CAN GO HOME TO YOUR PIGS' KNUCKLES AND SAUERKRAUT!
SO DON'T LOOK AT ME LIKE THAT ...I'M REALLY DOING YOU A FAVOR!
KLANK!
BWANNNG!
YOU'RE THE ONE I WANT! TELL YOUR MEN TO THROW DOWN THEIR ARMS..OR YOU'LL BE A MIGHTY SORRY LITTLE UBERGRUPPEN-FUEHRER!
KAMERAD! KAMERAD! YOU ARE RIGHT! THERE IS NO LONGER ANY USE IN FIGHTING FOR A LOST CAUSE!
THUS, A FEW BRIEF MOMENTS LATER...
IT'S OVER! COME AND COLLECT YOUR PRISONERS!
THAT'S THE LAST OF THEM! NOW, IT'S ON TO PARIS!
DER FUEHRER ALWAYS SAID THE ALLIES WOULD NEVER HAVE THE COURAGE TO STAND UP TO THE MASTER RACE!
AND, LIKE MIND-LESS PUPPETS, WE BELIEVED HIM!
THEN, AS THE PRISONERS ARE ROUNDED UP, ONE OF THE PARTISANS DETACHES HERSELF FROM HER GROUP, AND RUSHES TO CAPTAIN AMERICA, HER ADORING BLUE EYES SHINING WITH UNDISGUISED PRIDE ... AND SOME-THING MORE THAN PRIDE..!
YOU WERE WONDER-FUL! I'LL NEVER FORGET THESE WEEKS... WITH CAPTAIN AMERICA FIGHTING AT OUR SIDE!
I WON'T FORGET THEM, EITHER! BUT... YOU'VE GOT TO LEAVE THE PARTISANS! THIS ISN'T WOMAN'S WORK!
I CAN'T LEAVE! THIS WAR IS EVERYBODY'S WAR..! I WAS NEEDED ... AND I ANSWERED THE CALL ... JUST AS YOU DID, IN YOUR OWN WAY!
I KNOW! AND I KNOW I HAVEN'T THE RIGHT TO SPEAK TO YOU THIS WAY! IT'S JUST THAT YOU... YOU'VE COME TO MEAN SO MUCH TO ME..!
4.

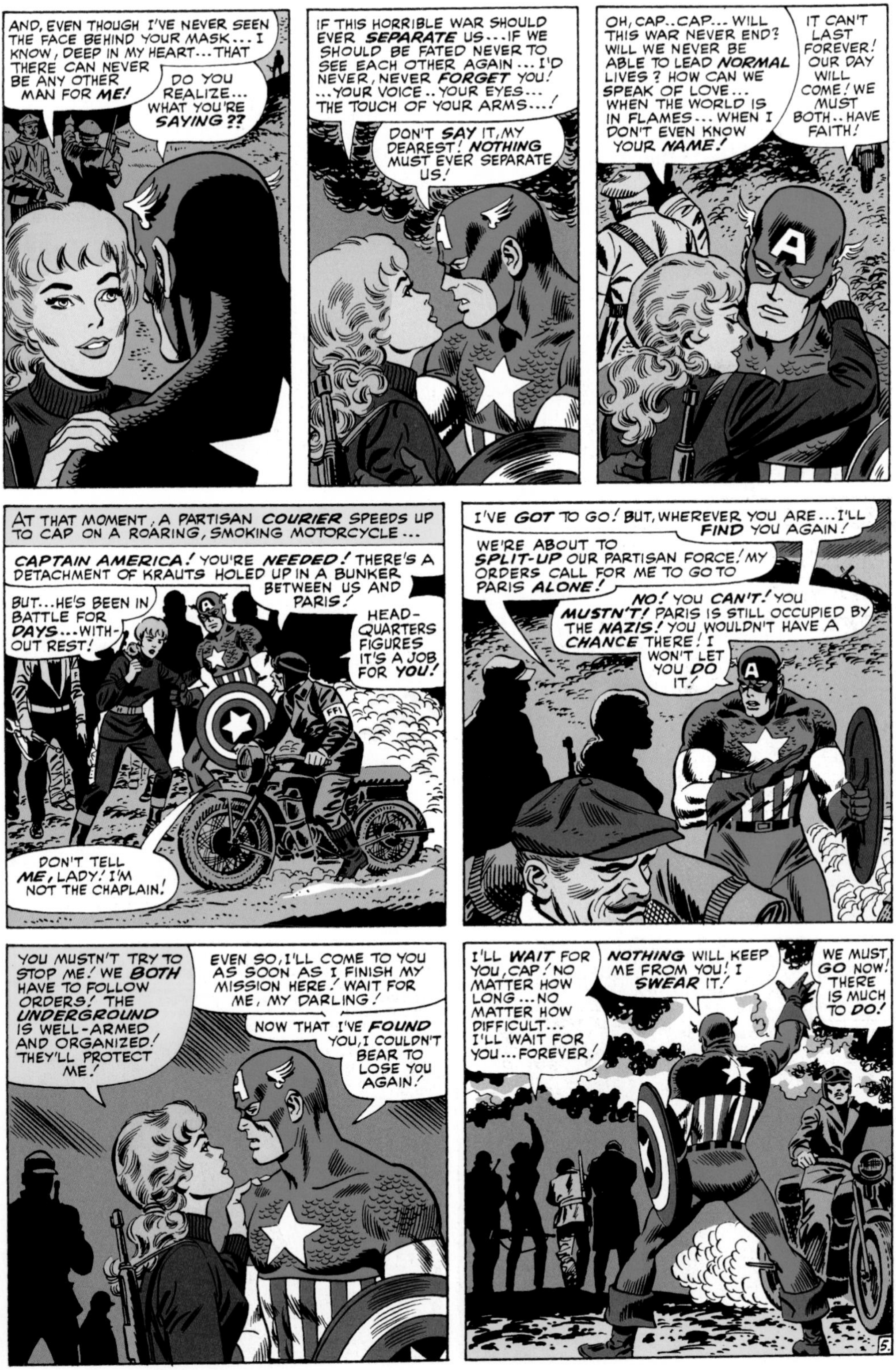
AND, EVEN THOUGH I'VE NEVER SEEN THE FACE BEHIND YOUR MASK... I KNOW, DEEP IN MY HEART... THAT THERE CAN NEVER BE ANY OTHER MAN FOR ME!
DO YOU REALIZE... WHAT YOU'RE SAYING??
IF THIS HORRIBLE WAR SHOULD EVER SEPARATE US... IF WE SHOULD BE FATED NEVER TO SEE EACH OTHER AGAIN... I'D NEVER, NEVER FORGET YOU! ...YOUR VOICE.. YOUR EYES... THE TOUCH OF YOUR ARMS...!
DON'T SAY IT, MY DEAREST! NOTHING MUST EVER SEPARATE US!
OH, CAP.. CAP... WILL THIS WAR NEVER END? WILL WE NEVER BE ABLE TO LEAD NORMAL LIVES? HOW CAN WE SPEAK OF LOVE... WHEN THE WORLD IS IN FLAMES... WHEN I DON'T EVEN KNOW YOUR NAME!
IT CAN'T LAST FOREVER! OUR DAY WILL COME! WE MUST BOTH.. HAVE FAITH!
AT THAT MOMENT, A PARTISAN COURIER SPEEDS UP TO CAP ON A ROARING, SMOKING MOTORCYCLE...
CAPTAIN AMERICA! YOU'RE NEEDED! THERE'S A DETACHMENT OF KRAUTS HOLED UP IN A BUNKER BETWEEN US AND PARIS!
BUT... HE'S BEEN IN BATTLE FOR DAYS... WITHOUT REST!
HEADQUARTERS FIGURES IT'S A JOB FOR YOU!
DON'T TELL ME, LADY! I'M NOT THE CHAPLAIN!
I'VE GOT TO GO! BUT, WHEREVER YOU ARE... I'LL FIND YOU AGAIN!
WE'RE ABOUT TO SPLIT-UP OUR PARTISAN FORCE! MY ORDERS CALL FOR ME TO GO TO PARIS ALONE!
NO! YOU CAN'T! YOU MUSTN'T! PARIS IS STILL OCCUPIED BY THE NAZIS! YOU WOULDN'T HAVE A CHANCE THERE! I WON'T LET YOU DO IT!
YOU MUSTN'T TRY TO STOP ME! WE BOTH HAVE TO FOLLOW ORDERS! THE UNDERGROUND IS WELL-ARMED AND ORGANIZED! THEY'LL PROTECT ME!
EVEN SO, I'LL COME TO YOU AS SOON AS I FINISH MY MISSION HERE! WAIT FOR ME, MY DARLING!
NOW THAT I'VE FOUND YOU, I COULDN'T BEAR TO LOSE YOU AGAIN!
I'LL WAIT FOR YOU, CAP! NO MATTER HOW LONG... NO MATTER HOW DIFFICULT... I'LL WAIT FOR YOU... FOREVER!
NOTHING WILL KEEP ME FROM YOU! I SWEAR IT!
WE MUST GO NOW! THERE IS MUCH TO DO!
5.

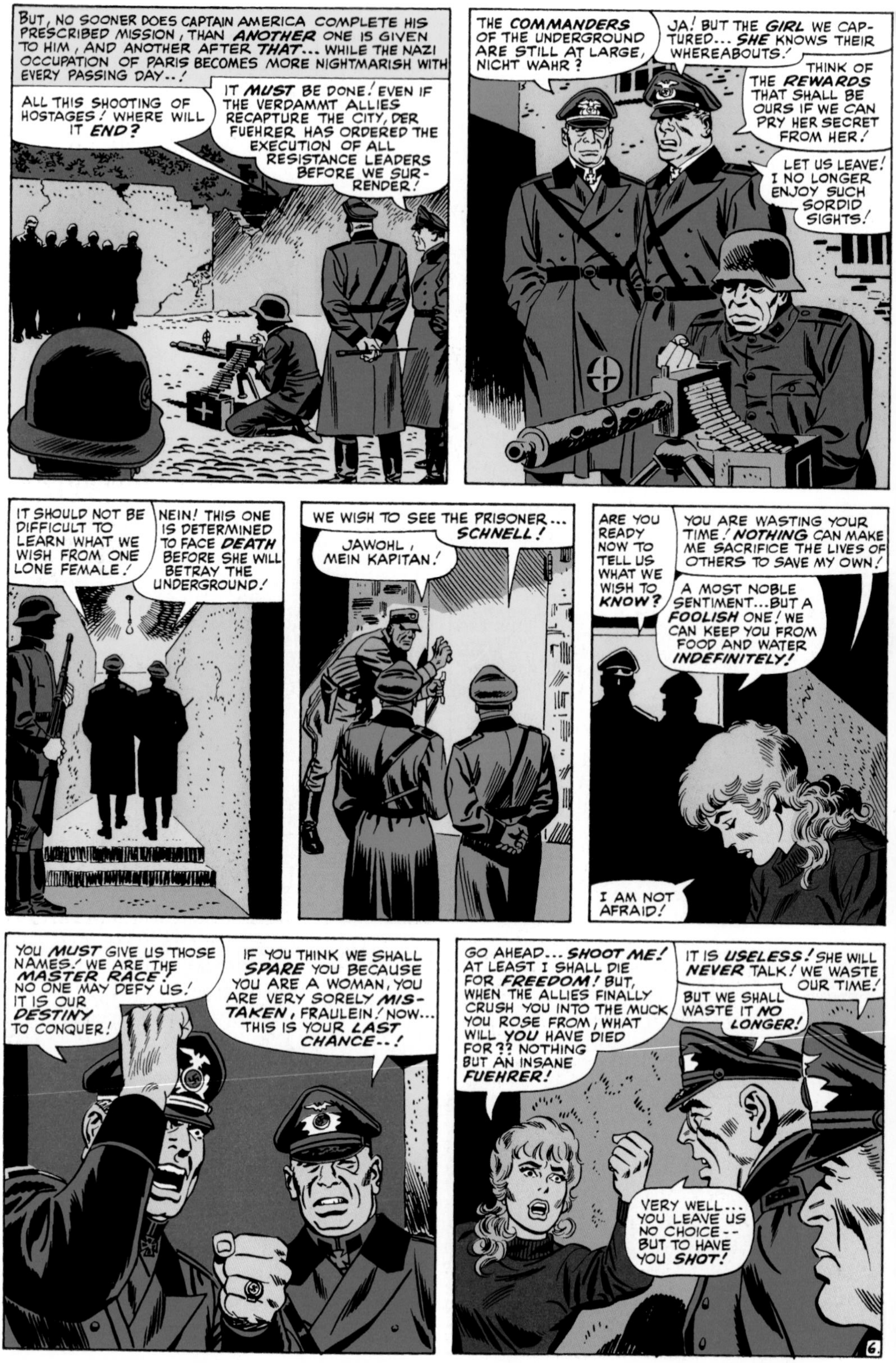

BUT, NO SOONER DOES CAPTAIN AMERICA COMPLETE HIS PRESCRIBED MISSION, THAN ANOTHER ONE IS GIVEN TO HIM, AND ANOTHER AFTER THAT... WHILE THE NAZI OCCUPATION OF PARIS BECOMES MORE NIGHTMARISH WITH EVERY PASSING DAY..!
ALL THIS SHOOTING OF HOSTAGES! WHERE WILL IT END?
IT MUST BE DONE! EVEN IF THE VERDAMMT ALLIES RECAPTURE THE CITY, DER FUEHRER HAS ORDERED THE EXECUTION OF ALL RESISTANCE LEADERS BEFORE WE SURRENDER!
THE COMMANDERS OF THE UNDERGROUND ARE STILL AT LARGE, NICHT WAHR?
JA! BUT THE GIRL WE CAPTURED... SHE KNOWS THEIR WHEREABOUTS!
THINK OF THE REWARDS THAT SHALL BE OURS IF WE CAN PRY HER SECRET FROM HER!
LET US LEAVE! I NO LONGER ENJOY SUCH SORDID SIGHTS!
IT SHOULD NOT BE DIFFICULT TO LEARN WHAT WE WISH FROM ONE LONE FEMALE!
NEIN! THIS ONE IS DETERMINED TO FACE DEATH BEFORE SHE WILL BETRAY THE UNDERGROUND!
WE WISH TO SEE THE PRISONER... SCHNELL!
JAWOHL, MEIN KAPITAN!
ARE YOU READY NOW TO TELL US WHAT WE WISH TO KNOW?
YOU ARE WASTING YOUR TIME! NOTHING CAN MAKE ME SACRIFICE THE LIVES OF OTHERS TO SAVE MY OWN!
A MOST NOBLE SENTIMENT...BUT A FOOLISH ONE! WE CAN KEEP YOU FROM FOOD AND WATER INDEFINITELY!
I AM NOT AFRAID!
YOU MUST GIVE US THOSE NAMES! WE ARE THE MASTER RACE! NO ONE MAY DEFY US! IT IS OUR DESTINY TO CONQUER!
IF YOU THINK WE SHALL SPARE YOU BECAUSE YOU ARE A WOMAN, YOU ARE VERY SORELY MISTAKEN, FRAULEIN! NOW... THIS IS YOUR LAST CHANCE--!
GO AHEAD... SHOOT ME! AT LEAST I SHALL DIE FOR FREEDOM! BUT, WHEN THE ALLIES FINALLY CRUSH YOU INTO THE MUCK YOU ROSE FROM, WHAT WILL YOU HAVE DIED FOR?? NOTHING BUT AN INSANE FUEHRER!
IT IS USELESS! SHE WILL NEVER TALK! WE WASTE OUR TIME!
BUT WE SHALL WASTE IT NO LONGER!
VERY WELL... YOU LEAVE US NO CHOICE-- BUT TO HAVE YOU SHOT!
6.

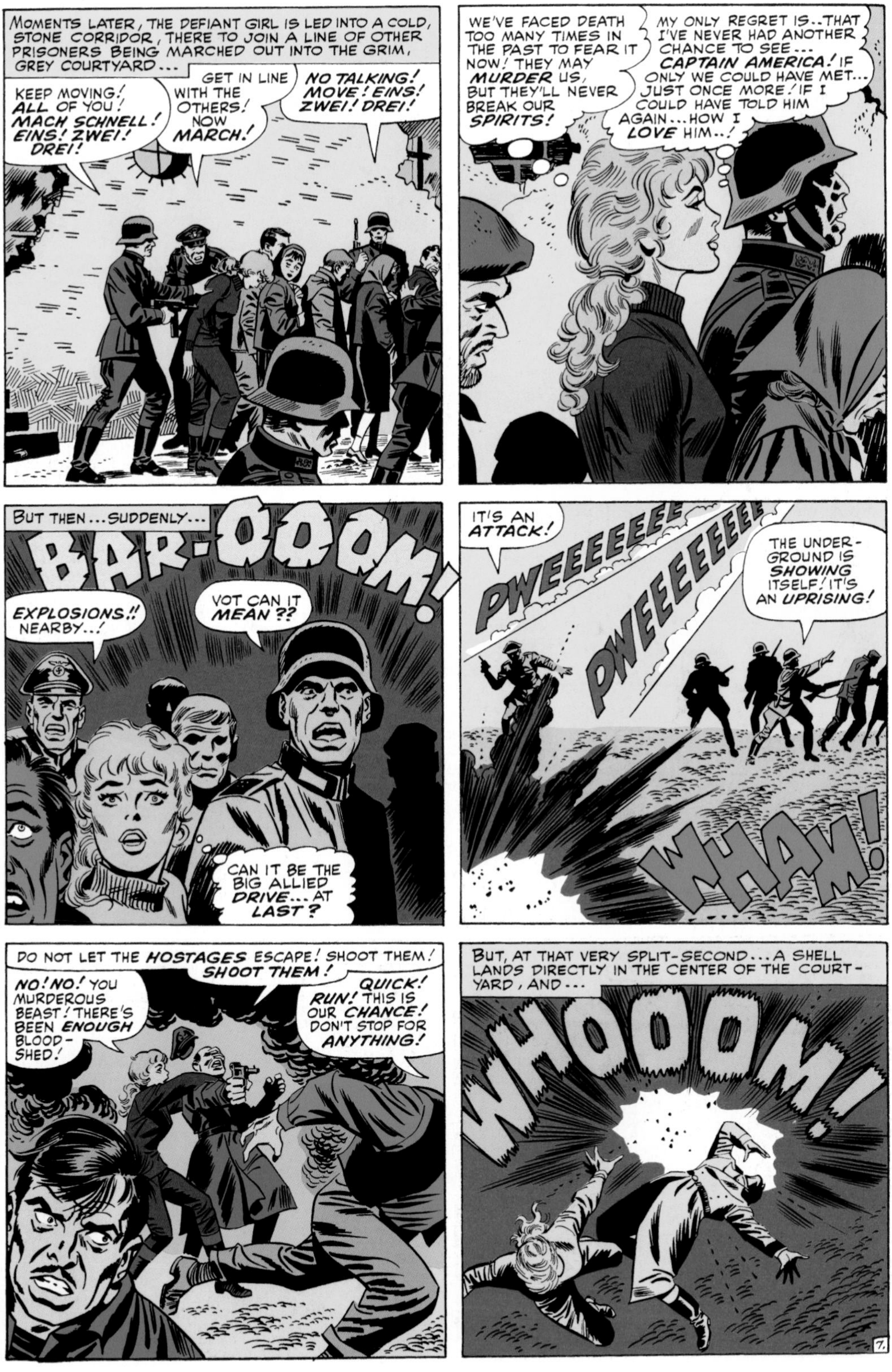
MOMENTS LATER, THE DEFIANT GIRL IS LED INTO A COLD, STONE CORRIDOR, THERE TO JOIN A LINE OF OTHER PRISONERS BEING MARCHED OUT INTO THE GRIM, GREY COURTYARD...
KEEP MOVING! ALL OF YOU! MACH SCHNELL! EINS! ZWEI! DREI!
GET IN LINE WITH THE OTHERS! NOW MARCH!
NO TALKING! MOVE! EINS! ZWEI! DREI!
WE'VE FACED DEATH TOO MANY TIMES IN THE PAST TO FEAR IT NOW! THEY MAY MURDER US, BUT THEY'LL NEVER BREAK OUR SPIRITS!
MY ONLY REGRET IS.. THAT I'VE NEVER HAD ANOTHER CHANCE TO SEE... CAPTAIN AMERICA! IF ONLY WE COULD HAVE MET... JUST ONCE MORE! IF I COULD HAVE TOLD HIM AGAIN... HOW I LOVE HIM..!
BUT THEN... SUDDENLY...
BAR-OOOM!
EXPLOSIONS!! NEARBY..!
VOT CAN IT MEAN ??
CAN IT BE THE BIG ALLIED DRIVE... AT LAST?
IT'S AN ATTACK!
PWEEEEEEE
PWEEEEEEEE
THE UNDER-GROUND IS SHOWING ITSELF! IT'S AN UPRISING!
WHAM!
DO NOT LET THE HOSTAGES ESCAPE! SHOOT THEM! SHOOT THEM!
NO! NO! YOU MURDEROUS BEAST! THERE'S BEEN ENOUGH BLOOD-SHED!
QUICK! RUN! THIS IS OUR CHANCE! DON'T STOP FOR ANYTHING!
BUT, AT THAT VERY SPLIT-SECOND... A SHELL LANDS DIRECTLY IN THE CENTER OF THE COURT-YARD, AND...
WHOOOM!
7.

MOMENTS LATER, THE REMAINING NAZI FORCES HAVE BEEN GIVEN THE ORDER... *EVACUATE PARIS!*

DEATH TO THE BOCHE!

THE KILLERS MUST NOT *ESCAPE!*

CRAK!

PTINNG!

PA-KOW!

STOP THEM! SMASH THEM! DESTROY THE NAZI MURDERERS!

DON'T LET THEM SURVIVE TO PLUNDER AND SACK *ANOTHER* TOWN!

KRAK!

PAKKA PAKKA KA-THOWW!

SURRENDER, NAZIS, SURRENDER..OR *DIE!*

BUDDA-BUDDA-BUDDA!

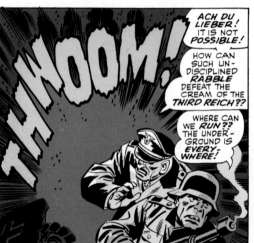

THWOOM!

ACH DU LIEBER! IT IS NOT *POSSIBLE!*

HOW CAN SUCH UN-DISCIPLINED *RABBLE* DEFEAT THE CREAM OF THE *THIRD REICH??*

WHERE CAN WE *RUN??* THE UNDER-GROUND IS *EVERY-WHERE!*

AND, THROUGHOUT THE BATTLE... DARTING, DASHING, FIGHTING, SHOUTING ENCOURAGEMENT AND LENDING INSPIRATION, THE FIGURE OF *CAPTAIN AMERICA* IS EVER IN THE FOREFRONT, UNTIL...

HOLD YOUR FIRE! IT IS THE AMERICAN ADVENTURER!

QUICK! WHICH ONE OF YOU IS *FRAN-COIS??*

SPEAK UP! EVERY MINUTE MAY BE *VITAL!*

I AM FRANCOIS! THE GIRL *TOLD* ME YOU WOULD COME...SOONER OR LATER!

BUT ALAS, MON AMI... YOU ARE *TOO LATE!*

TOO LATE?? WHAT DO YOU *MEAN??* OUT WITH IT, MAN!

SHE HAS BEEN *TAKEN*... BY THE ACCURSED *GESTAPO!* WE TRIED TO RESCUE HER...TIME AND AGAIN...BUT EACH TIME... WE *FAILED!*

BUT *CAPTAIN AMERICA* WON'T FAIL! WHERE IS THEIR *HEAD-QUARTERS??* HURRY...TELL ME! *TELL ME!*

8

MINUTES LATER, A NAZI STAFF CAR FRANTICALLY ATTEMPTS A DESPERATE ESCAPE DOWN A WRECKAGE-STREWN, SHELL-SCARRED BOULEVARD...

FASTER! FASTER, YOU DUMMKOPF! THE UNDERGROUND IS EVERYWHERE!

JUST ANOTHER FEW KILOMETERS, AND WE WILL BE SAFE!

BUT, THOSE FEW KILOMETERS ARE DESTINED TO BE FOREVER BEYOND THE REACH OF THE TWO FLEEING MEN...

A CAR! JUST WHAT I NEED!

IF ONE HAIR OF HER HEAD HAS BEEN HARMED... I'LL.. I'LL.. NO! I MUSTN'T EVEN THINK OF IT!

RRRRRRRR

MEANWHILE, A SCANT FEW HUNDRED YARDS AWAY, THE SPEARHEAD OF THE ALLIED COMBAT FORCES CAUTIOUSLY ENTERS THE SMOLDERING CITY OF PARIS...!

EVERYTHING LOOKS QUIET, SIR!

SO DOES A RATTLE-SNAKE, BEFORE IT STRIKES!

LOOK SHARP, SOLDIER! WE'RE NOT FIGHTING AMATEURS!

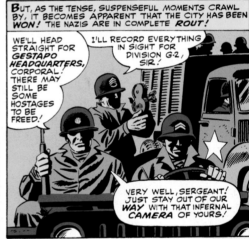

BUT, AS THE TENSE, SUSPENSEFUL MOMENTS CRAWL BY, IT BECOMES APPARENT THAT THE CITY HAS BEEN WON! THE NAZIS ARE IN COMPLETE ROUT!

WE'LL HEAD STRAIGHT FOR GESTAPO HEADQUARTERS, CORPORAL. THERE MAY STILL BE SOME HOSTAGES TO BE FREED!

I'LL RECORD EVERYTHING IN SIGHT FOR DIVISION G-2, SIR!

VERY WELL, SERGEANT! JUST STAY OUT OF OUR WAY WITH THAT INFERNAL CAMERA OF YOURS!

THUS, THE SCENE YOU ARE NOW BEHOLDING WAS RECORDED FOR POSTERITY...!

WHERE IS SHE?? WHAT DID YOU DO WITH HER?? TELL ME, OR...!

IT WAS A SHELL... IT HIT THE COURTYARD! WHEN THE SMOKE CLEARED... SHE WAS GONE! THEY WERE ALL GONE!

IT'S CAPTAIN AMERICA!

BRO-THER! THESE FILMS'LL MAKE ME FAMOUS!

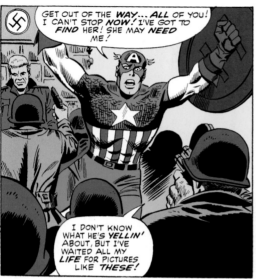

GET OUT OF THE *WAY*... *ALL* OF YOU! I CAN'T STOP *NOW*! I'VE GOT TO *FIND* HER! SHE MAY *NEED* ME!

I DON'T KNOW WHAT HE'S *YELLIN'* ABOUT, BUT I'VE WAITED ALL MY *LIFE* FOR PICTURES LIKE *THESE*!

AND, AS FATE WOULD HAVE IT, CAP'S DESPERATE CRIES ARE *DROWNED OUT* BY THE THUNDEROUS SHOUTS OF ELATION... THE SOUND OF COUNTLESS VOICES, CHEERING YELLING, LAUGHING... ACCLAIMING THE LIBERATION OF A *CITY*!

PARIS IS *FREE*! THE KRAUTS ARE ON THE *RUN*!

THERE'S *CAPTAIN AMERICA*! GRAB 'IM! HE'S GOTTA *CELEBRATE* WITH US!

NO! LET ME *GO*! *WAIT*... *STOP*..!

UH UH! THIS IS NO TIME FOR *MODESTY*, MISTER! WE GOT US A REAL GEN-U-WINE *HERO* NOW, AND WE AIN'T LETTIN' *GO*!

KEEP TOOTIN' THAT *BUGLE*, SOLDIER! LET'S MAKE 'EM HEAR US CLEAR BACK TO *BERLIN*!

♫♪ MADEMOISELLE FROM ARMENTIERES, PARLEE VOOO.. ♪♫

THAT'S *IT*, YOU GUYS! GET 'IM UP WHERE ALL THE JOES CAN *SEE* 'IM!

I..I *CAN'T* REFUSE THEM! IT'S THEIR MOMENT OF VICTORY...I MUSTN'T *SPOIL* IT!

C'MON, LET'S MARCH 'IM THROUGH THE TOWN! ..HERE WE *GO*, CAP!

GANG-WAY!

AND SO, THE COSTUMED FIGURE OF *CAPTAIN AMERICA* IS BORNE ALOFT ON THE SHOULDERS OF THE WILDLY CHEERING G.I.S...AS THE MASKED ADVENTURER'S HEART SLOWLY SINKS WITHIN HIM...!

IT'S ALL SO *HOPELESS*! HOW CAN I *EVER* FIND HER NOW?

PERHAPS *LATER*, WHEN THE NOISE AND EXCITEMENT DIE *DOWN*...!

BUT, SURELY SHE'LL LEARN THAT *I'M* IN PARIS...AND, EVEN IF I CAN'T FIND *HER*, SHE'S BOUND TO SEEK *ME* OUT!

ALL THAT NOISE! THE EXCITEMENT! IF ONLY I COULD REMEMBER ...WHAT IT'S ALL ABOUT!

EVERYTHING IS A *BLANK* IN MY MIND! WHO *AM* I? WHY AM I *HERE*..?

ALL I CAN REMEMBER IS ..AN *EXPLOSION*! A TERRIBLE ...EARTH-SHATTERING EXPLOSION!

I..I MUST HAVE HAD SOME SORT OF *SHOCK*! I'VE GOT TO BE PATIENT...MY MEMORY WILL RETURN SOON! IT...IT *HAS* TO RETURN ....IT *HAS* TO!

BUT, SOFTLY, THE LIGHT DRONE OF RAINDROPS BEGINS TO BEAT DOWN UPON THE STREETS OF NEW YORK, IN THE YEAR 1966, AS THE SOUND AND FURY OF THE SUDDEN STORM BEGINS TO FADE AWAY INTO WISPY NOTHINGNESS ...

AFTER ALL THESE YEARS...I STILL DON'T KNOW....IF SHE'S ALIVE OR DEAD! I STILL DON'T KNOW WHAT EVER *BECAME* OF HER..!

THEN, GENTLY,..A MEMORY-HAUNTED MAN CLOSES HIS WINDOW! THE PAST HAS VANISHED ONCE MORE ...AND HE KNOWS IT CAN NEVER RETURN!

NEXT ISSUE:
CAPTAIN AMERICA *MEETS* NICK FURY, AGENT OF SHIELD!

10

***Tales of Suspense* #60 page 1 original art**
by Jack Kirby & Chic Stone

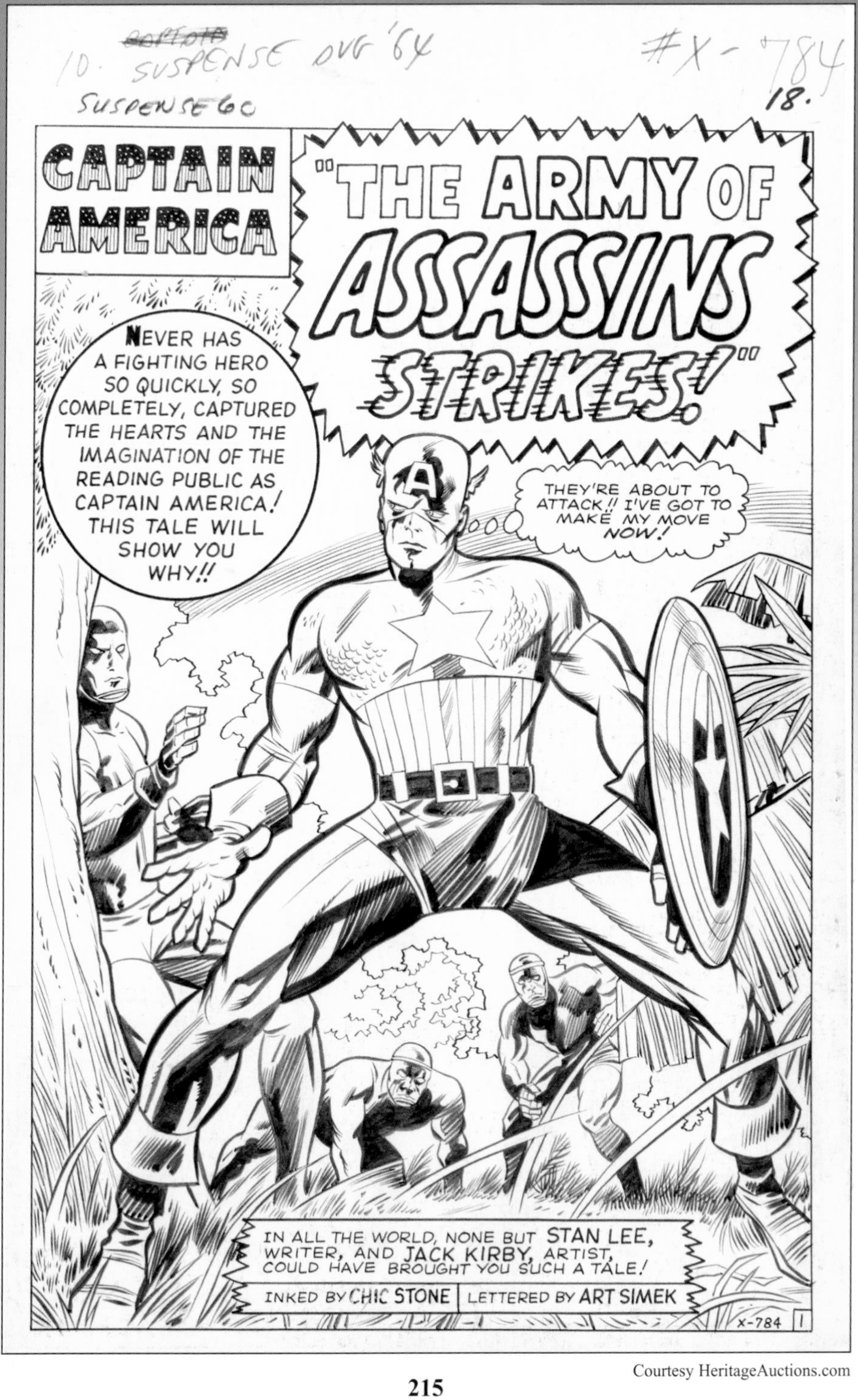

10. SUSPENSE AUG '64
#X-784
18.
SUSPENSE 60
CAPTAIN AMERICA
"THE ARMY OF ASSASSINS STRIKES!"
NEVER HAS A FIGHTING HERO SO QUICKLY, SO COMPLETELY, CAPTURED THE HEARTS AND THE IMAGINATION OF THE READING PUBLIC AS CAPTAIN AMERICA! THIS TALE WILL SHOW YOU WHY!!
THEY'RE ABOUT TO ATTACK!! I'VE GOT TO MAKE MY MOVE NOW!
IN ALL THE WORLD, NONE BUT STAN LEE, WRITER, AND JACK KIRBY, ARTIST, COULD HAVE BROUGHT YOU SUCH A TALE!
INKED BY CHIC STONE
LETTERED BY ART SIMEK
X-784
1

Courtesy HeritageAuctions.com

Tales of Suspense #75 page 1 original art
by Jack Kirby, Dick Ayers & John Tartaglione

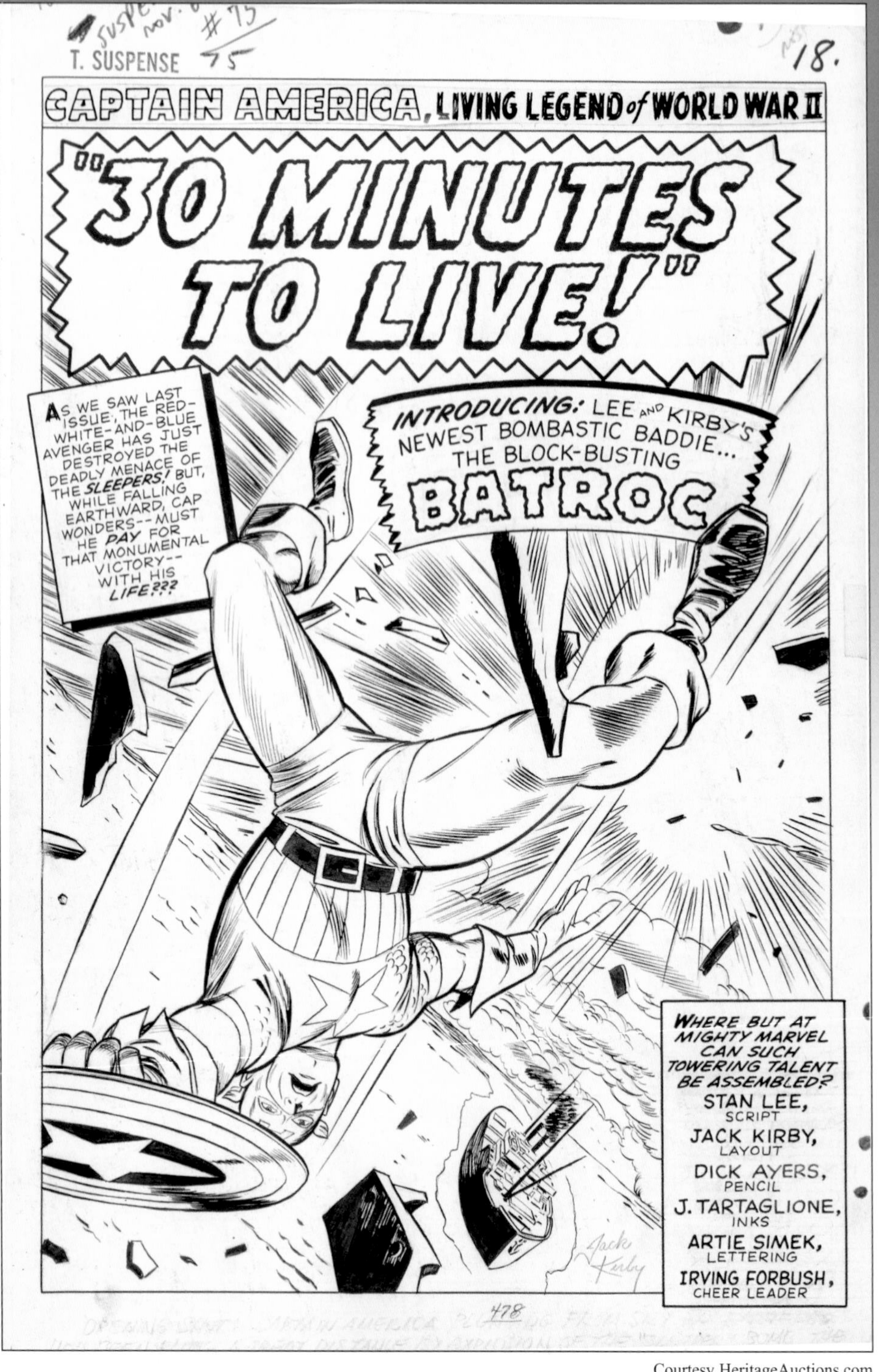
T. SUSPENSE
18.
CAPTAIN AMERICA, LIVING LEGEND of WORLD WAR II
"30 MINUTES TO LIVE!"
AS WE SAW LAST ISSUE, THE RED-WHITE-AND-BLUE AVENGER HAS JUST DESTROYED THE DEADLY MENACE OF THE SLEEPERS! BUT, WHILE FALLING EARTHWARD, CAP WONDERS--MUST HE PAY FOR THAT MONUMENTAL VICTORY--WITH HIS LIFE???
INTRODUCING: LEE AND KIRBY'S NEWEST BOMBASTIC BADDIE... THE BLOCK-BUSTING BATROC
WHERE BUT AT MIGHTY MARVEL CAN SUCH TOWERING TALENT BE ASSEMBLED?
STAN LEE, SCRIPT
JACK KIRBY, LAYOUT
DICK AYERS, PENCIL
J. TARTAGLIONE, INKS
ARTIE SIMEK, LETTERING
IRVING FORBUSH, CHEER LEADER
Jack Kirby

Courtesy HeritageAuctions.com